THE PEOPLE OF **AIRPORT**

Mel Bakersfeld
The airport's brilliant general manager, the man expected to keep everyone happy, keep bomb-carrying psychopaths off the planes, and always, somehow, keep the airport going.

Tanya Livingston
The passenger relations agent and attractive divorcée, whose visits to Mel Bakersfeld's executive suite weren't always strictly business.

Captain Vernon Demerest
The arrogant veteran pilot who was a superb performer in the cockpit or the bedroom—and well versed in the stewardess pregnancy program.

Keith Bakersfeld
The air traffic controller whose memory of one disaster was bringing him rapidly to the point of no return.

Gwen Meighen
The hot-tempered English brunette from "Stewardess Row," where liquor is served in pilfered two-ounce bottles and weekends are squeezed into twenty-four-hour layovers.

AIRPORT
"Another runaway . . . Superb storytelling."

ARTHUR HAILEY
AIRPORT

BANTAM BOOKS · TORONTO · NEW YORK · LONDON

All of the characters in this book are
fictitious, and any resemblance to actual
persons, living or dead, is purely coincidental.

AIRPORT

*A Bantam Book / published by arrangement with
Doubleday & Company, Inc.*

PRINTING HISTORY

Doubleday edition published March 1968

2nd printing	......March 1968	6th printing	.........July 1968
3rd printing	......March 1968	7th printing	.........July 1968
4th printing	........April 1968	8th printing	....September 1968
5th printing	.........June 1968	9th printing	......October 1968
	10th printing	.....October 1968	

Excerpt appeared in the CHICAGO TRIBUNE *March 1968*

Literary Guild edition published April 1968

Reader's Digest Condensed Book Club edition published April 1968

Dollar Book Club edition published January 1969

Bantam edition published July 1969

Bantam Books are published in Canada by Bantam Books
of Canada Ltd., registered user of the trademarks consisting of the word Bantam and the portrayal of a bantam.

PRINTED IN CANADA

Bantam Books of Canada Ltd.
888 DuPont Street, Toronto 4, Ontario

Oh! I have slipped the surly bonds of earth
And danced the skies on laughter-silvered wings

from *High Flight*
by John Gillespie Magee, Jr. (1922–1941)
sometime Flight Lieutenant, Royal Canadian Air Force

PART ONE

6:30 P.M.–8:30 P M (CST)

1

At half-past six on a Friday evening in January, Lincoln International Airport, Illinois, was functioning, though with difficulty.

The airport was reeling—as was the entire Midwestern United States—from the meanest, roughest winter storm in half a dozen years. The storm had lasted three days. Now, like pustules on a battered, weakened body, trouble spots were erupting steadily.

A United Air Lines food truck, loaded with two hundred dinners, was lost and presumably snowbound somewhere on the airport perimeter. A search for the truck—in driving snow and darkness—had so far failed to locate either the missing vehicle or its driver.

United's Flight 111—a non-stop DC-8 for Los Angeles, which the food truck was to service—was already several hours behind schedule. The food snafu would make it later still. Similar delays, for varying reasons, were affecting at least a hundred flights of twenty other airlines using Lincoln International.

Out on the airfield, runway three zero was out of use, blocked by an Aéreo-Mexican jet—a Boeing 707—its wheels deeply mired in waterlogged ground beneath snow, near the runway's edge. Two hours of intensive effort had failed to get the big jet moved. Now, Aéreo-Mexican, having exhausted its own local resources, had appealed to TWA for help.

Air Traffic Control, hampered by the loss of runway

three zero, had instituted flow control procedures, limiting the volume of incoming traffic from adjoining air route centers at Minneapolis, Cleveland, Kansas City, Indianapolis, and Denver. Despite this, twenty incoming flights were stacked up overhead, and orbiting, some nearing low fuel limits. On the ground, twice that number were readying for takeoff. But until the backlog of flights in the air could be reduced, ATC had ordered further delays of outbound traffic. Meanwhile, terminal gates, taxiways, and ground holding areas were increasingly crammed with waiting aircraft, many with engines running.

Air freight warehouses—of all airlines—were stacked to their palletized limits with shipments, their usual high speed transit impeded by the storm. Freight supervisors were nervously watching perishables—hothouse flowers from Wyoming for New England; a ton of Pennsylvania cheese for Anchorage, Alaska; frozen peas for Iceland; live lobsters—trans-shipped from the east for a polar route flight—destination Europe. The lobsters were for tomorrow's menus in Edinburgh and Paris where they would be billed as "fresh local seafood," and American tourists would order them unknowingly. Storm or not, contracts decreed that air freight perishables must arrive at destination fresh, and swiftly.

Causing special anxiety in American Airlines Freight was a shipment of several thousand turkey poults, hatched in incubators only hours earlier. The precise hatching-shipping schedule—like a complex order of battle—was set up weeks ago, before the turkey eggs were laid. It called for delivery of the live birds on the West Coast within forty-eight hours of birth, the limit of the tiny creatures' existence without their first food or water. Normally, the arrangement provided a near-hundred percent survival. Significant also—if the poults were fed en route, they would stink, and so would the airplane conveying them, for days afterward. Already the poults' schedule was out of joint by several hours. But an airplane had been diverted from passenger to freight service, and tonight the fledgling turkeys would have priority over everything else traveling, human VIPs included.

In the main passenger terminal, chaos predominated. Terminal waiting areas were jammed with thousands of passengers from delayed or canceled flights. Baggage, in piles, was everywhere. The vast main concourse had the combined appearance of a football scrimmage and Christmas Eve at Macy's.

High on the terminal roof, the airport's immodest slogan, LINCOLN INTERNATIONAL—AVIATION CROSSROADS OF THE WORLD, was entirely obscured by drifting snow.

The wonder was, Mel Bakersfeld reflected, that anything was continuing to operate at all.

Mel, airport general manager—lean, rangy, and a powerhouse of disciplined energy—was standing by the Snow Control Desk, high in the control tower. He peered out into the darkness. Normally, from this glass-walled room, the entire airport complex—runways, taxi strips, terminals, traffic of the ground and air—was visible like neatly aligned building blocks and models, even at night their shapes and movements well defined by lights. Only one loftier view existed—that of Air Traffic Control which occupied the two floors above.

But tonight only a faint blur of a few nearer lights penetrated the almost-opaque curtain of wind-driven snow. Mel suspected this would be a winter to be discussed at meteorologists' conventions for years to come.

The present storm had been born five days ago in the lee of the Colorado mountains. At birth it was a tiny low pressure area, no bigger than a foothills homestead, and most forecasters on their air route weather charts had either failed to notice, or ignored it. As if in resentment, the low pressure system thereupon inflated like a giant malignancy and, still growing, swung first southeast, then north.

It crossed Kansas and Oklahoma, then paused at Arkansas, gathering assorted nastiness. Next day, fat and monstrous, it rumbled up the Mississippi Valley. Finally, over Illinois the storm unloaded, almost paralyzing the state with blizzard winds, freezing temperatures, and a ten-inch snowfall in twenty-four hours.

At the airport, the ten-inch snow had been preceded

by a continuous, if somewhat lighter, fall. Now it was
being followed by more snow, whipped by vicious winds
which piled new drifts—at the same time that plows
were clearing the old. Maintenance snow crews were
nearing exhaustion. Within the past few hours several
men had been ordered home, overfatigued despite their
intermittent use of sleeping quarters provided at the airport for just this kind of emergency.

At the Snow Control Desk near Mel, Danny Farrow
—at other times an assistant airport manager, now snow
shift supervisor—was calling Maintenance Snow Center
by radiophone.

"We're losing the parking lots. I need six more Payloaders and a banjo team at Y-seventy-four."

Danny was seated at the Snow Desk, which was not
really a desk at all, but a wide, three-position console.
Confronting Danny and his two assistants—one on
either side—was a battery of telephones, Tel Autographs, and radios. Surrounding them were maps,
charts, and bulletin boards recording the state and location of every piece of motorized snow-fighting equipment, as well as men and supervisors. There was a
separate board for banjo teams—roving crews with individual snow shovels. The Snow Desk was activated only
for its one seasonal purpose. At other times of year, this
room remained empty and silent.

Danny's bald pate showed sweat globules as he
scratched notations on a large-scale airport grid map.
He repeated his message to Maintenance, making it
sound like a desperate personal plea, which perhaps it
was. Up here was the snow clearance command post.
Whoever ran it was supposed to view the airport as a
whole, juggling demands, and deploying equipment
wherever need seemed greatest. A problem though—
and undoubtedly a cause of Danny's sweating—was that
those down below, fighting to keep their own operations
going, seldom shared the same view of priorities.

"Sure, sure. Six more Payloaders." An edgy voice
from Maintenance, which was on the opposite side of
the airfield, rattled the speakerphone. "We'll get 'em

from Santa Claus. He ought to be around in this lot." A pause, then more aggressively, "Any other damnfool stupid notions?"

Glancing at Danny, Mel shook his head. He recognized the speakerphone voice as belonging to a senior foreman who had probably worked continuously since the present snowfall started. Tempers wore thin at times like this, with good reason. Usually, after an arduous, snow-fighting winter, airport maintenance and management had an evening stag session together which they called "kiss-and-make-up night." They would certainly need one this year.

Danny said reasonably, "We sent four Payloaders after that United food truck. They should be through, or almost."

"They might be—if we could find the frigging truck."

"You haven't located it *yet?* What are you guys doing —having a supper and ladies' night." Danny reached out, turning down the speakerphone volume as a reply slammed back.

"Listen, do you birds in the crummy penthouse have any idea what it's like out on the field? Maybe you should look out the windows once in a while. Anybody could be at the goddam North pole tonight and never know the difference."

"Try blowing on your hands, Ernie," Danny said. "It may keep 'em warm, and it'll stop you sounding off."

Mentally, Mel Bakersfeld filtered out most of the exchange, though he was aware that what had been said about conditions away from the terminal was true. An hour ago, Mel had driven across the airfield. He used service roads, but although he knew the airport layout intimately, tonight he had trouble finding his way and several times came close to being lost.

Mel had gone to inspect the Maintenance Snow Center and then, as now, activity had been intensive. Where the tower Snow Control Desk was a command post, the Maintenance Snow Center was a front line headquarters. From here, weary crews and supervisors came and went, alternately sweating and freezing, the tanks of regular workers swelled by auxiliaries—carpenters, electricians, plumbers, clerks, police. The auxiliaries were pulled from their regular airport duties and paid time-and-a-half until the snow emergency was over. But they knew what was expected, having rehearsed snow maneuvers, like weekend soldiers, on runways and taxi strips during summer and fall. It sometimes amused outsiders to see snow removal groups, plow blades down, blowers roaring, on a hot, sunny day. But if any expressed surprise at the extent of preparation, Mel Bakersfeld would remind them that removing snow from the airport's operating area was equal to clearing seven hundred miles of highway.

Like the Snow Desk in the control tower, the Maintenance Snow Center was activated for its winter function only. It was a big, cavernous room above an airport truck garage and, when in use, was presided over by a dispatcher. Judging from the present radio voice, Mel guessed that the regular dispatcher had been relieved for the time being, perhaps for some sleep in the "Blue Room," as Airport Standing Orders—with a trace of humor—called the snow crews' bunkhouse.

The maintenance foreman's voice came on the radiophone again. "We're worried about that truck too, Danny. The poor bastard of a driver could freeze out there. Though if he has any gumption, he isn't starving."

The UAL food truck had left the airline flight kitchen for the main terminal nearly two hours ago. Its route lay around the perimeter track, a journey which usually took fifteen minutes. But the truck had failed to arrive, and obviously the driver had lost his way and was snowbound somewhere in the airport boondocks. United flight dispatch had first sent out its own search party, without success. Now airport management had taken over.

Mel said, "That United flight finally took off, didn't it? Without food."

Danny Farrow answered without looking up. "I hear the captain put it to the passengers. Told them it'd take an hour to get another truck, that they had a movie and liquor aboard, and the sun was shining in California. Everybody voted to get the hell out. I would, too."

Mel nodded, resisting a temptation to take over and direct the search himself for the missing truck and driver. Action would be a therapy. The cold of several days, and dampness with it, had made Mel's old war injury ache again—a reminder of Korea which never left him—and he could feel it now. He shifted, leaning, letting the good foot take his weight. The relief was momentary. Almost at once, in the new position, the ache resumed.

He was glad, a moment later, that he had not inter- fered. Danny was already doing the right thing—intensi- fying the truck search, pulling plows and men from the terminal area and directing them to the perimeter road. For the time being, the parking lots would have to be abandoned, and later there would be plenty of beefs about *that*. But the missing driver must be saved first.

Between calls, Danny warned Mel, "Brace yourself for more complaints. This search'll block the perimeter road. We'll hold up all the other food trucks till we find the guy."

Mel nodded. Complaints were a stock-in-trade of an airport manager's job. In this case, as Danny predicted, there would be a flood of protests when other airlines realized their food trucks were not getting through, whatever the reason.

There were some who would find it hard to believe that a man could be in peril of death from exposure at a center of civilization like an airport, but it could happen just the same. The lonelier limits of the airport were no place to wander without bearings on a night like this. And if the driver decided to stay with his truck and keep the motor running for warmth, it could quickly be covered by drifts, with deadly carbon monoxide accu- mulating beneath.

With one hand, Danny was using a red telephone; with the other, leafing through emergency orders—Mel's orders, carefully drawn up for occasions such as this.

The red phone was to the airport's duty fire chief. Danny summarized the situation so far.

"And when we locate the truck, let's get an ambulance out there, and you may need an inhalator or heat, could be both. But better not roll until we know where exactly. We don't want to dig you guys out, too."

The sweat, in increasing quantity, was gleaming on Danny's balding head. Mel was aware that Danny disliked running the Snow Control Desk and was happier in his own department of airport planning, sifting logistics and hypotheses of aviation's future. Such things were comfortably projected well ahead, with time to think, not disconcertingly here-and-now like the problems of tonight. Just as there were people who lived in the past, Mel thought, for the Danny Farrows, the future was a refuge. But, unhappy or not, and despite the sweat, Danny was coping.

Reaching over Danny's shoulder, Mel picked up a direct line phone to Air Traffic Control. The tower watch chief answered.

"What's the story on that Aéreo-Mexican 707?"

"Still there, Mr. Bakersfeld. They've been working a couple of hours trying to move it. No luck yet."

That particular trouble had begun shortly after dark when an Aéreo-Mexican captain, taxiing out for takeoff, mistakenly passed to the right instead of left of a blue taxi light. Unfortunately, the ground to the right, which was normally grass covered, had a drainage problem, due to be worked on when winter ended. Meanwhile, despite the heavy snow, there was still a morass of mud beneath the surface. Within seconds of its wrong-way turn, the hundred and twenty ton aircraft was deeply mired.

When it became obvious that the aircraft could not get out, loaded, under its own power, the disgruntled passengers were disembarked and helped through mud and snow to hastily hired buses. Now, more than two hours later, the big jet was still stuck, its fuselage and tail blocking runway three zero.

Mel inquired, "The runway and taxi strip are still out of use?"

"Affirmative," the tower chief reported. "We're holding all outbound traffic at the gates, then sending them the long route to the other runways."

"Pretty slow?"

"Slowing us fifty percent. Right now we're holding ten flights for taxi clearance, another dozen waiting to start engines."

It was a demonstration, Mel reflected, of how urgently the airport needed additional runways and taxiways. For three years he had been urging construction of a new runway to parallel three zero, as well as other operational improvements. But the Board of Airport Commissioners, under political pressure from downtown, refused to approve. The pressure was because city councilmen, for reasons of their own, wanted to avoid a new bond issue which would be needed for financing.

"The other thing," the tower watch chief said, "is that with three zero out of use, we're having to route takeoffs over Meadowood. The complaints have started coming in already."

Mel groaned. The community of Meadowood, which adjoined the southwest limits of the airfield, was a constant thorn to himself and an impediment to flight operations. Though the airport had been established long before the community, Meadowood's residents complained incessantly and bitterly about noise from aircraft overhead. Press publicity followed. It attracted even more complaints, with increasingly bitter denunciations of the airport and its management. Eventually, after long negotiations involving politics, more publicity and —in Mel Bakerfeld's opinion—gross misrepresentation, the airport and the Federal Aviation Administration had conceded that jet takeoffs and landings directly over Meadowood would be made only when essential in special circumstances. Since the airport was already limited in its available runways, the loss in efficiency was considerable.

Moreover, it was also agreed that aircraft taking off toward Meadowood would—almost at once after becoming airborne—follow noise abatement procedures. This, in turn, produced protests from pilots, who considered the procedures dangerous. The airlines, however —conscious of the public furor and their corporate images—had ordered the pilots to conform.

Yet even this failed to satisfy the Meadowood residents. Their militant leaders were still protesting, organizing, and—according to latest rumors—planning legal harassment of the airport.

Mel asked the tower watch chief, "How many calls have there been?" Even before the answer, he decided glumly that still more hours of his working days were going to be consumed by delegations, argument, and the same insoluble discussions as before.

"I'd say fifty at least, we've answered; and there've been others we haven't. The phones start ringing right after every takeoff—our unlisted lines, too. I'd give a lot to know how they get the numbers."

"I suppose you've told the people who've called that we've a special situation—the storm, a runway out of use."

"We explain. But nobody's interested. They just want the airplanes to stop coming over. Some of 'em say that problems or not, pilots are still supposed to use noise abatement procedures, but tonight they aren't doing it."

"Good God!—if I were a pilot neither would I." How could anyone of reasonable intelligence, Mel wondered, expect a pilot, in tonight's violent weather, to chop back his power immediately after takeoff, and then go into a steeply banked turn on instruments—which was what noise abatement procedures called for.

"I wouldn't either," the tower chief said. "Though I guess it depends on your point of view. If I lived in Meadowood, maybe I'd feel the way they do."

"You wouldn't live in Meadowood. You'd have listened to the warnings we gave people, years ago, not to build houses there."

"I guess so. By the way, one of my people told me there's another community meeting over there tonight."

"In this weather?"

"Seems they still plan to hold it, and the way we heard, they're cooking up something new."

"Whatever it is," Mel predicted, "we'll hear about it soon."

Just the same, he reflected, if there *was* a public meeting at Meadowood, it was a pity to provide fresh ammunition so conveniently. Almost certainly the press and local politicians would be present, and the direct flights overhead, however necessary at this moment, would give them plenty to write and talk about. So the sooner the blocked runway—three zero—was back in use, the better it would be for all concerned.

"In a little while," he told the tower chief, "I'll go out on the field myself and see what's happening. I'll let you know what the situation is."

"Right."

Changing the subject, Mel inquired, "Is my brother on duty tonight?"

"Affirmative. Keith's on radar watch—west arrival."

West arrival, Mel knew, was one of the tough, tense positions in the tower. It involved supervising all incoming flights in the west quadrant. Mel hesitated, then remembered he had known the tower watch chief a long time. "Is Keith all right? Is he showing any strain?"

There was a slight pause before the answer. "Yes, he is. I'd say more than usual."

Between the two men was the knowledge that Mel's younger brother had lately been a source of anxiety to them both.

"Frankly," the tower chief said, "I wish I could let him take things easier. But I can't. We're short-staffed and everybody is under the gun." He added, "Including me."

"I know you are, and I appreciate your watching out for Keith the way you have."

"Well, in this job most of us have combat fatigue at one time or another." Mel could sense the other choosing his words carefully. "Sometimes it shows up in the mind, sometimes in the gut. Either way, when it happens we try to help each other."

"Thanks." The conversation had not eased Mel's anxiety. "I may drop in later."

"Right, sir." The tower chief hung up.

The "sir" was strictly a courtesy. Mel had no authority over ATC, which answered only to the Federal
Aviation Administration with headquarters in Washington. But relationships between controllers and airport
management were good, and Mel saw to it they stayed
that way.

An airport, any airport, was an odd complexity of
overlapping authority. No single individual had supreme
command, yet no one segment was entirely independent.
As airport general manager, Mel's was closest to an
over-all assignment, but there were areas where he knew
better than to intrude. Air Traffic Control was one, airline internal management another. He could, and did,
intervene in matters affecting the airport as a whole or
the welfare of people using it. He could peremptorily
order an airline to remove a door sign which was mis-
leading or failed to conform to terminal standards. But
what went on behind the doors was, within reason, the
airline's exclusive business.

This was why an airport manager needed to be a
tactician as well as versatile administrator.

Mel replaced the Snow Desk telephone. On another
line, Danny Farrow was arguing with the parking lot
supervisor, a harassed individual who for several hours
had been fielding irate complaints from marooned car
owners. People were asking: didn't whoever ran the
airport know it was snowing? And if they did, why
didn't someone get on the ball and move the stuff so a
man could drive his car anywhere at any time, as was
his democratic right?

"Tell 'em we declared a dictatorship." The non-cov-
ered lots, Danny insisted, would have to wait until priorities eased. He would send men and equipment when he
could. He was interrupted by a call from the tower
watch chief. A new weather forecast predicted a wind
shift in an hour. It would mean a change of runways,
and could they hurry the plowing of runway one seven,
left? He would do his best, Danny said. He'd check with
the Conga Line supervisor and call the tower back.

It was the kind of pressure, unremitting, which had
gone on for three days and nights since the present

snowfall started. The fact that the pressure had been met made all the more irritating a note, delivered to Mel by messenger, fifteen minutes ago. The note read:

> m —
>
> thought shd warn u—airlines snow
> committee (on vern demerest's urging
> . . . why does your bro-in-law dislike
> you?) filing critical report becos run-
> ways & taxiways snow clearance (v. d.
> says) lousy, inefficient . . .
>
> report blames airport (meaning u)
> for main hunk of flight delays . . . also
> claims stuck 707 wouldn't have if taxiway
> plowed sooner, better . . . so now
> all airlines being penalized, etc, etc,
> you get the drift . . . and where are you—
> in one? (drift, i mean) . . . climb out &
> buy me coffee soon.
>
> luv
>
> t

The "t" was for Tanya—Tanya Livingston, passenger relations agent for Trans America, and a special friend of Mel's. Mel read the note again, as he usually did messages from Tanya, which became clearer the second time around. Tanya, whose job straddled trouble-shooting and public relations, objected to capitals. ("Mel, doesn't it make sense? If we abolished capitals there'd be scads less trouble. Just look at the newspapers.") She had actually coerced a Trans America mechanic into chiseling all capitals from the typebars of her office typewriter. Someone higher up raised hob about that, Mel had heard, quoting the airline's rigid rule about willful damage to company property. Tanya had got away with it, though. She usually did.

The Vern Demerest in the note was Captain Vernon

Demerest, also of Trans America. As well as being one of the airline's more senior captains, Demerest was a militant campaigner for the Air Line Pilots Association, and, this season, a member of the Airlines Snow Committee at Lincoln International. The committee inspected runways and taxiways during snow periods and pronounced them fit, or otherwise, for aircraft use. It always included an active flying captain.

Vernon Demerest also happened to be Mel's brother-in-law, married to Mel's older sister, Sarah. The Bakersfeld clan, through precedent and marriage, had roots and branches in aviation, just as older families were once allied with seafaring. However, there was little cordiality between Mel and his brother-in-law, whom Mel considered conceited and pompous. Others, he knew, held the same opinion. Recently, Mel and Captain Demerest had had an angry exchange at a meeting of the Board of Airport Commissioners, where Demerest appeared on behalf of the pilots' association. Mel suspected that the critical snow report—apparently initiated by his brother-in-law—was in retaliation.

Mel was not greatly worried about the report. Whatever shortcomings the airport might have in other ways, he knew they were coping with the storm as well as any organization could. Just the same, the report was a nuisance. Copies would go to all airlines, and tomorrow there would be inquiring phone calls and memos, and a need for explanations.

Mel supposed he had better stay briefed, in readiness. He decided he would make an inspection of the present snow clearance situation at the same time that he was out on the airfield checking on the blocked runway and the mired Aéreo-Mexican jet.

At the Snow Desk, Danny Farrow was talking with Airport Maintenance again. When there was a moment's break, Mel interjected, "I'll be in the terminal, then on the field."

He had remembered what Tanya said in her note about having coffee together. He would stop at his own office first, then, on his way through the terminal, he would drop by Trans America to see her. The thought excited him.

2

Mel used the private elevator, which operated by pass-key only, to descend from the tower to the administrative mezzanine. Though his own office suite was silent, with stenographers' desks cleared and typewriters covered, the lights had been left on. He entered his own interior office. From a closet, near the wide mahogany desk he used in daytime, he took out a heavy topcoat and fur-lined boots.

Tonight Mel himself was without specific duties at the airport. This was as it should be. The reason he had stayed, through most of the three-day storm, was to be available for emergencies. Otherwise, he mused, as he pulled on the boots and laced them, by now he would have been home with Cindy and the children.

Or would he?

No matter how objective you tried to be, Mel reasoned, it was hard to be sure of your own real motives. Probably, if it had not been the storm, something else would have arisen to justify not going. Not going home, in fact, seemed lately to have become the pattern of his life. His job was a cause, of course. It provided plenty of reasons to remain extra hours at the airport, where lately there had been big problems facing him, quite apart from tonight's imbroglio. But—if he was honest with himself—the airport also offered an escape from the incessant wrangling between himself and Cindy which seemed to occur nowadays whenever they spent time together.

"Oh, hell!" Mel's exclamation cut across the silence of the office.

He plodded in the fur-lined boots toward his desk. A glance at a typed reminder from his secretary confirmed what he had just recalled. Tonight there was another of his wife's tedious charity affairs. A week ago, reluctantly, Mel had promised to attend. It was a cocktail party and dinner (so the typed note said), downtown at the swank Lake Michigan Inn. What the charity was, the note didn't specify, and, if it had ever been mentioned, he had since forgotten. It made no difference, though. The causes with which Cindy Bakersfeld involved herself were depressingly similar. The test of worthiness—as Cindy saw it—was the social eminence of her fellow committee members.

Fortunately, for the sake of peace with Cindy, the starting time was late—almost two hours from now and in view of tonight's weather, it might be even later. So he could still make it, even after inspecting the airfield. Mel could come back, shave and change in his office, and be downtown only a little late. He had better warn Cindy, though. Using a direct outside line, Mel dialed his home number.

Roberta, his elder daughter, answered.

"Hi," Mel said. "This is your old man."

Roberta's voice came coolly down the line. "Yes, I know."

"How was school today?"

"Could you be specific, Father? There were several classes. Which do you want to know about?"

Mel sighed. There were days on which it seemed to him that his home life was disintegrating all at once. Roberta, he could tell, was in what Cindy called one of her snotty moods. Did all fathers, he wondered, abruptly lose communication with their daughters at age thirteen? Less than a year ago, the two of them had seemed as close as father and daughter could be. Mel loved both his daughters deeply—Roberta, and her younger sister, Libby. There were times when he realized they were the only reasons his marriage had survived. As to Roberta, he had known that as a teen-ager she would develop interests which he could neither share nor wholly understand. He had been prepared for this. What he had not expected was to be shut out entirely or treated with a mixture of indifference and condescension. Though, to be objective, he supposed the increasing strife between Cindy and himself had not helped. Children were sensitive.

"Never mind," Mel said. "Is your mother home?"

"She went out. She said if you phoned to tell you you have to be downtown to meet her, and for once try not to be late."

Mel curbed his irritation. Roberta was undoubtedly repeating Cindy's words exactly. He could almost hear his wife saying them.

"If your mother calls, tell her I might have to be a little late, and that I can't help it." There was a silence, and he asked, "Did you hear me?"

"Yes," Roberta said. "Is there anything else, Father? I have homework to do."

He snapped back, "Yes, there is something else. You'll change your tone of voice, young lady, and show a little more respect. Furthermore, we'll end this conversation when I'm good and ready."

"If you say so, Father."

"And stop calling me Father!"

"Very well, Father."

Mel was tempted to laugh, then supposed he had better not. He asked, "Is everything all right at home?"

"Yes. But Libby wants to talk to you."

"In a minute. I was just going to tell you—because of the storm I may not be home tonight. There's a lot happening at the airport. I'll probably come back and sleep here."

Again a pause, as if Roberta was weighing whether or not she could get away with a smart answer: *So what else is new?* Apparently she decided not. "Will you speak to Libby now?"

"Yes, I will. Goodnight, Robbie."

"Goodnight."

There was an impatient shuffle as the telephone changed hands, then Libby's small breathless voice.

"Daddy, Daddy! Guess what!"

Libby was always breathless as if, to a seven-year-old, life were excitingly on the run and she must forever keep pace or be left behind.

"Let me think," Mel said. "I know—you had fun in the snow today."

"Yes, I did, But it wasn't that."

"Then I can't guess. You'll have to tell me."

"Well, at school, Miss Curzon said for homework we have to write down all the good things we think will happen next month."

He thought affectionately: he could understand Libby's enthusiasm. To her, almost everything was exciting and good, and the few things which were not were brushed aside and speedily forgotten. He wondered how much longer her happy innocence would last.

"That's nice," Mel said. "I like that."

"Daddy, Daddy! Will you help me?"

"If I can."

"I want a map of February."

Mel smiled. Libby had a verbal shorthand of her own which sometimes seemed more expressive than conventional words. It occurred to him that he could use a map of February himself.

"There's a calendar in my desk in the den." Mel told her where to find it and heard her small feet running from the room, the telephone forgotten. It was Roberta, Mel assumed, who silently hung up.

From the general manager's office suite, Mel walked onto the executive mezzanine which ran the length of the main terminal building. He carried the heavy topcoat with him.

Pausing, he surveyed the thronged concourse below, which seemed to have become even busier within the past half-hour. In waiting areas, every available seat was occupied. Newsstands and information booths were ringed by crowds, among them many military uniforms. In front of all airline passenger counters were line-ups, some extending around corners out of sight. Behind the counters, ticket agents and supervisors, their normal numbers swelled by colleagues from earlier shifts retained on overtime, had schedules and passage coupons spread out like orchestral scores.

Delays and reroutings which the storm had caused were taxing both scheduling and human patience. Immediately below Mel, at Braniff ticketing, a youngish man with long, blond hair and a yellow scarf was proclaiming loudly, "You've the effrontery to tell me I must

go to Kansas City to get to New Orleans. You people
are rewriting geography! You're mad with power!"

The ticket agent facing him, an attractive brunette in
her twenties, brushed a hand over her eyes before answering with professional patience, "We can route you
directly, sir, but we don't know when. Because of the
weather, the longer way will be faster and the fare is the
same."

Behind the yellow-scarfed man, more passengers with
other problems pressed forward urgently.

At the United counter, a small pantomime was being
played. A would-be passenger—a well-dressed businessman—leaned forward, speaking quietly. By the man's
expression and actions, Mel Bakersfeld could guess what
was being said. "I would very much like to get on that
next flight."

"I'm sorry, sir, the flight is fully booked. There's also
a long standby . . ." Before the ticket agent could complete his sentence, he glanced up. The passenger had
laid his briefcase on the counter in front of him. Gently,
but pointedly, he was tapping a plastic baggage tag
against a corner of the case. It was a 100,000-Mile Club
tag, one of those United issued to its favored friends—
an inner elite which all airlines had helped create. The
agent's expression changed. His voice became equally
low. "I think we'll manage something, sir." The agent's
pencil hovered, crossed out the name of another passenger—an earlier arrival whom he had been about to put
on the flight—and inserted the newcomer's name instead. The action was unobserved by those in line
behind.

The same kind of thing, Mel knew, went on at all
airline counters everywhere. Only the naïve or unin-
formed believed wait lists and reservations were operated with unwavering impartiality.

Mel observed that a group of new arrivals—presumably from downtown—was entering the terminal. They
were beating off snow from their clothing as they came
in, and judging from their appearance, it seemed that
the weather outside must be worsening. The newcomers
were quickly absorbed in the general crowds.

Few among the eighty thousand or so air travelers who thronged the terminal daily ever glanced up at the executive mezzanine, and fewer still were aware of Mel tonight, high above them, looking down. Most people who thought about airports did so in terms of airlines and airplanes. It was doubtful if many were even aware that executive offices existed or that an administrative machine—unseen, but complex and employing hundreds—was constantly at work, keeping the airport functioning.

Perhaps it was as well, Mel thought, as he rode the elevator down again. If people became better informed, in time they would also learn the airport's weaknesses and dangers, and afterward fly in and out with less assurance than before.

On the main concourse, he headed toward the Trans America wing. Near the check-in counters, a uniformed supervisor stepped forward. "Evening, Mr. Bakersfeld. Were you looking for Mrs. Livingston?"

No matter how busy the airport became, Mel thought, there would always be time for gossip. He wondered how widely his own name and Tanya's had been linked already.

"Yes," he said. "I was."

The supervisor nodded toward a door marked, AIRLINE PERSONNEL ONLY.

"You'll find her through there, Mr. Bakersfeld. We just had a bit of a crisis here. She's taking care of it."

3

In a small private lounge which was sometimes used for VIPs, the young girl in the uniform of a Trans America ticket agent was sobbing hysterically.

Tanya Livingston steered her to a chair. "Make yourself comfortable," Tanya said practically, "and take your time. You'll feel better afterward, and when you're ready we can talk."

Tanya sat down herself, smoothing her trim, tight uniform skirt. There was no one else in the room, and the only sound—apart from the crying—was the faint hum of air-conditioning.

There was fifteen years or so difference in age between the two women. The girl was not much more than twenty, Tanya in her late thirties. Watching, Tanya felt the gap to be greater than it was. It came, she supposed, from having been exposed to marriage, even though briefly and a long time ago—or so it seemed.

She thought: it was the second time she had been conscious of her age today. The first was while combing her hair this morning; she had seen telltale strands of gray among the short-cropped, flamboyant red. There was more of the gray than last time she had checked a month or so ago, and both occasions were reminders that her forties—by which time a woman ought to know where she was going and why—were closer than she liked to think about. She had another thought: in fifteen years from now, her own daughter would be the same age as the girl who was crying.

The girl, whose name was Patsy Smith, wiped reddened eyes with a large linen handkerchief which Tanya had given her. She spoke with difficulty, choking back more tears. "They wouldn't talk that way . . . so mean, rudely . . . at home . . . not to their wives."

"You mean passengers wouldn't?"

The girl nodded.

"Some would," Tanya said. "When you're married, Patsy, you may find out, though I hope not. But if you're telling me that men behave like adolescent boors when their travel plans get crossed up, I'll agree with you."

"I was doing my best . . . We all were . . . All day today; and yesterday . . . the day before . . . But the way people talk to you . . ."

"You mean they act as if you started the storm yourself. Especially to inconvenience them."

"Yes . . . And then that last man . . . Until him, I was all right . . ."

"What happened exactly? They called me when it was all over."

The girl was beginning to regain control of herself.

"Well . . . he had a ticket on Flight 72, and that was canceled because of weather. We got him a seat on 114, and he missed it. He said he was in the dining room and didn't hear the flight called."

"Flight announcements aren't made in the dining room," Tanya said. "There's a big notice saying so, and its on all the menus."

"I explained that, Mrs. Livingston, when he came back from the departure gate. But he was still nasty. He was going on as if it were my fault he'd missed the flight, not his. He said we were all inefficient and half asleep."

"Did you call your supervisor?"

"I tried to, but he was busy. We all were."

"So what did you do?"

"I got the passenger a seat—on the extra section, 2122."

"And?"

"He wanted to know what movie was showing on the flight. I found that out, and he said he'd seen it. He got nasty again. The movie he'd wanted to see was on the first flight which was canceled. He said, could I get him another flight which was showing the same movie as the first one? All the time, there were other passengers; they were pressing up against the counter. Some were making remarks out loud about how slow I was. Well, when he said that about the movie, that was when I . . ." The girl hesitated. "I guess something snapped."

Tanya prompted, "That was when you threw the timetable?"

Patsy Smith nodded miserably. She looked as if she were going to cry again. "Yes. I don't know what got into me, Mrs. Livingston . . . I threw it right over the counter. I told him he could fix his own flight."

"All I can say," Tanya said, "is that I hope you hit him."

The girl looked up. In place of tears, there was the beginning of a smile. "Oh, yes; I did." She thought, then giggled. "You should have seen his face. He was so surprised." Her expression became serious. "Then, after that . . ."

"I know what happened after that. You broke down, which was a perfectly natural thing to do. You were sent in here to finish your cry, and now you have, you're going home in a taxi."

The girl looked bemused. "You mean . . . that's all?"

"Certainly it's all. Did you expect us to fire you?"

"I . . . I wasn't sure."

"We might have to," Tanya said, "much as we'd dislike it, Patsy, if you did the same thing again. But you won't, will you? Not ever."

The girl shook her head firmly. "No, I won't. I can't explain, but having done it just once is enough."

"That's the end of it, then. Except that you might like to hear what happened after you left."

"Yes, please."

"A man came forward. He was one of those in the line-up, and he said he heard, and saw, the whole thing. He also said he had a daughter the same age as you, and if the first man had talked to his daughter the same way he talked to you, he would personally have punched him in the nose. Then the second man—the one from the line-up—left his name and address, and said if the man you had been talking to ever made any kind of complaint, to let him know and he would report what really happened." Tanya smiled. "So, you see—there are nice people, too."

"I know," the girl said. "There aren't many, but when you do get one like that, who's nice to you, and cheerful, you feel you want to hug him."

"Unfortunately we can't do that, any more than we should throw timetables. Our job is to treat everyone alike, and be courteous, even when passengers are not."

"Yes, Mrs. Livingston."

Patsy Smith would be all right, Tanya decided. Apparently, she hadn't thought of quitting, as some girls did who suffered similar experiences. In fact, now that she was over her emotion, Patsy seemed to have the kind of resilience which would be helpful to her in future.

God knows, Tanya thought, you needed resilience—and some toughness—in dealing with the traveling public, whatever job you held.

Take Reservations.

Downtown in reservation departments, she was aware, personal pressures would be even greater than at the airport. Since the storm began, reservation clerks would have made thousands of calls advising passengers of delays and rearrangements. It was a job the clerks all hated because people whom they called were invariably bad-tempered and frequently abusive. Airline delays seemed to arouse a latent savagery in those affected by them. Men talked insultingly to women telephonists, and even people who at other times were courteous and mild-mannered, turned snarly and disagreeable. New York-bound flights were worst of all. Reservation clerks had been known to refuse the assignment of telephoning news of delay or cancellation to a flight load of passengers destined for New York, preferring to risk their jobs rather than face the torrent of invective they knew awaited them. Tanya had often speculated on what it was about New York which infected those headed there with a kind of medicine-dance fervor to arrive.

But, for whatever reasons, she knew there would be resignations among airline staffs—in Reservations and elsewhere—when the present emergency was over. There always were. A few nervous breakdowns could be counted on, too, usually among the younger girls, more sensitive to passengers' rudeness and ill humor. Constant politeness, even when you were trained for it, was a strain which took a heavy toll.

She was glad, though, that Patsy Smith would not be among the casualties.

There was a knock at the outer door. It opened, and Mel Bakersfeld leaned in. He was wearing fleece-lined boots and carrying a heavy topcoat. "I was coming by," he told Tanya. "I can drop back later, if you like."

"Please stay." She smiled a welcome. "We've almost finished."

She watched him as he walked to a chair across the room. He looked tired, Tanya thought.

She switched her attention back, filled in a voucher, and handed it to the girl. "Give this to the taxi dispatcher, Patsy, and he'll send you home. Have a good night's rest, and we'll expect you back tomorrow, bright and breezy."

When the girl had gone, Tanya swung her chair around to face Mel's. She said brightly, "Hullo."

He put down a newspaper he had been glancing at, and grinned. "Hi!"

"You got my note?"

"I came to thank you for it. Though I might have made it here without." Gesturing to the door through which the girl had gone, he asked, "What was all that about? Battle fatigue?"

"Yes." She told him what had happened.

Mel laughed. "I'm tired, too. How about sending *me* off in a taxi?"

Tanya looked at him, inquiringly. Her eyes—a bright, clear blue—had a quality of directness. Her head was tilted, and an overhead light reflected red highlights from her hair. A slim figure, yet with a fullness which the trim airline uniform heightened . . . Mel was conscious, as at other times, of her desirability and warmth.

"I might consider it," she said. "If the taxi goes to my place, and you let me cook you dinner. Say, a Lamb Casserole."

He hesitated, weighing conflicting claims, then reluctantly shook his head. "I wish I could. But we've some trouble here, and afterward I have to be downtown." He got up. "Let's have coffee, anyway."

"All right."

Mel held the door open, and they went out into the bustling, noisy main concourse.

There was a press of people around the Trans America counter, even greater than when Mel had arrived. "I mustn't take long," Tanya said. "I've still two hours more on duty."

As they threaded their way through the crowds and increasing piles of luggage, she moderated her normally brisk pace to Mel's slower one. He was limping rather more than usual, she noticed. She found herself wanting to take his arm and help him, but supposed she had better not. She was still in Trans America uniform. Gossip spread fast enough without helping it actively. The two of them had been seen a good deal lately in each other's company, and Tanya was sure that the airport rumor machine—which operated like a jungle telegraph with IBM speed—had already taken note. Probably it was assumed that she and Mel were bedding down together, though, as it happened, that much was untrue.

They were headed for the Cloud Captain's Coffee Shop in the central lobby.

"About that Lamb Casserole," Mel said. "Could we make it another night? Say, the day after tomorrow?"

The sudden invitation from Tanya had surprised him. Although they had had several dates together—for drinks or dinner—until now she had not suggested visiting her apartment. Of course, going there could be for dinner only. Still . . . there was always the possibility that it might not.

Lately, Mel had sensed that if their meetings away from the airport continued, there could be a natural and obvious progression. But he had moved cautiously, instinct warning him that an affair with Tanya would be no casual romance but a deeply emotional involvement for them both. A consideration, also, was his own problems with Cindy. Those were going to take a lot of working out, if they could be worked out at all, and there was a limit to the number of complications a man could handle at one time. It was a strange commentary, he thought, that when a marriage was secure it seemed easier to manage an affair than when the same marriage was shaky. Just the same, Tanya's invitation seemed too enticing to pass up.

"The day after tomorrow is Sunday," she pointed out. "But I'll be off duty, and if you can manage it, I'll have more time."

Mel grinned. "Candles and wine?"

He had forgotten it would be Sunday. But he would have to come to the airport anyway because, even if the storm moved on, there would be aftereffects. As to Cindy, there had been several Sundays when she had been out, herself, without an announced reason.

Momentarily, Mel and Tanya separated as she dodged a hurrying, florid-faced man, followed by a redcap with a loaded luggage cart, topped by golf clubs and tennis rackets. Wherever that load was going, Tanya thought enviously, it was a long way south.

"Okay," she said when they rejoined. "Candles and wine."

As they entered the coffee shop, a pert hostess recognized Mel and ushered him, ahead of others, to a small table at the rear, marked RESERVED, which airport officials often used. About to sit down, he stumbled slightly and grasped Tanya's arm. The observant hostess flicked her eyes over them both with a half-smile. Rumor machine, stand by for a bulletin, Tanya thought.

Aloud, she said, "Did you ever see such crowds? This has been the wildest three days I remember."

Mel glanced around the packed coffee shop, its bedlam of voices punctuated by the clatter of dishes. He nodded toward the outer door through which they could both see a moving, surging swarm of people. "If you think this is a big horde tonight, wait until the civil version of the C-5A goes into service."

"I know—we can barely cope with the 747s; but a thousand passengers arriving all at once at a check-in counter . . . God help us!" Tanya shuddered. "Can you imagine what it'll be like when they collect their baggage? I don't even want to think about it."

"Nor do a good many other people—who *ought* to be thinking about it, right now." He was amused to find that their conversation had already drifted into aviation. Airplanes and airlines held a fascination for Tanya, and she liked talking about them. So did Mel, which was one of the reasons he enjoyed her company.

"Which people aren't thinking?"

"Those who control policy on the ground—airport

and air traffic. Most are acting as if today's jets will fly
forever. They seem to believe that if everybody keeps
quiet and still, the new, big airplanes will go away and
not bother us. That way we needn't have ground facilities to match them."

Tanya said thoughtfully, "But there's a lot of building
at airports. Wherever you go, you see it."

Mel offered her a cigarette and she shook her head
negatively. He lit one for himself before answering.

"Mostly the building going on is patchwork—changes
and additions to airports built in the 1950s or early
'60s. There's little that's farseeing. There are exceptions
—Los Angeles is one; Tampa, Florida, and Dallas-Fort
Worth are others; they'll be the first few airports in the
world ready for the new mammoth jets and supersonics.
Kansas City, Houston, and Toronto look good; San
Francisco has a plan, though it may get sunk politically.
In North America there's not much else that's impres-
sive."

"How about Europe?"

"Europe is routine," Mel said, "except for Paris—the
new Nord airport to replace Le Bourget will be among
the finest yet. London is the kind of inefficient mess
which only the English can create." He paused, considering. "We shouldn't knock other countries, though;
back home is bad enough. New York is frightening,
even with changes being made at Kennedy; there simply
isn't enough airspace above New York—I'm thinking of
traveling there by train in future. Washington, D.C., is
floundering—Washington National's a Black Hole of
Calcutta; Dulles was a giant step sideways. And Chicago
will wake up one day to find it let itself get twenty years
behind." He stopped, considering. "You remember a
few years ago, when the jets first started flying—what
conditions were like at airports which had been designed
for DC-4s and Constellations."

"I remember," Tanya said. "I worked at one. On
normal days you couldn't move for the crowds; on busy
days you couldn't breathe. We used to say it was like
holding the World Series in a sand lot."

"What's coming in the 1970s," Mel predicted, "is

going to be worse, far worse. And not just people congestion. We'll be choking on other things, too."

"Such as what?"

"Airways and traffic control for one, but that's another whole story. The really big thing, which most airport planning hasn't caught on to yet, is that we're moving toward the day—fast—when air freight business will be bigger than passenger traffic. The same thing's been true with every form of transportation, starting with the birchbark canoe. To begin with, people are carried, plus a little freight; but before long, there's more freight than people. In airline business we're already closer to that than is generally known. When freight does get to be top dog—as will happen in the next ten years or so—a lot of our present airport ideas will be obsolete. If you want a sign of the way things are moving, watch some of the young men who are going into airline management now. Not long ago, hardly anybody wanted to work in air freight departments; it was backroom stuff; passenger business had the glamour. Not any more! Now the bright boys are heading for air freight. They know that's where the future and the big promotions lie."

Tanya laughed. "I'll be old-fashioned and stick with people. Somehow freight . . ."

A waitress came to their table. "The special's off, and if we get many more people in here tonight, there won't be much else either."

They ordered coffee, Tanya cinnamon toast, and Mel a fried egg sandwich.

When the waitress had gone, Mel grinned. "I guess I started to make a speech. I'm sorry."

"Maybe you need the practice." She regarded him curiously. "You haven't made many lately."

"I'm not president of the Airport Operators Council any more. I don't get to Washington as much, or other places either." But it was not the whole reason for not making speeches and being less in the public eye. He suspected Tanya knew it.

Curiously, it was a speech of Mel's which had brought them together to begin with. At one of the rare interline meetings which airlines held, he had talked about coming developments in aviation, and the lag in ground organization compared with progress in the air. He had used the occasion as a dry run for a speech he intended to deliver at a national forum a week or so later. Tanya had been among the Trans America contingent, and next day had sent him one of her lower case notes:

> mr. b
>
> spch great. all'v us earthside slaves cheering u 4 admitting airport policy-makers asleep at drawing boards. somebody needed 2 say it. mind suggestion? wd all be more alive if fewer fax, more abt people. . . . passenger, once inside belly (air-plane or whale, remember jonah?) thinks only of self, not system much. i'll bet orville/wilbur felt same way once off ground. wright?
>
>   tl

As well as amusing him, the note had caused him to think. It was true, he realized—he *had* concentrated on facts and systems to the exclusion of people as individuals. He revised his speech notes, shifting the emphasis as Tanya suggested. The result was the most successful presentation he had ever made. It gained him an ovation and was widely reported internationally. Afterward he had telephoned Tanya to thank her. That was when they had started seeing each other.

The thought of Tanya's first message was a reminder of the note she had sent this evening. "I appreciate that tip about the snow committee report, though I'm curious how you managed to see it before I have."

"No mystery. It was typed in the Trans America office. I saw our Captain Demerest checking it, and chortling."

"Vernon showed it to you?"

"No, but he had it spread out, and I'm adept to reading upside down. Which reminds me, you didn't answer my question: Why does your brother-in-law dislike you?"

Mel grimaced. "I guess he knows I'm not overly keen on *him*."

"If you wanted to," Tanya said, "you could tell him now. There's the great man himself." She nodded toward the cashier's desk, and Mel turned his head.

Captain Vernon Demerest of Trans America was counting out change as he paid a bill. A tall, broad-shouldered, striking figure, he towered above others around him. He was dressed informally in a Harris tweed jacket and impeccably creased slacks, yet managed to convey an impression of authority—like a Regular Army General, Mel thought, temporarily in civilian clothes. Demerest's strong, aristocratic features were unsmiling as he addressed a four-striper Trans America captain—in uniform—who was with him. It appeared that Demerest was giving instructions; the other nodded. Captain Demerest glanced briefly around the coffee shop and, observing Mel and Tanya, gave a curt, cool nod. Then, checking his watch, and with a final word to the other captain, he strode out.

"He appeared in a hurry," Tanya said. "Though wherever he's going, it won't be for long. Captain D. is taking Flight Two to Rome tonight."

Mel smiled. *"The Golden Argosy?"*

"No less. I see, sir, you read our advertising."

"It's hard not to." Mel was aware, as were millions of others who admired the four-color double-page spreads in *Life, Look,* the *Post,* and other national magazines, that Trans America Flight Two—*The Golden Argosy* —was the airline's crack, prestige flight. He also knew that only the line's most senior captains ever commanded it.

"It seems to be agreed," Mel said, "that Vernon is one of the finest pilots extant."

"Oh yes, indeed. Extant and arrogant." Tanya hesitated, then confided, "If you're in a mood for gossip, you aren't alone in not caring for your brother-in-law. I heard one of our mechanics say not long ago, he was sorry there weren't propellers any more because he'd always hoped Captain Demerest would walk into one."

Mel said sharply, "That's a pretty savage thought."

"I agree. Personally, I prefer what Mr. Youngquist, our president, is supposed to have said. I understand his instructions about Captain Demerest are: 'Keep that bumptious bastard out of my hair, but book me on his flights.' "

Mel chuckled. Knowing both men, he felt sure the sally was true. He should not have let himself be drawn into a discussion about Vernon Demerest, he realized, but news of the adverse snow report and the nuisance effect it would have, still rankled. He wondered idly where his brother-in-law was going at the moment, and if it involved one of his amorous adventures, of which —reportedly—there were a good many. Looking toward the central lobby, Mel saw that Captain Demerest had already been swallowed up in the crowds outside.

Across the table, Tanya smoothed her skirt with a swift stroking gesture which Mel had noticed before and liked. It was a feminine habit and a reminder that few women looked as good in uniform, which often seemed to have a de-sexing effect, but with Tanya worked the opposite way.

Some airlines, Mel knew, let their senior passenger agents out of uniform, but Trans America liked the authority which its jaunty blue and gold commanded. Two gold rings edged with white, on Tanya's cuffs, proclaimed her job and seniority.

As if surmising his thoughts, she volunteered, "I may be out of uniform soon."

"Why?"

"Our District Transportation Manager is being transferred to New York. The Assistant D.T.M. is moving up, and I've applied for his job."

He regarded her with a mixture of admiration and curiosity. "I believe you'll get it. And that won't be the end, either."

Her eyebrows went up. "You think I might make vice-president?"

"I believe you could. That is, if it's the kind of thing you want. To be the lady executive; all that."

Tanya said softly, "I'm not sure if it's what I want, or not."

The waitress brought their order. When they were alone again, Tanya said, "Sometimes us working girls don't get a lot of choice. If you're not satisfied to stay in the job you have through pension time—and lots of us aren't—the only way out is up."

"You're excluding marriage?"

She selected a piece of cinnamon toast. "I'm not excluding it. But it didn't work for me once, and it may not again. Besides which, there aren't many takers—eligible ones—for used bride with baby."

"You might find an exception."

"I might win the Irish Sweep. Speaking from experience, Mel dear, I can tell you that men like their women unencumbered. Ask my ex-husband. If you can find him, that is; I never could."

"He left you after your baby was born?"

"Goodness, no! That way Roy would have had six months of responsibility. I think it was on a Thursday I told him I was pregnant; I couldn't have kept it to myself much longer. On Friday when I came home from work, Roy's clothes were gone. So was Roy."

"You haven't seen him since?"

She shook her head. "In the end, it made the divorce much simpler—desertion; no complications like another woman. I have to be fair, though. Roy wasn't all bad. He didn't empty our joint checking account, though he could have. I must admit I've sometimes wondered if it was kindness, or if he just forgot. Anyway, I had all that eighty dollars to myself."

Mel said, "You've never mentioned that before."

"Should I have?"

"For sympathy, maybe."

She shook her head. "If you understood me better, you'd know the reason I'm telling you now is because I don't need sympathy. Everything has worked out fine." Tanya smiled. "I may even get to be an airline vice-president. You just said so."

At an adjoining table, a woman said loudly, "Geez! Lookit the time!"

Instinctively, Mel did. It was three quarters of an hour since he had left Danny Farrow at the Snow Control Desk. Getting up from the table, he told Tanya, "Don't go away. I have to make a call."

There was a telephone at the cashier's counter, and Mel dialed one of the Snow Desk unlisted numbers. Danny Farrow's voice said, "Hold it," then, a few moments later, returned on the line.

"I was going to call you," Danny said. "I just had a report on that stuck 707 of Aéreo-Mexican."

"Go ahead."

"You knew Mexican had asked TWA for help?"

"Yes."

"Well, they've got trucks, cranes, God knows what out there now. The runway and taxiway are blocked off completely, but they still haven't shifted the damn airplane. The latest word is that TWA has sent for Joe Patroni."

Mel acknowledged, "I'm glad to hear it, though I wish they'd done it sooner."

Joe Patroni was airport maintenance chief for TWA, and a born trouble-shooter. He was also a down-to-earth, dynamic character and a close crony of Mel's.

"Apparently they tried to get Patroni right away," Danny said. "But he was at home and the people here had trouble reaching him. Seems there's a lot of phone lines down from the storm."

"But he knows now. You're sure of that?"

"TWA's sure. They say he's on his way."

Mel calculated. He knew that Joe Patroni lived at Glen Ellyn, some twenty-five miles from the airport, and even with ideal driving conditions the journey took forty minutes. Tonight, with snowbound roads and crawling traffic, the airline maintenance chief would be lucky to make it in twice that time.

"If anyone can get that airplane moved tonight," Mel conceded, "it'll be Joe. But meanwhile I don't want anybody sitting on his hands until he gets here. Make it clear to everyone that we need runway three zero usable, and urgently." As well as the operational need, he remembered unhappily that flights must still be taking off over Meadowood. He wondered if the community meeting, which the tower chief had told him about, was yet in session.

"I've been telling 'em," Danny confirmed. "I'll do it some more. Oh, a bit of good news—we found that United food truck."

"The driver okay?"

"He was unconscious under the snow. Motor still running, and there was carbon monoxide, the way we figured. But they got an inhalator on him, and he'll be all right."

"Good! I'm going out on the field now to do some checking for myself. I'll radio you from there."

"Wrap up well," Danny said. "I hear it's a lousy night."

Tanya was still at the table when Mel returned, though preparing to go.

"Hold on," he said, "I'm coming, too."

She motioned to his untouched sandwich. "How about dinner? If that's what it was."

"This will do for now." He bolted a mouthful, washed it down hastily with coffee, and picked up his topcoat. "Anyway, I'm having dinner downtown."

As Mel paid their check, two Trans America ticket agents entered the coffee shop. One was the supervising agent whom Mel had spoken to earlier. Observing Tanya, he came across.

"Excuse me, Mr. Bakersfeld . . . Mrs. Livingston, the D.T.M.'s looking for you. He has another problem."

Mel pocketed his change from the cashier. "Let me guess. Somebody else threw a timetable."

"No, sir." The agent grinned. "I reckon if there's another thrown this evening it'll be by me. This one's a stowaway—on Flight 80 from Los Angeles."

"Is that all?" Tanya appeared surprised. Aerial stowaways—though all airlines had them—were seldom a cause of great concern.

"The way I hear it," the agent said, "this one's a dilly. There's been a radio message from the captain, and a security guard has gone to the gate to meet the flight. Anyway, Mrs. Livingston, whatever the trouble is, they're calling for you." With a friendly nod, he went off to rejoin his companion.

Mel walked with Tanya from the coffee shop into the central lobby. They stopped at the elevator which would take Mel to the basement garage where his car was parked.

"Drive carefully out there," she cautioned. "Don't get in the way of any airplanes."

"If I do, I'm sure you'll hear about it." He shrugged into the heavy topcoat. "Your stowaway sounds interesting. I'll try to drop by before I leave, to find out what it's all about." He hesitated, then added, "It'll give me a reason to see you again tonight."

They were close together. As one, each reached out and their hands touched. Tanya said softly, "Who needs a reason?"

In the elevator, going down, he could still feel the warm smoothness of her flesh, and hear her voice.

4

Joe Patroni—as Mel Bakersfeld had learned—was on his way to the airport from his home at Glen Ellyn. The cocky, stocky Italian-American, who was airport maintenance chief for TWA, had left his suburban, ranch-style bungalow by automobile some twenty minutes earlier. The going was exceedingly slow, as Mel had guessed it would be.

At the moment, Joe Patroni's Buick Wildcat was halted in a traffic tie-up. Behind and ahead, as far as visibility extended, were other vehicles, also stopped. While waiting, his actions illuminated by the taillights of the car in front, Patroni lit a fresh cigar.

Legends had grown up around Joe Patroni; some professional, others personal.

He had begun his working life as a grease monkey in a garage. Soon after, he won the garage from his employer in a dice game, so that at the end of the game they reversed roles. As a result, young Joe became heir to various bad debts, including one which made him owner of an ancient, decrepit Waco biplane. With a mixture of resourcefulness and sheer mechanical ability, he repaired the airplane, then flew it successfully—without benefit of flying lessons, which he could not afford.

The airplane and its mechanical functioning absorbed Joe Patroni completely—so much so, that he enticed his former employer into another dice game and allowed him to win the garage back. Joe thereupon quit the garage and took a job as an airline mechanic. He studied at night school, became a lead mechanic, then a foreman with a reputation as a top-notch troubleshooter. His crew could change an engine faster than an airplane manufacturer said it could be done; and with absolute reliability. After a while, whenever there was pressure, or a difficult repair job, the word went out: *get Joe Patroni*.

A contributing reason for his success was that he never wasted time on diplomacy. Instead, he went directly to the point, both with people and airplanes. He also had a total disregard for rank, and was equally forthright with everyone, including the airline's senior executives.

On one occasion, still talked about when airline men reminisced, Joe Patroni walked off his job and, without word to anyone, or prior consultation, rode an airplane to New York. He carried a package with him. On arrival, he went by bus and subway to the airline's Olympian headquarters in midtown Manhattan where, without announcement or preamble, he strode into the president's office. Opening the package, he deposited an oily, disassembled carburetor on the immaculate presidential desk.

The president, who had never heard of Joe Patroni,

and whom no one ever got to see without prior appointment, was apoplectic until Joe told him, "If you want to
lose some airplanes in flight, throw me out of here. If
you don't, sit down and listen."

The president sat down—while Joe Patroni lighted a
cigar—and listened. Afterward, he called in his engineering vice-president who, later still, ordered a mechanical modification affecting carburetor icing in flight,
which Patroni had been urging—unsuccessfully at lower
level—for months.

Later, Patroni received official commendation, and
the incident became one more to add to an already
growing fund of Patroni stories. Soon after, Joe was
promoted to senior supervisor, and a few years later was
given the important post of maintenance chief at
Lincoln International.

On a personal level, another report said that Joe Patroni made love to his wife, Marie, most nights, the way
other men enjoyed a pre-dinner drink. This was true. In
fact, he had been thus engaged when the telephone message came from the airport about the mired Aéreo-Mexican jet which TWA had been asked to help extricate.

The same rumor continued: Patroni made love the
same way he did everything else—with a long, thin cigar
stuck jauntily in the side of his mouth. This was untrue,
at least nowadays. Marie, having coped with several
pillow fires during their early years of marriage—
drawing on her training as a TWA air hostess to extin-
guish them—had emphatically forbidden any more
cigars in bed. Joe complied with the edict because he
loved his wife. He had reason to. When he married her,
she was probably the most popular and beautiful hostess
in the entire airline system, and twelve years and three
children later she could still hold her own with most
successors. There were some who wondered aloud why
Marie—who had been pursued ardently by captains and
first officers—had ever chosen Joe Patroni at all. But
Joe, even as a young maintenance foreman, which he
was when they met, had a way with him, and had kept
Marie satisfied—in all important ways—ever since.

Another thing about Joe Patroni was that he never

panicked in emergencies. Instead, he quickly assessed each situation, deciding what priority the emergency rated, and whether or not he should complete other tasks before coping with it. In the case of the mired 707, instinct told him it was a moderate-to-acute crisis, which meant there was time to finish what he was doing, or have dinner, but not both. Accordingly, he abandoned dinner. Soon after, Marie raced to the kitchen in her robe and threw sandwiches together for Joe to eat during his twenty-five-mile drive to the airport. He nibbled on a sandwich now.

Being recalled to the airport after performing a full day's work was not a new experience, but tonight the weather was worse than any other occasion he remembered. Accumulated effects of the three-day storm were everywhere, making driving exacting and hazardous. Huge snowpiles lined the streets and, in the darkness, more snow was falling. Both on and off freeways, traffic was moving at a crawl, or not at all. Even with mud-snow tires, which Patroni's Buick Wildcat had, traction was poor. Windshield wipers and defrosters were barely coping with gusting snow outside and steam within, while headlight beams illuminated only short distances ahead. Stalled vehicles, some abandoned by their drivers, turned roads into obstacle courses. It was obvious that only those with good reason would be out on such a night.

Patroni checked his watch. Both his own car and the one immediately ahead had been stationary for several minutes. Farther ahead still, he could make out others, also stopped, and to his right was another halted lane of traffic. Moreover, for some time, no vehicles had come from the opposite direction, so obviously something had happened to obstruct all four lanes. If nothing more occurred in the next five minutes, he decided, he would get out of the car to investigate, though observing the slush, drifts, and still falling snow outside, he hoped he would not have to. There would be plenty of time to become cold and miserable—as he was undoubtedly going to be before the night was out—after arrival at the airport. Meanwhile, he turned up the volume of the car radio, which was tuned to a rock-and-roll station, and puffed at his cigar.

Five minutes went by. Ahead, Joe Patroni could see people getting out of cars and walking forward, and he prepared to join them. He had brought a fleece-lined parka and pulled it tightly around him, slipping the hood over his head. He reached for the heavy-duty electric lantern which he always carried. As he opened the car door, wind and snow rushed in. He eased out, closing the door quickly.

He plodded forward while other car doors slammed and voices called, "What happened?" Someone shouted, "There's been an accident. It's a real mess." As he progressed, flashing lights became visible ahead, and shadows moved and separated, becoming a cluster of people. A new voice said, "I'm telling you they won't clear that lot in a hurry. We'll all be stuck here for hours." A large, darker shadow loomed, partially lighted by sputtering red flares. It proved to be a massive tractor-trailer unit on its side. The cumbersome eighteen-wheeled vehicle was spread across the road, blocking all traffic movement. Part of its cargo—apparently cases of canned goods—had spewed out, and already a few opportunists were braving the snow and collecting cases, then hurrying with them to their cars.

Two state police patrol cars were at the scene. State troopers were questioning the truck driver, who appeared unhurt.

"All I did was touch the goddam brakes," the driver protested loudly. "Then she jackknifed, and rolled over like a whore in heat."

One of the policemen wrote in his notebook, and a woman murmured to a man beside her, "Do you think he's putting that last bit down?"

Another woman shouted, "Lotta good that'll do." Her voice was shrill against the wind. "Whyn't you cops get this thing moved?"

One of the state troopers walked across. Most of his uniform coat was already snow-covered. "If you'll give us a hand to lift, madam, we'd be glad to oblige."

A few people tittered, and the woman muttered, "Smart ass cops."

A tow truck, amber roof-beacon flashing, approached, moving slowly, on the opposite side of the obstruction. The driver was using the now unoccupied lanes on what would normally be the wrong side of the road. He stopped and got out, shaking his head doubtfully as he saw the size and position of the tractor-trailer.

Joe Patroni shoved forward. He puffed on his cigar, which glowed redly in the wind, and prodded the state trooper sharply on the shoulder. "Listen, son, you'll never move that rig with one tow truck. It'll be like hitching a tomtit to a brick."

The policeman turned. "Whatever it's like, mister, there's spilled gasoline around here. You'd better get that cigar out."

Patroni ignored the instruction, as he ignored almost all smoking regulations. He waved the cigar toward the over-turned tractor-trailer. "What's more, son, you'd be wasting everybody's time, including mine and yours, trying to get that hunk of junk right side up tonight. You'll have to drag it clear so traffic can move, and to do that you need two more tow trucks—one on this side to push, two over there to pull." He began moving around, using his electric lantern to inspect the big articulated vehicle from various angles. As always, when considering a problem, he was totally absorbed. He waved the cigar once more. "The two trucks together'll hitch on to three points. They'll pull the cab first, and faster. That'll overcome the jackknifing. The other truck . . ."

"Hold it," the state trooper said. He called across to one of the other officers. "Hank, there's a guy here sounds like he knows what he's talking about."

Ten minutes later, working with the police officers, Joe Patroni had virtually taken charge. Two additional tow trucks, as he had suggested, were being summoned by radio. While awaiting their arrival, the driver of the first tow truck was attaching chains, under Patroni's direction, to the axles of the capsized tractor-trailer. The situation had already assumed a proficient, get-on-with-it pattern—a trademark of any proceeding in which the energetic TWA maintenance chief became involved.

Patroni himself had remembered several times, with concern, his reason for being out at all tonight, and the fact that by now he was long overdue at the airport. But helping to clear the blocked highway, he calculated, was the fastest means of getting there. Obviously, his own car and others could not move forward until the wrecked tractor-trailer had been dragged clear from the center of the road. To go back and try an alternate route was equally impossible because traffic behind was backed up, with continuous lines of vehicles extending —so the police assured him—for miles to the rear.

He went back to his car to use the radio telephone he had installed at his employers' suggestion, and for which they picked up the monthly bills. He called the airline's maintenance department at the airport to report on his delay, and, in return, was informed of Mel Bakersfeld's message about the urgent need for runway three zero to be cleared and usable.

Joe Patroni gave some instructions over the telephone, but was aware that the most important thing was to be on the airfield himself as speedily as possible.

When he left the Buick for the second time, snow was still falling heavily. Dodging drifts which had formed around the line of waiting cars, he returned to the road block at a jog trot and was relieved to see that the first of the two extra tow trucks had arrived.

5

The elevator, which Mel Bakersfeld had taken after leaving Tanya, deposited him in the terminal basement. His official airport car—mustard yellow, and radio-equipped—was in a privileged parking stall close by.

Mel drove out, meeting the storm where the building exit joined an aircraft parking ramp outside. As he left the shelter of the terminal, wind and whirling snow slammed savagely against the car's windshield. The wiper blades slapped swiftly back and forth, though barely maintaining sufficient clear space for forward vision. Through a fractionally opened window, a blast of icy air and snow rushed in. Mel closed the window hastily. The transition from the terminal's warm snugness to the harshness of the night outside was startling.

Immediately ahead were airplanes parked at gate positions on the ramp. Through breaks in the snow, as the wind whipped and eddied around concourse buildings, Mel could see into the lighted interiors of several aircraft, which had passengers already seated. Obviously, several flights were ready to leave. These would be awaiting word from the tower to start engines, their continued delay a result of the blockage of runway three zero. Farther out on the airfield and runways, he could make out blurred shapes and navigation lights of other airplanes—recent arrivals, with engines running. These were in a holding area, which pilots called the penalty box, and would move in as gate positions became vacant. Undoubtedly, the same thing was happening in the other seven aircraft concourses grouped around the terminal.

The two-way radio in Mel's car, tuned to ground control frequency, crackled alive.

"Ground Control to Eastern seventeen," a controller intoned, "you are cleared to runway two five. Change frequency now for your airways clearance."

A burst of static. "Eastern seventeen. Roger."

A stronger voice rasped irritably. "Ground control from Pan Am fifty-four on outer taxiway to two five. There's a private Cessna in front—a twin-engine tortoise. I'm standing on my brakes to keep behind."

"Pan Am fifty-four, stand by." The briefest pause, then the controller's voice again: "Cessna seven three metro from ground control. Enter the next right intersection, hold, and let Pan American pass you."

Unexpectedly, a pleasant woman's voice responded.

"Ground control from Cessna seven three metro. I'm turning now. Go ahead, Pan Am, you great big bully."

A chuckle, then, "Thanks, honey. You can fix your lipstick while you wait."

The controller's voice rebuked. "Tower to all aircraft. Confine your messages to official business."

The controller was edgy, Mel could tell, despite the routine, studied calmness. But who wouldn't be tonight, with conditions and traffic the way they were? He thought uneasily again about his brother, Keith, involved with the unrelenting pressure of west arrival control.

The talk between tower and aircraft was continuous, with no gaps between transmissions. When one exchange ended, Mel snapped his own mike button down. "Ground control from mobile one. I'm at gate sixty-five, proceeding to runway three zero, site of the stuck 707."

He listened while the controller gave taxing instructions to two other flights which had just landed. Then: "Tower to mobile one. Roger, follow the Air Canada DC-9 pulling out of the gate ahead of you. Hold short of runway two one."

Mel acknowledged. He could see the Air Canada flight, at this moment easing out from a terminal gate, its high graceful tail an angular silhouette.

While still in the ramp area, he drove out toward the airfield carefully, watching for ramp lice—as airport men called the proliferation of vehicles which surrounded airplanes on the ground. As well as the usual ones, tonight there were several cherry pickers—trucks with high, maneuverable platforms at the end of steel, articulated arms. On the platforms, service crews were reaching out to clear snow from aircraft wings, and spraying glycol to retard ice formation. The men themselves were snow-covered in their exposed position.

Mel braked hastily, avoiding a speeding honey wagon, on its way from the ramp area to disgorge its malodorous four-hundred gallon load of contents pumped out from aircraft toilets. The load would eject into a shredding machine in a special building which other airport employees avoided, and then be pumped to city sewers. Most times the procedure worked efficiently, except when passengers reported losses of items—dentures, purses, wallets, even shoes—dropped accidentally in aircraft toilets. It happened once or twice a day. Then loads had to be sifted, while everyone hoped the missing item could be located quickly.

Even without incidents, Mel realized, this would be a busy night for sanitary crews. Airport managements knew from experience that demands on toilet facilities, on the ground and in the air, increased as weather worsened. Mel wondered how many people were aware that airport sanitary supervisors received hourly weather forecasts and made their plans—for extra cleaning and increased supplies—accordingly.

The Air Canada jet he was to follow had cleared the terminal and was increasing taxi speed. Mel accelerated to keep up. It was reassuring—with windshield wipers barely coping with the snow—to have the DC-9's tail-light as a reference point ahead. Through the rear mirror he could make out the shape of another, larger jet now following. On radio, the ground controller cautioned, "Air France four-o-four, there is an airport ground vehicle between you and Air Canada."

It took a quarter of an hour to reach the intersection where runway three zero was blocked by the Aéreo-Mexican 707. Before then, Mel had separated from the stream of taxiing aircraft which were destined for takeoff on the two other active runways.

He stopped the car and got out. In the dark and loneliness out here, the storm seemed even more wintry and violent than nearer the terminal. The wind howled across the deserted runway. If wolves appeared tonight, Mel thought, it would not be surprising.

A shadowy figure hailed him. "Is that Mr. Patroni?"

"No, it isn't." Mel found that he, too, had to shout to make himself heard above the wind. "But Joe Patroni's on the way."

The other man came closer. He was huddled into a parka, his face blue with cold. "When he gets here, we'll be glad to see him. Though I'm damned if I know what

Patroni'll do. We've tried about everything to get this bastard out." He gestured to the airplane looming, shadowy, behind them. "She's stuck, but good."

Mel identified himself, then asked, "Who are you?"

"Ingram, sir. Aéreo-Mexican maintenance foreman. Right now, I wish I had some other job."

As the two men talked, they moved nearer to the stalled Boeing 707, instinctively seeking shelter under the wings and fuselage, high above them. Under the big jet's belly, a red hazard light winked rhythmically. In its reflection Mel could see the mud beneath snow in which the aircraft's wheels were deeply mired. On the runway and adjoining taxiway, clustered like anxious relatives, were a profusion of trucks and service vehicles, including a fuel tanker, baggage tenders, a post office van, two crew buses, and a roaring power cart.

Mel pulled the collar of his topcoat tightly around him. "We need this runway urgently—tonight. What have you done so far?"

In the past two hours, Ingram reported, old-fashioned boarding ramps had been trundled from the terminal, manhandled to the aircraft, and passengers guided down them. It had been a slow, tricky job because steps were icing as fast as they were cleared. An elderly woman had been carried down by two mechanics. Babies were passed from hand to hand in blankets. Now, all passengers were gone—in buses, along with the stewardesses and the second officer. The captain and first officer remained.

"Since the passengers left—have you tried to get the airplane moving?"

The foreman nodded affirmatively. "Had the engines running twice. The captain's put on all the power he dare. But she won't come free. Just seems to dig herself in deeper."

"What's happening now?"

"We're taking off more weight, hoping that'll help." Most of the fuel, Ingram added, had been sucked out by tankers—a heavy load since tanks were full for takeoff. Baggage and freight compartments in the belly had been emptied. A post office truck was retrieving mailbags.

Mel nodded. The mail, he knew, would have come off anyway. The airport post office kept a minute-to-minute watch on airline schedules. They knew exactly where their mailbags were and, if delays occurred, postal employees quickly switched mail from one airline to another. Mail from the stranded jet, in fact, would fare better than passengers. In half an hour at most, it would be on its way by another flight, if necessary on an alternate route.

Mel asked, "Have you all the help you need?"

"Yes, sir—for all we can do now. I've got most of our crew from Aéreo-Mexican here—a dozen men. Right now, half of 'em are thawing out in one of the buses. Patroni may want more people, depending on what his ideas are." Ingram turned, surveying the silent aircraft gloomily. "But if you ask me, it's going to be a long job, and we'll need heavy cranes, jacks, and maybe pneumatic bags to lift the wings. For most of those, we'd have to wait until daylight. The whole thing could take most of tomorrow."

Mel said sharply, "It can't take most of tomorrow, or even tonight. This runway has to be cleared . . ." He stopped abruptly, shivering with a suddenness which startled him. The intensity was unexpected, almost eerie.

Mel shivered again. What was it? He assured himself: the weather—the fierce, harsh wind across the airport, driving the whirling snow. Yet, strangely, since leaving the car until this moment, his body had adjusted to the cold.

From the opposite side of the airfield, above the wind, he could hear the thunder of jet engines. They rose to a crescendo, then diminished as a flight took off. Another followed, and another. Over there, all was well.

And here?

It was true, wasn't it?—for the briefest instant he had had a premonition. A hint, no more; an intuition; the smell of greater trouble brewing. He should ignore it, of course; impulse, premonitions, had no place in pragmatic management. Except that once, long ago, he had had the selfsame feeling—a conviction of events accumulating, and progressing to some disastrous, unenvisaged end. Mel remembered the end, which he had been unable to avert . . . entirely.

He glanced at the 707 again. It was snow-covered now, its outline blurring. Commonsense told him: apart from the runway blockage and the inconvenience of takeoffs over Meadowood, the situation was harmless. There had been a mishap, with no injuries, no apparent damage. Nothing more.

"Let's go to my car," he told the Aéreo-Mexican foreman. "We'll get on the radio and find out what's happening."

On the way, he reminded himself that Cindy would shortly be waiting impatiently downtown.

Mel had left the car heater turned on, and inside the car it was comfortingly warm. Ingram grunted appreciatively. He loosened his coat and bent forward to hold his hands in the stream of warm air.

Mel switched the radio to the frequency of airport maintenance.

"Mobile one to Snow Desk. Danny, I'm at the blocked intersection of three zero. Call TWA maintenance and check on Joe Patroni. Where is he? When coming? Over."

Danny Farrow's voice crisped back through the speaker on the dash. "Snow Desk to mobile one. Wilco. And, Mel, your wife called."

Mel pressed the mike button. "Did she leave a number?"

"Affirmative."

"Mobile one to Snow Desk. Please call her, Danny. Tell her I'm sorry, I'll be a little late. But check on Patroni first."

"Understood. Stand by." The radio went silent.

Mel reached inside his topcoat for a pack of Marlboros. He offered them to Ingram.

"Thanks."

They lit up, watching the windshield wipers slap back and forth.

Ingram nodded toward the lighted cockpit of the Aéreo-Mexican jet. "Up there, that son-of-a-bitch of a captain is probably crying into his sombrero. Next time, he'll watch blue taxi lights like they was altar candles."

Mel asked, "Are your ground crews Mexicans or American?"

"We're all American. Only meatheads like us would work in this lousy weather. Know where that flight was going?"

Mel shook his head.

"Acapulco. Before this happened, I'd have given up six months' screwing to be on it." The foreman chuckled. "Can you imagine, though—getting aboard, and your ass all settled, then having to get off in this. You should have heard the passengers cursing, especially the women. I learned some new words tonight."

The radio came alive again.

"Snow Desk to mobile one," Danny Farrow said. "I talked with TWA about Joe Patroni. They've heard from him, but he's held up in traffic. He'll be another hour, at least. He sent a message. You read me so far?"

"We read," Mel said. "Let's have the message."

"Patroni warns not to get the airplane deeper in the mud than it is already. Says it can happen easily. So, unless the Aéreo-Mexican crowd are real sure of what they're doing, they should hold off any more tries until Joe gets there."

Mel glanced sideways at Ingram. "How does the Aéreo-Mexican crowd feel about that?"

The foreman nodded. "Patroni can have all the tries he wants. We'll wait."

Danny Farrow said, "Did you get that? Is it clear?"

Mel thumbed the mike button. "It's clear."

"Okay. There's more. TWA is rounding up some extra ground crew to help. And, Mel, your wife phoned again. I gave her your message." Mel sensed Danny hesitating, aware that others whose radios were on the airport maintenance frequency were listening, too.

Mel said, "She wasn't happy?"

"I guess not." There was a second's silence. "You'd better get to a phone when you can."

It was a safe bet, Mel thought, that Cindy had been

more than usually snippy with Danny, but, loyally, he
wasn't saying so.

As for the Aéreo-Mexican 707, obviously there was
nothing more to be done until Joe Patroni arrived. Patroni's advice about not getting the aircraft more deeply
mired made good sense.

Ingram was pulling on heavy mitts and refastening his
coat. "Thanks for the warm-up." He went out, into the
wind and snow, slamming the door quickly. A few moments later, Mel could see him plodding through deep
drifts toward the assembled vehicles on the taxiway.

On radio, the Snow Desk was speaking to Maintenance Snow Center. Mel waited until the exchange
finished, then held the transmit button down. "This is
mobile one, Danny. I'm going to the Conga Line."

He eased the car forward, picking his way carefully in
the blowing snow and darkness, with only widely spaced
runway lights to guide him.

The Conga Line, both spearhead and prime mover of
the airport snow-fighting system, was—at the moment
—on runway one seven, left. In a few minutes, Mel
thought grimly, he would find out for himself if there
was truth, or merely malice, in the critical report of
Captain Demerest's Airlines Snow Committee.

6

The subject of Mel's thoughts—Captain Vernon Demerest of Trans America—was, at the moment, some
three miles from the airport. He was driving his Mercedes 230 SL Roadster and, compared with the journey
he had made to the airport earlier from home, was
having little trouble negotiating local streets, which had
been recently plowed. Snow was still falling heavily,
abetted by a strong wind, but the fresh covering on the

ground was not yet deep enough to make conditions difficult.

Demerest's destination was a group of three-story apartment blocks, close to the airport, known colloquially to flying crews as Stewardess Row. It was here that many of the stewardesses based at Lincoln International—from all airlines—maintained apartments. Each apartment was usually shared by two or three girls, and the initiated also had a name for the individual ménages. They were known as stewardess nests.

The nests were often the scene of lively, off-duty parties, and sometimes headquarters for the amorous affairs which occurred, with predictable regularity, between stewardesses and male flying crews.

Taken as a whole, the stewardess nests were neither more nor less freewheeling than other apartments occupied by single girls elsewhere. The difference was that most of what transpired in the way of swinging, amoral activities, involved airline personnel.

There was good reason for this. Both the stewardesses and male crew members whom they met—captains, and first and second officers—were, without exception, high-caliber people. All had reached their jobs, which many others coveted, through a tough, exacting process of elimination in which those less talented were totally eclipsed. The comparative few who remained were the brightest and best. The result was a broth of sharp, enlightened personalities with a zest for life and the perceptiveness to appreciate one another.

Vernon Demerest, in his time, had appreciated many stewardesses, as they had appreciated him. He had, in fact, had a succession of affairs with beautiful and intelligent young women whom a monarch or a male movie idol might well have desired without attaining. The stewardesses whom Demerest and fellow pilots knew, and regularly made love to, were neither whores nor easy lays. They were, however, alive, responsive, and sexually endowed girls, who valued quality, and took it when so obviously and conveniently close to hand.

One who had taken it—so to speak—from Vernon Demerest, and seemed inclined to continue to, was a vivacious, attractive, English-born brunette, Gwen Meighen. She was a farmer's daughter who had left home to come to the United States ten years earlier at the age of eighteen. Before joining Trans America she was briefly a fashion model in Chicago. Perhaps because of her varied background, she combined an uninhibited sexuality in bed with elegance and style when out of it.

It was to Gwen Meighen's apartment that Vernon Demerest was headed now.

Later tonight, the two of them would leave for Rome on Trans America Flight Two. On the flight deck, Captain Demerest would command. In the passenger cabins, aft, Gwen Meighen would be senior stewardess. At the Rome end of the journey, there would be a three-day layover for the crew, while another crew—already in Italy for its own layover—would fly the airplane back to Lincoln International.

The word "layover" had long ago been adopted officially by airlines and was used deadpan. Possibly, whoever coined the term had a sense of humor; in any case, flying crews frequently gave it a practical application as well as its official one. Demerest and Gwen Meighen were planning a personal definition now. On arrival in Rome, they would leave immediately for Naples for a forty-eight-hour "layover" together It was a halcyon, idyllic prospect, and Vernon Demerest smiled appreciatively at the thought of it He was nearing Stewardess Row, and as he reminded himself of how well other things had gone this evening, his smile broadened.

He had arrived at the airport early, after leaving Sarah, his wife, who—placidly as usual—had wished him a pleasant trip. In an earlier age, Sarah might have busied herself with needlepoint or knitting during her liege's absence. As it was, he knew that as soon as he had left, she would become immersed in her curling club, bridge, and amateur oil painting which were the mainstays of her life.

Sarah Demerest's placidity, and her dullness which naturally went with it, were qualities her husband had come to accept and, in a perverse way, valued. Between

flying trips and affairs with more interesting women, he
thought of his sojourns at home, and sometimes spoke
of them to intimates, as "going into the hangar for a
stand down." His marriage had another convenience.
While it existed, the women he made love to could
become as emotional and demanding as they liked, but
he could never be expected to meet the ultimate demand
of matrimony. In this way, he had a perpetual protection against his own hasty action in the heat of passion.
As to sexual intimacy with Sarah, he still obliged her
occasionally, as one would play "throw the ball" with
an old dog. Sarah responded dutifully, with conventional body heavings and quickened breath, though he
suspected both were more from rote than passion, and
that if they quit copulation entirely she would not be
overly concerned. He was also sure that Sarah suspected
his philandering, if not in fact, then at least by instinct.
But, characteristically, she would prefer not to know, an
arrangement in which Vernon Demerest was happy to
cooperate.

Another thing which had pleased him this evening
was the Airlines Snow Committee report in which he
had delivered a verbal kick in the crotch, aimed at his
stuffed-shirt brother-in-law, Mel Bakersfeld.

The critical report had been solely Demerest's idea.
The other two airline representatives on the committee
had at first taken the view that the airport management
was doing its best under exceptional conditions. Captain
Demerest argued otherwise. The others had finally gone
along with him and agreed that Demerest would personally write the report, which he made as scathing as he
could. He had not bothered about accuracy or otherwise
of the indictment; after all, with so much snow around,
who could be sure of anything? He had, however, made
certain that the widely circulated report would cause a
maximum of embarrassment and irritation to Mel Bakersfeld. Copies were now being Xeroxed and would be
sent to regional vice-presidents of all airlines, as well as
airline headquarters, in New York and elsewhere.
Knowing how everyone enjoyed finding a scapegoat for

operational delays, Captain Demerest was confident that telephones and teletypes would be busy after its receipt.

A revenge, Vernon Demerest thought pleasurably—small but satisfying—had been exacted. Now, perhaps, his limping, quarter-cripple brother-in-law would think twice before antagonizing Captain Demerest and the Air Line Pilots Association, as Mel Bakersfeld had presumed to do—in public—two weeks ago.

Captain Demerest swung the Mercedes into an apartment building parking lot. He stopped the car smoothly and got out. He was a little early, he noticed—a quarter of an hour before the time he had said he would collect Gwen and drive her to the airport. He decided to go up, anyway.

As he entered the building, using the passkey Gwen had given him, he hummed softly to himself, then smiled, realizing the tune was *O Sole Mio*. Well, why not? It was appropriate. Naples . . . a warm night instead of snow, the view above the bay in starlight, soft music from mandolins, Chianti with dinner, and Gwen Meighen beside him . . . . all were less than twenty-four hours away. Yes, indeed!—*O Sole Mio*. He continued humming it.

In the elevator going up, he remembered another good thing. The flight to Rome would be an easy one.

Tonight, though Captain Demerest was in command of Flight Two—*The Golden Argosy*—he would do little of the work which the flight entailed. The reason was that he was flying as a line check captain. Another four-striper captain—Anson Harris, almost as senior as Demerest himself—had been assigned to the flight and would occupy the command pilot's left seat. Demerest would use the right seat—normally the first officer's position—from where he would observe and report on Captain Harris's performance.

The check flight arrangement had come up because Captain Harris had elected to transfer from Trans America domestic operations to international. However, before flying as a full-fledged international captain, he was required to make two flights over an overseas route with a regular line captain who also held instructor's qualifications. Vernon Demerest did.

After Captain Harris's two flights, of which tonight's would be the second, he would be given a final check by a senior supervisory captain before being accepted for international command.

Such checks—as well as regular six-monthly check flights, which all pilots of all airlines were required to undergo—entailed an aerial scrutiny of ability and flying habits. The checks took place on ordinary scheduled flights, and the only indication a passenger might have that one was in progress would be the presence of two four-striper captains on the flight deck up front.

Despite the fact that captains checked each other, the tests, both regular and special, were usually serious, exacting sessions. The pilots wanted them that way. Too much was at stake—public safety and high professional standards—for any mutual back-scratching, or for weaknesses to be overlooked. A captain being checked was aware that he must measure up to required standards in all respects. Failure to do so would mean an automatic adverse report which, if serious enough, could lead to an even tougher session with the airline's chief pilot, with the testee's job in jeopardy.

Yet, while performance standards were not relaxed, senior captains undergoing flight checks were treated by their colleagues with meticulous courtesy. Except by Vernon Demerest.

Demerest treated any pilot he was assigned to test, junior or senior to himself, in precisely the same way— like an errant schoolboy summoned to the headmaster's presence. Moreover, in the headmaster's role, Demerest was officious, arrogant, condescending, and tough. He made no secret of his conviction that no one else's ability as a pilot was superior to his own. Colleagues who received this brand of treatment raged inwardly, but had no choice but to sit and take it. Subsequently they vowed to one another that when Demerest's own time came they would give him the meanest, toughest check ride he had ever had. They invariably did, with a single consistent result—Vernon Demerest turned in a flawless performance which could not be faulted.

This afternoon, characteristically, Demerest prefaced his check session by telephoning Captain Anson Harris at home. "It'll be a bad night for driving," Demerest said without preamble. "I like my crew to be punctual, so I suggest you allow plenty of time to get to the airport."

Anson Harris, who in twenty-two unblemished years with Trans America had never been late for a single flight, was so outraged, he almost choked. Fortunately, before Harris could get any words out, Captain Demerest hung up.

Still fuming, but to make absolutely sure that Demerest would not catch him out, Captain Harris had arrived at the airport almost three hours ahead of flight time instead of the usual one hour. Captain Demerest, fresh from his stint with the Airlines Snow Committee, had encountered Harris in the Cloud Captain's Coffee Shop. Demerest was wearing a sports jacket and slacks; he kept a spare uniform in his airport locker and planned to change into it later. Captain Harris, a graying, grizzled veteran whom many younger pilots addressed as "sir," was in Trans America uniform.

"Hi, Anson." Vernon Demerest dropped into an adjoining seat at the counter. "I see you took my good advice."

Captain Harris's grip on his coffee cup tightened slightly, but all he said was, "Good evening, Vern."

"We'll start the pre-flight briefing twenty minutes earlier than usual," Demerest said. "I want to check your flight manuals."

Thank God, Harris thought, his wife had gone through his manuals only yesterday, inserting the very latest amendments. But he had better check his mail slot in the dispatch office. This bastard was likely to fault him for not making an amendment published only this afternoon. To give his hands—which were itching— something to do, Captain Harris filled and lit his pipe.

He was aware of Vernon Demerest looking at him critically.

"You're not wearing a regulation shirt."

For a moment, Captain Harris could not believe his colleague was serious. Then, as he realized he was, Harris's face suffused a deep plum red.

Regulation shirts were an irritant to Trans America pilots, as they were to pilots of other airlines. Obtainable through company sources, the official shirts cost nine dollars each, and were often ill fitting, their material of dubious quality. Though contrary to regulations, a much better shirt could be purchased independently for several dollars less, with the difference in appearance scarcely noticeable. Most pilots bought the unofficial shirts and wore them. *Vernon Demerest did too.* On several occasions Anson Harris had heard Demerest speak disdainfully of the company's shirts and point to the superior quality of his own.

Captain Demerest motioned to a waitress for coffee, then reassured Harris, "It's all right. I won't report on your wearing a non-reg shirt here. As long as you change it before you come on my flight."

Hold on! Anson Harris told himself. *Dear God in heaven, give me strength not to blow, which is probably what the ornery son-of-a-bitch wants. But why? Why?*

All right. All right, he decided; indignity or not, he would change his unofficial shirt for a regulation one. He would not give Demerest the satisfaction of having a single miniscule check point on which to fault him. It would be difficult to get a company shirt tonight. He would probably have to borrow one—exchange shirts with some other captain or first officer. When he told them why, they would hardly believe him. He hardly believed it himself.

But when Demerest's own check flight came up . . . *the next, and all others from this moment on . . . let him beware.* Anson Harris had good friends among the supervisory pilots. Let Demerest be wearing a regulation shirt; let him hew to regulations in every other trifling way . . . *or else.* Then Harris thought glumly: The foxy bastard will remember; he'll make sure he does.

"Hey, Anson!" Demerest seemed amused. "You've bitten off the end of your pipe."

And so he had.

Remembering, Vernon Demerest chuckled. Yes, it *would* be an easy flight tonight—for him.

His thoughts returned to the present as the apartment block elevator stopped at the third floor. He stepped into the carpeted corridor and turned to the left familiarly, heading for the apartment which Gwen Meighen shared with a stewardess of United Air Lines. The other girl, Demerest knew because Gwen had told him, was away on an overnight flight. On the apartment door bell he tapped out their usual signal, his initials in Morse . . . dit-dit-dit-dah dah-dit-dit . . . then went in, using the same key which opened the door below.

Gwen was in the shower. He could hear the water running. When he went to her bedroom door, she called out, "Vernon, is that you?" Even competing with the shower, her voice—with its flawless English accent, which he liked so much— sounded mellow and exciting. He thought: Small wonder Gwen had so much success with passengers. He had seen them appear to melt—the men especially—when her natural charm was turned toward them.

He called back, "Yes, honey."

Her filmy underthings were laid out on the bed—panties, sheer nylons; a transparent bra, flesh colored, with a girdle of the same material; a French silk, hand-embroidered slip. Gwen's uniform might be standard, but beneath it she believed in expensive individuality. His senses quickened; he moved his eyes away reluctantly.

"I'm glad you came early," she called again. "I want to have a talk before we leave."

"Sure, we've time."

"You can make tea, if you like."

"Okay."

She had converted him to the English habit of tea at all times of day, though he had scarcely ever drunk tea at all until knowing Gwen. But now he often asked for it at home, a request which puzzled Sarah, particularly when he insisted on it being correctly made—the pot warmed first, as Gwen had taught him, the water still boiling at the instant it touched the tea.

He went to the tiny kitchen, where he knew his way around, and put a kettle of water on the stove. He poured milk into a jug from a carton in the refrigerator, then drank some milk himself before putting the carton back. He would have preferred a Scotch and soda, but, like most pilots, abstained from liquor for twenty-four hours before a flight. Out of habit he checked his watch; it showed a few minutes before 8:00 P.M. At this moment, he realized, the sleek, long-range Boeing 707 jet which he would command on its five-thousand mile flight to Rome, was being readied for him at the airport.

He heard the shower stop. In the silence he began humming once again. Happily. *O Sole Mio.*

7

The blustering, biting wind across the airfield was as strong as ever, and still driving the heavily falling snow before it.

Inside his car, Mel Bakersfeld shivered. He was heading for runway one seven, left, which was being plowed, after leaving runway three zero and the stranded Aéreo-Mexican jet. Was the shivering due to the cold outside, Mel wondered, or to memory, which the scent of trouble a few minutes ago, plus the nagging reminder from the old injury of his foot, had triggered?

The injury had happened sixteen years ago off the coast of Korea when Mel had been a Navy pilot flying fighter missions from the carrier *Essex*. Through the previous twelve hours (he remembered clearly, even now) he had had a presentiment of trouble coming. It wasn't fear—like others, he had learned to live with that; rather, a conviction that something fateful, possibly final, was moving inexorably toward him. Next day, in a dogfight with a MIG-15, Mel's Navy F9F-5 had been shot down into the sea.

He managed a controlled ditching, but though unhurt himself, his left foot was trapped by a jammed rudder pedal. With the airplane sinking fast—an F9F-5 had the floating characteristics of a brick—Mel used a survival-kit hunting knife to slash desperately, wildly, at his foot and the pedal. Somehow, underwater, his foot came free. In intense pain, half-drowned, he surfaced.

He had spent the next eight hours in the sea before being picked up, unconscious. Later he learned he had severed the ligaments in front of his ankle, so that the foot extended from his leg in an almost straight line.

In time, Navy medics repaired the foot, though Mel had never flown—as a pilot—since then. But at intervals the pain still returned, reminding him that long ago, as on other later occasions, his instinct for trouble had been right. He had the same kind of instinct now.

Handling his car cautiously, being careful to retain his bearings in the darkness and restricted visibility, Mel was nearing runway one seven, left. This was the runway which, the tower chief had indicated, Air Traffic Control would seek to use when the wind shifted as was forecast to happen soon.

At the moment, on the airfield, two runways were in use: one seven, right, and runway two five.

Lincoln International had five runways altogether. Through the past three days and nights they had represented the front line of the battle between the airport and the storm.

The longest and widest of the five was three zero, the runway now obstructed by Aéreo-Mexican. (With a change of wind and an aircraft approaching from the opposite direction, it could also be runway one two. The figures indicated compass headings of 300 and 120 degrees.) This runway was almost two miles long and as wide as a short city block; an airport joke claimed that one end could not be seen from the other because of the earth's curvature.

Each of the other four runways was half a mile or so shorter, and less wide.

Without ceasing, since the storm began, the miles of runways had been plowed, vacuumed, brushed, and sanded. The motorized equipment—several million dollars' worth of roaring diesels—had stopped only minutes at a time, mainly for refueling or relieving crews. It was work which air travelers never saw at close hand because no aircraft used a fresh-cleared runway until the surface had been inspected and declared safe. Standards were exacting. Half an inch of slush or three inches of powdery snow were maximums allowable for jets. More than that would be sucked into engines and endanger operation.

It was a pity, Mel Bakersfeld reflected, that runway snow teams were not more on public view. The sight was spectacular and stirring. Even now, in storm and darkness, approaching the massed equipment from the rear, the effect was impressive. Giant columns of snow cascaded to the right in arcs of a hundred and fifty feet. The arcs were framed in vehicle searchlights, and shimmered from the added color of some twenty revolving beacons—one on the roof of each vehicle in the group.

Airport men called the group a Conga Line.

It had a head, a tail, a body, and an entourage, and it progressed down a runway with the precision of choreography.

A convoy leader was the head. He was a senior foreman from airport maintenance and drove an airport car—bright yellow, like all other equipment in the Line. The leader set the Conga Line pace, which was usually fast. He had two radios and remained permanently in touch with the Snow Desk and Air Traffic Control. By a system of lights, he could signal drivers following— green for "speed up," amber for "maintain pace," red for "slow down," and flashing red for "stop." He was required to carry in his head a detailed map of the airport, and must know precisely where he was, even on the darkest night, as now.

Behind the convoy leader, its driver, like an orchestra's first violinist, was the number one plow—tonight a mammoth Oshkosh with a big main blade ahead, and a wing blade to the side. To the rear of number one plow, and on its right, was number two. The first plow heaved the snow aside; the second accepted the load from the first and, adding more, heaved both lots farther.

Then came a Snowblast, in echelon with the plows, six hundred roaring horsepower strong. A Snowblast cost sixty thousand dollars and was the Cadillac of snow clearance. With mighty blowers it engulfed the snow which both plows piled, and hurled it in a herculean arc beyond the runway's edge.

In a second echelon, farther to the right, were two more plows, a second Snowblast.

After the plows and Snowblasts came the graders— five in line abreast, with plow blades down to clear any mounds the front plows missed. The graders towed re- volving brushes, each sixteen feet wide and indepen- dently diesel powered. The brushes scoured the runway surface like monstrous yard brooms.

Next were sanders. Where the eleven vehicles ahead had cleared, three hulking FWD trucks, with hoppers holding fourteen cubic yards apiece, spread sand out evenly.

The sand was special. Elsewhere around the airport, on roadways and areas which the public used, salt was added to the sand as a means of melting ice. But never for aeronautical areas. Salt corroded metal, shortening its life, and airplanes were treated with more respect than cars.

Last in the Conga Line itself—"tail-end Charlie"— was an assistant foreman in a second car. His job was to insure that the line stayed intact and to chivvy strag- glers. He was in radio touch with the convoy leader, often out of sight ahead in snow and darkness.

Finally came the entourage—a standby plow, in case one faltered in the Line; a service truck with a detail of mechanics; refueling tankers—diesel and gasoline; and —when summoned by radio at appointed times—a coffee and doughnut wagon.

Mel accelerated around the entourage and positioned his car alongside the assistant foreman's. His arrival was noticed. He heard the convoy leader notified by radio, "Mr. Bakersfeld just joined us."

The Line was moving fast—close to forty miles an hour instead of its usual twenty-five. The leader had probably speeded up because of the expected wind shift and the need to have the runway open soon.

Switching his radio to ATC ground frequency, Mel heard the convoy leader call the tower, ". . . on one seven, left, approaching intersection with runway two five. Request clearance over intersection."

Runway two five was an active runway, now in use.

"Convoy leader from ground control, hold short of the intersection. We have two flights on final approach. You may not, repeat, not, cross runway intersection. Acknowledge."

The voice from the tower was apologetic. Up there, they understood the difficulty of stopping a rolling Conga Line, and getting it started again. But the approaching flights had undoubtedly made a tricky instrument descent and now were close to landing, one behind the other. Only a desperate emergency would justify sending them round again on such a night.

Ahead of Mel, red lights were going on, flashing commandingly as the Conga Line slowed and stopped.

The assistant foreman, a cheerful young Negro, jumped from his car and came across to Mel's. As he opened the door, the wind swept in, but could only be felt, not heard, above the encompassing roar of idling diesels. The assistant put his mouth against Mel's ear. "Say, Mr. B., how's about joining the Line? One of the boys'll take care of your car."

Mel grinned. The pleasure he got, whenever he could spare time, from riding and occasionally handling heavy motorized equipment was well known around the airport. Why not? he reasoned. He had come out to inspect the snow clearance as a result of the adverse report by Vernon Demerest's Airlines Snow Committee. Clearly, the report was unjustified, and everything was going well. But maybe he should watch a few minutes longer from a ringside perch.

Nodding agreement, he shouted, "Okay, I'll ride the second Snowblast."

"Yessir!"

The assistant foreman, carrying a hand searchlight and leaning against the wind, preceded Mel past the now stationary lines of sand trucks and brushes. Mel observed that already fresh snow was starting to cover the runway area cleared only moments ago. To the rear, a figure ducked from a service truck and hastened to Mel's car.

"Better hurry, Mr. B. It's only a short stop." The young Negro flashed his light at the Snowblast cab, then held it steady, illuminating the way, as Mel clambered up. High above, the Snowblast driver opened the cab door and held it while Mel eased inside. On the way up, his impaired foot pained him sharply, but there was no time to wait. Ahead, the flashing red lights had already changed to green, and presumably the two approaching aircraft had now landed and were past the intersection. The Conga Line must hurry across before the next landing, perhaps only a minute or two away. Glancing to the rear, Mel could see the assistant foreman sprinting back toward his tail-end-Charlie car.

The Snowblast was already moving, picking up speed with a deep-throated roar. Its driver glanced sideways as Mel slipped into one of the two soft, padded seats.

"Hi, Mr. Bakersfeld."

"How are you, Will?" Mel recognized the man, who, when there was no snow emergency, was employed by the airport as a payroll clerk.

"I'm pretty good, sir. Tired some."

The driver was holding position carefully behind the third and fourth plows, their beacon lights just visible. Already the Snowblast's huge auger blades were engorging snow, cramming it to the blower. Once more, a continuous white stream was arcing outward, clear of the runway.

Up here was like the bridge of a ship. The driver held his main control wheel lightly, like a helmsman. A multitude of dials and levers, glowing in the darkness, were arranged for fingertip control. Circular, high-speed windshield wipers—as on a ship—provided ports of clear vision through encrusted snow.

"I guess everyone's tired," Mel said. "All I can tell you is that this can't last forever."

He watched the forward speed needle climb—from twenty-five to thirty, thirty to thirty-five. Swinging in his seat, Mel surveyed outside. From this position, at the center of the Conga Line, he could see the lights and shapes of the other vehicles. He noted approvingly that the formation was exact.

A few years ago, in a storm like this, an airport would have closed completely. Now it didn't, mainly because ground facilities—in this one area—had caught up with progress in the air. But of how many areas of aviation could the same thing be said? Mel reflected ruefully: very few.

"Oh, well," the driver said, "it makes a change from working an adding machine, and the longer this keeps up, the more extra pay there'll be when it's over." He touched a lever, tilting the cab forward to inspect the auger blades. With another control he adjusted the blades, then releveled the cab. "I don't have to do this; you know that, Mr. Bakersfeld, I volunteer. But I kinda like it out here. It's sort of . . ." He hesitated. "I dunno."

Mel suggested, "Elemental?"

"I guess so." The driver laughed. "Maybe I'm snow happy."

"No, Will, I don't believe you are." Mel swung forward, facing the way the Conga Line was moving. It *was* elemental here. More to the point, amid the air-fields loneliness there was a feeling of closeness to avia-tion, the real aviation which in its simplest sense was man against the elements. You lost that kind of feeling if you stayed too long in terminals and airline office buildings; there, the extraneous, non-essential things confused you. Maybe all of us in aviation management, Mel thought, should stand at the distant end of a runway once in a while, and feel the wind on our faces. It could help to separate detail from fundamentals. It might even ventilate our brains as well.

Sometimes in the past Mel had gone out onto the airfield when he needed to think, to reason quietly and alone. He had not expected to tonight, but found himself doing so now . . . wondering, speculating, as he had so often in recent days, about the airport's future and his own.

8

Less than a lustrum ago, the airport was considered among the world's finest and most modern. Delegations inspected it admiringly. Civic politicians were given to pointing with pride and would huff and puff about "air leadership" and "a symbol of the jet age." Nowadays the politicians still huffed and puffed, but with less reason. What most failed to realize was that Lincoln International, like a surprising number of other major airports, was close to becoming a whited sepulcher.

Mel Bakersfeld pondered the phrase *whited sepulcher* while riding in darkness down runway one seven, left. It was an apt definition, he thought. The airport's deficiencies were serious and basic, yet, since they were mostly out of public view, only insiders were aware of them.

Travelers and visitors at Lincoln International saw principally the main passenger terminal—a brightly lighted, air-conditioned Taj Mahal. Of gleaming glass and chrome, the terminal was impressively spacious, its thronged concourses adjoining elegant waiting areas. Opulent service facilities ringed the passenger area. Six specialty restaurants ranged from a gourmet dining room, with gold-edged china and matching prices, to a grab-it-and-run hot dog counter. Bars, cozily darkened or stand-up and neon lit, were plentiful as toilets. While waiting for a flight, and without ever leaving the terminal, a visitor could shop, rent a room and bed, and take a steam bath with massage, have his hair cut, suit pressed, shoes shined, or even die and have his burial arranged by Holy Ghost Memorial Gardens which maintained a sales office on the lower concourse.

Judged by its terminal alone, the airport was still spectacular. Where its deficiencies lay were in operating areas, notably runways and taxiways.

Few of the eighty thousand passengers who flew in and out each day were aware of how inadequate—and therefore hazardous—the runway system had become. Even a year previously, runways and taxiways were barely sufficient; now, they were dangerously overtaxed. In normally busy periods, on two main runways, a takeoff or landing occurred every thirty seconds. The Meadowood situation, and the consideration the airport showed to community residents, made it necessary, at peak periods, to use an alternative runway which bisected one of the other two. As a result, aircraft took off and landed on converging courses, and there were moments when air traffic controllers held their breath and prayed. Only last week Keith Bakersfeld, Mel's brother, had predicted grimly, "Okay, so we stay on our toes in the tower, and we cope with the hairy ones, and we haven't brought two airplanes together at that intersection yet. But someday there'll be a second's inattention or misjudgment, and one of us will. I hope to God it isn't me because when it happens it'll be the Grand Canyon all over again."

The intersection Keith had spoken of was the one which the Conga Line had just passed over. In the cab of the Snowblast, Mel glanced to the rear. The Conga Line was well clear of the intersection now, and, through a momentary gap in the snow, airplane navigation lights were visible on the other runway, moving swiftly as a flight took off. Then, incredibly, there were more lights only a few yards behind as another flight landed, it seemed at the same instant.

The Snowblast driver had turned his head also. He whistled. "Those two were pretty close."

Mel nodded. They *had* been close, exceptionally so, and for an instant his flesh had prickled with alarm. Obviously, what had happened was that an air traffic controller, instructing the pilots of both airplanes by radio, had cut tolerances exceedingly fine. As usual, the controller's skilled judgment had proven right, though only just. The two flights were safe—one now in the air, the other on the ground. But it was the need for a multiplicity of such hairbreadth judgments which created an unceasing hazard.

Mel had pointed out the hazard frequently to the Board of Airport Commissioners and to members of City Council, who controlled airport financing. As well as immediate construction of more runways and taxiways, Mel had urged purchase of additional land around the airport for long term development. There had been plenty of discussion, and sometimes angry argument, as a result. A few Board and Council members saw things the way Mel did, but others took a strongly counter view. It was hard to convince people that a modern jetport, built in the late 1950s, could so quickly have become inadequate to the point of danger. It made no difference that the same was true of other centers—New York, San Francisco, Chicago, and elsewhere; there were certain things which politicians simply did not want to see.

Mel thought: maybe Keith was right. Perhaps it would take another big disaster to arouse public awareness, just as the 1956 Grand Canyon disaster had spurred President Eisenhower and the Eighty-fourth Congress to revamp the airways. Yet, ironically, there was seldom any difficulty in getting money for non-operational improvements. A proposal to triple-deck all parking lots had won city approval without dissent. But that was something which the public—including those who had votes—could see and touch. Runways and taxiways were different. A single new runway cost several million dollars and took two years to build, yet few people other than pilots, air traffic controllers, and airport management, ever knew how good or bad a runway system was.

But at Lincoln International a showdown was coming soon. It had to. In recent weeks, Mel had sensed the signs, and when it happened the choice would be clear

—between advancement on the ground, matching new achievements in the air, or impotently drifting backward. In aviation, there was never a status quo.

There was another factor.

As well as the airport's future, Mel's personal future was at stake. Whichever way airport policies veered, so would his own prestige advance or lessen in places where it counted most.

Only a short time ago, Mel Bakersfeld had been a national spokesman for ground logistics of aviation, had been touted as the rising young genius in aviation management. Then, abruptly, a single, calamitous event had wrought a change. Now, four years later, the future was no longer clear, and there were doubts and questioning about Mel Bakersfeld, in others' minds as well as in his own.

The event which caused the change was the John F. Kennedy assassination.

"Here's the end of the runway, Mr. Bakersfeld. You riding back with us, or what?" The voice of the Snowblast driver broke in on Mel's reverie.

"Hm?"

The man repeated his question. Ahead of them, once more, warning lights were flashing on, the Conga Line showing. Half the width of a runway was cleared at one time. Now, the Line would reverse itself and go back the way it had come, clearing the remaining portion. Allowing for stops and starts, it took forty-five minutes to an hour to plow and sand a single runway.

"No," Mel said. "I'll get off here."

"Right, sir." The driver directed a signal light at the assistant foreman's car which promptly swung out of line. A few moments later, as Mel clambered down, his own car was waiting. From other plows and trucks, crews were descending and hurrying to the coffee wagon.

Driving back toward the terminal, Mel radioed the Snow Desk, confirming to Danny Farrow that runway one seven, left, would be usable shortly. Then, switching to ATC ground control, he turned the volume low, the subdued, level voices a background to his thoughts.

In the Snowblast cab he had been reminded of the event which, of all others he remembered, had struck with greatest impact.

It had been four years ago.

He thought, startled, was it really that long ago?—four years since the gray November afternoon when, dazedly, he had pulled the p.a. microphone across his desk toward him—the microphone, rarely used, which overrode all others in the terminal—and cutting in on a flight arrival bulletin, had announced to concourses which swiftly hushed, the shattering news which seconds earlier had flashed from Dallas.

His eyes, as he spoke then, had been on the photograph on the facing wall across his office, the photograph whose inscription read: *To my friend Mel Bakersfeld, concerned, as I am, with attenuating the surly bonds of earth—John F. Kennedy.*

The photograph still remained, as did many memories.

The memories began, for Mel, with a speech he had made in Washington, D.C.

At the time, as well as airport general manager, he had been president of the Airport Operators Council—the youngest leader, ever, of that small but influential body linking major airports of the world. AOC headquarters was in Washington, and Mel flew there frequently.

His speech was to a national planning congress.

Aviation, Mel Bakersfeld had pointed out, was the only truly successful international undertaking. It transcended ideological boundaries as well as the merely geographic. Because it was a means of intermingling diverse populations at ever-diminishing cost, it offered the most practical means to world understanding yet devised by man.

Even more significant was aerial commerce. Movement of freight by air, already mammoth in extent, was destined to be greater still. The new, giant jet airplanes, to be in service by the early 1970s, would be the fastest and cheapest cargo carriers in human history; within a decade, oceangoing ships might be dry-dock museum pieces, pushed out of business in the same way that passenger airplanes had clobbered the *Queen Mary* and *Elizabeth*. The effect could be a new, worldwide argosy of trade, with prosperity for now impoverished nations. Technologically, Mel reminded his audience, the airborne segment of aviation offered these things, and more, within the lifetimes of today's middle-aged people.

Yet, he had continued, while airplane designers wove the stuff of dreams into fabrics of reality, facilities on the ground remained, for the most part, products of shortsightedness or misguided haste. Airports, runway systems, terminals, were geared to yesterday, with scant —if any—provision for tomorrow; what was lost sight of, or ignored, was the juggernaut speed of aviation's progress. Airports were set up piecemeal, as individually as city halls, and often with as small imagination. Usually, too much was spent on showplace terminals, too little on operating areas. Coordinated, high-level planning, either national or international, was non-existent.

At local levels, where politicians were apathetic about problems of ground access to airports, the situation was as bad, or worse.

"We have broken the sound barrier," Mel declared, "but not the ground barrier."

He listed specific areas for study and urged international planning—U.S. led and presidentially inspired— for aviation on the ground.

The speech was accorded a standing ovation and was widely reported. It produced approving nods from such diverse sources as *The Times* of London, *Pravda,* and *The Wall Street Journal.*

The day after the speech, Mel was invited to the White House.

The meeting with the President had gone well. It had been a relaxed, good-humored session in the private study on the White House second floor. J.F.K., Mel found, shared many of his own ideas.

Subsequently, there were other sessions, some of them "brain trust" affairs involving Kennedy aides, usually when the Administration was considering aviation matters. After several such occasions, with informal aftermaths, Mel was at home in the White House, and less surprised than he had been at first to find himself there at all. As time went on, he drifted into one of those easygoing relationships which J.F.K. encouraged among those with expertise to offer him.

It was a year or so after their first encounter that the President sounded Mel out about heading the Federal Aviation Agency. (It was an Agency then, an Administration later.) Sometime during the Kennedy second term, which everyone assumed would be automatic, the incumbent FAA Administrator, Halaby, would move on to other things. How did Mel feel about implementing, from within, some of the measures he had advocated from without? Mel had replied that he was very interested indeed. He made it clear that if an offer were made, his answer would be yes.

Word filtered out, not from Mel, but through others who had had it from the top. Mel was "in"—a dues-paid member of the inner circle. His prestige, high before, went higher still. The Airport Operators Council re-elected him president. His own airport commissioners voted him a handsome raise. Barely in his late thirties, he was considered the Childe Roland of aviation management.

Six months later, John F. Kennedy made his fateful Texas journey.

Like others, Mel was first stunned, then later wept. Only later still, did it dawn on him that the assassin's bullets had ricocheted onto the lives of others, his own among them. He discovered he was no longer "in" in Washington. Najeeb Halaby did, in fact, move on from FAA—to a senior vice-presidency of Pan American—but Mel did not succeed him. By then, power had shifted, influences waned. Mel's name, he later learned, was not even on President Johnson's short list for the FAA appointment.

Mel's second tenure as AOC president ran out uneventfully and another bright young man succeeded him. Mel's trips to Washington ceased. His public appearances became limited to local ones, and, in a way, he found the change to be a relief. His own responsibilities at Lincoln International had already increased as air traffic proliferated beyond most expectations. He became intensely occupied with planning, coupled with efforts to persuade the Board of Airport Commissioners to his own viewpoints. There was plenty to think about, including troubles at home. His days and weeks and months were full.

And yet, there was a sense that time and opportunity had passed him by. Others were aware of it. Unless something dramatic occurred, Mel surmised, his career might continue, and eventually end, precisely where he was.

"Tower to mobile one—what is your position?" The radio enjoinder broke through Mel's thoughts, returning him abruptly to the present.

He turned up the radio volume and reported. By now, he was nearing the main passenger terminal, its lights becoming clearer, despite the still heavily falling snow. The aircraft parking areas, he observed, were as fully occupied as when he left, and there was still a line of arriving aircraft waiting for gate positions to be vacated.

"Mobile one, hold until the Lake Central Nord crosses ahead of you, then follow it in."

"This is mobile one. Roger."

A few minutes later, Mel eased his car into the terminal basement parking area.

Near his parking stall was a locked box with an airport telephone. He used one of his passkeys to open the box, and dialed the Snow Desk. Danny Farrow answered. Was there any fresh news, Mel inquired, about the mired Aéreo-Mexican jet?

"Negative," Danny said. "And the tower chief said to tell you that not being able to use runway three zero is still slowing traffic fifty percent. Also, he's getting more phone complaints from Meadowood every time there's a takeoff over there."

Mel said grimly, "Meadowood will have to suffer." Community meeting or not, there was nothing he could do to eliminate overhead noise for the time being. The most important thing at the moment was to reduce the lag in operations. "Where's Joe Patroni now?"

"Same place. Still held up."

"Can he make it for sure?"

"TWA says so. He has a phone in his car, and they've been in touch."

"As soon as Joe gets here," Mel instructed, "I want to be notified. Wherever I am."

"That'll be downtown, I guess."

Mel hesitated. There was no reason, he supposed, why he need remain at the airport any longer tonight. Yet again, unaccountably, he had the same sense of foreboding which had disturbed him on the airfield. He remembered his conversation earlier with the tower watch chief, the line of waiting aircraft on the ramp apron outside. He made a spontaneous decision.

"No, I won't be downtown. We need that runway badly, and I'm not leaving until I know positively that Patroni is out there on the field, in charge."

"In that case," Danny said, "I suggest you call your wife right now. Here's the number she's at."

Mel wrote it down, then depressed the receiver rest and dialed the downtown number. He asked for Cindy, and after a brief wait, heard her voice say sharply, "Mel, why aren't you here?"

"I'm sorry, I was held up. There've been problems at the airport. It's a pretty big storm . . ."

"Damn you, *get down here fast!*"

From the fact that his wife's voice was low, Mel deduced there were others within hearing. Just the same, she managed to convey a surprising amount of venom.

Mel sometimes tried to associate the voice of Cindy nowadays with the Cindy he remembered before their marriage fifteen years ago. She had been a gentler person then, it seemed to him. In fact, her gentleness had been one of the things which appealed to Mel when they first met in San Francisco, he on leave from the Navy and Korea. Cindy had been an actress at the time, though in a minor way because the career she had hoped for had not worked out, and clearly wasn't going to. She had had a succession of diminishingly small parts in summer stock and television, and afterward, in a moment of frankness, admitted that marriage had been a welcome release from the whole thing.

Years later, that story changed a little, and it became a favorite gambit of Cindy's to declare that she had sacrificed her career and probable stardom because of Mel. More recently, though, Cindy didn't like her past as an actress being mentioned at all. That was because she had read in *Town and Country* that actresses were seldom, if ever, included in *The Social Register,* and addition of her own name to the *Register* was something Cindy wanted very much indeed.

"I'm coming downtown to join you just as soon as I can," Mel said.

Cindy snapped, "That isn't good enough. You should be here already. You knew perfectly well that tonight was important to me, and a week ago you made a definite promise."

"A week ago I didn't know we were going to have the biggest storm in six years. Right now we've a runway out of use, there's a question of airport safety . . ."

"You've people working for you, haven't you? Or are the ones you've chosen so incompetent they can't be left alone?"

Mel said irritably, "They're highly competent. But I get paid to take some responsibility, too."

"It's a pity you can't act responsibly to me. Time and again I make important social arrangements which you enjoy demolishing."

Listening, as the words continued, Mel sensed that Cindy was getting close to boiling point. Without any effort, he could visualize her now, five feet six of imperious energy in her highest heels, clear blue eyes flashing, and her blonde coiffed head tilted back in that damnably attractive way she had when she was angry. That was one reason, Mel supposed, why, in their early years of marriage, his wife's temper outbursts seldom dismayed him. The more heated she became, it always seemed, the more desirable she grew. At such moments, he had invariably let his eyes rove upward, beginning at her ankles—not hurriedly, because Cindy possessed extraordinarily attractive ankles and legs; in fact, better than those of most other women Mel knew—to the rest of her which was just as proportionate and physically appealing.

In the past, when his eyes had made their appreciative assessment, some two-way physical communion sprang into being, prompting each to reach out, to touch one another, impulsively, hungrily. The result was predictable. Invariably, the origin of Cindy's anger was forgotten in a wave of sensuality which engulfed them. Cindy had an exciting, insistent savagery, and in their lovemaking would demand, *Hurt me, goddam you, hurt me!"* At the end, they would be spent and drained, so that picking up the skein of a quarrel was more than either had the wish or energy to do.

It was, of course, a way of shelving, rather than resolving, differences which—Mel realized, even early on —were fundamental. As the years passed, and passion lessened, accumulated differences became more sharply accented.

Eventually, they ceased entirely to use sex as a panacea and, in the past year or so, physical intimacy of any kind had become more and more occasional. Cindy, in fact, whose bodily appetites had always needed satisfying whatever the state of mind between them, appeared in recent months to have become indifferent altogether. Mel had wondered about that. Had his wife taken a lover? It was possible, and Mel supposed he ought to care. The sad thing was, it seemed easier not to be concerned.

Yet there were still moments when the sight or sound of Cindy in her willful anger could stir him physically, arousing old desires. He had that feeling now as he listened to her excoriating voice on the telephone.

When he was able to cut in, he said, "It isn't true that I enjoy demolishing your arrangements. Most of the time I go along with what you want, even though I don't think the things we go to are all that important. What I would enjoy are a few more evenings at home with the children."

"That's a lot of crap," Cindy said, "and you know it."

He felt himself tense, gripping the telephone more tightly. Then he conceded to himself: perhaps the last remark was true, to an extent. Earlier this evening he had been reminded of the times he had stayed at the airport when he could have gone home—merely because he wanted to avoid another fight with Cindy. Roberta and Libby had got left out of the reckoning then, as children did, he supposed, when marriages went sour. He should not have mentioned them.

But apart from that, tonight *was* different. He ought to stay on at the airport, at least until it became known for sure what was happening about the blocked runway.

"Look," Mel said, "let's make one thing clear. I haven't told you this before, but last year I kept some notes. You wanted me to come to fifty-seven of your charitable whingdings. Out of that I managed forty-five which is a whole lot more than I'd attend from choice, but it isn't a bad score."

"You bastard! I'm not a ball game where you keep a scorecard. I'm your wife."

Mel said sharply, "Take it easy!" He was becoming angry, himself. "Also, in case you don't know it, you're raising your voice. Do you want all those nice people around to know what kind of a heel you have for a husband?"

"I don't give a goddam!" But she said it softly, just the same.

"I do know you're my wife, which is why I intend to get down there just as soon as I can." What would happen, Mel wondered, if he could reach out and touch Cindy now? Would the old magic work? He decided not. "So save me a place, and tell the waiter to keep my soup warm. Also, apologize and explain why I'm late. I presume some of the people there have heard there *is* an airport." A thought struck him. "Incidentally, what's the occasion tonight?"

"I explained last week."

"Tell me again."

"It's a publicity party—cocktails and dinner—to promote the costume ball which is being given next month for the Archidona Children's Relief Fund. The press is here. They'll be taking photographs."

Now Mel knew why Cindy wanted him to hurry. With him there, she stood a better chance of being in the photographs—and on tomorrow's newspaper social pages.

"Most other committee members," Cindy insisted, "have their husbands here already."

"But not all?"

"I said most."

"And you did say the Archidona Relief Fund?"

"Yes."

"Which Archidona? There are two. One's in Ecuador, the other in Spain." At college, maps and geography had fascinated Mel, and he had a retentive memory.

For the first time, Cindy hesitated. Then she said testily, "What does it matter? This isn't the time for stupid questions."

Mel wanted to laugh out loud. *Cindy didn't know.* As usual, she had chosen to work for a charity because of *who* was involved, rather than what.

He said maliciously, "How many letters do you expect to get from this one?"

"I don't know what you mean."

"Oh, yes, you do."

To be considered for listing in *The Social Register,* a new aspirant needed eight sponsoring letters from people whose names already appeared there. At the last count Mel had heard, Cindy had collected four.

"By God, Mel, if you say anything—tonight or any other time . . ."

"Will the letters be free ones, or do you expect to pay for them like those other two?" He was aware of having an advantage now. It happened very rarely.

Cindy said indignantly, "That's a filthy allegation. It's impossible to buy your way in . . ."

"Nuts!" Mel said. "I get the canceled checks from our joint account. Remember?"

There was a silence. Then Cindy asserted, low-voiced and savagely, "Listen to me! You'd better get here tonight, and soon. If you don't come, or if you do come and embarrass me by saying anything of what you did just now, it'll be the end. Do you understand?"

"I'm not sure that I do." Mel spoke quietly. Instinct cautioned him that this was an important moment for them both. "Perhaps you'd better tell me exactly what you mean."

Cindy countered, "You figure it out."

She hung up.

On his way from the parking area to his office, Mel's fury seethed and grew. Anger had always come to him less quickly than to Cindy. He was the slow-burn type. But he was burning now.

He was not entirely sure of the focus of his anger. A good deal was directed at Cindy, but there were other factors, too: His professional failure, as he saw it, to prepare effectually for a new era of aviation; a seeming inability to infuse others any longer with his own convictions; high hopes, unfulfilled. Somehow, between them all, Mel thought, his personal and professional lives had become twin testaments to inadequacy. His marriage was on the rocks, or apparently about to go there; if and when it did, he would have failed his children, also. At the same time, at the airport, where he was trustee for thousands who passed through daily in good faith, all his efforts and persuasion had failed to halt deterioration. There, the high standards he had worked to build were eroding steadily.

En route to the executive mezzanine, he encountered no one he knew. It was just as well. If he had been spoken to, whatever question had been put, he would have snarled a heated answer. In his office, he peeled off the heavy outdoor clothing and let it stay on the floor where it fell. He lit a cigarette. It had an acrid taste, and he stubbed it out. As he crossed to his desk, he was aware that the pain in his foot had returned, increasingly.

There was a time—it seemed long ago—when on nights like this, if his wounded foot pained him, he would have gone home, where Cindy would have insisted he relax. He would have a hot bath first, then after, while he lay face downward on their bed, she would massage his back and neck with cool, firm fingers until pain ebbed out of him. It was unthinkable, of course, that Cindy would ever do the same thing again; but even if she did, he doubted that it would work. You could lose communication in other ways besides the spoken word.

Seated at his desk, Mel put his head in his hands.

As he had done on the airfield earlier, he shivered. Then, abruptly in the silent office, a telephone bell jangled. For a moment he ignored it. It rang again, and he realized it was the red alarm system telephone on a stand beside the desk. In two swift strides he reached it.

"Bakersfeld here."

He heard clicks and more acknowledgments as others came on the line.

"This is Air Traffic Control," the tower chief's voice announced. "We have an airborne emergency, category three."

9

Keith Bakersfeld, Mel's brother, was a third of the way through his eight-hour duty watch in the air traffic control radar room.

In radar control, tonight's storm was having a profound effect, though not a directly physical one. To a spectator, Keith thought, lacking an awareness of the complex story which a conglomeration of radarscopes was telling, it might have seemed that the storm, raging immediately outside, was a thousand miles away.

The radar room was in the control tower, one floor down from the glass-surrounded eyrie—the tower cab —from which ATC directed aircraft movement on the ground and immediate local flying. The radar section's jurisdiction extended beyond the airport, and radar controllers reached out to bridge the gap between local control and the nearest ATC regional center. The regional centers—usually miles from any airport—controlled main trunk airways and traffic coming on and off them.

In contrast to the top portion of the tower, the radar room had no windows. Day and night, at Lincoln International, ten radar controllers and supervisors labored in perpetual semidarkness under dim moonglow lights. Around them, tightly packed equipment—radarscopes, controls, radio communications panels—lined all four walls. Usually, controllers worked in shirtsleeves since the temperature, winter or summer, was maintained at an even seventy degrees to protect the delicate electronic gear.

The pervading tone in the radar room was calm. However, beneath the calmness, at all times, was a constant nervous strain. Tonight, the strain had been added to by the storm and, within the past few minutes, it had heightened further still. The effect was like stretching an already tensioned spring.

Cause of the added tension was a signal on a radarscope which, in turn, had triggered a flashing red light and alarm buzzer in the control room. The buzzer had now been silenced, but the distinctive radar signal remained. Known as a double blossom, it had flowered on the semidarkened screen like a tremulous green carnation and denoted an aircraft in distress. In this case, the aircraft was a U. S. Air Force KC-135, high above the airport in the storm, and seeking an immediate emergency landing. Keith Bakersfeld had been working the flatface scope on which the emergency signal appeared, and a supervisor had since joined him. Both were now transmitting urgent, swift decisions—by interphone to controllers at adjoining positions, and by radio to other aircraft.

The tower watch chief on the floor above had been promptly informed of the distress signal. He, in turn, had declared a category three emergency, alerting airport ground facilities.

The flatface scope, at the moment the center of attention, was a horizontal glass circle, the size of a bicycle tire, set into a tabletop console. Its surface was dark green, with brilliant green points of light showing all aircraft in the air within a forty-mile radius. As the aircraft moved, so did the points of light. Beside each light point was a small plastic marker, identifying it. The markers were known colloquially as "shrimp boats" and controllers moved them by hand as aircraft progressed and their positions on the screen changed. As more aircraft appeared, they were identified by voice radio and similarly tagged. New radar systems dispensed with shrimp boats; instead, identifying letter-number codes—including altitude—appeared directly on the radar screen. But the newer method was not yet in wide use and, like all new systems, had bugs which needed elimination.

Tonight there was an extraordinary number of aircraft on the screen, and someone had remarked earlier that the green pinpoints were proliferating like fecund ants.

Keith was seated closest to the flatface, his lean, spindly figure hunched forward in a gray steel chair. His body was tense; his legs, hooked underneath the chair, were as rigid as the chair itself. He was concentrating, his face strained and gaunt, as it had been for months. The green reflection of the scope accentuated, eerily, deep hollows beneath his eyes. Anyone who knew Keith well, but had not seen him for a year or so, would have been shocked both by his appearance and his change in manner. Once, he had exuded an amiable, relaxed good-nature; now, all signs of it were gone. Keith was six years younger than his brother, Mel, but nowadays appeared a good deal older.

The change in Keith Bakersfeld had been noticed by his colleagues, some of whom were working tonight at other control positions in the radar room. They were also well aware of the reason for the change, a reason which had evoked genuine sympathy. However, they were practical men with an exacting job, which was why the radar supervisor, Wayne Tevis, was observing Keith covertly at this moment, watching the signs of increasing strain, as he had for some time. Tevis, a lanky, drawling Texan, sat centrally in the radar room on a high stool from where he could peer down over the shoulders of operators at the several radarscopes serving special functions. Tevis had personally equipped the stool with castors, and periodically he rode it like a horse, propelling himself by jabs of his hand-tooled Texan boots wherever he was needed at the moment.

During the preceding hour, Wayne Tevis had at no point moved far away from Keith. The reason was that Tevis was ready, if necessary, to relieve Keith from radar watch, a decision which instinct told him might have to be made at any time.

The radar supervisor was a kindly man, despite his mild flamboyance. He dreaded what he might have to do, and was aware of how far-reaching, for Keith, its effect could be. Nevertheless, if he had to, he would do it.

His eyes on Keith's flatface scope, Tevis drawled, "Keith, old son, that Braniff flight is closing on Eastern. If you turn Braniff right, you can keep Eastern going on the same course." It was something which Keith should have seen himself, but hadn't.

The problem, which most of the radar room crew was working at feverishly, was to clear a path for the Air Force KC-135, which had already started down on an instrument landing approach from ten thousand feet. The difficulty was—below the big Air Force jet were five airline flights, stacked at intervals of a thousand feet, and orbiting a limited airspace. All were awaiting their turn to land. A few miles on either side were other columns of aircraft, similarly stacked and, lower still, were three more airliners, already on landing approaches. In between them all were busy departure corridors. Somehow, the military flight had to be threaded down through the stacked civilian airplanes without a collision occurring. Under normal conditions the assignment would test the strongest nerves. As it was, the situation was complicated by radio failure in the KC-135, so that voice contact with the Air Force pilot had been lost.

Keith Bakersfeld thumbed his microphone. "Braniff eight twenty-nine, make an immediate right turn, heading zero-niner-zero." At moments like this, even though pressures built to fever pitch, voices should stay calm. Keith's voice was highpitched and betrayed his nervousness. He saw Wayne Tevis glance at him sharply. But the blips on the radar screen, which had been uncomfortably close, began separating as the Braniff captain obeyed instructions. There were moments—this was one—when air traffic controllers thanked whatever gods they acknowledged for the swift, alert responses of airline pilots. The pilots might beef, and often did subsequently, at being given sudden course changes which required tight, abrupt turns and shook up passengers. But when a controller gave the order "*immediate*," they obeyed instantly and argued later.

In another minute or so the Braniff flight would have to be turned again, and so would Eastern, which was at the same level. Even before that, there must be new courses for two TWAs—one higher, the other lower—plus a Lake Central Convair, an Air Canada Vanguard, and a Swissair just coming on the screen. Until the KC-135 had come through, these and others must be given zigzag courses, though for brief distances only, since none must stray into adjoining airspaces. In a way, it was like an intricate chess game, except that all the pieces were at various levels and moving at several hundred miles an hour. Also as part of the game, pieces had to be raised or lowered while they still moved forward, yet none must come closer than three miles laterally or a thousand feet vertically from another, and none must go over the edge of the board. And while all of it happened, the thousands of passengers, anxious for their journeys to end, had to sit in their airborne seats—and wait.

In occasional moments of detachment, Keith wondered how the Air Force pilot, in difficulty and letting

down through storm and crowded airspace, was feeling
at this moment. Lonely, probably. Just as Keith himself
was lonely; just as all life was lonely, even with others
physically close beside you. The pilot would have a
co-pilot and crew, in the same way that Keith had fel-
low-workers who, at this moment, were near enough to
touch. But that was not the kind of nearness which
counted. Not when you were alone in that inner room of
the mind, where no one else could enter, and where you
lived—apart and solitary—with awareness, memory,
conscience, fear. Alone, from the moment you were
born until you died. Always, and forever, alone.

Keith Bakersfeld knew how much alone a single
human being could be.

In succession, Keith gave fresh courses to Swissair,
one of the TWAs, Lake Central, and Eastern. Behind
him he could hear Wayne Tevis trying to raise the Air
Force KC-135 on radio again. Still no response, except
that the distress radar blip, actuated by the KC-135
pilot, still blossomed on the scope. The position on the
blip showed the pilot was doing the right thing—following exactly the instructions he had been given before
the radio failure happened. In doing so, he would be
aware that air traffic control could anticipate his movements. He would also know that his position could be
seen by radar on the ground, and trusted that other
traffic would be routed out of his way.

The Air Force flight, Keith knew, had originated in
Hawaii and come non-stop after mid-air refueling over
the West Coast, its destination Andrews Air Force Base,
near Washington. But west of the Continental Divide
there had been an engine failure, and afterward electrical trouble, causing the airplane commander to elect
an unscheduled landing at Smoky Hill, Kansas. At
Smoky Hill, however, snow clearance of runways had
not been completed, and the KC-135 was diverted to
Lincoln International. Air Route Control nursed the
military flight northeast across Missouri and Illinois.
Then, thirty miles out, West Arrivals Control, in the
person of Keith Bakersfeld, took over. It was soon after-

ward that radio failure had been added to the pilot's other troubles.

Most times, when flying conditions were normal, military aircraft stayed clear of civil airports. But in a storm like tonight's help was asked—and given—without question.

In this darkened, tightly packed radar room, other controllers, as well as Keith, were sweating. Yet no hint of pressures or tension must be betrayed by controllers' voices when speaking with pilots in the air. The pilots had plenty to concern themselves with at any time. Tonight, buffeted by the storm, and flying solely on instruments with nil visibility outside their cockpits, demands upon their skill were multiplied. Most pilots had already flown extra time because of delays caused by heavy traffic; now they would have to stay even longer in the air.

From each radar control position a swift, quiet stream of radio orders was going out to hold even more flights clear of the danger area. The flights were awaiting their own turn to land and every minute or two were being joined by new arrivals coming off airways. *A controller, his voice low but urgent, called over his shoulder. "Chuck, I've got a hot one. Can you take Delta seven three?"* It was a controller's way of saying he was in trouble and had more than he could handle. *Another voice. "Hell!—I'm piled up, too . . . Wait! . . . Affirmative, I got it." A second's pause. "Delta seven three from Lincoln approach control. Turn left; heading one two zero. Maintain altitude, four thousand!"* Controllers helped each other when they could. A few minutes from now the second man might need help himself. *"Hey, watch that Northwest; he's coming through from the other side. Christ! it's getting like the Outer Drive at rush hour." . . . "American four four, hold present heading, what's your altitude?" . . . "That Lufthansa departure's way off course. Get him the hell out of the approach area!"* . . . Departing flights were being routed well around the trouble area, but arrivals were being held up, valuable landing time lost. Even later, when the

emergency would be over, everyone knew it would take
an hour or more to unravel the aerial traffic jam.

Keith Bakersfeld was trying hard to maintain his concentration, to retain a mental picture of his sector and
every aircraft in it. It required instant memorizing—
identifications, positions, types of aircraft, speeds, altitudes, sequence of landing . . . a detailed diagram, in
depth, with constant changes . . . a configuration which
was never still. Even at quieter times, mental strain was
unceasing; tonight, the storm was taxing cerebral effort
to its limit. A controller's nightmare was to "lose the
picture," a situation where an overtaxed brain rebelled
and everything went blank. It happened occasionally,
even to the best.

Keith had been the best. Until a year ago, he was one
whom colleagues turned to when pressures built to un-
reason. *Keith, I'm getting swamped. Can you take a
couple?* He always had.

But, lately, roles had changed. Now, colleagues
shielded him as best they could, though there was a limit
to how much any man could help another and do his
own job, too.

More radio instructions were needed. Keith was on
his own; Tevis, the supervisor, had propelled himself
and his high stool across the room to check another
controller. Keith's mind clicked out decisions. *Turn
Braniff left, Air Canada right, Eastern through a hundred and eighty degrees.* It was done; on the radar
screen, blips were changing direction. *The slower-
moving Lake Central Convair could be left another
minute. Not so, the Swissair jet; it was converging with
Eastern. Swissair must be given a new course immediately, but what? Think fast! Forty-five degrees right, but
for a minute only, then right again. Keep an eye on TWA
and Northwest! A new flight coming in from the west at
high speed—identify, and find more airspace. Concentrate, concentrate!*

Keith determined grimly: *He would not lose the
picture; not tonight, not now.*

There was a reason for not doing so; a secret he had
shared with no one, not even Natalie, his wife. Only

Keith Bakersfeld, and Keith alone, knew that this was the last time he would ever face a radarscope or stand a watch. Today was his last day with air traffic control. It would be over soon.

It was also the last day of his life.

"Take a break, Keith." It was the tower watch chief's voice.

Keith had not seen the tower chief come in. He had done so unobtrusively, and was standing by Wayne Tevis, the radar supervisor.

A moment earlier, Tevis had told the tower chief quietly, "Keith's all right, I reckon. For a few minutes I was worried, but he seemed to pull together." Tevis was glad he had not had to take the drastic action he had contemplated earlier, but the tower chief murmured, "Let's take him off a while, anyway"; and, as an afterthought, "I'll do it."

Glancing at the two men together, Keith knew at once why he was being relieved. There was still a crisis, and they didn't trust him. The work break was a pretext; he wasn't due for one for half-an-hour. Should he protest? For a controller as senior as himself, it was an indignity which others would notice. Then he thought: Why make an issue now? It wasn't worth it. Besides, a ten-minute break would steady him. Afterward, when the worst of the emergency was over, he could return to work for the remainder of his shift.

Wayne Tevis leaned forward. "Lee will take over, Keith." He motioned to another controller who had just returned from his own work break—a scheduled one.

Keith nodded, without comment, though he remained in place and continued to give radio instructions to aircraft while the new man got the picture. It usually took several minutes for one controller to hand over to another. The man coming in had to study the radar display, letting the over-all situation build in his mind. He also needed to become mentally tensed.

Getting tensed—consciously and deliberately—was a part of the job. Controllers called it "sharpening to an edge," and in Keith's fifteen years in air traffic control, he had watched it happen regularly, to others and to himself. You did it, because you had to, when you took over a duty, as now. At other times it became a reflex action, such as when controllers drove to work together —in car pools, as some did. On leaving home, conversation would be relaxed and normal. At that point in the journey, a casual question like, "Are you going to the ball game Saturday?" would elicit an equally casual answer—"Sure am," or "No, I can't make it this week." Yet, nearing the job, conversation tautened, so that the same question—a quarter mile from the airport—might produce a terse "affirmative" or "negative," and nothing more.

Coupled with tense mental sharpness was another requirement—a controlled, studied calmness at all times on duty. The two requirements—contradictory in terms of human nature—were exhausting mentally and, in the long run, took a toll. Many controllers developed stomach ulcers which they concealed through fear of losing their jobs. As part of the concealment, they paid for private medical advice instead of seeking free medical help to which their employment entitled them. At work, they hid bottles of Maalox—"'for the relief of gastric hyperacidity"—in their lockers and, at intervals, sipped the white, sweetish fluid surreptitiously.

There were other effects. Some controllers—Keith Bakersfeld knew several—were mean and irascible at home, or flew into rages, as a reaction to pent-up emotions at work. Coupled with irregular hours of working and sleeping, which made it difficult to regulate a household, the effect was predictable. Among air traffic controllers, the list of broken homes was long, divorce rates high.

"Okay," the new man said, "I have the picture."

Keith slid out from his seat, disconnecting his headset as the relieving controller took his place. Even before the newcomer was seated, he had begun transmitting fresh instructions to the lower TWA.

The tower chief told Keith, "Your brother said he might drop around later."

Keith nodded as he left the radar room. He felt no resentment against the tower chief, who had his own responsibilities to contend with, and Keith was glad he had made no protest about being relieved prematurely. More than anything else at the moment, Keith wanted a cigarette, some coffee, and to be alone. He was also glad —now the decision had been made for him—to be away from the emergency situation. He had been involved in too many in the past to regret missing the culmination of one more.

Air traffic emergencies of one kind or another occurred several times a day at Lincoln International, as they did at any major airport. They could happen in any kind of weather—on the clearest day, as well as during a storm like tonight's. Usually, only a few people knew about such incidents, because almost all were resolved safely, and even pilots in the air were seldom told the reason for delays or abrupt instructions to turn this way or that. For one thing, there was no need for them to know; for another, there was never time for radio small talk. Ground emergency staffs—crash crews, ambulance attendants, and police—as well as airport senior management, were always alerted, and the action they took depended on the category of emergency declared. Category one was the most serious, but was rarely invoked, since it signaled an actual crash. Category two was notification of imminent danger to life, or physical damage. Category three, as now, was a general warning to airport emergency facilities to stand by; they might be needed, or they might not. For controllers, however, any type of emergency involved additional pressures and aftereffects.

Keith entered the controllers' locker room which adjoined the radar control room. Now that he had a few minutes to think more calmly, he hoped, for the sake of everyone, that the Air Force KC-135 pilot, and all others in the air tonight, made it safely down through the storm.

The locker room, a small cubicle with a single window, had three walls of metal lockers, and a wooden bench down the center. A notice board beside the window held an untidy collection of official bulletins and notices from airport social groups. An unshaded light bulb in the ceiling seemed dazzling after the radar room's semidarkness. No one else was in the locker room, and Keith reached for the light switch and turned it off. There were floodlights on the tower outside, and enough light came in for him to see.

He lit a cigarette. Then, opening his locker, he took out the lunch pail which Natalie had packed before his departure from home this afternoon. As he poured coffee from a Thermos, he wondered if Natalie had put a note in with his meal, or, if not a note, some inconsequential item she had clipped from a newspaper or a magazine. She often did one of both, hoping, he supposed, that it might cheer him. She had worked hard at doing that, right from the beginning of his trouble. At first, she had used obvious ones, though Keith had always realized—in a detached, dispassionate kind of way—exactly what Natalie was doing, or trying to. More recently, there had been fewer notes and clippings.

Perhaps Natalie, too, had finally lost heart. She had had less to say lately, and he knew, from the redness of her eyes, there were times she had been crying.

Keith had wanted to help her when he saw it. But how could he—when he couldn't help himself?

A picture of Natalie was taped to the inside of his locker door—a snapshot, in color, which Keith had taken. He had brought it here three years ago. Now, the light from outside shone on the picture only dimly, but he knew it so well, he could see what was there, whether highlighted or not.

The picture showed Natalie in a bikini. She was seated on a rock, laughing, one slim hand held above her eyes to shield them from the sun. Her light brown hair streamed behind; her small, pert face showed the freckles which always appeared in summer. There was an impudent, pixyish quality to Natalie Bakersfeld, as well as strength of will, and the camera had caught both. In the rear of the picture was a blue-water lake, high firs, and a rocky outcropping. They had been on a motoring holiday in Canada, camping among the Haliburton lakes, and for once their children, Brian and

Theo, had been left behind in Illinois, with Mel and Cindy. The holiday proved to be one of the happier times that Keith and Natalie had ever known.

Perhaps, Keith thought, it wasn't a bad thing to be remembering it tonight.

Pushed in behind the photo was a folded paper. It was one of the notes he had been thinking about, which Natalie put occasionally in his lunch pail. This was one from a few months ago which, for some reason, he had saved. Though knowing what was there, he took the paper out and walked to the window to read. It was a clipping from a news magazine, with some lines below in his wife's handwriting.

Natalie had all kinds of odd interests, some far-ranging, which she encouraged Keith and the boys to share. This clipping was about continuing experiments, by U.S. geneticists. Human sperm, it reported, could now be fast frozen. The sperm was placed in a deep freeze for storage where it remained in good condition indefinitely. When thawed, it could be used for fertilization of women at any time—either soon or generations hence.

Natalie had written:

> The Ark could have been 50 percent smaller, if Noah .
> Had known the facts about frozen spermatazoa;
> It appears you can have babies by the score
> Merely by opening a refrigerator door.
> I'm glad we had our ration
> With love and passion.

She had been trying then; still trying desperately to return their lives . . . the two of them; and as a family . . . to the way they had been before. *With love and passion*.

Mel had joined forces, too, attempting with Natalie, to induce his brother to fight free from the tide-race of anguish and depression which engulfed him totally.

Even then a part of Keith had wanted to respond. Summoning, from some deep consciousness, a spark of spirit, he had sought to match their strength by drawing on his own; to respond to proffered love with love himself. But the effort failed. It failed—as he had known it would—because there was no feeling or emotion left within himself. Neither warmth, nor love, nor even anger to be kindled. Only bleakness, remorse, and all-enveloping despair.

Natalie realized their failure now; he was sure of that. It was the reason, he suspected, that she had been crying, somewhere out of sight.

And Mel? Perhaps Mel, too, had given up. Though not entirely—Keith remembered what the tower chief had told him. "Your brother said he might drop around . . ."

It would be simpler if Mel didn't. Keith felt unequal to the effort, even though they had been as close as brothers could be all their lives. Mel's presence might be complicating.

Keith was too drained, too weary, for complications any more.

He wondered again if Natalie had put in a note with his meal tonight. He took out the contents of the lunch pail carefully, hoping that she had.

There were ham and watercress sandwiches, a container of cottage cheese, a pear, and wrapping paper. Nothing more.

Now that he knew there was none, he wished desperately there had been some message; any message, even the most trifling. Then he realized—it was his own fault; there had been no time. Today, because of the preparations he needed to make, he had left home earlier than usual. Natalie, to whom he had given no advance warning, had been rushed. At one point, he had suggested not taking a lunch at all; he would get a meal, he said, at one of the airport cafeterias. But Natalie, who knew the cafeterias would be crowded and noisy, which Keith disliked, had said no, and gone ahead as quickly as she could. She had not asked why he wanted to leave early, though he knew she was curious. Keith was relieved that there had been no question. If there had been, he would have had to invent something, and he

would not have wanted the last words between them to
have been a lie.

As it was, there had been enough time. He had driven
to the airport business area and registered at the
O'Hagan Inn where, earlier in the day, he had made a
reservation by telephone. He had planned everything
carefully, using a plan worked out several weeks ago,
though he had waited—giving himself time to think
about it, and be sure—before putting the plan into
effect. After checking into his room, he had left the Inn
and arrived at the airport in time to go on duty.

The O'Hagan Inn was within a few minutes' drive of
Lincoln International. In a few hours from now, when
Keith's duty watch was ended, he could go there
quickly. The room key was in his pocket. He took it out
to check.

10

The information—which the tower watch chief had relayed earlier to Mel Bakersfeld—about a meeting of
Meadowood citizenry, was entirely accurate.

The meeting, in the Sunday school hall of Meadowood First Baptist Church—fifteen seconds, as a jet
flies, from the end of runway two five—had been in
session half-an-hour. Its proceedings had started later
than planned, since most of the six hundred adults who
were present had had to battle their way, in cars and on
foot, through deep snow. But somehow they had come.

It was a mixed assemblage, such as might be found in
any averagely prosperous dormitory community. Of the
men, some were medium-level executives, others arti-
sans, with a sprinkling of local tradespeople. In numbers, men and women were approximately equal. Since
it was Friday night, the beginning of a weekend, most

were casually dressed, though exceptions were half a dozen visitors from outside the community and several press reporters.

The Sunday school hall was now uncomfortably crowded, stuffy and smoke-filled. All available chairs were occupied, and at least a hundred people were standing.

That so many had turned out at all on such a night, leaving warm homes to do so, spoke eloquently of their mettle and concern. They were also, at the moment, unanimously angry.

The anger—almost as tangible as the tobacco smoke —had two sources. First was the long-standing bitterness with the airport's by-product—the thunderous, ear-assaulting noise of jet propulsion which assailed the homes of Meadowood, day and night, shattering peace and privacy, both waking and sleeping. Second was the immediate frustration that, through a large part of the meeting so far, those assembled had been unable to hear one another.

Some difficulty in hearing had been anticipated. After all, it was what the meeting was about, and a portable p.a. system had been borrowed from the church. What had not been expected, however, was that tonight jet aircraft would be taking off immediately overhead, rendering both human ears and the p.a. system useless. The cause, which the meeting neither knew nor cared about, was that runway three zero was blocked by the mired Aéreo-Mexican 707, and other aircraft were being instructed to use runway two five instead. The latter runway pointed directly at Meadowood, like an arrow; whereas runway three zero, when usable, at least routed takeoffs slightly to one side.

In a momentary silence the chairman, red-faced, shouted, "Ladies and gentlemen, for years we have tried reasoning with the airport management and the airline companies. We have pointed to the violation of our homes. We have proved, with independent testimony, that normal living—under the barrage of noise we are forced to endure—is impossible. We have pleaded that our very sanity is in danger and that our wives, our

children, and ourselves live on the edge of nervous
breakdowns, which some among us have suffered already."

The chairman was a heavy-jowled, balding man
named Floyd Zanetta, who was a printing firm manager
and Meadowood homeowner. Zanetta, sixtyish, was
prominent in community affairs, and in the lapel of his
sports jacket was a Kiwanis long-service badge.

Both · the chairman and an impeccably dressed
younger man were on a small raised platform at the
front of the hall. The younger man, seated, was Elliott
Freemantle, a lawyer. A black leather briefcase stood
open at his side.

Floyd Zanetta slammed a hand on the lectern in front
of him. "What do the airport and airlines do? I'll tell
you what they do. They pretend; pretend to listen. And
while they are pretending, they make promises and more
promises which they have no intention of fulfilling. The
airport management, the FAA, and the airlines are
cheats and liars . . ."

The word "liars" was lost.

It was engulfed in a shattering, almost unbelievable
crescendo of sound, a monstrous roar of power which
seemed to seize the building and shake it. As if protectively, many in the hall covered their ears. A few
glanced upward nervously. Others, their eyes transmitting anger, spoke heatedly to those beside them, though
only a lip reader could have known what was said; no
words were audible. A water pitcher near the chairman's lectern trembled. If Zanetta had not grasped it
quickly, it would have fallen to the floor and shattered.

As swiftly as it had begun and built, the roar lessened
and faded. Already miles away and several thousand
feet above, Flight 58 of Pan American was climbing
through storm and darkness, reaching for higher, clearer
altitudes, swinging onto course for Frankfurt, Germany.
Now, Continental Airlines 23, destination Denver, Colorado, was rolling on the farther end of runway two
five, cleared for takeoff—over Meadowood. Other
flights, already in line on an adjoining taxiway, were
waiting their turn to follow.

It had been the same way all evening, even before the Meadowood meeting started. And after it started, business had had to be conducted in brief intervals between the overwhelming din of takeoffs.

Zanetta continued hastily, "I said they are cheats and liars. What is happening here and now is conclusive evidence. At the very least we are entitled to noise abatement procedures, but tonight even this . . ."

"Mr. Chairman," a woman's voice cut in from the body of the hall, "we've heard all this before. We all know it, and going over it again won't change anything." All eyes had turned to the woman, who was now standing. She had a strong, intelligent face and shoulder-length brown hair which had fallen forward, so that she brushed it back impatiently. "What I want to know, and so do others, is what else can we do, and where do we go from here?"

There was an outburst of applause, and cheering.

Zanetta said irritably, "If you'll kindly let me finish . . ."

He never did.

Once again, the same encompassing roar dominated the Sunday school hall.

The timing, and the last remark, provided the only laughter, so far, of the evening. Even the chairman grinned ruefully as he raised his hands in a despairing gesture.

A man's voice called peevishly, "Get on with it!"

Zanetta nodded agreement. He continued speaking, picking his way—like a climber over rocks—between recurring peaks of sound from overhead. What the community of Meadowood must do, he declared, was to discard politeness and reasonable approaches to the airport authority and others. Instead, a purely legalistic attack must be the order from now on. The residents of Meadowood were citizens with legal rights, which were being infringed upon. Along with those legal rights went recourse to the courts; therefore, they must be prepared to fight in the courts, with toughness, even viciousness if necessary. As to what form a legalistic offensive should take, it so happened that a noted lawyer, Mr. Elliott

Freemantle, whose offices were downtown in the Loop, had consented to be present at the meeting. Mr. Freemantle had made a study of laws affecting excessive noise, privacy and airspace, and, very soon, those who had braved the weather to attend would have the pleasure of hearing this distinguished gentleman. He would, in fact, present a proposal . . .

As the clichés rolled on, Elliott Freemantle fidgeted. He passed a hand lightly over his barber-styled, gray-streaked hair, fingering the smoothness of his chin and cheeks—he had shaved an hour before the meeting—and his keen sense of smell confirmed that the exclusive face lotion, which he always used after shaving and sunlamp sessions, still lingered. He recrossed his legs, observing that his two-hundred dollar alligator shoes still gleamed with mirror clearness, and was careful not to spoil the crease in the trousers of his tailored Blue Spruce pebble-weave suit. Elliott Freemantle had long ago discovered that people preferred their lawyers unlike their doctors—to look prosperous. Prosperity in a lawyer conveyed an aura of success at the bar, success which those about to engage in litigation wanted for themselves.

Elliott Freemantle hoped that most of those in the hall would shortly become litigants, and that he would represent them. Meanwhile, he wished the old cluck of a chairman, Zanetta, would get the hell off his feet so that he, Freemantle, could take over. There was no surer way to lose the confidence of an audience, or a jury, than by letting them think faster than yourself, so that they became aware of what you were going to say before you said it. Freemantle's finely honed intuition told him this was what was happening now. It meant that when his own turn came, he would have to work that much harder to establish his competence and superior intellect.

Some among his legal colleagues might have questioned whether Elliott Freemantle's intellect was, in fact, superior. They might even have objected to the chairman's description of him as a gentleman.

Fellow lawyers sometimes regarded Freemantle as an

exhibitionist who commanded high fees mainly through a showman's instinct for attracting attention. It was conceded, though, that he had an enviable knack for latching early onto causes which later proved spectacular and profitable.

For Elliott Freemantle, the Meadowood situation seemed custom made.

He had read about the community's problem and promptly arranged, through contacts, to have his name suggested to several homeowners as the one lawyer who could most likely help them. As a result, a homeowners committee eventually approached him, and the fact that they did so, rather than the other way around, gave him a psychological advantage he had planned from the beginning. Meanwhile, he had made a superficial study of the law, and recent court decisions, affecting noise and privacy—a subject entirely new to him—and when the committee arrived, he addressed them with the assurance of a lifetime expert.

Later, he had made the proposition which resulted in this meeting tonight, and his own attendance.

Thank God! It looked as if Zanetta, the chairman, were finally through with his windy introduction. Banal to the last, he was intoning, ". . . and so it is my privilege and pleasure to present . . ."

Scarcely waiting for his name to be spoken, Elliott Freemantle bounded to his feet. He began speaking before Zanetta's buttocks had made contact with his chair. As usual, he dispensed with all preliminaries.

"If you are expecting sympathy from me, you can leave right now, because there won't be any. You won't get it at this session, or others we may have later. I am not a purveyor of crying towels, so if you need them, I suggest you get your own, or supply each other. My business is law. Law, and nothing else."

He had deliberately made his voice harsh, and he knew he had jolted them, as he intended to.

He had also seen the newspaper reporters look up and pay attention. There were three of them at the press table near the front of the hall—two young men from the big city dailies and an elderly woman from a local weekly. All were important to his plans, and he had taken the trouble to find out their names and speak to them briefly before the meeting started. Now, their pencils were racing. Good! Cooperation with the press always ranked high in any project of Elliott Freemantle's, and he knew from experience that the best way to achieve it was by providing a lively story with a fresh angle. Usually he succeeded. Newspaper people appreciated that—a lot more than free drinks or food—and the livelier and more colorful the story, the more friendly their reportage was inclined to be.

He returned his attention to the audience.

Only a shade less aggressively, he continued. "If we decide, between us, that I am to represent you, it will be necessary for me to ask you questions about the effect of airport noise on your homes, your families, your own physical and mental health. But do not imagine I shall be asking the questions because I care personally about these things, or you as individuals. Frankly, I don't. You may as well know that I am an extremely selfish man. If I ask these questions, it will be to discover to what extent wrong has been done you under the law. I am already convinced that some wrong has been done —perhaps considerable wrong—and, in that event, you are entitled to legal redress. But you may as well know that whatever I learn, and however deeply I become involved, I am not given to losing sleep about the welfare of my clients when I'm away from my office or the courts. But . . ." Freemantle paused dramatically, and stabbed a finger forward to underscore his words. "But, in my office and in the courts, as clients, you would have the utmost of my attention and ability, *on questions of law*. And on those occasions, if we work together, I promise you will be glad I am on your side and not against you."

Now he had the attention of everyone in the hall. Some, both men and women, were sitting forward in their chairs, striving not to miss any words as he paused —though for the minimum time—as aircraft continued overhead. A few faces had become hostile as he spoke, but not many. It was time, though, to relax the pressure a little. He gave a swift, short smile, then went on seriously.

"I inform you of these things so that we understand each other. Some people tell me that I am a mean, unpleasant man. Maybe they are right, though personally if ever I want a lawyer for myself I'll make sure of choosing someone who *is* mean and unpleasant, also tough—on my behalf." There were a few approving nods and smiles.

"Of course, if you want a nicer guy who'll hand you more sympathy, though maybe a bit less law"—Elliott Freemantle shrugged—"that's your privilege."

He had been watching the audience closely and saw a responsible-looking man, in heavy rimmed glasses, lean toward a woman and whisper. From their expressions, Freemantle guessed the man was saying, "This is more like it!—what we wanted to hear." The woman, probably the whisperer's wife, nodded agreement. Around the hall, other faces conveyed the same impression.

As usual on occasions like this, Elliott Freemantle had shrewdly judged the temper of the meeting and calculated his own approach. He sensed early that these people were weary of platitudes and sympathy—well-meaning but ineffective. His own words, blunt and brutal, were like a cold, refreshing douche. Now, before minds could relax and attention wander, he must take a new tack. The moment for specifics had arrived—tonight, for this group, a discourse on the law of noise. The trick to holding audience attention, at which Elliott Freemantle excelled, was to stay half a mental pace ahead; that much and no more, so that those listening could follow what was being said, but must remain sufficiently alert to do so.

"Pay attention," he commanded, "because I'm going to talk about your particular problem."

The law of noise, he declared, was increasingly under study by the nation's courts. Old concepts were changing. New court decisions were establishing that excessive noise could be an invasion of privacy as well as trespass on property rights. Moreover, courts were in a mood to grant injunctions and financial recompense where intrusion—including aircraft intrusion—could be proven.

Elliott Freemantle paused while another takeoff thundered overhead, then gestured upward. "I believe you will have no difficulty in proving it here."

At the press table, all three reporters made a note.

The United States Supreme Court, he went on, had already set a precedent. In *U.S. v. Causby* the court ruled that a Greensboro, North Carolina, chicken farmer was entitled to compensation because of "invasion" by military planes flying low above his house. In handing down the *Causby* decision, Mr. Justice William O. Douglas had stated, ". . . if the landowner is to have full enjoyment of the land, he must have exclusive control of the immediate reaches of the enveloping atmosphere." In another case reviewed by the Supreme Court, *Griggs* v. *County of Allegheny,* a similar principle was upheld. In state courts of Oregon and Washington, in *Thornburg* v. *Port of Portland* and *Martin* v. *Port of Seattle,* damages for excessive aircraft noise had been awarded, even though airspace directly above the plaintiffs had not been violated. Other communities had begun, or were contemplating, similar legal action, and some were employing sound trucks and movie cameras as aids to proving their case. The trucks took decibel readings of noise; the cameras recorded aircraft altitudes. The noise frequently proved greater, the altitudes lower, than airlines and airport management admitted. In Los Angeles, a homeowner had filed suit against L. A. International Airport, asserting that the airport, by permitting landings on a newly extended runway close to his home, had taken an easement on his property without due process of law. The homeowner was claiming ten thousand dollars which he believed to be equivalent to the decrease in value of his home. Elsewhere, more and more similar cases were being argued in the courts.

The recital was succinct and impressive. Mention of a specific sum—ten thousand dollars—evoked immediate interest, as Elliott Freemantle intended that it should. The entire presentation sounded authoritative, factual, and the product of years of study. Only Freemantle himself knew that his "facts" were the result, not of poring over law reports, but of two hours, the previous afternoon, spent studying newsclippings in a downtown newspaper morgue.

There were also several facts which he had failed to mention. The chicken farmer ruling of the Supreme Court was made more than twenty years earlier, and total damages awarded were a trifling three hundred and seventy-five dollars—the actual value of some dead chickens. The Los Angeles suit was merely a claim which had not yet come to trial and might never do so. A more significant case, *Batten* v. *U.S.*, on which the Supreme Court had ruled as recently as 1963, Elliott Freemantle knew about but conveniently ignored. In *Batten*, the court accepted that only an actual "physical invasion" could create liability; noise alone did not do so. Since, at Meadowood, there had been no such invasion, the *Batten* precedent meant that if a legal case was launched, it might well be lost before it was begun.

But lawyer Freemantle had no wish for this to be known, at least not yet; nor was he overly concerned whether a case, if brought to court, might eventually be won or lost. What he wanted was this Meadowood homeowners group as clients—at a whopping fee.

On the subject of fee, he had already counted the house and done some mental arithmetic. The result delighted him.

Of six hundred people in the hall, he estimated that five hundred, probably more, were Meadowood property owners. Allowing for the presence of husbands and wives together, it meant there was a minimum of two hundred and fifty prospective clients. If each of those two hundred and fifty could be persuaded to sign a one hundred dollar retainer agreement—which Elliott Freemantle hoped they would before the evening was over—a total fee in excess of twenty-five thousand dollars seemed decidedly within reach.

On other occasions he had managed precisely the same thing. It was remarkable what you could accomplish with audacity, particularly when people were white hot in pursuing their own interests. An ample supply of printed retainer forms was in his bag. *This memorandum of agreement between . . . . hereinafter known as plaintiff/s and Freemantle and Sye, attorneys at law . . . who will undertake plaintiff/s legal representation in promotion of a claim for damages sustained due to aircraft use of the Lincoln International Airport facility . . . Plaintiff/s agrees to pay the said Freemantle and Sye one hundred dollars, in four installments of twenty-five dollars, the first installment now due and payable, the balance quarterly on demand . . . Further, if the suit is successful Freemantle and Sye will receive ten percent of the gross amount of any damages awarded . . .*

The ten percent was a long shot because it was highly unlikely that there would ever be any damages to collect. Just the same, strange things sometimes happened in law, and Elliott Freemantle believed in covering all bases.

"I have informed you of the legal background," he asserted. "Now I intend to give you some advice." He flashed one of his rare, quick smiles. "This advice will be a free sample, but—like toothpaste—any subsequent tubes will have to be paid for."

There was a responsive laugh which he cut off brusquely with a gesture. "My advice is that there is little time for anything else but action. Action now."

The remark produced handclapping and more nods of approval.

There was a tendency, he continued, to regard legal proceedings as automatically slow and tedious. Often that was true, but on occasions, if determination and legal skill were used, the law could be harried along. In the present instance, legal action should be begun at once, before airlines and airport, by perpetuation of noise over a period of years, could claim custom and usage. As if to underline the point, still another aircraft thundered overhead. Before its sound could die, Elliott Freemantle shouted, "So I repeat—my advice to you is wait no longer! You should act tonight. Now!"

Near the front of the audience, a youngish man in an

alpaca cardigan and hopsack slacks sprang to his feet. "By God!—tell us how we start."

"You start—if you want to—by retaining me as your legal counsel."

There was an instant chorus of several hundred voices. "Yes, we want to."

The chairman, Floyd Zanetta, was now on his feet again, waiting for the shouting to subside. He appeared pleased. Two of the reporters had craned around and were observing the obvious enthusiasm throughout the hall. The third reporter—the elderly woman from the local weekly—looked up at the platform with a friendly smile.

It had worked, as Elliott Freemantle had known it would. The rest, he realized, was merely routine. Within the next half hour a good many of the retainer blanks in his bag would be signed, while others would be taken home, talked over, and most likely mailed tomorrow. These people were not afraid of signing papers, or of legal procedures; they had become accustomed to both in purchasing their homes. Nor would a hundred dollars seem an excessive sum; a few might even be surprised that the figure was that low. Only a handful would bother doing the mental arithmetic which Elliott Freemantle had done himself, and even if they objected to the size of the total amount, he could argue that the fee was justified by responsibility for the large numbers involved.

Besides, he would give them value for their money—a good show, with fireworks, in court and elsewhere. He glanced at his watch; better get on. Now that his own involvement was assured, he wanted to cement the relationship by staging the first act of a drama. Like everything else so far, it was something he had already planned and it would gain attention—much more than this meeting—in tomorrow's newspapers. It would also confirm to these people that he meant what he said about not wasting any time.

The actors in the drama would be the residents of Meadowood, here assembled, and he hoped that everyone present was prepared to leave this hall and to stay out late.

The scene would be the airport.

The time: tonight.

11

At approximately the same time that Elliott Freemantle was savoring success, an embittered, thwarted, former building contractor named D. O. Guerrero was surrendering to failure.

Guerrero was fifteen miles or so from the airport, in a locked room of a shabby walk-up apartment on the city's South Side. The apartment was over a noisome, greasy-spoon lunch counter on 51st Street, not far from the stockyards.

D. O. Guerrero was a gaunt, spindly man, slightly stoop-shouldered, with a sallow face and protruding, narrow jaw. He had deep-set eyes, pale thin lips, and a slight sandy mustache. His neck was scrawny, with a prominent Adam's apple. His hairline was receding. He had nervous hands, and his fingers were seldom still. He smoked constantly, usually lighting a fresh cigarette from the stub of the last. At the moment he needed a shave and a clean shirt, and was perspiring, even though the room in which he had locked himself was cold. His age was fifty; he looked several years older.

Guerrero was married, and had been for eighteen years. By some standards, the marriage was good, if unspectacular. D.O. (through most of his life he had been known by his initials) and Inez Guerrero accepted each other equably, and the idea of coveting some other partner seemed not to occur to them. D. O. Guerrero, in any case, had never been greatly interested in women; business, and financial maneuvering, occupied his thoughts far more. But in the past year, a mental gulf had opened between the Guerreros which Inez, though she tried, was unable to bridge. It was one result of a series of business disasters which reduced them from comparative affluence to near poverty, and eventually forced a succession of moves—first from their comfortable and spacious, if heavily mortgaged, suburban home to other quarters less pretentious, and later still to this seamy, drafty, cockroach-infested, two-room apartment.

Even though Inez Guerrero did not enjoy their situation, she might have made the best of it if her husband had not become increasingly moody, savagely bad tempered, and at times impossible to talk with. A few weeks ago, in a rage, he had struck Inez, bruising her face badly, and though she would have forgiven him, he would neither apologize nor discuss the incident later. She feared more violence and, soon after, sent their two teen-age children—a boy and a girl—to stay with her married sister in Cleveland. Inez herself stayed on, taking a job as a coffee-house waitress, and although the work was hard and the pay small, it at least provided money for food. Her husband seemed scarcely to notice the children's absence, or her own; his mood recently had been a deep and self-contained dejection.

Inez was now at her job. D. O. Guerrero was in the apartment alone. He need not have locked the door of the small bedroom where he was occupied, but had done so as an added guarantee of privacy, even though he would not be there for long.

Like others this night, D. O. Guerrero would shortly leave for the airport. He held a confirmed reservation, plus a validated ticket—for tonight—on Trans America Flight Two to Rome. At this moment, the ticket was in a pocket of his topcoat, also in the locked room, slung over a rickety wooden chair.

Inez Guerrero had no knowledge of the ticket to Rome, nor did she have the slightest inkling of her husband's motive in obtaining it.

The Trans America ticket was for a round trip excursion which normally cost four hundred and seventy-four dollars. However, by lying, D. O. Guerrero had obtained credit. He had paid forty-seven dollars down, acquired by pawning his wife's last possession of any value—her mother's ring (Inez had not yet missed it) —and promised to remit the balance, plus interest, in monthly installments over the next two years.

It was highly unlikely that the promise would ever be fulfilled.

No self-respecting finance company or bank would have loaned D. O. Guerrero the price of a bus ticket to Peoria, let alone an airline fare to Rome. They would have investigated his background thoroughly, and discovered that he had a long history of insolvency, a parcel of long-standing personal debts, and that his homebuilding company, Guerrero Contracting Inc., had been placed in bankruptcy a year earlier.

An even closer check into Guerrero's tangled finances might have disclosed that during the past eight months —using his wife's name—he had attempted to raise capital for a speculative land deal, but failed to do so. In course of this failure he had incurred even more debts. Now, because of certain fraudulent statements, as well as being an undischarged bankrupt, exposure, which seemed imminent, would involve criminal prosecution and almost certainly a prison term. Slightly less serious, but just as immediate, was the fact that the rent of this apartment, wretched as it was, was three weeks overdue, and the landlord had threatened eviction tomorrow. If evicted, they would have nowhere else to go.

D. O. Guerrero was desperate. His financial rating was minus zero.

Airlines, though, were notably easygoing about extending credit; also, if a debt went sour they were usually less tough in collection procedures than other agencies. This was calculated policy. It was based on the fact that fare-paying air travelers, over the years, had proven themselves an unusually honest cross-section of society, and bad debt losses of most airlines were remarkably low. Deadbeats like D. O. Guerrero troubled them rarely; therefore they were not geared—because it was not worth while—to defeat the kind of subterfuge he had used.

He avoided, by two simple means, more than a cursory credit investigation. First, he produced an "employer's reference" which he had typed himself on the letterhead of a defunct company he once operated (not the bankrupt one), the company's address being his own post office box. Second, in typing the letter he deliberately misspelled his surname, changing the initial from "G" to "B," so that a routine consumer credit check of "Buerrero" would produce no information, instead of the harmful data recorded under his correct name. For further identification he used his Social Security card and driver's license, on both of which he carefully changed the same initial beforehand, and had since changed it back again. Another point he remembered was to make sure that his signature on the time payment contract was indecipherable, so it was not clear whether he had signed "G" or "B."

The misspelling was perpetuated by the clerk who yesterday made out his airline ticket in the name of "D. O. Buerrero," and D. O. Guerrero had weighed this carefully in light of his immediate plans. He decided not to worry. If any query was raised afterward, the error of a single letter, both on the "employer's reference" and the ticket, would appear to be a genuine mistake. There was nothing to prove he had arranged it deliberately. In any case, when checking in at the airport later tonight, he intended to have the spelling corrected—on the Trans America flight manifest as well as on his ticket. It was important, once he was aboard, to be sure there was no confusion about his correct identity. That was part of his plan, too.

Another part of D. O. Guerrero's plan was to destroy Flight Two by blowing it up. He would destroy himself along with it, a factor which did not deter him since his life, he reasoned, was no longer of value to himself or others.

But his death could be of value, and he intended to make sure it was.

Before departure of the Trans America flight, he

would take out flight insurance for seventy-five thousand dollars, naming his wife and children as beneficiaries. He rationalized that he had done little for them until now, but his final act would be a single transcendent gesture on their behalf. He believed that what he was doing was a deed of love and sacrifice.

In his warped, perverted mind—driven by desperation—he had given no thought to other passengers who would be aboard Flight Two, nor to the aircraft's crew, all of whose deaths would accompany his own. With a psychopath's total lack of conscience he had considered others only to the extent that they might circumvent his scheme.

He believed he had anticipated all contingencies.

The business about his ticket would not matter once the aircraft was en route. No one could prove he had not intended to pay the installments he contracted for; and even if the fake "employer's reference" was exposed —as it probably would be—it demonstrated nothing except that he had obtained credit under false pretenses. That, in itself, would have no bearing on a subsequent insurance claim.

Another thing was that he deliberately bought a round-trip ticket to create the appearance of not only intending to complete the outward flight, but also to return. As to choosing a Rome flight, he had a second cousin in Italy whom he had never seen, but occasionally talked of visiting—a fact which Inez knew. So at least there would seem an element of logic to his choice.

D. O. Guerrero had had his plan in mind for several months while his fortunes were worsening. During that time he studied carefully the histories of air disasters where airliners were destroyed by individuals seeking to profit from flight insurance. The number of instances was surprisingly large. In all cases on record the motive had been exposed by post-crash investigation and, where conspirators remained alive, they were charged with murder. The flight insurance policies of those involved had been invalidated.

There was no means of knowing, of course, how many other disasters, where causes remained unknown, had been the result of sabotage. The key factor was the presence or absence of wreckage. Wherever wreckage was recovered, trained investigators pieced it together in an attempt to learn its secrets. They usually succeeded. If there was an explosion in mid-air, its traces remained, and the nature of the explosion could be determined. Therefore, D. O. Guerrero reasoned, his own plan must preclude the recovery of wreckage.

This was the reason he had selected Trans America's non-stop flight to Rome.

A large portion of the journey of Flight Two—*The Golden Argosy*—was above ocean, where wreckage from a disintegrated airplane would never be found.

Using one of the airline's own passenger brochures which conveniently showed air routes, aircraft speeds, and even had a feature called *Chart Your Own Position,* Guerrero calculated that after four hours' flying—allowing for average winds—Flight Two would be over mid-Atlantic. He intended to check the calculation and amend it, if necessary, as the journey progressed. He would do so, first by noting the exact time of takeoff, then by listening carefully to the announcements which captains always made over cabin p.a. systems about the aircraft's progress. With the information it would be a simple matter to decide if the flight was behind schedule, or ahead, and by how much. Finally, at approximately a point he had already decided on—eight hundred miles east of Newfoundland—he would trigger an explosion. It would send the aircraft, or what remained of it, plummeting toward the sea.

No wreckage could ever be found.

The debris of Flight Two would remain forever, hidden and secret, on the Atlantic Ocean floor. There would be no examination, no later exposure of the cause of the aircraft's loss. Those left might wonder, question, speculate; they might even guess the truth, but they could never *know.*

Flight insurance claims—in the absence of any evidence of sabotage—would be settled in full.

The single element on which everything else hinged was the explosion. Obviously it must be adequate to destroy the airplane, but—equally important—it must occur at the right time. For the second reason D. O. Guerrero had decided to carry the explosive device aboard and set it off himself. Now, within the locked bedroom, he was putting the device together, and despite his familiarity—as a building contractor—with explosives, was still sweating, as he had been since he started a quarter of an hour ago.

There were five main components—three cartridges of dynamite, a tiny blasting cap with wires attached, and a single cell transistor radio battery. The dynamite cartridges were Du Pont Red Cross Extra—small but exceedingly powerful, containing forty percent nitroglycerin; each was an inch and a quarter in diameter and eight inches long. They were taped together with black electrician's tape and, to conceal their purpose, were in a Ry-Krisp box, left open at one end.

Guerrero had also laid out several other items, carefully, on the ragged coverlet of the bed where he was working. These were a wooden clothespin, two thumbtacks, a square inch of clear plastic, and a short length of string. Total value of the equipment which would destroy a six and a half million dollar airplane was less than five dollars. All of it, including the dynamite—a "leftover" from D. O. Guerrero's days as a contractor—had been bought in hardware stores.

Also on the bed was a small, flat attaché case of the type in which businessmen carried their papers and books when traveling by air. It was in this that Guerrero was now installing the explosive apparatus. Later, he would carry the case with him on the flight.

It was all incredibly simple. It was so simple, in fact, Guerrero thought to himself, that most people, lacking a knowledge of explosives, would never believe that it would work. And yet it would—with shattering, devastating deadliness.

He taped the Ry-Krisp box containing the dynamite securely in place inside the attaché case. Close to it he fastened the wooden clothespin and the battery. The battery would fire the charge. The clothespin was the switch which, at the proper time, would release the current from the battery.

His hands were trembling. He could feel sweat, in rivulets, inside his shirt. With the blasting cap in place, one mistake, one slip, would blow himself, this room, and most of the building, apart, here and now.

He held his breath as he connected a second wire from the blasting cap and dynamite to one side of the clothespin.

He waited, aware of his heart pounding, using a handkerchief to wipe moisture from his hands. His nerves, his senses, were on edge. Beneath him, as he sat on the bed, he could feel the thin, lumpy mattress. The decrepit iron bedstead screeched a protest as he moved.

He resumed working. With exquisite caution, he connected another wire. Now, only the square inch of clear plastic was preventing the passage of an electric current and thereby an explosion.

The plastic, less than a sixteenth of an inch thick, had a small hole near its outer edge. D. O. Guerrero took the last item left on the bed—the string—and passed one end through the hole in the plastic, then tied it securely, being cautious not to move the plastic. The other end of the string he pushed through an inconspicuous hole, already drilled, which went through to the outside of the attaché case, emerging under the carrying handle. Leaving the string fairly loose inside the case, on the outside he tied a second knot, large enough to prevent the string from slipping back. Finally—also on the outside—he made a finger-size loop, like a miniature hangman's noose, and cut off the surplus string.

And that was it.

A finger through the loop, a tug on the string! Electric current would flow, and the explosion would be instant, devastating, final, for whomever or whatever was nearby.

Now that it was done, Guerrero relaxed and lit a cigarette. He smiled sardonically as he reflected again on how much more complicated the public—including writers of detective fiction—imagined the manufacture of a bomb to be. In stories he had read there were always elaborate mechanisms, clocks, fuses, which ticked or hissed or spluttered, and which could be circumvented if immersed in water. In reality, no complications were required—only the simple, homely components he had just put together. Nor could anything stop the detonation of his kind of bomb—neither water, bullets, nor bravery—once the string was pulled.

Holding the cigarette between his lips, and squinting through its smoke, D. O. Guerrero put some papers carefully into the attaché case, covering the dynamite, clothespin, wires, battery, and string. He made sure the papers would not move around, but that the string could move freely under them. Even if he opened the case for any reason, its contents would appear innocent. He closed the case and locked it.

He checked the cheap alarm clock beside the bed. It was a few minutes after 8 P.M., a little less than two hours to flight departure time. Time to go. He would take the subway uptown to the airline terminal, then board an airport bus. He had just enough money left for that, and to buy the flight insurance policy. The thought reminded him that he must allow sufficient time at the airport to get insurance. He pulled on his topcoat quickly, checking that the ticket to Rome was still in the inside pocket.

He unlocked the bedroom door and went into the mean, shabby living room, taking the attaché case with him, holding it gingerly.

One final thing to do! A note for Inez. He found a scrap of paper and a pencil and, after thinking for several seconds, wrote:

I won't be home for a few days. I'm going away.
I expect to have some good news soon which
will surprise you.

He signed it *D.O.*

For a moment he hesitated, softening. It wasn't much of a note to mark the end of eighteen years of marriage. Then he decided it would have to do; it would be a mistake to say too much. Afterward, even without wreckage from Flight Two, investigators would put the passenger list under a microscope. The note, as well as all other papers he had left, would be examined minutely.

He put the note on a table where Inez would be sure to see it.

As he went downstairs D. O. Guerrero could hear voices, and a jukebox playing, from the greasy-spoon lunch counter. He turned up the collar of his topcoat, with the other hand holding the attaché case tightly. Under the carrying handle of the case, the loop of string like a hangman's noose was close to his curled fingers.

Outside, as he left the South Side building and headed for the subway, it was still snowing.

PART TWO

8:30 P.M.–11 P.M. (CST)

1

Once more, Joe Patroni returned to the warmth of his car and telephoned the airport. The TWA maintenance chief reported that the road between himself and the airport was still blocked by the traffic accident which had delayed him, but the chances of getting through soon looked good. Was the Aéreo-Mexican 707, he inquired, still stuck in mud out on the airfield? Yes, he was informed, it was; furthermore, every few minutes, everyone concerned was calling TWA to ask where he was, and how much longer he would be, because his help was needed urgently.

Without waiting to warm himself fully, Patroni left the car and hurried back down the highway, through the still falling snow and deep slush underfoot, to where the accident had occurred.

At the moment, the scene around the wrecked tractor-trailer transport looked like a staged disaster for a wide screen movie. The mammoth vehicle still lay on its side, blocking all four traffic lanes. By now it was completely snow covered and, with none of its wheels touching ground, seemed like a dead, rolled-over dinosaur. Floodlights and flares, aided by the whiteness of the snow, made the setting seem like day. The floodlights were on the three tow trucks which Patroni had urged sending for, and all had now arrived. The brilliant red flares had been planted by state police, of whom several more had appeared, and it seemed that when a

121

state trooper lacked something to do, he lit another flare. As a result, the display of pyrotechnics was worthy of the Fourth of July.

The arrival of a TV camera crew, a few minutes earlier, had heightened the stage effect. The self-important crew had come with blaring horn and illegal flashing beacon, driving down a shoulder of the road in a maroon station wagon blazoned WSHT. Typically, the four young men who comprised the TV crew had taken over as if the entire event had been arranged for their convenience, and all further developments could now await their pleasure. Several state troopers, having ignored the illegal beacon on the station wagon, were engaged in waving the two trucks from their present positions into new ones, as the TV men directed.

Before he left to make his telephone call, Joe Patroni had carefully coaxed the two trucks into locations which would give them the best leverage, together, to move the disabled tractor-trailer. As he left, the truck drivers and helpers were connecting heavy chains which he knew would take several more minutes to secure. The state police had been glad of his aid, and a burly police lieutenant, by that time in charge at the scene, had told the tow truck drivers to take their instructions from Patroni. But now, incredibly, the chains were removed, except for one which a grinning tow truck operator was handling as photofloods and a portable TV camera focused on him.

Behind the camera and lights a crowd of people, even larger than before, had assembled from other blocked vehicles. Most were watching the TV filming interestedly, their earlier impatience and the cold bleak misery of the night apparently forgotten for the moment.

A sudden gust of wind slapped icy wet snow into Joe Patroni's face. Too late, his hand went to the neck of his parka. He felt some of the snow slide in, penetrate his shirt, and soak him miserably. Ignoring the discomfort, he strode toward the state police lieutenant and demanded, "Who in hell changed the trucks? The way they're lined now, you couldn't move a peck of coondirt. All they'll do is pull each other."

"I know, Mister." The lieutenant, tall, broad-shouldered, and towering above the short, stocky figure of Patroni, appeared fleetingly embarrassed. "But the TV guys wanted a better shot. They're from a local station, and it's for the news tonight—all about the storm. Excuse me."

One of the television men—himself huddled into a heavy coat—was beckoning the lieutenant into the filming. The lieutenant, head up, and ignoring the falling snow, walked with brisk authority toward the tow truck which was the center of the film shot. Two state troopers followed. The lieutenant, being careful to keep his face toward the camera, began giving instructions, with gestures, to the tow truck operator, instructions which were largely meaningless, but on screen would look impressive.

The maintenance chief, remembering his need to get to the airport speedily, felt his anger rise. He braced himself to race out, grab the TV camera and lights, and smash them all. He could do it, too; instinctively his muscles tightened, his breathing quickened. Then, with an effort, he controlled himself.

A trait of character of Joe Patroni's was a white-hot, violent temper; fortunately the violent part was not easily set off, but once it was, all reason and logic deserted him. The exercise of control over his temper was something he had tried to learn through his years of manhood. He had not always succeeded, though nowadays a single memory helped.

On one occasion he had failed to have control. The result, forever after, haunted him.

In the Army Air Forces of World War II, Joe Patroni had been a redoubtable amateur boxer. He fought as a middleweight and, at one point, came within sight of the Air Forces championship, within his division, of the European Theater.

In a bout staged in England shortly before the Normandy invasion, he had been matched against a crew chief named Terry O'Hale, a rough, tough Bostonian with a reputation for meanness in the ring, as well as out of it. Joe Patroni, then a young Pfc. aviation

mechanic, knew O'Hale and disliked him. The dislike
would not have mattered if O'Hale, as a calculated part
of his ring technique, had not whispered constantly,
*"You greasy dago wop . . . Whyn't you fighting for the
other side, you mother lovin' Eytie? . . . You cheer
when they shoot our ships down, dago boy?"* and other
pleasantries. Patroni had seen the gambit for what it was
—an attempt to get him rattled—and ignored it until
O'Hale landed two low blows near the groin in swift
succession, which the referee, circling behind, did not
observe.

The combination of insults, foul blows, and excruciating pain, produced the anger which Patroni's opponent had counted on. What he did not count on was that
Joe Patroni would deliver an onslaught so swift, savage,
and utterly without mercy that O'Hale went down
before it and, after being counted out, was pronounced
dead.

Patroni was exonerated. Although the referee had not
observed the low blows, others at ringside had. Even
without them, Patroni had done no more than was expected—fought to the limit of his skill and strength.
Only he was aware that for the space of seconds he had
been berserk, insane. Alone and later, he faced the realization that even if he had known O'Hale was dying, he
could not have stopped himself.

In the end, he avoided the cliché of abandoning
fighting, or "hanging up his gloves for good," as the
usual fiction sequence went. He had gone on fighting,
employing in the ring the whole of his physical resource,
not holding back, yet testing his own control to avoid
crossing the hairline between reason and berserk savagery. He succeeded, and knew that he had, because
there were tests of anger where reason struggled with
the wild animal inside him—and reason won. Then, and
only then, did Joe Patroni quit fighting for the remainder of his life.

But control of anger did not mean dismissing it entirely. As the police lieutenant returned from camera
range, Patroni confronted him heatedly. "You just
blocked this road an extra twenty minutes. It took ten

minutes to locate those trucks where they should be; it'll take another ten to get them back."

As he spoke, there was the sound of a jet aircraft overhead—a reminder of the reason for Joe Patroni's haste.

"Now listen, mister." The lieutenant's face suffused a deeper red than it already was from cold and wind. "Get through your head that I'm in charge here. We're glad to have help, including yours. But I'm the one who's making decisions."

"Then make one now!"

"I'll make what I'm . . ."

"No!—*you* listen to *me*." Joe Patroni stood glaring, uninhibited by the policeman's bulk above him. Something of the maintenance chief's contained anger, and a hint of authority, made the lieutenant hesitate.

"There's an emergency at the airport. I already explained it; and why I'm needed there." Patroni stabbed his glowing cigar through the air for emphasis. "Maybe other people have reasons for hightailing it out of here too, but mine's enough for now. There's a phone in my car. I can call my top brass, who'll call your brass, and before you know it, somebody'll be on that radio of yours asking why you're polishing your TV image instead of doing the job you're here for. So make a decision, the way you said! Do I call in, or do we move?"

The lieutenant glared wrathfully back at Joe Patroni. Briefly, the policeman seemed ready to vent his own anger, then decided otherwise. He swung his big body toward the TV crew. "Get all that crap out of here! You guys have had long enough."

One of the television men called over his shoulder, "We'll just be a few minutes more, chief."

In two strides the lieutenant was beside him. "You heard me! Right now!"

The policeman leaned down, his face still fierce from the encounter with Patroni, and the TV man visibly jumped. "Okay, okay." He motioned hastily to the others and the lights on the portable camera went out.

"Let's have those two trucks back the way they were!" The lieutenant began firing orders at the state troopers, who moved quickly to execute them. He returned to Joe Patroni and gestured to the overturned transport; it was clear that he had decided Patroni was more use as an ally than an antagonist. "Mister, you still think we have to drag this rig? You sure we can't get it upright?"

"Only if you want to block this road till daylight. You'd have to unload the trailer first, and if you do . . ."

"I know, I know! Forget it! We'll pull and shove now, and worry about damage later." The lieutenant gestured to the waiting line of traffic. "If you want to get moving right after, you'd better hustle your car out of line and move up front. You want an escort to the airport?"

Patroni nodded appreciatively. "Thanks."

Ten minutes later the last pindle tow hook snapped into place. Heavy chains from one tow truck were secured around the axles of the disabled transport tractor; a stout wire cable connected the chains to the tow truck winch. A second tow truck was connected to the toppled trailer. The third tow truck was behind the trailer, ready to push.

The driver from the big transport unit, which, despite its overturning, was only partially damaged, groaned as he watched what was happening. "My bosses ain't gonna like this! That's a near-new rig. You're gonna tear it apart."

"If we do," a young state trooper told him, "we'll be finishing what you started."

"Wadda you care? Ain't nothing to you I just lost a good job," the driver grumbled back. "Maybe I should try for a soft touch next time—like bein' a lousy cop."

The trooper grinned. "Why not? You're already a lousy driver."

"You figure we're ready?" the lieutenant asked Patroni.

Joe Patroni nodded. He was crouching, observing the tautness of chains and cables. He cautioned, "Take it slow and easy. Get the cab section sliding first."

The first tow truck began pulling with its winch; its wheels skidded on snow and the driver accelerated forward, keeping the tow chain straining. The overturned transport's front portion creaked, slid a foot or two with a protesting scream of metal, then stopped.

Patroni motioned with his hand. "Keep it moving! And get the trailer started!"

The chains and cable between the trailer axles and the second tow truck tightened. The third tow truck pushed against the trailer roof. The wheels of all three tow trucks skidded as they fought for purchase on the wet, packed snow. For another two feet the tractor and trailer, still coupled together, as they had been when they rolled over, moved sideways across the highway to an accompanying ragged cheer from the crowd of on-lookers. The TV camera was functioning again, its lights adding brightness to the scene.

A wide, deep gash in the road showed where the big transport had been. The tractor cab and the body of the loaded trailer were taking punishment, the trailer roof beginning to angle as one side of the trailer dragged against the road. The price to be paid—no doubt by insurers—for reopening the highway quickly would be a steep one.

Around the road blockage, two snowplows—one on either side like skirmishers—were attempting to clear as much as they could of the snow which had piled since the accident occurred. Everything and everyone, by this time, was snow covered, including Patroni, the lieu-tenant, state troopers, and all others in the open.

The truck motors roared again. Smoke rose from tires, spinning on wet, packed snow. Slowly, ponder-ously, the overturned vehicle shifted a few inches, a few feet, then slid clear across to the far side of the road. Within seconds, instead of blocking four traffic lanes, it obstructed only one. It would be a simple matter now for the three tow trucks to nudge the tractor-trailer clear of the highway onto the shoulder beyond.

State troopers were already moving flares, prepara-tory to untangling the monumental traffic jam which would probably occupy them for several hours to come. The sound, once again, of a jet aircraft overhead was a reminder to Joe Patroni that his principal business this night still lay elsewhere.

The state police lieutenant took off his cap and shook the snow from it. He nodded to Patroni. "I guess it's your turn, mister."

A patrol car, parked on a shoulder, was edging onto the highway. The lieutenant pointed to it. "Keep close up behind that car. I've told them you'll be following, and they've orders to get you to the airport fast."

Joe Patroni nodded. As he climbed into his Buick Wildcat, the lieutenant called after him, "And mister . . . Thanks!"

2

Captain Vernon Demerest stood back from the cupboard door he had opened, and emitted a long, low whistle.

He was still in the kitchen of Gwen Meighen's apartment on Stewardess Row. Gwen had not yet appeared after her shower and, while waiting, he had made tea as she suggested. It was while looking for cups and saucers that he had opened the cupboard door.

In front of him were four tightly packed shelves of bottles. All were miniature bottles of liquor—the ounce-and-a-half size which airlines served to passengers in flight. Most of the bottles had small airline labels above their brand names, and all were unopened. Making a quick calculation, Demerest estimated there were close to three hundred.

He had seen airline liquor in stewardesses' apartments before, but never quite so much at one time.

"We have some more stashed away in the bedroom," Gwen said brightly from behind him. "We've been saving them for a party. I think we've enough, don't you?"

She had come into the kitchen quietly, and he turned.

As always since the beginning of their affair, he found the first sight of her enchanting and refreshing. Unusual for one who never lacked confidence with women, he had at such moments a heady sense of wonder that he had ever possessed Gwen at all. She was in a trim uniform skirt and blouse which made her seem even younger than she was. Her eager, high-cheekboned face was tilted upward, her rich black hair lustrous under the kitchen lights. Gwen's deep dark eyes regarded him with smiling, frank approval. "You can kiss me hard," she said. "I haven't put on makeup yet."

He smiled, her clear melodious English voice delighting him again. As girls from upper-crust British private schools somehow managed to do, Gwen had captured all that was best in English intonation and avoided the worst. At times, Vernon Demerest encouraged Gwen to talk, merely for the joy of hearing her speak.

Not talking now, they held each other tightly, her lips responding eagerly to his.

After a minute or so, Gwen pushed herself away. "No!" she insisted firmly. "No, Vernon dear. Not here."

"Why not? We've time enough." There was a thickness to Demerest's voice, a rough impatience.

"Because I told you—I want to talk, and we don't have time for both." Gwen rearranged her blouse which had parted company with the skirt.

"Hell!" he grumbled. "You bring me to the boil, and then . . . Oh, all right; I'll wait till Naples." He kissed her more gently. "All the way to Europe you can think of me up there on the flight deck, turned to 'simmer.' "

"I'll bring you to the boil again. I promise." She laughed, and leaning close against him, passed her long slim fingers through his hair and around his face.

He groaned. "My God!—you're doing it right now."

"Then that's enough." Gwen took his hands, which were around her waist, and pushed them resolutely from her. Turning away, she moved to close the cupboard he had been looking into.

"Hey, wait a minute. What about all those?" Demerest pointed to the miniature liquor bottles with their airline labels.

"Those?" Gwen surveyed the four crowded shelves, her eyebrows arched, then switched to an expression of injured innocence. "They're just a few little old leftovers that passengers didn't want. Surely, Captain, sir, you're not going to report me for possession of leftovers."

He said skeptically, "That many?"

"Of course." Gwen picked up a bottle of Beefeater gin, put it down and inspected a Canadian Club whisky. "One nice thing about airlines is, they always buy the best brands. Care for one now?"

He shook his head. "You know better than that."

"Yes, I do; but you shouldn't sound so disapproving."

"I just don't want you to get caught."

"Nobody gets caught, and almost everybody does it. Look—every first class passenger is entitled to two of these little bottles, but some passengers use only one, and there are always others who won't have any."

"The rules say you turn back all the unused ones."

"Oh, for heaven's sake! So we do—a couple for appearances, but the rest the girls divide between them. The same thing goes for wine that's left over." Gwen giggled. "We always like a passenger who asks for more wine near the end of a trip. That way, we can officially open a fresh bottle, pour off one glass . . ."

"I know. And take the rest home?"

"You want to see?" Gwen opened another cupboard door. Inside were a dozen filled wine bottles.

Demerest grinned. "I'll be damned."

"This isn't all mine. My roommate and one of the girls next door have been saving theirs for the party we're planning." She took his arm. "You'll come, won't you?"

"If I'm invited, I guess."

Gwen closed both cupboard doors. "You will be."

They sat down in the kitchen, and she poured the tea he had made. He watched admiringly while she did it. Gwen had a way of making even a casual session like this seem an occasion.

He noticed with amusement that she produced cups from a pile in another cupboard, all bearing Trans America insignia. They were the kind the airline used in flight. He supposed he should not have been stuffy about the airline liquor bottles; after all, stewardess "perks" were nothing new. It was just that the size of the hoard amazed him.

All airline stewardesses, he was aware, discovered early in their careers that a little husbandry in airplane galleys could relieve their cost of living at home. Stewardesses learned to board their flights with personal hand baggage which was partially empty, using the space for surplus food—always of highest quality, since airlines purchased nothing but the best. A Thermos jug, brought aboard empty, was useful for carrying off spare liquids —cream or even decanted champagne. If a stewardess was really enterprising, Demerest was once assured, she could cut her weekly grocery bill in half. Only on international flights where, by law, all food—untouched or otherwise—was incinerated immediately after landing, were the girls more cautious.

All this activity was strictly forbidden by regulations of all airlines—but it still went on.

Another thing stewardesses learned was that no inventory check of removable cabin equipment was ever made at the termination of a flight. One reason was that airlines simply didn't have time; another, it was cheaper to accept some losses than make a fuss about them. Because of this, many stewardesses managed to acquire home furnishings—blankets, pillows, towels, linen napkins, glasses, silverware—in surprising quantity, and Vernon Demerest had been in stewardess nests where most items used in daily living seemed to have come from airline sources.

Gwen broke in on his thoughts. "What I was going to tell you, Vernon, is that I'm pregnant."

It was said so casually that at first the words failed to register. He reacted blankly. "You're what?"

"Pregnant—p-r-e-g-n . . ."

He snapped irritably, "I know how to spell it." His mind was still groping. "Are you sure?"

Gwen laughed—her attractive silvery laugh—and sipped her tea. He sensed she was making fun of him. He was also aware that she had never looked more lovely and desirable than at this moment.

"That line you just said, darling," she assured him, "is an old cliché. In every book I've ever read where there's a scene like this, the man asks, 'Are you sure?' "

"Well, goddammit, Gwen!" His voice rose. *"Are you?"*

"Of course. Or I wouldn't be telling you now." She motioned to the cup in front of him. "More tea?"

"No!"

"What happened," Gwen said calmly, "is perfectly simple. On that layover we had in San Francisco . . . you remember?—we stayed at that gorgeous hotel on Nob Hill; the one with the view. What was it called?"

"The Fairmont. Yes, I remember. Go on."

"Well, I'm afraid I was careless. I'd quit taking pills because they were making me overweight; then I thought I didn't need any other precautions that day, but it turned out I was wrong. Anyway, because I was careless, now I have a teensy-weensy little Vernon Demerest inside me who's going to get bigger and bigger."

There was a silence, then he said awkwardly, "I suppose I shouldn't ask this . . ."

She interrupted. "Yes, you should. You're entitled to ask." Gwen's deep dark eyes regarded him with open honesty. "What you want to know is, has there been anyone else, and am I positive it's you? Right?"

"Look, Gwen . . ."

She reached out to touch his hand. "You don't have to be ashamed of asking. I'd ask too, if things were the other way around."

He gestured unhappily. "Forget it. I'm sorry."

"But I want to tell you." She was speaking more hurriedly now, a shade less confidently. "There hasn't been anybody else; there couldn't be. You see . . . I happen to love you." For the first time her eyes were lowered. She went on, "I think I did . . . I know I did . . . love you, I mean—even before that time we had in San Francisco. When I've thought about it, I've been glad of that, because you ought to love someone if you're to have his baby, don't you think so?"

"Listen to me, Gwen." He covered her hands with his own. Vernon Demerest's hands were strong and sensitive, accustomed to responsibility and control, yet capable of precision and gentleness. They were gentle now. Women he cared about always had that effect on him, in contrast to the couth brusqueness with which he dealt with men. "We have to do some serious talking, and make some plans." Now that the first surprise was over, his thoughts were becoming orderly. It was perfectly clear what needed to be done next.

"You don't have to do anything." Gwen's head came up; her voice was under control. "And you can stop wondering whether I'm going to be difficult, or whether I'll make things awkward for you. I won't. I knew what I was getting into; that there was the chance this would happen. I didn't really expect it to, but it has. I had to tell you tonight because the baby's yours; it's part of you; you ought to know. Now you do, I'm also telling you you don't have to worry. I intend to work things out myself."

"Don't be ridiculous; of course I'll help. You don't imagine I'd walk away and ignore the whole bit." The essential thing, he realized, was speed; the trick with unwanted fetuses was to get the little beggars early. He wondered if Gwen had any religious scruples about abortions. She had never mentioned having a religion, but sometimes the most unlikely people were devout. He asked her, "Are you Catholic?"

"No."

Well, he reflected, that helped. Maybe, then, a quick flight to Sweden would be the thing; a few days there was all Gwen would need. Trans America would cooperate, as airlines always did, providing they were not officially involved—the word "abortion" could be hinted at, but must never be mentioned. That way, Gwen could fly deadhead on a Trans America flight to Paris, then go by Air France to Stockholm on a reciprocal employee pass. Of course, even when she got to Sweden, the medical fees would still be damnably expensive; there was a jest among airline people that the Swedes took their overseas abortion customers to the clinic and the cleaners at the same time. The whole thing was cheaper in Japan, of course. Lots of airline stewardesses flew to Tokyo and got abortions there for fifty dollars. The abortions were supposed to be therapeutic, but Demerest mistrusted them; Sweden—or Switzerland—were more reliable. He had once declared: when he got a stewardess pregnant, she went first class.

From his own point of view, it was a bloody nuisance that Gwen had got a bun in the oven at this particular time, just when he was building an extension on his house which, he remembered gloomily, had already gone over budget. Oh well, he would have to sell some stock—General Dynamics, probably; he had a nice capital gain there, and it was about time to take a profit. He would call his broker right after getting back from Rome—and Naples.

He asked, "You're still coming to Naples with me?"

"Of course; I've been looking forward to it. Besides, I bought a new negligee. You'll see it tomorrow night."

He stood up from the table and grinned. "You're a shameless hussy."

"A shameless *pregnant* hussy who shamelessly loves you. Do you love me?"

She came to him, and he kissed her mouth, face, and an ear. He probed her pinna with his tongue, felt her arms tighten in response, then whispered, "Yes, I love you." At the moment, he reflected, it was true.

"Vernon, dear."

"Yes?"

Her cheek was soft against his. Her voice came, muffled, from his shoulder. "I mean what I said. You don't have to help me. But if you really want to, that's different."

"I want to." He decided he would sound her out about an abortion, on their way to the airport.

Gwen disengaged herself and glanced at her watch; it was 8:20. "It's time, Captain, sir. We'd better go."

"I guess you know you really don't have to worry," Vernon Demerest said to Gwen as they drove. "Airlines are used to having their unmarried stewardesses get pregnant. It happens all the time. The last report I read, the national airline average was ten percent, per year."

Their discussion, he noted approvingly, was becoming increasingly matter-of-fact. Good!—it was important to steer Gwen away from any emotional nonsense about this baby of hers. If she did become emotional, Demerest knew, all sorts of awkward things could happen, impeding commonsense.

He was handling the Mercedes carefully, with the delicate yet firm touch which was second nature to him when controlling any piece of machinery, including a car or airplane. The suburban streets, which were newly cleared when he drove from the airport to Gwen's apartment, were thickly snow-covered again. Snow was still coming down continuously, and there were deepening drifts in wind-exposed places, away from the shelter of buildings. Captain Demerest warily skirted the larger drifts. He had no intention of getting stuck nor did he even want to get out of the car until the shelter of the enclosed Trans America parking lot was reached.

Curled into the leather bucket seat beside him, Gwen said incredulously, "Is that really true—that every year, ten out of every hundred stewardesses get pregnant?"

He assured her, "It varies slightly each year, but it's usually pretty close. Oh, the pill has changed things a bit, but the way I hear it, not as much as you'd expect. As a union officer I have access to that kind of information."

He waited for Gwen to comment. When she made none, he went on, "What you have to remember is that airline stewardesses are mostly young girls, from the country, or modest city homes. They've had a quiet upbringing, an average life. Suddenly, they have a glamour job; they travel, meet interesting people, stay in the best hotels. It's their first taste of *la dolce vita*." He grinned. "Once in a while that first taste leaves some sediment in the glass."

"That's a rotten thing to say!" For the first time since

he had known her, Gwen's temper flared. She said indignantly, "You sound so superior; just like a man. If I have any sediment in *my* glass, *or* in me, let me remind you that it's yours, and even if we didn't plan to leave it there, I think I'd find a better name for it than that. Also, if you're lumping me together with all those girls you talked about from the country and 'modest city homes,' I don't like that one damn bit either."

There was heightened color in Gwen's cheeks; her eyes flashed angrily.

"Hey!" he said. "I like your spirit."

"Well, keep on saying things like you did just now, and you'll see more of it."

"Was I that bad?"

"You were insufferable."

"Then I'm sorry." Demerest slowed the car and stopped at a traffic light which shone with myriad red reflections through the falling snow. They waited in silence until, with Christmas card effect, the color winked to green. When they were moving again, he said carefully, "I didn't mean to lump you with anybody, because you're an exception. You're a sophisticate who got careless. You said you did, yourself. I guess we were both careless."

"All right." Gwen's anger was dissipating. "But don't ever put me in bunches. I'm me; no one else."

They were quiet for several moments, then Gwen said thoughtfully, "I suppose we could call him that."

"Call who what?"

"You made me remember what I said earlier—about a little Vernon Demerest inside me. If we had a boy, we could call him Vernon Demerest, Junior, the way Americans do."

He had never cared much for his own name. Now he began to say, "I wouldn't want my son . . ." then stopped. This was dangerous ground.

"What I started to say, Gwen, was that airlines are used to this kind of thing. You know about the Three-Point Pregnancy Program?"

She said shortly, "Yes."

It was natural that Gwen did. Most stewardesses were

aware of what airlines would do for them if they became pregnant, providing the stewardess herself agreed to certain conditions. Within Trans America the system was referred to familiarly as the "3-PPP." Other airlines used differing names, and arrangements varied slightly, but the principle was the same.

"I've known girls who've used the 3-PPP," Gwen said. "I didn't think I'd ever need to."

"Most of the others didn't, I guess." He added: "But you wouldn't need to worry. It isn't something that airlines advertise, and it all works quietly. How are we for time?"

Gwen held her wrist watch under the light of the dash. "We're okay."

He swung the Mercedes into a center lane carefully, judging his traction on the wet, snowy surface, and passed a lumbering utilities truck. Several men, probably an emergency crew, were clinging to the sides of the truck as it moved along. They looked weary, wet, and miserable. Demerest wondered what the men's reaction would be if they knew that he and Gwen would be under warm Neapolitan sunshine only hours from now.

"I don't know," Gwen said; "I don't know if I could ever do it."

Like Demerest, Gwen knew the reasoning of management which lay behind airline pregnancy programs. No airline liked losing stewardesses for any reason. Their training was expensive; a qualified stewardess represented a big investment. Another thing: the right kind of girls, with good looks, style, and personality, were hard to find.

The way the programs worked was practical and simple. If a stewardess became pregnant, and did not plan to be married, obviously she could return to her job when her pregnancy was over, and usually her airline would be delighted to have her back. So, the arrangement was, she received official leave of absence, with her job seniority protected. As to her personal welfare, airline personnel departments had special sections which, among other things, would help make medical or nursing home arrangements, either where a girl lived or at some distant point, whichever she preferred. The airline helped psychologically, too, by letting the girl know that someone cared about her, and was looking out for her interest. A loan of money could sometimes be arranged. Afterward, if a stewardess who had had her child was diffident about returning to her original base, she would be quietly transferred to a new one of her own choosing.

In return for all this, the airline asked three assurances from the stewardess—hence the Three-Point Pregnancy Program.

First, the girl must keep the airline personnel department informed of her whereabouts at all times during her pregnancy.

Second, she must agree that her baby be surrendered for adoption immediately after birth. The girl would never know the baby's adoptive parents; thus the child would pass out of her life entirely. However, the airline guaranteed that proper adoption procedures would be followed, with the baby being placed in a good home.

Third—at the outset of the three-point program the stewardess must inform the airline of the name of the child's father. When she had done so, a representative from Personnel—experienced in such situations—promptly sought out the father with the objective of obtaining financial support for the girl. What the personnel man tried to obtain was a promise, in writing, of enough money to cover medical and nursing home expenses and, if possible, some or all of the stewardess's lost wages. Airlines preferred such arrangements to be amiable and discreet. If they had to, though, they could get tough, using their considerable corporate influence to bring pressure on non-cooperating individuals.

It was seldom necessary to be tough where the father of a stewardess's baby was a flying crew member—a captain, or first or second officer. In such cases, gentle company suasion, plus the father's wish to keep the whole thing quiet, were usually enough. As to keeping quiet, the company obliged. Temporary support payments could be made in any reasonable way, or, if preferred, the airline made regular deductions from the employee's pay checks. Just as considerately, to avoid awkward questions at home, such deductions appeared under the heading: "personal misc."

All money received by these means was paid, in its entirety, to the pregnant stewardess. The airline deducted nothing for its own costs.

"The whole point about the program," Demerest said, "is that you're not alone, and there's all kinds of help."

He had been careful of one thing—to avoid any reference, so far, to abortion. That was a separate subject because no airline would, or could, become directly involved in abortion arrangements. Advice on the subject was frequently given unofficially to those who sought it—by stewardess supervisors who learned, through experience of others, how such arrangements could be made. Their objective, if a girl was determined on abortion, was to insure its performance under safe medical conditions, avoiding at all costs the dangerous and disreputable practitioners whom desperate people sometimes resorted to.

Gwen regarded her companion curiously. "Tell me one thing. How is it you know so much about all this?"

"I told you, I'm a union officer . . ."

"You're part of the ALPA's for pilots. You don't have anything to do with stewardesses—not in that way, anyhow."

"Maybe not directly."

"Vernon, this has happened to you before . . . getting a stewardess pregnant . . . Vernon, hasn't it?"

He nodded reluctantly. "Yes."

"It must come pretty easily to you, knocking up stewardesses—those gullible country girls you were talking about. Or were they mostly from 'modest city homes'?" Gwen's voice was bitter. "How many have there been altogether? Two dozen, a dozen? Just give me an idea in round figures."

He sighed. "One; only one."

He had been incredibly lucky, of course. It could have been many more, but his answer was the truth.

Well . . . almost the truth; there was that other time, and the miscarriage, but that shouldn't count.

Outside the car, traffic density was increasing as they neared the airport, now less than a quarter mile away. The bright lights of the great terminal, though dimmed tonight by snow, still filled the sky.

Gwen said, "The other girl who got pregnant. I don't want to know her name . . ."

"I wouldn't tell you."

"Did she use the thingummy—the three-point program?"

"Yes."

"Did you help her?"

He answered impatiently, "I said earlier—what kind of a man do you think I am? Of course I helped her. If you must know, the company made deductions from my pay checks. That's how I knew about the way it's done."

Gwen smiled. " 'Personal misc.?' "

"Yes."

"Did your wife ever know?"

He hesitated before answering. "No."

"What happened to the baby?"

"It was adopted."

"What was it?"

"Just a baby."

"You know perfectly well what I mean. Was it a boy or a girl?"

"A girl, I think."

"You *think*."

"I know. It was a girl."

Gwen's questioning made him vaguely uncomfortable. It revived memories he would as soon forget.

They were silent as Vernon Demerest swung the Mercedes into the airport's wide and imposing main entry. High above the entry, soaring and floodlighted, were the futuristic parabolic arches—acclaimed achievement of a world-wide design contest—symbolizing, so it was said, the noble dreams of aviation. Ahead was an impressive, serpentine complex of roads, interchanges, flyovers, and tunnels, designed to keep the airport's unceasing vehicular traffic flowing at high speed, though tonight the effects of the three-day storm were making progress slower than usual. Great mounds of snow were occupying normally usable road space. Snowplows and dump trucks, trying to keep remaining areas open, were adding their own confusion.

After several brief hold-ups, Demerest turned onto the service road which would bring them to the Trans America main hangar area, where they would leave the car and take a crew bus to the terminal.

Gwen stirred beside him. "Vernon."

"Yes."

"Thank you for being honest with me." She reached out touching his nearer hand on the steering wheel. "I'll be all right. I expect it was just a bit much, all at once. And I *do* want to go with you to Naples."

He nodded and smiled, then took his hand off the wheel and clasped Gwen's tightly. "We'll have a great time, and I promise we'll both remember it."

He would do his best, he decided, to ensure the promise came true. For himself, it would not be difficult. He had been more attracted to Gwen, had felt more loving in her company, and closer in spirit, than with anyone else he remembered. If it were not for his marriage . . . He wondered, not for the first time, about breaking with Sarah, and marrying Gwen. Then he pushed the thought away. He had known too many others of his profession who had suffered upheaval—pilots who forsook wives of many years, for younger women. More often than not, all the men had in the end were shattered hopes and heavy alimony.

Sometime during their trip, though, either in Rome or Naples, he must have another serious discussion with Gwen. Their talk, so far, had not gone exactly as he would have liked, nor had the question of an abortion yet been raised.

Meanwhile—the thought of Rome reminded him—there was the more immediate matter of his command of Trans America Flight Two.

3

The key was to room 224 of the O'Hagan Inn.

In the semidarkened locker area adjoining the air traffic control radar room, Keith Bakersfeld realized he had been staring at the key and its identifying plastic tag for several minutes. Or had it been seconds only? It might have been. Just lately, like so much else, the passage of time seemed inconstant and disoriented. Sometimes at home recently, Natalie had found him standing quite still, looking into nothingness. And when she had asked, with concern, *Why are you there?*, only then had he become awakened to where he was, and had resumed movement and conscious thinking.

What had happened, he supposed—then and a moment ago—was that his worn, weary mind had switched itself off. Somewhere inside the brain's intricacies—of blood vessels, sinew, stored thought, and emotion—was a tiny switch, a self-defense mechanism like a thermal cutout in an electric motor, which worked when the motor was running too hot and needed to be saved from burning itself out. The difference, though, between a motor and a human brain, was that a motor stayed out of action if it needed to.

A brain would not.

The floodlights outside, on the face of the control tower, still reflected enough light inward through the locker room's single window for Keith to see. Not that he needed to see. Seated on one of the wooden benches, the sandwiches Natalie had made, untouched, beside him, he was doing nothing more than holding the O'Hagan Inn key and thinking, reflecting on the paradox of the human brain.

A human brain could achieve soaring imagery, conceive poetry and radarscopes, create the Sistine Chapel and a supersonic Concordé. Yet a brain, too—holding memory and conscience—could be compelling, self-tormenting, never resting; so that only death could end its persecution.

Death . . . with oblivion, forgetfulness; with rest at last.

It was the reason that Keith Bakersfeld had decided on suicide tonight.

He must go back soon to the radar room. There were still several hours of his shift remaining, and he had made a pact with himself to finish his air traffic control duty for tonight. He was not sure why, except that it seemed the right thing to do, and he had always tried to do the right thing, conscientiously. Perhaps being conscientious was a family trait; he and his brother Mel always seemed to have that much in common.

Anyway, when the duty was done—his final obligation finished—he would be free to go to the O'Hagan Inn, where he had registered late this afternoon. Once there, without wasting time, he would take the forty Nembutal capsules—sixty grains in all—which were in a drugstore pillbox in his pocket. He had husbanded the capsules, a few at a time, over recent months. They had been prescribed to give him sleep, and from each prescription which Natalie's druggist had delivered, he had carefully extracted half and hidden it. A few days ago he had gone to a library, checking a reference book on clinical toxicology to assure himself that the quantity of Nembutal he had was well in excess of a fatal dose.

His present duty shift would end at midnight. Soon after, when he had taken the capsules, sleep would come quickly and with finality.

He looked at his watch, holding its face toward the light from outside. It was almost nine o'clock. Should he return to the radar room now? No—stay a few minutes longer. When he went, he wanted to be calm, his nerves steady for whatever these last few hours of duty might contain.

Keith Bakersfeld fingered the O'Hagan Inn key again. Room 224.

It was strange about the coincidence of figures; that his room number tonight, allocated by chance, should have in it a "24." There were people who believed in

that kind of thing—numerology; the occult significance
of numbers. Keith didn't, though if he did, those third
and last figures, prefaced by a "2" could be taken to
mean 24 for the second time.

The first 24 had been a date, a year and a half ago.
Keith's eyes misted, as they had so many times before,
when he remembered. The date was seared—with self-
reproach and anguish—in his memory. It was the
wellspring of his darksome spirit, his utter desolation. It
was the reason he would end his life tonight.

A summer's day; morning. Thursday, June the twen-
ty-fourth.

It was a day for poets, lovers, and color photographers; the kind of day which people stored up in their
minds, to open like a scrapbook when they wanted to
remember, years later, all that was best of any time and
place. In Leesburg, Virginia, not far from historic Har-
pers Ferry, the sky was clear at dawn—CAVU, the
weather reports said, which is aviation shorthand for
"ceiling and visibility unlimited"; and conditions stayed
that way, except for a few cotton-wool tufts of scattered
cumulus by afternoon. The sun was warm, but not
oppressive. A gentle breeze from the Blue Ridge Mountains carried the scent of honeysuckle.

On his way to work that morning—driving to the
Washington Air Route Traffic Control Center at Leesburg—Keith Bakersfeld had seen wild roses blooming.
He thought of a line from Keats which he had learned in
high school—"*For Summer has o'erbrimmed . . .*" It
seemed appropriate to such a day.

He had driven, as usual, across the Virginia border
—from Adamstown, Maryland, where he and Natalie,
with their two boys shared a pleasant rented home. The
top of the Volkswagen convertible was down; he had
traveled without haste, enjoying the benevolence of air
and sun, and when the familiar low, modern buildings of
the Air Route Center came in sight, he had felt less
tense than usual. Afterward, he wondered if that, in
itself, had been a cause of the events which followed.

Even inside the Operations Wing—thick-walled and

windowless, where daylight never penetrated—Keith
had an impression that the glory of the summer's day
outside had somehow percolated inward. Among the
seventy or more shirtsleeved controllers on duty there
seemed a sense of lightness, in contrast to the pressure-
driven earnestness with which work proceeded on most
days of the year. One reason, perhaps, was that the
traffic load was less than usual, due to the exceptionally
clear weather. Many non-commercial flights—private,
military, even a few airliners—were operating on VFR
—"visual flight rules," or the see-and-be-seen method
by which aircraft pilots kept track of their own progress
through the air, without need to report by radio to ATC
air route controllers.

The Washington Air Route Center at Leesburg was
a key control point. From its main operations room all
air traffic on airways over six eastern seaboard states
was observed and directed. Added up, the control area
came to more than a hundred thousand square miles.
Within that area, whenever an aircraft which had filed
an instrument flight plan left an airport, it came under
Leesburg observation and control. It remained under
that control either until its journey was complete or it
passed out of the area. Aircraft coming into the area
were handed over from other control centers, of which
there were twenty across the continental United States.
The Leesburg center was among the nation's busiest. It
included the southern end of the "northeast corridor"
which daily accommodated the world's heaviest concentration of air traffic.

Oddly, Leesburg was distant from any airport, and
forty miles from Washington, D.C., from which the Air
Route Center took its name. The center itself was in
Virginia countryside—a cluster of low, modern buildings with a parking lot—and was surrounded on three
sides by rolling farmland. Nearby was a small stream
named Bull Run—its fame enshrined forever by two
battles of the Civil War. Keith Bakersfeld had once gone
to Bull Run after duty, reflecting on the strange and
diametric contrast between Leesburg's past and present.

This morning, despite awareness of the summer's day

outside, everything in the spacious, cathedral-like main
control room was operating as usual. The entire control
area—larger than a football field—was, as always,
dimly lighted to allow proper viewing of the several
dozen radar screens, arranged in tiers and rows under
overhanging canopies. The control room noise level was
what any newcomer noticed first. From a flight data
area, with great banks of computers, assorted electronic
gear and automatic teletypes, arose the continuous whir
and chatter of machinery. Nearby, from dozens of positions where controllers sat, directing aerial traffic, came
a ceaseless hum of voice radio exchanges on a host of
frequencies. The machinery and human voices merged,
producing a constant noise level which was all-per-
vading, yet strangely muted by acoustic, sound-ab-
sorbent walls and ceilings.

Above the working level of the control room was an
observation bridge, running the room's full width, where
occasional visitors were brought to watch proceedings
below. The control room activity looked, from this
eyrie, not unlike that of a stock exchange. Controllers
rarely glanced up at the bridge, being trained to ignore
anything which might diminish concentration on their
work, and since only a few especially privileged visitors
ever made it to the control room floor, controllers and
outsiders rarely met. Thus the work was not only high
pressure, but also monastic—the last condition added to
by the total absence of women.

In an annex to the control room Keith slipped off his
jacket, and came in wearing the crisp white shirt which
was like a uniform for air traffic controllers. No one
knew why controllers wore white shirts on duty; there
was no rule about it, but most of them did. As he passed
other control positions while heading for his own, a few
colleagues wished him a friendly "good morning," and
that was unusual too. Normally, the immediate sense of
pressure on entering the control area made it customary
to give a hurried nod or a brief "Hi!"—sometimes not
even that.

The control sector which Keith regularly worked
comprised a segment of the Pittsburgh-Baltimore area.

The sector was monitored by a team of three. Keith was radar controller, his job to maintain contact with aircraft and to issue radio instructions. Two assistant controllers handled flight data and airport communications; a supervisor coordinated activities of the other three. Today, in addition, the team had a trainee controller whom Keith had been instructing, at intervals, over the past several weeks.

Others of the team were drifting in at the same time as Keith Bakersfeld, taking position behind the men they were to relieve, and allowing a few minutes while they absorbed the "picture" in their minds. All through the big control room, at other positions, the same thing was happening.

Standing at his own sector, behind the radar controller about to go off duty, Keith already felt his mental acuity sharpen, his speed of thinking consciously accelerate. For the next eight hours, except for two brief work breaks, his brain must continue to operate that way.

Traffic, he observed, was averagely busy for the time of day, taking into account the widespread good weather. On the scope's dark surface, some fifteen pinpoints of bright green light—or "targets," as radarmen called them—indicated aircraft in the air. Allegheny had a Convair 440 at eight thousand feet, approaching Pittsburgh. Behind the Allegheny flight, at varying altitudes, was a National DC-8, an American Airlines 727, two private aircraft—a Lear jet and a Fairchild F-27—and another National, this time a prop-jet Electra. Several other flights, Keith noted, were due to come on the screen at any moment, both from other sectors and as a result of takeoffs from Friendship Airport, Baltimore. Going the opposite way, toward Baltimore, was a Delta DC-9, about to be taken over by Friendship approach control; behind this flight were a TWA, a Piedmont Airlines Martin, another private flight, two Uniteds, and a Mohawk. Height and distance separations of all aircraft were satisfactory, Keith observed, except that the two Uniteds heading for Baltimore were a little close. As if the controller still at the scope had read Keith's mind, he gave the second United a delaying diversionary course.

"I have the picture," Keith said quietly. The other controller nodded and moved out.

Keith's supervisor, Perry Yount, plugged in his headset above Keith's head and leaned over, making his own assessment of the traffic situation. Perry was a tall, lean Negro, a few years younger than Keith. He had a quick, retentive memory which could store a mass of flight data, then repeat it back, as a whole or in pieces, with computer accuracy. Perry was a comforting man to have around when there was trouble.

Keith had already accepted several new flights and handed over others when the supervisor touched his shoulder. "Keith, I'm running two positions this shift— this and the next one. We're a man short. You okay for a while?"

Keith nodded. "Roger." He radioed a course correction to an Eastern 727, then motioned toward the trainee controller, George Wallace, who had slipped into a seat beside him. "I've got George to keep an eye on me."

"Okay." Perry Yount unplugged his headset and moved to the adjacent console. The same kind of thing had happened occasionally before, and was handled without difficulty. Perry Yount and Keith had worked together for several years; each was aware that he could trust the other.

Keith told the trainee beside him, "George, start getting the picture."

George Wallace nodded and edged closer to the radarscope. He was in his mid-twenties, had been a trainee for almost two years; before that, he had served an enlistment in the U. S. Air Force. Wallace had already shown himself to have an alert, quick mind, plus the ability not to become rattled under tension. In one more week he would be a qualified controller, though for practical purposes he was fully trained now.

Deliberately, Keith allowed the spacing between an American Airlines BAC-400 and a National 727 to become less than it should be; he was ready to transmit quick instructions if the closure became critical. George Wallace spotted the condition at once, and warned Keith, who corrected it.

That kind of firsthand exercise was the only sure way the ability of a new controller could be gauged. Similarly, when a trainee was at the scope himself, and got into difficulties, he had to be given the chance to show resourcefulness and sort the situation out unaided. At such moments, the instructing controller was obliged to sit back, with clenched hands, and sweat. Someone had once described it as, "hanging on a brick wall by your fingernails." When to intervene or take over was a critical decision, not to be made too early or too late. If the instructor did take over, the trainee's confidence might be permanently undermined, and a potentially good controller lost. On the other hand, if an instructor failed to take over when he should, a ghastly mid-air collision could result.

The risks involved, and extra mental pressures, were such that many controllers refused to take them. They pointed out that the task of teaching their work to others carried neither official recognition nor extra pay. Moreover, if anything went wrong, the instructing controller was wholly responsible. Why suffer so much strain and liability for nothing?

Keith, however, had shown an aptitude as an instructor as well as patience in bringing trainees along. And although he, too, suffered and sweated at times, he did the job because he felt he should. At this moment, he took a personal pride in the way George Wallace had developed.

Wallace said quietly again, "I'd turn United 284 right until you get altitude separation with Mohawk."

Keith nodded agreement as he thumbed his microphone button. "United Flight 284, from Washington center. Turn right, heading zero six zero."

Promptly the reply crackled back. "Washington control, this is United 284. Roger; zero six zero." Miles distant, and high above in clear bright sunshine while passengers dozed or read, the powerful sleek jet would be easing into a smooth controlled turn. On the radarscope, the bright green half inch wide blip which was United 284 began moving in a new direction.

Below the control area, in a room devoted to rack upon rack of ponderously turning tape recorders, the exchange between ground and air had been recorded— for playback later if need arose. Every such conversation, from each position in the control room, was recorded and stored. Periodically, some of the tapes were replayed and listened to critically by supervisors. If a procedure was wrong, a controller heard about it; yet no controller knew when a recording of his own might be selected for analysis. On a door of the tape-recorder room was the grimly humorous reminder, *"Big Brother Is Listening."*

The morning progressed.

Periodically, Perry Yount appeared. He was still overseeing two positions and stayed long enough to assess the current traffic situation. What he saw seemed to satisfy him, and he spent less time behind Keith than at the other position, where several problems seemed to be occurring. Around mid-morning the air traffic volume eased slightly; it would pick up again before midday. Soon after 10:30 A.M. Keith Bakersfeld and George Wallace exchanged positions. The trainee was now at the scope, Keith checking from alongside. There was no need, Keith found, for intervention; young Wallace was proving competent and alert. As far as was possible in the circumstances, Keith relaxed.

At ten to eleven, Keith was aware of a need to visit the toilet. In recent months, he had had several bouts with intestinal flu; he had a suspicion that this was the beginning of another. He signaled Perry Yount and told him.

The supervisor nodded. "Is George doing okay?"

"Like a veteran." Keith said it loud enough so George could hear.

"I'll hold things down," Perry said. "You're relieved, Keith."

"Thanks."

Keith signed the sector log sheet and noted his time of checking out. Perry scribbled an initial on the next line of the log, accepting responsibility for monitoring Wallace. In a few minutes time, when Keith returned, they would follow the same procedure.

As Keith Bakersfeld left the control room, the supervisor was studying the scope, his hand lightly on George Wallace's shoulder.

The washroom Keith had gone to was on an upper level; a frosted-glass window admitted some of the brightness of the day outside. When Keith had finished, and freshened himself with a wash, he went to the window and opened it. He wondered if the weather was still as superb as when he had arrived earlier. It was.

From the rear of the building into which the window was set, he could see—beyond a service area—green meadows, trees, and wild flowers. The heat was greater now. All around was a drowsy hum of insects.

Keith stood looking out, aware of a reluctance to leave the cheerful sunlight and return to the control room's gloom. It occurred to him that lately he had had similar feelings at other times—too many times, perhaps; and he thought—if he was honest, it was not the gloom he minded so much, but the mental pressures. There was a time when the tensions and pressures of his job, unrelenting as they were, had never bothered him. Nowadays they did, and on occasions he had to force himself, consciously, to meet them.

While Keith Bakersfeld was standing at the window, thinking, a Northwest Orient 727 jet, en route from Minneapolis-St. Paul, was nearing Washington, D.C. Within its cabin a stewardess was bending over an elderly male passenger. His face was ashen; he seemed unable to speak. The stewardess believed he had had, or was having, a heart attack. She hurried to the flight deck to inform the captain. Moments later, acting on the captain's orders, the Northwest first officer asked Washington Air Route Center for special clearance down, with priority handling to Washington National Airport.

Keith wondered sometimes—as he was wondering now—how many more years he could force his occa-

sionally weary mind to go on. He had been a controller
for a decade and a half. He was thirty-eight.

The depressing thing was—in this business you could
be mentally drained, an old man, at age forty-five or
fifty, yet honorable retirement was another ten or fifteen
years away. For many air traffic controllers, those final
years proved an all-too-grueling trail, whose end they
failed to reach.

Keith knew—as most controllers did—that strains on
the human systems of those employed in air traffic
control had long been recognized. Official flight sur-
geons' files bulged with medical evidence. Case histories,
directly attributable to controllers' work, included hy-
pertension, heart attacks, gastric ulcers, tachycardia,
psychiatric breakdowns, plus a host of lesser ailments.
Eminent, independent medics, in scholarly research
studies, had confirmed such findings. In the words of
one: "A controller will spend nervous, sleepless hours
every night wondering how in the name of heaven he
kept all those planes from running into each other. He
managed not to cause a disaster today, but will he have
the same luck tomorrow? After a while, something
inside him—physical, mental, oftentimes both—inevitably breaks down."

Armed with this knowledge, and more, the Federal
Aviation Agency had urged Congress to allow air traffic
controllers to retire at age fifty, or after twenty years of
service. The twenty years, doctors declared, were equal
to forty in most other jobs. The FAA warned legisla-
tors: public safety was involved; controllers, after more
than twenty years of service, were potentially unsafe.
Congress, Keith remembered, had ignored the warning
and refused to act.

Subsequently, a Presidential Commission also turned
thumbs down on early retirement for controllers, and
the FAA—then a presidential agency—had been told to
cease and desist in its argument. Now, officially, it had.
Privately, however—as Keith and others knew—Washington FAA officials were as convinced as ever; they
predicted that the question would arise again, though

only after an air disaster, or a series, involving worn-out controllers, followed by press and public furor.

Keith's thoughts switched back to the countryside. It *was* glorious today; the fields inviting, even when viewed from a washroom window. He wished he could go out there and sleep in the sun. Well, he couldn't, and that was that. He supposed he had better get back to the control room. He would—in just a moment more.

The Northwest Orient 727 had already started down, on authority from Washington Center. At lower altitudes, other flights were being hurriedly diverted, or ordered to orbit, safe distances away. A slanting hole, through which Northwest would continue descending, was being cleared in the growing midday traffic. Approach control at Washington National Airport had been alerted; its function would come shortly when it accepted the Northwest jet from Washington Center. At this moment, responsibility for the Northwest flight and other aircraft devolved on the sector team next to Keith's—the extra sector which the young Negro, Perry Yount, was supervising.

Fifteen aircraft with combined speeds totaling seven thousand five hundred miles per hour were being juggled in an airspace a few miles wide. No airplane must come near another. The Northwest flight must be brought down, safely, through them all.

Similar situations happened several times a day; in bad weather it could be several times an hour. Sometimes emergencies came together, so that controllers numbered them—emergency one, emergency two, emergency three.

In the present situation, as always, Perry Yount— quiet-spoken, cool, and capable—was responding with experienced skill. Working with others in the sector team, he was coordinating emergency procedures— calmly, level voiced, so that from his tone no bystander listening would be aware that an emergency existed. Other aircraft could not hear transmissions to the Northwest flight, which had been instructed to switch to a separate radio frequency.

Everything was going well. The Northwest flight was steady on course, descending. In a few minutes, the emergency situation would be over.

Amid the pressures, Perry Yount even found time to slip across to the adjoining position—which normally would have his undivided attention—to check George Wallace. Everything looked good, though Perry knew he would be easier in mind when Keith Bakersfeld was back. He glanced toward the control room door. No sign of Keith yet.

Keith—still at the open window, still looking out at the Virginia countryside—was remembering Natalie. He sighed. Lately, there had been disagreements between them, triggered by his work. There were points of view which his wife could or would not see. Natalie was concerned about Keith's health. She wanted him to give up air traffic control; to quit, and choose some other occupation while some of his youth and most of his health remained. It had been a mistake, he realized now, to confide his doubts to Natalie, to describe what he had seen happen to other controllers whose work had made them prematurely old and ailing. Natalie had become alarmed, perhaps with reason. But there were considerations to giving up a job, walking away from years of training and experience; considerations which it was hard for Natalie—or for any woman, he supposed—to grasp.

Over Martinsburg, West Virginia—some thirty miles northwest of Washington Route Center—a private, four-place Beech Bonanza, at seven thousand feet, was leaving Airway V166 and entering Airway V44. The little Beech Bonanza, identifiable visually by its butterfly tail, was cruising at 175 mph, its destination Baltimore. It contained the Redfern family: Irving Redfern, a consulting engineer-economist, his wife Merry, and their two children—Jeremy, ten years old, and Valerie, nine.

Irving Redfern was a careful, thorough man. Today, because of favorable weather conditions, he could have flown using visual flight rules. However, he considered it more prudent to file an instrument flight plan and, since leaving his home airport of Charleston, West Virginia, had stayed on airways, remaining in touch with air traffic control. A few moments earlier, Washington Route Center had given him a new course on Airway V44. He had already turned on it and now his magnetic compass, which had been swinging slightly, was settling down nicely.

The Redferns were going to Baltimore partly for Irving Redfern's business, and partly for pleasure, which would include a family theatre outing tonight. While their father was concentrating on his flying, the children, with Merry, were chattering about what they would have for lunch at Friendship Airport.

The Washington Center controller who had given Irving Redfern his latest instructions was George Wallace, the almost-qualified trainee still filling in for Keith Bakersfeld. George had correctly identified the Redferns' Beechcraft on his radarscope, where it appeared as a bright green dot, though smaller and moving more slowly than most other traffic—at the moment, principally airline jets. There was nothing closing up on the Beechcraft, however, which appeared to have plenty of airspace all around it. Perry Yount, the sector supervisor, had by now returned to the adjoining position. He was helping sort out the aftermath confusion now that the critical Northwest Orient 727 had been handed over safely to Washington National Airport approach control. Periodically, Perry glanced across at George and once called out, "Is everything okay?" George Wallace nodded, though he was beginning to sweat a little. Today's heavier noontime traffic seemed to be building up earlier than usual.

Unknown to George Wallace or Perry Yount or Irving Redfern, an Air National Guard T-33 jet trainer was flying—at the moment idly in circles—a few miles north of Airway V44. The T-33 was from Martin Airport, near Baltimore, and its National Guard pilot was an automobile salesman named Hank Neel.

Lieutenant Neel, who was fulfilling his part-time military training requirements, had been sent up solo for

*VFR proficiency flying. Because he had been cautioned
to do only local flying in an authorized area northwest
of Baltimore, no flight plan had been filed; therefore,
Washington Air Route Center had no knowledge that
the T-33 was in the air. This would not have mattered,
except that Neel had become bored with his assignment
and was also a careless pilot. Looking out casually, as
he held the jet trainer in lazy circles, he realized he had
drifted south while practicing maneuvers, though in
reality he had come a good deal farther than he imagined. He was so far south that several minutes ago the
National Guard jet had entered George Wallace's radar
control area and now appeared on Wallace's screen at
Leesburg as a green dot, slightly larger than the Redfern
family's Beech Bonanza. A more experienced controller
would have recognized the dot instantly for what it was.
George, however, still busy with other traffic, had not
yet observed the extra, unidentified signal.*

*Lieutenant Neel, at fifteen thousand feet, decided he
would finish his flying practice with some aerobatics—
two loops, a couple of slow rolls—and then return to
base. He swung the T-33 into a steep turn and circled
again while he took the standard precaution of looking
for other airplanes above and below. He was now even
closer than before to Airway V44.*

The thing his wife failed to realize, Keith Bakersfeld
thought, was that a man couldn't just quit his job irre-
sponsibly, on a whim, even if he wanted to. Especially
when the man had a family to support, children to
educate. Especially when the job you possessed, the
skills you so patiently acquired, had fitted you for
nothing else. In some branches of government service,
employees could leave and utilize their proficiency elsewhere. Air Traffic controllers could not. Their work had
no counterpart in private industry; no one else wanted
them.

Being trapped that way—which was what it
amounted to, Keith recognized—was a disillusion which
came with other disillusions. Money was one. When you
were young, enthusiastic, wanting to be a part of avia-

tion, the civil service pay scale of an air traffic controller seemed adequate or better. Only later did it become clear how inadequate—in relation to the job's awesome responsibility—that pay scale was. The two most skillful specialists involved in air traffic nowadays were pilots and controllers. Yet pilots earned thirty thousand dollars a year while a senior controller reached his ceiling at ten thousand. No one believed pilots should earn less. But even pilots, who were notoriously selfish in taking care of themselves, believed air traffic controllers should earn more.

Nor was promotion—as in most other occupations—something an air traffic controller could look forward to. Senior supervisory posts were few; only a fortunate handful ever attained them.

And yet . . . unless you were reckless or uncaring—which controllers, by the nature of their work, were not—there was no way out. So there would be no quitting for himself, Keith decided. He must have another talk with Natalie; it was time she accepted that for better or worse, it was too late for change. He had no intention, at this stage, of scratching inadequately for some other kind of living.

He really must go back. Glancing at his watch, he realized guiltily that it was almost fifteen minutes since he left the control room. For part of the time he had been daydreaming—something he rarely did, and it was obviously the somniferous effect of the summer's day. Keith closed the washroom window. From the corridor outside, he hurried downward to the main control room.

High over Frederick County, Maryland, Lieutenant Neel straightened up his National Guard T-33 and eased on forward trim. Neel had completed his somewhat casual inspection and had seen no other aircraft. Now, beginning his first loop and slow roll, he put the jet trainer into a steep dive.

Entering the control room, Keith Bakersfeld was aware at once of an increased tempo. The hum of voices was louder than when he left. Other controllers were too preoccupied to glance up—as they had done earlier this morning—as he passed by them on the way to his own position. Keith scribbled a signature in the sector log and noted the time, then moved behind George Wallace, getting the picture, letting his eyes adjust to the control room semidarkness, in sharp contrast to the bright sunlight outside. George had murmured "Hi!" as Keith returned, then continued transmitting radio instructions to traffic. In a moment or two, when Keith had the picture, he would relieve George and slip into his seat. It had probably been good for George, Keith reasoned, to be on his own for a while; it would improve his confidence. From the adjoining sector console, Perry Yount had noted Keith's return.

Keith studied the radarscope and its moving pinpoints of light—the aircraft "targets" which George had identified, then noted on small movable markers on the screen. A bright green dot without identification caught Keith's eye. He asked George sharply, "What's the other traffic near the Beech Bonanza 403?"

Lieutenant Neel had finished his first loop and slow roll. He had climbed back to fifteen thousand feet, and was still over Frederick County, though a little farther south. He leveled the T-33 jet, then put the nose down sharply and began a dive into a second loop.

"What other traffic . . . ?" George Wallace's eyes followed Keith's across the radarscope. He gasped; then in a strangled voice—"My God!"

With a swift, single movement, Keith ripped the radio headset from George and shouldered him aside. Keith flung a frequency switch open, snapped a transmit button down. "Beech Bonanza NC-403, this is Washington Center. There is unidentified traffic to your left. Make an immediate right turn *now!*"

The National Guard T-33 was at the bottom of its dive. Lieutenant Neel pulled the control column back and, with full power on, began a fast, steep climb. Immediately above was the tiny Beech Bonanza, con-

*taining Irving Redfern and his family, cruising steadily
on Airway V44.*

In the control room . . . breathlessly . . . silently . . .
praying hard . . . they watched the closing, bright green
dots.

The radio crackled with a burst of static. "Washington Center, this is Beech . . ." Abruptly the transmission stopped.

*Irving Redfern was a consulting engineer-economist.
He was a competent amateur pilot, but not a commercial one.*

*An airline pilot, receiving the Washington Center
message, would have flung his aircraft instantly into a
steep right turn. He would have caught the urgency in
Keith's voice, would have acted, without waiting to trim,
or acknowledge, or—until later—question. An airline
pilot would have ignored all minor consequences except
the overriding urgency of escaping the nearby peril
which the route center message unmistakably implied.
Behind him, in the passenger cabin, scalding coffee
might have spilled, meals scattered, even minor injuries
resulted. Later there would have been complaints, apol-
ogies, denunciations, perhaps a Civil Aeronautics Board
inquiry. But—with ordinary luck—there could have
been survival. Quick action could have insured it. It
would have insured it for the Redfern family, too.*

*Airline pilots were conditioned by training and usage,
to swift, sure reflexes. Irving Redfern was not. He was a
precise, scholarly man, accustomed to think before
acting, and to following correct procedures. His first
thought was to acknowledge the Washington Center
message. Thus, he used up two or three seconds—all
the time he had. The National Guard T-33, swooping
upward from the bottom of its loop, struck the Redferns' Beech Bonanza on the left side, slicing off the
private aircraft's port wing with a single screeching rip
of metal. The T-33, mortally damaged itself, continued
upward briefly while its forward section disintegrated.
Scarcely knowing what was happening—he had caught*

*only the briefest glimpse of the other plane—Lieutenant
Neel ejected and waited for his parachute to open. Far
below, out of control and spinning crazily, the Beechcraft Bonanza, with the Redfern family still inside, was
plummeting to earth.*

Keith's hands were trembling as he tried again.
"Beech Bonanza NC-403, this is Washington Center.
Do you read?"

Beside Keith, George Wallace's lips moved silently.
His face was drained of color.

As they watched in horror, the dots on the radarscope
converged, blossomed suddenly, then faded.

Perry Yount, aware of something wrong, had joined
them. "What is it?"

Keith's mouth was dry. "I think we've had a mid-air."

It was then it happened: the nightmarish sound which
those who heard it wished that they had not, yet afterward would not be able to erase from memory.

*In the pilot's seat of the doomed, spinning Beech
Bonanza, Irving Redfern—perhaps involuntarily, perhaps as a last despairing act—pressed the transmit
button of his microphone and held it down. The radio
still worked.*

At Washington Center, the transmission was heard on
a console speaker which Keith had switched in when his
emergency transmissions began. At first there was a
burst of static, then immediately a succession of
piercing, frantic, chilling screams. Elsewhere in the
control room, heads turned. Faces nearby paled. George
Wallace was sobbing hysterically. Senior supervisors
came hurrying from other sections.

Suddenly, above the screaming clearly, a single voice
—terrified, forlorn, beseeching. At first, not every word
was audible. Only later, when the tape recording of the
last transmission was played and replayed many times,
were the full words put together, the voice identified as
that of Valerie Redfern, nine years old.

"*. . . Mummy! Daddy! . . . Do something! I don't*

want to die . . . Oh, Gentle Jesus, I've been good . . .
Please, I don't want . . ."

Mercifully, the transmission stopped.

The Beech Bonanza crashed and burned near the village of Lisbon, Maryland. What remained from the four bodies was unrecognizable and was buried in a common grave.

Lieutenant Neel landed safely by parachute, five miles away.

All three controllers involved in the tragedy—George Wallace, Keith Bakersfeld, Perry Yount—were at once suspended from duty, pending investigation.

Later, the trainee, George Wallace, was held technically not to blame, since he was not a qualified controller when the accident occurred. He was, however, dismissed from government service and barred forever for further employment in air traffic control.

The young Negro supervisor, Perry Yount, was held wholly responsible. The investigating board—taking days and weeks to play back tapes, examine evidence, and review decisions which Yount himself had had to make in seconds, under pressure—decided he should have spent less time on the emergency involving the Northwest Orient 727 and more in supervising George Wallace during the absence of Keith Bakersfeld. The fact that Perry Yount was doing double duty—which, had he been less cooperative, he could have refused—was ruled not relevant. Yount was officially reprimanded, and reduced in civil service grade.

Keith Bakersfeld was totally exonerated. The investigating board was at pains to point out that Keith had requested to be temporarily relieved from duty, that his request was reasonable, and he followed regulations in signing out and in. Furthermore, immediately on return, he perceived the possibility of a mid-air collision and tried to prevent it. For his quick thinking and action—though the attempt was unsuccessful—he was commended by the board.

The question of the length of Keith's absence from the control room did not arise initially. Near the end of

the investigation—perceiving the way things were going
for Perry Yount—Keith attempted to raise it himself,
and to accept the major share of blame. His attempt was
treated kindly, but it was clear that the investigating
board regarded it as a chivalrous gesture—and no more.
Keith's testimony, once its direction became clear, was
cut off summarily. His attempted intervention was not
referred to in the board's final report.

An independent Air National Guard inquiry produced evidence that Lieutenant Henry Neel had been
guilty of contributory negligence in failing to remain in
the vicinity of Middletown Air Base, and for allowing
his T-33 to drift near Airway V44. However, since his
actual position could not be proved conclusively, no
charges were preferred. The lieutenant went on selling
automobiles, and flying during weekends.

On learning of the investigating board's decision, the
supervisor, Perry Yount, suffered a nervous collapse. He
was hospitalized and placed under psychiatric care. He
appeared to be moving toward recovery when he received by mail, from an anonymous source, a printed
bulletin of a California rightwing group opposing—
among other things—Negro civil rights. The bulletin contained a viciously biased account of the Redfern
tragedy. It portrayed Perry Yount as an incompetent,
bumbling dullard, indifferent to his responsibilities, and
uncaring about the Redfern family's death. The entire
incident, the bulletin argued, should be a warning to
"bleeding heart liberals" who aided Negroes in attaining
responsible positions for which they were not mentally
equipped. A "housecleaning" was urged of other
Negroes employed in air traffic control, "before the
same thing happens again."

At any other time, a man of Perry Yount's intelligence would have dismissed the bulletin as a maniacal
diatribe, which it was. But because of his condition, he
suffered a relapse after reading it, and might have remained under treatment indefinitely if a government
review board had not refused to pay hospital bills for his
care, maintaining that his mental illness had not been
caused through government employment. Yount was

discharged from the hospital but did not return to air traffic control. When Keith Bakersfeld last heard of him, he was working in a Baltimore waterfront bar, and drinking heavily.

George Wallace disappeared from sight. There were rumors that the former trainee controller had re-enlisted —in the U. S. Army Infantry, not the Air Force—and was now in serious trouble with the Military Police. According to stories, Wallace repeatedly started fist fights and brawls in which he appeared to go out of his way to bring physical punishment on himself. The rumors were not confirmed.

For Keith Bakersfeld, it seemed for a while as if life would go on as usual. When the investigation ended, his temporary suspension was lifted; his qualifications and government service rating remained intact. He returned to work at Leesburg. Colleagues, aware that Keith's experience could easily have been their own, were friendly and sympathetic. His work, at first, went well enough.

After his abortive attempt to raise the subject before the investigating board, Keith confided to no one—not even to Natalie—the fact of his washroom loitering that fateful day. Yet the secret knowledge was seldom far from the forefront of his mind.

At home, Natalie was understanding and, as always, loving. She sensed that Keith had undergone a traumatic shock from which he would need time to recover, and she attempted to meet his moods—to talk or be animated when he felt like it, to stay silent when he did not. In quiet, private sessions Natalie explained to the boys, Brian and Theo, why they, too, should show consideration for their father.

In an abstracted way, Keith understood and appreciated what Natalie was trying to do. Her method might eventually have succeeded, except for one thing—an air traffic controller needed sleep. Keith was getting little sleep and, some nights, none.

On the occasions he did sleep, he had a persistent dream in which the scene in the Washington Center control room, moments before the mid-air collision, was

re-created . . . the merging pinpoints of light on the
radarscope . . . Keith's last desperate message . . . the
screams; the voice of little Valerie Redfern . . .

Sometimes the dream had variations. When Keith
tried to move toward the radarscope to seize George
Wallace's radio headset and transmit a warning, Keith's
limbs resisted, and would change position only with
frustrating slowness, as if the air surrounding them were
heavy sludge. His mind warned frantically: If he could
only move freely, the tragedy could be averted. . . .
Although his body strained and fought, he always
reached his goal too late. At other times he attained the
headset, but his voice would fail. He knew that if he
could articulate words, a warning would suffice, the situation could be saved. His mind would race, his lungs
and larynx strain, but no sound came.

But even with variations, the dream always ended the
same way—with the Beech Bonanza's last radio transmission as he heard it so many times during the inquiry,
on the played-back tape. And afterward, with Natalie
asleep beside him, he would lie awake, thinking, remembering, longing for the impossible—to change the shape
of things past. Later still, he would resist sleep, fighting
for wakefulness, so he would not endure the torture of
the dream again.

It was then that in the loneliness of night, his conscience would remind him of the stolen, wasted minutes
in the route center washroom; crucial minutes when he
could have returned to duty, and should have done, but
through idleness and self-concern had failed to do so.
Keith knew—as others did not—that the real responsibility for the Redfern tragedy was his own, not Perry
Yount's. Perry had been a circumstantial sacrifice, a
technical victim. Perry had been Keith's friend, had
trusted Keith that day to be conscientious, to come back
to the control room as quickly as he could. Yet Keith,
though knowing his friend was standing double duty,
aware of the extra pressures on him, had been twice as
long as he needed to be, and had let Perry down; so in
the end, Perry Yount stood accused and convicted in
Keith's place.

Perry for Keith—a sacrificial goat.

But Perry, though grievously wronged, was still alive. The Redfern family was dead. Dead because Keith doodled mentally, dallying in the sunshine, leaving a semi-experienced trainee too long with responsibilities which were rightly Keith's, and for which Keith was better qualified. There could be no question that had he returned sooner, he would have spotted the intruding T-33 long before it neared the Redferns' plane. The proof was that he *had* spotted it when he did return—too late to be of use.

Around and around . . . over and over in the night . . . as if committed to a treadmill . . . Keith's mind labored on, self-torturing, sick with grief, recrimination. Eventually he would sleep from exhaustion, usually to dream, and to awake again.

In daytime, as well as night, the memory of the Redferns persisted. Irving Redfern, his wife, their children —though Keith had never known them—haunted him. The presence of Keith's own children, Brian and Theo —alive and well—appeared a personal reproach. Keith's own living, breathing, seemed to him an accusation.

The effect of sleepless nights, the mental turmoil, showed quickly in his work. His reactions were slow, decisions hesitant. A couple of times, under pressure, Keith "lost the picture" and had to be helped. Afterward he realized he had been under close surveillance. His superiors knew from experience what might happen, had half-expected some such signs of strain.

Informal, friendly talks followed, in upper-level offices, which achieved nothing. Later, on a suggestion from Washington, and with Keith's consent, he was transferred from the East Coast to the Midwest—to Lincoln International for control tower duty. A change of locale, it was believed, would prove therapeutic. Officialdom, with a touch of humanity, was also aware that Keith's older brother, Mel, was general manager at Lincoln; perhaps Mel Bakersfeld's influence would be steadying too. Natalie, though loving Maryland, made the transition without complaint.

The idea hadn't worked.

Keith's sense of guilt persisted; so did the nightmares, which grew, and took on other patterns, though always the basic one remained. He slept only with the aid of barbiturates prescribed by a physician friend of Mel's.

Mel understood part of his brother's problem, but not all; Keith still kept the secret knowledge of his washroom dawdling at Leesburg solely to himself. Later, watching Keith's deterioration, Mel urged him to seek psychiatric help, but Keith refused. His reasoning was simple. Why should he seek some panacea, some ritualistic mumbo-jumbo to insulate his guilt, when the guilt was real, when nothing in heaven or earth or clinical psychiatry could ever change it?

Keith's dejection deepened until even Natalie's resilient nature rebelled against his moods Though aware that he slept badly, Natalie had no knowledge of his dreams. One day she inquired in anger and impatience, "Are we supposed to wear hair shirts for the rest of our lives? Are we never to have fun again, to laugh the way we used to? If you intend to go on this way, you'd better understand one thing—I don't, and I won't let Brian and Theo grow up around this kind of misery either."

When Keith hadn't answered, Natalie went on, "I've told you before: our lives, our marriage, the children, are more important than your work. If you can't take that kind of work any more—and why should you if it's that demanding?—then give it up now, get something else. I know what you always tell me: the money'll be less; you'd throw away your pension. But that isn't everything; we'd manage somehow. I'll take all the hardship you can give me, Keith Bakersfeld, and maybe I'd complain a little, but not much, because anything would be better than the way we are right now." She had been close to tears, but managed to finish. "I'm warning you I can't take much more. If you're going on like this, it may have to be alone."

It was the only time Natalie had hinted at the possibility of their marriage breaking up. It was also the first time Keith considered suicide.

Later, his idea hardened to resolve.

The door of the darkened locker room opened. A switch snapped on. Keith was back again in the control tower at Lincoln International, blinking in the overhead light's glare.

Another tower controller, taking his own work break, was coming in. Keith put away his untouched sandwiches, closed his locker, and walked back toward the radar room. The other man glanced at him curiously. Neither spoke.

Keith wondered if the crisis involving the Air Force KC-135, which had had radio failure, had ended yet. Chances were, it had; that the aircraft and its crew had landed safely. He hoped so. He hoped that something good, for someone, would survive this night.

As he went in, he touched the O'Hagan Inn key in his pocket to be sure, once again, that it was there. He would need it soon.

4

It was almost an hour since Tanya Livingston had left Mel Bakersfeld in the central lobby of the main terminal. Even now, though other incidents had intervened, she remembered the way their hands touched at the elevator, the tone he used when he had said, "It'll give me a reason to see you again tonight."

Tanya hoped very much that Mel remembered too, and—though she was aware he had to go downtown— that he would find time to stop by first.

The "reason" Mel referred to—as if he needed one —was his curiosity about the message received by Tanya while in the coffee shop. "There's a stowaway on Flight 80," a Trans America agent had told her. "They're calling for you," and "the way I hear it, this one's a dilly."

The agent had already been proved right.

Tanya was once more in the small, private lounge behind the Trans America check-in counters where earlier this evening she had comforted the distraught young ticket agent, Patsy Smith. But now, instead of Patsy, Tanya faced the little old lady from San Diego.

"You've done this before," Tanya said. "Haven't you?"

"Oh yes, my dear. Quite a few times."

The little old lady sat comfortably relaxed, hands folded daintily in her lap, a wisp of lace handkerchief showing between them. She was dressed primly in black, with an old-fashioned high-necked blouse, and might have been somebody's great-grandmother on her way to church. Instead she had been caught riding illegally, without a ticket, between Los Angeles and New York.

There had been stowaways, Tanya recalled reading somewhere, as long ago as 700 B.C., on ships of the Phoenicians which plied the eastern Mediterranean. At that time, the penalty for those who were caught was excruciating death—disembowelment of adult stowaways, while children were burned alive on sacrificial stones.

Since then, penalties had abated, but stowaways had not.

Tanya wondered if anyone, outside a limited circle of airline employees, realized how much of a stowaway epidemic there had been since jet airplanes increased the tempo and pressures of passenger aviation. Probably not. Airlines worked hard to keep the whole subject under wraps, fearing that if the facts became known, their contingent of nonpaying riders would be greater still. But there *were* people who realized how simple it all could be, including the little old lady from San Diego.

Her name was Mrs. Ada Quonsett. Tanya had checked this fact from a Social Security card, and Mrs. Quonsett would undoubtedly have reached New York undetected if she had not made one mistake. This was confiding her status to her seat companion, who told a stewardess. The stewardess reported to the captain, who radioed ahead, and a ticket agent and security guard were waiting to remove the little old lady at Lincoln International. She had been brought to Tanya, part of whose job as passenger relations agent was to deal with such stowaways as the airline was lucky enough to catch.

Tanya smoothed her tight, trim uniform skirt in the gesture which had become a habit. "All right," she said, "I think you'd better tell me about it."

The older woman's hands unfolded and the lace handkerchief changed position slightly. "Well, you see, I'm a widow and I have a married daughter in New York. Sometimes I get lonely and want to visit her. So what I do is go to Los Angeles and get on an airplane that's going to New York."

"Just like that? Without a ticket."

Mrs. Quonsett seemed shocked. "Oh, my dear, I couldn't possibly afford a ticket. I just have Social Security and this small pension my late husband left. It's all I can do to manage the bus fare from San Diego to Los Angeles."

"You *do* pay on the bus?"

"Oh, yes. The Greyhound people are very strict. I once tried buying a ticket to the first stop up the line, then staying on. But they make a check at every city, and the driver found my ticket wasn't good. They were quite unpleasant about it. Not like the airlines at all."

"I'm curious," Tanya said, "why you don't use San Diego airport."

"Well, I'm afraid, my dear, they know me there."

"You mean you've been caught at San Diego?"

The little old lady inclined her head. "Yes."

"Have you been a stowaway on other airlines? Besides ours?"

"Oh, yes. But I like Trans America best."

Tanya was trying hard to remain severe, though it was difficult when the conversation sounded as if they were discussing a stroll to the corner store. But she kept her face impassive as she asked, "Why do you like Trans America, Mrs. Quonsett?"

"Well, they're always so reasonable in New York.

When I've stayed with my daughter a week or two, and I'm ready to go home, I go to your airline offices and tell them."

"You tell them the truth? That you came to New York as a stowaway?"

"That's right, my dear. They ask me the date and the flight number—I always write it down so I'll remember. Then they look up some papers."

"The flight manifest," Tanya said. She wondered: was this conversation real or just imagination.

"Yes, dear, I think that's what it's called."

"Please go on."

The little old lady looked surprised. "There isn't anything else. After that, they just send me home. Usually the same day, on one of your airplanes."

"And that's everything? Nothing else is said?"

Mrs. Quonsett gave a gentle smile, as she might have done at a vicarage afternoon tea. "Well, I do sometimes get a little scolding. I'm told I've been naughty, and not to do it again. But that really isn't much, is it?"

"No," Tanya said. "It certainly isn't."

The incredible thing, Tanya realized, was that it was all so obviously true. As airlines were aware, it happened frequently. A would-be stowaway merely boarded an airplane—there were plenty of ways it could be done —and sat quietly, waiting for departure. As long as the stowaway stayed away from the first class compartment, where passengers could be identified easily, and unless the flight was full, detection was unlikely. It was true that stewardesses would count heads, and their tally might disagree with the gate agent's manifest. At that point a stowaway would be suspected, but the agent in charge would be faced with two choices. Either he could let the airplane go, recording on the manifest that the head and ticket counts did not agree, or a recheck could be made of the tickets of everyone aboard.

A recheck, if decided on, would take most of half an hour; meanwhile, the cost of holding a six-million-dollar jet airplane on the ground would soar. Schedules, both at origin and down the line, would be disrupted. Passengers with connections to make, or appointments, would grow angrily impatient, while the captain, conscious of his punctuality record, would fume at the agent. The agent would reason that he might have made a mistake anyway; moreover, unless he could show good reason for a delay, he would get a roasting later on from his District Transportation Manager. In the end, even if a stowaway was found, the loss in dollars and goodwill would far exceed the cost of providing a free ride for a single individual.

So what happened was that the airline did the only sensible thing—it closed the doors, and sent the airplane on its way.

That was usually the end of it. Once in flight, stewardesses were too busy to do a ticket check, and passengers would certainly not submit to the delay and annoyance of one at journey's end. Therefore the stowaway walked off, unquestioned and unhindered.

What the little old lady had told Tanya about returning was just as accurate. Airlines took the view that stowaway incidents should not happen and, when they did, it was their own fault for failing to prevent them. On the same basis, airlines accepted responsibility for insuring that stowaways were returned to their point of origin and—since there was no other way to convey them—offenders went back in regular seats, getting normal service, including airline meals.

"You're nice, too," Mrs. Quonsett said. "I can always tell nice people when I meet them. But you're a lot younger than the others in the airline—those I get to meet, I mean."

"You mean the ones who deal with cheats and stowaways."

"That's right." The little old lady seemed unabashed. Her eyes moved appraisingly. "I should say you're twenty-eight."

Tanya said shortly, "Thirty-seven."

"Well, you have a young mature look. Perhaps it comes from being married."

"Come off it," Tanya said. "That isn't going to help you."

"But you are married."

"I was. I'm not now."

"Such a pity. You could have beautiful children. With red hair like your own."

Red hair, perhaps, but not with the beginnings of gray, Tanya thought—the gray she had noticed again this morning. As to children, she might have explained that she did have a child, who was at home in their apartment and, she hoped, asleep. Instead, she addressed Mrs. Ada Quonsett sternly.

"What you've done is dishonest. You've defrauded; you've broken the law. I suppose you realize you can be prosecuted."

For the first time, a gleam of triumph crossed the older woman's innocent face. "But I won't be, will I? They never do prosecute anybody."

There was really no point in continuing, Tanya thought. She knew perfectly well, and so apparently did Mrs. Quonsett, that airlines never prosecuted stowaways, on the theory that publicity would be more harmful than otherwise.

There was just a chance, though, that some more questions might produce information useful in the future.

"Mrs. Quonsett," Tanya said, "since you've had so much free travel from Trans America, the least you can do is help us a little."

"I'll be glad to if I can."

"What I'd like to know is how you get aboard our flights."

The little old lady smiled. "Well, my dear, there are quite a few ways. I try to use different ones as much as I can."

"Please tell me about them."

"Well, most times I try to be at the airport early enough so I can get myself a boarding pass."

"Isn't that difficult to do?"

"Getting a boarding pass? Oh, no; it's very easy. Nowadays airlines use their ticket folders as passes. So I go to one of the counters and say I've lost my ticket folder, and please may I have another. I pick a counter where the clerks are busy, with a lot of people waiting. They always give me one."

Naturally they would, Tanya thought. It was a normal request which occurred frequently. Except that, unlike Mrs. Quonsett, most people wanted a fresh ticket folder for a legitimate reason.

"But it's just a blank folder," Tanya pointed out. "It isn't made out as a gate pass."

"I make it out myself—in the ladies' room. I always have some old passes with me, so I know what to write. And I keep a big black pencil in my purse." Depositing the lace handkerchief in her lap, Mrs. Quonsett opened her black beaded purse. "See?"

"I do see," Tanya said. She reached out, removing the crayon pencil. "Do you mind if I keep this?"

Mrs. Quonsett looked faintly resentful. "It's really mine. But if you want it, I suppose I can get another."

"Go on," Tanya said. "So now you have a boarding pass. What happens after that?"

"I go to where the flight is leaving from."

"The departure gate?"

"That's right. I wait until the young man checking the tickets is busy—he always is when a lot of people come together. Then I walk past him, and on to the airplane."

"Suppose someone tries to stop you?"

"No one does, if I have a pass."

"Not even the stewardesses?"

"They're just young girls, my dear. Usually they're talking to each other, or interested in the men. All they look at is the flight number, and I always get that right."

"But you said you don't always use a boarding pass."

Mrs. Quonsett blushed. "Then, I'm afraid, I have to tell a little white lie. Sometimes I say I'm going aboard to see my daughter off—most airlines let people do that, you know. Or, if the plane has come in from somewhere else, I say I'm going back to my seat, but I left my ticket on board. Or, I tell them my son just got on, but he dropped his wallet and I want to give it to him. I carry a wallet in my hand, and that works best of all."

"Yes," Tanya said, "I imagine it would. You seem to have thought everything out very carefully." She had plenty of material, she mused, for a bulletin to all gate agents and stewardesses. She doubted, though, if it would have much effect.

"My late husband taught me to be thorough. He was a teacher—of geometry. He always said you should try to think of every angle."

Tanya looked hard at Mrs. Quonsett. Was her leg being gently pulled?

The face of the little old lady from San Diego remained impassive. "There's one important thing I haven't mentioned."

On the opposite side of the room a telephone rang. Tanya got up to answer it.

"Is that old biddy still with you?" The voice was the District Transportation Manager's. The D.T.M. was responsible for all phases of Trans America operations at Lincoln International. Usually a calm, good-natured boss, tonight he sounded irascible. Clearly, three days and nights of flight delays, rerouting unhappy passengers, and endless needlings from the airline's Eastern head office were having their effect.

"Yes," Tanya said.

"Get anything useful out of her?"

"Quite a lot. I'll send you a report."

"When you do, use some goddam capitals for once, so I can read it."

"Yes, sir."

She made the "sir" sufficiently pointed, so there was a momentary silence at the other end. Then the D.T.M. grunted. "Sorry, Tanya! I guess I'm passing on to you what I've been getting from New York. Like the cabin boy kicking the ship's cat, only you're no cat. Can I do anything?"

"I'd like a one-way passage to Los Angeles, tonight, for Mrs. Ada Quonsett."

"Is that the old hen?"

"The same."

The D.T.M. said sourly, "I suppose, a company charge."

"I'm afraid so."

"What I hate about it is putting her ahead of honest-to-goodness fare-paying passengers who've been waiting hours already. But I guess you're right; we're better off to get her out of our hair."

"I think so."

"I'll okay a requisition. You can pick it up at the ticket counter. But be sure to alert Los Angeles, so they can have the airport police escort the old hag off the premises."

Tanya said softly, "She could be Whistler's Mother."

The D.T.M. grunted. "Then let Whistler buy her a ticket."

Tanya smiled and hung up. She returned to Mrs. Quonsett.

"You said there was an important thing—about getting aboard flights—that you hadn't told me."

The little old lady hesitated. Her mouth had tightened noticeably at the mention, during Tanya's conversation, of a return flight to Los Angeles.

"You've told me most of it," Tanya prompted. "You might as well finish. *If* there's anything else."

"There certainly is." Mrs. Quonsett gave a tight, prim nod. "I was going to say it's best not to choose the big flights—the important ones, I mean, that go non-stop across the country. They often get full, and they give people seat numbers, even in Economy. That makes it harder, though I did it once when I could see there weren't many others going."

"So you take flights that aren't direct. Don't you get found out at intermediate stops?"

"I pretend to be asleep. Usually they don't disturb me."

"But this time you were."

Mrs. Quonsett pressed her lips in a thin, reproving line. "It was that man sitting beside me. He was very mean. I confided in him, and he betrayed me to the stewardess. That's what you get for trusting people."

"Mrs. Quonsett," Tanya said. "I imagine you heard; we're going to send you back to Los Angeles."

There was the slightest gleam behind the elderly, gray eyes. "Yes, my dear. I was afraid that would happen.

But I'd like to get a cup of tea. So, if I can go now, and you'll tell me what time to come back . . ."

"Oh, no!" Tanya shook her head decisively. "You're not going anywhere alone. You can have your cup of tea, but an agent will be with you. I'm going to send for one now, and he'll stay with you until you board the Los Angeles flight. If I let you loose in this terminal I know exactly what would happen. You'd be on an airplane for New York before anybody knew it."

From the momentary hostile glare which Mrs. Quonsett gave her, Tanya knew she had guessed right.

Ten minutes later, all arrangements were complete. A single seat reservation had been made on Flight 103 for Los Angeles, leaving in an hour and a half. The flight was nonstop; there was to be no chance of Mrs. Quonsett getting off en route and heading back. D.T.M. Los Angeles had been advised by teletype; a memo was going to the crew of Flight 103.

The little old lady from San Diego had been handed over to a male Trans America agent—a recently recruited junior, young enough to be her grandson.

Tanya's instructions to the agent, Peter Coakley, were precise. "You're to stay with Mrs. Quonsett until flight time. She says she wants some tea, so take her to the coffee shop and she can have it; also something to eat if she asks, though there'll be dinner on the flight. But whatever she has, stay with her. If she needs the ladies' room, wait outside; otherwise, don't let her out of your sight. At flight time, take her to the departure gate, go aboard with her and hand her over to the senior stewardess. Make it clear that once aboard, she is not to be allowed off the airplane for any reason. She's full of little tricks and plausible excuses, so be careful."

Before leaving, the little old lady grasped the young agent's arm. "I hope you don't mind, young man. Nowadays an old lady needs support, and you do so remind me of my dear son-in-law. He was good-looking, too, though of course he's a lot older than you are now. Your airline does seem to employ nice people." Mrs. Quonsett glanced reproachfully at Tanya. "At least, most of them are."

"Remember what I said," Tanya cautioned Peter Coakley. "She's got a barrelful of tricks."

Mrs. Quonsett said severely, "That isn't very kind. I'm sure this young man will form his own opinion."

The agent was grinning sheepishly.

At the doorway, Mrs. Quonsett turned. She addressed Tanya. "Despite the way you've behaved, my dear, I want you to know that I don't bear any grudge."

A few minutes later, from the small lounge which she had used for tonight's two interviews, Tanya returned to the Trans America executive offices on the main mezzanine. The time, she noticed, was a quarter to nine. At her desk in the big outer office she speculated on whether the airline had heard the last, or not, of Mrs. Ada Quonsett. Tanya rather doubted it. On her capitalless typewriter she began a memo to the District Transportation Manager.

to: dtm
from: tanya liv'stn
sbject: whistler's mum

She stopped, wondering where Mel Bakersfeld was, and if he would come.

5

He simply couldn't, Mel Bakersfeld decided, go downtown tonight.

Mel was in his office, in the mezzanine administrative suite. His fingers drummed thoughtfully on the surface of his desk, from where he had been telephoning, obtaining latest reports on the airport's operating status.

Runway three zero was still out of use, still blocked by the mired Aéreo-Mexican jet. As a result, the gen-

eral runway availability situation was now critical, and
traffic delays—both in the air and on the ground—were
worsening. The possibility of having to declare the airport closed, some time within the next few hours, was
very real.

Meanwhile, aircraft takeoffs were continuing over
Meadowood, which was a hornet's nest all its own. The
airport switchboard, as well as air traffic control's, was
being swamped with bitterly complaining calls from
Meadowood householders—those who were at home. A
good many others, Mel had been informed, were at the
protest meeting he had heard about earlier this evening;
and now there was a rumor—which the tower chief had
passed along a few minutes ago—that some kind of
public demonstration was being planned, to take place
at the airport tonight.

Mel thought glumly: a bunch of demonstrators underfoot was all he needed.

One good thing was that the category three emergency had just been declared concluded, the air force
KC-135 which caused it, having landed safely. But one
emergency ended was no assurance another would not
begin. Mel had not forgotten the vague unease, the presentiment of danger he had felt while on the airfield an
hour ago. The feeling, impossible to define or justify,
still bothered him. Yet even without it, the other circumstances were enough to require his remaining here.

Cindy, of course—still waiting for him at her charity
whingding—would raise all hell. But she was angry,
anyway, because he was going to be late; he would have
to brace himself to absorb the extra wrath as a result of
not appearing at all. He supposed he might as well get
Cindy's first salvo over with. The slip of paper with the
downtown number where he had reached his wife earlier
was still in his pocket. He took it out, and dialed.

As before, it took several minutes for Cindy to come
to the telephone, and when she did, surprisingly, there
was none of the fire she had shown during their previous
conversation, only an icy chill. She listened in silence to
Mel's explanation—why it was essential he should
remain at the airport. Because of the lack of argument,
which he had not expected, he found himself flound-

ering, with labored excuses not wholly convincing to himself. He stopped abruptly.

There was a pause before Cindy inquired coldly, "Have you finished?"

"Yes."

She sounded as if she were talking to someone distasteful and remote. "I'm not surprised, because I didn't expect you to come. When you said you would, I assumed as usual you were lying."

He said heatedly, "I wasn't lying, and it isn't as usual. I told you earlier tonight, how many times I've been . . ."

"I thought you said you'd finished."

Mel stopped. What was the use? He conceded wearily, "Go on."

"As I was trying to say when you interrupted—also as usual . . ."

"Cindy, for God's sake!"

". . . knowing you were lying, gave me the chance to do some thinking." She paused "You say you're staying at the airport "

"Considering that's what this conversation is all about . . ."

"How long?"

"Until midnight; perhaps all night."

"Then I'll come out there. You can expect me."

"Listen, Cindy, it's no good. This isn't the time or place."

"Then we'll make it the time. And for what I have to say to you, any place is good enough."

"Cindy, please be reasonable. I agree there are things we have to discuss, but not . . ."

Mel stopped, realizing he was talking to himself. Cindy had hung up.

He replaced his own phone and sat in the silent office, meditatively. Then, not quite knowing why, he picked up the telephone again and, for the second time tonight, dialed home. Earlier, Roberta had answered. This time it was Mrs. Sebastiani, their regular babysitter.

"I was just calling to check," Mel said. "Is everything all right? Are the girls in bed?"

"Roberta is, Mr. Bakersfeld. Libby's just going."

"May I speak to Libby?"

"Well . . . just for a moment, if you promise to be very quick."

"I promise."

Mrs. Sebastiani, Mel perceived, was her usual didactic self. When on duty she exacted obedience, not just from children, but from entire families. He sometimes wondered if the Sebastianis—there was a mousy husband who appeared occasionally—ever had emotional marriage problems. He suspected not. Mrs. Sebastiani would never permit it.

He heard the patter of Libby's feet approach the phone.

"Daddy," Libby said, "does our blood keep going round inside forever and ever?"

Libby's questions were always intriguingly different. She opened new subjects as if they were presents under a Christmas tree.

"Not forever, dear; nothing's forever. Just so long as you live. Your blood has been going around for seven years, ever since your heart started pumping."

"I can feel my heart," Libby said. "In my knee."

He was on the point of explaining that hearts were not in knees, and about pulses and arteries and veins, then changed his mind. There was plenty of time for all that. As long as you could feel your heart—wherever it seemed to be—that was the important thing. Libby had an instinct for essentials; at times he had the impression that her little hands reached up and gathered stars of truth.

"Goodnight, Daddy."

"Goodnight, my love."

Mel was still not sure why he had called, but he felt better for having done so.

As to Cindy, when she determined to do something she usually did it, so it was entirely likely that she would arrive at the airport later tonight. And perhaps she was right. There were fundamental things they had to settle, notably whether their hollow shell of a marriage was to continue for the children's sake, or not. At least they would have privacy here, out of hearing of Roberta and Libby, who had overheard too many of their fights before.

At the moment there was nothing specific for Mel to do, except be available. He went out from his office onto the executive mezzanine, looking down on the continued bustling activity of the main terminal concourse.

It would not be many years, Mel reflected, before airport concourses changed dramatically. Something would have to be done soon to revise the present inefficient way in which people boarded airplanes and got off them. Simply walking on and off, individually, was far too cumbersome and slow. As each year passed, individual airplanes cost more and more millions of dollars; at the same time, the cost of letting them stay idle on the ground grew greater. Aircraft designers, airline planners, were striving to arrange more flying hours, which produced revenue, and fewer ground hours, which produced none at all.

Already plans were afoot for "people-pods"—based on American Airline-type "igloos" now used for pre-loading air freight. Most other airlines had their own variants of the igloo system.

Freight igloos were self-contained compartments, shaped to fit tightly in a jet plane fuselage. Each igloo was pre-loaded with freight of associated shapes and sizes, and could be lifted to fuselage level, and stowed inside a jet, in minutes. Unlike conventional passenger planes, the inside of a jet freighter was usually a hollow shell. Nowadays when an all-cargo plane arrived at an airport freight terminal, igloos already in the airplane were off-loaded, and new ones put in. With a minimum of time and labor, an entire jet could be swiftly unloaded, reloaded, and be ready again for takeoff.

"People-pods" would be an adaptation of the same idea, and Mel had seen drawings of the type now contemplated. They would comprise small, comfortable cabin sections complete with seats, which passengers would step into at an airport check-in point. The pods would then be whisked on conveyor lines—similar to present baggage conveyor systems—to ramp positions. While their occupants remained seated, the people-pods would be slid into an aircraft which might have arrived only a few minutes earlier, but had already discharged other people-pods containing incoming passengers.

When the pods were loaded and in place, windows in them would correspond with windows in the aircraft fuselage. Doors at the end of each pod would fold back so that stewardesses and passengers could pass through to other sections. Galley compartments, complete with fresh food and fresh stewardesses, would be inserted as separate pods.

A refinement of the system might eventually allow boarding of people-pods downtown, or permit interline transfers by passengers without ever leaving their seats.

A related concept was a "sky lounge" already under development in Los Angeles. Each lounge, holding forty passengers, would be part-bus, part-helicopter. On local routes it could travel suburban or downtown streets under its own power, then, at a local heliport become a pod beneath an outsize helicopter—the entire unit whisked to and from an airport.

And these things would happen, Mel Bakersfeld reflected. Or if not those precisely, then something similar, and soon. A fascination, for those who worked in the aviation milieu, was the speed with which fantastic dreams came true.

A shout, abruptly, from the concourse below, broke into his thoughts.

"Hey, Bakersfeld! Hey up there!"

Mel searched with his eyes, seeking the source of the voice. Locating it was made more difficult by the fact that fifty or so faces, their owners curious about who was being called, had simultaneously swung up. A moment later he identified the caller. It was Egan Jeffers, a tall, lean Negro in light tan slacks and a short-sleeved shirt. One sinewy brown arm gestured urgently.

"You get down here, Bakersfeld. You hear me! You got troubles."

Mel smiled. Jeffers, who held the terminal shoeshine concession, was an airport character. With a challenging, broad grin across his homely features, he could make the most outrageous statements and somehow get away with it.

"I hear you, Egan Jeffers. How about you coming up instead?"

The grin widened. "Nuts to that, Bakersfeld! I'm a lessee and don't forget it."

"If I do, I suppose you'll read me the Civil Rights Act."

"You said it, Bakersfeld. Now haul your ass down here."

"And you watch your language in my airport." Still amused, Mel turned away from the mezzanine rail and headed for the staff elevator. At the main concourse level, Egan Jeffers was waiting.

Jeffers operated four shoeshine parlors within the terminal. As concessions went, it was not a major one, and the airport's parking, restaurant, and newsstand concessions produced revenues which were astronomical by comparison. But Egan Jeffers, a one-time curbside bootblack, blithely behaved as if he alone kept the airport solvent.

"We gotta contract, me and this airport. Check?"

"Check."

"Down in all that fancy rig-y-marole it says I got the ex-clu-sive right to shine shoes in these here premises. *Ex-clu-sive*. Check?"

"Check."

"Like I said, man, you got trouble. Follow me, Bakersfeld."

They crossed the main concourse to a lower level escalator which Jeffers descended in long strides, two steps at a time. He waved genially to several people as they passed. Less athletically, favoring his weaker foot, Mel followed.

At the foot of the escalator, near the group of car-rental booths occupied by Hertz, Avis, and National, Egan Jeffers gestured. "There it is, Bakersfeld! Look at it! Taking the shoe polish outa the mouths of me and the boys who work for me."

Mel inspected the cause of complaint. At the Avis counter a bold display card read:

A SHINE WHILE YOU SIGN
With Our Compliments
* * *
We're Trying Harder Still!

Beneath, at floor level, was a rotating electric shoe polisher, positioned so that anyone standing at the counter could do what the notice said.

Mel was half amused; the other half of his mind accepted Egan Jeffers' complaint. Half-kidding or not, Jeffers was within his rights. His contract spelled out that no one else at the airport could shine shoes, just as Jeffers himself could not rent cars or sell newspapers. Each concessionaire received the same kind of protection in return for the substantial portion of his profits which the airport appropriated for itself.

With Egan Jeffers watching, Mel crossed to the car-rental booth. He consulted his pocket panic list—a slim booklet containing private telephone numbers of senior airport personnel. The Avis manager was listed. The girl behind the counter switched on an automatic smile as he approached. Mel instructed her, "Let me use your phone."

She protested, "Sir, it's not a public . . ."

"I'm the airport manager." Mel reached across, picked up the telephone and dialed. Not being recognized in his own airport was a frequent experience. Most of Mel's work kept him behind scenes, away from public areas, so that those who worked there seldom saw him.

Listening to the ringing tone, he wished that other problems could be settled as swiftly and simply as this one was going to be.

It took a dozen rings, then several minutes more of waiting, before the Avis manager's voice came on the line. "Ken Kingsley here."

"I might have needed a car," Mel said. "Where were you?"

"Playing with my kid's trains. Take my mind off automobiles—and people who call me about them."

"Must be great to have a boy," Mel said. "I just have girls. Is your boy mechanically minded?"

"An eight-year-old genius. Any time you need him to run that toy airport of yours, let me know."

"Sure will, Ken." Mel winked at Egan Jeffers. "There is one thing he might do now. He could set up a shoeshine machine at home. I happen to know where there's one surplus. So do you."

There was a silence, then the Avis manager sighed. "Why is it you guys always want to stifle a little honest sales promotion?"

"Mostly because we're mean and ornery. But we can make it stick. Remember that contract clause?—any change in display space must have prior approval of airport management. Then there's the one about not infringing on other lessees' business."

"I get it," Kingsley said. "Egan Jeffers has been beefing."

"Let's say he isn't cheering."

"Okay, you win. I'll tell my people to yank the damn thing. Is there any fat rush?"

"Not really," Mel said. "Any time in the next half hour will do."

"You bastard."

But he could hear the Avis man chuckling as he hung up.

Egan Jeffers nodded approvingly, his wide grin still in place. Mel brooded: I'm the friendly airport fun man; I make everybody happy. He wished he could do the same thing for himself.

"You handled that A-OK, Bakersfeld," Jeffers said. "Just stay on the ball so it don't happen again." At a businesslike pace, still beaming, he headed for the "up" escalator.

Mel followed more slowly. On the main concourse level, at the Trans America counters, a milling crowd was in front of two positions marked:

Special Check-in
Flight Two—*The Golden Argosy*
Rome Nonstop

Nearby, Tanya Livingston was talking animatedly with a group of passengers. She signaled Mel and, after a moment or two, came over to join him.

"I mustn't stop; it's like a madhouse here. I thought you were going downtown."

"My plans changed," Mel said. "For that matter, I thought you were going off duty."

"The D.T.M. asked if I'd stay. We're trying to get *The Golden Argosy* away on time. It's supposed to be for prestige, though I suspect the real reason is, Captain Demerest doesn't like to be kept waiting."

"You're letting prejudice carry you away." Mel grinned. "Though sometimes I do, too."

Tanya gestured down the concourse to a raised platform with a circular counter surrounding it, a few yards from where they were standing. "That's what your big fight with your brother-in-law was all about; why Captain Demerest is so mad at you. Isn't it?"

Tanya was pointing to the airport's insurance-vending booth. A dozen or more people were ranged around the circular counter, most of them completing application forms for air trip insurance. Behind the counter, two attractive girls, one a striking blonde with big breasts, were busy writing policies.

"Yes," Mel acknowledged, "that was most of our trouble—at least, recently. Vernon and the Air Line Pilots Association think we should abolish insurance booths at airports, and insurance policy vending machines. I don't. The two of us had a battle about it in front of the Board of Airport Commissioners. What Vernon didn't like, and still doesn't, is that I won."

"I heard," Tanya looked at Mel searchingly. "Some of us don't agree with you. This time we think Captain Demerest is right."

Mel shook his head. "Then we'll have to disagree. I've been over it all so many times; Vernon's arguments just don't make sense."

They hadn't made any more sense—in Mel's opinion —that day a month ago, at Lincoln International, when Vernon Demerest had appeared before an Airport Commissioners meeting. Vernon requested the hearing, and had represented the Air Line Pilots Association, which was waging a campaign to outlaw insurance vending at airports everywhere.

Mel remembered the details of the session clearly.

It was a regular Board of Airport Commissioners

meeting, on a Wednesday morning in the airport board room. All five commissioners were present: Mrs. Mildred Ackerman, an attractive brunette housewife who was rumored to be a mistress of the mayor, hence her appointment; and her four male colleagues—a university professor, who was Board chairman, two local businessmen, and a retired union official.

The Board room was a mahogany paneled chamber, in the terminal, on the executive mezzanine. At one end, on a raised platform, the commissioners sat in reclining leather chairs behind a handsome elliptical-shaped table. At a lower level was a second table, less elaborate. Here Mel Bakersfeld presided, flanked by his department heads. Alongside was a press table and, at the rear, a section for the public, since Board meetings were nominally open. The public section was rarely occupied.

Today the only outsider, apart from commissioners and staff, was Captain Vernon Demerest, smartly attired in Trans America uniform, his four gold stripes of rank bright under the overhead lights. He sat waiting in the public section, with books and papers spread over two other chairs beside him. Courteously, the Board elected to hear Captain Demerest first, ahead of its regular business.

Demerest rose. He addressed the Board with his usual self-assurance, and referred only occasionally to his notes. He was appearing, he explained, on behalf of the Air Line Pilots Association, of which he was a local council chairman. However, the views he would expound were equally his own, and were shared by most pilots of all airlines.

The commissioners settled back in their reclining chairs to listen.

Airport insurance vending, Demerest began, was a ridiculous, archaic hangover from flying's early days. The very presence of insurance booths and machines, their prominence in airport concourses, were insults to commercial aviation, which had a finer safety record, in relation to miles traveled, than any other form of transportation.

In a railway station or bus depot, or on boarding an

ocean liner, or driving his own car from a parking garage, did a departing traveler have special insurance policies, against death and mutilation, thrust beneath his nose with subtle sales pressure? Of course not!

Then why aviation?

Demerest answered his own question. The reason, he declared, was that insurance companies knew a rich bonanza when they saw it, "and never mind the consequences."

Commercial aviation was still sufficiently new so that many people thought of traveling by air as hazardous, despite the provable fact that an individual was safer in a commercial airliner than in his own home. This inherent mistrust of flying was magnified on the exceedingly rare occasions when an airline accident occurred. The impact was dramatic, and obscured the fact that far more deaths and injuries occurred in other, more accepted ways.

The truth about the safety of flying, Demerest pointed out, was attested by insurance companies themselves. Airline pilots, whose exposure to air travel was far greater than that of passengers, could buy standard life insurance at regular rates and, through their own group plans, at even lower rates than the general populace.

Yet other insurance companies, abetted by greedy airport managements, and with the docile acquiescence of airlines, continued to batten on the fears and gullibility of air travelers.

Listening, at the staff table, Mel conceded mentally that his brother-in-law was making a lucid presentation, though the reference to "greedy airport managements" had been unwise. The remark had produced frowns from several of the five commissioners, including Mrs. Ackerman.

Vernon Demerest seemed not to notice. "Now, madam and gentlemen, we come to the most significant, the vital point."

This, he declared, was the very real danger, to every air passenger and to all flying crews, created by irresponsible, casual sales of insurance policies at airport counters, and by vending machines . . . "policies promising vast sums, fortunes, in return for a mere few dollars' premium."

Demerest continued heatedly: "The system—if you choose to dignify a public disservice by calling it a system . . . and most pilots don't—offers a gilt-edged, open invitation to maniacs and criminals to engage in sabotage and mass murder. Their objectives need be only the simplest: personal reward for themselves or their expected beneficiaries."

"Captain!" The woman commissioner, Mrs. Ackerman, was leaning forward in her chair. From her voice and expression, Mel guessed she was doing a slow burn about the "greedy airport managements" remark. "Captain, we're hearing a whole lot of your opinions. Do you have any facts to back up all this?"

"Indeed I do, madam. There are many facts."

Vernon Demerest had prepared his case thoroughly. Using charts and graphs, he demonstrated that known in-flight disasters caused by bombings or other acts of violence averaged one and one half per year. Motives varied, but a consistent, prevalent cause was financial gain from flight insurance. As well, there had been additional bombing attempts which either failed or were prevented, and other disasters where sabotage was suspected but not proved.

He named classic incidents: Canadian Pacific Airlines, 1949 and 1965; Western Airlines, 1957; National Airlines, 1960 and a suspected sabotage in 1959; two Mexican airlines, 1952 and 1953; Venezuelan Airlines, 1960; Continental Airlines, 1962; Pacific Air Lines, 1964; United Air Lines, 1950, 1955, and a suspected sabotage in 1965. In nine of the thirteen incidents, all passengers and crew members perished.

It was true, of course, that where sabotage was exposed, any insurance policies which had been taken out by those involved were automatically invalidated. In short: sabotage didn't pay, and normal, informed people were aware of this. They also knew that even after an air disaster from which there were no survivors, providing wreckage was located, it was possible to tell whether an explosion had occurred and, usually, by what means.

But it was not normal people, Demerest reminded the commissioners, who committed bombings or savage acts of violence. It was the abnormal, the psychopaths, the criminally insane, the conscienceless mass killers. That kind of people were seldom well-informed, and even if they were, the pyschopathic mind had a way of perceiving only what it wanted to, of bending facts to suit what it was convenient to believe.

Mrs. Ackerman made an interjection again; this time her hostility to Demerest was unmistakable. "I'm not sure any of us, even you, Captain, have qualifications to discuss what goes on in the mind of psychopaths."

"I wasn't discussing it," Demerest said impatiently. "In any case, that isn't the point."

"Pardon me, you *were* discussing it. And I happen to think it is the point."

Vernon Demerest flushed. He was accustomed to command, not to being questioned. His temper, never far below the surface, flashed. "Madam, are you normally stupid or just being deliberately obtuse?"

The Board chairman rapped sharply with his gavel, and Mel Bakersfeld resisted the urge to laugh.

Well, Mel thought, we might as well finish right now. Vernon should stick to flying, which he was good at, and avoid diplomacy, where he had just struck out. The chances of the Airport Board doing anything which Captain Demerest wanted were, at this moment, minus nil—at least unless Mel helped Demerest out. For a moment he wondered if he should. He suspected Demerest realized he had gone too far. However, there was still time to turn what had just happened into a joke which everyone could laugh at, including Mildred Ackerman. Mel had a knack for doing that kind of thing, for making differences amenable, at the same time saving face for those on both sides. Also, he knew he was a favorite of Millie Ackerman's; they got on well together, and she always listened attentively to anything Mel might say.

Then he decided: the hell with it. He doubted if his

brother-in-law would do the same thing if their situations were reversed. Let Vernon get out of the mess himself. In any case, Mel was going to have his own say in a few minutes' time.

"Captain Demerest," the Board chairman observed coldly, "that last remark is uncalled for, out of order, and you will please withdraw it."

Demerest's features were still flushed. Momentarily he hesitated, then nodded. "Very well, I withdraw it." He glanced at Mrs. Ackerman. "I beg the lady's pardon. Perhaps she can understand that this is a subject which I, like most commercial flying crews, feel strongly about. When there's something which seems to me so obvious . . ." He left the sentence incomplete.

Mrs. Ackerman was glaring. The apology, such as it was, Mel thought, had been handled badly. Now it was too late to smooth things over, even if he wanted to.

One of the other commissioners asked, "Captain, what exactly do you want from us?"

Demerest took a pace forward. His voice became persuasive. "I'm appealing to you for abolition of insurance machines and over-the-counter insurance vending at this airport, and a promise that you will refuse to rent space, ever again, for the same purpose."

"You'd abolish insurance sales entirely?"

"At airports—yes. I may say, madam and gentlemen, that the Air Line Pilots Association is urging other airports to do the same thing. We're also asking Congress to take action to make airport insurance sales illegal."

"What would be the point of doing that in the United States, when air travel is international?"

Demerest smiled faintly. "This campaign is international, too."

"How international?"

"We have the active support of pilots' groups in forty-eight other countries. Most believe that if an example were set in North America, either by the U.S. or Canada, others would follow."

The same commissioner said skeptically, "I'd say you're all expecting quite a lot."

"Surely," the chairman interjected, "the public is entitled to buy air travel insurance if they want it."

Demerest nodded agreement. "Of course. No one is saying they can't."

"Yes, you are." It was Mrs. Ackerman again.

The muscles around Demerest's mouth tightened. "Madam, anyone can get all the travel insurance he wants. All he needs have is the elementary foresight to make arrangements in advance—through any insurance broker or even a travel agency." His glance took in the other commissioners. "Nowadays a good many people carry a blanket accident policy for travel; then they make all the trips they want, and they're insured permanently. There are plenty of ways of doing it. As an example, the major credit card companies—Diners, American Express, Carte Blanche—all offer permanent travel insurance to their card holders; it can be renewed automatically each year, and billed."

Most businessmen who traveled, Demerest pointed out, had at least one of the credit cards he had named, so abolition of airport insurance need impose no hardship nor inconvenience on business people.

"And with all these blanket policies, the rates are low. I know, because I have that kind of policy myself."

Vernon Demerest paused, then continued, "The important thing about all these insurance policies is that they go through channels. The applications are handled by experienced people; a day or so elapses between an application and the issuance of the policy. Because of this, there is a far better chance of the psychotic, the maniac, the unbalanced individual being noticed, his intentions questioned.

"Another thing to remember—an insane or unbalanced person is a creature of impulse. Where flight insurance is concerned, this impulse is catered to by the quickie, no-questions-asked policies available from airport vending machines and at insurance counters."

"I think we all get the point you're making," the chairman said sharply. "You're beginning to repeat yourself, Captain."

Mrs. Ackerman nodded. "I agree. Personally, I'd like to hear what Mr. Bakersfeld has to say."

The eyes of the commissioners swung toward Mel. He acknowledged. "Yes, I do have some observations. But I'd prefer to wait until Captain Demerest is completely finished."

"He's finished," Mildred Ackerman said. "We just decided."

One of the other commissioners laughed, and the chairman rapped with his gravel. "Yes, I really think so ... If you please, Mr. Bakersfeld."

As Mel rose, Vernon Demerest returned, glowering, to his seat.

"I may as well make it clear," Mel began, "that I take the opposite point of view to just about everything Vernon has said. I guess you could call it a family disagreement."

The commissioners, who were aware of Mel's relationship by marriage to Vernon Demerest, smiled, and already, Mel sensed, the tension of a few minutes earlier had lessened. He was used to these meetings and knew that informality was always the best approach. Vernon could have found that out, too—if he had taken the trouble to inquire.

"There are several points we ought to think about," Mel continued. "First, let's face up to the fact that most people have always had an inherent fear of flying, and I'm convinced that feeling will always exist, no matter how much progress we make, and however much we improve our safety record. Incidentally, the one point on which I agree with Vernon is that our safety record is exceedingly good already."

He went on: Because of this inherent fear, many passengers felt more comfortable, more reassured, with air trip insurance. They wanted it. They also wanted it to be obtainable at airports, a fact proven by the enormous volume of sales from vending machines and airport insurance booths. It was a matter of freedom that passengers should have the right, and the opportunity, to buy insurance or not. As for getting the insurance ahead of time, the plain fact was that most people didn't think of it. Besides, Mel added, if flight insurance were sold this way, a great deal of revenue to airports—including Lincoln International—would be lost. At the mention of airport revenue, Mel smiled. The airport commissioners smiled with him.

That was the crux of it, of course, Mel realized. Revenue from the insurance concessions was too important to lose. At Lincoln International, the airport gained half a million dollars annually from commissions on insurance sales, though few purchasers realized that the airport appropriated twenty-five cents from every premium dollar. Yet insurance represented the fourth largest concession, with only parking, restaurants, and auto rentals producing larger sums for the airport's coffers. At other big airports, insurance revenue was similar or higher. It was all very well, Mel reflected, for Vernon Demerest to talk about "greedy airport management," but that kind of money had a way of talking, too.

Mel decided not to put his thoughts into speech. His single brief reference to revenue was enough. The commissioners, who were familiar with the airport's financial affairs, would get the point.

He consulted his notes. They were notes which one of the insurance companies doing business at Lincoln International had supplied him with yesterday. Mel had not asked for the notes, nor had he mentioned to anyone outside his own office that today's insurance debate was coming up. But the insurance people had somehow learned, and it was extraordinary how they always did —then acted promptly to protect their interests.

Mel would not have used the notes if they had run counter to his own honestly held opinions. Fortunately, they did not.

"Now," Mel said, "about sabotage—potential and otherwise." He was aware of the board members listening intently.

"Vernon has talked quite a lot about that—but I must say, having listened carefully, that most of his remarks seemed to me to be overstatements. Actually, the proven incidents of air disasters because of insurance-inspired bombings have been very few."

In the spectator section, Captain Demerest shot to his feet. "Great God!—how many disasters do we need to have?"

The chairman rapped sharply with his gavel. "Captain . . . if you please!"

Mel waited until Demerest subsided, then continued calmly, "Since the question has been asked, the answer is 'none.' A more pertinent question is: Might not the disasters still have occurred, even if airport-purchased insurance had not been available?"

Mel paused, to let his point sink home, before continuing.

"It can be argued, of course, that if airport insurance had not been available, the disasters we are talking about might never have happened at all. In other words, these were crimes of impulse, triggered by the ease with which airport insurance can be bought. Similarly, it can be contended that even if the crimes were contemplated in advance, they might not have been carried through had flight insurance been less readily available. Those, I think, are Vernon's arguments—and the ALPA's."

Mel glanced briefly at his brother-in-law who gave no sign beyond a scowl.

"The glaring weakness of all those arguments," Mel maintained, "is that they are purely suppositional. It seems to me just as likely that someone planning such a crime would not be deterred by the absence of airport insurance, but would merely obtain their insurance elsewhere, which—as Vernon himself pointed out—is a simple thing to do."

Expressed another way, Mel pointed out, flight insurance appeared only a secondary motive of would-be saboteurs, and not a prime reason for their crime. The real motives, when aerial sabotage occurred, were based on age-old human weaknesses—love triangles, greed, business failures, suicide.

As long as there had been human beings, Mel argued, it had proven impossible to eliminate these motives. Therefore, those concerned with aviation safety and sabotage prevention should seek, not to abolish airport flight insurance, but to strengthen other precautionary measures in the air and on the ground. One such measure was stricter control of the sale of dynamite— the principal tool used by most aerial saboteurs to date. Another proposal was development of "sniffer" devices to detect explosives in baggage. One such device, Mel informed the attentive Airport Commissioners, was already in experimental use.

A third idea—urged by flight insurance companies— was that passengers' baggage be opened for examination *before* flight, in the same way that happened with Customs inspection now. However, Mel concluded, the last idea presented obvious difficulties.

There should be stricter enforcement, he claimed, of existing laws prohibiting the carrying of side arms on commercial airliners. And airplane design should be studied in relation to sabotage, with the objective that aircraft could better endure an internal explosion. In that connection, one idea—also advocated by the insurance vending companies—was for an inner skin of baggage compartments to be made stronger and heavier than at present, even at the price of increased weight and decreased airline revenue.

The FAA, Mel pointed out, had made a study of airport insurance and subsequently opposed any ban on airport sales. Mel glanced at Vernon Demerest, who was glowering. Both knew that the FAA "study" was a sore point with the airline pilots since it had been made by an insurance company executive—an aviation insurance man himself—whose impartiality was highly suspect.

There were several more points remaining in the insurance company notes which Mel had not yet touched on, but he decided he had said enough. Besides, some of the remaining arguments were less convincing. He even had serious doubts, now that he had made it, about the baggage compartment suggestion of a moment or two ago. Who would the extra weight be for, he wondered —the passengers, airlines, or mostly for the flight insurance companies? But the other arguments, he thought, were sound enough.

"So," he concluded, "what we have to decide is whether, because of supposition and very little else, we should deprive the public of a service which they so obviously want."

As Mel resumed his seat, Mildred Ackerman said promptly and emphatically, "I'd say no." She shot Vernon Demerest a glance of triumph.

With minimum formality the other commissioners agreed, then adjourned, leaving other business until afternoon.

In the corridor outside, Vernon Demerest was waiting for Mel.

"Hi, Vernon!" Mel spoke quickly, making an effort at conciliation before his brother-in-law could speak. "No hard feelings, I hope. Even friends and relatives have to differ now and then."

The "friends" was, of course, an overstatement. Mel Bakersfeld and Vernon Demerest had never liked each other, despite Demerest's marriage to Mel's sister, Sarah, and both men knew it; also, of late, the dislike had sharpened to open antagonism.

"You're damn right there are hard feellings," Demerest said. The peak of his anger had passed, but his eyes were hard.

The commissioners, now filing out from the Board room, looked curiously at them both. The commissioners were on their way to lunch. In a few minutes Mel would join them.

Demerest said contemptuously, "It's easy for people like you—ground-bound, desk-tied, with penguins' minds. If you were in the air as often as I am, you'd have a different point of view."

Mel said sharply, "I wasn't always flying a desk."

"Oh, for Christ's sake! Don't hand me that hero veteran crap. You're at zero-feet now; the way you think shows it. If you weren't, you'd see this insurance deal the way any self-respecting pilot does."

"You're sure you mean self-respecting, not self-adoring?" If Vernon wanted a slanging match, Mel decided, he could have one. There was no one else within hearing now. "The trouble with most of you pilots is you've become so used to thinking of yourselves as demigods and captains of the clouds, you've convinced yourselves your brains are something wonderful too. Well, except in a few specialized ways, they're not. Sometimes I think the rest of what you have has addled through sitting up in that rarefied air too long while automatic pilots do the work. So when someone comes up with an honest opinion which happens to run counter to your own, you behave like spoiled little children."

"I'll let all that stuff go," Demerest said, "though if anybody's childish it's you right now. What's more to the point is that you're dishonest."

"Now look, Vernon . . ."

"An honest opinion, you said." Demerest snorted in disgust. "Honest opinion, my eye! In there, you were using an insurance company poop sheet. You were reading from it! I could see from where I was sitting, and I know because I have a copy myself." He touched the pile of books and papers he was carrying. "You didn't even have the decency, or take the trouble, to prepare a case yourself."

Mel flushed. His brother-in-law had caught him out. He *should* have prepared his own case, or at least adapted the insurance company's notes and had them retyped. It was true he had been busier than usual for several days before the meeting, but that was no excuse.

"Some day you may regret this," Vernon Demerest said. "If you do, and I'm around, I'll be the one to remind you of today. Until then, I can do without seeing you any more than I have to."

Before Mel could reply, his brother-in-law had turned and gone.

Remembering, now, with Tanya beside him in the main terminal concourse, Mel wondered—as he had several times since—if he could not have handled the clash with Vernon a good deal better. He could still have differed with his brother-in-law; even now Mel saw no reason to change his point of view. But he could have done it more good-naturedly, avoiding the tactlessness which was a part of Vernon Demerest's makeup, but not of Mel's.

There had been no confrontation, since that day, between the two of them; the near-encounter with Demerest in the airport coffee shop tonight had been Mel's first sight of his brother-in-law since the airport commissioners' meeting. Mel had never been close to his older sister, Sarah, and they seldom visited each other's homes. Yet sooner or later, Mel and Vernon Demerest would have to meet, if not to resolve their differences, at least to shelve them. And, Mel thought, judging by the strongly worded snow committee report—unquestionably inspired by Vernon's antagonism—the sooner it happened, the better.

"I wouldn't have mentioned the insurance bit," Tanya said, "if I'd known it would send you so far away from me."

Though the recollections which had flashed through his mind occupied only seconds of time, Mel was conscious once again of Tanya's perceptiveness concerning himself. No one else that he could remember had ever had quite the same facility for divining his thoughts. It argued an instinctive closeness between them.

He was aware of Tanya watching his face, her eyes gentle, understanding, but beyond the gentleness was a woman's strength and a sensuality which instinct told him could leap to flame. Suddenly, he wanted their closeness to become closer still.

"You didn't send me far away," Mel answered. "You brought me nearer. At this moment I want you very much." As their eyes met directly, he added, "In every way."

Tanya was characteristically frank. "I want you too." She smiled slightly. "I have for a long time."

His impulse was to suggest that they both leave now, and find some quiet place together . . . Tanya's apartment perhaps . . . and hang the consequences! Then Mel accepted what he already knew; he couldn't go. Not yet.

"We'll meet later," he told her. "Tonight. I'm not sure how much later, but we will. Don't go home without me." He wanted to reach out, and seize and hold her, and press her body to his, but the traffic of the concourse was all around them.

She reached out, her fingertips resting lightly on his hand. The sense of contact was electric. "I'll wait," Tanya said. "I'll wait as long as you want."

A moment later she moved away, and was instantly swallowed up in the press of passengers around the Trans America counters.

6

Despite her forcefulness when she had talked with Mel a half-hour earlier, Cindy Bakersfeld was uncertain what to do next. She wished there were someone she could trust to advise her. Should she go to the airport tonight, or not?

Alone and lonely, with the cocktail party babel of the Friends of the Archidona Children's Relief Fund around her, Cindy brooded uneasily over the two courses of action she could take. Through most of the evening, until now, she had moved from group to group, chatting animatedly, meeting people she knew, or wanted to. But for some reason tonight—rather more than usual— Cindy was aware of being here unaccompanied. For the past few minutes she had been standing thoughtfully, preoccupied, by herself.

She reasoned again: She didn't feel like going unescorted into dinner, which would begin soon. So on the one hand she could go home; on the other, she could seek out Mel and face a fight.

On the telephone with Mel she had insisted she would go to the airport and confront him. But if she went, Cindy realized, it would mean a showdown—almost certainly irreversible and final—between them both. Commonsense told her that sooner or later the showdown must come, so better to have it now and done with; and there were other related matters which had to be resolved. Yet fifteen years of marriage were not to be shrugged off lightly like a disposable plastic raincoat. No matter how many deficiencies and disagreements there were—and Cindy could think of plenty—when two people lived together that long, there were connecting strands between them which it would be painful to sever.

Even now, Cindy believed, their marriage could be salvaged if both of them tried hard enough. The point was: Did they want to? Cindy was convinced she did— if Mel would meet some of her conditions, though in the past he had refused to, and she doubted very much if he would ever change as much as she would like. Yet without some changes, continuing to live together as they were would be intolerable. Lately there had not even been the consolation of sex which once upon a time made up for other inadequacies. Something had gone wrong there too, though Cindy was not sure what. Mel still excited her sexually; even now, just thinking about him in that way was enough to arouse her, and at this moment she was conscious of her body stirring. But somehow, when the opportunity was there, their mental separation inhibited them both. The result—at least in Cindy—was frustration, anger, and later a sexual appetite so strong that she had to have a man. Any man.

She was still standing alone, in the plush La Salle Salon of the Lake Michigan Inn, where tonight's reception for the press was being held. The buzz of conversation around her was mostly about the storm and the difficulty everyone had had in getting here; but at least —unlike Mel, Cindy thought—they had made it. Occasionally there was a mention of Archidona, reminding Cindy that she still hadn't found out which Archidona —Ecuador or Spain . . . *damn you, Mel Bakersfeld! Okay, so I'm not as smart as you are*—her charity was directed at.

An arm brushed against hers and a voice said amiably, "No drink, Mrs. Bakersfeld? Can I get you one?"

Cindy turned. The questioner was a newspaperman named Derek Eden, whom she knew slightly. His by-line appeared in the *Sun-Times* frequently. Like many of his kind, he had an easy, confident manner and air of mild dissipation. She was aware that each of them had taken note of the other on previous occasions.

"All right," Cindy said. "A Bourbon and water, go lightly on the water. And please use my first name; I think you know it."

"Sure thing, Cindy." The newspaperman's eyes were admiring and frankly appraising. Well, Cindy thought, why not? She knew she looked good tonight; she had dressed well and made up carefully.

"I'll be back," Derek Eden assured her, "so don't go away now I've found you." He headed purposefully for the bar.

Waiting, surveying the crowded La Salle Salon, Cindy caught the glance of an older woman in a flowered hat. At once Cindy smiled warmly and the woman nodded, but her eyes moved on. She was a society page columnist. A photographer was beside her and together they were planning pictures for what would probably be a full-page layout in tomorrow's paper. The woman in the flowered hat motioned several of the charity workers and their guests together, and they crowded in, smiling obligingly, trying to look casual, but pleased that they had been selected. Cindy knew why she had been passed over; alone she was not important enough, though she would have been if Mel were there. In the city's life, Mel rated. The galling thing was—socially, Mel didn't care.

Across the room the photographer's light gun flashed; the woman in the hat was writing names. Cindy could have cried. For *almost every charity* . . . she volunteered, worked hard, served on the meanest committees, did menial chores which more socially prominent women rejected; then to be left out like this . . .

Damn you again, Mel Bakersfeld! Damn the bitching snow! And screw that demanding, stinking marriage-wrecking airport!

The newspaperman, Derek Eden, was coming back

with Cindy's drink and one of his own. Threading his
way across the room, he saw her watching him and
smiled. He looked sure of himself. If Cindy knew men,
he was probably calculating what his chances were of
laying her tonight. Reporters, she supposed, knew all
about neglected, lonely wives.

Cindy did some calculating of her own concerning
Derek Eden. Early thirties, she thought; old enough to
be experienced, young enough to be taught a thing or
two and to get excited, which was what Cindy liked. A
good body from the outward look of him. He would be
considerate, probably tender; would give as well as take.
And he was available; even before he left to get the
drinks he had already made that clear. Communication
didn't take long between two reasonably sensitive people
with a similar idea.

A few minutes earlier she had weighed the alternatives of going home or to the airport. Now, it seemed,
there might be a third choice.

"There you are." Derek Eden handed her the drink.
She glanced at it; there was a lot of Bourbon, and he
had probably told the barman to pour heavily. Really!
—men were so obvious.

"Thank you." She sipped, and regarded him across
the glass.

Derek Eden raised his own drink and smiled. "Noisy
in here, isn't it?"

For a writer, Cindy thought, his dialogue was deplor-
ably unoriginal. She supposed she was expected to say
yes, then the next thing he would come up with would
be, *Why don't we go some place where it's quieter?* The
lines to follow were equally predictable.

Postponing her response, Cindy took another sip of
Bourbon.

She considered. Of course, if Lionel were in town she
would not have bothered with this man. But Lionel,
who was her storm anchor at other times, and who
wanted her to divorce Mel so that he, Lionel, could
marry her, Cindy . . . Lionel was in Cincinnati (or was
it Columbus?) doing whatever architects did when they

went on business trips, and wouldn't be back for another ten days, perhaps longer.

Mel didn't know about Cindy and Lionel, at least not specifically, though Cindy had an idea that Mel suspected she had a lover somewhere, stashed away. She also had a parallel notion that Mel didn't mind much. It gave him an excuse to concentrate on the airport, to the total exclusion of herself; that goddamned airport, which had been fifty times worse than a mistress in their marriage.

It had not always been that way.

Early in their marriage, soon after Mel left the Navy, Cindy had been proud of his ambitions. Later, when Mel was rapidly ascending the lower rungs of aviation management, she was happy when promotions, new appointments, came his way. As Mel's stature grew, so did Cindy's—especially socially, and in those days they had social engagements almost every evening. On behalf of them both, Cindy accepted invitations to cocktail parties, private dinners, opening nights, charity soirees . . . and if there were two the same night, Cindy was expert at judging which was more important, and turning down the other. That kind of socializing, getting to know prominent people, was important to a young man on the rise. Even Mel saw that. He went along with everything Cindy arranged, without complaining.

The trouble was, Cindy now realized, she and Mel had two different long-term aims. Mel saw their social life as a means to fulfilling his professional ambitions; his career was the essential, the socializing a tool which eventually he would dispense with. Cindy, on the other hand, envisaged Mel's career as a passport to an even greater—and higher level—social life. Looking back, it sometimes occurred to her that if they had understood each other's point of view better in the beginning, they might have compromised. Unfortunately, they hadn't.

Their differences began around the time that Mel—in addition to being general manager of Lincoln International—was elected president of the Airport Operators Council.

When Cindy learned that her husband's activity and

influence now extended to Washington, D.C., she had been overjoyed. His subsequent summons to the White House, the rapport with President Kennedy, led Cindy to assume they would plunge forthwith into Washington society. In roseate daydreams she saw herself strolling —and being photographed—with Jackie or Ethel or Joan, at Hyannis Port or on the White House lawn.

It hadn't happened; not any of it. Mel and Cindy had not become involved in Washington social life at all, although they could have done so quite easily. Instead, they began—at Mel's insistence—declining some invitations. Mel reasoned that his professional reputation was now such that he no longer needed to worry about being "in" socially, a status he had never cared for, anyway.

When she caught on to what was happening, Cindy exploded, and they had a first-class row. That was a mistake, too. Mel would sometimes respond to reason, but Cindy's anger usually made him stand firm to the point of obstinacy. Their dispute raged for a week, Cindy becoming bitchier as it progressed, thus making things worse. Being bitchy was one of Cindy's failings, and she knew it. Half the time she didn't intend to be that way, but sometimes, faced with Mel's indifference, her fiery temper got the better of her—as it had on the telephone tonight.

After the week-long argument, which never really ended, their quarrels became more frequent; they also stopped trying to conceal them from the children, which was impossible, anyway. Once—to the shame of them both—Roberta announced that in future after school she would be going to a friend's house first, "because when I stay home, I can't do my homework while you're fighting."

Eventually a pattern was established. Some evenings Mel accompanied Cindy to certain social events which he had agreed on in advance. Otherwise, he stayed longer hours at the airport and came home less frequently. Finding herself alone much more, Cindy concentrated on what Mel sneered at as her "junior league charities" and "silly social climbing."

Well, maybe at times, Cindy thought, it did look silly

to Mel. But she didn't have much else, and it so happened she enjoyed the social status competition—which was what it was, really. It was all very well for a man to criticize; men had plenty of activities to occupy their time. In Mel's case there was his career, his airport, his responsibilities. What was Cindy supposed to do? Stay home all day and dust the house?

Cindy had no illusions about herself so far as mental acuity went. She was no great intellect, and she knew that in lots of ways, mentally, she would never measure up to Mel. But then, that was nothing new. In their early years of marriage, Mel used to find her occasional mild stupidities amusing, though nowadays when he derided her—as he had taken to doing lately—he seemed to have forgotten that. Cindy was also realistic about her former career as an actress—she would never have made the grade to stardom, or have come close to it. It was true that, in the past, she sometimes implied that she might have done so if marriage had not ended her theatrical activity. But that was merely a form of self-defense, a need to remind others—including Mel—that she was an individual as well as being the airport manager's wife. Within herself Cindy knew the truth— that as a professional actress she would almost certainly not have risen above bit parts.

The involvement in social life, however—in the *mise en scène* of local society—was something Cindy could handle. It gave her a sense of identity and importance. And although Mel scoffed, and denied that what Cindy had done was an achievement, she *had* managed to climb, to be accepted by socially conspicuous people whom she would not have met otherwise, and to be involved in events like tonight's . . . except that on this occasion she needed Mel as escort, and Mel—thinking first of his goddamned airport, as always—had let her down.

Mel, who had so much in the way of identity and prestige, had never understood Cindy's need to carve out some kind of individuality for herself. She doubted if he ever would.

Just the same, Cindy had gone ahead. She also had

plans for the future which she knew would entail a monstrous family battle if she and Mel stayed married. It was Cindy's ambition to have her daughter Roberta, and later Libby, presented as debutantes at the Passavant Cotillion, glittering apex of the Illinois deb season. As the girls' mother, Cindy herself would garner social status.

She had once mentioned the notion casually to Mel, who reacted angrily, "Over my dead body!" Debutantes and their silly, simpering mothers, he advised Cindy, belonged to an age that was gone. Debutante balls, he declared—and thank goodness there were few of them left—were an anachronistic perpetuation of a snobbery and class structure which the nation was fortunately shedding, though—judging by people who still thought as Cindy did—not nearly fast enough. Mel wanted his children to grow up (he told Cindy) with the knowledge that they were equal to others, but not with some conceited, misguided notion that they were socially superior. And so on.

Unusual for Mel, whose policy declarations were normally brief and concise, he had gone on for some time.

Lionel, on the other hand, thought the whole thing was a good idea.

Lionel was Lionel Urquhart. At the moment he hovered alongside Cindy's life in the shape of a question mark.

Curiously, it was Mel who had brought Cindy and Lionel together to begin with. Mel had introduced them at a civic luncheon which Lionel was attending because of something architectural he had done for the city, and Mel was there because of the airport. The two men had known each other casually for years.

Afterward, Lionel telephoned Cindy, and they met a few times for luncheons and dinners, then more frequently, and eventually for the ultimate intimacy between a man and a woman.

Unlike many people who made a practice of extramarital sex, Lionel had taken the experience extremely seriously. He lived alone, having been separated from his wife for several years, but was not divorced. Now he wanted to get a divorce, and have Cindy do the same, so they could marry. By this time, he knew that Cindy's own marriage was shaky.

Lionel and his estranged wife had never had children —a fact, he confided to Cindy, that he greatly regretted. It was not too late, he declared, for Cindy and himself to have a child if they married soon. Also, he would be more than happy to provide a home for Roberta and Libby, and would do his best to be a substitute father.

Cindy had put off a decision for several reasons. Principally, she hoped that relations between herself and Mel would improve, making their marriage closer to what it used to be. She could not say with assurance that she was still in love with Mel; love, Cindy found, was something you became more skeptical about as you grew older. But at least she was used to Mel. He was there; so were Roberta and Libby; and, like many women, Cindy dreaded a major upheaval in her life.

Initially, too, she believed that a divorce and remarriage would be damaging to her socially. On this point, however, she had now changed her mind. Plenty of people had divorces without dropping out of sight socially, even temporarily, and one saw wives with old husbands one week, new ones the next. Cindy even had the impression sometimes that not to have been divorced, at least once, was somewhat square.

It was possible that marriage to Lionel might improve Cindy's status socially. Lionel was much more amenable to partying and entertaining than Mel. Also, the Urquharts were an old, respected city family. Lionel's mother still presided, dowager-like, over a decaying mansion near the Drake Hotel, where an antique butler ushered visitors in, and an arthritic maid brought afternoon tea on a silver tray. Lionel had taken Cindy there for tea one day. Afterward he reported that Cindy had made a good impression, and he was sure he could persuade his mother to sponsor Roberta and Libby as debutantes when the time came.

There and then—because her differences with Mel had grown even more intense—Cindy might have plunged ahead, committing herself to Lionel, except for one thing. Sexually, Lionel was a dying duck.

He tried hard, and occasionally he managed to surprise her, but most of the times they made love he was like a clock whose mainspring is running down. He said gloomily one night, after an abortive session in the bedroom of his apartment, which had been frustrating for both of them, "You should have known me when I was eighteen; I was a young ram." Unfortunately, Lionel was now a long way from eighteen; he was forty-eight.

Cindy envisaged that if she married Lionel, such limited sex as they now enjoyed as lovers would drift into nothingness when they came to live together. Of course, Lionel would try to make up in other ways—he was kind, generous, considerate—but was that enough? Cindy was far from being on the wane sexually; she had always been strongly sensual, and lately her desire and sexual appetite seemed to have grown. But even if Lionel failed in that area, she wasn't batting any better with Mel right now, so what was the difference? Overall, Lionel would give her more.

Perhaps the answer was to marry Lionel Urquhart and do some bedding down on the side. The latter might be difficult, especially when she was newly married, but if she was cautious it could be managed. Other people she knew of—men and women, some in high places—did the same thing to keep themselves satiated physically, and their marriages intact. After all, she had succeeded in deceiving Mel. He might suspect her in a general sense, but Cindy was positive that Mel had no definite knowledge about Lionel or anyone else.

Now, how about tonight? Should she go to the airport for a showdown with Mel, as she had considered earlier? Or should she let herself get involved for the evening with this newspaperman, Derek Eden, who was standing beside her waiting for an answer to his question.

It occurred to Cindy that perhaps she could manage both.

She smiled at Derek Eden. "Tell me again. What was it you said?"

"I said it was noisy in here."

"Yes, it is."

"I wondered if we might skip the dinner and go somewhere quieter."

Cindy could have laughed aloud. Instead, she nodded. "All right."

She glanced around at the other hosts and guests of the Archidona Children's Relief Fund press party. The photographers had stopped taking pictures; so there was really no point in staying any longer. She could slip out quietly, and not be noticed.

Derek Eden asked, "Do you have a car here, Cindy?"

"No, do you?" Because of the weather, Cindy had come in a taxi.

"Yes."

"All right," she said, "I won't leave here with you. But if you're waiting in your car, outside, I'll come through the main doors in fifteen minutes."

"Better make it twenty minutes. I'll need to make a couple of phone calls."

"Very well."

"Do you have any preference? I mean where we'll go?"

"That's entirely up to you."

He hesitated, then said, "Would you like dinner first?"

She thought amusedly: the "first" was a message—to make quite sure she understood what she was getting into.

"No," Cindy said. "I haven't time. I have to be somewhere else later."

She saw Derek Eden's eyes glance down, then return to her face. She sensed the intake of his breath, and had the impression that he was marveling at his own good fortune. "You're the greatest," he said. "I'll only believe my good luck when you come out through those doors."

With that, he turned away and slipped quietly from the La Salle Salon. A quarter of an hour later, unnoticed, Cindy followed him.

She collected her coat and, as she left the Lake Michigan Inn, drew it closely around her. Outside it was

still snowing, and an icy, shrieking wind swept across
the open spaces of the Lakeshore and the Outer Drive.
The weather made Cindy remember the airport. A few
minutes ago she had made a firm resolve: she would still
go there, later tonight; but it was early yet—not quite
half-past nine—and there was plenty of time—for everything.

A porter forsook the shelter of the Inn doorway and
touched his hat. "Taxi, ma'am?"

"I don't think so."

At that moment the lights of a car in the parking lot
came on. It moved forward, skidding once on the loose
snow, then came toward the door where Cindy was
waiting. The car was a Chevrolet, several models old.
She could see Derek Eden at the wheel.

The porter held the car door open and Cindy got in.
As the door slammed closed, Derek Eden said, "Sorry
about the car being cold. I had to call the paper, then
make some arrangements for us. I got here just ahead of
you."

Cindy shivered, and pulled her coat even tighter.
"Wherever we're going, I hope it's warm."

Derek Eden reached across and took her hand. Since
the hand was resting on her knee, he held that too.
Briefly she felt his fingers move, then he returned his
hand to the wheel. He said softly, "You'll be warm. I
promise."

7

Forty-five minutes before its scheduled departure time
of 10 P.M., Trans America Airline Flight Two—*The
Golden Argosy*, Captain Vernon Demerest commanding
—was in the final stages of preparation for its five-thou-
sand-mile, non-stop journey to Rome.

General preparations for the flight had been under way for months and weeks and days. Others, more immediate, had continued for the past twenty-four hours.

An airline flight from any major terminal is, in effect, like a river joining the sea. Before it reaches the sea, a river is fed by tributaries, originating far back in time and distance, each tributary joined along its length by others, either greater or smaller. At length, at the river's mouth, the river itself is the sum of everything which flowed into it. Translated into aviation terms, the river at the sea is an airliner at its moment of takeoff.

The aircraft for Flight Two was a Boeing 707-320B Intercontinental Jetliner, registered number N-731-TA. It was powered by four Pratt & Whitney turbofan jet engines, providing a cruising speed of six hundred and five miles per hour. The aircraft's range, at maximum weight, was six thousand miles, or the straight line distance from Iceland to Hong Kong. It carried a hundred and ninety-nine passengers and twenty-five thousand U.S. gallons of fuel—enough to fill a good-size swimming pool. The aircraft's cost to Trans America Airlines was six and a half million dollars.

The day before yesterday N-731-TA had flown from Düsseldorf, Germany, and, two hours out from Lincoln International, an engine overheated. As a precaution, the captain ordered it shut down. None of the aircraft's passengers were aware that they were operating with three engines instead of four; if necessary, the aircraft could have flown on one. Nor was the flight even late arriving.

Trans America Maintenance, however, was advised by company radio. As a result, a crew of mechanics was waiting, and whisked the airplane to a hangar as soon as passengers and freight were disembarked. Even while taxiing to the hangar, diagnostic specialists were at work, seeking out the airplane's trouble, which they located quickly.

A pneumatic duct—a stainless steel pipe around the affected engine—had cracked and broken in flight. The immediate procedure was for the engine to be removed and a replacement installed. That was relatively simple. More complicated was the fact that for several minutes before the overheating engine was shut down, extremely hot air must have escaped into the engine nacelle. This heat could conceivably have damaged one hundred and eight pairs of wires from the aircraft's electrical system.

Close examination of the wires showed that while some had been heated, none apparently had suffered damage. If a similar condition had occurred within an automobile, bus, or truck, the vehicle would have been put back into service without question. But airlines took no such chances. It was decided that all one hundred and eight pairs of wires must be replaced.

The work of replacement was highly skilled, but exacting and tedious because only two men at a time could operate in the confined space of the engine nacelle. Moreover, each pair of wires must be identified, then connected painstakingly to cannon plugs. A non-stop, day-and-night effort was planned, with teams of electrical mechanics relieving each other.

The entire job would cost Trans America Airlines thousands of dollars in skilled man-hours and lost revenue while the big aircraft was unproductive on the ground. But the loss was accepted without question, as all airlines accepted such losses in pursuit of high safety standards.

The Boeing 707—N-731-TA—which was to have flown to the West Coast and back before its flight to Rome, was taken out of service. Operations was advised, and hastily shuffled schedules to help bridge the gap. A connecting flight was canceled and several dozen passengers transferred to competitive airlines. There was no substitute aircraft. When it came to multimillion-dollar jets, airlines did not carry spares.

Operations, however, urged Maintenance to have the 707 ready for Flight Two to Rome, which was then thirty-six hours away from scheduled departure. An operations vice-president in New York personally called the Trans America base maintenance chief, and was told: "If we can get it ready for you, we will." A top-notch foreman and a crack crew of mechanics and electricians were already on the job, all of them aware of the importance of finishing quickly. A second crew, to relieve the others through the night, was being rounded up. Both crews would work extra hours until the job was done.

Contrary to general belief, aircraft mechanics took a close interest in the operational flights of airplanes they serviced. After a complex job, or a rush one such as this, they would follow the progress of a particular airplane to learn how their work had stood up. It was a source of satisfaction to them when, as usually happened, the airplane functioned well. Months later they might say to each other, observing an airplane taxiing in, "There's old 842. Remember that time . . . and the trouble we had with her. I guess we cured it."

Through the critical day and a half following discovery of the trouble with N-731-TA, work on the airplane, though slow by its nature, continued as speedily as possible.

At length, three hours from Flight Two's departure time, the last of the hundred-odd pairs of wires was reconnected.

It took another hour to replace the engine cowlings and for an engine run-up on the ground. Then, before the airplane could be accepted for service, an air test was required. By this time, urgent calls from Operations demanded: Would N-731-TA be ready for Flight Two or not? If not, would Maintenance for Chrissake say so, so Sales could be informed of a possible long delay, and passengers notified before they left their homes.

His fingers crossed, and touching wood, the maintenance chief replied that, barring complications on the air test, the aircraft would be available on time.

It was—but only just. The chief Trans America pilot at the base, who had been standing by for just that purpose, test flew the airplane, barreling up through the storm to clearer altitudes above. He reported on return: "You guys down here'd never know it, but the moon's still there," then certified N-731-TA as completely airworthy. Executive pilots like that kind of assignment; it helped build up their needed flying hours without going far from their desks.

There was so little time left when the chief pilot landed, that he taxied the airplane directly to gate forty-seven of the terminal, where—as Flight Two, *The Golden Argosy*—it was to load.

Thus Maintenance had come through—as Maintenance did so often—but no corners had been cut.

Once the airplane was at its gate, knots of workers bustled in and around it like scurrying elves.

Food was a major item to go aboard. Seventy-five minutes before departure time, Departure Control called the caterer's flight kitchen, ordering food for the flight, according to the number of passengers expected. Tonight the first-class section of Flight Two would have only two vacant seats; the economy section would be three quarters full. First-class, as usual, was allocated six meals extra; economy had the same number of meals as passengers. Thus, first-class passengers could have a second dinner if they asked for it; economy passengers couldn't.

Despite the exact count, a last-minute passenger would always get a meal. Spare meals—including Kosher meals—were available in lockers near the departure gate. If an unexpected passenger went aboard as doors were closing, his food tray was passed in after him.

Liquor stocks, requiring a signed stewardess receipt, came aboard too. Liquor for first-class passengers were free; tourist passengers paid a dollar a drink (or the equivalent in foreign currency) unless they took advantage of a piece of inside information. The information was that stewardesses were issued almost no change, sometimes none, and where a stewardess could not make change, her instructions were to give the passenger his or her drinks free. Some regular travelers had drunk free for years in tourist class, merely by proffering a fifty- or twenty-dollar bill and insisting they had nothing smaller.

At the same time that the food and liquor went aboard, other commissary supplies were checked and replenished. There were several hundred items, ranging from babies' diapers, blankets, pillows, airsick bags, and a Gideon Bible to accessories like "Tray, beverage service, 8-hole, qty. 5." All were expendable. At the conclusion of a flight, airlines never bothered checking inventories. Whatever was missing was replaced without question, which was why passengers who walked from an airplane with anything portable were seldom stopped.

Included in commissary supplies were magazines and newspapers. Newspapers were usually available on flights—with an exception. The Trans America commissary had a standing order: if a newspaper front page featured an air disaster, the newspapers were not to go aboard, but were thrown away. Most other airlines had the same rule.

Tonight, on Flight Two, there were plenty of newspapers. The principal news was weather—the effect, on the entire Midwest, of the three-day winter storm.

Baggage was now coming aboard Flight Two as passengers were beginning to check in. When a passenger saw his bag disappear at the check-in counter it went, by a series of conveyor belts, to a room deep below the departure gates which baggage men privately called "the lion's den." It acquired that name because (so baggage men confided after several drinks) only the brave or innocent would allow a bag they cared about to enter here. Some bags as saddened owners could testify— came into the lion's den and were never seen again.

In the den, an attendant on duty watched each bag arrive. According to its destination label, he flicked a lever on a panel and, a moment later, an automatic arm reached out and grabbed the bag, setting it beside others for the same flight. From this point, and others, a crew of several men transferred all bags to the proper airplanes.

It was an excellent system—when it worked. Unfortunately, it often didn't.

Baggage handling—airlines conceded privately—was the least efficient part of air travel. In an age where human ingenuity could place a capsule the size of a houseboat in outer space, it was a fact that an airline passenger's bag could not be counted on to arrive safely at Pine Bluff, Arkansas, or Minneapolis-St. Paul, or even at the same time as the passenger. An astounding amount of airline baggage—at least one bag in every hundred—went to wrong destinations, was delayed, or lost entirely. Executives pointed woefully to the many opportunities for human error which existed with baggage handling. Efficiency experts periodically examined airline baggage systems, and periodically they were improved. Yet no one had come up with a system which was infallible, or even close to it. The result was that all airlines employed staffs, at every major terminal, whose job was solely to trace missing baggage. Such staffs were seldom idle.

An experienced, cagey traveler did the best he could by making sure that the tags which agents or porters put on his bags when he checked in showed his correct destination. Often they didn't. With surprising frequency, wrong tags were slapped on in haste, and had to be changed when the error was pointed out. Even then, when the bags disappeared from sight, there was the sense of having entered a lottery, and at that point the traveler could only pray that some day, somewhere, he would be reunited with his luggage again.

Tonight, at Lincoln International—though no one knew it yet—the baggage for Flight Two was already incomplete. Two bags, which should have gone to Rome, were at this moment being loaded aboard a flight for Milwaukee.

Freight was now going aboard Flight Two in a steady stream. So was mail. Tonight there were nine thousand pounds of mail in colored nylon bags, some for Italian cities for onward transmission to faraway places, whose names read like pages from Marco Polo . . . Zanzibar, Khartoum, Mombassa, Jerusalem, Athens, Rhodes, Calcutta . . .

The heavier-than-usual mail load was a bonus for Trans America. A flight of British Overseas Airways Corporation, scheduled to leave shortly before Trans America Flight Two, had just announced a three-hour delay. The post office ramp supervisor, who kept con-

stant watch on schedules and delays, promptly ordered a
switch of mail from the BOAC airliner to Trans
America. The British airline would be unhappy because
carriage of mail was highly profitable, and competition
for post office business keen. All airlines kept uniformed
representatives at airport post offices, their job to keep
an eye on the flow of mail and insure that their own
airline got a "fair share"—or more—of the outgoing
volume. Post office supervisors sometimes had favorites
among the airline men, and saw to it that business came
their way. But in cases of delay, friendships didn't
count. At such moments there was an inflexible rule:
the mail went by the faster route.

Inside the terminal, at lower level, and a few hundred
feet from the Boeing 707 aircraft which was now Flight
Two, was Trans America Control Center (Lincoln International). The center was a bustling, jam-packed,
noisy conglomeration of people, desks, telephones, teletypes, Tel Autographs, private line TV, and information
boards. Its personnel were responsible for directing the
preparation of Flight Two and all other Trans America
flights. On occasions like tonight, with schedules chaotic
because of the storm, the atmosphere was pandemonic,
the scene resembling an old-time newspaper city room,
as seen by Hollywood.

In a corner of the control center was the Load
Control Desk—the desk top invisible beneath a sea of
paper—occupied by a young, bearded man with the
improbable name of Fred Phirmphoot. In his spare
time Phirmphoot was an amateur abstract painter; recently he had taken to throwing paint on canvas, then
riding over it with a child's tricycle. He was reputed to
dabble—at weekends—with LSD, and also suffered
from body odor. The last was a constant annoyance to
his fellow workers in the control center—hot and stuffy
tonight despite the cold, bitter weather outside—and
more than once Fred Phirmphoot had been told that he
should take a bath more often.

Yet, paradoxically, Phirmphoot had a keen mathema-
tician's mind, and his superiors swore that he was one of
the best load control men in the business. At the

moment he was masterminding the loading of Flight Two.

An airplane (Fred Phirmphoot would occasionally explain to his bored beat friends), "She's a bird that's a teeter-totter, man. If you ain't hep, that airplane chick'll teeter or totter, maybe the twain; but me, baby, I don't let it none."

The trick was to distribute weight correctly through the airplane so that its fulcrum point and center of gravity were at predetermined places; hence, the aircraft would be balanced, and stable in the air. Fred Phirmphoot's job was to calculate how much could be stowed aboard Flight Two (and other flights) and where. No mailbag, no individual piece of freight, went into any position in the aircraft hold without his say-so. At the same time, he was concerned with cramming in as much as possible. "Illinois to Rome, man," Fred was apt to declare, "that's long spaghetti. It don't pay off in marmalade."

He worked with charts, manifests, tabulations, an adding machine, last-minute messages, a walkie-talkie, three telephones—and an uncanny instinct.

The ramp supervisor had just asked, by walkie-talkie, for permission to load another three hundred pounds of mail in the forward compartment.

"Roger-dodger," Fred Phirmphoot acknowledged. He shuffled papers, checking the passenger manifest which had lengthened in the past two hours. Airlines allowed an average weight for passengers—a hundred and seventy pounds in winter, ten pounds less in summer. The average always worked out, with one exception: when a football team was traveling. The husky ballplayers threw all calculations out of joint, and at that time load dispatchers added their own estimates, which varied according to how well they knew the team. Baseball and hockey players were no problem; being smaller they fitted the average. Tonight the manifest showed that Flight Two had only normal passengers.

"It's okay for the mail, baby," Fred Phirmphoot replied into the walkie-talkie, "but I want that coffin moved back to the rear compartment; from the look of the weight slip, that dead guy was a fatso. Also, there's a packaged generator from Westinghouse. Locate that midships; the rest of the freight can fit around it."

Phirmphoot's problems had just been added to by an order from the Crew of Flight Two that an extra two thousand pounds of fuel were to be added for taxiing and ground running, in addition to the normal reserve for that purpose. Out on the airfield tonight, all aircraft were being subjected to long delays, with engines running, before takeoff. A jet engine, operating at ground level, drank fuel like a thirsty elephant, and Captains Demerest and Harris didn't want to waste precious gallonage which they might require on the way to Rome. At the same time, Fred Phirmphoot had to calculate that all that extra fuel, which was now being pumped into the wing tanks of N-731-TA, might not be burned before takeoff; therefore, some of it could be added to the total takeoff weight. The question was, how much?

There were safety limits for gross weights at takeoff, yet with every airline flight the objective was to carry as much as possible, to earn maximum revenue. Fred Phirmphoot's dirty fingernails danced over his adding machine, making hasty computations. He pondered the result, fingering his beard, his body odor rather worse than usual.

The decision about extra fuel was one of many decisions which Captain Vernon Demerest had been making for the past half hour. Or rather, he had been letting Captain Anson Harris make the decisions, then—as check captain with the final responsibility—Demerest approved them. Vernon Demerest was enjoying his passive role tonight—having someone else do most of the work, yet relinquishing none of his own authority. So far Demerest had not faulted any of Anson Harris's decisions, which was not surprising since Harris's experience and seniority were almost as great as Demerest's own.

Harris had been dour and huffy when they met for the second time tonight in the crew room at the Trans America hangar. Demerest noted with amusement that Anson Harris was wearing a regulation shirt, though it was on the small side, and every now and then Harris's hand would go up to ease the collar. Captain Harris had managed to switch shirts with an obliging first officer who later related the story zestfully to his own captain.

But after a few minutes, Harris relaxed. A professional to his bushy, graying eyebrows, he was aware that no flight crew could function efficiently with hostility in the cockpit.

In the crew room both captains inspected their mail slots, and there was a pile of mail as usual, some of it company bulletins which must be read before tonight's flight. The remainder—memos from the chief pilot, medical branch, the research department, cartographer's office, and the rest, they would take home to go through later.

While Anson Harris inserted a couple of amendments in his flight manuals—which Demerest had announced his intention of checking—Vernon Demerest studied the Crew Schedule Board.

The Schedule Board was made up monthly. It showed the dates on which captains and first and second officers would fly, and on which routes. There was a similar board for stewardesses in their crew room down the hall.

Every pilot bid, each month, for the route he wanted to fly, and those who were most senior got first choice. Demerest invariably got what he bid for; so did Gwen Meighen, whose seniority among the stewardesses was correspondingly high. It was the bidding system which made it possible for pilots and stewardesses to make mutual layover plans much as Demerest and Gwen had done in advance of tonight.

Anson Harris had finished the hasty amending of his flight manuals.

Vernon Demerest grinned. "I guess your manuals are okay, Anson. I've changed my mind; I won't inspect them."

Captain Harris gave no sign, except a tightening around his mouth.

The second officer for the flight, a young two-striper named Cy Jordan, had joined them. Jordan was flight engineer; also a qualified pilot. He was lean and angular, with a hollow-cheeked, mournful face, and always looked as if he needed a good meal. Stewardesses heaped extra food upon him, but it never seemed to make any difference.

The first officer who usually flew as second-in-command to Demerest, tonight had been told to stay home, though under his union contract he would receive full pay for the round-trip flight. In the first officer's absence, Demerest would do some of the first officer duties, Jordan the rest. Anson Harris would do most of the flying.

"Okay," Demerest told the other two, "let's get moving."

The crew bus, snow-covered, its windows steamed inside, was waiting at the hangar door. The five stewardesses for Flight Two were already in the bus, and there was a chorus of "Good evening, Captain . . . good evening, Captain," as Demerest and Anson Harris clambered in, followed by Jordan. A gust of wind, and snow flurries, accompanied the pilots. The bus driver hastily closed the door.

"Hi, girls!" Vernon Demerest waved cheerfully, and winked at Gwen. More conventionally, Anson Harris added a "Good evening."

The wind buffeted the bus as the driver felt his way warily around the plowed perimeter track, the snowbanks high on either side. Word had filtered around the airport of the experience of the United Air Lines food truck earlier in the evening, and all vehicle drivers were being cautious as a result. As the crew bus neared its destination, the bright terminal lights were a beacon in the darkness. Farther out on the airfield a steady stream of aircraft was taking off and landing.

The bus stopped, and the crew scrambled out, diving for the shelter of the nearest door. They were now in the Trans America wing of the terminal, at lower level. The passenger departure gates—including gate forty-seven, where Flight Two was being readied—were above.

The stewardesses went off to complete their own preflight procedures while the three pilots headed for the Trans America international dispatch office.

The dispatcher, as always, had prepared a folder with the complex information which the flight crew would need. He spread it out on the dispatch office counter and the three pilots pored over it. Behind the counter a half-dozen clerks were assembling world-wide information on airways, airport conditions, and weather which other international flights of Trans America would require tonight. A similar dispatch room for domestic flights was down the hall.

It was at that point that Anson Harris tapped a preliminary load report with his pipestem and asked for the extra two thousand pounds of fuel for taxiing. He glanced at the second officer, Jordan, who was checking fuel consumption graphs, and Demerest. Both nodded agreement, and the dispatcher scribbled an order which would be relayed to the ramp fueling office.

The company weather forecaster joined the other four. He was a pale young man, scholarly behind rimless glasses, who looked as if he rarely ventured out into the weather personally.

Demerest inquired, "What have the computers given us tonight, John? Something better than here, I hope."

More and more, airline weather forecasts and flight plans were being spewed out by computers. Trans America and other airlines still maintained a personal element, with individuals liaising between computers and flight crews, but predictions were that the human weathermen would disappear soon.

The forecaster shook his head as he spread out several facsimile weather charts. "Nothing better until you're over mid-Atlantic, I'm afraid. We have some improved weather coming in here soon, but since you're going east you'll catch up with what's already left us. The storm we're in now extends all the way from here to Newfoundland, and beyond." He used a pencil point to trace the storm's wide swathe. "Along your route, incidentally, Detroit Metropolitan and Toronto airports are both below limits and have closed down."

The dispatcher scanned a teletype slip which a clerk had handed him. He interjected, "Add Ottawa; they're closing right now."

"Beyond mid-Atlantic," the weatherman said, "everything looks good. There are scattered disturbances across southern Europe, as you can see, but at your altitudes they shouldn't bother you. Rome is clear and sunny, and should stay that way for several days."

Captain Demerest leaned over the southern Europe map. "How about Naples?"

The weatherman looked puzzled. "Your flight doesn't go there."

"No, but I'm interested."

"It's in the same high pressure system as Rome. The weather will be good."

Demerest grinned.

The young forecaster launched into a dissertation concerning temperatures, and high and low pressure areas, and winds aloft. For the portion of the flight which would be over Canada he recommended a more northerly course than usual to avoid strong headwinds which would be encountered farther south. The pilots listened attentively. Whether by computer or human calculation, choosing the best altitudes and route was like a game of chess in which intellect could triumph over nature. All pilots were trained in such matters; so were company weather forecasters, more attuned to individual airline needs than their counterparts in the U. S. Weather Bureau.

"As soon as your fuel load permits," the Trans America forecaster said, "I'd recommend an altitude of thirty-three thousand feet."

The second officer checked his graphs; before N-731-TA could climb that high, they would have to burn off some of their initially heavy fuel load.

After a few moments the second officer reported, "We should be able to reach thirty-three thousand around Detroit."

Anson Harris nodded. His gold ballpoint pen was racing as he filled in a flight plan which, in a few minutes' time, he would file with air traffic control. ATC would then tell him whether or not the altitudes he sought were available and, if not, what others he might have. Vernon Demerest, who normally would have pre-

pared his own flight plan, glanced over the form when
Captain Harris finished, then signed it.

All preparations for Flight Two, it seemed, were
going well. Despite the storm, it appeared as if *The
Golden Argosy,* pride of Trans America, would depart
on time.

It was Gwen Meighen who met the three pilots as
they came aboard the aircraft. She asked, "Did you
hear?"

Anson Harris said, "Hear what?"

"We're delayed an hour. The gate agent just had
word."

"Damn!" Vernon Demerest said. "Goddam!"

"Apparently," Gwen said, "a lot of passengers are on
their way, but have been held up—I guess because of
the snow. Some have phoned in, and Departure Control
decided to allow them extra time."

Anson Harris asked, "Is boarding being delayed
too?"

"Yes, Captain. The flight hasn't been announced. It
won't be for another half-hour, at least."

Harris shrugged. "Oh, well; we might as well relax."
He moved toward the flight deck.

Gwen volunteered, "I can bring you all coffee, if you
like."

"I'll get coffee in the terminal," Vernon Demerest
said. He nodded to Gwen. "Why don't you come with
me?"

She hesitated. "Well, I could."

"Go ahead," Harris said. "One of the other girls can
bring mine, and there's plenty of time."

A minute or two later, Gwen walked beside Vernon
Demerest, her heels clicking as she kept pace with his
strides down the Trans America departure wing. They
were heading for the main terminal concourse.

Demerest was thinking: the hour's delay might not be
a bad thing after all. Until this moment, with the essential business of Flight Two to think about, he had
pushed all thoughts of Gwen's pregnancy from his mind.
But, over coffee and a cigarette, there would be a
chance to continue the discussion they had begun ear-

lier. Perhaps, now, the subject which he had not broached before—an abortion—could be brought into the open.

8

Nervously, D. O. Guerrero lit another cigarette from the stub of his previous one. Despite his efforts to control the motion of his hands, they trembled visibly. He was agitated, tense, anxious. As he had earlier, while putting his dynamite bomb together, he could feel rivulets of perspiration on his face and beneath his shirt.

The cause of his distress was time—the time remaining between now and the departure of Flight Two. It was running out, remorselessly, like sand from an hourglass; and much—too much—of the sand was gone.

Guerrero was in a bus en route to the airport. Half an hour ago the bus had entered the Kennedy Expressway, from which point, normally, there would have been a swift, fifteen-minute ride to Lincoln International. But the expressway, like every other highway in the state, was impeded by the storm, and jammed with traffic. At moments the traffic was halted, at other times merely inching along.

Before departure from downtown, the dozen or so bus passengers—all destined for Flight Two—had been told of their flight's delay by one hour. Even so, at the present rate of progress, it appeared as if it might take another two hours, perhaps three, to get to the airport.

Others in the bus were worried, too.

Like D. O. Guerrero, they had checked in at the Trans America downtown terminal in the Loop. Then, they had been in plenty of time, but now, in view of the mounting delay, were wondering aloud whether Flight Two would wait for them indefinitely, or not.

The bus driver was not encouraging. In reply to questions, he declared that usually, if a bus from a downtown terminal was late, a flight was held until the bus arrived. But when conditions got really bad, like tonight, anything could happen. The airline might figure that the bus would be held up for hours more—as it could be—and that the flight should go. Also, the driver added, judging by the few people in the bus, it looked as if most passengers for Flight Two were out at the airport already. That often happened with international flights, he explained; relatives came to see passengers off, and drove them out by car.

The discussion went back and forth across the bus, though D. O. Guerrero, his spindly body hunched into his seat, took no part in it. Most of the other passengers appeared to be tourists, with the exception of a voluble Italian family—a man and woman with several children —who were talking animatedly in their own language.

"If I were you, folks, I wouldn't worry," the bus driver had announced a few minutes earlier. "The traffic ahead looks as if it's loosenin' up some. We might just make it."

So far, however, the speed of the bus had not increased.

D. O. Guerrero had a double seat section, three rows back from the driver, to himself. The all-important attaché case was held securely on his lap. He eased forward, as he had done several times already, straining to peer ahead into the darkness beyond the bus; all he could see, through the twin arcs cleared by the big, slapping windshield wipers, was what appeared to be an endless string of vehicle lights, disappearing into the falling snow. Despite his sweating, his pale, thin lips were dry; he moistened them with his tongue.

For Guerrero, "just making it" to the airport in time for Flight Two would simply not do. He needed an extra ten or fifteen minutes, at least, to buy flight insurance. He cursed himself for not having gone out to the airport sooner, and bought the flight insurance he needed in plenty of time. In his original plan, purchasing the insurance at the last minute, and thus minimizing any chance of inquiry, seemed a good idea. What he had not foreseen was the kind of night this had turned out to be—though he ought to have foreseen it, remembering the time of year. It was just that kind of thing—overlooking some significant, variable factor—which had dogged D. O. Guerrero through his business enterprises, and time after time brought grandiose schemes to naught. The trouble was, he realized, whenever he made plans, he convinced himself that everything would go exactly as he hoped; therefore he failed to allow for the unexpected. More to the point, he thought bitterly, he never seemed able to learn from past experience.

He supposed that when he got to the airport—assuming Flight Two had not already left—he could go to the Trans America flight counter and announce himself as being present. Then he would insist on being allowed time to buy flight insurance before the flight took off. But it would involve the one thing he desperately wanted to avoid: drawing attention to himself, in the same way that he had drawn attention already—and for the stupidest omission he could possibly have made.

He had failed to bring any baggage, other than the small, slim attaché case in which he was carrying the dynamite bomb.

At the check-in counter downtown the ticket agent had asked, "Is that your baggage, sir?" He pointed to a large pile of suitcases belonging to a man in line behind.

"No." D. O. Guerrero hesitated, then held up the small attaché-briefcase. "I . . . er. . . . don't have anything except this."

The agent's eyebrows went up. "No baggage for a trip to Rome, sir? You really are traveling light." He motioned to the attaché case. "Do you wish to check that?"

"No, thank you." All D. O. Guerrero wanted at that moment was his airline ticket, and to get away from the counter, and secure an inconspicuous seat on the airport bus. But the agent glanced curiously at him a second time, and Guerrero knew that, from this moment onward, he would be remembered. He had stamped

himself indelibly on the ticket agent's memory—all
because he forgot to bring a suitcase, which he could so
easily have done. Of course, the reason he had not done
so was instinctive. D. O. Guerrero knew—as others
did not—that Flight Two would never reach its
destination; therefore no baggage was necessary. But he
ought to have had baggage, as a cover. Now, at the
inquiry which would inevitably follow the flight's loss,
the fact that one passenger—himself—had boarded
without baggage, would be remembered and commented
on. It would underscore whatever other suspicions about
D. O. Guerrero investigators might, by that time, have.

But if there were no wreckage, he reminded himself,
what could they prove?

Nothing! The flight insurance people would have to
pay.

Would the bus *never* get to the airport?

The children from the Italian family were running
noisily up and down the aisle of the bus. A few seats
back, the mother was still jabbering in Italian to the
husband; she held a baby which was crying lustily. Neither the woman nor the man seemed aware of the baby's
crying.

Guerrero's nerves were stretched and raw. He wanted
to seize the baby and throttle it; to shout to the others,
Shut up! Shut up!

Couldn't they sense? . . . Didn't the fools know that
this was no time for stupid chattering? . . . No time,
when Guerrero's whole future—at least, his family's
future . . . the success of the plan so painstakingly
worked out . . . everything, *everything,* was predicated
on getting to the airport with time to spare.

One of the running children—a boy of five or six,
with an attractive, intelligent face—stumbled in the aisle
and fell sideways into the empty seat beside D. O.
Guerrero. In regaining his balance, the boy's hand went
out, striking the attaché case still on Guerrero's lap. The
case slipped sideways and Guerrero grabbed it. He managed to stop it before it fell, then turned to the child, his
face contorted to a snarl, his hand raised to strike.

Wide-eyed, the boy regarded him. He said softly, "*Scusi*."

With an effort, Guerrero controlled himself. Others in the bus might be watching. If he were not careful, he would draw attention to himself again. Groping for some of the words he had picked up from Italians who had worked for him on construction projects, he said awkwardly, "*É troppo rumorosa*."

The child nodded gravely. "*Si*." He stood where he was.

"All right," Guerrero said. "That's all. Get lost! *Se ne vada!*"

"*Si*," the boy said again. His eyes were uncomfortably direct, and for a moment Guerrero was reminded that this child, and others, would be aboard Flight Two. Well, it made no difference. There was no point in becoming sentimental; nothing would change his intentions now. Besides, when it happened, when he pulled the string of the attaché case and the airplane ripped apart, everything would be over quickly, before anyone—especially the children—had time to know.

The boy turned away, and went back in the bus to his mother.

At last!—the bus was moving faster . . . now it was speeding up! Ahead, through the windshield, D. O. Guerrero could see that the traffic had thinned, other lights in front were moving quickly. They might . . . just might . . . arrive at the airport in time for him to buy flight insurance without any need to arouse attention. But it was going to be close. He hoped the insurance booth would not be busy.

He noticed that the children from the Italian family had returned to their seats, and he congratulated himself about not attracting attention a moment ago. If he had struck the child—as he almost had—people would have made a fuss. At least he had avoided that. It was still a pity that he had got himself noticed when checking in, though when he thought about it, he supposed that no irreparable harm had been done.

Or had it?

A new worry nagged him.

Supposing the ticket agent who had been curious about the absence of any baggage remembered the incident again, after the bus had gone. Guerrero knew he had appeared nervous at the time; supposing the agent had noticed, had later become suspicious. The agent would talk to someone else, a supervisor perhaps, who might already have telephoned the airport. Even at this moment, someone—the police?—might be waiting for the bus to arrive; to interrogate D. O. Guerrero; to open and inspect his single, small attaché case with the damning evidence inside. For the first time Guerrero wondered what would happen if he were caught. It would mean arrest, imprisonment. Then he thought: before he would allow that to happen . . . if he were accosted, if exposure seemed imminent . . . he would pull the loop of string on the outside of the case and blow himself, along with everyone nearby, to pieces. His hand went out. Beneath the attaché case handle he touched the loop of string and held it. It was reassuring . . . Now, for the moment, he would try to think of something else.

He wondered if Inez had yet found his note.

She had.

Inez Guerrero came tiredly into the miserable 51st Street apartment, and slipped off her shoes, which had been hurting, and her coat and kerchief, which were soaked from melted snow. She was aware of a cold coming, and an all-engulfing weariness. Her work as a waitress had been harder than usual today, the customers meaner, the tips smaller. Besides, she was not yet accustomed to it, which took a greater toll.

Two years ago, when the Guerreros lived comfortably in a congenial home in the suburbs, Inez, though never beautiful, had been a pleasant-appearing, well-preserved woman. Since then, ravages of time and circumstance had come swiftly to her face, so that where once she seemed younger than she was, now she looked considerably older. Tonight, if Inez had been in a house of her own, she would have sought the solace of a hot bath, which always seemed to relax her in times of trouble—

of which there had been plenty in the Guerreros' married life. Although there was a bathroom of sorts down the hall, which three apartments shared, it was unheated and drafty, with old paint peeling, and a gas water heater which had to be appeased with quarters. The thought of it defeated her. She decided she would sit still for a while in the shabby living room, then go to bed. She had no idea where her husband was.

It was some time before she noticed the note on the living-room table.

I won't be home for a few days. I'm going away.
I expect to have some good news soon which
will surprise you.

Few things surprised Inez where her husband was concerned; he had always been unpredictable and, more recently, irrational. Good news would certainly be a surprise, but she couldn't bring herself to believe that there would be any. Inez had watched too many of her husband's ambitious schemes totter and collapse to believe in the likelihood of one more possibility succeeding.

But the first part of the note puzzled her. Where was D.O. going "for a few days"? Equally mystifying: What did he intend to use for money? The night before last the Guerreros pooled the last of the money they had in the world. The total was twenty-two dollars and some cents. Besides the money, they had only one thing left worth pawning; it belonged to Inez—her mother's ring, and so far she had resisted parting with it. It might have to go soon.

Of the twenty-two dollars-odd, Inez had taken fourteen, to use for food and as a token payment toward the rent. She had seen the desperation in D.O.'s face as he pocketed the remaining eight dollars and small change.

Inez decided to stop puzzling, and to go to bed as she had planned. She was too weary even to worry about how her children were faring, though she had not heard from her sister in Cleveland—with whom the children were staying—for more than a week. She turned out the single light in the living room and went into the cramped, shabby bedroom.

She had trouble finding her nightgown. Some of the contents of the rickety dressing chest seemed to have been moved around. Eventually she found the night-gown in a drawer with three of D.O.'s shirts; they were the last he had, so wherever he had gone, he had not taken a change of clothing. Under one of the shirts a folded sheet of yellow paper caught her eye. She took it out and opened it.

The yellow sheet was a printed form which had been filled in by typewriter; what Inez was holding was a carbon copy. When she saw what it was, she sat down, unbelieving, on the bed. To make sure she had not misunderstood, she read the contents of the form again.

It was a time-payment contract between Trans America Airlines and D. O. "Buerrero"—the name, she noticed, was misspelled. The contract acknowledged that "Buerrero" had received a round-trip ticket to Rome, economy class; that he had made a down pay-ment of forty-seven dollars, and hereby promised to pay the balance of four hundred and twenty-seven dollars, plus interest, in installments over twenty-four months.

It didn't make sense.

Inez stared dazedly at the yellow form. Within her mind, questions chased one another.

Why did D.O. need an air ticket at all? And if a ticket, why to Rome? And what about the money? He couldn't possibly pay the installments, though that part, at least, was understandable. There had been plenty of other obligations D. O. Guerrero incurred that he couldn't meet; debts never disturbed him, as they did Inez. But apart from the debt, where had the forty-seven dollars down payment come from? The form acknowl-edged receipt; the money had been paid. Yet two nights ago, D.O. declared that he had no more money than they pooled, and whatever else he might do, Inez knew he never lied to her.

Yet that forty-seven dollars came from somewhere. Where?

Suddenly, she remembered the ring; it was gold with

a single diamond in a platinum setting. Until a week or two ago, Inez wore it regularly, but recently her hands had swollen and she took the ring off, leaving it in a small box in one of the bedroom drawers. For the second time tonight she searched the drawers. The box was there—empty. Obviously, to get the forty-seven dollars, D.O. had pawned the ring.

Her first reaction was regret. To Inez, the ring had meant something; it was a last tenuous link between herself and the past, her scattered family, her dead mother whose memory she revered. More realistically: the ring, though not exceptionally valuable, had been a last resort. While it was there, there was the knowledge that however bad things became, the ring would always provide a few days more of living. Now it was gone, and along with it, the minor reassurance.

Yet knowing where the down payment came from for the airline ticket, still provided no answer to the question—why? Why an air journey? Why to Rome?

Still seated on the bed, Inez applied herself to thinking carefully. For the moment, she ignored her tiredness.

Inez was not a highly intelligent woman. If she had been, probably she would not have endured marriage to D. O. Guerrero for almost twenty years; and even now, if better equipped mentally, she would have been more than a coffeehouse waitress at a paltry wage. But occasionally, through slow, careful reasoning aided by instinct, Inez could reach right conclusions. Especially where her husband was concerned.

Now, instinct more than reason warned her that D. O. Guerrero was in trouble—more serious trouble than they had yet encountered. Two things convinced her: his irrationality of late, and the length of his intended journey; in the Guerrero's present circumstances, only some monumental, desperate undertaking could require a trip to Rome. She went to the living room and returned with the note, which she read again. Over the years there had been many notes; Inez sensed that this one did not mean what it said.

Beyond that, her reasoning failed to go. But she had

the feeling, a conviction growing as each minute passed, that there must be something, *ought* to be something, she should do.

It did not occur to Inez to abdicate entirely; to abandon D.O. to the outcome of whatever new folly he might have begun. She was essentially a simple soul with an uncomplicated nature. Eighteen years ago she accepted D. O. Guerrero "for better or worse." That it had turned out to be mostly "worse" did not, as Inez saw it, change her responsibility as a wife.

Her cautious, measured reasoning continued. She supposed the first thing to do was find out if D.O. had already left by air; if not, perhaps there was time to stop him. Inez had no idea how much of a start D.O. had, or how many hours ago his note to her was written. She looked again at the yellow time-payment form; it said nothing about when the flight would be, or its departure time, though she could telephone the airline—Trans America. As quickly as she could, Inez began putting on the clothes which, a few minutes earlier, she had taken off.

Her outdoor shoes hurt her feet again, and her coat was still sodden and uncomfortable as she went down the narrow stairs from the apartment to the street. In the mean lower hallway, snow had blown under the outer door and covered the bare boards of the floor. Outside, Inez saw, the snow was even deeper than when she came in. The cold, bleak wind assaulted her as she left the building's shelter, whipping more snow into her face.

There was no telephone in the Guerreros' apartment, and although Inez could have used a pay phone in the lunch counter on the lower floor, she wanted to avoid a meeting with the proprietor, who was also the building landlord. He had threatened eviction tomorrow if the Guerreros' arrears of rent were not paid in full. That was something else which Inez had pushed from her mind tonight, and which—if D.O. failed to return by morning—she would have to face alone.

A drugstore, with a pay phone, was a block and a

half away. Picking her way through deep snow on un-
cleared sidewalks, Inez headed there.

The time was a quarter to ten.

The drugstore telephone was in use by two teen-age
girls, and Inez waited almost ten minutes for it to be
free. Then, when she dialed the Trans America number,
a recording informed her that all lines to Reservations
were busy, and would she please wait. She waited while
the recording repeated itself several times before a brisk
woman's voice declared that she was Miss Young, and
could she help?

"Please," Inez said, "I want to ask about flights to
Rome."

As if a button had been pressed, Miss Young replied
that Trans America had direct non-stop flights from
Lincoln International to Rome on Tuesdays and Fridays; through New York there were connections daily,
and did the caller wish to make a reservation now?

"No," Inez said. "No, I'm not going. It's about my
husband. Did you say there was one on Fridays . . . a
flight . . . tonight?"

"Yes, madam—our Flight Two, *The Golden Argosy.*
It departs at ten o'clock local time, except that tonight
the flight has been delayed one hour, due to weather
conditions."

Inez could see the drugstore clock. By now, it was
nearly five past ten.

She said quickly, "You mean the flight hasn't gone
yet?"

"No, madam, not yet."

"Please . . ." As she often did, Inez found herself
groping for words. "Please, it's important for me to find
out if my husband is on that flight. His name is D. O.
Guerrero, and . . ."

"I'm sorry; we're not permitted to give out that information." Miss Young was polite but firm.

"I don't think you understand, miss. It's my husband
I'm asking about. This is his wife."

"I do understand, Mrs. Guerrero, and I'm sorry; but
it's a company rule."

Miss Young, and others like her, were well drilled in

the rule and understood its reason. Many businessmen took secretaries or mistresses along on air trips, listing them as wives, to take advantage of family plan fare reductions. In the past, a few suspicious, genuine wives had checked up, causing trouble for the airlines' customers—the men. Later, it was the men who complained bitterly about breaches of confidence, with the result that airlines nowadays made a policy of not disclosing passenger names.

Inez began, "Isn't there any way . . ."

"There really isn't."

"Oh, dear."

"Do I understand," Miss Young inquired, "that you think your husband might be leaving on Flight Two, but you're not sure?"

"Yes, that's right."

"Then the only thing you might do, Mrs. Guerrero, is to go out to the airport. Probably the flight hasn't boarded yet; so if your husband is there, you could see him. Even if the flight has boarded, they might help you at the departure gate. But you'd have to hurry."

"All right," Inez said. "If that's the only thing, I suppose I'd better try." She had no idea how she would get to the airport—more than twenty miles away—in less than an hour, in the storm.

"Just a moment." Miss Young sounded hesitant, her voice more human, as if some of Inez's distress had penetrated through the phones. "I really shouldn't do this, Mrs. Guerrero, but I'll give you a little tip."

"Please."

"At the airport, when you get to the departure gate, don't say you *think* your husband is aboard. Say you know he's aboard and you'd like to speak to him. If he isn't, you'll find out. If he is, it will make it easier for the gate agent to tell you what you want to know."

"Thank you," Inez said. "Thank you very much."

"You're entirely welcome, madam." Miss Young was her machine-like self once more. "Good night, and thank you for calling Trans America."

Replacing the telephone, Inez remembered something she had noticed coming in. A taxi was parked outside;

now she saw the driver. In a yellow, peaked cap, he was at the drugstore soda fountain, in conversation with another man.

A taxi would be costly, but if she was to get to the airport by 11 P.M., it was probably the only means.

Inez crossed to the soda fountain and touched the driver on the arm. "Excuse me."

The cab driver turned. "Yeah, waddya want?" He had a mean, flabby face, and needed a shave.

"I was wondering how much it would cost for a taxi to the airport."

The driver inspected her through narrowed, calculating eyes. "From here, maybe nine, ten dollars on the meter."

Inez turned away. It was too much—more than half the small amount of money she had remaining; and she was not even sure that D.O. would be on the flight.

"Hey, you! Hold it!" The cabbie downed a Coke he had been drinking and hurried after Inez. He caught her at the door. "How much dough ya got?"

"It isn't that." Inez shook her head. "It's just . . . it's more than I can afford."

The cabbie snorted, "Suma you people think ya can get them kinda rides for peanuts. 'S long drag out there."

"Yes, I know."

"Why you wanna go? Whyn't yer get th' bus?"

"It's important; I have to be there . . . ought to be there . . . by eleven o'clock."

"Here," the cab driver said, "maybe it's bargain night. I'll take yer for seven, even."

"Well . . ." Inez still hesitated. Seven dollars was most of what she had planned to offer the apartment landlord tomorrow in an attempt to appease him about the arrears of rent. She would have no wages from the coffee house until the end of next week.

The cab driver said impatiently, " 'S th' best offer you'll get. You wanna take it, or not?"

"Yes," Inez said. "Yes, I'll take it."

"Okay, lessgo."

While Inez climbed into the cab unaided, the driver

smirked as he used a whisk broom to clear snow from the windshield and windows. When Inez approached him in the drugstore, he was already off duty and, since he lived near the airport, was about to dead-head home. Now, he had a fare. Also, he lied in declaring the meter fare to the airport to be nine or ten dollars; it was actually less than seven. But the lie made it possible to concoct what his passenger believed to be a deal, so now he could drive with his flag up, and pocket the seven dollars for himself. High-flagging was illegal, but no cop, the driver reasoned, would be likely to spot him on a lousy night like this.

Thus, the cab driver thought smugly, in a single move he had managed to cheat both this stupid old crone of a passenger and his son-of-a-bitch employer.

As they moved off, Inez asked anxiously, "Are you sure you can get there by eleven o'clock?"

Over his shoulder the driver snarled, "I said so, didn't I, so lemme do the drivin'."

Just the same, he conceded to himself, he was not certain that they would. The roads were bad, the other traffic slow. They might just make it, but it was going to be close.

Thirty-five minutes later, the taxi containing Inez was crawling tediously along the snowbound, still-plugged Kennedy Expressway. Sitting tensely on the back seat, her fingers working nervously, Inez was wondering how much longer the journey would last.

At the same moment, the airport bus containing the contingent of Flight Two passengers swung on to the departure ramp entrance at Lincoln International. The bus, after shaking itself free from the slow-moving traffic nearer town, had continued to make good time; now, the clock above the terminal showed a quarter to eleven.

As the bus stopped, D. O. Guerrero was first to alight.

9

"Bring along that portable public address system," Elliott Freemantle commanded. "We may be glad of it."

The Meadowood community meeting in the Sunday school hall of Meadowood First Baptist Church was sizzling with excitement which Lawyer Freemantle had skillfully generated. The meeting was also about to move on to Lincoln International Airport.

"Don't hand me any bilgewater about it being too late, or not wanting to go," Elliott Freemantle had exhorted his audience of six hundred a few minutes earlier. He stood before them confidently, impeccable as ever in his elegant Blue Spruce suit and gleaming alligator shoes; not a single barber-styled hair was out of place, and he radiated confidence. The meeting was enthusiastically with him now, and the rougher tongued he was, it seemed, the more they liked him.

He continued, "And don't let's have a lot of footling excuses for not going. I don't want to hear about babysitters, mothers-in-law left alone, or stews on the stove simmering, because I couldn't care less; neither—at this moment—should you. If your car's stuck in the snow, leave it there and ride in someone else's. The point is: I'm going to the airport tonight, on your behalf, to make myself obnoxious." He paused as another aircraft thundered overhead. "By God!—it's time somebody did." The last remark had caused applause and laughter.

"I need your support, and I want you there—all of you. Now I'll ask you a plain, straight question: Are you coming?"

The hall resounded to a roar of, "Yes!" People were on their feet, cheering.

"All right," Freemantle said, and the hall had hushed. "Let's get a few things clear before we go."

He had already told them, he pointed out, that legal proceedings must be the basis of any action to gain relief for Meadowood community from its overwhelming airport noise. Such legal proceedings, however, should not be the kind which nobody noticed, or which took place in some out-of-the-way, unpeopled courtroom. Instead, they must be conducted in the spotlight of public attention and public sympathy.

"How do we get that kind of attention and sympathy?" Lawyer Freemantle paused, then answered his own question.

"We get it by making our point of view known in such a way that it becomes newsworthy. Then, and only then, can the attention-getting media—press, radio, and television—feature our viewpoint prominently, in the kind of way we want."

The press were good friends, he declared. "We do not ask them to share our point of view, merely to report it fairly, which—in my experience—they always do. But it helps out reporter friends if a cause can engender some drama; that way, they get a better story."

The three reporters at the press table were grinning as Freemantle added, "We'll see if we can stage some drama for them tonight."

While Elliott Freemantle was speaking, he was also observing shrewdly the progress of the legal forms, retaining himself as legal counsel for individual homeowners, which were now circulating through the hall. Many of the forms—at least a hundred, he estimated—had been signed and passed forward. He had watched ballpoint pens appear, husbands and wives bend over the documents to sign jointly, thus committing each family to payment of a hundred dollars. Lawyer Freemantle did some happy calculation: a hundred completed retainers meant ten thousand dollars for himself. Not a bad fee for—so far—an evening's work, and in the end the total fee would be a great deal more.

While the forms were still circulating, he decided, he would continue talking for a few minutes longer.

As to what was going to happen at the airport tonight, he instructed his listeners, they were to leave that to him. He hoped there would be a confrontation with the airport's management; in any case, he intended to stage a demonstration—within the airport terminal—which people would remember.

"All I ask is that you stay together and that you raise your voices only when I tell you."

Emphatically, he cautioned, there would be no disorder. No one must be able to say next day that the Meadowood anti-noise delegation violated any law.

"Of course"—Freemantle smiled suggestively—"we may get in the way and cause some inconvenience; I understand that the airport is extremely busy tonight. But we can't help that."

There was laughter again. He sensed that people were ready to go.

Still another aircraft reverberated overhead, and he waited until the sound had died.

"Very well! Let us be on our way!" Lawyer Freemantle raised his hands like a jet-age Moses, and mix-quoted: "For I have promises to keep, with much ado before I sleep."

The laughter changed to renewed cheering, and people began moving toward the doors.

It was then that he had noticed the portable p.a. system, borrowed from the Meadowood First Baptist Church, and instructed that it be brought along. Floyd Zanetta, the meeting's chairman—virtually ignored since Elliott Freemantle eclipsed him in attention—hurried to comply.

Freemantle himself was stuffing signed retainer forms into his briefcase. A quick count showed that he had underestimated earlier—there were over a hundred and sixty forms, or more than sixteen thousand dollars' worth of collectible fees. In addition, many who had come forward to shake his hand within the past few minutes, assured him they would mail their own forms, along with checks, in the morning. Lawyer Freemantle glowed.

He had no real plan as to what would happen at the airport, any more than he had arrived tonight with a fixed idea about how to take over this meeting. Elliott Freemantle disliked fixed ideas. He preferred to improvise, to get situations rolling, then direct them this way or that, to his own advantage. His freewheeling methods had worked once already this evening; he saw no reason why they should not do so again.

The main thing was to keep these Meadowood home-owners convinced that they had a dynamic leader who would eventually produce results. Furthermore, they must remain convinced until the four quarterly payments, which the legal retainer agreements called for, were made. After that, when Elliott Freemantle had his money in the bank, the opinions were less important.

So he had to keep this situation lively, he reasoned, for ten or eleven months—and he would do it. He would give these people all the dynamism they could want. There would be need for some more meetings and demonstrations like tonight's because those made news. Too often, court proceedings didn't. Despite what he had said a few minutes ago about legal proceedings being a base, any sessions in court were likely to be unspectacular and possibly unprofitable. Of course, he would do his best to introduce some histrionics, though quite a few judges nowadays were wise to Lawyer Freemantle's attention-creating tactics, and curtailed them sternly.

But there were no real problems, providing he remembered—as he always did in these affairs—that the most important factor was the care and feeding of Elliott Freemantle.

He could see one of the reporters, Tomlinson of the *Tribune*, using a pay phone just outside the hall; another reporter was nearby. Good! It meant that downtown city desks were being alerted, and would cover whatever happened at the airport. There would also, if earlier arrangements Freemantle had made worked out, be some TV coverage, too.

The crowd was thinning. Time to go!

10

Near the airport's floodlighted main entrance, the flashing red beacon of the state police patrol car died.

The patrol car, which had preceded Joe Patroni from the site of the wrecked tractor-trailer, slowed, and the state trooper at the wheel pulled over to the curb, waving the TWA maintenance chief past. Patroni accelerated. As his Buick Wildcat swept by, Patroni waved his cigar in salutation and honked his horn twice.

Although the last stage of Joe Patroni's journey had been accomplished with speed, over-all it had taken more than three hours to cover a distance—from his home to the airport—which normally took forty minutes. Now, he hoped, he could make good some of the lost time.

Fighting the snow and slippery road surface, he cut swiftly through the stream of terminal-bound traffic and swung onto a side road to the airport's hangar area. At a sign, "TWA Maintenance," he wheeled the Buick sharply right. A few hundred yards farther on, the airline's maintenance hangar loomed towering and massive. The main doors were open; he drove directly in.

Inside the hangar a radio-equipped pickup truck, with driver, was waiting; it would take Patroni onto the airfield—to the mired Aéreo-Mexican jet, still obstructing runway three zero. Stepping from his car, the maintenance chief paused only long enough to relight his cigar —ignoring "no smoking" regulations—then hoisted his stocky figure into the truck cab. He instructed the driver, "Okay, son, push that needle round the dial."

The truck raced away, Patroni obtaining radio clearance from the tower as they went. Once away from the lighted hangar area, the driver stayed close to taxi lights, the only guide—in the white-tinted gloom—to where paved surfaces began and ended. On instructions from the tower they halted briefly near a runway while a DC-9 of Delta Air Lines landed in a flurry of snow and rolled by with a thunder of reversed jet thrust. The ground controller cleared them across the runway, then added, "Is that Joe Patroni?"

"Yep."

There was an interval while the controller dealt with other traffic, then: "Ground control to Patroni. We have a message from the airport manager's office. Do you read?"

"This's Patroni. Go ahead."

"Message begins: Joe, I'll bet you a box of cigars against a pair of ball tickets that you can't get that stuck airplane clear of three zero tonight, and I'd like you to win. Signed, Mel Bakersfeld. End of message."

Joe Patroni chuckled as he depressed the transmit button. "Patroni to ground control. Tell him he's on."

Replacing the radio mike, he urged the truck driver, "Keep her moving, son. Now I got me an incentive."

At the blocked intersection of runway three zero, the Aéreo-Mexican maintenance foreman, Ingram—whom Mel Bakersfeld had talked with earlier—approached the pickup as it stopped. The foreman was still huddled into a parka, shielding his face as best he could from the biting wind and snow.

Joe Patroni bit off the end of a fresh cigar, though this time without lighting it, and descended from the truck cab. On the way out from the hangar he had changed from the overshoes he had been wearing into heavy fleece-lined boots; high as the boots were, the deep snow came over them.

Patroni pulled his own parka around him and nodded to Ingram. The two men knew each other slightly.

"Okay," Patroni said; he had to shout to make himself heard above the wind. "Gimme the poop."

As Ingram made his report, the wings and fuselage of the stalled Boeing 707 loomed above them both, like an immense ghostly albatross. Beneath the big jet's belly a red hazard light still winked rhythmically, and the collection of trucks and service vehicles, including a crew bus and roaring power cart, remained clustered on the taxiway side of the aircraft.

The Aéreo-Mexican maintenance foreman summarized what had been done already: the removal of passengers, and the first abortive attempt to get the airplane moving under its own power. Afterward, he informed Joe Patroni, as much weight as had been taken off as possible—freight, mail, baggage, with most of the fuel load being sucked out by tankers. Then there had been a second attempt to blast the airplane out, again with its own jets, which also ended in failure.

Chewing his cigar instead of smoking it—one of Patroni's rare concessions to fire precaution, since the smell of aviation kerosene was strong—the TWA maintenance chief moved closer to the aircraft. Ingram followed, and the two were joined by several ground crewmen who emerged from the shelter of the crew bus. As Patroni surveyed the scene, one of the crewmen switched on portable floodlights which were rigged in a semicircle in front of the airplane's nose. The lights revealed that the main landing gear was partially out of sight, embedded in a covering of black mud beneath snow. The aircraft had stuck in an area which was normally grass-covered, a few yards off runway three zero, near an intersecting taxiway—the taxiway which the Aéreo-Mexican pilot had missed in the dark and swirling snow. It was sheer bad luck, Patroni realized, that at that point the ground must have been so waterlogged that not even three days of snow and freezing temperatures had been sufficient to harden it. As a result, the two attempts to blast the airplane free with its own power had merely succeeded in settling it deeper. Now, nacelles of the four jet engines beneath the wings were uncomfortably close to ground level.

Ignoring the snow, which swirled about him like a scene from *South with Scott,* Patroni considered, calculating the possibilities of success.

There was still a worthwhile chance, he decided, of getting the airplane out by use of its own engine power. It would be the fastest way, if it could be done. If not, they would have to employ giant lifting bags—eleven altogether, made of nylon fabric—placed under wings and fuselage, and inflated by pneumatic blowers. When the bags were in place, heavy-duty jacks would be used to raise the aircraft's wheels, then a solid floor built under them. But the process would be long, difficult, and wearying. Joe Patroni hoped it could be avoided.

He announced, "We gotta dig deep and wide in front of the gear. I want two six-foot-wide trenches down to where the wheels are now. Coming forward from the wheels, we'll level the trenches at first, then slope 'em up gradually." He swung to Ingram. "That's a lot of digging."

The foreman nodded. "Sure is."

"When we've finished that part, we'll start the engines and pull full power with all four." Patroni motioned to the stalled, silent aircraft. "That should get her moving forward. When she's rolling, and up the slope of the trenches, we'll swing her this way." Stomping with the heavy boots he had put on in the truck, he traced an elliptical path through the snow between the soft ground and the taxiway paved surface. "Another thing—let's lay big timbers, as many as we can, in front of the wheels. You got any at all?"

"Some," Ingram said. "In one of the trucks."

"Unload 'em, and send your driver around the airport to round up as many as he can. Try all the airlines, and airport maintenance."

The ground crewmen nearest Patroni and Ingram hailed others, who began scrambling from the crew bus. Two of the men rolled back a snow-covered tarpaulin on a truck containing tools and shovels. The shovels were passed around among figures, moving and shadowy outside the semicircle of bright lights. The blowing snow, at times, made it difficult for the men to see each other. They waited for orders to begin.

A boarding ramp, leading to the forward cabin door of the 707, had been left in place. Patroni pointed to it. "Are the flyboys still aboard?"

Ingram grunted. "They're aboard. The goddam captain and first officer."

Patroni looked at him sharply. "They been giving you trouble?"

"It wasn't what they gave me," Ingram said sourly, "it's what they wouldn't. When I got here, I wanted 'em to pull full power, the way you just said. If they'd done it the first time, I reckon she'd have come out; but they didn't have the guts, which is why we got in deeper. The captain's made one big screwup tonight, and knows it. Now he's scared stiff of standing the ship on its nose."

Joe Patroni grinned. "If I were him, I might feel the same way." He had chewed his cigar to shreds; he threw it into the snow and reached inside his parka for another. "I'll talk to the captain later. Is the interphone rigged?"

"Yeah."

"Call the flight deck, then. Tell 'em we're working, and I'll be up there soon."

"Right." As he moved closer to the aircraft, Ingram called to the twenty or so assembled ground crewmen, "Okay, you guys; let's get digging!"

Joe Patroni seized a shovel himself and, within minutes, the group was shifting mud, earth, and snow.

When he had used the fuselage interphone to speak to the pilots in their cockpit high above, Ingram—with the aid of a mechanic—began groping through icy mud, with cold numbed hands, to lay the first of the timbers in front of the aircraft's wheels.

Across the airfield occasionally, as the snow gusted and limits of visibility changed, the lights of aircraft taking off and landing could be seen, and the whine-pitched roar of jet engines was carried on the wind to the ears of the men working. But close alongside, runway three zero remained silent and deserted.

Joe Patroni calculated: It would probably be an hour before the digging would be complete and the Boeing 707's engines could be started in an attempt to taxi the big airliner out. Meanwhile, the men now excavating the twin trenches, which were beginning to take shape, would have to be relieved in shifts, to warm themselves in the crew bus, still parked on the taxiway.

It was ten-thirty now. With luck, he thought, he might be home in bed—with Marie—soon after midnight.

To bring the prospect nearer, also to keep warm, Patroni threw himself even harder into shoveling.

11

In the Cloud Captain's Coffee Shop, Captain Vernon Demerest ordered tea for Gwen, black coffee for himself. Coffee—as it was supposed to do—helped keep him alert; he would probably down a dozen more cups between here and Rome. Although Captain Harris would be doing most of the flying of Flight Two tonight, Demerest had no intention of relaxing mentally. In the air, he rarely did. He was aware, as were most veteran pilots, that aviators who died in their beds of old age were those who throughout their careers had been ready to cope instantly with the unexpected.

"We're both unusually quiet," Gwen said in her gentle English voice. "We scarcely said a word coming into the terminal."

It was just a few minutes since they left the departure concourse, after announcement of the one hour flight delay. They had managed to snare a booth near the rear of the coffee shop, and now Gwen was looking into the mirror of her compact, patting her hair into place where it flowed superbly from beneath the smart Trans America stewardess cap. Her dark, expressive eyes switched briefly from the mirror to Vernon Demerest's face.

"I wasn't talking," Demerest said, "because I've been thinking; that's all."

Gwen moistened her lips, though not applying lipstick—airlines had strict rules against stewardesses applying make-up in public. In any case, Gwen used very little; her complexion was the milk and roses kind which so many English girls seemed born with.

"Thinking about what? Your traumatic experience— the announcement we're to be parents?" Gwen smiled mischievously, then recited, "Captain Vernon Waldo Demerest and Miss Gwendolyn Aline Meighen announce the approaching arrival of their first child, a . . . what? . . . We don't know, do we? We won't for another seven months. Oh well, it isn't long to wait."

He remained silent while their coffee and tea was set before them, then protested, "For God's sake, Gwen, let's be serious about this."

"Why should we be? Especially if I'm not. After all, if anyone's worrying, it ought to be me."

He was about to object again when Gwen reached for his hand under the table. Her expression changed to

sympathy. "I'm sorry. I suppose it really is a bit shattering—for both of us."

It was the opening Demerest had been waiting for.
He said carefully, "It needn't be shattering. What's
more, we don't have to be parents unless we choose to
be."

"Well," Gwen said matter-of-factly, "I was wondering when you'd get around to it." She snapped her
compact closed, and put it away. "You almost did in the
car, didn't you? Then thought better of it."

"Thought better of what?"

"Oh really, Vernon! Why pretend? We both know
perfectly well what it is you're talking about. You want
me to have an abortion. You've been thinking about it
ever since I told you I was pregnant. Well, haven't
you?"

He nodded reluctantly. "Yes." He still found Gwen's
directness disconcerting.

"What's the matter? Did you think I'd never heard
about abortions before?"

Demerest glanced over his shoulder, wondering if
they could be overheard, but the clatter of the coffee
shop, the buzz of conversation generally, were all-per-
vading.

"I wasn't sure how you'd feel."

"I'm not sure either." It was Gwen's turn to be serious. She was looking down at her hands, the long
slender fingers he admired so much now clasped in front
of her. "I've thought about it. I still don't know."

He felt encouraged. At least there was no slammed
door, no blank refusal.

He tried to make himself the voice of reason. "It's
really the only sensible thing to do. Maybe in some ways
it's unpleasant to think of, but at least it's over quickly,
and if it's done properly, therapeutically, there's no
danger involved, no fear of complications."

"I know," Gwen said. "It's all terribly simple. Now
you have it; now you don't." She looked at him directly.
"Right?"

"Right."

He sipped his coffee. Perhaps this was going to be easier than he had thought.

"Vernon," Gwen said softly, "have you considered that what's inside me is a human being; that it's alive, a person—even now? We made love. It's us, you and me; a part of us." Her eyes, more troubled than he had yet seen them, searched his face for a response.

He said emphatically, his voice deliberately harsh, "That isn't true. A fetus at this stage is not a human being; nor is it a person, not yet. It could be later, but it isn't now. It doesn't have life or breath or feeling. An abortion—particularly this soon—isn't the same as taking a human life."

Gwen reacted with the same quick temper she had shown in the car on their way to the airport. "You mean it might not be such a good thing later on? If we waited, then had an abortion, it might not be so ethical when the baby was perfectly formed, its fingers and toes all there. To kill it then might be a little worse than now. Is that it, Vernon?"

Demerest shook his head. "I didn't say that."

"But you implied it."

"If I did, I didn't mean to. In any case, you're twisting words around."

Gwen sighed. "I'm being womanly."

"No one's more entitled to be." He smiled; his eyes moved over her. The thought of Naples, with Gwen . . . a few hours from now . . . still excited him.

"I do love you, Vernon. I really do."

Under the table he retrieved her hand. "I know. It's why this is hard for us both."

"The thing is," Gwen said slowly, as if thinking aloud, "I've never conceived a child before, and until it happens a woman always wonders if she can. When you find out, as I have, that the answer's yes, in a way it's a gift, a feeling . . . that only a woman knows . . . that's great and wonderful. Then suddenly in our kind of situation, you're faced with ending it all, of squandering what was given." Her eyes were misty. "Do you understand, Vernon? Really understand?"

He answered gently, "Yes, I think so."

"The difference between you and me is that you've had a child."

He shook his head. "I've no children. Sarah and I . . ."

"Not in your marriage. But there *was* a child; you told me so. A little girl; the one from the 3-PPP Program"—Gwen gave the ghost of a smile—"who was adopted. Now, whatever happens there's always someone, somewhere, that's you again."

He remained silent.

Gwen asked, "Do you ever think about her? Don't you ever wonder where she is, what she's like?"

There was no reason to lie. "Yes," he said. "Sometimes I do."

"You've no means of finding out?"

He shook his head. He had once inquired, but was told that when an adoption was sealed, they threw away the files. There was no way to know—ever.

Gwen drank from her teacup. Over its rim she surveyed the crowded coffee shop. He sensed that her composure had returned; the trace of tears was gone.

She said with a smile, "Oh dear, what a lot of trouble I'm causing you."

He answered, and meant it: "It isn't my worrying that matters. It's what's best for you."

"Well, I suppose in the end I'll do what's sensible. I'll have an abortion. I just have to think it through, talk it out, first."

"When you're ready, I'll help. But we shouldn't lose much time."

"I suppose not."

"Look, Gwen," he assured her, "the whole thing is fast, and I promise you it'll be medically safe." He told her about Sweden; that he would pay whatever the clinic cost; that the airline would cooperate in getting her there.

She acknowledged, "I'll make up my mind, for sure, before we get back from this trip."

He picked up their check, and they rose to leave. It was nearing time for Gwen to be on hand to greet passengers boarding Flight Two.

As they left the coffee shop, she said, "I guess I'm pretty lucky you're the way you are. Some men would have walked away and left me."

"I won't leave you."

But he *would* leave her; he knew that now. When Naples and the abortion were over, he would finish with Gwen, break off their affair—as considerately as he could, but completely and definitely just the same. It would not be too difficult. There might be an uncomfortable moment or two when Gwen learned of his intention, but she was not the kind to make a fuss; she had demonstrated that already. In any event, he could handle the situation, which would not be a new one. Vernon Demerest had disentangled himself successfully from amorous affairs before.

It was true that this time there was a difference. No one before had ever had quite the same effect on him as Gwen. No other woman had stirred him quite so deeply. No one else—at least, whom he remembered—had caused him to enjoy her company, just being with her, quite so much. Parting, for himself, would not be easy, and he knew he would be tempted, later on, to change his mind.

But he would not. Through all his life so far, once he had decided on a course of action, Vernon Demerest had seen it through. Self-discipline was a habit he enforced.

Besides, commonsense told him that if he did not break with Gwen soon, the time might come when he could not, when—self-discipline or not—he could never bring himself to give her up. If that happened, it would entail a need for permanence and, along with that, the kind of catastrophic upheaval—marital, financial, emotional—which he was determined to avoid. Ten or fifteen years ago, maybe; not now.

He touched Gwen's arm. "You go on. I'll follow in a minute."

Ahead of them, as the crowds in the central concourse parted briefly, he had observed Mel Bakersfeld. Vernon Demerest had no particular objection to being seen with Gwen; just the same, there was no sense in advertising their relationship around the family.

His brother-in-law, he noticed, was talking earnestly with Lieutenant Ned Ordway, the efficient, amiable Negro who commanded the airport police detachment. Perhaps Mel would be too absorbed to notice his sister's husband, which was perfectly all right with Demerest, who had no particular wish for a meeting, though at the same time he had no intention of avoiding one.

Gwen disappeared into the crowd; his last glimpse of her was of shapely, nylon-sheathed legs, and ankles equally as attractive and proportionate. *O Sole Mio . . .* hurry up!

Damn! Mel Bakersfeld had seen him.

"I was looking for you," Lieutenant Ordway had told Mel a few minutes earlier. "I've just heard we're having visitors—several hundred."

Tonight the airport police chief was in uniform; a tall, striking figure who looked like an African emperor, though for one so big, he spoke with surprising softness.

"We already have visitors." Mel glanced around the crowded, bustling concourse. He had been passing through on the way to his office on the executive mezzanine. "Not hundreds; thousands."

"I don't mean passengers," Ordway said. "The ones I'm talking about may cause us more trouble."

He told Mel about the Meadowood mass meeting to protest airport noise; now the meeting had adjourned and most of its members were on their way to the airport. Lieutenant Ordway had learned about the meeting, and its intended follow-up, from a TV news crew which had requested permission to set up cameras inside the terminal. After talking with the TV people, Ordway telephoned a friend on the *Tribune* city desk downtown, who read him the gist of a news story which a reporter at the original meeting had just phoned in.

"Hell!" Mel grumbled. "Of all the nights to choose! As if we don't have enough trouble already."

"I guess that's the idea; they'll get noticed more that way. But I thought you'd better be warned because they'll probably want to see you, and maybe someone from the FAA."

Mel said sourly, "The FAA goes underground when they hear of something like this. They never come out until the all clear's sounded."

"How about you?" The policeman grinned. "You plan to start tunneling?"

"No. You can tell them I'll meet a delegation of half a dozen, though even that's a waste of time tonight. There's nothing I can do."

"You realize," Ordway said, "that providing they don't create a disturbance or damage property, there's nothing I can do legally to keep the rest of them out."

"Yes, I realize it, but I'm not going to talk to a mob, though just the same, let's not look for trouble. Even if we get pushed around a little, make sure we don't do any pushing ourselves unless we have to. Remember that the press will be here, and I don't want to create any martyrs."

"I already warned my men. They'll make with the jokes and save the jujitsu."

"Good!"

Mel had confidence in Ned Ordway. The policing of Lincoln International was handled by a self-administering detachment of the city force, and Lieutenant Ordway represented the best type of career policeman. He had been in charge of the airport police detail a year, and would probably move on to a more important assignment downtown soon. Mel would be sorry to see him go.

"Apart from this Meadowood thing," Mel inquired, "how's everything else been?" He was aware that Ordway's force of a hundred policemen, like most others at the airport, had done extra hours of duty since the storm began.

"Mostly routine. More drunks than usual, and a couple of fist fights. But that figures because of all the flight delays and your busy bars."

Mel grinned. "Don't knock the bars. The airport takes a percentage from every drink, and we need the revenue."

"So do airlines, I guess. At least judging by the passengers they try to sober up, so they can put them aboard. I have my usual beef about that."

"Coffee?"

"Right. The moment a passenger in his cups shows up at an airline check-in counter, somebody from passenger relations gets assigned to pour coffee into him. Airlines never seem to learn that when the coffee's in, all you have is a wide-awake drunk. Mostly, that's when they call us."

"You can handle it."

Ordway's men, Mel was aware, were expert at dealing with airport drunks, who were rarely charged unless they became obstreperous. Mostly they were salesmen and businessmen from out of town, sometimes exhausted after a grueling, competitive week, whom a few drinks on the way home hit hard. If flight crews wouldn't allow them aboard—and captains, who had the last word on such matters, were usually adamant about it—the drunks were escorted to the police detention building and left to sober up. Later, they were allowed to go—usually sheepishly.

"Oh, there is one thing," the police chief said. "The parking lot people think we have several more dumped cars. In this weather it's hard to be sure, but we'll check it out as soon as we can."

Mel grimaced. Worthless cars abandoned on parking lots were currently a plague at every big city airport. Nowadays, when an old jalopy became useless, it was surprisingly hard to get rid of it. Scrap and salvage dealers were jammed to the limits of their yards and wanted no more—unless car owners paid. So an owner was faced with the alternatives of paying for disposal, renting storage, or finding a place to abandon his vehicle where it could not be traced back to him. Airports had become obvious dumping grounds.

The old cars were driven into airport parking lots, then license plates and other obvious identification quietly removed. Engine serial numbers could not be removed, of course, but the time and trouble involved in tracing them was never worth while. It was simpler for the airport to do what the ex-owner would not—pay for the car to be taken away and junked, and as quickly as possible since it was occupying revenue parking space. Recently, at Lincoln International, the monthly bill for old car disposal had become formidable.

Through the shifting throng in the concourse, Mel caught sight of Captain Vernon Demerest.

"Aside from that," Ordway said genially, "we're in great shape for your Meadowood visitors. I'll let you know when they get here." With a friendly nod, the policeman moved on.

Vernon Demerest—in Trans America uniform, his bearing confident as usual—was coming Mel's way. Mel felt a surge of irritation, remembering the adverse snow committee report which he had heard about, but still hadn't seen.

Demerest seemed disinclined to stop until Mel said, "Good evening, Vernon."

"Hi." The tone was indifferent.

"I hear that you're an authority, now, on snow clearance."

"You don't have to be an authority," Vernon Demerest said brusquely, "to know when there's a lousy job being done."

Mel made an effort to keep his tone moderate. "Have you any idea how much snow there's been?"

"Probably better than you. Part of my job is studying weather reports."

"Then you're aware we've had ten inches of snow on the airport in the past twenty-four hours; to say nothing of what was there already."

Demerest shrugged. "So clear it."

"It's what we're doing."

"Goddamned inefficiently."

"The maximum recorded snowfall here—ever," Mel persisted, "was twelve inches in the same period. That was an inundation, and everything closed down. This time we've come near to it, but we haven't closed. We've fought to stay open, and we've managed it. There isn't an airport anywhere that could have coped better

than we have with this storm. We've had every piece of
snow-moving machinery manned around the clock."

"Maybe you haven't got enough machinery."

"Good God, Vernon! Nobody has enough equipment
for the kind of storm we've had these past three days.
Anybody could use more, but you don't buy snow-
clearing machinery for occasional maximum situations
—not if you've any economic sense. You buy for op-
timums, then when an emergency hits, you use everything you have, deploying it to best advantage. That's
what my men have been doing, and they've done
damned well!"

"Okay," Demerest said, "you have your opinion, I
have mine. I happen to think you've done an incompetent job. I've said so in my report."

"I thought it was a committee report. Or did you
elbow the others out so you could take a personal stab
at me?"

"How the committee works is our business. The
report is what matters. You'll get your copy tomorrow."

"Thanks a lot." His brother-in-law, Mel noticed, had
not bothered to deny that the report was directed personally. Mel went on, "Whatever it is you've written
won't change anything, but if it gives you satisfaction,
it'll have a nuisance value. Tomorrow I'll have to waste
time explaining how ignorant—in some areas—you
really are."

Mel had spoken heatedly, not bothering to conceal
his anger, and for the first time Demerest grinned. "Got
under your skin a little, eh? Well, that's too bad about
the nuisance value and your precious time. I'll remember it tomorrow while I'm enjoying Italian sunshine." Still grinning, he walked away.

He had not gone more than a few yards when the grin
changed to a scowl.

The cause of Captain Demerest's displeasure was the
central lobby insurance booth—tonight, clearly doing a
brisk business. It was a reminder that Demerest's
victory over Mel Bakersfeld had been picayune, a pin-
prick only. A week from now, the adverse snow committee report would be forgotten, but the insurance

counter would still be here. So the real victory was still
with his smooth, smug brother-in-law, who had defeated
Demerest's arguments in front of the Board of Airport
Commissioners, and made him look a fool.

Behind the insurance counters two young girls—one
of them the big-breasted blonde—were rapidly writing
policies for applicants, while another half dozen people
waited in line. Most of those waiting were holding cash
in their hands—representing more quick profits for the
insurance companies, Demerest reflected sourly—and
he had no doubt the automatic vending machines in
various locations in the terminal were just as busy.

He wondered if any of his own Flight Two passen-
gers-to-be were among those in line. He was tempted to
inquire and, if so, do some proselytizing of his own; but
he decided not. Vernon Demerest had tried the same
thing once before—urging people at an insurance
counter not to buy airport flight insurance, and telling
them why; and afterward there had been complaints,
resulting in a sharply worded reprimand to him from
Trans America management. Though airlines did not
like airport insurance vending any more than aircrews
did, the airlines were subject to differing pressures
which forced them to stay neutral. For one thing, airport managements claimed they needed the insurance
companies' revenue; if they didn't get it from that
source, they pointed out, maybe the airlines would have
to make up the difference in higher landing fees. For
another, airlines were not eager to offend passengers,
who might resent not being able to buy insurance in a
way they had become used to. Therefore the pilots alone
had taken the initiative—along with the abuse.

Preoccupied with his thoughts, Captain Demerest had
paused for a few seconds, watching the insurance booth
activity. Now he saw a newcomer join the queue—a
nervous-looking man—spindly and stoop-shouldered,
and with a small, sandy mustache. The man carried a
small attaché case and seemed to be worrying about the
time; he cast frequent glances at the central lobby clock,
comparing it with his own watch. He was clearly unhappy about the length of the line-up ahead of him.

Demerest thought disgustedly: the man had left himself with too little time; he should forget about insurance
and get aboard his flight.

Then Demerest reminded himself: he should be back
on the flight deck of Flight Two. He began to walk
quickly toward the Trans America departure concourse;
at any moment now the first boarding announcement
would be made. Ah!—there it was.

*"Trans America Airlines announces the departure of
Flight Two,* The Golden Argosy, *for Rome . . ."*

Captain Demerest had stayed in the terminal longer
than he intended. As he hurried, the announcement,
clear and audible above the babel in the concourses,
continued.

12

". . . Flight Two, The Golden Argosy, *for Rome. The
flight is now ready for boarding. All passengers holding
confirmed reservations . . ."*

An airport flight departure announcement meant diverse things to those who heard it. To some, it was a
routine summons, a prefix to another tedious, work-
oriented journey which—had free choice been theirs—
they would not have made. For others, a flight announcement spelled a beginning of adventure; for others
still, the nearing of an end—the journey home. For
some it entailed sadness and parting; for others, in
counterpoint, the prospect of reunion and joy. Some
who heard flight announcements heard them always for
other people. Their friends or relatives were travelers; as
to themselves, the names of destinations were wistful
not-quite-glimpses of faraway places they would never
see. A handful heard flight announcements with fear;
few heard them with indifference. They were a signal

that a process of departure had begun. An airplane was ready; there was time to board, but no time to be tardy; only rarely did airliners wait for individuals. In a short time the airplane would enter man's unnatural element, the skies; and because it was unnatural there had always been, and would forever remain, a component of adventure and romance.

There was nothing romantic about the mechanics of a flight announcement. It originated in a machine which in many ways resembled a juke box, except that push buttons instead of coins were required to actuate it. The push buttons were on a console in Flight Information Control—a miniature control tower (each airline had its own F.I.C. or equivalent)—located above the departure concourse. A woman clerk pushed the buttons in appropriate sequence; after that the machinery took over.

Almost all flight announcements—the exceptions were those for special situations—were pre-recorded on cartridge tapes. Although, to the ear, each announcement seemed complete in itself, it never was, for it consisted of three separate recordings. The first recording named the airline and flight; the second described the loading situation, whether preliminary, boarding, or final; the third recording specified gate number and concourse. Since the three recordings followed one another without a pause, they sounded—as they were intended to—continuous.

People who disliked quasi-human automation were sometimes cheered when flight announcement machines went wrong. Occasionally part of the machinery would jam, with such results as passengers for half a dozen flights being misdirected to the same gate. The resultant debacle, involving a thousand or more confused, impatient passengers, was an airline agent's nightmare.

Tonight, for Flight Two, the machinery worked.

"*. . . passengers holding confirmed reservations please proceed to gate forty-seven, the Blue Concourse 'D'.*"

By now, thousands in the terminal had heard the announcement of Flight Two. Some who heard were more concerned than others. A few, not yet concerned, would be, before the night was done.

More than a hundred and fifty Flight Two passengers heard the announcement. Those who had checked in, but had not reached gate forty-seven, hastened toward it, a few recent arrivals still knocking snow from their clothing as they went.

Senior Stewardess Gwen Meighen was pre-boarding several families with small children when the announcement echoed down the boarding walkway. She used the flight deck interphone to notify Captain Anson Harris, and prepared herself for an influx of passengers within the next few minutes. Ahead of the passengers, Captain Vernon Demerest ducked aboard and hurried forward, closing the flight deck door behind him.

Anson Harris, working with Second Officer Cy Jordan, had already begun the pre-flight check.

"Okay," Demerest said. He slipped into the first officer's righthand seat, and took the check list clipboard. Jordan returned to his regular seat behind the other two.

Mel Bakersfeld, still in the central concourse, heard the announcement and remembered that *The Golden Argosy* was Vernon Demerest's flight. Mel genuinely regretted that once again an opportunity to end, or even lessen, the hostility between himself and his brother-in-law had ended in failure. Now, their personal relationship was—if possible—worse than before. Mel wondered how much of the blame was his own; some, certainly, because Vernon seemed to have a knack for probing out the worst in Mel, but Mel honestly believed that most of their quarrel was of Vernon's making. Part of the trouble was that Vernon saw himself as a superior being, and resented it when others didn't. A good many pilots whom Mel knew—especially captains—felt that way about themselves.

Mel still seethed when he remembered Vernon, after the airport commissioners' meeting, asserting that people like Mel were "ground-bound, desk-tied, with penguins' minds." As if flying an airplane, Mel thought, were something so damned extra-special compared with other occupations!

Just the same, Mel wished that tonight for a few hours he was a pilot once again, and was about to leave —as Vernon was leaving—on a flight for Rome. He remembered what Vernon had said about enjoying Italian sunshine tomorrow. Mel could do with a little of that, a little less, at this moment, of aviation's logistics of the ground. Tonight the surly bonds of earth seemed surlier than usual.

Police Lieutenant Ned Ordway, who had left Mel Bakersfeld a few minutes earlier, heard the announcement of Flight Two through the opened doorway of a small security office just off the main concourse. Ordway was in the office receiving a telephoned report from his desk sergeant at airport police headquarters. According to a radio message from a patrol car, a heavy influx of private automobiles, crammed with people, was coming into the parking lots, which were having difficulty accommodating them. Inquiries had revealed that most of the cars' occupants were from Meadowood community—members of the anti-noise demonstration which Lieutenant Ordway had already heard about. As per the lieutenant's orders, the desk sergeant said, police reinforcements were on their way to the terminal.

A few hundred feet from Lieutenant Ordway, in a passenger waiting area, the little old lady from San Diego, Mrs. Ada Quonsett, paused in her conversation with young Peter Coakley of Trans America, while both listened to the announcement of Flight Two.

They were seated, side by side, on one of a series of black, leather padded benches. Mrs. Quonsett had been describing the virtues of her late husband in the same kind of terms which Queen Victoria must have used when speaking of Prince Albert. "Such a dear person, so very wise, and handsome. He came to me in later life, but I imagine, when he was young, he must have been very much like you."

Peter Coakley grinned sheepishly, as he had done many times in the past hour and a half. Since leaving Tanya Livingston, with instructions to remain with the old lady stowaway until the departure of her return flight for Los Angeles, their talk had consisted chiefly of a monologue by Mrs. Quonsett in which Peter Coakley was compared frequently and favorably with the late Herbert Quonsett. It was a subject of which Peter was becoming decidedly weary. He was unaware that that was what Ada Quonsett astutely intended.

Surreptitiously, Peter Coakley yawned; this was not the kind of work he had expected when he became a Trans America passenger agent. He felt an absolute fool, sitting here in uniform, playing dry nurse to a harmless, garrulous old dame who could have been his great-grandmother. He hoped this duty would be over soon. It was bad luck that Mrs. Quonsett's flight to Los Angeles, like most others tonight, was being further delayed by the storm; otherwise the old girl would have been on her way an hour ago. He hoped to goodness that the L.A. flight would be called soon. Meanwhile, the announcement about Flight Two, which was continuing, made a welcome, if brief, respite.

Young Peter Coakley had already forgotten Tanya's cautioning words: "Remember . . . she's got a barrelful of tricks."

"Fancy that!" Mrs. Quonsett said when the announcement ended. "A flight to Rome! An airport is so interesting, don't you think, especially for a young, intelligent person like you? Now there was a place—Rome —which my late, dear husband wanted us both to visit." She clasped her hands, a wispy lace handkerchief between them, and sighed. "We never did."

While she talked, Ada Quonsett's mind was ticking like a fine Swiss watch. What she wanted was to give this child in a man's uniform the slip. Although he was plainly becoming bored, boredom itself was not enough; he was still here. What she had to do was develop a situation in which boredom would become carelessness. But it needed to be soon.

Mrs. Quonsett had not forgotten her original objective—to stow away on a flight to New York. She had listened carefully for New York departure announcements, and five flights of various airlines had been called, but none was at the right moment, with any reasonable chance of getting away from her young custodian, unnoticed. Now, she had no means of knowing if there would be another New York departure before the Trans America flight to Los Angeles—the flight which she was supposed to go on, but didn't want to.

Anything, Mrs. Quonsett brooded, would be better than going back to Los Angeles tonight. Anything!— even . . . a sudden thought occurred to her . . . even getting aboard that flight to Rome.

She hesitated. Why not? A lot of things she had said tonight about Herbert were untrue, but it *was* true that they had once looked at some picture postcards of Rome together . . . If she got no farther than Rome airport, she would at least have been there; it would be something to tell Blanche when she finally got to New York. Just as satisfying, it would be spitting in the eye of that red-headed passenger agent bitch . . . But could she manage it? And what was the gate number they had just announced? Wasn't it . . . gate forty-seven in the Blue Concourse "D"? Yes, she was sure it was.

Of course, the flight might be full, with no space for a stowaway or anyone else, but that was always a chance you took. Then for a flight to Italy, she supposed, people needed passports to get aboard; she would have to see how that worked out. And even now, if there was a flight announcement for New York . . .

The main thing was not just to sit here, but to do *something*.

Mrs. Quonsett fluttered her frail, lined hands. "Oh dear!" she exclaimed. "Oh dear!" The fingers of her right hand moved, hovering near the top of her old-fashioned, high-necked blouse. She dabbed at her mouth with the lace handkerchief and emitted a soft, low moan.

A look of alarm sprang to the young ticket agent's face. "What is it, Mrs. Quonsett? What's wrong?"

Her eyes closed, then opened; she gave several short gasps. "I'm so sorry. I'm afraid I don't feel at all well."

Peter Coakley inquired anxiously, "Do you want me to get help? A doctor?"

"I don't want to be a nuisance."

"You won't be . . :"

"No." Mrs. Quonsett shook her head weakly. "I think I'll just go to the ladies' room. I expect I'll be all right."

The young ticket agent appeared doubtful. He didn't want the old girl dying on him, though she looked ready for it. He asked uneasily, "Are you sure?"

"Yes, quite sure." Mrs. Quonsett decided she didn't want to attract attention here, not in the main part of the terminal. There were too many people nearby who would be watching. "Please help me up . ., . thank you . . . now, if you'll just give me your arm. I believe the ladies' room is over there." On the way, she threw in a couple of low moans, producing anxious glances from Peter Coakley. She reassured him, "I've had an attack like this before. I'm sure I'll feel better soon."

At the door to the women's room she released young Coakley's arm. "You're very kind to an old lady. So many young people nowadays . . . Oh, dear! . . ." She cautioned herself: that was enough; she must be careful not to overdo it. "You'll wait here for me? You won't go away?"

"Oh, no. I won't go."

"Thank you." She opened the door and went in.

There were twenty or thirty women inside; everything at the airport was busy tonight, Mrs. Quonsett thought, including washrooms. Now she needed an ally. She looked the field over carefully before selecting a youngish secretary-type woman in a beige suit, who didn't seem in a hurry. Mrs. Quonsett crossed to her.

"Excuse me, I'm not feeling very well. I wonder if you'd help me." The little old lady from San Diego fluttered her hands and closed and opened her eyes, as she had for Peter Coakley.

The younger woman was concerned at once. "Of course I'll help. Would you like me to take you . . ."

"No . . . please." Mrs. Quonsett leaned against a

washbasin, apparently for support. "All I want is to
send a message. There's a young man outside the door
in airline uniform—Trans America. His name is Mr.
Coakley. Please tell him . . . yes, I would like him to get
a doctor after all."

"I'll tell him. Will you be all right until I get back?"

Mrs. Quonsett nodded. "Yes, thank you. But you will
come back . . . and tell me."

"Of course."

Within less than a minute the younger woman had
returned. "He's sending for a doctor right away. Now, I
think you should rest. Why don't . . ."

Mrs. Quonsett stopped leaning on the basin. "You
mean he's already gone?"

"He went immediately."

Now all she had to do, Mrs. Quonsett thought, was
get rid of this woman. She closed and opened her eyes
again. "I know it's asking a great deal . . . you've
already been so good . . . but my daughter is waiting for
me by the main door, near United Air Lines."

"You'd like me to get her for you? Bring her here?"

Mrs. Quonsett touched the lace handkerchief to her
lips. "I'd be so grateful, though really it's an imposi-
tion."

"I'm sure you'd do as much for me. How will I know
your daughter?"

"She's wearing a long mauve coat and a small white
hat with yellow flowers. She has a little dog—a French
poodle."

The secretary-type woman smiled. "That should be
easy. I won't be long."

"It *is* so good of you."

Ada Quonsett waited only a moment or two after the
woman had gone. Mrs. Quonsett hoped, for her temporary helper's sake, she did not spend too much time
searching for an imaginary figure in a mauve coat,
accompanied by a non-existent French poodle.

Smiling to herself, the little old lady from San Diego
left the washroom, walking spryly. No one accosted her
as she moved away and was absorbed in the surging
terminal crowds.

Now, she thought, which was the way to the Blue Concourse "D," and gate forty-seven?

To Tanya Livingston, the Flight Two announcement was like a scoreboard change at a quadruple-header ball game. Four Trans America flights were, at the moment, in various stages of departure; in her capacity as passenger relations agent, Tanya was liaising with them all. As well, she had just had an irritating session with a passenger from an incoming flight from Kansas City.

The aggressive, fast-talking passenger complained that his wife's leather traveling case, which appeared on the arrivals carousel with a rip in its side, had been damaged as a result of careless handling. Tanya did not believe him—the rip looked like an old one—but, as Trans America and other airlines invariably did, she offered to settle the claim on the spot, for cash. The difficulty had been in arriving at an agreeable sum. Tanya offered thirty-five dollars, which she considered to be more than the bag's value; the passenger held out for forty-five. Finally they settled at forty dollars, though what the complainant didn't know was that a passenger relations agent had authority to go to sixty dollars to get rid of a nuisance claim. Even when suspecting fraud, airlines found it cheaper to pay up quickly than enter into a prolonged dispute. In theory, ticket agents were supposed to note damaged bags at check-in, but seldom did; as a result, passengers who knew the ropes sometimes replaced worn-out luggage in that way.

Though the money was not her own, Tanya always hated parting with it when, in her opinion, the airline was being cheated.

Now, she turned her attention to helping round up stragglers for Flight Two, some of whom were still coming in. Fortunately, the bus with downtown check-ins had arrived several minutes earlier, and most of its passengers had by now been directed to Concourse "D," gate forty-seven. In a minute or two, Tanya decided, in case there were any last-minute passenger problems during boarding, she would go to gate forty-seven herself.

D. O. Guerrero heard the announcement of Flight Two while in line at the insurance counter in the terminal central concourse.

It was Guerrero, appearing hurried and nervous, whom Captain Vernon Demerest had seen arrive there, carrying his small attaché case which contained the dynamite bomb.

Guerrero had come directly from the bus to the insurance counter, where he was now fifth in line. Two people at the head of the line were being dealt with by a pair of girl clerks who were working with maddening slowness. One of the clerks—a heavy-chested blonde in a low-cut blouse—was having a prolonged conversation with her present customer, a middle-aged woman. The clerk was apparently suggesting that the woman take out a larger policy than had been asked for; the woman was being indecisive. Obviously, it would take at least twenty minutes for Guerrero to reach the head of the line, but by then Flight Two would probably be gone. Yet he *had* to buy insurance; he *had* to be aboard.

The p.a. announcement had said that the flight was being boarded at gate forty-seven. Guerrero should be at the gate *now*. He felt himself trembling. His hands were clammy on the attaché case handle. He checked his watch again, for the twentieth time, comparing it with the terminal clock. Six minutes had gone by since the announcement of Flight Two. The final call . . . the airplane doors closing . . . could come at any moment. He would have to do *something*.

D. O. Guerrero pushed his way roughly to the head of the line. He was past caring about being noticed, or offending. A man protested, "Hey, buddy, we're waiting too." Guerrero ignored him. He addressed the big-breasted blonde. "Please . . . my flight has been called —the one to Rome. I need insurance. I can't wait."

The man who had spoken before interjected, "Then go without. Another time, get here sooner."

Guerrero was tempted to retort: *There won't be an-*

other time. Instead, he addressed himself to the blonde again. "Please!"

To his surprise, she smiled warmly; he had been expecting a rebuff. "You did say Rome?"

"Yes, yes. The flight's been called."

"I know. She smiled again. "Trans America Flight Two. It is called *The Golden Argosy.*"

Despite his anxiety, he was aware that the girl had a sexy European accent, probably Hungarian.

D. O. Guerrero made an effort to speak normally. "That's right."

The girl turned her smile on the others who were waiting. "This gentleman really does not have much time. I'm sure you will not mind if I oblige him first."

So much had gone wrong tonight that he could scarcely believe his good luck. There was some muttered grumbling in the line of people waiting, but the man who had done the talking until now was silent.

The girl produced an insurance application form. She beamed at the woman she had been dealing with. "This will only take a moment." Then she turned her smile again on D. O. Guerrero.

For the first time he realized how effective the smile was, and why there had been no real protest from the others. When the girl looked at him directly, Guerrero —who was seldom affected by women—had the feeling he was going to melt. She also had the biggest tits he had ever seen.

"My name is Bunnie," the girl said in her European accent. "What is yours?" Her ballpoint pen was poised.

As a vendor of airport flight insurance, Bunnie Vorobioff was a remarkable success.

She had come to the United States, not from Hungary as D. O. Guerrero had supposed, but from Glauchau in the southern portion of East Germany, via the Berlin Wall. Bunnie (who was then Gretchen Vorobioff, the homely, flat-chested daughter of a minor Communist official and a Young Communist herself) crossed the wall at night with two male companions. The young men were caught by searchlights, shot and killed; their bodies hung for twenty-four hours on barbed wire, in public view. Bunnie avoided the searchlights and small arms fire and survived, survival being a quality which seemed to come to her naturally.

Later, on arrival as a U.S. immigrant at age twenty-one, she had embraced American free enterprise and its goodies with the enthusiasm of a religious convert. She worked hard as a hospital aide, in which she had some training, and moonlighted as a waitress. Into the remaining time she somehow crammed a Berlitz course in English, and also managed to get to bed—occasionally to sleep, more often with interns from the hospital. The interns repaid Gretchen's sexual favors by introducing her to silicone breast injections, which started casually and ended by being a joyous group experiment to see just how big her breasts would get. Fortunately, before they could become more than gargantuan, she exercised another new-found freedom by quitting her hospital job for one with more money. Somewhere along the way she was taken to Washington, D.C., and toured the White House, the Capitol, and the Playboy Club. After the last, Gretchen further Americanized herself by adopting the name Bunnie.

Now, a year and a half later, Bunnie Vorobioff was totally assimilated. She was in an Arthur Murray dancing class, the Blue Cross and Columbia Record Club, had a charge account at Carson Pirie Scott, subscribed to *Reader's Digest* and *TV Guide,* was buying the *World Book Encyclopedia* on time, owned a wig and a Volkswagen, collected trading stamps, and was on pills.

Bunnie also loved contests of all kinds, especially those which held a hope of tangible reward. Along these lines, a reason she enjoyed her present job more than any other she had had so far, was that periodically her insurance company employers held sales contests for its staff, with merchandise prizes. One such contest was in progress now. It would end tonight.

The contest was the reason why Bunnie had reacted so agreeably when D. O. Guerrero announced that he was on his way to Rome. At this moment Bunnie needed forty more points to win her objective in the present sales contest—an electric toothbrush. For a while tonight she had despaired of completing her total of points before the deadline, since insurance policies she had sold today were mostly for domestic flights; these produced lower premiums and earned fewer contest points. However, if a maximum size policy could be sold for an overseas flight, it would earn twenty-five contest points, bringing the remainder within easy reach. The question was: How big an insurance policy did this Rome passenger want and, assuming it was less than the maximum, could Bunnie Vorobioff sell him more?

Usually she could. Bunnie merely turned on her most sexy smile, which she had learned to use like an instant warming oven, leaned close to the customer so that her breasts bemused him, then announced how much more benefit could be had for an additional small sum of money. Most times the ploy worked and was the reason for Bunnie's success as an insurance saleswoman.

When D. O. Guerrero had spelled out his name, she asked, "What kind of policy were you considering, sir?"

Guerrero swallowed. "Straight life—seventy-five thousand dollars."

Now that he had said it, his mouth was dry. He had a sudden fear that his words had alerted everyone in the line-up; their eyes were boring into his back. His entire body was trembling; he was sure it would be noticed. To cover up, he lit a cigarette, but his hand was shaking so much that he had trouble bringing match and cigarette together. Fortunately, the girl, with her pen hovering over the entry "principal sum," appeared not to notice.

Bunnie pronounced, "That would cost two dollars and fifty cents."

"What? . . . Oh, yes." Guerrero managed to light the cigarette, then dropped the match. He reached into his pocket for some of the small amount of money he had remaining.

"But it is quite a tiny policy." Bunnie Vorobioff had still not marked in the principal sum. Now she leaned forward, bringing her breasts nearer to the customer. She could see him looking down at them with fascination; men always did. Some, she sensed at times, wanted to reach out and touch. Not this man, though.

"Tiny?" Guerrero's speech was awkward, halting. "I thought . . . it was the biggest."

Even to Bunnie, the man's nervousness was now apparent. She supposed it was because he would be flying soon. She directed a dazzling smile across the counter.

"Oh no, sir; you could buy a three hundred thousand dollar policy. Most people do, and for just ten dollars premium. Really, it isn't much to pay for all that protection, is it?" She kept her smile switched on; the response could mean a difference of nearly twenty contest points; it might gain or lose her the electric toothbrush.

"You said . . . ten dollars?"

"That's right—for three hundred thousand dollars."

D. O. Guerrero thought: *He hadn't known.* All along, he had believed that seventy-five thousand dollars was the top limit for airport-purchase insurance for an overseas flight. He had obtained the information from an insurance application blank which, a month or two ago, he had picked up at another airport. Now he remembered—the earlier blank came from an automatic vending machine. It had not occurred to him that over-the-counter policies could be that much greater.

Three hundred thousand dollars!

"Yes," he said eagerly. "Please . . . yes."

Bunnie beamed. "The full amount, Mr. Guerrero?"

He was about to nod assent when the supreme irony occurred to him. He probably did not possess ten dollars. He told Bunnie, "Miss . . . wait!" and began searching his pockets, pulling out whatever money he could find.

The people in line behind were becoming restive. The man who had objected to Guerrero to begin with, protested to Bunnie, "You said he'd just take a minute!"

Guerrero had found four dollars and seventy cents.

Two nights ago, when D. O. Guerrero and Inez had pooled their last remaining money, D.O. had taken eight dollars, plus small change, for himself. After pawning Inez's ring and making the down payment on the Trans America ticket, there had been a few dollars

left; he wasn't sure how many, but since then he had
paid for meals, subway fares, the airport bus . . . He had
known that he would need two and a half dollars for
flight insurance, and had kept it carefully in a separate
pocket. But beyond that he hadn't bothered, aware that
once aboard Flight Two, money would be of no further
use.

"If you don't have cash," Bunnie Vorobioff said,
"you can give me a check."

"I left my checkbook home." It was a lie; there were
checks in his pocket. But if he wrote a check, it would
bounce and invalidate the insurance.

Bunnie persisted, "How about your Italian money,
Mr. Guerrero? I can take lire and give you the proper
rate."

He muttered, "I don't have Italian money," then
cursed himself for having said it. *Downtown he had
checked in without baggage for a flight to Rome. Now,
insanely, he had demonstrated before onlookers that he
had no money, either American or Italian.* Who would
board an overseas flight unequipped and penniless,
except someone who knew the flight would never reach
its destination?

Then D. O. Guerrero reminded himself . . . except in
his own mind . . . the two incidents—downtown and
here—were unconnected. They would not be connected
until afterward, and by then it wouldn't matter.

He reasoned, as he had on the way out: It was not
the strength of suspicion which was important. The
crucial factor would still be the absence of wreckage, the
absence of proof.

Surprisingly, despite his latest gaffe, he discovered he
was growing more confident.

He added some dimes and pennies to the pile of
change on the insurance counter. Then, miraculously, in
an inside pocket, he found a five-dollar bill.

Not concealing his excitement, Guerrero exclaimed,
"That's it! I have enough!" There was even a dollar or
so in small change left over.

But even Bunnie Vorobioff was doubtful now. Instead of writing the three hundred thousand dollar policy which the man was waiting for, she hesitated.

While he had searched his pockets, she had been watching the customer's face.

It was strange, of course, that this man was going overseas without money, but, after all, that was his own business; there could be plenty of reasons for it. What really bothered her was his eyes; they held a hint of frenzy, desperation. Both were qualities which Bunnie Vorobioff recognized from her past. She had seen them in others. At moments—though it seemed long ago— she had been close to them herself.

Bunnie's insurance company employers had a standing instruction: If a purchaser of flight insurance seemed irrational, unusually excited, or was drunk, the fact was to be reported to the airline on which he was traveling. The question for Bunnie was: Was this an occasion to invoke the rule?

She wasn't sure.

The company standing instruction was sometimes discussed, among themselves, by flight insurance sales clerks. Some of the girls resented or ignored it, arguing that they were hired to sell insurance, not to act as unpaid, unqualified psychologists. Others pointed out that many people who bought flight insurance at an airport were nervous to begin with; how could anyone, without special training, decide where nervousness ended and irrationality began? Bunnie herself had never reported a keyed-up passenger, though she knew a girl who had, and the passenger turned out to be an airline vice president, excited because his wife was going to have a baby. There had been all kinds of trouble over *that*.

Still Bunnie hesitated. She had covered her hesitation by counting the man's money on the counter. Now she wondered if Marj, the other clerk working beside her, had noticed anything unusual. Apparently not. Marj was busy writing a policy, earning *her* contest points.

In the end, it was Bunnie Vorobioff's past which swayed her decision. Her formative years . . . occupied Europe, her flight to the West, the Berlin Wall . . . had taught her survival, and conditioned her to something else: to curb curiosity, and not to ask unnecessary questions. Questions had a way of leading to involvement, and involvement—in other people's problems—was something to be avoided when one had problems of one's own.

Without further questioning, at the same time solving her problem of how to win an electric toothbrush, Bunnie Vorobioff wrote a flight insurance policy, for three hundred thousand dollars, on D. O. Guerrero's life.

Guerrero mailed the policy to his wife, Inez, on his way to gate forty-seven and Flight Two.

13

U. S. Customs Inspector Harry Standish did not hear the announcement of Flight Two's impending departure, but knew it had been made. Flight announcements were not relayed to the Customs Hall, since only international arriving passengers came there, so Standish obtained his information on the telephone, from Trans America Airlines. He had been informed that Flight Two was beginning to load at gate forty-seven and would depart at its rescheduled time of 11 P.M.

Standish was watching the clock and would go to gate forty-seven in a few minutes, not on official business, but to say goodbye to his niece, Judy—his sister's child —who was leaving for a year's schooling in Europe. Standish had promised his sister, who lived in Denver, that he would see Judy off. Earlier this evening, in the terminal, he had spent some time with his niece—a pleasant, self-possessed girl of eighteen—and had said he would drop around for a final goodbye before her flight took off.

Meanwhile, Inspector Standish was trying to clear up a tiresome problem near the end of what had been an exceptionally harassing day.

"Madam," he said quietly to the haughty, angular woman whose several suitcases were spread open on the Customs inspection table between them, "are you quite sure you don't wish to change your story?"

She snapped back, "I suppose you're suggesting I should lie, when I've already told you the truth. Really! —you people are so officious, so disbelieving, I sometimes wonder if we're not living in a police state."

Harry Standish ignored the second remark, as Customs officers were trained to ignore the many insults they received; and answered politely, "I'm not suggesting anything, madam. I merely asked if you wished to amend your statement about these items—the dresses, the sweaters, and the fur coat."

The woman, whose American passport showed that she was Mrs. Harriet Du Barry Mossman who lived in Evanston, and had just returned from a month in England, France, and Denmark, replied acidly, "No, I don't. Furthermore, when my husband's lawyer hears of this interrogation . . ."

"Yes madam," Harry Standish said. "In that case, I wonder if you'd mind signing this form. If you like, I'll explain it to you."

The dresses, sweaters, and fur coat were spread out on top of the suitcases. Mrs. Mossman had been wearing the coat—a sable jacket—until a few minutes ago when Inspector Standish arrived at Customs inspection station number eleven; he had asked her to take the coat off so that he could look at it more closely. Shortly before that, a red light on a wall panel near the center of the big Customs Hall had summoned Standish. The lights—one for each station—indicated that an inspecting officer had a problem and needed supervisory help.

Now, the young Customs man who had dealt with Mrs. Mossman originally was standing at Inspector Standish's side. Most of the other passengers, who had arrived aboard a Scandinavian Airlines DC-8 from

Copenhagen, had cleared Customs and had left. Only this well-dressed American woman posed a problem, insisting that all she had bought in Europe was some perfume, costume jewelry, and shoes. The total declared value was ninety dollars—ten dollars less than the free exemption she was allowed. The young officer had been suspicious.

"Why should I sign anything?" Mrs. Harriet Du Barry Mossman demanded.

Standish glanced at an overhead clock; it was a quarter to eleven. He still had time to finish this and reach Flight Two before it left. He answered patiently, "To make things easier for yourself, madam. We're merely asking you to confirm in writing what you've already told us. You say the dresses were purchased. . ."

"How many times must I tell you? They were bought in Chicago and New York before I left for Europe; so were the sweaters. The coat was a gift—purchased in the United States. I received it six months ago."

Why, Harry Standish wondered, did people do it? All the statements just made, he knew with certainty, were lies.

To begin with, the dresses—six, all of good quality—had had their labels removed. No one did that innocently; women were usually proud of the labels in quality clothes. More to the point—the workmanship of the dresses was unmistakably French; so was the styling of the fur coat—though a Saks Fifth Avenue label had been sewn unskillfully in the coat lining. What people like Mrs. Mossman failed to realize was that a trained Customs man didn't need to see labels to know where garments originated. Cutting, stitching—even the way a zipper was put in—were like familiar handwriting, and equally distinctive.

The same thing was true of the three expensive sweaters. They also were without labels, and were unmistakably from Scotland, in typical British "drab" shades, not available in the United States. When a U.S. store ordered similar sweaters, the Scottish mills made them in much brighter colors, which the North American market favored. All this, and much else, Customs officers learned as part of their training.

Mrs. Mossman asked, "What happens if I sign the form?"

"Then you may go, madam."

"And take my things with me? All my things?"

"Yes."

"Supposing I refuse to sign?"

"Then we shall be obliged to detain you here while we continue the investigation."

There was the briefest hesitation, then: "Very well. You fill out the form; I'll sign."

"No, madam; *you* fill it out. Now here, please describe the items, and alongside where you say they were obtained. Please give the name of the stores; also from whom you received the fur coat as a gift . . ."

Harry Standish thought: He would have to leave in a minute; it was ten to eleven now. He didn't want to reach Flight Two after the doors were closed. But first he had a hunch . . .

He waited while Mrs. Mossman completed the form and signed it.

Commencing tomorrow, an investigative officer would begin checking out the statement Mrs. Mossman had just made. The dresses and sweaters would be requisitioned and taken to the stores where she claimed they were purchased; the fur jacket would be shown to Saks Fifth Avenue, who would undoubtedly disown it . . . Mrs. Mossman—though she didn't know it yet—was in for a great deal of trouble, including some heavy Customs duty to be paid, and almost certainly a stiff fine.

"Madam," Inspector Standish said, "is there anything else you wish to declare?"

Mrs. Mossman snapped indignantly, "There certainly isn't!"

"You're sure?" It was Customs Bureau policy to give travelers the utmost opportunity to make voluntary declarations. People were not to be entrapped unless they brought it on themselves.

Not deigning to reply, Mrs. Mossman inclined her head disdainfully.

"In that case, madam," Inspector Standish said, "will you kindly open your handbag?"

For the first time the haughty woman betrayed uncertainty. "But surely, purses are never inspected. I've been through Customs many times . . ."

"Normally they are not. But we do have the right."

Asking to see the contents of a woman's handbag was a rarity; like a man's pockets, a handbag was considered personal and almost never looked into. But when an individual chose to be difficult, Customs men could be difficult too.

Reluctantly, Mrs. Harriet Du Barry Mossman unclipped her purse.

Harry Standish inspected a lipstick and a gold compact. When he probed the powder in the compact, he extracted a diamond and ruby ring: he blew the powder on the ring away. There was a tube of hand lotion, partially used. Unrolling the tube, he could see that the bottom had been opened. When he pressed the tube near the top, there was something hard inside. He wondered when would-be smugglers would come up with something original. Such old tricks! He had seen them all many times.

Mrs. Mossman was noticeably pale. Her hauteur had disappeared.

"Madam," Inspector Standish said, "I have to leave for a short while, but I'll be back. In any case, this is going to take some time." He instructed the young Customs officer beside him, "Inspect everything else very carefully. Check the linings of the bag and cases, the seams and hems of all the clothes. Make a list. You know what to do."

He was leaving when Mrs. Mossman called after him. "Officer!"

He stopped. "Yes, madam."

"About the coat and dresses . . . perhaps I did make a mistake . . . I was confused. I did buy them, and there are some other things . . ."

Standish shook his head. What people never seemed to learn was that there had to be a cut-off point somewhere; after that, cooperation was too late. He saw that the young officer had found something else.

"Please! . . . I beg of you . . . my husband . . ." As

the Inspector turned away, the woman's face was white and drawn.

Walking briskly, Harry Standish used a short cut, below the public portion of the terminal, to reach Concourse "D" and gate forty-seven. As he went, he reflected on the foolishness of Mrs. Harriet Du Barry Mossman and the many like her. Had she been honest about the coat and dresses, and declared them, the duty payable would not have been great, especially for someone who was clearly well-to-do. The young Customs officer, though noticing the sweaters, probably would not have bothered with them; and certainly her handbag would not have been inspected. Customs men were aware that most returning travelers did a little smuggling, and were often tolerant about it. Also, if asked, they would help people lump high-duty items under their duty-free exemption, charging duty on other articles which were entitled to lower rates.

The people who got nabbed, hit hard, and were sometimes prosecuted, were invariably the greedy ones like Mrs. Mossman, who tried to get away with everything. What had depressed Harry Standish today was the number of others of her kind.

He was relieved to see that the doors of Trans America Flight Two had not yet closed, and a few remaining passengers were still being checked in. His U.S. Customs uniform was a passport anywhere within the airport, and the busy gate agent barely glanced up as Inspector Standish went past. The gate agent, Standish noticed, was being helped by a red-headed woman passenger relations agent whom he knew as Mrs. Livingston.

The inspector entered the walkway to the tourist section; a stewardess was at the rear airplane doorway. He smiled. "I'll only be a moment. Don't take off with me aboard."

He found his niece, Judy, in an aisle seat of a three-seat section. She was keeping a baby amused, the baby belonging to a young couple in the two seats alongside. Like all airplane tourist sections, this one already seemed cramped and crowded, the seats oppressively close to one another. On the few air journeys Inspector Standish made himself, he traveled tourist, but always had a sense of claustrophobia. Tonight he didn't envy any of these people the monotonous ten-hour journey which lay ahead of them.

"Uncle Harry!" Judy said. "I thought you weren't going to make it." She handed the baby back to its mother.

"I just came to say God bless!" he told her. "Have a good year, and when you come back don't try any smuggling."

She laughed. "I won't. Goodbye, Uncle Harry."

His niece put her face up to be kissed, and he bussed her affectionately. He felt good about Judy. He had a feeling she would not grow up to be a Mrs. Mossman.

Leaving the aircraft, with a friendly nod to the stewardesses, the Customs inspector paused a moment at the concourse gate, watching. The last moments before departure of any flight, especially one for some far distant place, always fascinated him, as it did many people. The final call . . . *"Trans America Airlines announce the immediate departure of Flight Two, The Golden Argosy . . ."* . . . was just coming over the p.a. system.

The knot of people waiting to board had been reduced to two. The redheaded passenger agent, Mrs. Livingston, was gathering up her papers as the regular gate agent dealt with the last arrival but one—a tall blond man, hatless, and wearing a camel-hair coat. Now, the blond man left the agent's desk and entered the tourist section walkway. Mrs. Livingston left too, walking away from the departure gate, toward the main section of the terminal.

While he had been watching, Inspector Standish was aware, almost subconsciously, of someone else nearby, facing a window which looked away from the departure gate. Now the figure turned. He saw that it was an old lady; she appeared small, demure, and frail. She was dressed primly in black in an old-fashioned style, and carried a black beaded purse. She looked as if she needed somebody to take care of her, and he wondered why someone so old, and apparently alone, was here so late at night.

Moving with surprising spryness, the old lady crossed to where the Trans America ticket agent was dealing with the last Flight Two passenger. Standish heard some, though not all, of what was said; the old lady's words were punctuated by noise from outside, from the aircraft engines, which were being started. "Excuse . . . my son just boarded . . . blond hair, no hat, camel-hair coat . . . forgot his wallet . . . all his money." The old lady, Standish observed, was holding what looked like a man's billfold.

The gate agent glanced up impatiently. He appeared harassed; gate men usually were at the last moments of departure. The agent put out his hand to take the wallet, then, observing the old lady, changed his mind and said something quickly. He pointed to the tourist boarding walkway and Standish heard, "Ask a stewardess." The old lady smiled and nodded, and entered the walkway. A moment later she was out of sight.

All that Customs Inspector Standish had observed had taken only moments—perhaps less than a minute. Now, he saw a newcomer arrive—a stoop-shouldered, spindly man, hurrying down Concourse "D" toward gate forty-seven. The man had a gaunt face and a slight sandy mustache. He was carrying a small attaché case.

Standish had been about to turn away, but something about the man attracted his attention. It was the way the newcomer was holding his case—under his arm, protectively. Harry Standish had watched people, many times, doing the same thing as they came through Customs. It was a giveaway that whatever was inside the case was something they wanted to conceal. If this man had been coming in from overseas, Standish would have had him open the case, and would have examined its contents. But the man was going *out* of the United States.

Strictly speaking, it was none of Harry Standish's business.

Yet something . . . instinct, a sixth sense which Customs men developed, plus a personal connection, through Judy, with Flight Two . . . something kept the inspector watching, his eyes directed at the small attaché case which the spindly man still cradled.

The feeling of confidence which returned to D. O. Guerrero at the insurance counter had remained. As he approached gate forty-seven, observing that he was still in time for Flight Two, he had a conviction that most of his difficulties were over; from now on, he assured himself, everything would work out as he had foreseen. In keeping with this belief, there was no problem at the gate. As he had planned from the beginning, at this point he drew attention to the minor discrepancy between the name "Buerrero" on his ticket and "Guerrero" on his passport. Barely glancing at the passport, the gate agent corrected both the ticket and his passenger list, then apologized, "Sorry, sir; sometimes our reservation machines get careless." Now, Guerrero noted with satisfaction, his name was recorded properly; later, when Flight Two was reported missing, there would be no doubt about his own identification.

"Have a pleasant flight, sir." The gate agent returned his ticket folder and motioned toward the tourist section walkway.

As D. O. Guerrero went aboard, still holding his attaché case carefully, the starboard engines were already running.

His numbered seat—by a window in a three-seat section—had been allocated when he checked in downtown. A stewardess directed him to it. Another male passenger, already in the aisle seat, stood up partially as Guerrero squeezed by. The center seat, between them, was unoccupied.

D. O. Guerrero balanced his case cautiously on his knees as he strapped himself in. His seat was midway in the tourist section, on the left side. Elsewhere in the cabin, other passengers were still settling down, arranging hand baggage and clothing; a few people were blocking the center aisle. One of the stewardesses, her lips moving silently, and looking as if she wished everyone would keep still, was making a count of heads.

Relaxing for the first time since leaving the South

Side apartment, D. O. Guerrero leaned back in his seat and closed his eyes. His hands, steadier than at any other time this evening, were firmly on the attaché case. Without opening his eyes, his fingers groped under the handle and located the all-important loop of string. The feel of it was reassuring. He would sit precisely like this, he decided, when in approximately four hours from now he would pull the string, releasing the electrical current which would fire the massive charge of dynamite within the case. When the moment came, he wondered, how much would he have time to know? In answer, he reasoned: there would be an instant . . . one fleeting particle of a second only . . . when he would savor, triumphantly, the knowledge of success. Then, mercifully, no more . . .

Now that he was aboard and ready, he wished the flight would go. But when he opened his eyes, the same stewardess was still counting.

There were two stewardesses, at the moment, in the tourist cabin. The little old lady from San Diego, Mrs. Ada Quonsett, had been observing them both, intermittently, peering through the slightly opened door of a toilet where she was hiding.

The pre-takeoff head count by a stewardess, now being made, was something which Mrs. Quonsett knew about; she was also aware that this was the moment when anyone who was aboard illegally was closest to exposure. But if a stowaway could survive the count, chances were that she (or he) would not be detected until much later, if at all.

Fortunately, the stewardess now making the head count was not the one whom Mrs. Quonsett encountered when she came aboard.

Mrs. Quonsett had had a few anxious moments outside while she cautiously watched the redheaded passenger agent bitch, whom she had been distressed to find on duty at gate forty-seven. Fortunately, the woman had left just before the flight finished loading, and getting past the male gate agent proved easy.

After that, Mrs. Quonsett repeated her story about

the wallet to the stewardess on duty at the aircraft doorway. The stewardess, who was trying to cope with queries from several other people milling in the entranceway, declined to accept the wallet when she learned there was "a lot of money in it"—a reaction Mrs. Quonsett had counted on. Also as expected, the little old lady was told she could take the wallet to her son herself, if she was quick.

The tall blond man who, all unknowingly, had been a "son" to Mrs. Quonsett, was getting into a seat near the front of the cabin. Mrs. Quonsett moved in his direction, but only briefly. She was watching covertly, waiting for the attention of the stewardess near the door to be diverted. Almost at once it was.

Mrs. Quonsett had left her plans flexible. There was a seat close by, which she could have occupied; however, a sudden movement by several passengers at once left a clear path to one of the aircraft toilets. A moment or two later, through the partially opened toilet door, she saw the original stewardess go forward out of sight and another stewardess begin the head count, starting at the front.

When the second stewardess—still counting—neared the back of the airplane, Mrs. Quonsett emerged from the toilet and walked quickly past with a muttered, "Excuse me." She heard the stewardess cluck her tongue impatiently. Mrs. Quonsett sensed that she had now been included in the count—but that was all.

A few rows forward, on the left side, there was an unoccupied seat in the middle of a section of three. In her experience as an aerial stowaway, the little old lady from San Diego had learned to seek such seats because most passengers disliked them; therefore they were the last to be chosen from seat selection boards and, where an airplane was less than full, were usually left empty.

Once in the seat, Mrs. Quonsett kept her head down, trying to be as inconspicuous as possible. She had no illusion that she could avoid discovery indefinitely. At Rome there would be Immigration and Customs formalities, making it impossible for her to walk away unimpeded, as she was accustomed to doing after her illegal flights to New York; but, with luck, she would have the thrill of reaching Italy, plus an agreeable journey back. Meanwhile, on this flight, there would be a good meal, a movie, and, later, perhaps, a pleasant conversation with her two seat companions.

Ada Quonsett wondered about her seat companions. She had noticed that both were men, but for the time being avoided looking at the man on her right since it would mean turning her face toward the aisle and the stewardesses, both of whom were now moving back and forth, making another head count. Mrs. Quonsett took covert stock, however, of the man on her left, a survey made easier by the fact that he was reclining and had his eyes closed. He was a gaunt, thin man, she observed, with a sallow face and scrawny neck, who looked as if a hearty meal might do him good. He had a small sandy mustache.

On his knees, Mrs. Quonsett noticed, the man on her left had an attaché case and, despite the fact that his eyes were closed, he was holding it firmly.

The stewardesses had finished their head count. Now a third stewardess appeared from the first class compartment forward, and the three of them were holding a hurried consultation.

The man on Mrs. Quonsett's left had opened his eyes. He was still gripping the case tightly. The little old lady from San Diego—an habitually curious soul—wondered what was inside.

Walking back toward the Customs Hall—this time through the passenger section of the terminal—Inspector Harry Standish was still thinking about the man with the attaché case. Standish could not have questioned the man; outside a Customs enclosure a Customs officer had no right to interrogate anyone, unless believing they had evaded Customs inspection. The man at the departure gate quite obviously had not.

What Standish could do, of course, was telegraph the man's description to Italian Customs, advising that he might be carrying contraband. But Standish doubted if he would. There was little cooperation between Customs

departments internationally, only an intense professional
rivalry. Even with Canadian Customs, close at hand, the
same thing was true; incidents were on record where
U.S. Customs had been tipped of that illegal diamond
shipments were being smuggled into Canada, but—as a
matter of policy—Canadian authorities were never told.
Instead, U.S. agents spotted the suspects on arrival in
Canada and tailed them, only making an arrest if they
crossed the United States border. The U.S. reasoning
was: the country which seized that kind of contraband
kept it all, and Customs departments were averse to
sharing loot.

No, Inspector Standish decided, there would be no
telegram to Italy. He would, however, tell Trans America Airlines of his doubts and leave a decision to them.

Ahead of him he had seen Mrs. Livingston, the passenger relations agent who had been at the Flight Two
departure gate. She was talking with a Skycap and a
group of passengers. Harry Standish waited until the
Skycap and passengers had gone.

"Hullo, Mr. Standish," Tanya said. "I hope things are
quieter in Customs than around here."

"They aren't," he told her, remembering Mrs. Harriet
Du Barry Mossman, no doubt still being questioned in
the Customs Hall.

As Tanya waited for him to speak again, Standish
hesitated. Sometimes he wondered if he was becoming
too much the super sleuth, too aware of the keenness of
his instincts. Most times, though, his instincts proved
right.

"I was watching your Flight Two load," Standish
said. "There was something bothered me." He described
the gaunt, spindly man and the suspicious way he had
been clasping an attaché case.

"Do you think he's smuggling something?"

Inspector Standish smiled. "If he were arriving from
abroad, instead of leaving, I'd find out. All I can tell
you, Mrs. Livingston, is that there's something in that
case which he'd prefer other people not to know about."

Tanya said thoughtfully, "I don't quite know what I

can do." Even if the man *was* smuggling she was not convinced it was the airline's business.

"Probably there's nothing to do. But you people cooperate with us, so I thought I'd pass the information on."

"Thank you, Mr. Standish. I'll report it to our D.T.M., and perhaps he'll want to notify the captain."

As the Customs inspector left, Tanya glanced at the overhead terminal clock; it showed a minute to eleven. Heading for Trans America Administration on the executive mezzanine, she reasoned: it was too late now to catch Flight Two at the departure gate; if the flight had not yet left the gate, it certainly would within the next few moments. She wondered if the District Transportation Manager was in his office. If the D.T.M. thought the information important, he might notify Captain Demerest by radio while Flight Two was still on the ground and taxiing. Tanya hurried.

The D.T.M. was not in his office, but Peter Coakley was.

Tanya snapped, "What are you doing here?"

The young Trans America agent, whom the little old lady from San Diego had eluded, described sheepishly what had happened.

Peter Coakley had already received one dressing down. The doctor, summoned to the women's washroom on a fool's errand, had been articulate and wrathful. Young Coakley clearly expected more of the same from Mrs. Livingston. He was not disappointed.

Tanya exploded, "Damn, damn, damn!" She remonstrated, "Didn't I warn you she had a barrelful of tricks?"

"Yes, you did, Mrs. Livingston. I guess I . . ."

"Never mind that now! Get on the phone to each of our gates. Warn them to be on the lookout for an old, innocent-looking woman in black—you know the description. She's trying for New York, but may go a roundabout way. If she's located, the gate agent is to detain her and call here. She is not to be allowed on any flight, no matter what she says. While you're doing that, I'll call the other airlines."

"Yes, ma'am."

There were several telephones in the office. Peter Coakley took one, Tanya another.

She knew by memory the airport numbers of TWA, American, United, and Northwest; all four airlines had direct New York flights. Talking first with her opposite number in TWA, Jenny Henline, she could hear Peter Coakley saying, "Yes, very old . . . in black . . . when you see her, you won't believe it . . ."

A contest of minds had developed, Tanya realized, between herself and the ingenious, slippery Ada Quonsett. Who, in the end, Tanya wondered, would outwit the other?

For the moment she had forgotten both her conversation with Customs Inspector Standish and her intention to locate the D.T.M.

Aboard Flight Two, Captain Vernon Demerest fumed, "What in hell's the holdup?"

Engines numbers three and four, on the starboard side of aircraft N-731-TA, were running. Throughout the airplane their subdued but powerful jet thrumming could be felt.

The pilots had received ramp supervisor's clearance by interphone, several minutes ago, to start three and four, but were still awaiting clearance to start engines one and two, which were on the boarding side and normally not activated until all doors were closed. A red panel light had winked off a minute or two earlier, indicating that the rear fuselage door was closed and secure; immediately after, the rear boarding walkway was withdrawn. But another bright red light, still glowing, showed that the forward cabin door had not been closed, and a glance backward through the cockpit windows confirmed that the front boarding walkway was still in place.

Swinging around in his right-hand seat, Captain Demerest instructed Second Officer Jordan, "Open the door."

Cy Jordan was seated behind the other two pilots at a complex panel of instruments and engine controls. Now he half rose and, extending his long, lean figure, released the flight deck door which opened outward. Through the doorway, in the forward passenger section, they could see a half dozen figures in Trans America uniform, Gwen Meighen among them.

"Gwen!" Demerest called. As she came into the flight deck, "What the devil's happening?"

Gwen looked worried. "The tourist passenger count won't tally. We've made it twice; we still can't agree with the manifest and tickets."

"Is the ramp supervisor there?"

"Yes, he's checking our count now."

"I want to see him."

At this stage of any airline flight there was always a problem of divided authority. Nominally the captain was already in command, but he could neither start engines nor taxi away without authorization from the ramp supervisor. Both the captain and ramp chief had the same objective—to make an on-schedule departure. However, their differing duties sometimes produced a clash.

A moment later, the uniformed ramp supervisor, a single silver stripe denoting his rank, arrived on the flight deck.

"Look, chum," Demerest said, "I know you've got problems, but so have we. How much longer do we sit here?"

"I've just ordered a ticket recheck, captain. There's one more passenger in the tourist section than there ought to be."

"All right," Demerest said. "Now I'll tell *you* something. Every second we sit here we're burning fuel on three and four, *which you gave the okay to start* . . . precious fuel which we need in the air tonight. So unless this airplane leaves right now, I'm shutting everything down and we'll send for Fueling to top off our tanks. There's another thing you ought to know: air traffic control just told us they have a temporary gap in traffic. If we taxi out right away, we can be off the ground fast; in ten minutes from now that may have changed. Now, you make the decision. What's it to be?"

Torn between dual responsibilities, the ramp supervisor hesitated. He knew the captain was right about burning fuel; yet to stop engines now, and top off tanks, would mean a further half hour's costly delay on top of the hour which Flight Two was late already. On the other hand, this was an important international flight on which the head count and ticket collection *ought* to agree. If there was really an unauthorized person aboard, and he was found and taken off, later the ramp supervisor could justify his decision to hold. But if the difference in tallies turned out to be a clerical error—as it might—the D.T.M. would roast him alive.

He made the obvious decision. Calling through the flight deck door, he ordered, "Cancel the ticket recheck. This flight is leaving now."

As the flight deck door closed, a grinning Anson Harris was on the interphone to a crewman on the ground below. "Clear to start two?"

The reply rattled back, "Okay to start two."

The forward fuselage door was closed and secured; in the cockpit, its red indicator light winked out.

Number two engine fired and held at a steady roar.

"Okay to start one?"

"Okay to start one."

The forward boarding walkway, like a severed umbilical cord, was gliding back toward the terminal.

Vernon Demerest was calling ground control on radio for permission to taxi.

Number one engine fired and held.

In the left seat, Captain Harris, who would taxi out and fly the takeoff, had his feet braced on the rudder pedal toe brakes.

It was still snowing hard.

"Trans America Flight Two from ground control. You are clear to taxi . . ."

The engine tempo quickened.

Demerest thought: *Rome . . . and Naples . . . here we come!*

It was 11 P.M., Central Standard Time.

In Concourse "D," half running, half stumbling, a figure reached gate forty-seven.

Even if there had been breath to ask, questions were unneeded.

The boarding ramps were closed. Portable signs denoting the departure of Flight Two, *The Golden Argosy,* were being taken down. A taxiing aircraft was leaving the gate.

Helplessly, not knowing what she should do next, Inez Guerrero watched the airplane's lights recede.

PART THREE

11 P.M.–1:30 A.M. (CST)

1

As always at the beginning of a flight, Senior Stewardess Gwen Meighen experienced a sense of relief as the forward cabin door slammed closed and, a few moments later, the aircraft began moving.

An airliner in a terminal was like a dependent relative, subject to the whims and succor of its family. Such life as it had was never independent. Its identity was blurred; supply lines hobbled it; strangers, who would never join its airborne complement, moved in and out.

But when doors were sealed as the airplane prepared for takeoff, it became once more an entity. Crew members were most keenly aware of the change; they were returned to a familiar, self-contained environment in which they could function with skill and independence for which they had been trained. No one impeded them; nothing was underfoot, except what they were used to and at home with. Their tools and equipment were the finest; their resources and limitations were inventoried and known. Self-reliance returned. The camaraderie of the air—intangible, yet real to all who shared it—was theirs once more.

Even passengers—the more sensitive ones—were attuned to a mental transformation and, once in the air, awareness of the change increased. At high altitude, looking down, concerns of the everyday world seemed less important. Some, more analytical than others, saw the new perspective as a shedding of the pettiness of earth.

Gwen Meighen, occupied with pre-takeoff rituals, had
no time for such analysis. While four of the five stewardesses busied themselves with housekeeping chores
around the airplane, Gwen used the p.a. system to
welcome passengers aboard. With her soft English
voice, she did the best she could with the treacly, insin-
cere paragraph from her stewardess manual, which the
company insisted must be read on every flight.

*"On behalf of Captain Demerest and your crew . . .
our most sincere wish that your flight will be pleasant
and relaxing . . . shortly we shall have the pleasure of
serving . . . if there is anything we can do to make your
flight more enjoyable . . ."*

Gwen wondered sometimes when airlines would
realize that most passengers found such announcements,
at the beginning and end of every flight, a boring intrusion.

More essential were the announcements about emergency exits, oxygen masks, and ditching. With two of
the other stewardesses demonstrating, she accomplished
them quickly.

They were still taxiing, Gwen observed—tonight
more slowly than usual, taking longer to reach their
takeoff runway. No doubt the reason was traffic and the
storm. From outside she could hear an occasional
splatter of wind-driven snow on windows and fuselage.

There was one more announcement to be made—that
which aircrews liked least. It was required before
takeoffs at Lincoln International, New York, Boston,
Cleveland, San Francisco, and other airports with residential areas nearby.

*"Shortly after takeoff you will notice a marked de-
crease in engine noise, due to a reduction in power. This
is perfectly normal and is done as a courtesy to those
who live near the airport and in the direct flight path."*

The second statement was a lie. The power reduction
was neither normal nor desirable. The truth was: it was
a concession—some said a mere public relations gesture
—involving risk to aircraft safety and human life. Pilots
fought noise abatement power restrictions bitterly.
Many pilots, at risk of their careers, refused to observe
them.

Gwen had heard Vernon Demerest parody, in private, the announcement she had just made . . . "Ladies and gentlemen, at the most critical point of takeoff, when we need our best power and have a hundred other things to do in the cockpit, we are about to throttle back drastically, then make a steep climbing turn at high gross weight and minimum speed. This is an exceedingly foolish maneuver for which a student pilot would be thrown out of flying school. However, we are doing it on orders from our airline employers and the Federal Aviation Administration because a few people down below, who built their houses long after the airport was established, are insisting that we tiptoe past. They don't give a damn about air safety, or that we are risking your lives and ours. So hang on tight, folks! Good luck to us all, and please start praying."

Gwen smiled, remembering. There were so many things she appreciated about Vernon. He was energetically alive; he possessed strong feelings; when something interested him, he became actively involved. Even his failings—the abrasive manner, his conceit—were masculine and interesting. He could be tender, too—and was, in lovemaking, though responding eagerly to passion as Gwen had cause to know. Of all the men she knew, there was no one whose child she would bear more gladly than Vernon Demerest's. In the thought there was a bitter sweetness.

Replacing the p.a. microphone in its forward cabin niche, she was aware that the aircraft's taxiing pace had slowed; they must be near the takeoff point. These were the last few minutes she would have—for several hours to come—with any opportunity for private thoughts. After takeoff there would be no time for anything but work. Gwen had four stewardesses to supervise, as well as her own duties in the first class cabin. A good many overseas flights had male stewards directing cabin service, but Trans America encouraged senior women staffers like Gwen to take charge when they proved themselves capable.

Now the aircraft had stopped. From a window Gwen could see the lights of another aircraft ahead, several others in line behind. The one ahead was turning onto a runway; Flight Two would be next. Gwen pulled down a folding seat and strapped herself in. The other girls had found seats elsewhere.

She thought again: a bitter sweetness, and always the same single question recurring. Vernon's child, and her own—an abortion or not? . . . Yes or no? To be or not to be? . . . *They were on the runway* . . . Abortion or no abortion? . . . *The engines' tempo was increasing. They were rolling already, wasting no time; in seconds, no more, they would be in the air* . . . Yes or no? To permit to live or condemn to die? How, between love and reality, conscience and commonsense, did anyone decide?

As it happened, Gwen Meighen need not have made the announcement about power reduction.

On the flight deck, taxiing out, Captain Harris told Demerest gruffly, "I plan to ignore noise abatement procedures tonight."

Vernon Demerest, who had just copied their complicated route clearance, received by radio—a task normally performed by the absent First Officer—nodded. "Damn right! I would too."

Most pilots would have let it go at that, but, characteristically, Demerest pulled the flight log toward him and made an entry in the "Remarks" column: "N.A.P. not observed. Reason: weather, safety."

Later, there might be trouble about that log entry, but it was the kind of trouble Demerest enjoyed and would meet head on.

The cockpit lights were dimmed. Pre-takeoff checks had been completed.

They had been lucky in the temporary traffic lull; it had allowed them to reach their takeoff point, at the head of runway two five, quickly, and without the long ground hiatus which had plagued most other flights tonight. Already though, for others following, the delay was building up again. Behind Trans America Flight Two was a growing line of waiting aircraft and a procession of others taxiing out from the terminal. On radio, the ATC ground controller was issuing a swift stream of instructions to flights of United Air Lines, Eastern, American, Air France, Flying Tiger, Lufthansa, Braniff, Continental, Lake Central, Delta, TWA, Ozark, Air Canada, Alitalia, and Pan Am, their assorted destinations like an index of world geography.

Flight Two's additional fuel reserves, ordered by Anson Harris to allow for extra ground running time, had not, after all, been needed. But even with the heavy fuel load, they were still within safe takeoff limits, as Second Officer Jordan had just calculated, spreading out his graphs once more, as he would many times tonight and tomorrow before the flight ended.

Both Demerest's and Harris's radios were now switched to runway control frequency.

On runway two five, immediately ahead of Trans America, a British VC-10 of BOAC, received word to go. It moved forward, with lumbering slowness at first, then swiftly. Its company colors—blue, white, and gold —gleamed briefly in the reflection of other aircrafts' lights, then were gone in a flurry of whirling snow and black jet exhaust. Immediately the ground controller's voice intoned, "Trans America Two, taxi into position, runway two five, and hold; traffic landing on runway one seven, left."

One seven, left, was a runway which directly bisected runway two five. There was an element of danger in using the two runways together, but tower controllers had become adept at spacing aircraft—landing and taking off—so that no time was wasted, but no two airplanes reached the intersection at the same moment. Pilots, uncomfortably aware of the danger of collision when they heard by radio that both runways were in use, obeyed controllers' orders implicitly.

Anson Harris swiftly and expertly jockeyed Flight Two on to runway two five.

Peering out, through snow flurries, Demerest could see the lights of an airplane, about to touch down on one seven. He thumbed his mike button. "Trans America Two, Roger. In position and holding. We see the landing traffic."

Even before the landing aircraft had bisected their

own runway, the controller's voice returned. "Trans America Two, cleared for takeoff. Go, man, go!"

The final three words were not in any air traffic control manual, but to controller and pilots they had identical meaning: *Get the hell moving, now! There's another flight landing right after the last.* Already a fresh set of lights—ominously close to the airfield—was approaching runway one seven.

Anson Harris had not waited. His outspread fingers slid the four main throttles forward to their full extent. He ordered, "Trim the throttles," and briefly held his toe brakes on, allowing power to build, as Demerest set pressure ratios evenly for all four engines. The engines' sound deepened from a steady whine to a thunderous roar. Then Harris released the brakes and N-731-TA leaped forward down the runway.

Vernon Demerest reported to the tower, "Trans America Two on the roll," then applied forward pressure to the control yoke while Harris used nose wheel steering with his left hand, his right returning to the throttles.

Speed built. Demerest called, "Eighty knots." Harris nodded, released nose wheel steering and took over the control yoke . . . Runway lights flashed by in swirling snow. Near crescendo, the big jet's power surged . . . At a hundred and thirty-two knots, as calculated earlier, Demerest called out "V-one"—notification to Harris that they had reached "decision speed" at which the takeoff could still be aborted and the aircraft stopped. Beyond V-one the takeoff must continue . . . Now they were past V-one . . . Still gathering speed, they hurtled through the runways' intersection, glimpsing to their right a flash of landing lights of the approaching plane; in mere seconds the other aircraft would cross where Flight Two had just passed. Another risk—skillfully calculated—had worked out; only pessimists believed that one day such a risk might not . . . As speed reached a hundred and fifty-four knots, Harris began rotation, easing the control column back. The nose wheel left the runway surface; they were in lift-off attitude, ready to quit the ground. A moment later, with speed still increasing, they were in the air.

Harris said quietly, "Gear up."

Demerest reached out, raising a lever on the central instrument panel. The sound of the retracting landing gear reverberated through the aircraft, then stopped with a thud as the doors to the wheel wells closed.

They were going up fast—passing through four hundred feet. In a moment, the night and clouds would swallow them.

"Flaps twenty."

Still performing first officer duty, Demerest obediently moved the control pedestal flap selector from thirty degrees to twenty. There was a brief sensation of sinking as the wing flaps—which provided extra lift at takeoff —came partially upward.

"Flaps up."

Now the flaps were fully retracted.

Demerest noted, for his report later, that at no point during takeoff could he have faulted Anson Harris's performance in the slightest degree. He had not expected to. Despite the earlier needling, Vernon Demerest was aware that Harris was a top-grade captain, as exacting in performance—his own and others—as Demerest was himself. It was the reason Demerest had known in advance that their flight to Rome tonight would be, for himself, an easy journey.

Only seconds had passed since leaving the ground; now, still climbing steeply, they passed over the runway's end, the lights below already dimming through cloud and falling snow. Anson Harris had ceased looking out and was flying on instruments alone.

Second Officer Cy Jordan was reaching forward from his flight engineer's seat, adjusting the throttles to equalize the power of all four engines.

Within the clouds there was a good deal of buffeting; at the outset of their journey, the passengers behind were getting a rough ride. Demerest snapped the "No Smoking" light switch off; the "Fasten Seat Belts" sign would remain on until Flight Two reached more stable air. Later, either Harris or Demerest would make an announcement to the passengers; but not yet. At the moment, flying was more important.

Demerest reported to departure control. "Turning portside one eight zero; leaving fifteen hundred feet."

He saw Anson Harris smile at his use of the words "turning portside" instead of "turning left." The former was correct but unofficial. It was one of Demerest's own phrases; many veteran pilots had them—a minor rebellion against ATC officialese which nowadays all flying people were supposed to hew to. Controllers on the ground frequently learned to recognize individual pilots by such personal idioms.

A moment later Flight Two received radio clearance to climb to twenty-five thousand feet. Demerest acknowledged while Anson Harris kept the aircraft climbing. Up there in a few minutes from now they would be in clear, calm air, the storm clouds far below, and high above, in sight, the stars.

The "turning portside" phrase *had* been noticed on the ground—by Keith Bakersfeld.

Keith had returned to radar watch more than an hour ago, after the time spent in the controllers' locker room, alone, remembering the past and reaffirming his intention of tonight.

Several times since then Keith's hand had gone instinctively into his pocket, touching the key of his covertly rented room at the O'Hagan Inn. Otherwise, he had concentrated on the radarscope in front of him. He was now handling arrivals from the east and the continuing heavy traffic volume demanded intensive concentration.

He was not concerned directly with Flight Two; however, the departure controller was only a few feet away and in a brief interval between his own transmissions Keith heard the "turning portside" phrase and recognized it, along with his brother-in-law's voice. Until then, Keith had no idea that Vernon Demerest was flying tonight; there was no reason why he should. Keith and Vernon saw little of each other. Like Mel, Keith had never achieved any close rapport with his brother-in-law, though there had been none of the friction between them which marred relations between Demerest and Mel.

Shortly after Flight Two's departure, Wayne Tevis, the radar supervisor, propelled his castor-equipped chair across to Keith.

"Take five, buddyboy," Tevis said in his nasal Texan drawl. "I'll spell you. Your big brother dropped in."

As he unplugged his headset and turned, Keith made out the figure of Mel behind him in the shadows. He remembered his earlier hope that Mel would not come here tonight; at the time Keith feared that a meeting between the two of them might be more than he could handle emotionally. Now he found that he was glad Mel had come. They had always been good friends as well as brothers, and it was right and proper there should be a leave-taking, though Mel would not know that it was that—at least, until he learned tomorrow.

"Hi," Mel said. "I was passing by. How have things been?"

Keith shrugged. "I guess, all right."

"Coffee?" Mel had picked up two take-out coffees from one of the airport restaurants on his way. They were in a paper bag; he offered one of the cups to Keith and took the other himself.

"Thanks." Keith was grateful for the coffee as well as for the break. Now that he was away from the radarscope, if only briefly, he realized that his own mental tension had been accumulating again within the past hour. He observed, as if watching someone else, that his hand holding the coffee cup was not entirely steady.

Mel glanced around the busy radar room. He was careful not to look too obviously at Keith whose appearance—the gaunt, strained face with deep hollows beneath the eyes—had shocked him. Keith's appearance had deteriorated over recent months; tonight, Mel thought, his brother looked worse than at any time before.

His mind still on Keith, he nodded toward the profusion of radar equipment. "I wonder what the old man would have thought of all this."

The "old man" was—had been—their father, Wally (Wild Blue) Bakersfeld, stick-and-goggles aviator, stunt flier, crop duster, night mail carrier, and parachute jumper—the last when he needed money badly enough. Wild Blue had been a contemporary of Lindbergh, a crony of Orville Wright, and had flown to the end of his life, which terminated abruptly in a filmed Hollywood stunt sequence—an airplane crash, intended to be simulated, but which turned out to be real. It happened when Mel and Keith were in their teens, but not before Wild Blue had inculcated in both boys an acceptance of aviation as their way of life, which persisted into adulthood. In Keith's case, Mel sometimes thought, the father had done his younger son a disservice.

Keith shook his head without answering Mel's question, which didn't matter because it had been only rhetorical, Mel marking time while wondering how best to approach what was uppermost in his mind. He decided to do it directly.

Keeping his voice low, Mel said, "Keith, you're not well; you're looking damned awful. I know it, you know it; so why pretend? If you'll let me, I'd like to help. Can we talk—about whatever the trouble is? We've always been honest with each other."

"Yes," Keith acknowledged, "we've always been that." He sipped his coffee, not meeting Mel's eyes.

The reference to their father, though casual, had moved Keith strangely. He remembered Wild Blue well; he had been a poor provider—the Bakersfeld family was perpetually short of money—but a genial man with his children, especially if the talk was about flying, as the two boys usually wanted it to be. Yet in the end it was not Wild Blue who had been a father figure to Keith, but Mel; Mel Bakersfeld who possessed the sound sense and stability, as far back as Keith remembered, which their father lacked. It was Mel who always looked out for Keith, though never being ostentatious about it, or overprotective as some older brothers were, robbing a younger boy of dignity. Mel had a facility, even then, for doing things for people and making them feel good at the same time.

Mel had shared things with Keith, had been considerate and thoughtful, even in small ways. He still was. Bringing the coffee tonight was an example, Keith thought, then checked himself: Don't wax sentimental over a carton of coffee just because this is a last meeting. This time, Keith's aloneness, his anguish and guilt were beyond Mel's fixing. Even Mel could not bring back to life little Valerie Redfern and her parents.

Mel motioned with his head and they moved to the corridor outside the radar room.

"Listen, old chum," Mel said. "You need a break from all this—a long one; perhaps more than a break. Maybe you need to get away for good."

For the first time Keith smiled. "You've been listening to Natalie."

"Natalie's apt to talk a lot of sense."

Whatever Keith's other problems might be, Mel reflected, he had been outstandingly fortunate in Natalie. The thought of his sister-in-law reminded Mel of his own wife, Cindy, who presumably was still on her way to the airport. Comparing your own marriage unfavorably with someone else's was disloyal, Mel supposed; at times, though, it was hard not to do it. He wondered if Keith really knew just how lucky—at least in that important area—he had been.

"There's something else," Mel said. "I haven't brought it up before, but maybe now's the time. I don't think you've ever told me the whole of what happened at Leesburg—that day, the accident. Maybe you didn't tell anyone, because I've read all the testimony. *Is* there something else; that you've never told?"

Keith hesitated only momentarily. "Yes."

"I figured there might be." Mel chose his words carefully; he sensed that what was passing between them could be of critical importance. "But I also figured if you wanted me to know, you'd tell me; and if you didn't, well, it was none of my business. Sometimes, though, if you care about someone enough—say, like a brother—you ought to make it your business, whether they want you to butt in or not. So I'm making this mine now." He added softly, "You hear me?"

"Yes," Keith said, "I hear you." He thought: He could stop this conversation, of course; perhaps he should stop it now, at once—since it was pointless—by excusing himself and going back to the radarscope. Mel would assume they could resume later, not knowing that for the two of them together, there would be no later.

"That day at Leesburg," Mel insisted. "The part you've never told—it has something to do with the way you feel, the way you *are,* right now. Hasn't it?"

Keith shook his head. "Leave it alone, Mel. Please!"

"Then I'm right. There *is* a relationship, isn't there?"

What was the point of denying the obvious? Keith nodded. "Yes."

"Won't you tell me? You have to tell someone; sooner or later you have to." Mel's voice was pleading, urgent. "You can't live with this thing—whatever it is —inside you forever. Who better to tell than me? I'd understand."

You can't live with this . . . Who better to tell than me?

It seemed to Keith that his brother's voice, even the sight of Mel, was coming to him through a tunnel, from the distant end, far away. At the farther end of the tunnel, too, were all the other people—Natalie, Brian, Theo, Perry Yount, Keith's friends—with whom he had lost communication long since. Now, of them all, Mel alone was reaching out, striving to bridge the gap between them . . . but the tunnel was long, their apartness —after all the length of time that Keith had been alone —too great.

And yet . . .

As if someone else were speaking, Keith asked, "You mean tell you here? Now?"

Mel urged, "Why not?"

Why not, indeed? Something within Keith stirred; a sense of wanting to unburden, even though in the end it could change nothing . . . Or could it? Wasn't that what the Confessional was all about; a catharsis; an exorcism of sin through acknowledgment and contrition? The difference, of course, was that the Confessional gave forgiveness and expiation, and for Keith there could be no expiation—ever. At least . . . he hadn't thought so. Now he wondered what Mel might say.

Somewhere in Keith's mind a door, which had been closed, inched open.

"I suppose there's no reason," he said slowly, "why I shouldn't tell you. It won't take long."

Mel remained silent. Instinct told him that if wrong words were spoken they could shatter Keith's mood, could cut off the confidence which seemed about to be given, which Mel had waited so long and anxiously to hear. He reasoned: if he could finally learn what bedeviled Keith, between them they might come to grips with it. Judging by his brother's appearance tonight, it had better be soon.

"You've read the testimony," Keith said. His voice was a monotone. "You just said so. You know most of what happened that day."

Mel nodded.

"What you don't know, or anybody knows except me; what didn't come out at the inquiry, what I've thought about over and over . . ." Keith hesitated; it seemed as if he might not continue.

"For God's sake! For your own reason, for Natalie's sake, for mine—go on!"

It was Keith's turn to nod. "I'm going to."

He began describing the morning at Leesburg a year and a half before; the air traffic picture when he left for the washroom; supervisor Perry Yount; the trainee controller left in immediate charge. In a moment, Keith thought, he would admit how he had loitered; how he failed the others through indifference and negligence; how he returned to duty too late; how the accident, the multiple tragedy of the Redferns' deaths, had been solely his own doing; and how others were blamed. Now that at last he was doing what he had longed to, without knowing it, there was a sense of blessed relief. Words, like a cataract long damned, began tumbling out.

Mel listened.

Abruptly, a door farther down the corridor opened. A voice—the tower watch chief's—called, "Oh, Mr. Bakersfeld!"

His footsteps echoing along the corridor, the tower chief walked toward them. "Lieutenant Ordway has been trying to reach you, Mr. Bakersfeld; so has the Snow Desk. They both want you to call." He nodded. "Hi, Keith!"

Mel wanted to cry out, to shout for silence or delay, plead to be alone with Keith for a few minutes more. But he knew it was no good. At the first sound of the tower chief's voice Keith had stopped in mid-sentence as if a switch were snapped to "off."

Keith had not, after all, reached the point of describing his own guilt to Mel. As he responded automatically to the tower chief's greeting, he wondered: Why had he begun at all? What could he have hoped to gain? There could never be any gain, never any forgetting. No confession—to whomever made—would exorcise memory. Momentarily he had grasped at what he mistook for a faint flicker of hope, even perhaps reprieve. As it had to be, it proved illusory. Perhaps it was as well that the interruption occurred when it did.

Once more, Keith realized, a mantle of loneliness, like an invisible thick curtain, surrounded him. Inside the curtain he was alone with his thoughts, and inside his thoughts was a private torture chamber where no one, not even a brother, could reach through.

From that torture chamber . . . waiting, always waiting . . . there could be only one relief. It was the way he had already chosen, and would carry through.

"I guess they could use you back inside, Keith," the tower watch chief said. It was the gentlest kind of chiding. Keith had already had one work-break tonight; another inevitably threw a heavier load on other people. It was also a reminder to Mel, perhaps unintended, that as airport general manager his writ did not run here.

Keith mumbled something and gave a distant nod. With a sense of helplessness, Mel watched his brother return to the radar room. He had heard enough to know that it was desperately important he should hear more. He wondered when that would be, and how. A few minutes ago he had broken through Keith's reserve, his secrecy. Would it happen again? With despair, Mel doubted it.

For sure, there would be no more confidences from Keith tonight.

"I'm sorry, Mr. Bakersfeld." As if belatedly guessing Mel's thoughts, the tower chief spread his hands. "You try to do the best for everybody. It isn't always easy."

"I know." Mel felt like sighing, but restrained himself. When something like this happened, you could only hope for the right occasion to occur again; meanwhile you got on with other things you had to do.

"Tell me, please," Mel said, "what were those messages again?"

The tower chief repeated them.

Instead of telephoning the Snow Control Desk, Mel walked down one floor of the control tower and went in. Danny Farrow was still presiding over the busy snow clearance command console.

There was a query about priorities in clearing the aircraft parking areas of competing airlines, which Mel settled, then checked on the situation concerning the blocked runway, three zero. There was no change, except that Joe Patroni was now on the airfield and had taken charge of attempts to move the mired Aéreo-Mexican 707, which was still preventing the runway being used. A few minutes earlier, Patroni had reported by radio that he expected to make a new attempt to move the aircraft within an hour. Knowing Joe Patroni's reputation as a top-notch troubleshooter, Mel decided there was nothing to be gained by demanding a more detailed report.

At the Snow Desk Mel remembered the message to call Police Lieutenant Ordway. Assuming that the lieutenant was still in the terminal, Mel had him paged and, a few moments later, Ordway came on the line. Mel expected the lieutenant's call to be about the anti-noise delegation of Meadowood residents. It wasn't.

"The Meadowood people are starting to come in, but they haven't been a problem and they haven't asked for you yet," Ned Ordway said when Mel raised the question. "I'll let you know when they do."

What he had called about, the policeman reported, was a woman who had been picked up by one of his men. She was crying, and apparently wandering aimlessly in the main terminal. "We couldn't get any sense out of her, but she wasn't doing anything wrong so I didn't want to take her to the station house. She seemed upset enough without that."

"What did you do?"

Ordway said apologetically, "There aren't many quiet places around here tonight, so I put her in the anteroom outside your office. I thought I'd let you know in case you got back and wondered."

"That's all right. Is she alone?"

"One of my men was with her, though he may have left by now. But she's harmless; I'm sure of that. We'll check on her again soon."

"I'll be back at my office in a few minutes," Mel said. "I'll see if I can do any good myself." He wondered if he would have more success talking with the unknown woman than he had had with Keith; he doubted if he could do worse. The thought of Keith, who seemed close to breaking point, still troubled Mel deeply.

As an afterthought, he asked, "Did you find out the woman's name?"

"Yes, we got that much. It's a Spanish-sounding name. Just a minute; I have it written down."

There was a pause, then Lieutenant Ordway said, "Her name is Guerrero. Mrs. Inez Guerrero."

Tanya Livingston said incredulously, "You mean Mrs. Quonsett's aboard Flight Two?"

"I'm afraid there's no doubt of it, Mrs. Livingston. There was a little old lady, exactly the way you've described her." The gate agent who had supervised boarding of *The Golden Argosy* was in the D.T.M.'s office with Tanya and young Peter Coakley, the latter still mortified at having been bamboozled by Mrs. Ada Quonsett while she was in his charge.

The gate agent had come to the office a few minutes ago in response to Coakley's telephoned warning, to all

Trans America gate positions, about the elusive Mrs. Quonsett.

"It just didn't occur to me there was anything wrong," the gate agent said. "We let other visitors aboard tonight; they came off." He added defensively, "Anyway, I'd been under pressure all evening. We were short staffed, and apart from the time you were there helping, I was doing the work of two people. You know that."

"Yes," Tanya said, "I know." She had no intention of passing out blame. If anyone was responsible for what had happened, it was Tanya herself.

"It was just after you left, Mrs. Livingston. The old lady said something about her son, I think it was, leaving his wallet. She even showed it to me. It had money in it, she said, which was why I didn't take it."

"She'd already figured that. It's one of her regular gags."

"I didn't know it, so I let her go aboard. From then until a few minutes ago when I got the phone call, I never gave her another thought."

"She fools you," Peter Coakley said. He gave a sideways glance at Tanya. "She sure fooled me."

The agent shook his head. "If I didn't have to believe it, I wouldn't, even now. But she's aboard, all right." He described the discrepancy between the tourist section head count and the ticket tally, then afterward, the ramp supervisor's decision to let the aircraft go, rather than incur further delay.

Tanya said quickly, "I suppose there's no doubt Flight Two's already taken off."

"Yes, they have. I checked on my way here. Even if they hadn't, I doubt they'd bring the aircraft back in, especially tonight."

"No they wouldn't." Nor was there the slightest chance, Tanya knew, of *The Golden Argosy* changing course and returning for a landing, merely because of Ada Quonsett. The time and cost to disembark one stowaway would run to thousands of dollars—far more than to take Mrs. Quonsett to Rome and bring her back.

"Is there a refueling stop?" Sometimes, Tanya knew, Europe-bound flights made non-scheduled stops for fuel at Montreal or Newfoundland. If so, there would be a chance to pull Mrs. Quonsett off, robbing her of the satisfaction of getting all the way to Italy.

"I asked Operations about that," the agent answered. "The flight plan shows they're going right through. No stops."

Tanya exclaimed, "Damn that old woman!"

So Ada Quonsett was going to get her ride to Italy and back, with probably a night's lodging in between, and with meals supplied—all at airline expense. Tanya thought angrily: she had underestimated the old lady's determination not to be sent back to the West Coast; she had erred also in assuming that Mrs. Quonsett would head only for New York.

Barely fifteen minutes earlier Tanya had thought of the developing contest between herself and Ada Quonsett as a battle of wits. If it was, without doubt the little old lady from San Diego had won.

With uncharacteristic savageness, Tanya wished that the airline would make an exception and prosecute Mrs. Quonsett. But she knew they wouldn't.

Young Peter Coakley started to say something.

Tanya snapped, "Oh, shut up!"

The District Transportation Manager returned to his office a few minutes after Coakley and the gate agent left. The D.T.M., Bert Weatherby, was a hard-working, hard-driving executive in his late forties, who had come up the hard way, beginning as a ramp baggage handler. Normally considerate, and with a sense of humor, to-night he was tired and testy from three days of continuous strain. He listened impatiently to Tanya's report in which she accepted the main responsibility herself, mentioning Peter Coakley only incidentally.

Running a hand through his sparse graying hair, the D.T.M. observed, "I like to check that there's still some left up there. It's things like this that are making the rest of it fall out." He considered, then rasped, "You got us into this mess; you'd better do the salvaging. Talk to Flight Dispatch; ask them to call the captain of Flight

Two on company radio and fill him in on what happened. I don't know what he can do. Personally, I'd like to throw the old hag out at thirty thousand feet, but that'll be up to him. By the way, who is the captain?"

"Captain Demerest."

The D.T.M. groaned. "It would be. He'll probably think it's all a great joke because management boobed. Anyway, advise him the old biddy's to be detained on board after landing, and is not to be allowed off without escort. If the Italian authorities want to jail her, so much the better. Then get a signal off to our station manager in Rome. When they arrive it'll be his baby, and I hope he's got more competent people around him than I have."

"Yes, sir," Tanya said.

She started to tell the D.T.M. of the other matter concerning Flight Two—the suspicious-looking man with an attaché case whom Customs Inspector Standish had seen going aboard. Before she could finish, the D.T.M. cut her off.

"Forget it! What do the Customs people want us to do—their job? As long as the airline's not involved, I don't give a damn what the guy's carrying. If Customs here want to know what's in his case, let them ask Italian Customs to check, not us. I'll be damned if I'll interrogate, and maybe offend, a fare-paying passenger for something that's none of our business."

Tanya hesitated. Something about the man with the attaché case—even though she hadn't actually seen him —bothered her. There were instances she had heard of where . . . Of course, the idea was absurd . . .

"I was wondering," she said. "He might not be smuggling at all."

The D.T.M. snapped, "I said forget it."

Tanya left. Back at her desk, she began writing the message to Captain Demerest of Flight Two concerning Mrs. Ada Quonsett.

2

In a taxi en route to the airport from downtown, Cindy Bakersfeld leaned back against the rear seat and closed her eyes. She was neither aware, nor cared, that outside it was still snowing, nor that the taxi was moving slowly in heavy traffic. She was in no hurry. A wave of physical pleasure and contentment (Was the right word euphoria? Cindy wondered) swept over her.

The cause was Derek Eden.

Derek Eden, who had been at the Archidona Relief Fund cocktail party (Cindy still didn't know *which* Archidona); who had brought her a triple-strength Bourbon, which she hadn't drunk, then had propositioned her in the most unimaginative way. Derek Eden, until today only a slightly known *Sun-Times* reporter with a second-grade by-line; Derek Eden with the dissolute face, the casual air, the nondescript unpressed clothes; Derek Eden and his beat-up filthy-inside-and-out Chevrolet; Derek Eden, who had caught Cindy in a barriers-down moment, when she needed a man, any man, and she hadn't hoped for much; Derek Eden who had proved to be the finest and most exciting lover she had ever known.

Never, never before had Cindy experienced anyone like him. Oh, God!, she thought; if ever there was sensual, physical perfection, she attained it tonight. More to the point; now that she had known Derek Eden . . . dear Derek . . . she wanted him again—often. Fortunately, it was unmistakable that he now felt the same way about her.

Still leaning back in the rear of the taxi, she relived mentally the past two hours.

They had driven, in the awful old Chevrolet, from the Lake Michigan Inn to a smallish hotel near the Merchandise Mart. A doorman accepted the car disdainfully —Derek Eden didn't seem to notice—and inside, in the

lobby, the night manager was waiting. Cindy gathered
that one of the phone calls which her escort had made
was to here. There was no formality of checking in, and
the night manager showed them directly to a room on
the eleventh floor. After leaving the key, and with a
quick "goodnight," he left.

The room was so-so; old fashioned, spartan, and with
cigarette burns on the furniture, but clean. It had a
double bed. Beside the bed, on a table, was an unopened bottle of Scotch, some mixes and ice. A card on
the liquor tray read, *"With the manager's compliments";*
Derek Eden inspected the card, then put it in his pocket.

When Cindy inquired, later on, Derek explained,
"Sometimes a hotel will oblige the press. When they do,
we don't make any promises; the paper wouldn't go for
it. But maybe sometimes a reporter or a deskman will
put the hotel's name in a story if it's an advantage; or if
the story's a bad one—like a death; hotels hate that—
we might leave it out. As I say, no promises. You do the
best you can."

They had a drink, and chatted, then another, and
during the second drink he began to kiss her. It was
soon after that she became aware of the gentleness of
his hands, which he passed through her hair quite a lot
to begin with, in a way which she could feel through her
entire body; then the hands began exploring slowly, oh,
so slowly . . . and it was also then that Cindy began to
realize this might be something special.

While he was undressing her, demonstrating a finesse
which he had lacked earlier, he whispered, "Don't let's
hurry, Cindy—either of us." But soon after, when they
were in bed, and wonderfully warm, as Derek Eden
promised in the car they would be, she *had* wanted to
hurry, and cried out, "Yes, yes! . . . Oh, please! I can't
wait!" But he insisted gently, "Yes, you can. You
must." And she obeyed him, being utterly, deliciously in
his control, while he led her, as if by the hand like a
child, close to the brink, then back a pace or two while
they waited with a feeling like floating in air; then near
once more, and back, and the same again and again, the
bliss of it all near-unendurable; and finally when neither

of them could wait longer, there was a shared crescendo like a hymn of heaven and a thousand sweet symphonies; and if Cindy had been able to choose a moment for dying, because nothing afterward could ever be that moment's equal, she would have chosen then.

Later, Cindy decided that one of the things she liked about Derek Eden was his total lack of humbug. Ten minutes after their supreme moment, at a point where Cindy's normal breathing was returning and her heart regaining its regular beat, Derek Eden propped himself on an elbow and lighted cigarettes for them both.

"We were great, Cindy." He smiled. "Let's play a return match soon, and lots of others after that." It was, Cindy realized, an admission of two things: that what they had experienced was solely physical, a sensual adventure, and neither should pretend that it was more; yet together they had attained that rare Nirvana, an absolute sexual compatibility. Now, what they had available, whenever needed, was a private physical paradise, to be nurtured and increasingly explored.

The arrangement suited Cindy.

She doubted if she and Derek Eden would have much in common outside a bedroom, and he was certainly no prize to be exhibited around the social circuit. Without even thinking about it, Cindy knew she would have more to lose than gain by being seen publicly in Derek's company. Besides, he had already intimated that his own marriage was solid, though Cindy guessed he wasn't getting as much sex at home as he needed, a condition with which she sympathized, being in the same situation herself.

Yes, Derek Eden was someone to be treasured—but not to become involved with emotionally. She *would* treasure him. Cindy resolved not to be demanding, nor let their love-making become too frequent. A single session like tonight's would last Cindy a long time, and could be relived just by thinking about it. Play a little hard-to-get, she told herself; see to it that Derek Eden went on wanting her as much as she wanted him. That way, the whole thing could last for years.

Cindy's discovery of Derek had also, in a strange

way, provided her with a freedom she had not possessed before.

Now that she had better-than-average sex available as it were, on a separate shelf, she could view the choice between Mel and Lionel Urquhart more objectively.

Her marriage to Mel had, in some ways, already terminated. Mentally and sexually they were estranged; their slightest disagreement resulted in bitter quarreling. All that Mel appeared to think about nowadays was his damned airport. Each day, it seemed, thrust Mel and Cindy farther apart.

Lionel, who was satisfactory in all respects except in bed, wanted divorces all around so that he could marry Cindy.

Mel detested Cindy's social ambitions. Not only would he do nothing to advance them; he impeded them. Lionel, on the other hand, was well established in Illinois society, saw nothing unusual in Cindy's social aims and would, and could, help her fulfill them.

Until now, Cindy's choice had been complicated by the remembrance of her fifteen years of marriage to Mel and the good times together, mental and physical, they had once enjoyed. She had hoped vaguely that the past —including the satisfactions of sex—might somehow be rekindled. It was, she admitted to herself, a delusive hope.

Lionel, as a sexual partner, had little or nothing to offer. Neither—at least for Cindy, any more—had Mel.

But if sex were eliminated—an elimination which Derek Eden, like a secretly stabled stallion, had now made possible—Lionel, as a competitor to Mel, came out far ahead.

In the taxi, Cindy opened her eyes and mused.

She wouldn't make any firm decision until she had talked with Mel. Cindy didn't like decisions, anyway, and invariably put them off until they could be delayed no longer. Also, there were still imponderables involved: the children; memories of the years with Mel, which hadn't *all* been bad; and when you once cared deeply for someone, you never shook it off entirely. But she was glad she had decided, after all, to come out here tonight.

For the first time since leaving downtown Cindy leaned forward, peering out into the darkness to see if she could determine where they were. She couldn't. Through misted windows she could see snow and many other cars, all moving slowly. She guessed they were on the Kennedy Expressway, but that was all.

She was aware of the cab driver's eyes watching her in his rearview mirror. Cindy had no idea what kind of man the driver was; she hadn't taken notice when she got into the cab back at the hotel, which she and Derek left separately since they decided they might as well start being discreet immediately. Anyway, tonight all faces and bodies merged into the face and body of Derek Eden.

"That's Portage Park over there, madam," the driver said. "We're getting close to the airport. Won't be long."

"Thank you."

"Lotsa traffic going out there besides us. Guess those airport people must have had their problems, what with the big storm and all."

Who the hell cares?, Cindy thought. *And didn't anyone ever think or talk of anything besides that cruddy airport?* But she kept quiet.

At the main terminal entrance Cindy paid off the cab and hurried inside to avoid wet snow which gusted under canopies and swirled along sidewalks. She threaded the crowds in the main concourse, moving around one sizable group which seemed to intend some kind of demonstration because several people were helping assemble a portable public address system. A Negro police lieutenant, whom Cindy had met several times with Mel, was talking to two or three men from the group who appeared to be leaders. The policeman was shaking his head vigorously. Not really curious—nothing about this place really interested her—Cindy moved on, heading for the airport administrative offices on the mezzanine.

Lights were on in all the offices, though most were unoccupied and there was none of the clatter of typewriters or hum of conversation, as during daytime working hours. At least some people, Cindy thought, had sense enough to go home at night.

The only person in sight was a middle-aged woman, in drab clothes, in the anteroom to Mel's office. She was seated on a settee from where she seemed to be looking vacantly into space, and took no notice as Cindy came in. The woman's eyes were red as if she had been crying. Judging by her clothes and shoes, which were sodden, she had been outside in the storm.

Cindy gave the other woman only a mildly curious glance before going into Mel's office. The office was empty, and Cindy sat down in a chair to wait. After a few moments she closed her eyes and resumed her pleasant thoughts about Derek Eden.

Mel hurried in—he was limping more than usual, Cindy noticed—about ten minutes later.

"Oh!" He appeared surprised when he saw Cindy, and went back to close the door. "I really didn't think you'd come."

"I suppose you'd have preferred me not to."

Mel shook his head. "I still don't think there's anything to be gained by it—at least, not for what you seem to have in mind." He looked at his wife appraisingly, wondering what her real purpose was in coming here tonight. He had learned long ago that Cindy's motives were usually complicated, and frequently quite different from what they appeared to be. He had to admit, though, that she looked her best tonight; positively glamorous, with a kind of radiance about her. Unfortunately, the glamour no longer affected him personally.

"Suppose you tell me," Cindy said, "what you think I have in mind."

He shrugged. "I got the impression that what you wanted was a fight. It occurred to me that we had enough of them at home without arranging another here."

"Perhaps we'll *have* to arrange something here; since you're hardly ever home any more."

"I might be home, if the atmosphere were more congenial."

They had been talking for just a few seconds, Cindy realized, and already were sniping at each other. It seemed impossible nowadays for the two of them to hold a conversation without that happening.

Just the same, she could not resist answering, "Oh, really! That isn't usually the reason you give for not being at home. You're always claiming how all-fired important it is for you to be here at the airport—if necessary, twenty-four hours a day. So many important things—or so you say—are always happening."

Mel said curtly, "Tonight they are."

"But not other times?"

"If you're asking whether I've sometimes stayed here in preference to coming home, the answer's yes."

"At least this is the first time you've been honest about it."

"Even when I do come home, you insist on dragging me to some stupid stuffed-shirt affair like tonight's."

His wife said angrily, "So you never did intend to come tonight!"

"Yes, I did. I told you so. But . . ."

"But nothing!" Cindy could feel the short fuse of her temper burning. "You counted on something turning up to prevent you, the way it always does. So that you could weasel out and have an alibi; so you could convince yourself, even if you don't convince me, because I think you're a liar and a fake."

"Take it easy, Cindy."

"I won't take it easy."

They glared at each other.

What happened to them, Mel wondered, that they had come to this?—squabbling like ill-bred children; dealing in pettiness; exchanging vicious gibes; and in all of it, he himself no better than Cindy. Something happened when they quarreled which demeaned them both. He wondered if it was always this way when things were sour with two people who had lived together for a long time. Was it because they knew, and therefore could probe painfully, each other's weaknesses? He had once heard someone say that a disintegrating marriage brought out the worst in both partners. In his own and Cindy's case it was certainly true.

He tried to speak more reasonably. "I don't think I'm a liar, or a fake. But maybe you have a point about my counting on something turning up, enough to keep me away from the social things, which you know I hate. I just hadn't thought of it that way."

When Cindy remained silent, he went on, "You can believe it or not, but I did intend to meet you tonight downtown—at least I think so. Maybe I didn't really, the way you said; I don't know. But I do know that I didn't arrange the storm, and, since it started, a lot of things have happened that—for real this time—have kept me here." He nodded toward the outer office. "One of them is that woman sitting out there. I told Lieutenant Ordway I'd talk to her. She seems to be in some sort of trouble."

"Your wife's in trouble," Cindy said. "The woman out there can wait."

He nodded. "All right."

"We've had it," Cindy said. "You and me. Haven't we?"

He waited before answering, not wanting to be hasty, yet realizing that now this had come up, it would be foolish to avoid the truth. "Yes," he said finally. "I'm afraid we have."

Cindy shot back, "If only you'd change! If you'd see things my way. It's always been what *you* want to do, or don't. If you'd only do what *I* want . . ."

"Like being out six nights a week in black tie, and white tie on the seventh?"

"Well, why not?" Emotionally, imperiously, Cindy faced him. He had always admired her in that kind of spunky mood, even when it was directed at himself. Even now . . .

"I guess I could say the same kind of thing," he told her. "About changing; all that. The trouble is, people don't change—not in what they are basically; they adapt. It's that—two people adapting to each other— that marriage is supposed to be about."

"The adapting doesn't have to be one-sided."

"It hasn't been with us," Mel argued, "no matter what you think. I've tried to adapt; I guess you have, too. I don't know who's made the most effort; obviously I think it's me, and you think it's you. The main thing is: though we've given it plenty of time to work, it hasn't."

Cindy said slowly, "I suppose you're right. About the last bit, anyway. I've been thinking the same way too." She stopped, then added, "I think I want a divorce."

"You'd better be quite sure. It's fairly important." Even now, Mel thought, Cindy was hedging about a decision, waiting for him to help her with it. If what they had been saying were less serious, he would have smiled.

"I'm sure," Cindy said. She repeated, with more conviction. "Yes, I'm sure."

Mel said quietly, "Then I think it's the right decision for us both."

For a second Cindy hesitated. "You're sure, too?"

"Yes," he said. "I'm sure."

The lack of argument, the quickness of the exchange, seemed to bother Cindy. She asked, "Then we've made a decision?"

"Yes."

They still faced each other, but their anger was gone.

"Oh hell!" Mel moved, as if to take a pace forward. "I'm sorry, Cindy."

"I'm sorry, too." Cindy stayed where she was. Her voice was more assured. "But it's the most sensible thing, isn't it?"

He nodded. "Yes. I guess it is."

It was over now. Both knew it. Only details remained to be attended to.

Cindy was already making plans. "I shall have custody of Roberta and Libby, of course, though you'll always be able to see them. I'll never be difficult about that."

"I didn't expect you would be."

Yes, Mel mused, it was logical that the girls would go

with their mother. He would miss them both, Libby especially. No outside meetings, however frequent, could ever be a substitute for living in the same house day by day. He remembered his talks with his younger daughter on the telephone tonight; what was it Libby had wanted the first time? *A map of February*. Well, he had one now; it showed some unexpected detours.

"And I'll have to get a lawyer," Cindy said. "I'll let you know who it is."

He nodded, wondering if all marriages went on to terminate so matter-of-factly once the decision to end them had been made. He supposed it was the civilized way of doing things. At any rate, Cindy seemed to have regained her composure with remarkable speed. Seated in the chair she had been occupying earlier, she was inspecting her face in a compact, repairing her make-up. He even had the impression that her thoughts had moved away from here; at the corners of her mouth there was the hint of a smile. In situations like this, Mel thought, women were supposed to be more emotional than men, but Cindy didn't show any signs of it, yet he himself was close to tears.

He was aware of sounds—voices and people moving —in the office outside. There was a knock. Mel called, "Come in."

It was Lieutenant Ordway. He entered, closing the door behind him. When he saw Cindy, he said, "Oh, excuse me, Mrs. Bakersfeld."

Cindy glanced up, then away, without answering. Ordway, sensitive to atmosphere, stood hesitantly. "Perhaps I should come back."

Mel asked, "What is it, Ned?"

"It's the anti-noise demonstration; those Meadowood people. There are a couple of hundred in the main concourse; more coming in. They all wanted to see you, but I've talked them into sending a delegation, the way you suggested. They selected half a dozen, and there are three newspaper reporters; I said the reporters could come too." The policeman nodded toward the ante-room. "They're all waiting outside."

He would have to see the delegation, Mel knew. He had never felt less like talking to anyone.

"Cindy," he pleaded, "this won't take long. Will you wait?" When she didn't answer, he added, "Please!"

She continued to ignore them both.

"Look," Ordway said, "if this is a bad time, I'll tell these people they'll have to come back some other day."

Mel shook his head. The commitment had been made; it was his own suggestion. "You'd better bring them in." As the policeman turned away, Mel added, "Oh, I haven't talked to that woman . . . I've forgotten her name."

"Guerrero," Ordway said. "And you don't have to. She looked as if she was leaving when I came in."

A few moments later the half dozen people from Meadowood—four men and two women—began filing in. The press trio followed. One of the reporters was from the *Tribune*—an alert, youngish man named Tomlinson who usually covered the airport and general aviation beat for his paper; Mel knew him well and respected his accuracy and fairness. Tomlinson's by-line also appeared occasionally in national magazines. The other two reporters were also known slightly to Mel— one a young man from the *Sun-Times*, the other an older woman from a local weekly.

Through the open doorway, Mel could see Lieutenant Ordway talking to the woman outside, Mrs. Guerrero, who was standing, fastening her coat.

Cindy remained where she was.

"Good evening." Mel introduced himself, then motioned to settees and chairs around his office. "Please sit down."

"Okay, we will," one of the men in the delegation said. He was expensively well-dressed, with precisely combed, graystreaked hair, and seemed to be the group's leader. "But I'll tell you we're not here to get cozy. We've some plain, blunt things to say and we expect the same kind of answers, not a lot of double-talk."

"I'll try not to give you that. Will you tell me who you are?"

"My name is Elliott Freemantle. I'm a lawyer. I represent these people, and all the others down below."

"All right, Mr. Freemantle," Mel said. "Why don't you begin?"

The door to the anteroom was still open. The woman who had been outside, Mel noticed, had gone. Now, Ned Ordway came in, closing the office door.

3

Trans America Airlines Flight Two was twenty minutes out of Lincoln International, and in a steady climb which would continue until reaching thirty-three thousand feet near Detroit, in eleven more minutes. Already the flight was on its airway and great circle course for Rome. For the past several minutes the aircraft had been in smooth air, the storm clouds and accompanying turbulence now far below. A three-quarter moon hung above and ahead like a lopsided lantern; all around, the stars were sharp and clear.

On the flight deck, initial pressures were over. Captain Harris had made a progress announcement to the passengers over the p.a. system. The three pilots were settling down to routines of their long flight.

Under the second officer's table, behind Captain Harris and Demerest, a chime sounded loudly. At the same instant, on a radio panel forward of the throttles, an amber light winked on. Both chime and light indicated a radio call on Selcal radio system through which most airliners could be called individually, as if by private telephone. Each aircraft, of Trans America and other major airlines, had its own separate call code, transmitted and received automatically. The signals which had just been actuated for aircraft N-731-TA would be seen or heard on no other flight.

Anson Harris switched from the radio to which he had been listening on air route control frequency, and acknowledged, "This is Trans America Two."

"Flight Two, this is Trans America dispatcher, Cleveland. I have a message for the captain from D.T.M., LIA. Advise when ready to copy."

Vernon Demerest, Harris observed, had also changed radio frequencies. Now Demerest pulled a notepad toward him and nodded.

Harris instructed, "We're ready, Cleveland. Go ahead."

The message was that which Tanya Livingston had written concerning Flight Two's stowaway, Mrs. Ada Quonsett. As it progressed, with the description of the little old lady from San Diego, both captains began smiling. The message ended by asking confirmation that Mrs. Quonsett was aboard.

"We will check and advise," Harris acknowledged. When the transmission ended, he clicked the radio controls back to air route control frequency.

Vernon Demerest, and Second Officer Jordan who had heard the message from an overhead speaker near his seat, were laughing aloud.

The second officer declared, "I don't believe it!"

"I believe it." Demerest chuckled. "All those boobs on the ground, and some ancient old duck fooled them all!" He pushed the call button for the forward galley phone. "Hey!" he said, when one of the stewardesses answered. "Tell Gwen we want her in the office."

He was still chuckling when the flight deck door opened. Gwen Meighen came in.

Demerest read Gwen the Selcal message with Mrs. Quonsett's description. "Have you seen her?"

Gwen shook her head. "I've hardly been back in tourist yet."

"Go back," Demerest told her, "and see if the old woman's there. She shouldn't be hard to spot."

"If she is, what do you want me to do?"

"Nothing. Just come back and report."

Gwen was gone only a few minutes. When she returned, she was laughing like the others.

Demerest swung around in his seat. "Is she there?"

Gwen nodded. "Yes, in seat fourteen-B. She's just the way the message said, only more so."

The second officer asked, "How old?"

"At least seventy-five; probably nearer eighty. And she looks like something out of Dickens."

Over his shoulder, Anson Harris said, "More like *Arsenic and Old Lace.*"

"Is she *really* a stowaway, Captain?"

Harris shrugged. "On the ground they say so. And I guess it explains why your head count was wrong."

"We can easily find out for sure," Gwen volunteered. "All I have to do is go back again and ask to see her ticket counterfoil."

"No," Vernon Demerest said. "Let's not do that."

As best they could in the darkened cockpit, the others regarded him curiously. After a second or so, Harris returned his eyes to the flight instruments; Second Officer Jordan swung back to his fuel charts.

"Hold on," Demerest told Gwen. While she waited, he made a check point report on company radio.

"All we were told to do," Demerest said when he had finished the report, "was to see if the old lady's aboard. Okay, she is; and that's what I'll tell Flight Dispatch. I guess they'll have someone waiting for her at Rome; we can't do anything about that, even if we wanted to. But if the old girl's made it this far, and since we're not turning back, why make her next eight hours miserable? So leave her alone. Maybe, just before we get to Rome, we'll let her know she's been found out; then it won't be a whole big shock. But for the time being, let her enjoy her flight. Give Grandma some dinner, and she can watch the movie in peace."

"You know," Gwen said; she was watching him thoughtfully. "There are times when I quite like you."

As Gwen left the flight deck, Demerest—still chuckling—changed radio channels and reported back himself to the Cleveland dispatcher.

Anson Harris, who had his pipe alight, looked up from adjusting the auto-pilot and said drily, "I didn't

think you were much of a one for the old ladies." He
emphasized the "old."

Demerest grinned. "I prefer younger ones."

"So I'd heard."

The stowaway report, and his reply, had put Demerest in a thoroughly good humor. More relaxed than
earlier, he added, "Opportunities change. Pretty soon
you and I will have to settle for the not-so-young ones."

"I already have." Harris puffed at his pipe. "For
quite some time."

Both pilots had one earpiece of their radio headsets
pushed upward. They could converse normally, yet hear
radio calls if any came in. The noise level of the flight
deck—persistent but not overwhelming—was sufficient
to give the two of them privacy.

"You've always played it straight down the line,
haven't you?" Demerest said. "With your wife, I mean.
No mucking around; on layovers I've seen you reading
books."

This time Harris grinned. "Sometimes I go to a
movie."

"Any special reason?"

"My wife was a stewardess—on DC-4s; that was how
we met. She knew what went on: the sleeping around,
pregnancies, abortions, all that stuff. Later, she got to be
a supervisor and had to deal with a lot of it in her job.
Anyway, when we were married I made her a promise
—the obvious one. I've always kept it."

"I guess all those kids you had helped."

"Maybe."

Harris made another minute adjustment to the auto-
pilot. As they talked, the eyes of both pilots, out of
training and habit, swept the illuminated banks of instruments in front of them, as well as those to each side
and above. An incorrect instrument reading would show
at once if anything in the aircraft was malfunctioning.
Nothing was.

Demerest said, "How many children is it? Six?"

"Seven." Harris smiled. "Four we planned, three we
didn't. But it all worked out."

"The ones you didn't plan—did you ever consider doing anything about them? Before they were born."

Harris glanced sharply sideways. "Abortion?"

Vernon Demerest had asked the question on impulse. Now he wondered why. Obviously, his two conversations earlier with Gwen had begun the train of thought about children generally. But it was uncharacteristic of him to be doing so much thinking about something— like an abortion for Gwen—which was essentially simple and straightforward. Just the same, he was curious about Harris's reaction.

"Yes," Demerest said. "That's what I meant."

Anson Harris said curtly, "The answer's no." Less sharply, he added, "It happens to be something I have strong views about."

"Because of religion?"

Harris shook his head negatively. "I'm an agnostic."

"What kind of views, then?"

"You sure you want to hear?"

"It's a long night," Demerest said. "Why not?"

On radio they listened to an exchange between air route control and a TWA flight, Paris-bound, which had taken off shortly after Trans America Flight Two. The TWA jet was ten miles behind, and several thousand feet lower. As Flight two continued to climb, so would TWA.

Most alert pilots, as a result of listening to other aircraft transmissions, maintained a partial picture of nearby traffic in their minds. Demerest and Harris both added this latest item to others already noted. When the ground-to-air exchange ended, Demerest urged Anson Harris, "Go ahead."

Harris checked their course and altitude, then began refilling his pipe.

"I've studied a lot of history. I got interested in college and followed through after. Maybe you've done the same."

"No," Demerest said. "Never more than I had to."

"Well, if you go through it all—history, that is—one thing stands out. Every bit of human progress has happened for a single, simple reason: the elevation of the status of the individual. Each time civilization has stumbled into another age that's a little better, a bit more enlightened, than the one before it, it's because people cared more about other people and respected them as individuals. When they haven't cared, those have been the times of slipping backward. Even a short world history—if you read one—will prove it's true."

"I'll take your word for it."

"You don't have to. There are plenty of examples. We abolished slavery because we respected individual human life. For the same reason we stopped hanging children, and around the same time we invented habeas corpus, and now we've created justice for all, or the closest we can come to it. More recently, most people who think and reason are against capital punishment, not so much because of those to be executed, but for what taking a human life—any human life—does to society, which is all of us."

Harris stopped. Straining forward against his seat harness, he looked outward from the darkened cockpit to the night surrounding them. In bright moonlight he could see a swirl of darkened cloudtops far below. With a forecast of unbroken cloud along the whole of their route until mid-Atlantic, there would be no glimpses tonight of lights on the ground. Several thousand feet above, the lights of another aircraft, traveling in an opposite direction, flashed by and were gone.

From his seat behind the other two pilots, Second Officer Cy Jordan reached forward, adjusting the throttle settings to compensate for Flight Two's increased altitude.

Demerest waited until Jordan had finished, then protested to Anson Harris, "Capital punishment is a long way from abortion."

"Not really," Harris said. "Not when you think about it. It all relates to respect for individual human life; to the way civilization's come, the way it's going. The strange thing is, you hear people argue for abolition of capital punishment, then for legalized abortion in the same breath. What they don't see is the anomaly of raising the value of human life on one hand, and lowering it on the other."

Demerest remembered what he had said to Gwen this evening. He repeated it now. "An unborn child doesn't have life—not an individual life. It's a fetus; it isn't a person."

"Let me ask you something," Harris said. "Did you ever see an aborted child? Afterward, I mean."

"No."

"I did once. A doctor I know showed it to me. It was in a glass jar, in formaldehyde; my friend kept it in a cupboard. I don't know where he got it, but he told me that if the baby had lived—not been aborted—it would have been a normal child, a boy. It was a fetus, all right, just the way you said, except it had been a human being, too. It was all there; everything perfectly formed; a good-looking face, hands, feet, toes, even a little penis. You know what I felt when I saw it? I felt ashamed; I wondered where the hell was I; where were all other decent-minded, sensitive people when this kid, who couldn't defend himself, was being murdered? Because that's what happened; even though, most times, we're afraid to use the word."

"Hell! I'm not saying a baby should be taken out when it's that far along."

"You know something?" Harris said. "Eight weeks after conception, everything's present in a fetus that's in a full-term baby. In the third month the fetus *looks* like a baby. So where do you draw the line?"

Demerest grumbled, "You should have been a lawyer, not a pilot." Just the same, he found himself wondering how far Gwen was along, then reasoned: if she conceived in San Francisco, as she assured him, it must be eight or nine weeks ago. Therefore, assuming Harris's statements to be true, there was almost a shaped baby now.

It was time for another report to air route control. Vernon Demerest made it. They were at thirty-two thousand feet, near the top of their climb, and in a moment or two would cross the Canadian border and be over southern Ontario. Detroit and Windsor, the twin cities straddling the border, were ordinarily a bright splash of light, visible for miles ahead. Tonight there was only darkness, the cities shrouded and somewhere down below to starboard. Demerest remembered that Detroit Metropolitan Airport had closed shortly before their own takeoff. Both cities, by now, would be taking the full brunt of the storm, which was moving east.

Back in the passenger cabins, Demerest knew, Gwen Meighen and the other stewardesses would be serving a second round of drinks and, in first class, hot hors d'oeuvres on exclusive Rosenthal china.

"I warned you I had strong feelings," Anson Harris said. "You don't need a religion, to believe in human ethics."

Demerest growled, "Or to have screwball ideas. Anyway, people who think like you are on the losing side. The trend is to make abortion easier; eventually, maybe, wide open and legal."

"If it happens," Harris said, "we'll be a backward step nearer the Auschwitz ovens."

"Nuts!" Demerest glanced up from the flight log, where he was recording their position, just reported. His irritability, seldom far below the surface, was beginning to show. "There are plenty of good arguments in favor of easy abortion—unwanted children who'll be born to poverty and never get a chance; then the special cases —rape, incest, the mother's health."

"There are always special cases. It's like saying, 'okay, we'll permit just a little murder, providing you make out a convincing argument.'" Harris shook his head, dissenting. "Then you talked about unwanted children. Well, they can be stopped by birth control. Nowadays everyone gets that opportunity, at every economic level. But if we slip up on that, and a human life starts growing, that's a new human being, and we've no moral right to condemn it to death. As to what we're born into, that's a chance we all take without knowing it; but once we have life, good or bad, we're entitled to keep it, and not many, however bad it is, would give it up. The answer to poverty isn't to kill unborn babies, but to improve society."

Harris considered, then went on, "As to economics, there are economic arguments for everything. It makes economic logic to kill mental deficients and mongoloids right after birth; to practice euthanasia on the terminally ill; to weed out old and useless people, the way they do in Africa, by leaving them in the jungle for hyenas to eat. But we don't do it because we value human life and dignity. What I'm saying, Vernon, is that if we plan to progress we ought to value them a little more."

The altimeters—one in front of each pilot—touched thirty-three thousand feet. They were at the top of their climb. Anson Harris eased the aircraft into level flight while Second Officer Jordan reached forward again to adjust the throttles.

Demerest said sourly to Harris, "Your trouble is cobwebs in the brain." He realized he had started the discussion; now, angrily, he wished he hadn't. To end the subject, he reached for the stewardess call button. "Let's get some hors d'oeuvres before the first class passengers wolf them all."

Harris nodded. "Good idea."

A minute or two later, in response to the telephoned order, Gwen Meighen brought three plates of aromatic hors d'oeuvres, and coffee. On Trans America, as on most airlines, captains got the fastest service.

"Thanks, Gwen," Vernon Demerest said; then, as she leaned forward to serve Anson Harris, his eyes confirmed what he already knew. Gwen's waist was as slim as ever, no sign of anything yet; nor would there be, no matter what was going on inside. The heck with Harris and his old woman's arguments! Of course Gwen would have an abortion—just as soon as they got back.

Some sixty feet aft of the flight deck, in the tourist cabin, Mrs. Ada Quonsett was engaged in spirited conversation with the passenger on her right, whom she had discovered was an amiable, middle-aged oboe player from the Chicago Symphony. "What a wonderful thing to be a musician, and *so* creative. My late husband loved classical music. He fiddled a little himself, though not professionally, of course."

Mrs. Quonsett was feeling warmed by a Dry Sack sherry for which her oboist friend had paid, and he had just inquired if she would like another. Mrs. Quonsett beamed, "Well, it's exceedingly kind of you, and perhaps I shouldn't, but I really think I will."

The passenger on her left—the man with the little sandy mustache and scrawny neck—had been less communicative; in fact, disappointing. Mrs. Quonsett's several attempts at conversation had been rebuffed by monosyllabic answers, barely audible, while the man sat, mostly expressionless, still clasping his attaché case on his knees.

For a while, when they had all ordered drinks, Mrs. Quonsett wondered if the left-seat passenger might unbend. But he hadn't. He accepted Scotch from the stewardess, paid for it with a lot of small change that he had to count out, then tossed the drink down almost in a gulp. Her own sherry mellowed Mrs. Quonsett immediately, so that she thought: Poor man, perhaps he has problems, and I shouldn't bother him.

She noticed, however, that the scrawny-necked man came suddenly alert when the captain made his announcement, soon after takeoff, about their speed, course, time of flight and all those other things which Mrs. Quonsett rarely bothered listening to. The man on her left, though, scribbled notes on the back of an envelope and afterward got out one of those *Chart Your Own Position* maps, which the airline supplied, spreading it on top of his attaché case. He was studying the map now, and making pencil marks, in between glances at his watch. It all seemed rather silly and childish to Mrs. Quonsett, who was quite sure that there was a navigator up front, taking care of where the airplane ought to be, and when.

Mrs. Quonsett then returned her attention to the oboist who was explaining that not until recently, when he had been in a public seat during a Bruckner symphony performance, had he realized that at a moment when his section of the orchestra was going "pom-tid-dey-pom-pom," the cellos were sounding "ah-diddleyah-dah." He mouthed both passages in tune to illustrate his point.

"Really! How remarkably interesting; I'd never thought of that," Mrs. Quonsett exclaimed. "My late husband would have so enjoyed meeting you, though of course you are very much younger."

She was now well into the second sherry and enjoying herself thoroughly. She thought: she had chosen such a nice flight; such a fine airplane and crew, the stewardesses polite and helpful, and with delightful passengers, except for the man on her left, who didn't really matter. Soon, dinner would be served and later, she had learned, there was to be a movie with Michael Caine, one of her favorite stars. What more could anyone possibly ask?

Mrs. Quonsett had been wrong in assuming that there was a navigator up front on the flight deck. There wasn't. Trans America, like most major airlines, no longer carried navigators, even on overseas flights, because of the multitude of radar and radio systems available on modern jet aircraft. The pilots, aided by constant air route control surveillance, did what little navigation was needed.

However, had there been an old-time air navigator aboard Flight Two, his charted position of the aircraft would have been remarkably similar to that which D. O. Guerrero had achieved by rough-and-ready reckoning. Guerrero had estimated several minutes earlier that they were close to Detroit; the estimate was right. He knew, because the captain had said so in his announcement to passengers, that their subsequent course would take them over Montreal; Fredericton, New Brunswick; Cape Ray; and later St. John's, Newfoundland. The captain had even been helpful enough to include the aircraft's ground speed as well as airspeed, making Guerrero's further calculations just as accurate.

The east coast of Newfoundland, D. O. Guerrero calculated, would be passed over in two-and-a-half hours from the present time. However, before then, the captain would probably make another position an-

nouncement, so the estimate could be revised if necessary. After that, as already planned, Guerrero would
wait a further hour to ensure that the flight was well
over the Atlantic Ocean before pulling the cord on his
case and exploding the dynamite inside. At this
moment, in anticipation, his fingers clasping the attaché
case tensed.

Now that the time of culmination was so close, he
wanted it to come quickly. Perhaps, after all, he
thought, he would not wait the full time. Once they had
left Newfoundland, really any time would do.

The shot of whisky had relaxed him. Although most
of his earlier tension had disappeared on coming
aboard, it had built up again soon after takeoff, particularly when the irritating old cat in the next seat had tried
to start a conversation. D. O. Guerrero wanted no conversation, either now or later; in fact, no more communication with anyone else in this life. All that he wanted
was to sit and dream—of three hundred thousand dollars, a larger sum than he had ever possessed at one
time before, and which would be coming to Inez and the
two children, he presumed, in a matter of days.

Right now he could have used another whisky, but
had no money left to pay for it. After his unexpectedly
large insurance purchase, there had been barely enough
small change for the single drink; so he would have to
do without.

As he had earlier, he closed his eyes. This time he
was thinking of the effect on Inez and the children when
they heard about the money. They ought to care about
him for what he was doing, even though they wouldn't
know the whole of it—that he was sacrificing himself,
giving his own life for them. But perhaps they might
guess a little. If they did, he hoped they would be appreciative, although he wondered about that, knowing from
experience that people could be surprisingly perverse in
reactions to what was done on their behalf.

The strange thing was: In all his thoughts about Inez
and the children, he couldn't quite visualize their faces.
It seemed almost as though he were thinking about
people whom he had never really known.

He compromised by conjuring up visions of dollar signs, followed by threes, and endless zeros. After a while he must have dropped off to sleep because, when he opened his eyes a quick glance at his watch showed that it was twenty minutes later, and a stewardess was leaning over from the aisle. The stewardess—an attractive brunette who spoke with an English accent—was asking, "Are you ready for dinner, sir? If so, perhaps you'd like me to take your case."

4

Almost from their initial moment of meeting, Mel Bakersfeld had formed an instinctive dislike of the lawyer, Elliott Freemantle, who was leading the delegation of Meadowood residents. Now, ten minutes or so after the delegation filed into Mel's office, the dislike was sharpening to downright loathing.

It seemed as if the lawyer was deliberately being as obnoxious as possible. Even before the discussion opened, there had been Freemantle's unpleasant remark about not wanting "a lot of doubletalk," which Mel parried mildly, though resenting it. Since then, every rejoinder of Mel's had been greeted with equal rudeness and skepticism. Mel's instinct cautioned him that Freemantle was deliberately baiting him, hoping that Mel would lose his temper and make intemperate statements, with the press recording them. If it was the lawyer's strategy, Mel had no intention of abetting it. With some difficulty, he continued to keep his own manner reasonable and polite.

Freemantle had protested what he termed, "the callous indifference of this airport's management to the health and well-being of my clients, the good citizen families of Meadowood."

Mel replied quietly that neither the airport nor the airlines using it had been callous or indifferent. "On the contrary, we have recognized that a genuine problem about noise exists, and have done our best to deal with it."

"Then your best, sir, is a miserable, weak effort! And you've done *what?*" Lawyer Freemantle declared, "So far as my clients and I can see—and hear—you've done no more than make empty promises which amount to nothing. It's perfectly evident—and the reason we intend to proceed to law—is that no one around here really gives a damn."

The accusation was untrue, Mel countered. There had been a planned program of avoiding takeoffs on runway two five—which pointed directly at Meadowood —whenever an alternate runway could be used. Thus, two five was used mostly for landings only, creating little noise for Meadowood, even though entailing a loss in operating efficiency for the airport. In addition, pilots of all airlines had instructions to use noise abatement procedures after any takeoff in the general direction of Meadowood, on whatever runway, including turns away from Meadowood immediately after leaving the ground. Air traffic control had cooperated in all objectives.

Mel added, "What you should realize, Mr. Freemantle, is that this is by no means the first meeting we have had with local residents. We've discussed our mutual problems many times."

Elliott Freemantle snapped, "Perhaps at the other times there was not enough plain speaking."

"Whether that's true or not, you seem to be making up for it now."

"We intend to make up for a good deal—of lost time, wasted effort and bad faith, the latter not on my clients' part."

Mel decided not to respond. There was nothing to be gained, for either side, by this kind of harangue—except, perhaps, publicity for Elliott Freemantle. Mel observed that the reporters' pencils were racing; one thing which the lawyer clearly understood was what made lively copy for the press.

As soon as he decently could, Mel resolved, he would cut this session short. He was acutely conscious of Cindy, still seated where she had been when the delegation came in, though now appearing bored, which was characteristic of Cindy whenever anything came up involving airport affairs. This time, however, Mel sympathized with her. In view of the seriousness of what they had been discussing, he was finding this whole Meadowood business an intrusion himself.

In Mel's mind, too, was his recurring concern for Keith. He wondered how things were with his brother, over in air traffic control. Should he have insisted that Keith quit work for tonight, and pursued their discussion which—until the tower watch chief's intervention cut it off—had seemed to be getting somewhere? Even now, perhaps, it was not too late . . . But then there was Cindy, who certainly had a right to be considered ahead of Keith; and now this waspish lawyer, Freemantle, still ranting on . . .

"Since you chose to mention the so-called noise abatement procedures," Elliott Freemantle inquired sarcastically, "may I ask what happened to them tonight?"

Mel sighed. "We've had a storm for three days." His glance took in the others in the delegation. "I'm sure you're all aware of it. It's created emergency situations." He explained the blockage of runway three zero, the temporary need for takeoffs on runway two five, with the inevitable effect on Meadowood.

"That's all very well," one of the other men said. He was a heavy-jowled, balding man whom Mel had met at other discussions about airport noise. "We know about the storm, Mr. Bakersfeld. But if you've living directly underneath, knowing *why* airplanes are coming over doesn't make anyone feel better, storm or not. By the way, my name is Floyd Zanetta. I was chairman of the meeting . . ."

Elliott Freemantle cut in smoothly. "If you'll excuse me, there's another point before we go on." Obviously the lawyer had no intention of relinquishing control of the delegation, even briefly. He addressed Mel, with a sideways glance at the press. "It isn't solely noise that's filling homes and ears of Meadowood, though that's bad enough—shattering nerves, destroying health, depriving children of their needed sleep. But there is a physical invasion . . ."

This time Mel interrupted. "Are you seriously suggesting that as an alternative to what's happened tonight, the airport should close down?"

"Not only am I suggesting that you do it; we may compel you. A moment ago I spoke of a physical invasion. It is that which I will prove, before the courts, on behalf of my clients. And we will win!"

The other members of the delegation, including Floyd Zanetta, gave approving nods.

While waiting for his last words to sink home, Elliott Freemantle deliberated. He supposed he had gone almost far enough. It was disappointing that the airport general manager hadn't blown a fuse, as Freemantle had been carefully goading him to do. The technique was one which he had used before, frequently with success, and it was a good technique because people who lost their tempers invariably came off worse in press reports, which was what Freemantle was mainly concerned about. But Bakersfeld, though clearly annoyed, had been too smart to fall for that ploy. Well, never mind, Elliott Freemantle thought; he had been successful just the same. He, too, had seen the reporters industriously getting his words down—words which (with the sneer and hectoring tone removed) would read well in print; even better, he believed, than his earlier speech at the Meadowood meeting.

Of course, Freemantle realized, this whole proceeding was just an exercise in semantics. Nothing would come of it. Even if the airport manager, Bakersfeld, could be persuaded to their point of view—a highly unlikely happening—there was little or nothing he could do about it. The airport was a fact of life and nothing would alter the reality of it being where and how it was. No, the value of being here at all tonight was partly in gaining public attention, but principally (from Lawyer Freemantle's viewpoint) to convince the Meadowood populace that they had a stalwart champion, so that those legal retainer forms (as well as checks) would keep on flowing into the offices of Freemantle and Sye.

It was a pity, Freemantle thought, that the remainder of the crowd from Meadowood, who were waiting downstairs, could not have heard him up here, dishing out the rough stuff—on their behalf—to Bakersfeld. But they would read about it in tomorrow's papers; also, Elliott Freemantle was not at all convinced that what was happening here and now would be the last Meadowood item on tonight's airport agenda. He had already promised the TV crews, who were waiting down below because they couldn't make it in here with their equipment, a statement when this present session was over. He had hopes that by now—because he had suggested it —the TV cameras would be set up in the main terminal concourse, and even though that Negro police lieutenant had forbidden any demonstration there, Freemantle had an idea that the TV session, astutely managed, might well develop into one.

Elliott Freemantle's statement of a moment ago had concerned legal action—the action which, he had assured Meadowood residents earlier this evening, would be his principal activity on their behalf. "My business is law," he had told them. "Law and nothing else." It was not true, of course; but then, Elliott Freemantle's policies were apt to back and fill as expediency demanded.

"What legal action you take," Mel Bakersfeld pointed out, "is naturally your own affair. All the same, I would remind you that the courts have upheld the rights of airports to operate, despite adjoining communities, as a matter of public convenience and necessity."

Freemantle's eyebrows shot up. "I didn't realize that you are a lawyer too."

"I'm not a lawyer. I'm also quite sure you're aware of it."

"Well, for a moment I was beginning to wonder." Elliott Freemantle smirked. "Because I am, you see; and with some experience in these matters. Furthermore, I assure you that there are legal precedents in my clients' favor." As he had at the meeting earlier, he rattled off the impressive-sounding list of cases—*U.S.* v.

Causby, Griggs v. *County of Allegheny, Thornburg* v. *Port of Portland, Martin* v. *Port of Seattle.*

Mel was amused, though he didn't show it. The cases were familiar to him. He also knew of others, which had produced drastically different judgments, and which Elliott Freemantle was either unaware of or had cagily avoided mentioning. Mel suspected the latter, but had no intention of getting into a legal debate. The place for that, if and when it happened, was in court.

However, Mel saw no reason why the lawyer—whom he now disliked even more intensely—should have everything his own way. Speaking to the delegation generally, Mel explained his reason for avoiding legal issues, but added, "Since we are all here, there are some things I would like to say to you on the subject of airports and noise generally."

Cindy, he observed, was yawning.

Freemantle responded instantly. "I doubt if that will be necessary. The next step so far as we are concerned..."

"Oh!" For the first time Mel dispensed with mildness, and bore down heavily. "Am I to understand that after I've listened patiently to you, you and your group are not prepared to extend the same courtesy?"

The delegate, Zanetta, who had spoken before, glanced at the others. "I do think we ought..."

Mel said sharply, "Let Mr. Freemantle answer."

"There's really no need"—the lawyer smiled suavely —"for anyone to raise their voice, or be discourteous."

"In that case, why have you been doing both those things ever since you came in?"

"I'm not aware..."

"Well, I *am* aware."

"Aren't you losing your temper, Mr. Bakersfeld?"

"No," Mel smiled. "I'm sorry to disappoint you, but I'm not." He was conscious of having seized an advantage, catching the lawyer by surprise. Now he went on, "You've had a good deal to say, Mr. Freemantle, and not much of it politely. But there are a few things I'd like to get on the record, too. Also, I'm sure the press will be interested in both sides even if no one else is."

"Oh, we're interested all right. It's just that we've heard all the wishy-washy excuses already." As usual, Elliott Freemantle was recovering fast. But he admitted to himself that he had been lulled by Bakersfeld's earlier mild manner, so that the sharp counterattack caught him unawares. He realized that the airport general manager was more astute than he appeared.

"I didn't say anything about excuses," Mel pointed out. "I suggested a review of airport noise situations generally."

Freemantle shrugged. The last thing he wanted was to open up some new approach which might be newsworthy and, therefore, divert attention from himself. At the moment, though, he didn't see how he could prevent it.

"Ladies and gentlemen," Mel began, "when you first came here tonight something was said about plain, blunt speaking on both sides. Mr. Freemantle has had his turn at that; now I will be equally candid."

Mel sensed he had the full attention of the two women and four men in the delegation; also of the press. Even Cindy was watching him covertly. He continued to speak quietly.

"All of you know, or should, the measures which we have taken at Lincoln International Airport to make life easier, more bearable, from the point of view of aircraft noise, for those who live in the airport vicinity. Some of these measures have been mentioned already, and there are others, such as using remote airport areas for the testing of engines, and even then during proscribed hours only."

Elliott Freemantle, already fidgeting, cut in. "But you've admitted that these so-called systems fail to work."

Mel snapped back, "I admitted nothing of the kind. Most of the time they *do* work—as well as any compromise can. Tonight I've admitted that they are not working because of exceptional circumstances, and frankly if I were a pilot, taking off in weather like this, I'd be reluctant to reduce power right after takeoff, and make a climbing turn too. Furthermore, this kind of condition is bound to recur from time to time."

"Most of the time!"

"No, sir! And please allow me to finish!" Without pausing, Mel went on, "The fact is: airports—here and elsewhere—have come close to doing as much as they can in the way of noise reduction. You may not like hearing this, and not everyone in this business admits it, but the truth is: there isn't a lot more that anyone can do. You simply cannot tiptoe a three hundred thousand pound piece of high-powered machinery into any place. So when you do bring a big jet airplane in—or take it out—inevitably it shakes hell out of a few people who are nearby." There were several quick smiles, though not from Elliott Freemantle, who was scowling. Mel added, "So if we need airports—and obviously we do —somebody, somewhere has to put up with some noise, or move away."

It was Mel's turn to see the reporters' pencils racing with his words.

"It's true," Mel continued, "that aircraft manufacturers are working on noise reduction devices, but— again to be honest with you—few people in the aviation industry take them seriously, and certainly they do not represent a major effort like, for example, development of a new aircraft. At best, they'll be palliatives. If you don't believe me, let me remind you that even though trucks have been in use for many years more than airplanes, no one has yet invented a really effective truck muffler.

"Another thing to bear in mind is that by the time one type of jet engine gets quieted a little—if it ever does—there'll be new, more powerful engines in use which, even with suppressors fitted, will be noisier than the first engine was to begin with. As I said," Mel added, "I am being absolutely frank."

One of the women in the delegation murmured gloomily, "You sure are."

"Which brings me," Mel said, "to the question of the future. There are new breeds of aircraft coming—another family of jets after the Boeing 747s, including behemoths like the Lockheed 500, which will come into use soon; then shortly afterward, the supersonic transports—the Concordé, and those to follow. The Lockheed 500 and its kind will be subsonic—that is, they'll operate at less than the speed of sound, and will give us the kind of noise we have now, only more of it. The supersonics will have a mighty engine noise too, *plus* a sonic boom as they breach the sound barrier, which is going to be more of a problem than any other noise we've had so far.

"You may have heard or read—as I have—optimistic reports that the sonic booms will occur high, far from cities and airports, and that the effect on the ground will be minor. Don't believe it! We're in for trouble, all of us —people in homes, like you; people like me, who run airports; airlines, who'll have a billion dollars invested in equipment which they must use continuously, or go bankrupt. Believe me, the time is coming when we'll wish we had the simplicity of the kind of noise we're talking about tonight."

"So what are you telling my clients?" Elliott Freemantle inquired sarcastically. "To go jump in the lunatic asylum now rather than wait until you and your behemoths drive them there?"

"No," Mel said firmly, "I'm not telling them that. I'm merely saying candidly—the way you asked me to—that I haven't any simple answers; nor will I make you promises that the airport cannot keep. Also I'm saying that in my opinion, airport noise is going to become greater, not less. However, I'd like to remind all of you that this problem isn't new. It's existed since trains started running, and since trucks, buses, and automobiles joined them; there was the same problem when freeways were built through residential areas; and when airports were established, and grew. All these things are for the public good—or so we believe—yet all of them create noise and, despite all kinds of efforts, they've continued to. The thing is: trucks, trains, freeways, airplanes, and the rest are here. They're part of the way we live, and unless we change our way of life, then their noise is something we have to live with too."

"In other words, my clients should abandon any idea of serenity, uninterrupted sleep, privacy and quietness for the remainder of their natural lives?"

"No," Mel said. "I think, in the end, they'll have to move. I'm not speaking officially, of course, but I'm convinced that eventually this airport and others will be obliged to make multibillion-dollar purchases of residential areas surrounding them. A good many of the areas can become industrial zones where noise won't matter. And of course, there would be reasonable compensation to those who owned homes and were forced to leave them."

Elliott Freemantle rose and motioned others in the delegation to do the same.

"That last remark," he informed Mel, "is the one sensible thing I've heard this evening. However, the compensation may start sooner than you think, and also be larger." Freemantle nodded curtly. "You will be hearing from us. We shall see you in court."

He went out, the others following.

Through the door to the anteroom Mel heard one of the two women delegates exclaim, "You were magnificent, Mr. Freemantle. I'm going to tell everyone so."

"Well, thank you. Thank you very . . ." The voices faded.

Mel went to the door, intending to close it.

"I'm sorry about that," he said to Cindy. Now that the two of them were alone again, he was not sure what else they had to say to each other, if anything.

Cindy said icily, "It's par for the course. You should have married an airport."

At the doorway, Mel noticed that one of the men reporters had returned to the anteroom. It was Tomlinson of the *Tribune*.

"Mr. Bakersfeld, could I see you for a moment?"

Mel said wearily, "What is it?"

"I got the impression you weren't too smitten with Mr. Freemantle."

"Is this for quotation?"

"No, sir."

"Then your impression was right."

"I thought you'd be interested in this," the reporter said.

"This" was one of the legal retainer forms which Elliott Freemantle had distributed at the Meadowood community meeting.

As Mel read the form, he asked, "Where did you get it?"

The reporter explained.

"How many people were at the meeting?"

"I counted. Roughly six hundred."

"And how many of these forms were signed?"

"I can't be sure of that, Mr. Bakersfeld. My guess would be a hundred and fifty were signed and turned in. Then there were other people who said they'd send theirs by mail."

Mel thought grimly: now he could understand Elliott Freemantle's histrionics; also why and whom the lawyer was trying to impress.

"I guess you're doing the same arithmetic I did," the reporter, Tomlinson, said.

Mel nodded. "It adds up to a tidy little sum."

"Sure does. I wouldn't mind a piece of it myself."

"Maybe we're both in the wrong business. Did you cover the Meadowood meeting too?"

"Yes."

"Didn't anyone over there point out that the total legal fee was likely to be at least fifteen thousand dollars?"

Tomlinson shook his head. "Either no one thought of it, or they didn't care. Besides, Freemantle has quite a personality; hypnotic, I guess you'd call it. He had 'em spellbound, like he was Billy Graham."

Mel handed back the printed retainer form. "Will you put this in your story?"

"I'll put it in, but don't be surprised if the city desk kills it. They're always wary about professional legal stuff. Besides, I guess if you come right down to it, there's nothing really wrong."

"No," Mel said, "it may be unethical, and I imagine the bar association wouldn't like it. But it isn't illegal. What the Meadowood folk should have done, of course, was get together and retain a lawyer as a group. But if people are gullible, and want to make lawyers rich, I guess it's their own affair."

Tomlinson grinned. "May I quote some of that?"

"You just got through telling me your paper wouldn't print it. Besides, this is off the record. Remember?"

"Okay."

If it would have done any good, Mel thought, he would have sounded off, and taken a chance on being quoted or not. But he knew it wouldn't do any good. He also knew that all over the country, ambulance chasing lawyers like Elliott Freemantle were busily signing up groups of people, then harassing airports, airlines, and —in some cases—pilots.

It was not the harassing which Mel objected to; that, and legal recourse, were everyone's privilege. It was simply that in many instances the homeowner clients were being misled, buoyed up with false hopes, and quoted an impressive-sounding, but one-sided selection of legal precedents such as Elliott Freemantle had used tonight. As a result, a spate of legal actions—costly and time-consuming—was being launched, most of which were foredoomed to fail, and from which only the lawyers involved would emerge as beneficiaries.

Mel wished that he had known earlier what Tomlinson had just told him. In that case he would have loaded his remarks to the delegation, so as to convey a warning about Elliott Freemantle, and what the Meadowood residents were getting into. Now it was too late.

"Mr. Bakersfeld," the *Tribune* reporter said, "there are some other things I'd like to ask you—about the airport generally. If you could spare a few minutes . . ."

"Any other time I'll be glad to." Mel raised his hands in a helpless gesture. "Right now there are fifteen things happening at once."

The reporter nodded. "I understand. Anyway, I'll be around for a while. I hear Freemantle's bunch are cooking up something down below. So if there's a chance later . . ."

"I'll do my best," Mel said, though he had no intention of being available any more tonight. He respected

Tomlinson's wish to dig below the surface of any story which he covered; just the same, Mel had seen enough of delegations *and* reporters for one evening.

As to whatever else it was that Freemantle and the Meadowood people were "cooking up down below," he would leave any worrying about that, Mel decided, to Lieutenant Ordway and his policemen.

5

When Mel turned, after closing the door of his office as the *Tribune* reporter left, Cindy was standing, pulling on her gloves. She remarked acidly, "Fifteen things happening, I believe you said. Whatever the other fourteen are, I'm sure they'll all take priority over me."

"That was a figure of speech," Mel protested, "as you know perfectly well. I already said I'm sorry. I didn't know this was going to happen—at least, not all at once."

"But you love it, don't you? All of it. Much more than me, home, the children, a decent social life."

"Ah!" Mel said. "I wondered when you'd get to that." He stopped. "Oh, hell! Why are we fighting again? We settled everything, didn't we? There's no need to fight any more."

"No," Cindy said. She was suddenly subdued. "No, I suppose not."

There was an uncertain silence. Mel broke it first.

"Look, getting a divorce is a pretty big thing for both of us; for Roberta and Libby, too. If you've any doubts . . ."

"Haven't we been over that already?"

"Yes; but if you want to, we'll go over it fifty times again."

"I don't want to." Cindy shook her head decisively.

"I haven't any doubts. Nor have you, not really. Have you?"

"No," Mel said. "I'm afraid I haven't."

Cindy started to say something, then stopped. She had been going to tell Mel about Lionel Urquhart, but decided against it. There was plenty of time for Mel to find that out for himself, later. As to Derek Eden, whom Cindy had been thinking about during most of the time that the Meadowood delegation had been in the office, she had no intention of disclosing his existence to Mel *or* Lionel.

There was a knock—light but definite—on the anteroom door.

"Oh, God!" Cindy muttered. "Isn't there *any* privacy?"

Mel called out irritably, "Who is it?"

The door opened. "Just me," Tanya Livingston said. "Mel, I need some advice . . ." As she saw Cindy, she stopped abruptly. "Excuse me. I thought you were alone."

"He will be," Cindy said. "In hardly any time at all."

"Please, no!" Tanya flushed. "I can come back, Mrs. Bakersfeld. I didn't know I was disturbing you."

Cindy's eyes flicked over Tanya, still in Trans America uniform.

"It's probably time we were disturbed," Cindy said. "After all, it's been a good three minutes since the last people left, and that's longer than we usually have together." She swung toward Mel. "Isn't it?"

He shook his head, without answering.

"By the way." Cindy turned back to Tanya. "I'm curious about one thing. How you were so sure who I am."

Momentarily, Tanya had lost her usual poise. Recovering it, she gave a small smile. "I suppose I guessed."

Cindy's eyebrows went up. "Am I supposed to do the same?" She glanced at Mel.

"No," he said. He introduced them.

Mel was aware of Cindy appraising Tanya Livingston. He had not the slightest doubt that his wife was already forming some conclusion about Tanya and him-

self; Mel had long ago learned that Cindy's instincts
about men-women relationships were uncannily
accurate. Besides, he was sure that his own introduction
of Tanya had betrayed something. Husbands and wives
were too familiar with each other's nuances of speech
for that not to happen. It would not even surprise him if
Cindy guessed about his own and Tanya's rendezvous
for later tonight, though perhaps, he reflected, that was
carrying imagination too far.

Well, whatever Cindy knew or guessed, he supposed
it didn't really matter. After all, she was the one who
had asked for a divorce, so why should she object to
someone else in Mel's life, however much or little Tanya
meant, and he wasn't sure of that himself? But then, Mel
reminded himself, that was a logical way of thinking.
Women—including Cindy, and probably Tanya—were
seldom logical.

The last thought proved right.

"How nice for you," Cindy told him with pseudo
sweetness, "that it isn't just dull old delegations who
come to you with problems." She eyed Tanya. "You did
say you have a problem?"

Tanya returned the inspection levelly. "I said I
wanted some advice."

"Oh, really! What kind of advice? Was it business,
personal? . . . Or perhaps you've forgotten."

"Cindy," Mel said sharply, "that's enough! You've no
reason . . ."

"No reason for what? And why is it enough?" His
wife's voice was mocking; he had the impression that in
a perverse way she was enjoying herself. "Aren't you
always telling me I don't take enough interest in your
problems? Now I'm all agog about your friend's
problem . . . that is, if there is one."

Tanya said crisply, "It's about Flight Two." She
added. "That's Trans America's flight to Rome, Mrs.
Bakersfeld. It took off half an hour ago."

Mel asked, "What about Flight Two?"

"To tell the truth"—Tanya hesitated—"I'm not really
sure."

"Go ahead," Cindy said. "Think of something."

Mel snapped, "Oh, shut up!" He addressed Tanya, "What is it?"

Tanya glanced at Cindy, then told him of her conversation with Customs Inspector Standish. She described the man with the suspiciously held attaché case, whom Standish suspected of smuggling.

"He went aboard Flight Two?"

"Yes."

"Then even if your man *was* smuggling," Mel pointed out, "it would be into Italy. The U.S. Customs people don't worry about that. They let other countries look out for themselves."

"I know. That's the way our D.T.M. saw it." Tanya described the exchange between herself and the District Transportation Manager, ending with the latter's irritable but firm instruction, "Forget it!"

Mel looked puzzled. "Then I don't see why . . ."

"I told you I'm not sure, and maybe this is all silly. But I kept thinking about it, so I started checking."

"Checking what?"

Both of them had forgotten Cindy.

"Inspector Standish," Tanya said, "told me that the man—the one with the attaché case—was almost the last to board the flight. He must have been because I was at the gate, and I missed seeing an old woman . . ." She corrected herself. "That part doesn't matter. Anyway, a few minutes ago I got hold of the gate agent for Flight Two and we went over the manifest and tickets together. He couldn't remember the man with the case, but we narrowed it down to five names."

"And then?"

"Just on a hunch I called our check-in counters to see if anyone remembered anything about any of those five people. At the airport counters, nobody did. But downtown, one of the agents did remember the man—the one with the case. So I know his name; the description fits . . . everything."

"I still don't see what's so extraordinary. He had to check in somewhere. So he checked in downtown."

"The reason the agent remembered him," Tanya said,

"is that he didn't have any baggage, except the little case. Also, the agent said, he was extremely nervous."

"Lots of people are nervous . . ." Abruptly Mel stopped. He frowned. "No baggage! For a flight to Rome!"

"That's right. Except for the little bag the man was carrying, the one Inspector Standish noticed. The agent downtown called it a briefcase."

"But nobody goes on that kind of journey without baggage. It doesn't make sense."

"That's what I thought." Again Tanya hesitated. "It doesn't make sense unless . . ."

"Unless what?"

"Unless you happen to know already that the flight you're on will never get to where it's supposed to be going. If you knew that, you'd also know that you wouldn't need any baggage."

"Tanya," Mel said softly, "what are you trying to say?"

She answered uncomfortably, "I'm not sure; that's why I came to you. When I think about it, it seems silly and melodramatic, only . . ."

"Go on."

"Well, supposing that man we've been talking about isn't smuggling at all; at least, in the way we've all assumed. Supposing the reason for him not having any luggage, for being nervous, for holding the case the way Inspector Standish noticed . . . suppose instead of having some sort of contraband in there . . . he has a bomb."

Their eyes held each other's steadily. Mel's mind was speculating, assessing possibilities. To him, also, the idea which Tanya had just raised seemed ridiculous and remote. Yet . . . in the past, occasionally, such things had happened. The question was: How could you decide if this was another time? The more he thought about it, the more he realized that the entire episode of the man with the attaché case could so easily be innocent; in fact, probably was. If that proved true after a fuss had been created, whoever began the fuss would have made a fool of himself. It was human not to want to do that; yet, with the safety of an airplane and passengers involved, did making a fool of oneself matter? Obviously not. On the other hand, there ought to be a stronger reason for the drastic actions which a bomb scare would involve than merely a possibility, plus a hunch. Was there, Mel wondered, some way conceivably in which a stronger hint, even corroboration, might be found?

Offhand, he couldn't think of one.

But there *was* something he could check. It was a long shot, but all that was needed was a phone call. He supposed that seeing Vernon Demerest tonight, with the reminder of the clash before the Board of Airport Commissioners, had made him think of it.

For the second time this evening, Mel consulted his pocket panic-list of telephone numbers. Then, using an internal airport telephone on his desk, he dialed the insurance vending booth in the main concourse. The girl clerk who answered was a long-time employee whom Mel knew well.

"Marj," he said, when he had identified himself, "have you written many policies tonight on the Trans America Flight Two?"

"A few more than usual, Mr. Bakersfeld. But then we have on all flights; this kind of weather always does that. On Flight Two, I've had about a dozen, and I know Bunnie—that's the other girl on with me—has written some as well."

"What I'd like you to do," Mel told her, "is read me all the names and policy amounts." As he sensed the girl hesitate, "If I have to, I'll call your district manager and get authority. But you know he'll give it to me, and I'd like you to take my word that this is important. Doing it this way, you can save me time."

"All right, Mr. Bakersfeld; if you say it's okay. But it will take a few minutes to get the policies together."

"I'll wait."

Mel heard the telephone put down, the girl apologize to someone at the insurance counter for the interruption. There was a rustling of papers, then another girl's voice inquiring, "Is something wrong?"

Covering the telephone mouthpiece, Mel asked Tanya, "What's that name you have—the man with the case?"

She consulted a slip of paper. "Guerrero, or it may be Buerrero; we had it spelled both ways." She saw Mel start. "Initials D.O."

Mel's hand still cupped the telephone. His mind was concentrating. The woman who had been brought to his office half an hour ago was named Guerrero; he remembered Lieutenant Ordway saying so. She was the one whom the airport police had found wandering in the terminal. According to Ned Ordway, the woman was distressed and crying; the police couldn't get any sense from her. Mel was going to try talking to her himself, but hadn't gotten around to it. He had seen the woman on the point of leaving the outer office as the Meadowood delegation came in. Of course, there might be no connection . . .

Through the telephone, Mel could still hear voices at the insurance booth and, in the background, the noise of the main terminal concourse.

"Tanya," he said quietly, "about twenty minutes ago there was a woman in the outside office—middle-aged, shabbily dressed; she looked wet and draggle-tailed. I believe she left when some other people came in, but she might be still around. If she's anywhere outside, bring her in. In any case, if you find her, don't let her get away from you." Tanya looked puzzled. He added, "Her name is Mrs. Guerrero."

As Tanya left the office, the girl clerk at the insurance booth came back on the line. "I have all those policies, Mr. Bakersfeld. Are you ready if I read the names?"

"Yes, Marj. Go ahead."

He listened carefully. As a name near the end occurred, he had a sudden sense of tension. For the first time his voice was urgent. "Tell me about that policy. Did you write it?"

"No. That was one of Bunnie's. I'll let you speak to her."

He listened to what the other girl had to say and asked two or three questions. Their exchange was brief.

He broke the connection and was dialing another number as Tanya returned.

Though her eyes asked questions which for the moment he ignored, she reported immediately, "There's no one on the mezzanine. There are still a million people down below, but you'd never pick anyone out. Should we page?"

"We can try, though I don't have a lot of hope." On the basis of what he had learned, Mel thought, not much was getting through to the Guerrero woman, so it was unlikely that a p.a. announcement would do so now. Also, by this time she could have left the airport and be halfway to the city. He reproached himself for not having tried to talk with her, as he had intended, but there had been the other things: the delegation from Meadowood; his anxiety about his brother, Keith—Mel remembered that he had considered going back to the control tower . . . well, that would have to wait now . . . then there had been Cindy. With a guilty start because he hadn't noticed before, he realized that Cindy was gone.

He reached for the p.a. microphone on his desk and pushed it toward Tanya.

There was an answer from the number he had dialed, which was airport police headquarters. Mel said crisply, "I want Lieutenant Ordway. Is he still in the terminal?"

"Yes, sir." The police desk sergeant was familiar with Mel's voice.

"Find him as quickly as you can; I'll hold. And by the way, what was the first name of a woman called Guerrero, whom one of your people picked up tonight? I think I know, but I want to make sure."

"Just a minute, sir. I'll look." A moment later he said, "It's Inez; Inez Guerrero. And we've already called the lieutenant on his beeper box."

Mel was aware that Lieutenant Ordway, like many others at the airport, carried a pocket radio receiver which gave a "beep" signal if he was required urgently. Somewhere, at this moment, Ordway was undoubtedly hastening to a phone.

Mel gave brief instructions to Tanya, then pressed the

"on" switch of the p.a. microphone, which overrode all others in the terminal. Through the open doors to the anteroom and mezzanine he heard an American Airlines flight departure announcement halt abruptly in mid-sentence. Only twice before, during the eight years of Mel's tenure as airport general manager, had the mike and override switch been used. The first occasion—branded in Mel's memory—had been to announce the death of President Kennedy; the second, a year later, was when a lost and crying child wandered directly into Mel's office. Usually there were regular procedures for handling lost children, but that time Mel had used the mike himself to locate the frantic parents.

Now he nodded to Tanya to begin her announcement, remembering that he was not yet sure why they wanted the woman, Inez Guerrero, or even that—for certain—there was anything wrong at all. Yet instinct told him that there was; that something serious had happened, or was happening; and when you had a puzzle of that kind, the smart and urgent thing to do was gather all the pieces that you could, hoping that somehow, with help from other people, you could fit them together to make sense.

"Attention please," Tanya was saying in her clear, unaffected voice, now audible in every corner of the terminal. "Will Mrs. Inez Guerrero, or Buerrero, please come immediately to the airport general manager's office on the administrative mezzanine of the main terminal building. Ask any airline or airport representative to direct you. I will repeat . . ."

There was a click in Mel's telephone. Lieutenant Ordway came on the line.

"We want that woman," Mel told him. "The one who was here—Guerrero. We're announcing . . ."

"I know," Ordway said. "I can hear."

"We need her urgently; I'll explain later For now, take my word . . ."

"I already have. When did you last see her?"

"In my outer office. When she was with you."

"Okay. Anything else?"

"Only that this may be big. I suggest you drop everything; use all your men. And whether you find her or not, get up here soon."

"Right." There was another click as Ordway hung up.

Tanya had finished her announcement; she pushed the "off" button of the microphone. Outside, Mel could hear another announcement begin, "Attention Mr. Lester Mainwaring. Will Mr. Mainwaring and all members of his party report immediately to the main terminal entrance?"

"Lester Mainwaring" was an airport code name for "policeman." Normally, such an announcement meant that the nearest policeman on duty was to go wherever the message designated. "All members of his party" meant every policeman in the terminal. Most airports had similar systems to alert their police without the public being made aware.

Ordway was wasting no time. Undoubtedly he would brief his men about Inez Guerrero as they reported to the main entrance.

"Call your D.T.M.," Mel instructed Tanya. "Ask him to come to this office as quickly as he can. Tell him it's important." Partly to himself, he added, "We'll start by getting everybody here."

Tanya made the call, then reported, "He's on his way." Her voice betrayed nervousness.

Mel had gone to the office door. He closed it.

"You still haven't told me," Tanya said, "what it was you found out."

Mel chose his words carefully.

"Your man Guerrero, the one with no luggage except the little attaché case, and whom you think might have a bomb aboard Flight Two, took out a flight insurance policy just before takeoff for three hundred thousand dollars. The beneficiary is Inez Guerrero. He paid for it with what looked like his last small change."

"My God!" Tanya's face went white. She whispered, "Oh, dear God . . . no!"

6

There were times—tonight was one—when Joe Patroni was grateful that he worked in the maintenance bailiwick of aviation, and not in sales.

The thought occurred to him as he surveyed the busy activity of digging beneath, and around the mired Aéreo-Mexican jet which continued to block runway three zero.

As Patroni saw it, airline sales forces—in which category he lumped all front office staff and executives—comprised inflatable rubber people who connived against each other like fretful children. On the other hand, Patroni was convinced that those in engineering and maintenance departments behaved like mature adults. Maintenance men (Joe was apt to argue), even when employed by competing airlines, worked closely and harmoniously, sharing their information, experience, and even secrets for the common good.

As Joe Patroni sometimes confided privately to his friends, an example of this unofficial sharing was the pooling of information which came to maintenance men regularly through conferences held by individual airlines.

Patroni's employers, like most major scheduled airlines, had daily telephone conferences—known as "briefings"—during which all regional headquarters, bases, and outfield stations were connected through a continent-wide closed-circuit hook-up. Directed by a head office vice-president, the briefings were, in fact, critiques and information exchanges on the way the airline had operated during the past twenty-four hours. Senior people throughout the company's system talked freely and frankly with one another. Operations and sales departments each had their own daily briefing; so did maintenance—the latter, in Patroni's opinion, by far the most important.

During the maintenance sessions, in which Joe Patroni took part five days a week, stations reported one by one. Where delays in service—for mechanical reasons —had occurred the previous day, those in charge were required to account for them. Nobody bothered making excuses. As Patroni put it: "If you goofed, you say so." Accidents or failures of equipment, even minor, were reported; the objective, to pool knowledge and prevent recurrence. At next Monday's session, Patroni would report tonight's experience with the Aéreo-Mexican 707, and his success or failure, however it turned out. The daily discussions were strictly no-nonsense, largely because the maintenance men were tough cookies who knew they couldn't fool one another.

After each official conference—and usually unknown to senior managements—unofficial ones began. Patroni and others would exchange telephone calls with cronies in maintenance departments of competing airlines. They would compare notes about one another's daily conferences, passing on what information seemed worth while. Rarely was any intelligence withheld.

With more urgent matters—especially those affecting safety—word was passed from airline to airline in the same way, but without the day's delay. If Delta, for example, had a rotor blade failure on a DC-9 in flight, maintenance departments of Eastern, TWA, Continental, and others using DC-9s, were told within hours; the information might help prevent similar failures on other aircraft. Later, photographs of the disassembled engine, and a technical report, would follow. If they wished, foremen and mechanics from other airlines could widen their knowledge by dropping over for a look-see at the failed part, and any engine damage.

Those who, like Patroni, worked in this give-and-take milieu were fond of pointing out that if sales and administration departments of competing airlines had occasion to consult, their people seldom went to one another's headquarters, but met on neutral ground. Maintenance men, in contrast, visited competitors' premises with the assurance of a common freemasonry. At other times, if one maintenance department was in trouble, others helped as they were able.

This second kind of help had been sent, tonight, to Joe Patroni.

In the hour and a half since work began in the latest attempt to move the stranded jet from alongside runway three zero, Patroni's complement of help had almost doubled. He had begun with the original small crew of Aéreo-Mexican, supplemented by some of his own people from TWA. Now, digging steadily with the others, were ground crews from Braniff, Pan Am, American, and Eastern.

As the various newcomers had arrived, in an assortment of airline vehicles, it became evident that news of Patroni's problem had spread quickly on the airport grapevine, and, without waiting to be asked, other maintenance departments had pitched in. It gave Joe Patroni a good, appreciative feeling.

Despite the extra help, Patroni's estimate of an hour's preparatory work had already been exceeded. Digging of twin trenches, floored by heavy timbers, in front of the airliner's main landing gear had gone ahead steadily —though slowly because of the need for all the men working to seek shelter periodically, to warm themselves. The shelter and the warmth, of a sort, were in two crew buses. As the men entered, they beat their hands and pinched their faces, numb from the biting wind still sweeping icily across the snow-covered airfield. The buses and other vehicles, including trucks, snow clearance equipment, a fuel tanker, assorted service cars, and a roaring power cart—most with beacon lights flashing—were still clustered on the taxiway close by. The whole scene was bathed by floodlights, creating a white oasis of snow-reflected light in the surrounding darkness.

The twin trenches, each six feet wide, now extended forward and upward from the big jet's main wheels to the firmer ground onto which Patroni hoped the airplane could be moved under its own power. At the deepest level of the trenches was a mess of mud beneath snow, which had originally trapped the momentarily strayed airliner. The mud and slush now mingled, but became less viscous as both trenches angled upward. A third trench, less deep, and narrower than the other two,

had been dug to allow passage of the nosewheel. Once
the firmer ground was reached, the aircraft would be
clear of runway three zero, over which one of its wings
now extended. It could also be maneuvered with reasonable ease onto the solid surface of the adjoining taxiway.

Now the preparatory work was almost complete, the
success of what came next would depend on the aircraft's pilots, still waiting on the Boeing 707's flight
deck, high above the current activity. What they would
have to judge was how much power they could safely
use to propel the aircraft forward, without upending it
on its nose.

Through most of the time since he arrived, Joe Patroni had wielded a shovel with the rest of the men
digging. Inactivity came hard to him. Sometimes, too, he
welcomed the chance to keep himself fit; even now,
more than twenty years since quitting the amateur
boxing ring, he was in better shape physically than most
men years his junior. The airline ground crewmen enjoyed seeing Patroni's cocky, stocky figure working with
them. He led and exhorted . . . *"Keep moving, son, or
we'll figure we're gravediggers, and you the corpse."* . . .
*"The way you guys keep heading for that bus, looks like
you've got a woman stashed there."* . . . *"If you lean on
that shovel any more, Jack, you'll freeze solid like Lot's
wife."* . . . *"Men, we want this airplane moved before
it's obsolete."*

So far, Joe Patroni had not talked with the captain
and first officer, having left that to the Aéreo-Mexican
foreman, Ingram, who had been in charge before Patroni's arrival. Ingram had passed up a message on the
aircraft interphone, telling the pilots what was happening below.

Now, straightening his back, and thrusting his shovel
at Ingram, the maintenance chief advised, "Five minutes
more should do it. When you're ready, get the men and
trucks clear." He motioned to the snow-shrouded airplane. "When this one comes out, she'll be like a cork
from a champagne bottle."

Ingram, huddled into his parka, still pinched and cold
as he had been earlier, nodded.

"While you're doing that," Patroni said, "I'll yak with the fly boys."

The old-fashioned boarding ramp which had been trundled from the terminal several hours ago to disembark the stranded passengers was still in place near the aircraft's nose. Joe Patroni climbed the ramp, its steps covered in deep snow, and let himself into the front passenger cabin. He went forward to the flight deck—with relief, lighting his inevitable cigar as he went.

In contrast to the cold and wind-blown snow outside, the pilots' cockpit was snug and quiet. One of the communications radios was tuned to soft music of a commercial station. As Patroni entered, the Aéreo-Mexican first officer, in shirt-sleeves, snapped a switch and the music stopped.

"Don't worry about doing that." The chunky maintenance chief shook himself like a bull terrier while snow cascaded from his clothing. "Nothing wrong with taking things easy. After all, we didn't expect you to come down and shovel."

Only the first officer and captain were in the cockpit. Patroni remembered hearing that the flight engineer had gone with the stewardesses and passengers to the terminal.

The captain, a heavy-set, swarthy man who resembled Anthony Quinn, swiveled around in his port-side seat. He said stiffly, "We have our job to do. You have yours." His English was precise.

"That's right," Patroni acknowledged. "Only trouble is, our job gets fouled up and added to. By other people."

"If you are speaking of what has happened here," the captain said, *"Madre de Dios!"*—you do not suppose that I placed this airplane in the mud on purpose."

"No, I don't." Patroni discarded his cigar, which was maimed from chewing, put a new one in his mouth, and lit it. "But now it's there, I want to make sure we get it out—this next time we try. If we don't, the airplane'll be in a whole lot deeper; so will all of us, including you." He nodded toward the captain's seat. "How'd you like me to sit there and drive it out?"

The captain flushed. Few people in any airline talked as casually to four-stripers as Joe Patroni.

"No, thank you," the captain said coldly. He might have replied even more unpleasantly, except that at the moment he was suffering acute embarrassment for having got into his present predicament at all. Tomorrow in Mexico City, he suspected, he would face an unhappy, searing session with his airline's chief pilot. He raged inwardly: *Jesucristo y por la amor de Dios!*

"There's a lotta half-frozen guys outside who've been busting their guts," Patroni insisted. "Getting out now's tricky. I've done it before. Maybe you should let me again."

The Aéreo-Mexican captain bridled. "I know who you are, Mr. Patroni, and I am told that you are likely to help us move from this bad ground, where others have failed. So I have no doubt that you are licensed to taxi airplanes. But let me remind you there are two of us here who are licensed to *fly* them. It is what we are paid for. Therefore we shall remain at the controls."

"Suit yourself." Joe Patroni shrugged, then waved his cigar at the control pedestal. "Only thing is, when I give the word, open those throttles all the way. And I mean all the way, and don't chicken out."

As he left the cockpit, he ignored angry glares from both pilots.

Outside, digging had stopped; some of the men who had been working were warming themselves again in the crew buses. The buses and other vehicles—with the exception of the power cart, which was needed for starting engines—were being removed some distance from the airplane.

Joe Patroni closed the forward cabin door behind him and descended the ramp. The foreman, huddled deeper than ever into his parka, reported, "Everything's set."

Remembering his cigar was still lighted, Patroni puffed at it several times, then dropped it into the snow where it went out. He motioned to the silent jet engines. "Okay, let's light up all four."

Several men were returning from the crew bus. A quartet put their shoulders to the ramp beside the aircraft and shoved it clear. Two others responded to the foreman's shout against the wind, "Ready to start engines!"

One of the second pair stationed himself at the front of the aircraft, near the power cart. He wore a telephone headset plugged into the fuselage. The second man, with flashlight signal wands, walked forward to where he could be seen by the pilots above.

Joe Patroni, with borrowed protective head pads, joined the crewman with the telephone headset. The remainder of the men were now scrambling from the sheltering buses, intent on watching what came next.

In the cockpit, the pilots completed their checklist.

On the ground below, the crewman with the telephone set began the jet starting ritual. "Clear to start engines."

A pause. The captain's voice. "Ready to start, and pressurize the manifold."

From the power cart blower, a stream of forced air hit the air turbine starter of number three engine. Compressor vanes turned, spun faster, whined. At fifteen percent speed, the first officer fed in aviation kerosene. As the fuel ignited, a smoke cloud belched back and the engine took hold with a deep-throated bellow.

"Clear to start four."

Number four engine followed three. Generators on both engines charging.

The captain's voice. "Switching to generators. Disconnect ground power."

Above the power cart, electric lines came down. "Disconnected. Clear to start two."

Number two took hold. Three engines now. An encompassing roar. Snow streaming behind.

Number one fired and held.

"Disconnect air."

"Disconnected."

The umbilical air hose slipped down. The foreman drove the power cart away.

Floodlights ahead of the aircraft had been moved to one side.

Patroni exchanged headsets with the crewman near

the front of the fuselage. The maintenance chief now had the telephone set, and communication with the pilots.

"This's Patroni. When you're ready up there, let's roll her out."

Ahead of the aircraft nose, the crewman with the lighted wands held them up, ready to be a guide along an elliptical path beyond the trenches, also cleared at Joe Patroni's direction. The crewman was ready to run if the 707 came out of the mud faster than expected.

Patroni crouched close to the nosewheel. If the airplane moved quickly, he, too, was vulnerable. He held a hand near the interphone plug, ready to disconnect. He watched the main landing gear intently for a sign of forward movement.

The captain's voice. "I am opening up."

The tempo of the jets increased. In a roar like sustained thunder, the airplane shook, the ground beneath it trembled. But the wheels remained still.

Patroni cupped his hands around the interphone mouthpiece. "More power! Throttles forward all the way!"

The engine noise heightened but only slightly. The wheels rose perceptibly, but still failed to move forward.

"Goddamit! All the way!"

For several seconds, the engine tempo remained as it was, then abruptly lessened. The captain's voice rattled the interphone; it had a sarcastic note. *"Patroni, por favor,* if I open my throttles all the way, this airplane will stand on its nose. Instead of a stranded 707, we shall both have a wrecked one."

The maintenance chief had been studying the landing gear wheels, which had now settled back, and the ground around them. "It'll come out, I tell you! All it needs is the guts to pull full power."

"Look to your own guts!" the captain snapped back. "I am shutting the engines down."

Patroni shouted into the interphone. "Keep those motors running; hold 'em at idle! I'm coming up!" Moving forward under the nose, he motioned urgently for the boarding ramp to be repositioned. But even as it was being pushed into place, all four engines quieted and died.

When he reached the cockpit, both pilots were unfastening their seat harnesses.

Patroni said accusingly, "You chickened out!"

The captain's reaction was surprisingly mild. *"Es posible.* Perhaps it is the only intelligent thing I have done tonight." He inquired formally, "Does your maintenance department accept this airplane?"

"Okay." Patroni nodded. "We'll take it over."

The first officer glanced at his watch and made an entry in a log.

"When you have extricated this airplane, in whatever way," the Aéreo-Mexican captain stated, "no doubt your company will be in touch with my company. Meanwhile, *buenas noches.*"

As the two pilots left, their heavy topcoats buttoned tightly at the neck, Joe Patroni made a swift, routine check of instruments and control settings. A minute or so later he followed the pilots down the outside ramp.

The Aéreo-Mexican foreman, Ingram, was waiting below. He nodded in the direction of the departing pilots, now hurrying toward one of the crew buses. "That was the same thing they done to me; not pulling enough power." He motioned gloomily toward the aircraft's main landing gear. "That's why she went in deep before; now she's dug herself in deeper still."

It was what Joe Patroni had feared.

With Ingram holding an electric lantern, he ducked under the fuselage to inspect the landing gear wheels; they were back in mud and slush again, almost a foot deeper than before. Patroni took the light and shone it under the wings; all four engine nacelles were disquietingly closer to the ground.

"Nothing but a sky hook'll help her now," Ingram said.

The maintenance chief considered the situation, then shook his head. "We got one more chance. We'll dig some more, bring the trenches down to where the wheels are now, then start the engines again. Only this time I'll drive."

The wind and snow still howled around them.

Shivering, Ingram acknowledged doubtfully, "I guess you're the doctor. But better you than me."

Joe Patroni grinned. "If I don't blast her out, maybe I'll blow her apart."

Ingram headed for the remaining crew bus to call out the men; the other bus had taken the Aéreo-Mexican pilots to the terminal.

Patroni calculated: there was another hour's work ahead before they could try moving the aircraft again. Therefore runway three zero would have to continue out of use for at least that long.

He went to his radio-equipped pickup to report to air traffic control.

7

The theory that an overburdened, exhausted mind can exercise its own safety valve by retreating into passive semiawareness was unknown to Inez Guerrero. Nevertheless, for her, the theory had proved true. At this moment she was a mental walking-wounded case.

The events of tonight affecting her personally, coupled with her accumulated distress and weariness of weeks, had proved a final crushing defeat. It prompted her mind—like an overloaded circuit—to switch off. The condition was temporary, not permanent, yet while it remained Inez Guerrero had forgotten where she was, or why.

The mean, uncouth taxi driver who had brought her to the airport had not helped. When bargaining downtown, he agreed to seven dollars as the price of the ride. Getting out, Inez proffered a ten dollar bill—almost the last money she had—expecting change. Mumbling that he had no change but would get some, the cabbie drove off. Inez waited for ten anxious minutes, watching the terminal clock which was nearing 11 P.M.—the time of Flight Two's departure—before it dawned on her that the man had no intention of returning. She had noticed neither the taxi number nor the driver's name—something the driver had gambled on. Even if she had, Inez Guerrero was not the kind who complained to authority; the driver had correctly guessed that, too.

Despite the initial slowness of her journey from downtown, she could have reached Flight Two before it left—but for the time spent waiting for the non-appearing change. As it was, she arrived at the departure gate to see the airplane taxiing away.

Even then, to find out if her husband, D.O., was really aboard, Inez had the presence of mind to use the subterfuge which the Trans America inquiries girl, Miss Young, suggested on the telephone. A uniformed agent was just leaving gate forty-seven, where Flight Two had been. Inez accosted him.

As Miss Young advised, Inez avoided asking a direct question, and made the statement, "My husband is on that flight which just left." She explained that she had missed seeing her husband, but wanted to be sure he was safely aboard. Inez unfolded the yellow time-payment contract which she had discovered at home among D.O.'s shirts, and showed it to the Trans America agent. He barely glanced at it, then checked the papers he was holding.

For a moment or two Inez wondered hopefully if she had made a mistake in presuming that D.O. was leaving on the flight; the idea of his going to Rome at all still seemed fantastic. Then the agent said, yes, there was a D. O. Guerrero aboard Flight Two, and he, the agent, was sorry that Mrs. Guerrero had missed seeing her husband, but everything was in a mixup tonight because of the storm, and now if she would please excuse him . . .

It was when the agent had gone and Inez realized that despite the press of people around her in the terminal, she was utterly alone, that she began to cry.

At first the tears came slowly; then, as she remembered all that had gone wrong, they streamed in great heaving sobs which shook her body. She cried for the past and for the present; for the home she had had and lost; for her children whom she could no longer keep with her; for D.O. who, despite his faults as a husband, and the failure to support his family, was at least familiar, but now had deserted her. She wept for what she herself had been and had become; for the fact that she had no money, nowhere to go but to the mean, cockroach-infested rooms downtown, from which she would be evicted tomorrow, having nothing left—after the taxi ride and driver's theft—from the pathetically small amount with which she had hoped to stave off the landlord . . . she was not even sure if she had enough small change to return downtown. She cried because her shoes still hurt her feet; for her clothes which were shabby and sodden; for her weariness, and because she had a cold and a fever which she could feel getting worse. She cried for herself and all others for whom every hope was gone.

It was then, to avoid stares of people who were watching, that she began walking aimlessly through the terminal, still weeping as she went. Somewhere near that time, too, the defensive machinery of her mind took over, inducing a protective numbness, so that her sorrow persisted but its reasons, for a while, were mercifully blurred.

Soon after, an airport policeman found her and, with a sensitivity for which police are not always credited, placed her in as obscure a corner as he could find while telephoning his superiors for instructions. Lieutenant Ordway happened to be nearby and dealt with the matter personally. It was he who decided that Inez Guerrero, though incoherent and upset, was harmless, and had ordered her taken to the airport general manager's office—the only place Ned Ordway could think of which was quiet, yet less intimidating than police headquarters.

Inez had gone docilely, in an elevator and along a mezzanine, only half-knowing that she was being taken anywhere at all, and not caring; and after, had sat quietly in a seat she was guided to, her body, if not her mind, grateful for the rest. She had been aware of people coming and going, and some had spoken, but she had brought neither the sight nor sound of them into focus, the effort seeming too much.

But after a while, her resilience—which is another word for strength of the human spirit, which all possess, however burdened or humble—brought her back to a realization, even though vague, that she must move on, because life moved on, and always had and would, no matter how many defeats it wrought, or dreary or empty as it might seem.

So Inez Guerrero stood up, still not sure where she was or how she had come there, but prepared to go.

It was then that the Meadowood delegation, escorted by Lieutenant Ordway, entered the anteroom to Mel Bakersfeld's office, where Inez was. The delegation continued into the other room, then Ned Ordway had returned to speak with Inez Guerrero, and Mel observed the two of them together briefly before the door to his office closed.

Inez, through her miasma of uncertainty, was also conscious of the big Negro policeman, whom she had a feeling she had seen somewhere before, quite recently, and he had been kind then, as he was being kind now, leading her with quiet, not-quite-questions, so that he seemed to understand, without her ever saying so, that she had to return downtown and wasn't sure she had enough money for it. She started to fumble with her purse, intending to count what was there, but he stopped her. Then, with his back to the other room, he slipped three one-dollar bills into her hand, and came with her outside, pointing the way down to where, he said, she would find a bus, and added that what he had given her would be enough for the fare, with something over for wherever she had to go when she got to the city.

The policeman had gone then, returning in the direction from which he had come, and Inez did what she was told, going down some stairs; then almost at the big door through which she was to go for the bus, she had

seen a familiar sight—a hot dog counter; and at that
moment she realized how hungry and thirsty she was, on
top of everything else. She had groped in her purse, and
found thirty-five cents, and bought a hot dog, and coffee
in a paper cup, and somehow the sight of those two very
ordinary things was reassuring. Not far from the food
counter, she found a seat and tucked herself into a
corner. She wasn't sure how long ago that was but now,
with the coffee gone and the hot dog eaten, awareness
which earlier had started to come back, was receding
from her once more in a comfortable way. There was
something comforting, too, about the crowds around
her, the noises, and loudspeaker announcements. Twice
Inez thought she heard her own name on the loud-
speakers, but knew it was imagination and couldn't be
true because no one would call her, or even know that
she was here.

She realized dimly that sometime soon she would
have to move on, and knew that tonight especially it
would entail an effort. But for a while, she thought, she
would sit here quietly, where she was.

8

With one exception, those summoned to the airport general manager's office on the administrative mezzanine
arrived there quickly. The calls made to them—some by
Mel Bakersfeld, others by Tanya Livingston—had
stressed urgency, and the need to leave whatever they
were doing.

The District Transportation Manager of Trans America—Tanya's boss, Bert Weatherby—arrived first.

Lieutenant Ordway, having started his policemen
searching for Inez Guerrero, though still not knowing
why, was close behind. For the time being Ordway had

abandoned to their own devices the sizable group of Meadowood residents, still milling in the main concourse, listening to Lawyer Freemantle expound their case before TV cameras.

As the D.T.M., Weatherby, entered Mel's office through the anteroom door, he inquired briskly, "Mel, what's all this about?"

"We're not sure, Bert, and we haven't a lot to go on yet, but there's a possibility there could be a bomb aboard your Flight Two."

The D.T.M. looked searchingly at Tanya, but wasted no time in asking why she was there. His gaze swung back to Mel. "Let's hear what you know."

Addressing both the D.T.M. and Ned Ordway, Mel summarized what was known or conjectured so far: the report of Customs Inspector Standish concerning the passenger with the attaché case, clasped in a way which Standish—an experienced observer—believed to be suspicious; Tanya's identification of the man with the case as one D. O. Guerrero, or perhaps Buerrero; the downtown agent's revelation that Guerrero checked in without any baggage other than the small case already mentioned; Guerrero's purchase at the airport of three hundred thousand dollars' worth of flight insurance, which he barely had enough money to pay for, so that he appeared to be setting out on a five-thousand mile journey, not only without so much as a change of clothing, but also without funds; and finally—perhaps coincidentally, perhaps not—Mrs. Inez Guerrero, sole beneficiary of her husband's flight insurance policy, had been wandering through the terminal, apparently in great distress.

While Mel was speaking, Customs Inspector Harry Standish, still in uniform, came in, followed by Bunnie Vorobioff. Bunnie entered uncertainly, glancing questioningly around her at the unfamiliar people and surroundings. As the import of what Mel was saying sank in, she paled and appeared scared.

The one non-arrival was the gate agent who had been in charge at gate forty-seven when Flight Two left. A staff supervisor whom Tanya had spoken to a few min-

utes ago informed her that the agent was now off duty
and on his way home. She gave instructions for a message to be left, and for the agent to check in by telephone as soon as he arrived. Tanya doubted if anything
would be gained by bringing him back to the airport
tonight; for one thing, she already knew that the agent
did not remember Guerrero boarding. But someone else
might want to question him by phone.

"I called everyone here who's involved so far," Mel
informed the D.T.M., "in case you or someone else have
questions. What we have to decide, I think—and it's
mainly your decision—is whether or not we have
enough to warn your captain of Flight Two." Mel was
reminded again of what he had temporarily pushed from
mind: that the flight was commanded by his brother-in-
law, Vernon Demerest. Later, Mel knew, he might have
to do some reconsidering about certain implications. But
not yet.

"I'm thinking now." The D.T.M. looked grim; he
swung to Tanya. "Whatever we decide, I want Operations in on this. Find out if Royce Kettering is still on
the base. If so, get him here fast." Captain Kettering
was Trans America's chief pilot at Lincoln International; it was he who earlier tonight had test-flown aircraft N-731-TA, before—as Flight Two, *The Golden
Argosy*—it took off for Rome.

"Yes, sir," Tanya said.

While she was on one telephone, another rang. Mel
answered.

It was the tower watch chief. "I have the report you
wanted on Trans America Two." One of Mel's calls for
a few minutes ago had been to air traffic control, requesting information on the flight's takeoff time and
progress.

"Go ahead."

"Takeoff was 11:13 local time." Mel's eyes swung to
a wall clock. It was now almost ten minutes after midnight; the flight had been airborne nearly an hour.

The tower chief continued, "Chicago Center handed
off the flight to Cleveland Center at 12:27 EST, Cleveland handed it to Toronto at 01:03 EST; that's seven

minutes ago. At the moment, Toronto Center reports the aircraft's position as near London, Ontario. I have more information—course, height, speed—if you want it."

"That's enough for now," Mel said. "Thanks."

"One other thing, Mr. Bakersfeld." The tower chief summarized Joe Patroni's latest bulletin about runway three zero; the runway would be out of use for at least another hour. Mel listened impatiently; at the moment, other things seemed more important.

When he hung up, Mel repeated the information about Flight Two's position to the D.T.M.

Tanya came off the other phone. She reported, "Operations found Captain Kettering. He's coming."

"That woman—the passenger's wife," the D.T.M. said. "What was her name?"

Ned Ordway answered. "Inez Guerrero."

"Where is she?"

"We don't know." The policeman explained that his men were searching the airport, although the woman might be gone. He added that city police headquarters had been alerted, and all buses from the airport to downtown were now being checked on arrival.

"When she was here," Mel explained, "we had no idea . . ."

The D.T.M. grunted. "We were all slow." He glanced at Tanya, then at Customs Inspector Standish, who so far had not spoken. The D.T.M., Tanya knew, was remembering ruefully his own instructions to "Forget it!"

Now he informed her, "We'll have to tell the captain of the flight something. He's entitled to know as much as we do, even though so far we're only guessing."

Tanya asked, "Shouldn't we send a description of Guerrero? Captain Demerest may want to have him identified without his knowing."

"If you do," Mel pointed out, "we can help. There are people here who've seen the man."

"All right," the D.T.M. acknowledged, "we'll work on that. Meanwhile, Tanya, call our dispatcher. Tell him there's an important message coming in a few minutes, and to get a Selcal circuit hooked into Flight Two.

I want this kept private, not broadcast for everybody. At least, not yet."

Tanya returned to the telephone.

Mel asked Bunnie, "Are you Miss Vorobioff?"

As she nodded nervously, the eyes of the others turned to her. Automatically, those of the men dropped to Bunnie's capacious breasts; the D.T.M. seemed about to whistle, but changed his mind.

Mel said, "You realize which man we're talking about?"

"I . . . I'm not sure."

"It's a man named D. O. Guerrero. You sold him an insurance policy tonight, didn't you?"

Bunnie nodded again. "Yes."

"When you wrote the policy, did you get a good look at him?"

She shook her head. "Not really." Her voice was low. She moistened her lips.

Mel seemed surprised. "I thought on the phone . . ."

"There were many other people," Bunnie said defensively.

"But you told me you remembered this one."

"It was someone else."

"And you don't recall the man Guerrero?"

"No."

Mel looked baffled.

"Let me, Mr. Bakersfeld." Ned Ordway took a pace forward; he put his face near the girl's. "You're afraid of getting involved, aren't you?" Ordway's voice was a harsh, policeman's voice, not at all the gentle tone he used earlier tonight with Inez Guerrero.

Bunnie flinched, but didn't answer.

Ordway persisted, "Well, aren't you? Answer me."

"I don't know."

"Yes, you do! You're afraid to help anyone for fear of what it might do to you. I know your kind." Ordway spat out the words contemptuously. This was a savage, tough side of the lieutenant's nature which Mel had never seen before. "Now you hear me, baby. If it's trouble you're scared of, you're buying it right now. The way to get out of trouble—*if you can*—is to answer questions. *And answer fast!* We're running out of time."

Bunnie trembled. She had learned to fear police inter-rogation in the grim school of Eastern Europe. It was a conditioning never totally erased. Ordway had recog-nized the signs.

"Miss Vorobioff," Mel said. "There are almost two hundred people aboard the airplane we're concerned with. They may be in great danger. Now, I'll ask you again. Did you get a good look at the man Guerrero?"

Slowly, Bunnie nodded. "Yes."

"Describe him, please."

She did so, haltingly at first, then with more confidence.

While the others listened, a picture of D. O. Guerrero emerged: gaunt and spindly; a pale, sallow face with protruding jaw; long scrawny neck; thin lips; a small sandy mustache; nervous hands with restless fingers. When she got down to it, Bunnie Vorobioff proved her-self a keen observer.

The D.T.M., now seated at Mel's desk, wrote the description, incorporating it with a message for Flight Two which he was drafting.

When Bunnie came to the part about D. O. Guerrero barely having enough money—and no Italian money; the man's nervous tension, the fumbling with dimes and pennies; his excitement on discovering a five-dollar bill in an inside pocket, the D.T.M. looked up with a mix-ture of disgust and horror. *"My God!* And you *still* issued a policy. Are you people *mad?"*

"I thought . . ." Bunnie started to say.

"You thought! But you didn't *do* anything, did you?"

Her face drained and white, Bunnie Vorobioff shook her head.

Mel reminded the D.T.M., "Bert, we're wasting time."

"I know, I know! Just the same . . ." The D.T.M. clenched the pencil he had been using. He muttered. "It isn't just *her,* or even the people who employ her. It's *us* —the airlines; we're as much to blame. We agree with the pilots about airport flight insurance, but haven't the guts to say so. We let them do our dirty work . . ."

Mel said tersely to Customs Inspector Standish, "Harry, is there anything you'd add to the description of Guerrero?"

"No," Standish said. "I wasn't as near to him as this young lady, and she saw some things I didn't. But I did watch the way he held the case, as you know, and I'd say this: If what you think is in there really is, don't anyone try to grab that case away from him."

"So what do you suggest?"

The Customs man shook his head. "I'm no expert, so I can't tell you; except, I guess you'd have to get it by some kind of trickery. But if it's a bomb, it has to be self-contained in the case, and that means somewhere there's a trigger, and the chances are it'll be the kind of trigger he can get to quickly. He's possessive about the case now. If someone tried to take it away, he'd figure he was found out and had nothing to lose." Standish added grimly, "A trigger finger can get mighty itchy."

"Of course," Mel said, "we still don't know if the man's an ordinary eccentric, and all he's got in there are his pajamas."

"If you're asking my opinion," the Customs inspector said, "I don't think so. I wish I did, because I've got a niece on that flight."

Standish had been conjecturing unhappily: If anything went wrong, how in God's name would he break the news to his sister in Denver? He remembered his last sight of Judy: that sweet young girl, playing with the baby from the next seat. She had kissed him. *Goodbye, Uncle Harry!* Now, he wished desperately that he had been more definite, had acted more responsibly, about the man with the attaché case.

Well, Standish thought, though it might be late, at least he would be definite now.

"I'd like to say something else." The eyes of the others swung to him.

"I have to tell you this because we haven't time to waste on modesty: I'm a good judge of people, mostly on first sight, and usually I can smell the bad ones. It's an instinct, and don't ask me how it works because I couldn't tell you, except that in my job some of us get to be that way. I spotted that man tonight, and I said he was 'suspicious'; I used that word because I was thinking of smuggling, which is the way I'm trained. Now, knowing what we do—even little as it is—I'd make it stronger. The man Guerrero is dangerous." Standish eyed the Trans America D.T.M. "Mr. Weatherby—get that word 'dangerous' across to your people in the air."

"I intend to, Inspector." The D.T.M. looked up from his writing. Most of what Standish had been saying was already included in the message for Flight Two.

Tanya, still on the telephone, was talking with Trans America's New York dispatcher by tie line. "Yes, it will be a long message. Will you put someone on to copy, please?"

A sharp knock sounded on the office door and a tall man with a seamed, weatherworn face and sharp blue eyes came in from the anteroom. He carried a heavy topcoat and wore a blue serge suit which might have been a uniform, but wasn't. The newcomer nodded to Mel, but before either could speak, the D.T.M. cut in.

"Royce, thanks for coming quickly. We seem to have some trouble." He held out the notepad on which he had been writing.

Captain Kettering, the base chief pilot for Trans America, read the draft message carefully, his only reaction a tightening at the mouth as his eyes moved down the page. Like many others, including the D.T.M., it was unusual for the chief pilot to be at the airport this late at night. But exigencies of the three-day storm, with the need for frequent operating decisions, had kept him here.

The second telephone rang, cutting through the temporary silence. Mel answered it, then motioned to Ned Ordway who took the receiver.

Captain Kettering finished reading. The D.T.M. asked, "Do you agree to sending that? We've dispatch standing by with a Selcal hook-up."

Kettering nodded. "Yes, but I'd like you to add:

'Suggest return or alternate landing at captain's discretion,' and have the dispatcher give them the latest weather."

"Of course," The D.T.M. penciled in the extra words, then passed the pad to Tanya. She began dictating the message.

Captain Kettering glanced at the others in the room. "Is that everything we know?"

"Yes," Mel said. "It is, so far."

"We may know more soon," Lieutenant Ordway said. He had returned from the telephone. "We just found Guerrero's wife."

The message from D.T.M. Lincoln International was addressed, CAPTAIN, TRANS AMERICA FLIGHT TWO, and began:

> UNCONFIRMED POSSIBILITY EXISTS THAT MALE TOURIST PASSENGER D. O. GUERRERO ABOARD YOUR FLIGHT MAY HAVE EXPLOSIVE DEVICE IN HIS POSSESSION. PASSENGER WITH NO LUGGAGE AND APPARENTLY WITHOUT FUNDS INSURED SELF HEAVILY BEFORE DEPARTURE. WAS OBSERVED BEHAVING SUSPICIOUSLY WITH ATTACHE TYPE BRIEFCASE CARRIED AS HAND BAGGAGE. DESCRIPTION FOLLOWS . . .

As the D.T.M. had foreseen, it took several minutes for a connection to be established, through company radio, with Flight Two. Since the earlier Selcal message to the flight, concerning its stowaway Mrs. Ada Quonsett, the aircraft had moved out of Trans America's Cleveland dispatch area into that of New York. Now, company messages must be passed through a New York dispatcher for relaying to the flight.

The message, as Tanya dictated it, was being typed by a girl clerk in New York. Alongside the clerk a Trans America dispatcher read the first few lines, then reached for a direct phone to an operator at ARINC—a private communications network maintained cooperatively by all major airlines.

The ARINC operator—at another location in New York—set up a second circuit between himself and Trans America dispatch, then punched into a transmitter keyboard a four-letter code, AGFG, specifically assigned to aircraft N-731-TA. Once more, like a telephone call to a single number on a party line, an alerting signal would be received aboard Flight Two only.

A few moments later the voice of Captain Vernon Demerest, responding from high above Ontario, Canada, was audible in New York. "This is Trans America Two answering Selcal."

"Trans America Two, this is New York dispatch. We have an important message. Advise when ready to copy."

A brief pause, then Demerest again. "Okay, New York. Go ahead."

"CAPTAIN, FLIGHT TWO," the dispatcher began. "UNCONFIRMED POSSIBILITY EXISTS . . ."

Inez had still been sitting quietly, in her corner near the food counter, when she felt her shoulder shaken.

"Inez Guerrero! Are you Mrs. Guerrero?"

She looked up. It took several seconds to collect her thoughts, which had been vague and drifting, but she realized that it was a policeman who was standing over her.

He shook her again and repeated the question.

Inez managed to nod. She became aware that this was a different policeman from the earlier one. This one was white, and neither as gentle nor as softly spoken as the other.

"Let's move it, lady!" The policeman tightened his grip on her shoulder in a way which hurt, and pulled her abruptly to her feet. "You hear me?—let's go! They're screamin' for you upstairs, and every cop in the joint's bin searchin' for you."

Ten minutes later, in Mel's office, Inez was the pivot of attention. She occupied a chair in the room's center to which she had been guided on arrival. Lieutenant

Ordway faced her. The policeman who had escorted Inez in was gone.

The others who had been present earlier—Mel, Tanya, Customs Inspector Standish, Bunnie Vorobioff, the Trans America D.T.M., Weatherby, and the chief pilot, Captain Kettering, were ranged about the room. All had remained at Mel's request.

"Mrs. Guerrero," Ned Ordway said. "Why is your husband going to Rome?"

Inez stared back bleakly and didn't answer. The policeman's voice sharpened, though not unkindly. "Mrs. Guerrero, please listen to me carefully. There are some important questions which I have to ask. They concern your husband, and I need your help. Do you understand?"

"I . . . I'm not sure."

"You don't have to be sure about *why* I'm asking the questions. There'll be time for that later. What I want you to do is help me by answering. Will you? Please."

The D.T.M. cut in urgently. "Lieutenant, we haven't got all night. That airplane is moving away from us at six hundred miles an hour. If we have to, let's get tough."

"Leave this to me, Mr. Weatherby," Ordway said sharply. "If we all start shouting, it'll take a lot more time to get a great deal less."

The D.T.M. continued to look impatient, but kept quiet.

"Inez," Ordway said; ". . . is it okay if I call you Inez?"

She nodded.

"Inez, *will* you answer my questions?"

"Yes . . . if I can."

"Why is your husband going to Rome?"

Her voice was strained, barely more than a whisper. "I don't know."

"Do you have friends there; relatives?"

"No . . . There is a distant cousin in Milan, but we have never seen him."

"Do your husband and the cousin correspond?"

"No."

"Can you think of any reason why your husband would go to visit the cousin—suddenly?"

"There is no reason."

Tanya interjected, "In any case, Lieutenant, if anyone was going to Milan they wouldn't use our Rome flight. They'd fly Alitalia, which is direct and cheaper—and Alitalia has a flight tonight, too."

Ordway nodded. "We can probably rule out the cousin." He asked Inez, "Does your husband have business in Italy?"

She shook her head.

"What *is* your husband's business?"

"He is . . . was . . . a contractor."

"What kind of contractor?"

Slowly but perceptibly, Inez's grasp of things was coming back. "He built buildings, houses, developments."

"You said 'was.' Why isn't he a contractor now?"

"Things . . . went wrong."

"You mean financially?"

"Yes, but . . . why are you asking?"

"Please believe me, Inez," Ordway said, "I've a good reason. It concerns your husband's safety, as well as others'. Will you take my word?"

She looked up. Her eyes met his. "All right."

"Is your husband in financial trouble now?"

She hesitated only briefly. "Yes."

"Bad trouble?"

Inez nodded slowly.

"Is he broke? In debt?"

Again a whisper." Yes."

"Then where did he get money for his fare to Rome?"

"I think . . ." Inez started to say something about her ring which D.O. had pawned, then remembered the Trans America Airlines time payment contract. She took the now-creased yellow sheet from her purse and gave it to Ordway who glanced over it. The D.T.M. joined him.

"It's made out to 'Buerrero,'" the D.T.M. said. "Though the signature could be anything."

Tanya pointed out, "Buerrero is the name we had at first on the flight manifest."

Ned Ordway shook his head. "It isn't important now, but it's an old trick if anyone has a lousy credit rating. They use a wrong first letter so the bad rating won't show up in inquiry—at least, not in a hurry. Later, if the mistake's discovered, it can be blamed on whoever filled out the form."

Ordway swung sternly back to Inez. He had the yellow printed sheet in hand. "Why did you agree to this when you knew your husband was defrauding?"

She protested, "I didn't know."

"Then how is it you have this paper now?"

Haltingly, she related how she had found it earlier this evening, and had come to the airport, hoping to intercept her husband before departure.

"So until tonight you had no idea that he was going?"

"No, sir."

"Anywhere at all?"

Inez shook her head.

"Even now, can you think of any reason for him going?"

She looked bewildered. "No."

"Does your husband ever do irrational things?"

Inez hesitated.

"Well," Ordway said, "does he?"

"Sometimes, lately . . ."

"He *has* been irrational?"

A whisper. "Yes."

"Violent?"

Reluctantly, Inez nodded.

"Your husband was carrying a case tonight," Ordway said quietly. "A small attaché case, and he seemed specially cautious about it. Have you any idea what might be inside?"

"No, sir."

"Inez, you said your husband was a contractor—a building contractor. In the course of his work did he ever use explosives?"

The question had been put so casually and without preamble, that those listening seemed scarcely aware it had been asked. But as its import dawned, there was a sudden tenseness in the room.

"Oh, yes," Inez said. "Often."

Ordway paused perceptibly before asking, "Does your husband know a lot about explosives?"

"I think so. He always liked using them. But . . ." Abruptly, she stopped.

"But what, Inez?"

Suddenly there was a nervousness to Inez Guerrero's speech which had not been there before. "But . . . he handles them very carefully." Her eyes moved around the room. "Please . . . what is this about?"

Ordway said softly, "You have an idea, Inez; haven't you?"

When she didn't answer, almost with indifference he asked, "Where are you living?"

She gave the address of the South Side apartment and he wrote it down. "Is that where your husband was this afternoon; earlier this evening?"

Thoroughly frightened now, she nodded.

Ordway turned to Tanya. Without raising his voice, he asked, "Get a line open, please, to police headquarters downtown; this extension"—he scribbled a number on a pad. "Ask them to hold."

Tanya went quickly to Mel's desk.

Ordway asked Inez, "Did your husband have any explosives in the apartment?" As she hesitated, he bore in with sudden toughness. "You've told the truth so far; don't lie to me now! Did he?"

"Yes."

"What kind of explosives?"

"Some dynamite . . . and caps . . . They were left over."

"From his contracting work?"

"Yes."

"Did he ever say anything about them? Give a reason for keeping them?"

Inez shook her head. "Only, that . . . if you knew how to handle them . . . they were safe."

"Where were the explosives kept?"

"Just in a drawer."

"In a drawer where?"

"The bedroom." An expression of sudden shock crossed Inez Guerrero's face. Ordway spotted it.

"You thought of something then! What was it?"

"Nothing!" Panic was in her eyes and voice.

"Yes, you did!" Ned Ordway leaned forward, close to Inez, his face aggressive. For the second time in this room tonight he exhibited nothing of kindness; only the rough, tough savagery of a policeman who needed an answer and would get it. He shouted, "Don't try holding back or lying! It won't work. Tell me what it was you thought." As Inez whimpered: "Never mind that! Tell me!"

"Tonight . . . I didn't think of it before . . . the things . . ."

"The dynamite and caps?"

"Yes."

"You're wasting time! What about them?"

Inez whispered, "They were gone!"

Tanya said quietly, "I have your call, Lieutenant. They're holding."

No one among the others spoke.

Ordway nodded, his eyes still fixed on Inez. "Did you know that tonight, before your husband's flight took off, he insured himself heavily—very heavily indeed—naming you as beneficiary?"

"No, sir. I swear I don't know anything . . ."

"I believe you," Ordway said. He stopped, considering, and when he spoke again his voice grated harshly.

"Inez Guerrero, listen to me carefully. We believe your husband has those explosives, which you've told us about, with him tonight. We think he carried them onto that Rome flight, and, since there can be no other explanation for having them there, that he intends to destroy the airplane, killing himself and everyone else aboard. Now, I've one more question, and before you answer, think carefully, and remember those other people—innocent people, including children—who are on that flight, too. Inez, you know your husband; you know him as well as anyone alive. Could he . . . for the insurance money; for you . . . could he do what I have just said?"

Tears streamed down Inez Guerrero's face. She seemed near collapse, but nodded slowly.

"Yes." Her voice was choked. "Yes, I think he could."

Ned Ordway turned away. He took the telephone from Tanya and began speaking rapidly in a low tone. He gave information, interspersed with several requests. Once Ordway paused, swinging back to Inez Guerrero. "Your apartment is going to be searched, and we'll get a warrant if necessary. But it will be easier if you consent. Do you?"

Inez nodded dully.

"Okay," Ordway said into the telephone, "she agrees." A minute or so later he hung up.

Ordway told the D.T.M. and Mel, "We'll collect the evidence in the apartment, if there's any there. Apart from that, at the moment, there isn't a lot we can do."

The D.T.M. said grimly, "There isn't a lot any of us can do, except maybe pray." His face strained and gray, he began writing a new message for Flight Two.

9

The hot hors d'oeuvres, which Captain Vernon Demerest had called for, had been served to the pilots of Flight Two. The appetizing assortment on a tray, brought by one of the stewardesses from the first class galley, was disappearing fast. Demerest grunted appreciatively as he bit into a lobster-and-mushroom tartlet garnished with Parmesan cheese.

As usual, the stewardesses were pursuing their campaign to fatten the skinny young second officer, Cy Jordan. Surreptitiously they had slipped him a few extra hors d'oeuvres on a separate plate behind the two captains and now, while Jordan fiddled with fuel crossfeed valves, his cheeks bulged with chicken livers in bacon.

Soon, all three pilots, relaxing in turn in the dimly lighted cockpit, would be brought the same delectable entree and dessert which the airline served its first class passengers. The only things the passengers would get, which the crew did not, were table wine and champagne.

Trans America, like most airlines, worked hard at providing an excellent cuisine aloft. There were some who argued that airlines—even international airlines—should concern themselves solely with transportation, gear their in-flight service to commuter standards, and dispense with frills, including meals of any higher quality than a box lunch. Others, however, believed that too much of modern travel had become established at box lunch level, and welcomed the touch of style and elegance which good airborne meals provided. Airlines received remarkably few complaints about food service. Most passengers—tourist and first class—welcomed the meals as a diversion and consumed them zestfully.

Vernon Demerest, searching out with his tongue the last succulent particles of lobster, was thinking much the same thing. At that moment the Selcal call chime sounded loudly in the cockpit and the radio panel warning light flashed on.

Anson Harris's eyebrows went up. A single call on Selcal was out of the ordinary; two within less than an hour were exceptional.

"What we need," Cy Jordan said from behind, "is an unlisted number."

Demerest reached out to switch radios. "I'll get it."

After the mutual identification between Flight Two and New York dispatch, Vernon Demerest began writing on a message pad under a hooded light. The message was from D.T.M. Lincoln International, and began: UNCONFIRMED POSSIBILITY EXISTS . . . As the wording progressed, Demerest's features, in the light's reflection, tautened. At the end he acknowledged briefly and signed off without comment.

Demerest handed the message pad to Anson Harris, who read it, leaning toward a light beside him. Harris whistled softly. He passed the pad over his shoulder to Cy Jordan.

The Selcal message ended: SUGGEST RETURN OR ALTERNATE LANDING AT CAPTAIN'S DISCRETION.

As both captains knew, there was a question of command to be decided. Although Anson Harris had been flying tonight as captain, with Demerest performing first officer duty, Vernon Demerest—as check pilot—had overriding authority if he chose to exercise it.

Now, in response to Harris's questioning glance, Demerest said brusquely, "You're in the left seat. What are we waiting for?"

Harris considered only briefly, then announced, "We'll turn back, but making a wide slow turn; that way, passengers shouldn't notice. Then we'll have Gwen Meighen locate this guy they're worried about, because it's a sure thing one of us can't show up in the cabin, or we'll alert him." He shrugged. "After that, I guess we play it by ear."

"Okay," Demerest assented. "You get us faced around; I'll handle the cabin end." He depressed the stewardess call button, using a three-ring code to summon Gwen.

On a radio frequency he had been using earlier, Anson Harris called air route control. He announced laconically, "This is Trans America Two. We seem to have a problem here. Request clearance back to Lincoln, and radar vector from present position to Lincoln."

Harris's swift reasoning had already ruled out landing at an alternate airport. Ottawa, Toronto, and Detroit, they had been informed at briefing, were closed to air traffic because of the storm. Besides, to deal with the man they were concerned about back in the cabin, the crew of Flight Two needed time. Returning to Lincoln International would provide it.

He had no doubt that Demerest had reached the same conclusion.

From Toronto Air Route Center, more than six miles below, a controller's voice responded. "Trans America

Two, Roger." A brief pause, then: "You may begin a left turn now to heading two seven zero. Stand by for an altitude change."

"Roger, Toronto. We are commencing the turn. We'd like to make it wide and gradual."

"Trans America Two. A wide turn approved."

The exchange was low key, as such exchanges usually were. Both in the air and on the ground there was mutual awareness that most would be gained by calm, least by dramatics or excitement. By the nature of Flight Two's request, the ground controller was instantly aware that an emergency—real or potential—existed. Jetliners, in flight at cruising altitude, did not abruptly reverse course without a major reason. But the controller also knew that if and when the captain was ready, he would officially declare an emergency and report its cause. Until then, the controller would not waste the time of the crew—undoubtedly occupied with urgent business of their own—by asking needless questions.

Whatever help was sought from air route control, however, would be given without query, and as speedily as possible.

Even now, on the ground, procedural wheels were turning. At Toronto Air Route Center, located in a handsome modern building some fourteen miles beyond the city limits, the controller receiving Flight Two's transmission had summoned a supervisor. The supervisor was liaising with other sectors, clearing a path ahead of Flight Two, as well as altitudes immediately below—the last as a precaution. Cleveland Center, which earlier had passed the flight to Toronto Center and now would receive it back, had been alerted also. Chicago Center, which would take over from Cleveland, was being notified.

On the flight deck of Flight Two, a new air route control message was coming in. "Begin descent to flight level two eight zero. Report leaving flight level three three zero."

Anson Harris acknowledged. "Toronto Center, this is Trans America Two. We are beginning descent now."

On Harris's orders, Second Officer Jordan was reporting to Trans America dispatch, by company radio, the decision to return.

The door from the forward cabin opened. Gwen Meighen came in.

"Listen," she said, "if it's more hors d'oeuvres, I'm sorry, but you can't have them. In case you hadn't noticed, we happen to have a few passengers aboard."

"I'll deal with the insubordination later," Demerest said. "Right now"—he mimicked Gwen's English accent —"we've got a spot o' bother."

Superficially, little had changed on the flight deck since a few moments ago when the message from D.T.M. Lincoln had come in. Yet, subtly, the relaxed mood prevailing earlier had vanished. Despite their studied composure, the three-man crew was all-professional and sharp, their minds at peak acuity, each sensing the adjustment in the other two. It was to achieve such moments, responsively and quickly, that years of training and experience marked the long route to airline captaincy. Flying itself—controlling an airplane—was not a difficult achievement; what commercial pilots were paid high salaries for was their reserve of resourcefulness, airmanship, and general aviation wisdom. Demerest, Harris, and—to a lesser extent—Cy Jordan, were summoning their reserves now. The situation aboard Flight Two was not yet critical; with luck, it might not be critical at all. But if a crisis arose, mentally the crew was ready.

"I want you to locate a passenger," Demerest told Gwen. "He isn't to know that you're looking for him. We have a description here. You'd better read the whole thing." He handed her the pad with the Selcal message. She moved nearer, holding it under the hooded light beside him.

As the aircraft rolled slightly, Gwen's hand brushed Vernon Demerest's shoulder. He was conscious of her closeness and a faint familiar perfume. Glancing sideways, he could see Gwen's profile in the semidarkness. Her expression as she read was serious, but not dismayed; it reminded him of what he had admired so much earlier this evening—her strength in no way less-

ening her femininity. In a swift, fleeting second he remembered that twice tonight Gwen had declared she
loved him. He had wondered then: had he ever truly
been in love himself? When you kept tight rein on personal emotions, you were never absolutely sure. But at
this moment, instinct told him, his feeling about Gwen
was the closest to loving he would ever know.

Gwen was reading the message again, more slowly.

Momentarily he felt a savage anger at this new circumstance which was contriving to delay their plans—
his own and Gwen's—for Naples. Then he checked
himself. This was a moment for professionalism only.
Besides, what was happening now would merely mean
delay, perhaps for a full twenty-four hours after their
return to Lincoln; but eventually the flight would go. It
did not occur to him that the bomb threat might not be
disposed of quickly, or that it would fail to end as
tamely as most others.

Alongside Demerest, Anson Harris was still holding
the aircraft in its gentle turn, using only the slightest
amount of bank. It was a perfect turn, exactly executed,
as demonstrated by each pilot's needle and ball indicator—the granddaddy of aviation flight instruments, still
used on modern jets, as it was used in Lindbergh's *Spirit
of St. Louis,* and airplanes long before. The needle was
tilted, the ball dead center. But only compass and gyro
betrayed the extent of the turn—that Flight Two was
coming around a hundred and eighty degrees in course.
Harris had declared that passengers would be unaware
of the course reversal, and he would be right—unless
someone, peering through a cabin window, happened to
be familiar with positions of stars and moon in relation
to westerly and easterly courses. Then they would observe the change, but that was a chance which had to be
taken; fortunately, the ground being obscured by cloud
meant that no one could see and identify cities. Now
Harris was beginning to lose height also, the aircraft's
nose lowered slightly, with throttles pulled back the
barest amount, so that the note of engines would change
no more than was usual during any flight. Harris was

concentrating, flying with textbook precision, ignoring Gwen and Demerest.

Gwen handed the message pad back.

"What I want you to do," Demerest instructed her, "is go back and locate this man. See if there's any sign of the bag, and whether there's a good chance of getting it away from him. You realize that one of us from here can't go back—at least for now—in case we scare him."

"Yes," Gwen said. "I understand that. But I don't need to go either."

"Why?"

She said quietly, "I know where he is already. In seat fourteen-A."

Vernon Demerest regarded her searchingly. "I don't have to tell you that this is important. If you've any doubt, go back and make sure."

"I haven't any doubt."

Half an hour or so ago, Gwen explained, after serving dinners in first class, she had gone aft into the tourist section to help out there. One of the passengers—in a window seat on the left—had been dozing. When Gwen spoke to him he awakened instantly. He was nursing a small attaché case on his knees and Gwen suggested that she take it, or that he put it down, while having dinner. The passenger refused. He continued to hold the case where it was, and she noticed that he clasped it as if it were important. Later, instead of letting down the folding table from the back of the seat ahead, he used the case, still held on his lap, to support his dinner tray. Accustomed to passengers' peculiarities, Gwen thought no more of it, though she remembered the man well. The description in the message fitted him exactly.

"Another reason I remember is that he's sitting right alongside the old lady stowaway."

"He's in a window seat, you say?"

"Yes."

"That makes it harder—to reach across and grab." Demerest was remembering the portion of the D.T.M.'s message: IF SUPPOSITION TRUE, LIKELY THAT TRIGGER FOR EXPLOSIVES WILL BE ON OUTSIDE OF CASE AND EASILY REACHABLE. THEREFORE USE EXTREME CAUTION

IN ATTEMPTING TO SEIZE CASE FORCIBLY. He guessed
that Gwen, too, was thinking of that warning.

For the first time a feeling, not of fear but doubt,
intruded on his reasoning. Fear might come later, but
not yet. *Was* there a possibility that this bomb scare
might prove to be more than a scare? Vernon Demerest
had thought and talked of this kind of situation often
enough, yet could never really believe it would happen
to himself.

Anson Harris was easing out of the turn as gently as
he had gone into it. They were now headed around
completely.

The Selcal chime sounded again. Demerest motioned
to Cy Jordan, who switched radios and answered, then
began copying down a message.

Anson Harris was talking once more with Toronto
Air Route Center.

"I wonder," Vernon Demerest said to Gwen, "if
there's any chance of getting those other two passengers
alongside Guerrero out of their seats. That way he'd be
left there, in the three-seat section, on his own. Then
maybe one of us could come from behind, lean over and
grab."

"He'd suspect," Gwen said emphatically. "I'm sure he
would. He's edgy now. The moment we got those other
people out, whatever excuse we used, he'd know something was wrong and he'd be watching and waiting."

The second officer passed over the Selcal message he
had been copying. It was from D.T.M. Lincoln. Using
the hooded light, Gwen and Demerest read it together.

NEW INFORMATION INDICATES EARLIER POSSI-
BILITY OF EXPLOSIVE DEVICE IN POSSESSION OF
PASSENGER GUERRERO IS NOW STRONG PROBA-
BILITY   REPEAT   STRONG   PROBABILITY. PAS-
SENGER   BELIEVED   MENTALLY   DISTURBED,
DESPERATE. REPEAT PREVIOUS WARNING TO AP-
PROACH WITH EXTREME CAUTION. GOOD LUCK.

"I like that last bit," Cy Jordan said. "That's real
nice, wishing us that."

Demerest said brusquely, "Shut up!"

For several seconds—apart from routine flight deck sounds—there was silence.

"If there were some way," Demerest said slowly, ". . . some way we could trick him into letting go of that case. All we'd need would be a few seconds to have our hands on it, then get it clear away . . . if we were quick, two seconds would be enough."

Gwen pointed out, "He wouldn't even put it down . . ."

"I know! I know! I'm thinking, that's all." He stopped. "Let's go over it again. There are two passengers between Guerrero and the aisle. One of them . . ."

"One of them is a man; he has the aisle seat. In the middle is the old lady, Mrs. Quonsett. Then Guerrero."

"So grandma's right beside Guerrero; right alongside the case."

"Yes, but how does it help? Even if we could let her know, she couldn't possibly . . ."

Demerest said sharply, "You haven't said anything to her yet? She doesn't know we're on to her?"

"No. You told me not to."

"Just wanted to be sure."

Again they were silent. Vernon Demerest concentrated, thinking, weighing possibilities. At length he said carefully, "I have an idea. It may not work, but at the moment it's the best we have. Now listen, while I tell you exactly what to do."

In the tourist section of Flight Two most passengers had finished dinner, and stewardesses were briskly removing trays. The meal service had gone faster than usual tonight. One reason was that due to the delayed takeoff, some passengers had eaten in the terminal and now, because of the lateness of the hour, they had either declined dinner or merely nibbled at it.

At the three-seat unit where Mrs. Ada Quonsett was still chatting with her new friend, the oboe player, one of the tourist cabin stewardesses—a pert young blonde —asked, "Have you finished with your trays?"

"Yes, I have, miss," the oboist said.

Mrs. Quonsett smiled warmly. "Thank you, my dear; you may take mine. It was very nice."

The dour man on Mrs. Quonsett's left surrendered his tray without comment.

It was only then that the little old lady from San Diego became aware of the other stewardess standing in the aisle.

She was one whom Mrs. Quonsett had observed several times previously, and appeared to be in charge of the other girls. She had deep black hair, an attractive, high-cheekboned face, and strong dark eyes which at the moment were focused, directly and coolly, on Ada Quonsett.

"Pardon me, madam. May I see your ticket?"

"My ticket? Why, of course." Mrs. Quonsett affected surprise, though she guessed immediately what lay behind the request. Obviously her stowaway status was either suspected or known. But she had never given up easily, and even now her wits were working. A question was: how much did this girl know?

Mrs. Quonsett opened her purse and pretended to search among its papers. "I know I had it, my dear. It must be here somewhere." She glanced up, her expression innocent. "That is, unless the ticket man took it when I came aboard. Perhaps he kept it and I didn't notice."

"No," Gwen Meighen said, "he wouldn't have. If it was a round-trip ticket, you'd be holding a return flight coupon. And if it was one-way, you'd still have the ticket stub and boarding folder."

"Well, it certainly seems strange . . ." Mrs. Quonsett continued fumbling in her purse.

Gwen inquired coldly, "Shall I look?" From the beginning of their exchange, she had shown none of her customary friendliness. She added, "If there's a ticket in your purse, I'll find it. If there isn't, it will save us both wasting time."

"Certainly not," Mrs. Quonsett said severely. Then, relenting: "I realize you mean no harm, my dear, but I have private papers here. You, being English, should respect privacy. You *are* English, aren't you?"

"Whether I am or not doesn't matter. At this moment we're talking about your ticket. That is, *if* you have one." Gwen's voice, pitched louder than usual, was audible several seats away. Heads of other passengers were turning.

"Oh, I have a ticket. It's just a question of where it is." Mrs. Quonsett smiled engagingly. "About your being English, though, I could tell you were from the very first moment you spoke. So many English people —people like you, my dear—make our language sound delightful. It's such a pity so few of us Americans can do the same. My late husband always used to say . . ."

"Never mind what he said. What about your ticket?"

It was hard for Gwen to be as rude and unpleasant as she was being. In the ordinary way she would have dealt with this old woman firmly, yet remained friendly and good-natured; Gwen also had a reluctance to bully someone more than twice her own age. But before she left the flight deck, Vernon had been explicit in his instructions.

Mrs. Quonsett looked a little shocked. "I'm being patient with you, young lady. But when I do discover my ticket I shall certainly have something to say about your attitude . . ."

"Will you really, Mrs. Quonsett?" Gwen saw the old woman start at the use of her name, and for the first time there was a weakening behind the prim façade. Gwen persisted, "You *are* Ada Quonsett, aren't you?"

The little old lady patted her lips with a lace handkerchief, then sighed. "Since you know I am, there's no point in denying it, is there?"

"No, because we know all about you. You've got quite a record, Mrs. Quonsett."

More passengers were watching and listening now; one or two had left their seats to move closer. Their expressions were sympathetic for the old lady, critical of Gwen. The man in the aisle seat, who had been talking with Mrs. Quonsett when Gwen arrived, shifted uncomfortably. "If there's some misunderstanding, perhaps I can help . . ."

"There's no misunderstanding," Gwen said. "Are you traveling with this lady?"

"No."

"Then there's nothing you need concern yourself about, sir."

So far, Gwen had not let herself look directly at the man seated farthest away, by the window, whom she knew to be Guerrero. Nor had he looked at her, though she could tell by the inclination of his head that he was listening intently to everything that was being said. Also without being obvious, she observed that he was still clasping the small attaché case on his knees. At the thought of what the case might contain she experienced a sudden, icy fear. She felt herself tremble, with a premonition of something terrible to come. She wanted to run, return to the flight deck and tell Vernon to handle this himself. But she didn't, and the moment of weakness passed.

"I said we know all about you, and we do," Gwen assured Mrs. Quonsett. "You were caught earlier today as a stowaway on one of our flights from Los Angeles. You were placed in custody, but you managed to slip away. Then, by lying, you got aboard this flight."

The little old lady from San Diego said brightly, "If you know so much, or think you do, it won't do any good arguing about it." Well, she decided, it was no good worrying now. After all, she had expected to get caught; at least she hadn't been until she'd had an adventure and a good dinner. Besides, what did it matter? As the redheaded woman back at Lincoln admitted, airlines never prosecuted stowaways.

She was curious, though, about what came next. "Are we going to turn back?"

"You're not that important. When we land in Italy you'll be handed over to the authorities." Vernon Demerest had warned Gwen to let it be thought that Flight Two was proceeding on to Rome, certainly not to admit that they were already turned around and heading back. He also impressed on her that she must be rough with the old lady, which Gwen had not enjoyed. But it was necessary to make an impression on the passenger Guerrero, to carry out Demerest's next step.

Though Guerrero didn't know it—and if all went well, he would not know until too late to make any difference—this entire performance was solely for his benefit.

"You're to come with me," Gwen instructed Mrs. Quonsett. "The captain has had a signal about you, and he has to make a report. Before he does, he wants to see you." She asked the man in the aisle seat, "Will you let this woman out, please?"

For the first time the old lady looked nervous. "The captain wants me?"

"Yes, and he doesn't like to be kept waiting."

Hesitantly, Mrs. Quonsett released her seat belt. As the oboe player moved out, unhappily, to let her pass, she stepped uncertainly into the aisle. Taking her arm, Gwen propelled her forward, conscious of hostile glances all around—directed at herself—as they went.

Gwen resisted an impulse to turn, to see if the man with the case was watching too.

"I'm Captain Demerest," Vernon Demerest said. "Please come in—as far forward as you can. Gwen, shut the door and let's see if we can squeeze everybody in." He smiled at Mrs. Quonsett. "I'm afraid they don't design flight decks for entertaining visitors."

The old lady from San Diego peered toward him. After the bright lights of the passenger cabin from which she had just come, her eyes were not yet adjusted to the cockpit's semidarkness. All she could make out were shadowy figures, seated, surrounded by dozens of redly glowing dials. But there had been no mistaking the friendliness of the voice. Its effect and tone were far different from what she had braced herself to expect.

Cy Jordan pushed an armrest upward on an empty crew seat behind Anson Harris. Gwen—gently, in contrast to her behavior of a few minutes ago—guided the old lady into the seat.

There was still no turbulence outside, which made it easy to move around. Though losing height, they were still far above the storm, and despite the airplane's speed of more than five hundred miles an hour, it was riding easily as if on a calm, untroubled sea.

"Mrs. Quonsett," Vernon Demerest said, "whatever

happened outside just now, you can forget it. It's not the reason you were brought here." He asked Gwen, "Were you pretty rough with her?"

"I'm afraid so."

"Miss Meighen was acting on my orders. I told her to do exactly what she did. We knew one particular person would be watching and listening. We wanted it to look good, to have a plausible reason for bringing you here."

The big shadowy figure speaking from the right-hand seat was becoming clearer to Ada Quonsett now. From what she could see of his face, he seemed a kind man, she thought. At the moment, of course, she had no idea what he was talking about. She looked about her. It was all very interesting. She had never been on a flight deck before. It was much more crowded and a smaller space than she expected. It was also warm, and the three men whom she could now see were all in shirtsleeves. This would certainly be something else to tell her daughter in New York—if she ever got there.

"Grandma," the man who had introduced himself as the captain said, "do you get frightened easily?"

It seemed an odd question, and she thought about it before answering. "Not easily, I think. I get nervous sometimes, though not as much as I used to. When you get older there isn't a lot left to be frightened of."

The captain's eyes were fixed searchingly on her face. "I've decided to tell you something, then ask for your help. We don't have too much time, so I'll make it fast. I suppose you've noticed the man sitting next to you, back in the cabin—on the window side."

"The skinny one, with the little mustache?"

"Yes," Gwen said. "That's him."

Mrs. Quonsett nodded. "He's a strange one. He won't talk to anybody, and he has a little case with him that he won't let go of. I think he's worried about something."

"We're worried, too," Vernon Demerest said quietly. "We've reason to believe that in that case he has a bomb. We want to get it away from him. That's why I need your help."

One of the surprising things about being up here with the pilots, Ada Quonsett thought, was how quiet it was.

In the silence which followed what had just been said, she could hear a message coming in on an overhead speaker near where she was seated. "Trans America Two, this is Toronto Center. Your position is fifteen miles east of Kleinburg beacon. Advise your flight level and intentions."

The man in the other front seat, on the left, whose face she hadn't yet seen, was answering. "Toronto Center from Trans America Two. Leaving flight level two niner zero. Request continued slow descent until we advise. No change in our intentions to return for landing at Lincoln."

"Roger, Trans America. We are clearing traffic ahead of you. You may continue slow descent."

A third man, at a little table to her right, facing still more dials, leaned across to the one who had been speaking. "I make it an hour and seventeen minutes in. That's using forecast winds, but if the front's moved faster than expected, it could be less."

"We *are* going back, aren't we?" Mrs. Quonsett found it hard to restrain the excitement in her voice.

Demerest nodded. "But you're the only one who knows, besides ourselves. For the time being you must keep it a secret, and above all, Guerrero—that's the man with the case—mustn't find out."

Ada Quonsett thought breathlessly: was this really happening to her? It was all quite thrilling, like something on TV. It *was* a little frightening perhaps, but she decided not to think too much about that. The main thing was—she was here, a part of it all, hobnobbing with the captain, sharing secrets, and what would her daughter say about *that*?

"Well, will you help us?"

"Oh, of course. I expect you want me to see if I can get that case away . . ."

"No!" Vernon Demerest swung farther around, leaning over the back of his seat for emphasis. He said sternly, "You must not so much as put your hands on that case, or even near it."

"If you say so," Mrs. Quonsett acknowledged meekly, "I won't."

"I do say so. And remember, it's important that

Guerrero have no idea we know about his case or what's inside. Now, as I did with Miss Meighen a little while ago, I'm going to tell you exactly what to do when you go back to the cabin. Please listen carefully."

When he had finished, the little old lady from San Diego permitted herself a small, brief smile. "Oh, yes; yes, I think I can do that."

She was getting out of her seat, with Gwen about to open the flight deck door for them to go, when Demerest asked, "That flight from Los Angeles you stowed away on—they said you were trying to reach New York. Why?"

She told him about being lonely sometimes on the West coast, and wanting to visit her married daughter in the east.

"Grandma," Vernon Demerest said, "if we pull this off I'll personally guarantee that not only will any trouble you're in be taken care of, but this airline will give you a ticket to New York, and back, first class."

Mrs. Quonsett was so touched, she almost cried.

"Oh, thank you! Thank you!" For once she found it hard to speak. What a remarkable man, she thought; such a kind, dear man!

Her genuine emotion as she was about to leave the flight deck helped Mrs. Quonsett in her progress through the first class compartment and then into the tourist cabin. With Gwen Meighen grasping her arm tightly and shoving her along, the old lady dabbed at her eyes with her lace handkerchief, giving a tearful, credible performance of acute distress. She reminded herself, almost gleefully beneath her tears, that it was her second performance tonight. The first, when she pretended to be ill, had been staged in the terminal for the young passenger agent, Peter Coakley. She had been convincing then, so why not now?

The performance was sufficiently authentic for one passenger to ask Gwen heatedly, "Miss, whatever she's done, do you have to be so rough?"

Gwen replied tartly, already aware that she was

within hearing of the man Guerrero, "Sir, please don't interfere."

As they passed into the tourist cabin, Gwen closed the draw curtain in the doorway separating the two passenger sections. That was part of Vernon's plan. Looking back the way they had come, toward the front of the aircraft, Gwen could see the flight deck door slightly ajar. Behind it, she knew, Vernon was waiting, watching. As soon as the curtain between first class and tourist was closed, Vernon would move aft and stand behind it, watching through a chink which Gwen was careful to leave open. Then, when the proper moment came, he would fling the curtain aside and rush through swiftly.

At the thought of what was going to happen within the next few minutes—whatever the outcome—once more an icy fear, a sense of premonition, came to Gwen. Once more she conquered it. Reminding herself of her responsibilities to the crew, and to the other passengers—who were oblivious of the drama being played out in their midst—she escorted Mrs. Quonsett the remaining distance to her seat.

The passenger Guerrero glanced up quickly, then away. The small attaché case, Gwen saw, was still in the same position on his knees, his hands holding it. The man from the aisle seat next to Mrs. Quonsett's—the oboe player—stood up as they approached. His expression sympathetic, he moved out to let the old lady in. Unobtrusively, Gwen moved in front of him, blocking his return. The aisle seat must remain unoccupied until Gwen moved out of the way. Gwen's eyes caught a flicker of movement through the chink she had left in the doorway curtain. Vernon Demerest was in position and ready.

"Please!" Still standing in the aisle, Mrs. Quonsett turned pleadingly, tearfully to Gwen. "I beg of you— ask the captain to reconsider. I don't want to be handed over to the Italian police . . ."

Gwen said harshly, "You should have thought of that before. Besides, I don't tell the captain what to do."

"But you can ask him! He'll listen to you."

D. O. Guerrero turned his head, took in the scene, then looked away.

Gwen seized the old lady's arm. "I'm telling you—get into that seat!"

Ada Quonsett's voice became a wail. "All I'm asking is to be taken back. Hand me over there, not in a strange country!"

From behind Gwen the oboe player protested, "Miss, can't you see the lady's upset?"

Gwen snapped, "Please keep out of this. This woman has no business here at all. She's a stowaway."

The oboist said indignantly, "I don't care what she is. She's still an old lady."

Ignoring him, Gwen gave Mrs. Quonsett a shove which sent her staggering. "You heard me! Sit down and be quiet."

Ada Quonsett dropped into her seat. She screamed, "You hurt me! You hurt me!"

Several passengers were on their feet, protesting.

D. O. Guerrero continued to look straight ahead. His hands, Gwen saw, were still on the attaché case.

Mrs. Quonsett wailed again.

Gwen said coldly, "You're hysterical." Deliberately, hating what she had to do, she leaned into the section of seats and slapped Mrs. Quonsett hard across the face. The slap resounded through the cabin. Passengers gasped. Two other stewardesses appeared incredulous. The oboist seized Gwen's arm; hastily she shook herself free.

What happened next occurred so swiftly that even those closest to the scene were uncertain of the sequence of events.

Mrs. Quonsett, in her seat, turned to D. O. Guerrero on her left. She appealed to him, "Sir, please help me! Help me!"

His features rigid, he ignored her.

Apparently overcome by grief and fear, she reached toward him, flinging her arms hysterically around his neck. "Please, please!"

Guerrero twisted his body away, trying to release

himself. He failed. Instead, Ada Quonsett wound her arms around his neck more tightly. "Oh, help me!"

Red-faced and close to choking, D. O. Guerrero put up both hands to wrench her away. As if in supplication, Ada Quonsett eased her grasp and seized his hands.

At the same instant, Gwen Meighen leaned forward toward the inside seat. She reached out and in a single even movement—almost without haste—she grasped the attaché case firmly and removed it from Guerrero's knees. A moment later the case was free and in the aisle. Between Guerrero and the case, Gwen and Ada Quonsett were a solid barrier.

The curtain across the doorway from the first class cabin swept open. Vernon Demerest, tall and impressive in uniform, hurried through.

His face showing relief, he held out his hand for the attaché case. "Nice going, Gwen. Let me have it."

With ordinary luck the incident—except for dealing with Guerrero later—would have ended there. That it did not was solely due to Marcus Rathbone.

Rathbone, until that moment, was an unknown, unconsidered passenger, occupying seat fourteen-D across the aisle. Although others were unaware of him, he was a self-important, pompous man, constantly aware of himself.

In the small Iowa town where he lived he was a minor merchant, known to his neighbors as a "knocker." Whatever others in his community did or proposed, Marcus Rathbone objected to. His objections, small and large, were legendary. They included the choice of books in the local library, a plan for a community antennae system, the needed disciplining of his son at school, and the color of paint for a civic building. Shortly before departing on his present trip he had organized the defeat of a proposed sign ordinance which would have beautified his town's main street. Despite his habitual "knocking," he had never been known to propose a constructive idea.

Another peculiarity was that Marcus Rathbone despised women, including his own wife. None of his objections had ever been on their behalf. Consequently, the humiliation of Mrs. Quonsett a moment earlier had not disturbed him, but Gwen Meighen's seizure of D. O. Guerrero's attaché case did.

To Marcus Rathbone this was officialdom in uniform —and a woman at that!—impinging on the rights of an ordinary traveler like himself. Indignantly, Rathbone rose from his seat, interposing himself between Gwen and Vernon Demerest.

At the same instant, D. O. Guerrero, flushed and mouthing incoherent words, scrambled free from his seat and the grasp of Ada Quonsett. As he reached the aisle, Marcus Rathbone seized the case from Gwen and —with a polite bow—held it out. Like a wild animal, with madness in his eyes, Guerrero grabbed it.

Vernon Demerest flung himself forward, but too late. He tried to reach Guerrero, but the narrowness of the aisle and the intervening figures—Gwen, Rathbone, the oboe player—defeated him. D. O. Guerrero had ducked around the others and was heading for the aircraft's rear. Other passengers, in seats, were scrambling to their feet. Demerest shouted desperately, "Stop that man! He has a bomb!"

The shout produced screams, and an exodus from seats which had the effect of blocking the aisle still further. Only Gwen Meighen, scrambling, pushing, clawing her way aft, managed to stay close to Guerrero.

At the end of the cabin—like an animal still, but this time cornered—Guerrero turned. All that remained between him and the aircraft's tail were three rear toilets; light indicators showed that two were empty, one was occupied. His back to the toilets, Guerrero held the attaché case forward in front of him, one hand on its carrying handle, the other on a loop of string now visible beneath the handle. In a strained voice, somewhere between a whisper and a snarl, he warned, "Stay where you are! Don't come closer!"

Above the heads of the others, Vernon Demerest shouted again. "Guerrero, listen to me! Do you hear me? Listen!"

There was a second's silence in which no one moved,

the only sound the steady background whine of the plane's jet engines. Guerrero blinked, continuing to face the others, his eyes roving and suspicious.

"We know who you are," Demerest called out, "and we know what you intended. We know about the insurance and the bomb, and they know on the ground, too, so it means your insurance is no good. Do you understand?—your insurance is invalid, canceled, worthless. If you let off that bomb you'll kill yourself for nothing. No one—least of all your family—will gain. In fact, your family will lose because they'll be blamed and hounded. Listen to me! Think."

A woman screamed. Still Guerrero hesitated.

Vernon Demerest urged, "Guerrero, let these people sit down. Then, if you like, we'll talk. You can ask me questions. I promise that until you're ready, no one will come close." Demerest was calculating: If Guerrero's attention could be held long enough, the aisle might be cleared. After that, Demerest would try to persuade Guerrero to hand over the case. If he refused, there was still a chance that Demerest could leap forward, throw himself bodily onto Guerrero and wrest the case free before the trigger could be used. It would be a tremendous risk, but there was nothing better.

People were easing nervously back into their seats.

"Now that I've told you what we know, Guerrero; now *you* know that it isn't any good going on, I'm asking you to give me that case." Demerest tried to keep his tone reasonable, sensing it was important to keep talking. "If you do as I say, I give you my solemn word that no one in this airplane will harm you."

D. O. Guerrero's eyes mirrored fear. He moistened thin lips with his tongue. Gwen Meighen was closest to him.

Demerest said quietly, "Gwen, take it easy. Try to get in a seat." If he had to leap, he wanted no one in the way.

Behind Guerrero the door of the occupied toilet opened. An owlish young man with thick glasses came out. He stopped, peering short-sightedly. Obviously he had heard nothing of what was going on.

Another passenger yelled, "Grab the guy with the case! He's got a bomb!"

At the first "click" of the toilet door, Guerrero half turned. Now he lunged, thrusting the man with glasses aside, and entered the toilet which the newcomer had vacated.

As Guerrero moved, Gwen Meighen moved too, remaining close behind him. Vernon Demerest, several yards away, was struggling fiercely aft, down the still crowded aisle.

The toilet door was closing as Gwen reached it. She thrust a foot inside and shoved. Her foot stopped the door from closing, but the door refused to move. Despairing, as pain shot through her foot, she could feel Guerrero's weight against the other side.

In D. O. Guerrero's mind the last few minutes had been a jumbled blur. He had not fully comprehended everything that had occurred, nor had he heard all that Demerest said. But one thing penetrated. He realized that like so many of his other grand designs, this one, too, had failed. Somewhere—as always happened with whatever he attempted—he had bungled. All his life had been a failure. With bitterness, he knew his death would be a failure too.

His back was braced against the inside of the toilet door. He felt pressure on it, and knew that at any moment the pressure would increase so that he could no longer hold the door closed. Desperately he fumbled with the attaché case, reaching for the string beneath the handle which would release the square of plastic, actuating the clothespin switch and detonating the dynamite inside. Even as he found the string and tugged, he wondered if the bomb he had made would be a failure also.

In his last split second of life and comprehension, D. O. Guerrero learned that it was not.

10

The explosion aboard Trans America Flight Two, *The Golden Argosy,* was instantaneous, monstrous, and over-whelming. In the airplane's confined space it struck with the din of a hundred thunderclaps, a sheet of flame, and a blow like a giant sledge hammer.

D. O. Guerrero died instantly, his body, near the core of the explosion, disintegrating utterly. One moment he existed; the next, there were only a few small, bloody pieces of him left.

The aircraft fuselage blew open.

Gwen Meighen, who, next to Guerrero, was nearest the explosion, received its force in her face and chest.

An instant after the dynamite charge ripped the air-craft skin, the cabin decompressed. With a second roar and tornado force, air inside the aircraft—until this moment maintained at normal pressure—swept through the ruptured fuselage to dissipate in the high altitude near-vacuum outside. Through the passenger cabins a dark engulfing cloud of dust surged toward the rear. With it, like litter in a maelstrom, went every loose object, light and heavy—papers, food trays, liquor bot-tles, coffeepots, hand luggage, clothing, passengers' be-longings—all whirling through the air as if impelled toward a cyclopean vacuum cleaner. Curtains tore away. Internal doors—flight deck, storage, and toilets —wrenched free from locks and hinges and were swept rearward with the rest.

Several passengers were struck. Others, not strapped in their seats, clung to any handhold as the wind and suction drew them inexorably toward the rear.

Throughout the aircraft, emergency compartments above each seat snapped open. Yellow oxygen masks came tumbling down, each mask connected by a short plastic tube to a central oxygen supply.

Abruptly the suction lessened. The aircraft's interior

was filled with mist and a savage, biting cold. Noise
from engines and wind was overwhelming.

Vernon Demerest, still in the aisle of the tourist cabin
where he had held himself by instinctively seizing a
seatback, roared, "Get on oxygen!" He grabbed a mask
himself.

Through knowledge and training, Demerest realized
what most others did not: The air inside the cabin was
now as rarefied as that outside, and insufficient to support life. Only fifteen seconds of full consciousness remained to everyone, unless oxygen was used at once
from the aircraft's emergency system.

Even in five seconds, without the aid of oxygen, a
degree of lessened judgment would occur.

In another five seconds a state of euphoria would
make many decide not to bother with oxygen at all.
They would lapse into unconsciousness, not caring.

Airlines had long been urged, by those who understood the hazards of decompression, to make pre-flight
announcements about oxygen equipment more definite
than they were. Passengers should be told, it was
argued: *The instant an oxygen mask appears in front of
you, grab it, stick your face into it, and ask questions
after. If there is a real decompression, you haven't a
single second to spare. If it's a false alarm, you can
always take the mask off later; meanwhile it will do no
harm.*

Pilots who took decompression tests were given a
simple demonstration of the effect of oxygen lack at
high altitudes. In a decompression tank, with an oxygen
mask on, they were told to begin writing their signatures, and part way through the exercise their masks
were removed. The signatures tailed off into a scrawl, or
nothingness. Before unconsciousness occurred, the
masks were put back on.

The pilots found it hard to believe what they saw on
the page before them.

Yet airline managements, theorizing that more
definite oxygen advice might create alarm among passengers, persisted in the use of innocuous flight announcements only. Smiling stewardesses, seeming either

bored or amused, casually demonstrated the equipment while an unseen voice—hurrying to get finished before takeoff—parroted phrases like: *In the unlikely event . . . and . . . Government regulations require that we inform you.* No mention was ever made of urgency, should the equipment be required for use.

As a result, passengers became as indifferent to emergency oxygen facilities as airlines and their staffs appeared to be. The overhead boxes and monotonous, always-alike demonstrations were (passengers reasoned) something dreamed up by a bunch of regulation-obsessed civil servants. (Yawn!) Obviously the whole thing was largely a charade, insisted on by the same kind of people who collected income taxes and disallowed expense accounts. *So what the hell!*

Occasionally, on regular flights, oxygen mask housings opened accidentally, and masks dropped down in front of passengers. When this happened, most passengers stared curiously at the masks but made no attempt to put them on. Precisely that reaction—though the emergency was real—had occurred aboard Flight Two.

Vernon Demerest saw the reaction and in a flash of sudden anger remembered his own, and other pilots', criticisms of soft-pedaled oxygen announcements. But there was no time to shout another warning, nor even to think of Gwen, who might be dead or dying only a few feet away.

Only one thing mattered: somehow to get back to the flight deck, and help save the airplane if he could.

Breathing oxygen deeply, he planned his movement forward in the aircraft.

Above every seat section in the tourist cabin, four oxygen masks had dropped—one for the occupant of each seat, plus a spare to be grabbed if necessary by anyone standing in the aisle. It was one of the spares which Demerest had seized and was using.

But to reach the flight deck he must abandon this mask and use a portable one that would permit him to move forward freely.

He knew that two portable oxygen cylinders were stowed, farther forward, in an overhead rack near the

first class cabin bulkhead. If he could make it to the
portable cylinders, either one would sustain him for the
remaining distance from the bulkhead to the flight deck.

He moved forward to the bulkhead one seat section
at a time, using one spare hanging mask after another as
he went.

A couple of seat sections ahead, he could see that all
four masks were being used by seated passengers; the
three seat occupants, including a teen-age girl, had one
mask each; the fourth mask was being held by the teen-
ager over the face of an infant on its mother's lap alongside. The girl seemed to have taken charge and was
motioning to others near her what to do. Demerest
swung toward the opposite side of the cabin, saw a
spare mask hanging, and taking a deep breath of
oxygen, he let go the one he had and reached for the
other spare. He made it, and breathed deeply once
again. He still had more than half the tourist cabin
length to go.

He had made one more move when he felt the aircraft roll sharply to the right, then dive steeply down.

Demerest hung on. He knew that, for the moment,
there was nothing he could do. What happened next was
dependent on two things: how much damage the explosion had done, and the skill of Anson Harris, at the
flight controls, alone.

On the flight deck, the events of the last few seconds
had occurred with even less warning than at the rear.
After the departure of Gwen Meighen and Mrs. Quonsett, followed by Vernon Demerest, the two remaining
crew members—Anson Harris and Second Officer Cy
Jordan—had no knowledge of what was going on in the
passenger cabins behind them until the dynamite blast
rocked the aircraft, followed an instant later by explosive decompression.

As in the passenger compartments, the cockpit filled
with a thick, dark cloud of dust, almost immediately
sucked out as the flight deck door smashed free from its
lock and hinges, and flew outward. Everything loose on
the flight deck was snatched up, to be carried back,
joining the debris-laden whirlwind.

Under the flight engineer's table, a warning horn began blaring intermittently. Over both front seats, bright yellow lights flashed on. Both horn and lights were signals of dangerously low pressure.

A fine mist—deathly cold—replaced the cloud of dust. Anson Harris felt his eardrums tighten painfully.

But even before that, he had reacted instantly—the effect of training and experience of many years.

On the long, uphill road to airline captaincy, pilots spent arduous hours in classrooms and simulators, studying and practicing airborne situations, both normal and emergency. The objective was to instill quick, correct reactions at all times.

The simulators were located at important air bases and all major scheduled airlines had them.

From outside, a simulator looked like the nose of an aircraft, with the rest of the fuselage chopped off; inside, was everything included in a normal flight deck.

Once inside a simulator, pilots remained shut up for hours, imitating the precise conditions of a long distance flight. The effect, when the outside door was closed, was uncanny; even motion and noise were present, creating the physical effect of being airborne. All other conditions paralleled reality. A screen beyond the forward windows could conjure up airports and runways, enlarging or receding to simulate takeoff and landing. The only difference between a simulator flight deck and a genuine one was that the simulator never left the ground.

Pilots in a simulator conversed with a nearby control room, as they would on radio in the air. Within the control room, skilled operators duplicated air traffic control procedures and other flight conditions. The operators could also feed in adverse situations, without warning, to pilots. These ranged through multiple engine failure, to fire, violent weather, electrical and fuel problems, explosive decompression, instrument malfunction, and other assorted unpleasantness. Even a crash could be reproduced; sometimes simulators were used in reverse to find out what had caused one.

Occasionally an operator would feed in several emergencies at once, causing pilots to emerge later, exhausted and sweat-drenched. Most pilots coped with such tests; the few who didn't had the fact noted in their records, were re-examined, and afterward watched carefully. The simulator sessions continued, several times a year, through every stage of a pilot's career until retirement.

The result was: When a real emergency occurred, airline pilots knew exactly what to do, and did it, without fumbling or loss of precious time. It was one of many factors which made travel by scheduled airlines the safest means of transportation in human history. It had also conditioned Anson Harris to instant action, directed toward the salvation of Flight Two.

In the drill for explosive decompression one rule was fundamental: the crew took care of themselves first. Vernon Demerest observed the rule; so did Anson Harris and Cy Jordan.

They must be on oxygen at once—even ahead of passengers. Then, with full mental faculties assured, decisions could be made.

Behind each pilot's seat a quick-don oxygen mask— resembling a baseball catcher's mask—was hanging. As he had practiced countless times, Harris ripped off his radio headset, then reached over his shoulder for the mask. He tugged, so that a holding clip snapped open, and slapped the mask on. As well as a connection to the airplane's oxygen supply, it contained a microphone. For listening, now his headset was removed, Harris changed a selector, actuating a speaker overhead.

Behind him, Cy Jordan, with identical swift movements, did the same.

In another reflex movement, Anson Harris took care of passengers. Cabin oxygen systems worked automatically in event of pressure failure; but as a precaution— in case they didn't—over the pilots' heads was an override switch. It ensured positive release of passenger masks and sent oxygen flowing into them. Harris flipped the switch.

He dropped his right hand to the throttles, pulling all four off. The aircraft slowed.

It must be slowed still more.

Left of the throttles was a speed brake handle. Harris

pulled it fully toward him. Along the top surface of both wings, spoilers rose up, inducing drag, and causing further slowing.

Cy Jordan silenced the warning horn.

So far, all procedures had been automatic. Now, a moment for decision had arrived.

It was essential that the aircraft seek a safer altitude below. From its present height of twenty-eight thousand feet, it must descend some three and a half miles to where the air was denser so that passengers and crew could breathe and survive without supplemental oxygen.

The decision Harris had to make was—should the descent be slow, or a high-speed dive?

Until the past year or two, the instruction to pilots in event of explosive decompression was: dive immediately. Tragically, however, the instruction had resulted in at least one aircraft breaking apart when a slower descent might have saved it. Nowadays, pilots were cautioned: *Check for structural damage first. If the damage is bad, a dive may worsen it, so go down slowly.*

Yet that policy, too, had hazards. To Anson Harris, they were instantly apparent.

Undoubtedly Flight Two had sustained structural damage. The sudden decompression proved it, and the explosion which had occurred just before—though still less than a minute ago—might already have done great harm. In other circumstances, Harris would have sent Cy Jordan to the rear to learn how bad the damage was, but since Demerest was gone, Jordan must stay.

But however serious the structural damage, there was another factor, perhaps more cogent. The air temperature outside the aircraft was minus fifty degrees centigrade. Judging by the near-paralyzing cold which Harris felt, the inside temperature must also be near that. In such intense cold, no one without protective clothing could survive for more than minutes.

So which was the lesser gamble—to freeze for sure, or take a chance and go down fast?

Making a decision which only later events could prove right or wrong, Harris called on interphone to Cy Jordan, "Warn air traffic control! We're diving!"

At the same moment, Harris banked the aircraft

steeply to the right and selected landing gear "down."
Banking before the dive would have two effects: Passengers or stewardesses who were not strapped in seats, or
who were standing, would be held where they were by
centrifugal force; whereas, a straight dive would throw
them to the ceiling. The turn would also head Flight
Two away from the airway they had been using, and—
hopefully—other traffic below.

Putting the landing gear down would further reduce
forward speed, and make the dive steeper.

On the overhead speaker, Harris could hear Cy Jor-
dan's voice intoning a distress call. "Mayday, mayday.
This is Trans America Two. Explosive decompression.
We are diving, diving."

Harris pushed the control yoke hard forward. Over
his shoulder he shouted, "Ask for ten!"

Cy Jordan added, "Request ten thousand feet."

Anson Harris clicked a radar transponder switch to
seventy-seven—a radar S-O-S. Now, on all monitoring
screens on the ground, a double blossom signal would
be seen, confirming both their distress and identity.

They were going down fast, the altimeter unwinding
like a clock with a wild mainspring . . . Passing through
twenty-six thousand feet . . . twenty-four . . . twenty-
three . . . Climb and descent meter showed eight thousand feet descent a minute . . . Toronto Air Route
Center on the overhead speaker: "All altitudes below
you are clear. Report your intentions when ready. We
are standing by." . . . Harris had eased out of the turn,
was diving straight ahead . . . No time to think about the
cold; if they could get low enough fast enough, there
might be survival—if the aircraft held together . . .
Already Harris was aware of trouble with rudder
control and elevators; rudder movement was stiff; stabilizer trim, not responding . . . Twenty-one thousand feet
. . . twenty . . . nineteen . . . From the feel of the
controls, the explosion had done damage to the tail; how
bad, they would discover when he tried to pull out in a
minute or less from now. It would be the moment of
greatest strain. If anything critical gave way, they would
continue plummeting in . . . Harris would have been
glad of some help from the right seat, but it was too late

for Cy Jordan to move there. Besides, the second officer was needed where he was—shutting air inlets, throwing in all the heat they had, watching for fuel system damage or fire warnings . . . Eighteen thousand feet . . . seventeen . . . When they reached fourteen thousand, Harris decided, he would start pulling out of the dive, hoping to level at ten . . . Passing through fifteen thousand . . . fourteen . . . Begin easing out *now!*

Controls were heavy, but responding . . . Harris pulled back hard on the control yoke. The dive was flattening, control surfaces holding, the aircraft coming out . . . Twelve thousand feet; descending more slowly now . . . eleven thousand . . . ten, five . . . *ten!*

They were level! So far, everything had held together. Here, the normal air was breathable and would sustain life, extra oxygen not necessary. The outside air temperature gauge showed minus five centigrade—five degrees below freezing; still cold, but not the killing cold of altitudes above.

From beginning to end, the dive had taken two and a half minutes.

The overhead speakers came alive. "Trans America Two, this is Toronto Center. How are you doing?"

Cy Jordan acknowledged. Anson Harris cut in. "Level at ten thousand, returning to heading two seven zero. We have structural damage due to explosion, extent unknown. Request weather and runway information—Toronto, Detroit Metropolitan, and Lincoln." In his mind, Harris had an instant picture of airports large enough to accommodate the Boeing 707, and with the special landing requirements he would need.

Vernon Demerest was clambering over the smashed flight deck door and other debris outside. Hurrying in, he slid into his seat on the right side.

"We missed you," Harris said.

"Can we maintain control?"

Harris nodded. "If the tail doesn't fall off, we may stay lucky." He reported the impeded rudder and stabilizer trim. "Somebody let off a firecracker back there?"

"Something like that. It's made a bloody great hole. I didn't stop to measure."

Their casualness, both men knew, was on the surface

only. Harris was still steadying the aircraft, seeking an even altitude and course. He said considerately, "It was a good scheme, Vernon. It could have worked."

"It could have, but it didn't." Demerest swung around to the second officer. "Get back in tourist. Check on damage, report by interphone. Then do all you can for the people. We'll need to know how many are hurt, and how badly." For the first time he permitted himself an anguished thought. "And find out about Gwen."

The airport reports, which Anson Harris had asked for, were coming in from Toronto center: Toronto airport still closed; deep snow and drifts on all runways. Detroit Metropolitan—all runways closed to regular traffic, but plows will vacate runway three left if essential for emergency approach and landing; runway has five to six inches level snow, with ice beneath. Detroit visibility, six hundred feet in snow flurries. Lincoln International—all runways plowed and serviceable; runway three zero temporarily closed, due to obstruction. Lincoln visibility one mile; wind northwest, thirty knots, and gusting.

Anson Harris told Demerest, "I don't intend to dump fuel."

Demerest, understanding Harris's reasoning, nodded agreement. Assuming they could keep the airplane under control, any landing they made would be tricky and heavy, due to the large fuel load which in other circumstances would have carried them to Rome. Yet, in their present situation, to dump unwanted fuel could be an even greater hazard. The explosion and damage at the rear might have set up electrical short circuits, or metal friction, which even now could be producing sparks. When dumping fuel in flight, a single spark could turn an aircraft into a flaming holocaust. Both captains rationalized: better to avoid the fire risk and accept the penalty of a difficult landing.

Yet the same decision meant that a landing at Detroit —the nearest large airport—could be attempted only in desperation. Because of their heavy weight, they would have to land fast, requiring every available foot of runway and the last ounce of braking power. Runway three left—Detroit Metropolitan's longest, which they would need—had *ice beneath snow,* in the circumstances the worst possible combination.

There was also the unknown factor—wherever Flight Two landed—of how limited their control might be, due to rudder and stabilizer trim problems, which they already knew about, though not their extent.

For a landing, Lincoln International offered the best chance of safety. But Lincoln was at least an hour's flying time away. Their present speed—two hundred and fifty knots—was far slower than they had been moving at the higher altitude, and Anson Harris was holding the speed down, in the hope of avoiding further structural damage. Unfortunately, even that involved a penalty. At their present low level of ten thousand feet there was considerable buffeting and turbulence from the storm, now all around them instead of far below.

The crucial question was: Could they remain in the air another hour?

Despite everything that had happened, less than five minutes had passed since the explosion and explosive decompression.

Air route control was asking again: "Trans America Two, advise your intentions."

Vernon Demerest replied, requesting a direct course for Detroit while the extent of damage was still being checked. Landing intentions, either at Detroit Metropolitan or elsewhere, would be notified within the next few minutes.

"Roger, Trans America Two. Detroit has advised they are removing snowplows from runway three left. Until informed otherwise, they will prepare for an emergency landing."

The intercom bell chimed and Demerest answered. It was Cy Jordan calling from the rear, shouting to make himself heard above a roar of wind. "Captain, there's a great hole back here, about six feet wide behind the rear door. Most else around the galley and toilets is a shambles. But as far as I can see, everything's holding together. The rudder power boost is blown to hell, but control cables look okay."

"What about control surfaces? Can you see anything?"

"It looks like the skin is bulged into the stabilizer, which is why the stabilizer's jammed. Apart from that, all I can see outside are some holes and bad dents, I guess from debris blowing back. But nothing's hanging loose—at least, that shows. Most of the blast, I'd say, went sideways."

It was this effect which D. O. Guerrero had not allowed for. He had blundered and miscalculated from the beginning. He bungled the explosion, too.

His greatest error was in failing to recognize that any explosion would be drawn outward and would largely dissipate, the moment the hull of a pressurized aircraft was pierced. Another error was in not realizing how stoutly a modern jetliner was built. In a passenger jet, structural and mechanical systems duplicated each other, so that no single malfunction or damage should result in destruction of the whole. An airliner could be destroyed by a bomb, but only if the bomb were detonated—either by plan or chance—in some vulnerable location. Guerrero made no such plan.

Demerest queried Cy Jordan, "Can we stay in the air an hour?"

"My guess is, the airplane can. I'm not sure about the passengers."

"How many are hurt?"

"I can't say yet. I checked structural damage first, the way you said. But things don't look good."

Demerest ordered, "Stay there as long as you need to. Do what you can." He hesitated, dreading what the answer to his next question might be, then asked, "Have you seen any sign of Gwen?" He still didn't know whether or not Gwen had been sucked out with the initial blast. In the past it had happened to others, including stewardesses who were near the site of an explosive decompression, unprotected. And even if that had not happened, Gwen had still been closest to the detonated bomb.

Cy Jordan answered, "Gwen's here, but in pretty bad shape, I think. We've got about three doctors, and they're working on her and the others. I'll report when I can."

Vernon Demerest replaced the interphone. Despite his last question and its answer, he was still denying himself the indulgence of private thoughts or personal emotion; there would be time for those later. Professional decisions, the safety of the airplane and its complement, came first. He repeated to Anson Harris the gist of the second officer's report.

Harris considered, weighing all factors. Vernon Demerest had still given no indication of taking over direct command, and obviously approved of Harris's decisions so far, else he would have said so. Now, Demerest appeared to be leaving the decision about where to land to Harris also.

Captain Demerest—even in utmost crisis—was behaving exactly as a check pilot should.

"We'll try for Lincoln," Harris said. The safety of the aircraft was paramount; however bad conditions might be in the passenger cabin, they would have to hope that most people could manage to hold on.

Demerest nodded acknowledgment and began notifying Toronto Center of the decision; in a few minutes, Cleveland Center would take them over. Demerest requested that Detroit Metropolitan still stand by in case of a sudden change of plan, though it wasn't likely. Lincoln International was to be alerted that Flight Two would require a straight-in emergency approach.

"Roger, Trans America Two. Detroit and Lincoln are being advised." A change of course followed. They were nearing the western shore of Lake Huron, the U.S.-Canadian border close.

On the ground, both pilots knew, Flight Two was now the center of attention. Controllers and supervisors in contiguous air route centers would be working intensely, coordinating removal of all traffic from the aircraft's path, sectors ahead warned of their approach, and airways cleared. Any request they made would be acted on with first priority.

As they crossed the border, Toronto Center signed off, adding to the final exchange, "Goodnight and good luck."

Cleveland Air Route Center responded to their call a moment later.

Glancing back toward the passenger cabins, through the gap where the flight deck door had been, Demerest could see figures moving—though indistinctly, because immediately after the door had gone, Cy Jordan had dimmed the first class cabin lights to avoid reflection on the flight deck. It appeared, though, as if passengers were being ushered forward, indicating that someone in the rear had taken charge—presumably Cy Jordan, who should be reporting again at any moment. The cold was still biting, even on the flight deck; back there it must be colder still. Once more, with a second's anguish, Demerest thought of Gwen, then ruthlessly cleared his mind, concentrating on what must be decided next.

Though only minutes had elapsed since the decision to risk another hour in the air, the time to begin planning their approach and landing at Lincoln International was now. As Harris continued flying, Vernon Demerest selected approach and runway charts and spread them on his knees.

Lincoln International was home base for both pilots, and they knew the airport—as well as runways and surrounding airspace—intimately. Safety and training, however, required that memory should be supplemented and checked.

The charts confirmed what both already knew.

For the high speed, heavy weight landing they must execute, the longest possible length of runway was required. Because of doubtful rudder control, the runway should be the widest, too. It must also be directly into wind which—the Lincoln forecast had said—was northwest at thirty knots, and gusting. Runway three zero answered all requirements.

"We need three zero," Demerest said.

Harris pointed out, "That last report said a temporary closing, due to obstruction."

"I heard," Demerest growled. "The damn runway's

been blocked for hours, and all that's in the way is a stuck Mexican jet." He folded a Lincoln approach chart and clipped it to his control yoke, then exclaimed angrily, "Obstruction hell! We'll give 'em fifty more minutes to pry it loose."

As Demerest thumbed his mike button to inform air route control, Second Officer Cy Jordan—white-faced and shaken—returned to the flight deck.

11

In the main terminal of Lincoln International, Lawyer Freemantle was puzzled.

It was most peculiar, he thought, that no one in authority had yet objected to the big, increasingly noisy demonstration of Meadowood residents who, at this moment, were monopolizing a large segment of the central concourse.

Earlier this evening, when Elliott Freemantle had asked the Negro police lieutenant for permission to hold a public censure meeting, he had been firmly refused. Yet here they were, with a curious crowd of spectators —and not a policeman in sight!

Freemantle thought again: it didn't make sense.

Yet what had happened was incredibly simple.

After the interview with the airport general manager, Bakersfeld, the delegation, led by Elliott Freemantle, had returned from the administrative mezzanine to the main concourse. There, the TV crews, whom Freemantle had talked with on the way in, had set up their equipment.

The remaining Meadowood residents—already at least five hundred strong, with more coming in—were gathering around the TV activity.

One of the television men told him, "We're ready if you are, Mr. Freemantle."

Two TV stations were represented, both planning separate film interviews for use tomorrow. With customary shrewdness, Freemantle had already inquired which TV shows the film was destined for, so that he could conduct himself accordingly. The first interview, he learned, was for a prime-time, popular show which liked controversy, liveliness, and even shock treatment. He was ready to supply all three.

The TV interviewer, a handsome young man with a Ronald Reagan haircut, asked, "Mr. Freemantle, why are you here?"

"Because this airport is a den of thieves."

"Will you explain that?"

"Certainly. The homeowners of Meadowood community are having thievery practiced on them. Thievery of their peace, their right to privacy, of their work-earned rest, and of their sleep. Thievery of enjoyment of their leisure; thievery of their mental and physical health, and of their children's health and welfare. All these things —basic rights under our Constitution—are being shamelessly stolen, without recompense or recognition, by the operators of Lincoln Airport."

The interviewer opened his mouth to smile, showing two rows of faultless teeth. "Counselor, those are fighting words."

"That's because my clients and I are in a fighting mood."

"Is that mood because of anything which has happened here tonight?"

"Yes, sir. We have seen demonstrated the callous indifference of this airport's management to my clients' problems."

"Just what are your plans?"

"In the courts—if necessary the highest court—we shall now seek closure of specific runways, even the entire airport during nighttime hours. In Europe, where they're more civilized about these things, Paris airport, for example, has a curfew. Failing that, we shall demand proper compensation for cruelly wronged homeowners."

"I assume that what you're doing at this moment means you're also seeking public support."

"Yes, sir."

"Do you believe the public *will* support you?"

"If they don't, I invite them to spend twenty-four hours living in Meadowood—providing their eardrums and sanity will stand it."

"Surely, Counselor, airports have official programs of noise abatement."

"A sham, sir! A fake! A public lie! The general manager of this airport confessed to me tonight that even the paltry, so-called noise abatement measures are not being observed."

And so on.

Afterward, Elliott Freemantle wondered if he should have qualified the statement about noise abatement procedures—as Bakersfeld had done—by referring to exceptional conditions of tonight's storm. But semi-truth or not, the way he had said it was stronger, and Freemantle doubted if it would be challenged. Anyway, he had given good performances—in the second interview as well as the first. Also during both filmings, the cameras panned several times over the intent, expressive faces of the assembled Meadowood residents. Elliott Freemantle hoped that when they saw themselves on their home screens tomorrow, they would remember who had been responsible for all the attention they were receiving.

The number of Meadowooders who had followed him to the airport—as if he were their personal Pied Piper —astonished him. Attendance at the meeting in the Sunday school hall at Meadowood had been roughly six hundred. In view of the bad night and lateness of the hour, he had thought they would be doing well if half that number made the farther trek to the airport; but not only did most of the original crowd come; some must have telephoned friends and neighbors who had joined them. He had even had requests for more copies of the printed forms retaining himself as legal counsel, which he was happy to pass out. Some revised mental arithmetic convinced him that his first hope of a fee from Meadowood totaling twenty-five thousand dollars might well be exceeded.

After the TV interviews, the *Tribune* reporter, Tomlinson—who had been taking notes during the filming —inquired, "What comes next, Mr. Freemantle? Do you intend to stage some kind of demonstration here?"

Freemantle shook his head. "Unfortunately the management of this airport does not believe in free speech, and we have been denied the elementary privilege of a public meeting. However"—he indicated the assembled Meadowooders—"I do intend to report to these ladies and gentlemen."

"Isn't that the same thing as a public meeting?"

"No, it is not."

Just the same, Elliott Freemantle conceded to himself, it would be a fine distinction, especially since he had every intention of turning what followed into a public demonstration if he could. His objective was to get started with an aggressive speech, which the airport police would dutifully order him to stop. Freemantle had no intention of resisting, or of getting arrested. Merely being halted by the police—if possible in full oratorical flow—would establish him as a Meadowood martyr and, incidentally, create one more color story for tomorrow's papers. (The morning papers, he imagined, had already closed with the earlier reports about himself and Meadowood; editors of the afternoon editions would be grateful for a new lead.)

Even more important, Meadowood homeowners would be further convinced that they had hired a strong counsel and leader, well worth his fee—the first installment checks for which, Lawyer Freemantle hoped, would start flooding in right after tomorrow.

"We're all set to go," Floyd Zanetta, chairman of the earlier Meadowood meeting, reported.

While Freemantle and the *Tribune* newsman had been speaking, several of the Meadowood men had hastily assembled the portable p.a. system, brought from the Sunday school hall. One of the men now handed Freemantle a hand microphone. Using it, he began to address the crowd.

"My friends, we came here tonight in a mood of reason and with constructive thoughts. We sought to communicate that mood and thoughts to this airport's management, believing we had a real and urgent problem, worthy of careful consideration. On your behalf I attempted—in reasoned but firm terms—to make that problem known. I hoped to report back to you—at best, some promise of relief; at least, some sympathy and understanding. I regret to tell you that your delegation received none. Instead, we were accorded only hostility, abuse, and an uncaring, cynical assurance that in future the airport's noise above and around your homes is going to get worse."

There was a cry of outrage. Freemantle raised a hand. "Ask the others who were with me. *They* will tell you." He pointed to the front of the crowd. "Did this airport's general manager, or did he not, inform us that there was worse to come?" At first a shade reluctantly, then more definitely, those who had been in the delegation nodded.

Having skillfully misrepresented the honest frankness which Mel Bakersfeld had shown the delegation, Elliott Freemantle continued, "I see others, as well as my Meadowood friends and clients, who have stopped, with curiosity, to discover what is going on. We welcome their interest. Let me inform you . . ." He continued in his customary, haranguing style.

The crowd, sizable before, was now larger still, and continuing to grow. Travelers on their way to departure gates were having trouble getting through. Flight announcements were being drowned out by the noise. Among the Meadowooders, several had raised hastily scrawled signs which read: AIRLANES OR PEOPLE FIRST? . . . OUTLAW JETS FROM MEADOWOOD! . . . NIX NOXIOUS NOISE . . . MEADOWOOD PAYS TAXES TOO . . . IMPEACH LINCOLN!

Whenever Freemantle paused, the shouts and general uproar grew louder. A gray-haired man in a windbreaker yelled, "Let's give the airport a taste of their own noise." His words produced a roar of approval.

Without question, Elliott Freemantle's "report" had

by now developed into a full-scale demonstration. At any moment, he expected, the police would intervene.

What Lawyer Freemantle did not know was that while the TV sessions were taking place and Meadowood residents assembling, the airport management's concern about Trans America Flight Two was beginning. Shortly after, every policeman in the terminal was concentrating on a search for Inez Guerrero, and thus the Meadowood demonstration escaped attention.

Even after Inez was found, Police Lieutenant Ordway remained occupied with the emergency session in Mel Bakersfeld's office.

As a result, after another fifteen minutes, Elliott Freemantle was becoming worried. Impressive as the demonstration was, unless halted officially, it would have little point. *Where in God's name,* he thought, *were the airport police, and why weren't they doing their job?*

It was then that Lieutenant Ordway and Mel Bakersfeld came down together from the administrative mezzanine.

Several minutes earlier the meeting in Mel's office had broken up. After the interrogation of Inez Guerrero and dispatch of the second warning message to Flight Two, there was nothing to be gained by retaining everyone together. Tanya Livingston, with the Trans America D.T.M. and chief pilot, returned anxiously to the airline's offices in the terminal, to await any fresh news there. The others—with the exception of Inez Guerrero, who was being held for questioning by downtown police detectives—returned to their own bailiwicks. Tanya had promised to notify Customs Inspector Standish, who was distressed and anxious about his niece aboard Flight Two, immediately there was any new development.

Mel, not certain where he would keep his own vigil, left his office with Ned Ordway.

Ordway saw the Meadowood demonstration first and caught sight of Elliott Freemantle. "That damn lawyer! I told him there'd be no demonstrations here." He hurried toward the concourse crowd. "I'll break this up fast."

Alongside, Mel cautioned, "He may be counting on you doing that—just so he can be a hero."

As they came nearer, Ordway shouldering his way ahead through the crowd, Elliott Freemantle proclaimed, "Despite assurances from the airport management earlier this evening, heavy air traffic—deafening and shattering as always—is still continuing at this late hour. Even now . . ."

"Never mind that," Ned Ordway cut in brusquely. "I already told you there would be no demonstrations in this terminal."

"But, Lieutenant, I assure you this is not a demonstration." Freemantle still held the microphone, so that his words carried clearly. "All that's happened is that I granted a television interview after a meeting with the airport management—I might say a highly unsatisfactory meeting—then reported to these people . . ."

"Report some place else!" Ordway swung around, facing others nearest him. "Now, let's break this up!"

There were hostile glances and angry mutterings among the crowd. As the policeman turned back to Elliott Freemantle, photographers' flash bulbs popped. TV floodlights, which had been turned off, went bright once more as television cameras focused on the two. At last, Elliott Freemantle thought, everything was going just the way he wanted.

On the fringe of the crowd, Mel Bakersfeld was talking with one of the TV men and Tomlinson of the *Tribune*. The reporter was consulting his notes and reading a passage back. As he listened, Mel's face suffused with anger.

"Lieutenant," Elliott Freemantle was saying to Ned Ordway, "I have the greatest respect for you and for your uniform. Just the same, I'd like to point out that we did hold a meeting some place else tonight—at Meadowood—but because of noise from this airport, we couldn't hear ourselves."

Ordway snapped back, "I'm not here for a debate, Mr. Freemantle. If you don't do as I say, you'll be arrested. I'm ordering you to get this group out of here."

Someone in the crowd shouted, "Suppose we won't go?"

Another voice urged, "Let's stay here! They can't arrest all of us."

"No!" Elliott Freemantle held up a hand self-righteously. "Please listen to me! There will be no disorder; no disobedience. My friends and clients—this police officer has ordered us to desist and leave. We will comply with his order. We may consider it a grave restriction of free speech" . . . . there were responsive cheers and booing . . . "but let it not be said that at any point we failed to respect the law." More crisply, he added, "I shall have a statement for the press outside."

"One moment!" Mel Bakersfeld's voice cut sharply across the heads of others. He thrust his way forward. "Freemantle, I'm interested to know what will be in that press statement of yours. Will it be more misrepresentation. Another dose of distorted law reports to delude people who don't know any better? Or just plain, old-fashioned fabrication which you're so expert at?"

Mel spoke loudly, his words carrying to those nearby. There was a buzz of interested reaction. People who had begun drifting away, stopped.

Elliott Freemantle reacted automatically. "That's a malicious, libelous statement!" An instant later, scenting danger, he shrugged. "However, I shall let it pass."

"Why? If it *is* libelous, you should know how to handle it." Mel faced the lawyer squarely. "Or perhaps you're afraid of it proving true."

"I'm afraid of nothing, Mr. Bakersfeld. The fact is, we've been told by this policeman that the party's over. Now, if you'll excuse me . . ."

"I said it was over for you," Ned Ordway pointed out. "What Mr. Bakersfeld does is something again. He has authority here." Ordway had moved beside Mel; together they blocked the lawyer's way.

"If you were a real policeman," Freemantle objected, "you'd treat us both equally."

Mel said unexpectedly, "I think he's right." Ordway glanced at him curiously. "You *should* treat us both equally. And instead of closing this meeting, I think you should allow me the same privilege of talking to these people which Mr. Freemantle just had. That is, if you want to be a real policeman."

"I guess I want to be." The big Negro police lieutenant, towering above the other two, was grinning. "I'm beginning to see it your way—and Mr. Freemantle's."

Mel observed blandly to Elliott Freemantle, "You see, he's come around. Now, since we're all here, we may as well clear up a few things." He held out his hand. "Let me have that microphone."

Mel's anger of a minute or two ago was now less apparent. When the *Tribune* reporter, Tomlinson, had read back from his notes the gist of what Elliott Freemantle stated in his TV interviews and later, Mel reacted heatedly. Both Tomlinson and the TV producer asked Mel to comment on what had been said. He assured them that he would.

"Oh no!" Freemantle shook his head decisively. The danger which he scented a few moments earlier was suddenly close and real. Once before, tonight, he had underestimated this man Bakersfeld; he had no intention of repeating that mistake. Freemantle himself now had the assembled Meadowood residents firmly under control; it was essential to his purpose that they remain that way. All he wanted at this moment was for everyone to disperse quickly.

He declared loftily, "More than enough has been said." Ignoring Mel, he passed the microphone to one of the Meadowood men and indicated the p.a. equipment. "Let's get all this apart and be on our way."

"I'll take that." Ned Ordway reached over and intercepted the microphone. "And leave the rest where it is." He nodded to several other policemen who had appeared on the fringes of the crowd. They moved in. While Freemantle watched helplessly, Ordway handed the microphone to Mel.

"Thank you." Mel faced the crowd of Meadowooders —many of their faces hostile—and others who, passing through the terminal, had stopped to listen. Though it was twenty minutes after midnight, and now Saturday morning, the heavy traffic in the main concourse showed no sign of lessening. Because of many delayed flights, pressures would probably continue through the remainder of the night, merging with a heightened weekend activity until schedules got back to normal. If one of the Meadowood objectives was to create a nuisance effect, Mel thought, it was succeeding. The extra thousand or so people were taxing available space in the concourse, arriving and departing passengers having to fight their way around like a flood tide encountering a sudden sandbank. Obviously the situation must not continue for more than a few minutes.

"I'll be brief," Mel said. He spoke into the microphone, telling them who and what he was.

"Earlier tonight I met a delegation representing all of you. I explained some of the airport's problems; also that we understood and sympathized with yours. I expected what I said to be passed along, if not exactly, then at least in substance. Instead, I find that I have been misrepresented and you have been deceived."

Elliott Freemantle emitted a roar of rage. "That's a lie!" His face was flushed. For the first time tonight his impeccably styled hair was disarrayed.

Lieutenant Ordway grasped the lawyer firmly by the arm. "Hush up, now! You had your turn."

In front of Mel a broadcast microphone had joined the hand mike he was using. The TV lights were on as he continued.

"Mr. Freemantle accuses me of lying. He's been strong in his use of words tonight." Mel consulted a note in his hand. "I understand they include 'thievery,' 'indifference,' that I met your delegation with 'hostility and abuse'; further, that the noise abatement measures we are trying to enforce are a 'sham, a fake, and a public lie.' Well, we'll see what *you* think about who's lying—or misrepresenting—and who is not."

He had made an error earlier, Mel realized, in speaking to the small delegation and not to this main group. His objectives had been to achieve understanding, yet avoid disruption in the terminal. Both objectives had failed.

But at least he would aim for understanding now.

"Let me outline this airport's policy on noise suppression."

For the second time tonight Mel described the operating limitations on pilots and their employer airlines. He added, "At normal times these restrictions are enforced. But in difficult weather, such as tonight's storm, pilots must be given leeway, and aircraft safety must côme first."

As to runways: "Wherever possible we avoid takeoffs over Meadowood from runway two five." Yet, he explained, there was occasional need to use that runway when runway three zero was out of commission, as at present.

"We do our best for you," Mel insisted, "and we are not indifferent, as has been alleged. But we are in business as an airport and we cannot escape our basic responsibilities, plus our concern for aviation safety."

The hostility among his audience was still apparent, but now there was interest as well.

Elliott Freemantle—glaring at Mel and fuming—was aware of the interest too.

"From what I've heard," Mel said, "Mr. Freemantle chose not to pass on some observations I offered to your delegation on the general subject of airport noise. My remarks were made"—he consulted his notes again—"not in 'uncaring cynicism,' as has been suggested, but in an attempt at honest frankness. I intend to share that frankness with you here."

Now, as earlier, Mel admitted there was little more in the area of noise reduction which could be done; glum expressions appeared when he described the expected greater noise from new aircraft soon to be in use. But he sensed there was appreciation for objective honesty. Beyond a few scattered remarks, there were no interruptions, his words remaining audible above the background noises of the terminal.

"There are two other things which I did not mention to your delegation, but now I intend to." Mel's voice hardened. "I doubt if you will like them."

The first point, he informed them, concerned Meadowood community.

"Twelve years ago your community didn't exist. It was a parcel of empty land—of low value until the airport's growth and closeness sent surrounding values soaring. To that extent your Meadowood is like thousands of communities which have mushroomed around airports everywhere in the world."

A woman shouted, "When we came to live here, we didn't know about jet noise."

"But *we* did!" Mel pointed a finger at the woman. "Airport managements knew that jet airplanes were coming, and knew what jet noise would be like, and we warned people, and local zoning commissions, and pleaded with them in countless Meadowoods *not to build homes*. I wasn't at this airport then, but there are records and pictures in our files. This airport put up signs where Meadowood is now: AIRPLANES WILL TAKE OFF AND LAND OVER THIS ROUTE. Other airports did the same. And everywhere the signs appeared, real estate developers and salesmen tore them down. Then they sold land and houses to people like you, keeping quiet about the noise to come, and airport expansion plans—which usually they knew of—and I guess in the end the real estate people outwitted us all."

This time there was no rejoinder, only a sea of thoughtful faces, and Mel guessed that what he had said had struck home. He had a sense of keen regret. These were not antagonists whom he wanted to defeat. They were decent people with a real and pressing problem; neighbors for whom he wished he could do more.

He caught sight of Elliott Freemantle's sneering features. "Bakersfeld, I suppose you think that's pretty clever." The lawyer turned away, shouting over nearer heads without benefit of amplifier. "Don't believe all that! You're being softened up! If you stick with me, we'll take these airport people, and we'll take them good!"

"In case any of you didn't hear," Mel said into the microphone, "that was Mr. Freemantle advising you to stick with him. I have something to say about that, too."

He told the now attentive crowd, "Many people—people like you—have had advantage taken of them by

being sold land or homes in areas which should not have
been developed, or should have been developed for industrial use where airport noise doesn't matter. You
haven't lost out entirely, because you have your land
and homes; but chances are, their values have decreased."

A man said gloomily, "Damn right!"

"Now there's another scheme afoot to part you from
your money. Lawyers all over North America are hot-
footing it to airport dormitory communities because
'thar's gold in that thar noise.' "

Lawyer Freemantle, his face flushed and distorted,
shrilled, "You say one more word—I'll sue you!"

"For what" Mel shot back. "Or have you guessed
already what I'm going to say?" Well, he thought,
maybe Freemantle would launch a libel action later,
though he doubted it. Either way, Mel felt some of his
old recklessness—a decision for plain speaking, and
never mind the consequences—take command. It was a
feeling which, in the past year or two, he had experienced rarely.

"Residents in the communities I spoke of," Mel
argued, "are being assured that airports can be sued—
successfully. Homeowners near airports are being promised there's a pot of dollars at every runway's end. Well,
I'm not saying airports can't be sued, nor am I saying
there aren't some fine, sound lawyers engaged in anti-
airport litigation. What I'm warning you is that there are
a good many of the other kind, too."

The same woman who had called out before asked—
more mildly this time—"How are we supposed to know
which is which?"

"It's difficult without a program; in other words,
unless you happen to know some airport law. If you
don't, you can be bamboozled by a one-sided list of
legal precedents." Mel hesitated only briefly before
adding, "I've heard a few specific law decisions mentioned tonight. If you wish, I'll tell you another side to
them."

A man at the front said, "Let's hear your version,
mister."

Several people were looking curiously at Elliott Free-mantle.

Mel had hesitated, realizing that this had already gone on longer than he intended. He supposed, though, that a few minutes more would make no difference.

On the fringes of the crowd he caught sight of Tanya Livingston.

"The legal cases which you and I have both heard referred to glibly," Mel said, "are old hat to people who run airports. The first, I think, was *U.S.* v. *Causby.*"

That particular case—a pillar of Lawyer Freemantle's presentation to the Meadowood group—was, Mel explained, a decision more than twenty years old. "It concerned a chicken farmer and military airplanes. The airplanes repeatedly flew over the farmer's house, as low as sixty-seven feet—a whole lot lower than any airplane ever comes near Meadowood. The chickens were frightened; some died."

After years of litigation the case found its way to the U.S. Supreme Court. Mel pointed out: "The total damages awarded were less than four hundred dollars—the value of the dead chickens."

He added, "There was no pot of dollars for the farmer, nor is there—in that legal precedent—for you."

Mel could see Elliott Freemantle, his face alternately crimson and white with rage. Ned Ordway was once more holding the lawyer by the arm.

"There *is* one legal case," Mel observed, "which Mr. Freemantle has chosen not to mention. It's an important one—also involving a Supreme Court ruling—and well known. Unfortunately for Mr. Freemantle, it doesn't support his arguments, but runs counter to them."

The case, he explained, was *Batten* v. *Batten* in which, in 1963, the Supreme Court ruled that only an actual "physical invasion" created liability. Noise alone was not enough.

Mel continued, "Another ruling, along the same lines, was *Loma Portal Civic Club* v. *American Airlines*—a 1964 decision of the California Supreme Court." In this, he reported, the Court ruled that property owners were not entitled to restrict the flight of aircraft over houses near an airport. Public interest in continuance of air travel, the California court laid down, was paramount and overwhelming . . .

Mel had quoted the legal cases unhesitatingly, without reference to notes. Clearly his audience was impressed. Now he smiled. "Legal precedents are like statistics. If you manipulate them, you can prove anything." He added, "You don't have to take my word for what I've told you. Look it up. It's all on record."

A woman near Elliott Freemantle grumbled at him, "You didn't tell us all that. You just gave your side."

Some of the hostility directed at Mel earlier was now being transferred toward the lawyer.

Freemantle shrugged. After all, he decided, he still had more than a hundred and sixty signed retainer forms, which he had been careful to transfer to a locked bag in the trunk of his car. Nothing that was said here could undo the fact of those.

A moment or two later he began to wonder.

Mel Bakersfeld was being asked by several people about legal contract forms which they had signed this evening. Their voices betrayed doubt. Obviously Mel's manner, as well as what he said, had made a strong impression. The crowd was dividing into small groups, most in animated discussion.

"I've been asked about a certain contract," Mel announced. Within the crowd, other voices silenced as he added, "I think you know the contract I mean. I have seen a copy of it."

Elliott Freemantle pushed forward. "So what! You aren't a lawyer; we've settled that once before. Therefore you're no authority on contracts." This time Freemantle was close enough to the microphone for his words to carry.

Mel snapped back, "I live with contracts! Every lessee in this airport—from the biggest airline to a headache pill concessionaire—operates under a contract approved by me, and negotiated by my staff."

He swung back to the crowd. "Mr. Freemantle points out, correctly, that I am not a lawyer; so I'll give you a businessman's advice. In certain circumstances the con-

tracts you signed tonight could be enforceable. A
contract is a contract. You *could* be taken to debtor's
court; the money might be collected. But my opinion is
that, providing you serve proper notice immediately,
neither thing will happen. For one thing, you have received no goods; no service has been rendered. For
another, each of you would have to be sued separately."
Mel smiled. "That, in itself, would be an undertaking.

"One more thing." He looked directly at Elliott Freemantle. "I do not believe that any court would look
favorably on a total legal fee in the region of fifteen
thousand dollars for legal service which, at best, was
nebulous."

The man who had spoken earlier asked, "So what do
we do?"

"If you've genuinely changed your mind, I suggest
that today or tomorrow you write a letter. Address it to
Mr. Freemantle. In it, state that you no longer want
legal representation as arranged, and why. Be sure to
keep a copy. Again, in my opinion—that's the last you'll
ever hear."

Mel had been blunter than he at first intended, and he
had also been excessively reckless, he supposed, in
going quite this far. If Elliott Freemantle chose, he
could certainly make trouble. In a matter in which the
airport—and therefore Mel—had active interest, Mel
had interposed between clients and lawyer, casting
doubt upon the latter's probity. Judging by the hatred in
the lawyer's eyes, he would be delighted to do any harm
to Mel he could. Yet instinct told Mel that the last thing
Freemantle wanted was a searching public scrutiny of
his client recruiting methods and working habits. A trial
judge, sensitive about legal ethics, might ask awkward
questions, later still, so might the Bar Association,
which safeguarded the legal profession's standards. The
more Mel thought about it, the less inclined he was to
worry.

Though Mel didn't know it, Elliott Freemantle had
reached the same conclusion.

Whatever else Freemantle might be, he was a pragma-
tist. He had long ago recognized that in life there were-

gambits which you won, others that you lost. Sometimes the loss was sudden and illogical. A chance, a quirk, a nettle in the grass, could turn an almost-grasped success into mortifying defeat. Fortunately for people like Freemantle, the reverse was sometimes true.

The airport manager, Bakersfeld, had proven to be a nettle—carelessly grasped—which should have been avoided. Even after their first brush, which Elliott Freemantle now realized could have been a warning to him, he had continued to underestimate his opponent by remaining at the airport instead of quitting while ahead. Another thing Freemantle had discovered too late was that Bakersfeld, while shrewd, was a gambler too. Only a gambler would have gone out on such a limb as Bakersfeld had a moment ago. And only Elliott Freemantle —at this point—knew that Bakersfeld had won.

Freemantle *was* aware that the Bar Association might regard this night's activity unfavorably. More to the point: He had had a brush with an association investigating committee once already, and had no intention of provoking another.

Bakersfeld had been right, Elliott Freemantle thought. There would be no attempted debt collecting, through the courts, on the basis of the signed legal retainer forms. The hazards were too great, the spoils uncertain.

He would not give up entirely, of course. Tomorrow, Freemantle decided, he would draft a letter to all Meadowood residents who had signed the forms; in it he would do his best to persuade them that retention of himself as legal counsel, at the individual fee specified, should continue. He doubted, though, if many would respond. The suspicion which Bakersfeld had effectively implanted—*damn his guts!*—was too great. There might be some small pickings left, from a few people who would be willing to continue, and later it would be necessary to decide if they were worth while. But the prospect of a big killing was gone.

Something else, though, he supposed, would turn up soon. It always had.

Ned Ordway and several other policemen were now

dispersing the crowd; normal traffic through the concourse was resuming. The portable p.a. system was at last being disassembled and removed.

Mel Bakersfeld noticed that Tanya, whom he had caught sight of a moment or two ago, was making her way in his direction.

A woman—one of the Meadowood residents whom Mel had noticed several times before—confronted him. She had a strong intelligent face and shoulder-length brown hair.

"Mr. Bakersfeld," the woman said quietly. "We've all talked a lot, and we understand a few things better than we did. But I still haven't heard anything that I can tell my children when they cry, and ask why the noise won't stop so they can sleep."

Mel shook his head regretfully. In a few words the woman had pointed up the futility of everything which had happened tonight. He knew he had no answer for her. He doubted—while airports and dwellings remained in proximity—if there would ever be one.

He was still wondering what to say when Tanya handed him a folded sheet of paper.

Opening it, he read the message which showed signs of being hastily typed:

> flight 2 had mid-air explosion.
> structural damage & injuries.
> now heading here 4 emergency
> landing, est. arrival 0130.
> capt. says must have runway
> three zero. tower reports runway still
> blocked.

12

In the bloody shambles which was the rear of the tourist cabin of Flight Two, Dr. Milton Compagno, general practitioner, was exerting the utmost of his professional skill in an attempt to save Gwen Meighen's life. He was not sure he would succeed.

When the initial explosion from D. O. Guerrero's dynamite bomb occurred, Gwen—next to Guerrero himself—was closest to the explosion's center.

In other circumstances she would have been killed instantly, as was D. O. Guerrero. Two things—for the moment—saved her.

Interposed between Gwen and the explosion were Guerrero's body and the aircraft toilet door. Neither was an effective shield, yet the two together were sufficient to delay the blast's initial force the fraction of a second.

Within that fractional time the airplane's skin ripped, and the second explosion—explosive decompression—occurred.

The dynamite blast still struck Gwen, hurling her backward, gravely injured and bleeding, but its force now had an opposing force—the outward rush of air through the hole in the fuselage at the aircraft's rear. The effect was as if two tornadoes met head on. An instant later the decompression triumphed, sweeping the original explosion out with it into the high-altitude, darkened night.

Despite the forcefulness of the explosion, injuries were not widespread.

Gwen Meighen, the most critically hurt, lay unconscious in the aisle. Next to her, the owlish young man who had emerged from the toilet and startled Guerrero, was wounded, bleeding badly, and dazed, but still on his feet and conscious. A half dozen passengers nearby sustained cuts and contusions from splinters and bomb fragments. Others were struck, and stunned or bruised by hurtling objects impelled toward the aircraft's rear by the explosive decompression, but none of the latter injuries was major.

At first, after decompression, all who were not secure in seats were impelled by suction toward the gaping hole in the aircraft's rear. From this danger, too, Gwen Meighen was in gravest peril. But she had fallen so that an arm instinctively or accidentally—encircled a seat base. It prevented her from being dragged farther, and her body blocked others.

After the initial outrush of air, the suction lessened.

Now, the greatest immediate danger for all—injured or not—was lack of oxygen.

Although oxygen masks dropped promptly from their housings, only a handful of passengers had grasped and put them on at once.

Before it was too late, however, a few people had acted. Stewardesses, responding to their training, and wherever they happened to be, seized masks and motioned others to do likewise. Three doctors, traveling with their wives as members of an off-season vacation tour, realized the need for speed, donned masks themselves and gave hasty instructions to those around them. Judy, the alert, eighteen-year-old niece of Customs Inspector Standish, placed a mask over the face of the baby in the seat beside her, as well as over her own. She then immediately signaled the baby's parents, and others across the aisle, to use oxygen. Mrs. Quonsett, the old lady stowaway, having observed oxygen demonstrations many times during her illegal flights, knew what to do. She took a mask herself and handed one to her friend, the oboe player, whom she pulled back into his seat beside her. Mrs. Quonsett had no idea if she was going to live or die, and found herself not greatly worried; but whatever happened, she intended to know what was going on until the very last moment.

Someone thrust a mask at the young man near Gwen who had been wounded. Though swaying, and scarcely aware of what was happening, he managed to hold it to his face.

Even so, barely half the passengers were on oxygen at the end of fifteen seconds—the critical time. By then, those not breathing oxygen were lapsing into drowsy stupor; in another fifteen seconds, most were unconscious.

Gwen Meighen received no oxygen, nor immediate help. The unconsciousness, caused by her injuries, deepened.

Then, on the flight deck, Anson Harris, accepting the

risk of further structural damage and possible total destruction of the aircraft, made his decision for a high speed dive, saving Gwen and others from asphyxiation.

The dive began at twenty-eight thousand feet altitude; it ended, two and a half minutes later, at ten thousand feet.

A human being can survive without oxygen for three to four minutes without damage to the brain.

For the first half of the dive—for a minute and a quarter, down to nineteen thousand feet—the air continued to be rarefied, and insufficient to support life. Below that point, increasing amounts of oxygen were present and breathable.

At twelve thousand feet regular breathing was possible. By ten—with little time to spare, but enough— consciousness returned to all aboard Flight Two who had lost it, excepting Gwen. Many were unaware of having been unconscious at all.

Gradually, as initial shock wore off, passengers and the remaining stewardesses took stock of their situation. The stewardess who was second in seniority after Gwen —a pert blonde from Oak Lawn, Illinois—hurried toward the injured at the rear. Though her face paled, she called urgently, "Is there a doctor, please?"

"Yes, miss." Dr. Compagno had already moved from his seat without waiting to be called. A small, sharp-featured man who moved impatiently and talked quickly with a Brooklyn accent, he surveyed the scene hurriedly, conscious of the already biting cold, the wind streaming noisily through the gaping hole in the fuselage. Where the toilets and rear galley had been was a twisted mess of charred and bloodstained wood and metal. The back of the fuselage to the interior of the tail was open, with control wires and structural assemblies exposed.

The doctor raised his voice to make himself heard above the noise of wind and engines, constant and encompassing now that the cabin was no longer sealed.

"I suggest you move as many people as you can nearer the front. Keep everyone as warm as possible. We'll need blankets for those who are hurt."

The stewardess said doubtfully, "I'll try to find

some." Many of the blankets normally stored in overhead racks had been swept out, along with passengers' extra clothing and other objects, in the whirlwind of decompression.

The two other doctors from Dr. Compagno's tour party joined him. One instructed another stewardess, "Bring us all the first aid equipment you have." Compagno—already on his knees beside Gwen—was the only one of the three with a medical bag.

Carrying a bag with emergency supplies wherever he went was characteristic of Milton Compagno. So was taking charge now, even though—as a G.P.—he was outranked professionally by the other two doctors who were internists.

Milton Compagno never considered himself off duty. Thirty-five years ago, as a young man who had fought an upward battle from a New York slum, he hung out a shingle in Chicago's Little Italy, near Milwaukee and Grand Avenues. Since then—as his wife told it, usually with resignation—the only time he ceased practicing medicine was while he slept. He enjoyed being needed. He acted as if his profession were a prize he had won, which, if not guarded, would slip away. He had never been known to refuse to see a patient at any hour, or to fail to make a house call if sent for. He never drove past an accident scene as did many of his medical brethren, fearing malpractice suits; he always stopped, got out of his car, and did what he could. He kept conscientiously up to date. Yet the more he worked, the more he seemed to thrive. He gave the impression of running through each day as if he planned to assuage the world's ailments in a lifetime, of which too little was left.

The journey to Rome—many years postponed—was to visit the birthplace of his parents. With his wife, Dr. Compagno was to be away a month, and because he was growing old, he had agreed that the time should be a total rest. Yet he fully anticipated that somewhere en route, or perhaps in Italy (never mind regulations about not being licensed) he would be needed. If so, he was ready. It did not surprise him that he was needed now.

He moved first to Gwen who was clearly most critical

among those hurt. He told his colleagues, over his shoulder, "You attend to the others."

In the narrow aisle, Dr. Compagno turned Gwen over partially, leaning forward to detect if she was breathing. She was, but her breath was light and shallow. He called to the stewardess he had been speaking to, "I need oxygen down here." While the girl brought a portable bottle and mask, he checked Gwen's mouth for an unobstructed airway; there were smashed teeth, which he removed, and a good deal of blood; he made sure the bleeding was not preventing respiration. He told the stewardess, "Hold the mask in place." The oxygen hissed. Within a minute or two a vestige of color returned to Gwen's skin, which had been ominously white.

Meanwhile, he began to control bleeding, extensive around the face and chest. Working quickly, he used a hemostat to clamp off a facial artery—worst site of external hemorrhage—and pressure dressings elsewhere. He had already detected a probable fracture of the clavicle and left arm, which would need to be splinted later. He was distressed to see what appeared to be splinters from the explosion in the patient's left eye; he was less sure about the right.

Second Officer Jordan, having moved carefully around Dr. Compagno and Gwen, took charge of the remaining stewardesses and was supervising the movement of passengers forward in the aircraft. As many tourist passengers as possible were being moved into the first class section, some squeezed in, two to a seat, others directed to the small, semicircular first class lounge, where spare seats were available. Such extra clothing as remained was distributed among those who appeared to need it most, without regard to ownership. As always, in such situations, people showed a willingness to help one another, unselfishness, and even flashes of humor.

The other two doctors were bandaging passengers who had received cuts, none excessively serious. The young man with glasses, who was behind Gwen at the moment of the explosion, had a deep gash in one arm, but it could be repaired and would heal. He had other

minor cuts about the face and shoulders. For the time
being, pressure dressings were applied to his injured
arm, and he was given morphine, while being made as
comfortable and warm as possible.

Both the medical attention and movement of passengers was being made more difficult by heavy buffeting
which the aircraft, at its present low altitude, was taking
from the storm. There was constant turbulence, punctuated every few minutes by violent pitching or sideways
movements. Several passengers were finding airsickness
added to their other troubles.

After reporting to the flight deck for the second time,
Cy Jordan returned to Dr. Compagno.

"Doctor, Captain Demerest asked me to say he's
grateful for everything you and the other doctors are
doing. When you can spare a moment, he'd appreciate it
if you'd come to the flight deck to tell him what to radio
ahead about casualties."

"Hold this dressing," Dr. Compagno ordered. "Press
down hard, right there. Now I want you to help me with
a splint. We'll use one of those leather magazine covers,
with a towel under it. Get the biggest cover you can
find, and leave the magazine in."

A moment later: "I'll come when I can. You can say
to your captain that I think, as soon as possible, he
should make an announcement to the passengers.
People are getting over their shock. They could use
some reassurance."

"Yes, sir." Cy Jordan looked down at the still unconscious figure of Gwen, his normally mournful, hollow-
cheeked face accentuated by concern. "Is there a chance
for her, Doc?"

"There's a chance, son, though I wouldn't say it was
the best. A lot depends on her own strength."

"I always figured she had a lot of that."

"A pretty girl, wasn't she?" Amid the torn flesh,
blood, and dirty, tousled hair, it was difficult to be sure.

"Very."

Compagno remained silent. Whatever happened, the
girl on the floor would not be pretty any more—not
without plastic surgery.

"I'll give the captain your message, sir." Looking a little sicker than before, Cy Jordan went forward to the flight deck.

Vernon Demerest's voice came calmly on the cabin p.a. system a few moments later.

"Ladies and gentlemen, this is Captain Demerest . . ." To overcome the roar of wind and engines, Cy Jordan had turned the volume control to "full." Each word rang clearly.

"You know we've had trouble—bad trouble. I won't attempt to minimize it. I won't make any jokes either, because up here on the flight deck we don't see anything that's funny, and I imagine you feel the same way. We've all come through an experience which none of us in the crew has ever had before, and I hope will never have again. But we *have* come through. Now, we have the airplane under control, we're turned around, and expect to land at Lincoln International in about three quarters of an hour."

In the two passenger cabins, where first and tourist class now mingled without distinction, movement and conversation stopped. Eyes instinctively went to the overhead speakers as everyone within hearing strained to miss nothing of what was said.

"You know, of course, that the airplane is damaged. But it's also true that the damage could have been a whole lot worse."

On the flight deck, with the p.a. mike in hand, Vernon Demerest wondered how specific—and how honest—he should be. On his own regular flights he always kept captain-to-passengers announcements to the barest terse minimum. He disapproved of "long-playing captains" who bombarded their captive audience with assorted commentaries from a flight's beginning to its end. He sensed, though, that this time he should say more, and that passengers were entitled to be told the true situation.

"I won't conceal from you," Demerest said into the microphone, "that we have a few problems still ahead of us. Our landing will be heavy, and we're not sure how the damage we've suffered will affect it. I'm telling you this because right after this announcement the crew will start giving instructions on how to sit, and how to brace yourselves, just before we land. Another thing you'll be told is how to get out of the airplane in a hurry, if we need to, right after landing. If that should happen, please act calmly but quickly, and obey instructions given you by any member of the crew.

"Let me assure you that on the ground everything necessary is being done to help us." Remembering their need for runway three zero, Demerest hoped it was true. He also decided there was no point in going into detail about the problem of the jammed stabilizer; most passengers wouldn't understand it anyway. With a touch of lightness in his voice, he added, "In one way you're lucky tonight because instead of one experienced captain on the flight deck, it just so happens you have two—Captain Harris and myself. We're a couple of ancient pelicans with more years of flying than we sometimes like to think about—except right now when all that combined experience comes in mighty useful. We'll be helping each other, along with Second Officer Jordan, who'll also be spending part of his time back with you. Please help us too. If you do, I promise you we'll come through this together—safely."

Demerest replaced the p.a. mike.

Without taking his eyes from the flight instruments, Anson Harris remarked, "That was pretty good. You should be in politics."

Demerest said sourly, "Nobody'd vote for me. Most times, people don't like plain talking and the truth." He was remembering bitterly the Board of Airport Commissioners meeting at Lincoln International where he urged curtailment of airport insurance vending. Plain speech there had proved disastrous. He wondered how the members of the Board, including his smooth, smug brother-in-law, would feel after learning about D. O. Guerrero's purchase of insurance and his maniacal intention to destroy Flight Two. Probably, Demerest thought, they would be complacent as ever, except that now instead of saying *It will never happen,* they would say, *What occurred was exceptional; the odds are*

against it happening again. Well, assuming Flight Two
made it back safely, and whatever was said or wasn't,
sure as hell he was going to create another big fight
about airport insurance vending. The difference was:
this time more people would listen. Tonight's near disaster, however it turned out, was certain to attract a lot
of press attention; he would make the most of it. He
would talk bluntly to reporters about flight insurance,
about the Lincoln airport commissioners, and not least
about his precious brother-in-law, Mel Bakersfeld.
Trans America's public relations flacks would do their
damnedest, of course, to keep him incommunicado "in
the interests of company policy." Just let them try!

The radio crackled alive. "Trans America Two, this
is Cleveland Center. Lincoln advises runway three zero
still temporarily out of use. They are attempting to clear
obstruction before you arrive. Failing that, will land you
on two five."

Harris's face went grim as Demerest acknowledged.
Runway two five was two thousand feet shorter, as well
as narrower, and at the moment with a bad crosswind.
Using it would compound the hazards they already
faced.

Demerest's expression clearly reflected his reaction to
the message.

They were still being thrown about severely by the
storm. Most of Harris's time was occupied by holding
the aircraft reasonably steady.

Demerest swung around to the second officer. "Cy, go
back with the passengers again, and take charge. See
that the girls demonstrate the landing drill, and that
everybody understands it. Then pick some key people
who look reliable. Make sure they know where emergency exits are and how to use them. If we run out of
runway, which'll be for sure if we use two five, everything may come apart in a hurry. If that happens we'll
all try to make it back there and help, but there may not
be time."

"Yes, sir." Once more, Jordan eased out of his flight
engineer's seat.

Demerest, still anxious for news of Gwen, would have

preferred to go himself, but at this stage neither he nor Harris could leave the flight deck.

As Cy Jordan left, Dr. Compagno arrived. It was now easier to move into and from the flight deck, since Jordan had moved the smashed entrance door to one side.

Milton Compagno introduced himself briskly to Vernon Demerest. "Captain, I have the report of injuries you asked for."

"We're grateful to you, Doctor. If you hadn't been here . . ."

Compagno waved a hand in dismissal. "Let's do all that later." He opened a leather-covered notebook where a slim gold pencil marked a page. It was characteristic that he had already obtained names, and recorded injuries and treatment. "Your stewardess, Miss Meighen, is the most badly hurt. She has multiple lacerations of the face and chest, with considerable bleeding. There is a compound fracture of the left arm and, of course, shock. Also, please notify whoever is making arrangements on the ground that an ophthalmic surgeon should be available immediately."

Vernon Demerest, his face paler than usual, had been steeling himself to copy the doctor's information onto the flight log clipboard. Now, with sudden shock, he stopped.

"An ophthalmic surgeon! You mean . . . her eyes?"

"I'm afraid so," Dr. Compagno said gravely. He corrected himself. "At least, her left eye has splinters, whether wood or metal I've no means of knowing. It will require a specialist to decide if the retina is affected. The right eye, as far as I can tell, is unharmed."

"Oh, God!" Feeling physically sick, Demerest put a hand to his face.

Dr. Compagno shook his head. "It's too early to draw conclusions. Modern ophthalmic surgery can do extraordinary things. But time will be important."

"We'll send all you've told us on company radio," Anson Harris assured him. "They'll have time to be ready."

"Then I'd better give you the rest."

Mechanically, Demerest wrote down the remainder of the doctor's report. Compared with Gwen's injuries, those of other passengers were slight.

"I'd better get back," Dr. Compagno said. "To see if there's any change."

Demerest said abruptly, "Don't go."

The doctor stopped, his expression curious.

"Gwen . . . that is, Miss Meighen . . ." Demerest's voice sounded strained and awkward, even to himself. "She was . . . is . . . pregnant. Does it make any difference?"

He saw Anson Harris glance sideways in startled surprise.

The doctor answered, a shade defensively, "I had no means of knowing. The pregnancy can't be very far advanced."

"No," Demerest avoided the other man's eyes. "It isn't." A few minutes earlier he had resolved not to ask the question. Then he decided that he had to know.

Milton Compagno considered. "It will make no difference to her own ability to recover, of course. As to the child, the mother was not deprived of oxygen long enough to do harm . . . no one was. She has no abdominal injuries." He stopped, then went on fussily, "So there should be no effect. Providing Miss Meighen survives—and with prompt hospital treatment her chances are fair to good—the baby should be born normally."

Demerest nodded without speaking. Dr. Compagno, after a moment's hesitation, left.

Briefly, between the two captains, there was a silence. Anson Harris broke it. "Vernon, I'd like to rest before I make the landing. Will you fly for a while?"

Demerest nodded, his hands and feet moving automatically to the controls. He was grateful for the absence of questioning or comment about Gwen. Whatever Harris was thinking or wondering, he had the decency to keep it to himself.

Harris reached for the clipboard containing Dr. Compagno's information. "I'll send that." He switched radio receivers to call Trans America dispatch.

For Vernon Demerest the act of flying was a physical relief after the shock and emotion of what he had just heard. Possibly Harris had considered that, possibly not. Either way, it made sense that whoever was in command for the landing should conserve his energies.

As to the landing, hazardous as it was going to be, Anson Harris obviously assumed he would make it. Demerest—on the basis of Harris's performance so far—saw no reason why he should not.

Harris completed his radio call, then eased his seat rearward and allowed his body to rest.

Beside him, Vernon Demerest tried to concentrate solely on flying. He did not succeed. To a pilot of experience and skill, total concentration during level flight—even in difficult circumstances, as now—was neither usual nor necessary. Though he tried to banish or postpone them, thoughts of Gwen persisted.

Gwen . . . whose chance of remaining alive was "fair to good," who tonight had been bright and beautiful and full of promise, would never go to Naples now, as they had planned . . . Gwen, who an hour or two ago had told him in her clear, sweet English voice, *I happen to love you* . . . Gwen, whom he loved in return, despite himself, and why not face it?

With grief and anguish he visualized her—injured, unconscious, *and carrying his child*; the child he urged her to dispose of like an unwanted litter . . . She had replied with spirit, *I was wondering when you'd get around to it* . . . Later she had been troubled. *It's a gift . . . that's great and wonderful. Then suddenly, in our kind of situation you're faced with ending it all, of squandering what was given.*

But eventually, after his persuading, she conceded, *Well, I suppose in the end I'll do what's sensible. I'll have an abortion.*

There would be no abortion now. In the kind of hospital Gwen was going to, it would not be permitted unless as a direct choice between saving the mother or the unborn child. From what Dr. Compagno had said, there seemed no likelihood of that; and afterward it would be too late.

So if Gwen came through, the baby would be born. Was he relieved or sorry? Vernon Demerest wasn't sure.

He remembered something else, though, that Gwen had said. *The difference between you and me is that you've had a child . . . whatever happens there's always someone, somewhere that's you again.*

She had been speaking of the child whom he had never known, even by name; the girl child, born in the limbo of the Trans America 3-PPP arrangements, who had disappeared from sight immediately and forever. Tonight, under questioning, he admitted that sometimes he wondered about her. What he had not admitted was that he wondered, and remembered, more often than he cared to.

His unknown daughter was eleven years old; Demerest knew her birthday, though he tried not to remember it, but always did, wishing the same thing each year: that there was something he could do—even a simple thing like sending a greeting . . . He supposed it was because he and Sarah had never had a child (though both had wanted children) whose birthday he could share . . . At other times he asked himself questions to which he knew there could be no answers: Where was his daughter? What was she like? Was she happy? Sometimes he looked at children in the streets; if their ages seemed right, he speculated on whether, by merest chance . . . then chided himself for foolishness. Occasionally the thought haunted him that his daughter might be ill-treated, or need help which he had no knowledge or means to give . . . At the instinctive reminder, now, Vernon Demerest's hands tightened on the control yoke.

For the first time he realized: he could never endure the same uncertainty again. His own nature demanded positiveness. He could, and would, have gone through with the abortion because that was final, definite; moreover, nothing Anson Harris had said earlier on that subject had changed his mind. True, he might have doubts, or even sorrow, afterward. But he would *know*.

The overhead radio speaker cut abruptly through his thoughts. "Trans America Two, this is Cleveland

Center. Turn left on heading two zero five. Begin descent, when ready, to six thousand. Advise when leaving ten."

Demerest's hand pulled back all four throttles to begin losing altitude. He reset the flight path indicator and eased into the turn.

"Trans America Two coming on course two zero five," Anson Harris was advising Cleveland. "We are leaving ten thousand now."

The buffeting increased as they descended, but with every minute they were nearer destination and the hope of safety. They were also nearing the air route boundary point where, at any moment, Cleveland would hand them over to Chicago Center. After that, there would be thirty minutes flying before entering the approach control of Lincoln International.

Harris said quietly, "Vernon, I guess you know how badly I feel about Gwen." He hesitated. "Whatever's between the two of you is none of my business, but if there's anything I can do as a friend . . ."

"There's nothing," Demerest said. He had no intention of unburdening himself to Anson Harris, who was a competent pilot, but still, in Demerest's eyes, an old maid.

Demerest regretted now that he had revealed as much as he did a few minutes ago, but emotion got the better of him—something which happened rarely. Now, he let his face resume a scowl, his shield against disclosing personal feelings.

"Passing through eight thousand feet," Anson Harris told air route control.

Demerest continued to hold the aircraft in a steady descent, on course. His eyes swept the flight instruments in consistent sequence.

He remembered something about the child—his child —who had been born eleven years ago. For weeks before the birth, he debated with himself whether he should confess his infidelity to Sarah, with the suggestion that they adopt the baby as their own. In the end, his courage had failed him. He dreaded his wife's shocked reaction; he feared that Sarah would never accept the child, whose presence she would regard as a permanent reproach.

Long after, and too late, he realized he had done Sarah an injustice. True, she would have been shocked and hurt, just as she would be shocked and hurt now, if she learned about Gwen. But afterward, in a short time, Sarah's habit of coping would have taken over. For all Sarah's placidity and what Demerest thought of as her dullness, despite her suburban bourgeois activities—the curling club and amateur oil painting—his wife had a core of sane solidity. He supposed it was why they had stayed married; why, even now, he could not contemplate divorce.

Sarah would have worked something out. She would have made him squirm and suffer for a while, perhaps for a long time. But she would have agreed to the adoption, and the one who would not have suffered at all would have been the child. Sarah would have seen to that; she was that kind of person. He thought: if only . . .

Demerest said aloud, "Life's full of goddamned 'if onlys.' "

He leveled out at six thousand feet, advancing the throttles to maintain speed. The jet whine rose in pitch.

Harris had been busy changing radio frequencies and —now they had passed the handoff point—reporting to Chicago Center. He asked, "Did you say something?" Demerest shook his head.

The storm's turbulence was as bad as ever, the aircraft still being thrown around.

"Trans America Two, we have you in radar contact," a new voice from Chicago Center rasped.

Harris was still attending to communications.

Vernon Demerest reasoned: So far as Gwen was concerned, he might just as well make a decision now.

All right, he decided; he would face Sarah's tears and denunciations, and perhaps her anger, but he would tell her about Gwen.

He would admit his responsibility for Gwen's pregnancy.

At home, the resulting hysteria might last several days and the aftereffects for weeks or even months, during which time he would suffer mightily. But when the worst was over they would work something out. Strangely—and he supposed it showed his confidence in Sarah—he had not the slightest doubt they would.

He had no idea what they might do, and a good deal would depend on Gwen. Despite what the doctor had just said about the seriousness of Gwen's injuries, Demerest had a conviction she would come through. Gwen had spunk and courage; even unconsciously she would fight to live, and eventually, whatever impairment she suffered, would adjust to it. She would also have her own ideas about the baby. She might not give it up easily or at all. Gwen was not one to be pushed around, or to be told what to do. She did her own thinking.

The result might be that he would have two women on his hands—plus child—instead of one. *That* would take some working out!

It would also pose the question just how far would Sarah go?

God!—what a mess.

But now that his own first decision was taken, he had the conviction that something good might result. He reflected grimly: For all it was going to cost him, in anguish and hard cash, it better had.

The altimeter showed they were maintaining six thousand feet.

There would be the child, of course. Already he was beginning to think of that part in a new and different way. Naturally, he wouldn't let himself get sickly sentimental, the way some people—Anson Harris, for example—were about children; but it would be his child, after all. The experience would certainly be new.

What was it Gwen had said in the car on their way to the airport tonight? . . . *a little Vernon Demerest inside me. If we had a boy we could call him Vernon Demerest, Junior, the way Americans do.*

Maybe it wasn't such a bad idea. He chuckled.

Harris glanced sideways. "What are you laughing at?"

Demerest exploded. "I'm not laughing! Why the hell

would *I* laugh? What is there for any of us to laugh about?"

Harris shrugged, "I thought I heard you."

"That's the second time you've heard things that didn't happen. After this check ride I suggest you have an ear checkup."

"There's no need to be unpleasant."

"Isn't there? *Isn't there?*" Demerest came angrily alert. "Maybe what this whole situation needs is for someone to get unpleasant."

"If that's true," Harris said, "there's no one better qualified than you."

"Then when you're through with damnfool questions, start flying again, and let me talk to those duffers on the ground."

Anson Harris slid his seat forward. "If you want to, why not?" He nodded. "I have it."

Relinquishing the controls, Demerest reached for the radio mike. He felt better, stronger, for a decision taken. Now he would contend with more immediate things. He let his voice grate harshly. "Chicago Center, this is Captain Demerest of Trans America Two. Are you still listening down there, or have you taken sleeping pills and quit?"

"This is Chicago Center, Captain. We're listening, and no one's quit." The controllers voice held a note of reproach; Demerest ignored it.

"Then why in blazes aren't we getting action? This flight is in serious trouble. We need help."

"Stand by, please." There was a pause, then a new voice. "This is Chicago Center supervisor. Captain, Trans America Two, I heard your last transmission. Please understand we're doing everything we can. Before you came into our area we had a dozen people working, clearing other traffic. They're still doing it. We're giving you priority, a clear radio frequency, and a straight-in course for Lincoln."

Demerest barked, "It isn't enough." He paused, holding down the mike button, then continued. "Chicago supervisor, listen carefully. A straight-in course to Lincoln is no good if it ends on runway two

five, or any runway except three zero. Don't tell me
three zero's out of use; I've heard it already, and I know
why. Now, write this down, and see that Lincoln understands it too: This airplane is heavily loaded; we'll be
landing very fast. As well as that, we've structural
damage including unserviceable stabilizer trim and
doubtful rudder control. If we're brought in on two five,
there'll be a broken airplane and dead people before the
next hour is over. So call Lincoln, mister, and turn the
screws. Tell them I don't care how they do it—they can
blow apart what's blocking three zero if they have to—
but we need that runway. Do you understand?"

"Yes, Trans America Two, we understand very well."
The supervisor's voice was unruffled, but a shade more
human than before. "Your message is being passed to
Lincoln now."

"Good." Demerest held the transmit button down
again. "I have another message. This one is to Mel
Bakersfeld, airport general manager at Lincoln. Give
him the previous message, then add this—personal from
his brother-in-law: 'You helped make this trouble, you
bastard, by not listening to me about airport flight insurance. Now you owe it to me and all others on this flight
to climb off your penguin's butt and get that runway
clear.' "

This time the supervisor's voice was doubtful. "Trans
America Two, we've copied your message. Captain, are
you sure you want us to use those words?"

"Chicago Center," Demerest's voice slammed back,
"you're damn right you'll use those words! I'm ordering
you to send that message—fast, and loud, and clear."

13

On ground control radio in his speeding car, Mel Bakersfeld could hear airport emergency vehicles being
summoned and positioned.

"Ground control to city twenty-five."

Twenty-five was the call sign of the airport fire chief.
"This is city twenty-five rolling. Go ahead ground."

"Further information. Category two emergency in approximately thirty-five minutes. The flight in question is disabled and landing on runway three zero, if runway open. If not open, will use runway two five."

Whenever they could, airport controllers avoided naming, on radio, an airline involved in any accident, or a potential one. The phrase "the flight in question" was used as a cover. Airlines were touchy about such things, taking the view that the fewer times their name was repeated in that kind of context, the better.

Just the same, Mel was aware, what had happened tonight would get plenty of publicity, most likely worldwide.

"City twenty-five to ground control. Is the pilot requesting foam on runway?"

"No foam. Repeat, no foam."

The absence of foam meant that the aircraft had serviceable landing gear and would not require a belly landing.

All emergency vehicles, Mel knew—pumpers, salvage trucks, and ambulances—would be following the fire chief, who also had a separate radio channel to communicate with them individually. When an emergency was notified, no one waited. They observed the principle: better to be ready too soon than too late. Emergency crews would now take up position between the two runways, ready to move to either as necessary. The procedure was no improvisation. Every move for situations like this was detailed in an airport emergency master plan.

When there was a break in transmissions, Mel thumbed on his own radio mike.

"Ground control from mobile one."

"Mobile one, go ahead."

"Has Joe Patroni, with stalled aircraft on runway three zero, been advised of new emergency situation?"

"Affirmative. We are in radio touch."

"What is Patroni's report on progress?"

"He expects to move the obstructing aircraft in twenty minutes."

"Is he certain?"

"Negative."

Mel Bakersfeld waited before transmitting again. He was heading across the airfield for the second time tonight, one hand on the wheel, the other on the microphone—driving as fast as he dared in the continued blowing snow and restricted visibility. Taxi and runway lights, guidelines in the dark, flashed by. Beside him on the car's front seat were Tanya Livingston and the *Tribune* reporter, Tomlinson.

A few minutes ago, when Tanya had handed Mel her note about the explosion aboard Flight Two, and the flight's attempt to reach Lincoln International, Mel had broken free instantly from the crowd of Meadowood residents. With Tanya beside him, he headed for the elevators which would take him to the basement garage two floors below, and his official airport car. Mel's place now was on runway three zero, if necessary to take charge. Shouldering his way through the crowd in the main concourse, he had caught sight of the *Tribune* reporter and said tersely, "Come with me." He owed Tomlinson a favor in return for the reporter's tip-off about Elliott Freemantle—both the legal contract form and the lawyer's mendacious statements later, which Mel had been able to repudiate. When Tomlinson hesitated, Mel snapped, "I haven't time to waste. But I'm giving you a chance you may be sorry for not taking." Without further questioning, Tomlinson fell in step beside him.

Now, as they drove, Mel accelerating ahead of taxiing aircraft where he could, Tanya repeated the substance of the news about Flight Two.

"Let me get this straight," Tomlinson said. "There's only one runway long enough, and facing the right direction?"

Mel said grimly, "That's the way it is. Even though there should be two." He was remembering bitterly the proposals he had made, over three successive years, for an additional runway to parallel three zero. The airport needed it. Traffic volume and aircraft safety cried out for implementation of Mel's report, particularly since the runway would take two years to build. But other influences proved stronger. Money had not been found, the new runway had not been built. Nor had construction—despite Mel's further pleas—yet been approved.

With a good many projects, Mel could swing the Board of Airport Commissioners his way. In the case of the proposed new runway, he had canvassed them individually and received promises of support, but later the promises were withdrawn. Theoretically, airport commissioners were independent of political pressure; in fact, they owed their appointments to the mayor and, in most cases, were political partisans themselves. If pressure was put on the mayor to delay an airport bond issue because of other projects, similarly financed and more likely to swing votes, the pressure penetrated through. In the case of the proposed new runway it not only penetrated, but three times had proved effective. Ironically, as Mel remembered earlier tonight, triple-decking of the airport's public parking lots—less necessary, but more visible—had *not* been held up.

Briefly, and in plain words, which until now he had reserved for private sessions, Mel described the situation, including its political overtones.

"I'd like to use all that as coming from you." Tomlinson's voice held the controlled excitement of a reporter who knew he was on to a good story. "May I?"

There would be the devil to pay after it appeared in print, Mel realized; he could imagine the indignant telephone calls from City Hall on Monday morning. But someone should say it. The public ought to know how serious the situation was.

"Go ahead," Mel said. "I guess I'm in a quoting mood."

"That's what I thought." From the far side of the car the reporter regarded Mel quizzically. "If you don't mind my saying so, you've been in great form tonight. Just now, and with the lawyer and those Meadowood people. More like your old self. I haven't heard you speak out like that in a long while."

Mel kept his eyes on the taxiway ahead, waiting to pass an Eastern DC-8, which was turning left. But he was thinking: Had his demeanor of the past year or two, the absence of his old fiery spirit, been so obvious that others had noticed it also?

Beside him, close enough so that Mel was conscious of her nearness and warmth, Tanya said softly, "All the time we're talking . . . about runways, the public, Meadowood, other things . . . I'm thinking about those people on Flight Two. I wonder how they're feeling, if they're afraid."

"They're afraid, all right," Mel said. "If they've any sense, and provided they know what's happening. I'd be afraid, too."

He was remembering his own fear when he had been trapped in the sinking Navy airplane, long ago. As if triggered by memory, he felt a surge of pain around the old wound in his foot. In the past hour's excitement he had adjusted to ignoring it, but as always, with tiredness and overstrain, the effect forced itself on him in the end. Mel compressed his lips tightly and hoped that soon the seizure would lessen or pass.

He had been waiting for another gap in ground-to-ground radio exchanges. As one occurred, Mel depressed his mike button once more.

"Mobile one to ground control. Do you have report on how critical is the requirement of the flight in distress for runway three zero?"

"Mobile one, we understand very critical. Is that Mr. Bakersfeld?"

"Yes, it is."

"Stand by, sir. We're getting more information now."

Still driving, nearing runway three zero, Mel waited. What came next would determine whether or not to follow the drastic course of action he was contemplating.

"Ground control to mobile one. Following message just received, via Chicago Center, from flight in question. Message begins. Straight-in course to Lincoln no good if ends on runway two five. Airplane heavily loaded, will be landing very fast . . ."

The trio in the car listened tensely to the report of Vernon Demerest's message. At the words, "If we're brought in on two five there'll be a broken airplane and dead people," Mel heard Tanya's sharp intake of breath, felt her shudder beside him.

He was about to acknowledge when ground control transmitted again.

"Mobile one—Mr. Bakersfeld, there is an addition to previous message, personal to you, from your brother-in-law. Can you reach a phone?"

"Negative," Mel said. "Read it now, please."

"Mobile one"—he sensed the controller hesitate— "the language is very personal."

The controller was aware—as Mel was—that many ears around the airport would be listening.

"Does it concern the present situation?"

"Affirmative."

"Then read it."

"Yes, sir. Message begins. 'You helped make this trouble, you bastard, by not listening to me about airport flight insurance . . .' "

Mel's mouth tightened, but he waited to the end, then acknowledged noncommittally, "Roger, out." He was sure that Vernon had enjoyed sending the message, as much as anything could be enjoyed aboard Flight Two at present, and would be even more pleased to learn the way it was received.

The extra message was unnecessary, though. Mel had already made his decision on the basis of the first.

His car was now speeding down runway three zero. The circle of floodlights and vehicles surrounding the mired Aéreo-Mexican 707 jet were coming into sight. Mel noted approvingly that the runway was only lightly snow-covered. Despite the blockage of one portion, the remainder had been kept plowed.

He switched his radio to the frequency of airport maintenance.

"Mobile one to Snow Desk."

"This is Snow Desk." Danny Farrow's voice sounded tired, which was not surprising. "Go ahead."

"Danny," Mel said, "break the Conga Line. Send the

Oshkosh plows and heavy graders across to runway three zero. They're to head for where the stuck airplane is, and await instructions. Get them started now, then call me back."

"Roger, wilco." Danny seemed about to add a question, then apparently changed his mind. A moment later, on the same frequency, the occupants of the car heard him issue orders to the Conga Line convoy leader.

The *Tribune* reporter leaned forward around Tanya.

"I'm still fitting pieces together," Tomlinson said. "That bit about flight insurance . . . Your brother-in-law's an Air Line Pilots Association wheel, isn't he?"

"Yes." Mel halted the car on the runway, a few feet short of the circle of lights around the big, stalled aircraft. There was plenty of action, he could see; beneath the aircraft fuselage, and on both sides, men were digging feverishly. The stocky form of Joe Patroni was visible directing activities. In a moment Mel would join him, after the return radio call from Danny Farrow at the Snow Desk.

The reporter said thoughtfully, "I think I heard something awhile back. Didn't your brother-in-law make a big play to cancel insurance vending here—the way ALPA wants to—and you turned him down?"

"I didn't turn him down. The airport board did, though I agreed with them."

"If it isn't an unfair question, has what's happened tonight made you change your mind?"

Tanya protested, "Surely this isn't the time . . ."

"I'll answer that," Mel said. "I haven't changed my mind, at least not yet. But I'm thinking about it."

Mel reasoned: the time for a change of heart about flight insurance—if there was to be one—was not now, in the height of emotion and the wake of tragedy. In a day or two, what had occurred tonight would be seen in better perspective. Mel's own decision—whether to urge the airport board to revise its policy, or not—should be made then. Meanwhile, no one could deny that tonight's events added strength to Vernon Demerest's—and the Air Line Pilots Association—arguments.

Possibly, Mel supposed, a compromise might be

worked out. An ALPA spokesman once confided to him that the pilots did not expect their anti-airport insurance campaign to be won, either outright or quickly; success would take years and "would have to be cut like bologna—a slice at a time." One slice at Lincoln International might be to prohibit use of non-supervised insurance vending machines, as some airports had already done. One state—Colorado—had outlawed the machines by Legislative Act. Other states, Mel knew, were considering similar legislation, though there was nothing to stop airports, meanwhile, from acting on their own.

It was the insurance vending machine system which Mel liked least, even though D. O. Guerrero's huge insurance policy tonight had not been bought that way. Then, if over-the-counter sales remained—for a few more years until public opinion could be molded—there would have to be more safeguards . . .

Even though Mel had resolved not to make a firm decision, it was obvious to himself which way his reasoning was going.

The radio, still tuned to airport maintenance frequency, had been busy with calls between vehicles. Now it announced, "Snow Desk to mobile one."

Mel responded, "Go ahead, Danny."

"Four plows and three graders, with convoy leader, are on their way to runway three zero as instructed. What orders, please?"

Mel chose his words carefully, aware that somewhere in an electronic maze beneath the control tower they were being recorded on tape. Later he might have to justify them. He also wanted to be sure there was no misunderstanding.

"Mobile one to Snow Desk. All plows and graders, under direction of convoy leader, will stand by near Aéreo-Mexican aircraft which is blocking runway three zero. Vehicles are not, repeat not, initially to obstruct the aircraft, which in a few minutes will attempt to move under its own power. But if that attempt fails, plows and graders will be ordered in to push the aircraft sideways, and to clear the runway. This will be done at any cost, and with all speed. Runway three zero must be open for use in approximately thirty minutes, by which time the obstructing aircraft and all vehicles must be clear. I will coordinate with air traffic control to decide at what time the plows will be ordered in, if necessary. Acknowledge, and confirm that these instructions are understood."

Inside the car the reporter, Tomlinson, whistled softly. Tanya turned toward Mel, her eyes searching his face.

On radio there were several seconds' silence, then Danny Farrow's voice. "I guess I understand. But I'd better be sure." He repeated the gist of the message, and Mel could imagine Danny sweating again, as he had been earlier.

"Roger," Mel acknowledged. "But be clear about one thing. If those plows and graders go in, I'll give the order; no one else."

"It's clear," Danny radioed. "And better you than me. Mel, I guess you've figured what that equipment of ours'll do to a 707."

"It'll move it," Mel said tersely. "Right now that's the important thing." There was, Mel knew, other motorized equipment in Airport Maintenance, capable of the same kind of brute force clearing job; but using the Conga Line units, already on the runways, would be surer and faster. He signed off, and replaced the radio mike.

Tomlinson said incredulously, "Move it! A six-million dollar airplane shoved sideways by snowplows! My God, you'll tear it to pieces! And afterward, the owners and insurers'll do the same to you."

"I wouldn't be surprised," Mel said. "Of course, a lot depends on your point of view. If the owners and insurers were on that other flight coming in, they might be cheering."

"Well," the reporter conceded, "I'll grant you there are some decisions take a lot of guts."

Tanya's hand reached down beside her and found Mel's. She said softly, emotion in her voice, "I'm cheering—for what you're doing now. Whatever happens after, I'll remember."

The plows and graders which Mel had summoned were coming into sight, traveling fast down the runway, roof beacons flashing.

"It may never happen." Mel squeezed Tanya's hand before releasing it, then opened the car door. "We've twenty minutes to hope it won't."

When Mel Bakersfeld approached him, Joe Patroni was stomping his feet in an effort to be warm; the effort was largely unsuccessful despite the fleece-lined boots and heavy parka the TWA maintenance chief was wearing. Apart from the brief time Patroni had spent on the aircraft flight deck when the Aéreo-Mexican captain and first officer departed, he had been continuously out in the storm since his arrival on the scene more than three hours ago. As well as being cold and physically tired from his various exertions of the day and night, his failure to move the stranded jet despite two attempts so far, had made his temper ready to erupt.

It almost did, at the news of Mel's intention.

With anyone else, Joe Patroni would have stormed and ranted. Because Mel was a close friend, Patroni removed the unlighted cigar he had been chewing, and eyed Mel unbelievingly. "Shove an undamaged airplane with snowplows! Are you out of your mind?"

"No," Mel said. "I'm out of runways."

Mel felt a momentary depression at the thought that no one in authority, other than himself, seemed to understand the urgency of clearing three zero, at any cost. Obviously, if he went ahead as he intended, there would be few who would support his action afterward. On the other hand, Mel had not the least doubt there would be plenty of people tomorrow with hindsight—including Aéreo-Mexican officials—who would assert he could have done this or that, or that Flight Two should have landed on runway two five after all. Obviously his decision was to be a lonely one. It did not change Mel's conviction that it should be made.

At the sight of the assembled plows and graders, now deployed in line on the runway, to their right, Patroni dropped his cigar altogether. As he produced another he growled, "I'll save you from your own insanity. Keep those Dinky Toys of yours out of my hair and away from this airplane. In fifteen minutes, maybe less, I'll drive it out."

Mel shouted to make himself heard above the wind and roaring engines of vehicles around them. "Joe, let's be clear about one thing. When the tower tells us we're running out of time, that's it; there'll be no argument. People's lives are involved on the flight that's coming in. If you've engines running, they're to be shut down. At the same time all equipment and the men must move clear immediately. Make sure in advance that all your people understand. The plows will move on my order. If and when they do, they won't waste time."

Patroni nodded gloomily. Despite his outburst, Mel thought, the maintenance chief's usual cocky self-assurance seemed abated.

Mel returned to his car. Tanya and the reporter, huddled in their coats, had been standing outside, watching the work of digging around the aircraft. They got into the car with him, grateful for the warmth inside.

Once more, Mel called ground control on radio, this time asking for the tower watch chief. After a brief pause, the tower chief's voice came on the air.

In a few words Mel explained his intention. What he sought from air traffic control now was an estimate of how long he could wait before ordering the plows and graders to move. Once they did, it would take only minutes to have the obstructing aircraft clear.

"The way it looks now," the tower chief said, "the flight in question will be here sooner than we thought. Chicago Center expects to hand over to our approach control in twelve minutes from now. After that we'll be controlling the flight for eight to ten minutes before landing, which would make time of touchdown, at latest, 0128."

Mel checked his watch in the dim light from the dash. It showed 1:01 A.M.

"A choice of which runway to use," the tower chief said, "will have to be made no later than five minutes before landing. After that, they'll be committed; we can't turn them."

So what it meant, Mel calculated, was that his own final decision must be made in another seventeen minutes, perhaps less, depending on the handover time from Chicago Center to Lincoln approach control. There was even less time remaining than he had told Joe Patroni.

Mel found he, too, was beginning to sweat.

Should he warn Patroni again, informing him of the reduced time? Mel decided not. The maintenance chief was already directing operations at the fastest pace he could. Nothing would be gained by harassing him further.

"Mobile one to ground control," Mel radioed. "I'll need to be kept informed of exact status of the approaching flight. Can we hold this frequency clear?"

"Affirmative," the tower chief said. "We've already moved regular traffic to another frequency. We'll keep you informed."

Mel acknowledged and signed off.

Beside him, Tanya asked, "What happens now?"

"We wait." Mel checked his watch again.

A minute went by. Two.

Outside they could see men working, still digging feverishly near the front and on each side of the mired aircraft. With a flash of headlights, another truck arrived; men jumped down from its tailgate and hastened to join the others. Joe Patroni's stocky figure was moving constantly, instructing and exhorting.

The plows and graders were still in line, waiting. In a way, Mel thought, like vultures.

The reporter, Tomlinson, broke the silence inside the car.

"I was just thinking. When I was a kid, which isn't all that long ago, most of this place was fields. In summer there were cows and corn and barley. There was a grass airfield; small; nobody thought it would amount to much. If anyone traveled by air, they used the airport in the city."

"That's aviation," Tanya said. She felt a momentary relief at being able to think and talk of something other than what they were waiting for. She went on, "Somebody told me once that working in aviation makes a lifetime seem longer because everything changes so often and so fast."

Tomlinson objected, "Not everything's fast. With airports, the changes aren't fast enough. Isn't it true, Mr. Bakersfeld, that within three to four years there'll be chaos?"

"Chaos is always relative," Mel said; the focus of his mind was still on the scene he could see through the car windshield. "In a good many ways we manage to live with it."

"Aren't you dodging the question?"

"Yes," he conceded. "I suppose I am."

It was scarcely surprising, Mel thought. He was less concerned with aviation philosophy at this moment than with the immediacy of what was happening outside. But he sensed Tanya's need for a lessening of tension, even if illusory his awareness of her feelings was part of the empathy they seemed increasingly to share. He reminded himself, too, that it was a Trans America flight they were waiting for, and which might land safely or might not. Tanya was a part of Trans America, had helped with the flight's departure. In a real sense, of the three of them she had the most direct involvement.

With an effort he concentrated on what Tomlinson had said.

"It's always been true," Mel declared, "that in aviation, progress in the air has been ahead of progress on the ground. We sometimes think we'll catch up; in the mid-1960s we almost did but by and large we never do. The best we can manage, it seems, is not to lag too far behind."

The reporter persisted, "What *should* we do about airports? What *can* we do?"

"We can think more freely, with more imagination, for one thing. We should get rid of the railway station mind."

"You believe we still have it?"

Mel nodded. "Unfortunately, in a good many places. All our early airports were imitation railway stations because designers had to draw on experience from somewhere, and railroad experience was all they had. Afterward, the habit remained. It's the reason, nowadays, we have so many 'straight line' airports, where terminals stretch on and on, and passengers must walk for miles."

Tomlinson asked, "Isn't some of that changing?"

"Slowly, and in just a few places." As always, despite the pressures of the moment, Mel was warming to his theme. "A few airports are being built as circles—like doughnuts with car parking inside, instead of somewhere out beyond; with minimum distances for people to walk with aids like high-speed horizontal elevators; with airplanes brought close to passengers instead of the other way around. What it means is that airports are finally being thought of as special and distinct also as units instead of separate components. Creative ideas, even outlandish ones, are being listened to. Los Angeles is proposing a big, offshore seadrome; Chicago, a man-made airport island in Lake Michigan; nobody's scoffing. American Airlines has a plan for a giant hydraulic lift to stack airplanes one above the other for loading and unloading. But the changes are slow, they're not coordinated; we build airports like an unimaginative, patchwork quilt. It's as if phone subscribers designed and made their own telephones, then plugged them into a world-wide system."

The radio cut abruptly across Mel's words. "Ground control to mobile one and city twenty-five. Chicago Center now estimates handoff of the flight in question to Lincoln approach control will be 0117."

Mel's watch showed 1:06 A.M. The message meant that Flight Two was already a minute earlier than the tower chief had forecast. A minute less for Joe Patroni to work only eleven minutes to Mel's own decision.

"Mobile one, is there any change in the status of runway three zero?"

"Negative; no change."

Mel wondered: was he cutting things too fine? He was tempted to direct the snowplows and graders to move now, then restrained himself. Responsibility was a two-way street, especially when it came to ordering the near-destruction of a six-million dollar aircraft on the ground. There was still a chance that Joe Patroni might make it, though with every second the possibility was lessening. In front of the stalled 707, Mel could see, some of the floodlights and other equipment were being moved clear. But the aircraft's engines had not yet been started.

"Those creative people," Tomlinson queried, "the ones you were talking about. Who are they?"

With only half his mind, Mel acknowledged, "It's hard to make a list."

He was watching the scene outside. The remainder of the vehicles and equipment in front of the stalled Aéreo-Mexican 707 had now been moved clear, and Joe Patroni's stocky, snow-covered figure was climbing the boarding ramp, positioned near the aircraft's nose. Near the top, Patroni stopped, turned, and gestured; he appeared to be shouting to others below. Now Patroni opened the front fuselage door and went inside; almost at once another, slighter figure climbed the ramp and followed him. The aircraft door slammed. Others below trundled the ramp away.

Inside the car, the reporter asked again, "Mr. Bakersfeld, could you name a few of those people—the most imaginative ones about airports and the future?"

"Yes," Tanya said, "couldn't you?"

Mel thought: it would be like a parlor game while the house was burning. All right, he decided if Tanya wanted him to, he would play.

"I can think of some," Mel said. "Fox of Los Angeles; Joseph Foster of Houston, now with ATA of America. Alan Boyd in government; and Thomas Sullivan, Port of New York Authority. In the airlines: Halaby of Pan Am; Herb Godfrey of United. In Canada, John C. Parkin. In Europe—Pierre Cot of Air France; Count Castell in Germany. There are others."

"Including Mel Bakersfeld," Tanya injected. "Aren't you forgetting him?"

Tomlinson, who had been making notes, grunted. "I already put him down. It goes without saying."

Mel smiled. But did it, he wondered, go without saying? Once, not long ago, the statement would have been true; but he knew that on the national scene he had slipped from view. When that happened, when you left the mainstream for whatever reason, you were apt to be forgotten quickly; and later, even if you wanted to, sometimes you never did get back. It was not that he was doing a less important job at Lincoln International, or doing it less well; as an airport general manager, Mel knew he was as good as ever, probably better. But the big contribution which he had once seemed likely to make no longer was in view. He realized that this was the second time tonight the same thought had occurred to him. Did it matter? Did he care? He decided; Yes, he did!

"Look!" Tanya cried out. "They're starting the engines."

The reporter's head came up; Mel felt his own excitement sharpen.

Behind number three engine of the Aéreo-Mexican 707, a puff of white-gray smoke appeared. Briefly it intensified, then whirled away as the engine fired and held. Now snow was streaming rearward in the jet blast.

A second puff of smoke appeared behind number four engine, a moment later to be whisked away, snow following.

"Ground control to mobile one and city twenty-five." Within the car the radio voice was so unexpected that Mel felt Tanya give a startled jump beside him. "Chicago Center advises revised handoff time of the flight in question will be 0116 . . . seven minutes from now."

Flight Two, Mel realized, was still coming in faster than expected. It meant they had lost another minute.

Again Mel held his watch near the light of the dash.

On the soft ground near the opposite side of the runway from their car, Patroni now had number two engine started. Number one followed. Mel said softly, "They could still make it." Then he remembered that all engines had been started twice before tonight, and both attempts to blast the stuck airplane free had failed.

In front of the mired 707 a solitary figure with flashlight signal wands had moved out ahead to where he could be seen from the aircraft flight deck. The man with the wands was holding them above his head, indicating "all clear." Mel could hear and feel the jet engines' thrum, but sensed they had not yet been advanced in power.

Six minutes left. *Why hadn't Patroni opened up?*

Tanya said tensely, "I don't think I can bear the waiting."

The reporter shifted in his seat. "I'm sweating too."

Joe Patroni was opening up! This was it! Mel could hear and feel the greater all-encompassing roar of engines. Behind the stalled Aéreo-Mexican jet, great gusts of snow were blowing wildly into the darkness beyond the runway lights.

"Mobile one," the radio demanded sharply, "this is ground control. Is there any change in status of runway three zero?"

Patroni, Mel calculated by his watch, had three minutes left.

"The airplane's still stuck." Tanya was peering intently through the car windshield. "They're using all the engines, but it isn't moving."

It was straining forward, though; that much Mel could see, even through the blowing snow. But Tanya was right. The aircraft wasn't moving.

The snowplows and heavy graders had shifted closer together, their beacons flashing brightly.

"Hold it!" Mel said on radio. "Hold it! Don't commit that flight coming in to runway two five. One way or the other, there'll be a change in three zero status any moment now."

He switched the car radio to Snow Desk frequency, ready to activate the plows.

14

Ordinarily, after midnight, pressures in air traffic control
relented slightly. Tonight they hadn't. Because of the
storm, airlines at Lincoln International were continuing
to dispatch and receive flights which were hours late.
More often than not, their lateness was added to by the
general runway and taxiway congestion still prevailing.

Most members of the earlier eight-hour watch in air
traffic control had ended their shift at midnight and
gone wearily home. Newcomers on duty had taken their
place. A few controllers, because of staff shortage and
illness of others, had been assigned a spreadover shift
which would end at 2 A.M. They included the tower
watch chief; Wayne Tevis, the radar supervisor; and
Keith Bakersfeld.

Since the emotion-charged session with his brother,
which ended abruptly and abortively an hour and a half
ago, Keith had sought relief of mind by concentrating
intensely on the radar screen in front of him. If he could
maintain his concentration, he thought, the remaining
time—the last he would ever have to fill—would pass
quickly. Keith had continued handling east arrivals,
working with a young assistant—a radar handoff man
—seated on his left. Wayne Tevis was still supervising,
riding his castor-equipped stool around the control
room, propelled by his Texan boots, though less energetically, as Tevis's own duty shift neared an end.

In one sense, Keith had succeeded in his concentration; yet in a strange way he had not. It seemed almost
as if his mind had split into two levels, like a duplex,
and he was able to be in both at once .On one level he
was directing east arrivals traffic—at the moment,
without problems. On the other, his thoughts were personal and introspective. It was not a condition which
could last, but perhaps, Keith thought, his mind was like

a light bulb about to fail and, for its last few minutes, burning brightest.

The personal side of his thoughts was dispassionate now, and calmer than before; perhaps the session with Mel had achieved that, if nothing more. All things seemed ordained and settled. Keith's duty shift would end; he would leave this place; soon after, all waiting and all anguish would be over. He had the conviction that his own life and others' were already severed; he no longer belonged to Natalie or Mel, or Brian and Theo . . . or they to him. He belonged to the already dead—to the Redferns who had died together in the wreck of their Beech Bonanza; to little Valerie . . . her family. *That was it!* Why had he never thought of it that way before; realized that his own death was a debt he owed the Redferns? With continued dispassion, Keith wondered if he were insane; people who chose suicide were said to be, but either way it made no difference. His choice was between torment and peace; and before the light of morning, peace would come. Once more, as it had intermittently in the past few hours, his hand went into his pocket, fingering the key to room 224 of the O'Hagan Inn.

All the while, on the other mental level, and with traces of his old flair, he coped with east arrivals.

Awareness of the crisis with Trans America Flight Two came to Keith gradually.

Lincoln air traffic control had been advised of Flight Two's intention to return there—almost an hour ago, and seconds after Captain Anson Harris's decision was made known. Word had come by "hot line" telephone directly from Chicago Center supervisor to the tower watch chief, after similar notification through Cleveland and Toronto centers. Initially there had been little to do at Lincoln beyond advising the airport management through the Snow Desk, of the flight's request for runway three zero.

Later, when Flight Two had been taken over from Cleveland, by Chicago Center, more specific preparations were begun.

Wayne Tevis, the radar supervisor, was alerted by the

tower chief, who went personally to the radar room to inform Tevis of Flight Two's condition, its estimated arrival time, and the doubt about which runway—two five or three zero—was to be used for landing.

At the same time, ground control was notifying airport emergency services to stand by and, shortly after, to move with their vehicles onto the airfield.

A ground controller talked by radio telephone with Joe Patroni to check that Patroni had been advised of the urgent need for runway three zero. He had.

Contact was then established, on a reserve radio frequency, between the control tower and the flight deck of the Aéreo-Mexican jet which blocked the runway. The setup was to ensure that when Patroni was at the aircraft's controls, there could be instant two-way communication, if needed.

In the radar room, when he had listened to the tower chief's news, Wayne Tevis's initial reaction was to glance at Keith. Unless duties were changed around, it would be Keith, in charge of east arrivals, who would accept Flight Two from Chicago Center, and monitor the flight in.

Tevis asked the tower chief quietly, "Should we take Keith off; put someone else on?"

The older man hesitated. He remembered the earlier emergency tonight involving the Air Force KC-135. He had removed Keith from duty then, on a pretext, and afterward wondered if he had been too hasty. When a man was teeter-tottering between self-assurance and the loss of it, it was easy to send the scales the wrong way without intending to. The tower chief had an uneasy feeling, too, of having blundered into something private between Keith and Mel Bakersfeld when the two of them were talking earlier in the corridor outside. He could have left them alone for a few minutes longer, but hadn't.

The tower watch chief was tired himself, not only from the trying shift tonight, but from others which preceded it. He remembered reading somewhere recently that new air traffic systems, being readied for the mid-1970s, would halve controllers' work loads, thereby reducing occupational fatigue and nervous breakdowns. The tower chief remained skeptical. He doubted if, in air traffic control, pressures would ever lighten; if they eased in one way, he thought, they would increase in another. It made him sympathize with those who, like Keith—still gaunt, pale, strained—had proved victims of the system.

Still in an undertone, Wayne Tevis repeated, "Do I take him off, or not?"

The tower chief shook his head. Low-voiced, he answered, "Let's not push it. Keep Keith on, but stay close."

It was then that Keith, observing the two with heads together, guessed that something critical was coming up. He was, after all, an old hand, familiar with signals of impending trouble.

Instinct told him, too, that the supervisors' conversation was in part, about himself. He could understand why. Keith had no doubt he would be relieved from duty in a few minutes from now, or shifted to a less vital radar position. He found himself not caring.

It was a surprise when Tevis—without shuffling duties—began warning all watch positions of the expected arrival of Trans America Two, in distress, and its priority handling.

Departure control was cautioned: Route all departures well clear of the flight's anticipated route in.

To Keith, Tevis expounded the runway problem—the uncertainty as to which runway was to be used, and the need to postpone a decision until the last possible moment.

"You work out your own plan, buddy boy," Tevis instructed in his nasal Texas drawl. "And after the handover, stay with it. We'll take everything else off your hands."

At first, Keith nodded agreement, no more perturbed than he had been before. Automatically, he began to calculate the flight pattern he would use. Such plans were always worked out mentally. There was never time to commit them to paper; besides, the need for improvisation usually turned up.

As soon as he received the flight from Chicago Center, Keith reasoned, he would head it generally toward runway three zero, but with sufficient leeway to swing the aircraft left—though without drastic turns at low altitude—if runway two five was forced on them as the final choice.

He calculated: He would have the aircraft under approach control for approximately ten minutes. Tevis had already advised him that not until the last five, probably, would they know for sure about the runway. It was slicing things fine, and there would be sweating in the radar room, as well as in the air. But it could be managed—just. Once more, in his mind, Keith went over the planned flight path and compass headings.

By then, more definite reports had begun to filter, unofficially, through the tower. Controllers passed information to each other as work gaps permitted . . . The flight had had a mid-air explosion. It was limping in with structural damage and injured people . . . Control of the airplane was in doubt. The pilots needed the longest runway—which might or might not be available . . . Captain Demerest's warning was repeated: . . . *on two five a broken airplane and dead people* . . . The captain had sent a savage message to the airport manager. Now, the manager was out on three zero, trying to get the runway cleared . . . The time available was shortening.

Even among the controllers, to whom tension was as commonplace as traffic, there was now a shared nervous anxiety.

Keith's radar handoff man, seated alongside, passed on the news which came to him in snatches. As he did, Keith's awareness and apprehension grew. *He didn't want this, or any part of it!* There was nothing he sought to prove, or could; nothing he might retrieve, even if he handled the situation well. And if he didn't, if he mishandled it, he might send a planeload of people to their deaths, *as he had done once before*.

Across the radar room, on a direct line, Wayne Tevis took a telephone call from the tower watch chief. A few minutes ago the chief had gone one floor above, into the tower cab, to remain beside the ground controller.

Hanging up, Tevis propelled his chair alongside Keith. "The old man just had word from center. Trans America Two—three minutes from handoff."

The supervisor moved on to departure control, checking that outward traffic was being routed clear of the approaching flight.

The man on Keith's left reported that out on the airfield they were still trying frantically to shift the stranded jet blocking runway three zero. They had the engines running, but the airplane wouldn't move. Keith's brother (the handoff man said) had taken charge, and if the airplane wouldn't move on its own, was going to smash it to pieces to clear the runway. But everybody was asking: was there time?

If Mel thought so, Keith reasoned, there probably was. Mel coped, he managed things; he always had. Keith couldn't cope—at least not always, and never in the same way as Mel. It was the difference between them.

Almost two minutes had gone by.

Alongside Keith, the handoff man said quietly, "They're coming on the scope." On the edge of the radarscope Keith could see the double blossom radar distress signal—unmistakably Trans America Two.

Keith wanted out! He couldn't do it! Someone else must take over; Wayne Tevis could himself. There was still time.

Keith swung away from the scope looking for Tevis. The supervisor was at departure control, his back toward Keith.

Keith opened his mouth to call. To his horror, no words came. He tried again . . . the same.

He realized: It was as in the dream, his nightmare; his voice had failed him . . . But this was no dream; this was reality! *Wasn't it?* . . . Still struggling to articulate, panic gripped him.

On a panel above the scope, a flashing white light indicated that Chicago Center was calling. The handoff man picked up a direct line phone and instructed, "Go ahead, center." He turned a selector, cutting in a speaker overhead so that Keith could hear.

"Lincoln, Trans America Two is thirty miles southeast of the airport. He's on a heading of two five zero."

"Roger, center. We have him in radar contact. Change him to our frequency." The handoff man replaced the phone.

Center, they knew, would now be instructing the flight to change radio frequency, and probably wishing them good luck. It usually happened that way when an aircraft was in trouble; it seemed the least that anyone could do from the secure comfort of the ground. In this isolated, comfortably warm room of low-key sounds, it was difficult to accept that somewhere outside, high in the night and darkness, buffeted by wind and storm, its survival in doubt, a crippled airliner was battling home.

The east arrivals radio frequency came alive. A harsh voice, unmistakably Vernon Demerest's; Keith hadn't thought about that until this moment. "Lincoln approach control, this is Trans America Two, maintaining six thousand feet, heading two five zero."

The handoff man was waiting expectantly. It was Keith's moment to acknowledge, to take over. *But he wanted out!* Wayne Tevis was still turned away! Keith's speech wouldn't come.

"Lincoln approach control," the voice from Trans America Two grated again, "where in hell are you?"

Where in hell . . .

Why wouldn't Tevis turn?

Keith seethed with sudden rage. *Damn Tevis! Damn air traffic control! Damn his dead father, Wild Blue Bakersfeld, who led his sons into a vocation Keith hadn't wanted to begin with! Damn Mel, with his infuriating self-sufficient competence! Damn here and now! Damn everything!* . . .

The handoff man was looking at Keith curiously. At any moment Trans America Two would call again. Keith knew that he was trapped. Wondering if his voice would work, he keyed his mike.

"Trans America Two," Keith said, "this is Lincoln approach control. Sorry about the delay. We're still hoping for runway three zero; we shall know in three to five minutes."

A growled acknowledgment, "Roger, Lincoln. Keep us informed."

Keith was concentrating now; the extra level of his mind had closed. He forgot Tevis, his father, Mel, himself. All else was excluded but the problem of Flight Two.

He radioed clearly and quietly, "Trans America Two, you are now twenty-five miles east of the outer marker. Begin descent at your discretion. Start a right turn to heading two six zero . . ."

One floor above Keith, in the glass-walled tower cab, the ground controller had advised Mel Bakersfeld that handoff from Chicago Center had occurred.

Mel radioed back, "Snowplows and graders have been ordered to move, and clear the Aéreo-Mexican aircraft from the runway. Instruct Patroni to shut down all engines immediately. Tell him—if he can, get clear himself; if not, hold on tight. Stand by for advice when runway is clear."

On a second frequency, the tower chief was already informing Joe Patroni.

15

Even before it happened, Joe Patroni knew he was running out of time.

He had deliberately not started the engines of the Aéreo-Mexican 707 until the latest possible moment, wanting the work of clearing under and around the aircraft to continue as long as it could.

When he realized that he could wait no longer, Patroni made a final inspection. What he saw gave him grave misgivings.

The landing gear was still not as clear from surrounding earth, mud, and snow as it should be. Nor
were the trenches, inclining upward from the present
level of the main wheels to the hard surface of the
nearby taxiway, as wide or deep as he had wanted.
Another fifteen minutes would have done it.

Patroni knew he didn't have the time.

Reluctantly he ascended the boarding ramp, to make
his second attempt at moving the mired aircraft, now
with himself at the controls.

He shouted to Ingram, the Aéreo-Mexican foreman,
"Get everybody clear! We're starting up."

From under the aircraft, figures began to move out.

Snow was still falling, but more lightly than for several hours.

Joe Patroni called again from the boarding ramp. "I
need somebody with me on the flight deck, but let's
keep the weight down. Send me a skinny guy who's
cockpit qualified."

He let himself into the aircraft's forward door.

Inside, through the flight deck windows, Patroni
could see Mel Bakersfeld's airport car, its bright yellow
coloring reflected through the darkness. The car was
parked on the runway, to the left. Near it was the line of
snowplows and graders—a reminder, if he needed one,
that he had only a few minutes more.

The maintenance chief had reacted with shocked
disbelief when Mel announced his plan to shove the
Aéreo-Mexican aircraft clear of runway three zero by
force, if necessary. The reaction was natural, but was
not through indifference to the safety of those aboard
Trans America Flight Two. Joe Patroni lived with
thoughts of aircraft safety, which was the object of his
daily work. It was simply that the idea of reducing an
undamaged aircraft to a pile of scrap metal, or something close to it, was near-impossible for him to grasp.
In Patroni's eyes, an aircraft—any aircraft—represented
devotion, skill, engineering know-how, hours of labor,
and sometimes love. Almost anything was better than its
deliberate destruction. *Almost* anything.

Patroni intended to save the airplane if he could.

Behind him, the fuselage door opened, and slammed closed.

A young mechanic, small and spare, came forward to the flight deck, shedding snow. Joe Patroni had already slipped off his parka and was strapping himself into the left seat.

"What's your name, son?"

"Rolling, sir."

Patroni chuckled. "That's what we're trying to get this airplane doin'. Maybe you're an omen."

As the mechanic removed his own parka and slid into the right seat, Patroni looked through the window behind his left shoulder. Outside, the boarding ramp was being trundled clear.

The interphone chimed, and Patroni answered. The foreman, Ingram, was calling from below. "Ready to start when you are."

Joe Patroni glanced sideways. "All set, son?"

The mechanic nodded.

"Number three starter switch—ground start."

The mechanic snapped a switch; Patroni ordered on interphone, "Pressurize the manifold!"

From a power cart below, air under pressure whined. The maintenance chief moved a start level to "idle"; the young mechanic, monitoring instruments, reported, "Light-up on number three." The engine note became a steady roar.

In smooth succession, engines four, two, and one followed.

On interphone, Ingram's voice was diminished by a background of wind and jet whine. "Power cart's clear. So's everything else down here."

"Okay," Patroni shouted back. "Disconnect interphone, and get the hell clear yourself."

He told his cockpit companion, "Sit tight, son, and hang on." The maintenance chief shifted his cigar, which contrary to regulations he had lighted a few minutes earlier, so that it was now jauntily in a corner of his mouth. Then, with chunky fingers spread, he eased the four main throttles forward.

With power at midpoint, the clamor of all four engines grew.

Ahead of the aircraft, in the snow, they could see a ground crewman with raised, lighted signal wands. Patroni grinned, "If we come out fast, I hope that guy's a good runner."

All brakes were off, flaps slightly down to engender lift. The mechanic held the control yoke back. Patroni worked the rudder controls alternately, hoping by sideways strain to help the airplane forward.

Glancing left, he saw Mel Bakersfeld's car was still in position. From an earlier calculation, Joe Patroni knew there could be only minutes—perhaps less than a minute—left.

Now, power was past three quarters. From the high-pitched note of engines, he could tell it was more power than the Aéreo-Mexican captain had used during the earlier attempt to get free. Vibration told why. Normally, at this setting, the airplane would be unimpeded, bowling fast down a runway. Because it was not, it was shaking severely, with every portion of its upper area straining forward, resisting the anchoring effect of the wheels below. The airplane's inclination to stand on its nose was unmistakable. The mechanic glanced uneasily sideways.

Patroni saw the glance and grunted. "She'd better come out now, or she's a dead duck."

But the aircraft was not moving. Obstinately, as it had for hours, and through two earlier attempts, it was remaining stuck.

In the hope of rocking the wheels free, Patroni slackened engine power, then increased it.

Still the aircraft failed to move.

Joe Patroni's cigar, moist from previous chewing, had gone out. Disgustedly, he flung it down and reached for another. His breast pocket was empty; the cigar had been his last.

He swore, and returned his right hand to the throttles. Moving them still farther forward, he snarled, "Come out! Come out, you son of a bitch!"

"Mr. Patroni!" the mechanic warned. "She won't take much more."

Abruptly, the overhead radio speakers came alive. The tower chief's voice. "Joe Patroni, aboard Aéreo-

Mexican. This is ground control. We have a message from Mr. Bakersfeld: 'There is no more time. Stop all engines.' Repeat—stop all engines."

Glancing out, Patroni saw the plows and graders were already moving. They wouldn't close in, he knew, until the aircraft engines were stopped. But he remembered Mel's warning: *When the tower tells us we're out of time, there'll be no argument.*

He thought: *Who's arguing?*

The radio again, urgently: "Joe Patroni, do you read? Acknowledge."

"Mr. Patroni!" the mechanic shouted. "Do you hear? We have to shut down!"

Patroni shouted back, "Can't hear a damn thing, son. Guess there's too much noise."

As any seasoned maintenance man knew, you always had a minute more than the panic-prone sales types in the front office said you had.

In the worst way, though, he needed a cigar. Suddenly Joe Patroni remembered—hours ago, Mel Bakersfeld bet him a box of cigars he couldn't get this airplane free tonight.

He called across the cockpit, "I gotta stake in this, too. Let's go for broke." In a single, swift motion he shoved the throttles forward to their limit.

The din and vibration had seemed great before; now they were overwhelming. The airplane shuddered as if it might fall apart. Joe Patroni kicked the rudder pedals hard again.

Around the cockpit, engine warning lights flashed on. Afterward, the mechanic described the effect as "like a pinball machine at Vegas."

Now, alarm in his voice, he called, "Exhaust gas temperature seven hundred."

The radio speakers were still emitting orders, including something about Patroni getting clear himself. He supposed he would have to. His hand tensed to close the throttles.

Suddenly the airplane shifted forward. At first, it moved slowly. Then, with startling speed, they were hurtling toward the taxiway. The mechanic shouted a warning. As Patroni snatched back all four throttles, he commanded, "Flaps up!" Glancing below and ahead, both men had an impression of blurred figures running.

Fifty feet from the taxiway, they were still moving fast. Unless turned promptly, the airplane would cross the hard surface and roll into piled snow on the other side. As he felt the tires reach pavement, Patroni applied left brakes hard and slammed open the two starboard throttles. Brakes and engines responded, and the aircraft swung sharply left, in a ninety-degree arc. Halfway around, he slid back the two throttles and applied all brakes together. The Aéreo-Mexican 707 rolled forward briefly, then slowed and halted.

Joe Patroni grinned. They had stopped with the aircraft parked neatly, in the center of the taxiway paralleling runway three zero.

The runway, two hundred feet away, was no longer blocked.

In Mel Bakersfeld's car, on the runway, Tanya cried, "He's done it! He's done it!"

Beside her, Mel was already radioing the Snow Desk, ordering plows and graders to get clear.

Seconds earlier, Mel had been calling angrily to the tower, demanding for the third time that Joe Patroni stop engines immediately. Mel had been assured the messages were relayed, but Patroni ignored them. The heat of Mel's anger still remained; even now, he could cause Joe Patroni serious trouble for the latter's failure to obey, or even acknowledge, an airport management order in a matter of urgency and safety. But Mel knew he wouldn't. Patroni had gotten away with it, and no one with sense quarreled with that kind of success. Also, Mel knew, after tonight there would be one more item to add to the Patroni legend.

The plows and graders were already moving.

Mel switched his radio back to tower frequency. "Mobile one to ground control. Obstructing aircraft has been moved from runway three zero. Vehicles following. I am inspecting for debris."

Mel shone a spotlight from his car over the runway

surface. Tanya and the reporter, Tomlinson, peered
with him. Sometimes incidents like tonight's resulted in
work crews leaving tools or debris—a hazard to aircraft
taking off or landing. The light showed nothing beyond
an irregular surface of snow.

The last of the snowplows was turning off at the
nearest intersection. Mel accelerated and followed. All
three in the car were emotionally drained from tensions
of the past few minutes, but aware that a greater cause
for tension was still to come.

As they swung left, behind the plows, Mel reported,
"Runway three zero clear and open."

16

Trans America Flight Two, *The Golden Argosy,* was
ten miles out, in cloud, at fifteen hundred feet.

Anson Harris, after another brief respite, had resumed flying.

The Lincoln International approach controller—with
a voice vaguely familiar to Vernon Demerest, though he
hadn't stopped to think about it—had guided them thus
far on a series of courses, with gentle turns as they
descended.

They had been, both pilots realized, skillfully positioned so that a final commitment toward either of the
two possible runways could be made without major maneuvering. But the commitment would have to be made
at any moment.

Tension of the pilots grew as that moment approached.

A few minutes earlier, Second Officer Cy Jordan had
returned to the flight deck, on Demerest's orders, to
prepare an estimate of gross landing weight, allowing for
the fuel they had used, and that remaining. Now, having
done everything else necessary at his flight engineer's

position, Jordan had gone back to his emergency landing station in the forward passenger compartment.

Anson Harris, aided by Demerest, had already gone through emergency trim procedures in preparation for landing with their jammed stabilizer.

As they finished, Dr. Compagno appeared briefly behind them. "I thought you'd like to know—your stewardess, Miss Meighen, is holding her own. If we can get her to a hospital soon, I'm fairly sure she'll come through."

Demerest, finding it hard to conceal his sudden emotion, had resorted to not speaking. It was Anson Harris who half-turned and acknowledged, "Thank you, Doctor. We've only a few minutes to go."

In both passenger cabins, all precautions which could be taken were complete. The injured, with the exception of Gwen Meighen, had been strapped in seats. Two of the doctors had stationed themselves on either side of Gwen, ready to support her as they landed. Other passengers had been shown how to brace themselves for what might prove an exceptionally heavy landing, with unknown consequences.

The old lady stowaway, Mrs. Quonsett, a little frightened at last, was tightly clutching the hand of her oboe player friend. Weariness, too, was creeping over her from the exertions of an exceedingly full day.

A short time earlier her spirits had been buoyed by a brief message from Captain Demerest, relayed through a stewardess. The captain thanked her, the stewardess said, for what she had done to help; since Mrs. Quonsett had kept her part of their bargain, after they landed Captain Demerest would keep his by arranging passage for her to New York. How wonderful of that dear man, Ada Quonsett thought, to remember that when he had so much else to think of! . . . But now she wondered: would she be around to make the trip at all?

Judy, the niece of Customs Inspector Standish, had once more been holding the baby whose parents were in the seats beside her. Now she passed the child back to its mother. The baby—least concerned of anyone aboard the airplane—was asleep.

On the flight deck, in the right-hand seat, Vernon Dem-

erest checked the weight information the second
officer had given him against a weight-airspeed plaque
on the pilots' instrument panel. He announced tersely,
"Bug speed 150 knots."

It was the speed at which they must pass over the
airfield boundary, allowing both for weight and the
jammed stabilizer.

Harris nodded. Looking glum, he reached out to set a
warning pointer on his airspeed indicator. Demerest did
the same.

Even on the longest runway their landing would be
risky.

The speed—more than 170 miles per hour—was dia-
bolically fast for landing. Both pilots knew that it would
mean an exceptionally long run after touchdown, with
slow deceleration because of their heavy weight. Thus
their weight became a dual liability. Yet to approach at
anything less than the speed which Demerest had just
computed would be suicidal; the aircraft would stall,
and plummet earthward out of control.

Demerest reached for his radio mike.

Before he could transmit, the voice of Keith Bakersfeld announced, "Trans America Two, turn right on
heading two eight five. Runway three zero is open."

"Jesus Christ!" Demerest said. "And about time!"

He keyed his mike and acknowledged.

Together, both pilots ran through a pre-landing check
list.

There was a "thud" through the airplane as their
landing gear went down.

"I'm going in low," Harris said, "and we'll touch
down early. We're still going to need every bit of real
estate they have down there."

Demerest grunted agreement. He was peering ahead,
straining to penetrate cloud and darkness, to catch a
glimpse of the airport lights which must be visible soon.
His thoughts, despite his own outward calm, were on
the damage to the plane. They still didn't know exactly
how bad it was, or how it might have worsened during
the rough flight in. There was that damned great hole;
then there would be the heavy, fast landing . . . *God!*—
the whole tail assembly might come off . . . If it does,

Demerest thought, at a hundred and fifty knots we've had it . . . *That son-of-a-bitch who had set off the bomb!* A pity he had died! Demerest would like to have his hands on him now, to personally rip out his stinking life . . .

Beside him, Anson Harris, making an Instrument Landing System approach, increased the rate of descent from seven hundred to eight hundred feet per minute.

Demerest wished desperately he were flying himself. With anyone else but Harris—with a younger or less senior captain—Demerest would have taken full command. As it was, he couldn't fault Harris for a thing . . . He hoped the landing would be the same way . . . His thoughts went back to the passenger cabin. *Gwen, we're almost in! Keep on living!* His conviction about their child, that he and Gwen and Sarah would work out something, was as strong as ever.

On radio, Keith Bakersfeld's voice reported, "Trans America Two, your course and descent look fine. There is medium to light snow on runway. Wind northwest, thirty knots. You are number one to land."

Seconds later they emerged from cloud to see runway lights dead ahead.

"Lincoln approach control," Demerest radioed, "we have the runway in sight."

"Roger, Flight Two." Relief in the controller's voice was unmistakable. "The tower clears you to land; monitor their frequency when ready. Good luck, and out."

Vernon Demerest clicked his mike button twice—an airman's shorthand "thank you."

Anson Harris ordered crisply, "Landing lights on. Fifty degrees flap."

Demerest complied.

They were coming down fast.

Harris warned, "I may need help with rudder."

"Right." Demerest set his feet on the rudder pedals. When speed came off, the rudder—because of the destroyed boost mechanism—would be stiff, like a car's power steering which had failed, only more so. After landing, both pilots might need to exert force, together, to maintain directional control.

They zoomed over the airfield edge, runway lights

strung ahead like strands of converging pearls. On either side were piled banks of snow; beyond them, darkness. Harris had made his approach as low as he dared; the nearness to the ground revealed their exceptional speed. To both pilots, the mile and three quarters of runway in front had never looked shorter.

Harris flared out, leveling the aircraft, and closed all four throttles. The jet thrum lessened; an urgent, shrieking wind replaced it. As they crossed the runway's edge, Vernon Demerest had a blurred impression of clustered emergency vehicles which would, he knew, follow them down the runway. He thought: *We damned well might need them! Hang on, Gwen!*

They were still floating, their speed scarcely diminished.

Then the aircraft was down. Heavily. Still traveling fast.

Swiftly, Harris raised wing spoilers and slammed thrust reverse levers upward. With a roar, the jet engines reversed themselves, their force—acting as a brake—now exerted in an opposite direction to the airplane's travel.

They had used three quarters of the runway and were slowing, but not enough.

Harris called, "Right rudder!" The aircraft was veering to the left. With Demerest and Harris shoving together, they maintained direction. But the runway's forward limit—with piled snow and a cavern of darkness beyond—was coming up fast.

Anson Harris was applying toe brakes hard. Metal was straining, rubber screaming. Still the darkness neared. Then they were slowing . . . gradually . . . slowing more . . .

Flight Two came to rest three feet from the runway's end.

17

By the radar room clock, Keith Bakersfeld could see that another half hour of his shift remained. He didn't care.

He pushed back his chair from the radar console, unplugged his headset, and stood up. He looked around him, knowing it was for the last time.

"Hey!" Wayne Tevis said. "What gives?"

"Here," Keith told him. "Take this. Somebody else may need it." He thrust the headset at Tevis, and went out.

Keith knew he should have done it years ago.

He felt a strange lightheadedness, almost a sense of relief. In the corridor outside he wondered why.

It was not because he had guided in Flight Two; he had no illusions about that. Keith had performed competently, but anyone else on duty could have done as well, or better. Nor—as he had known in advance—did anything done tonight wipe out, or counterbalance, what had gone before.

It didn't matter, either, that he had overcome his mental block of ten minutes ago. Keith hadn't cared at the time; he simply wanted out. Nothing that had happened since had changed his mind.

Perhaps, he thought, there had been a purging in his own sudden anger of a few minutes ago, in the admission, never faced before even in private thoughts, of how much he hated aviation, and always had. Now, fifteen years late, he wished he had faced the fact long ago.

He entered the controllers' locker room, with its wooden benches and cluttered notice board. Keith opened his locker and put on his outdoor clothes. There were a few personal things on the locker shelves; he ignored them. All he wanted was the color snapshot of Natalie; he peeled it carefully from the inside surface of the metal door . . . Natalie in a bikini; laughing; her impudent pixyish face, and freckles; her hair streaming . . . When he looked at it, he wanted to cry. Behind the photograph was her note he had treasured:

> *I'm glad we had our ration*
> *With love and passion.*

Keith pocketed both. Someone else could clear the other things out. There was nothing he wanted to remind him of this place—ever.

He stopped.

He stood there, realizing that without intending to, he had come to a new decision. He wasn't sure of everything the decision involved, or how it might seem tomorrow, or even if he could live with it beyond then. If he couldn't live with it, there was still an escape clause; a way out—the drugstore pillbox in his pocket.

For tonight, the main thing was: he was not going to the O'Hagan Inn. He was going home.

But there was one thing he knew: If there was to be a future, it must be removed from aviation. As others who had quit air traffic control before him had discovered, that could prove the hardest thing of all.

And even if that much could be overcome—*face it now,* Keith told himself—there would be times when he would be reminded of the past. Reminded of Lincoln International; of Leesburg; of what had happened at both places. Whatever else you escaped, if you had a whole mind, there was no escaping memory. The memory of the Redfern family who had died . . . of little Valerie Redfern . . . would never leave him.

Yet memory could adapt—couldn't it?—to time, to circumstance, to the reality of living here and now. The Redferns were dead. The Bible said: *Let the dead bury their dead.* What had happened, was done.

Keith wondered if . . . from now on . . . he could remember the Redferns with sadness, but do his best to make the living—Natalie, his own children—his first concern.

He wasn't sure that it would work. He wasn't sure

that he had the moral or the physical strength. It had been a long time since he was sure of anything. But he could try.

He took the tower elevator down.

Outside, on his way to the FAA parking lot, Keith stopped. On sudden impulse, knowing he might regret it later, he took the pillbox from his pocket and emptied its contents into the snow.

18

From his car, which he had parked on the nearby taxiway after quitting runway three zero, Mel Bakersfeld could see that the pilots of Trans America Flight Two were wasting no time in taxiing to the terminal. The aircraft's lights, now halfway across the airfield, were still visible, moving fast. On his radio, switched to ground control, Mel could hear other flights being halted at taxiway and runway intersections to let the damaged airliner pass. The injured were still aboard. Flight Two had been instructed to head directly for gate forty-seven where medical help, ambulances, and company staff were waiting.

Mel watched the aircraft's lights diminish, and merge with the galaxy of terminal lights beyond.

Airport emergency vehicles, which had not after all been required, were dispersing from the runway area.

Tanya and the *Tribune* reporter, Tomlinson, were both on their way back to the terminal. They were driving with Joe Patroni, who had handed over the Aéreo-Mexican 707 for someone else to taxi to the hangars.

Tanya wanted to be at gate forty-seven for the disembarking of passengers from Flight Two. It was likely she would be needed.

Before leaving, she had asked Mel quietly, "Are you still coming home?"

"If it isn't too late," he said, "I'd like to."

He watched while Tanya pushed a strand of red hair back from her face. She had looked at him with her direct, clear eyes and smiled. "It's not too late."

They agreed to meet at the main terminal entrance in three quarters of an hour.

Tomlinson's purpose was to interview Joe Patroni, and after that the crew of Trans America Flight Two. The crew—and Patroni, no doubt—would be heroes within a few hours. The dramatic story of the flight's peril and survival, Mel suspected, would eclipse his own pronouncements on the more mundane subject of the airport's problems and deficiencies.

Though not entirely, perhaps. Tomlinson, to whom Mel had entrusted his opinions, was a thoughtful, intelligent reporter who might decide to link present dramatics with the equally serious long-term view.

The Aéreo-Mexican 707, Mel saw, was now being moved away. The airplane appeared undamaged, but would undoubtedly be washed down and inspected thoroughly before resuming its interrupted flight to Acapulco.

The assortment of service vehicles which had stayed with the aircraft during its ordeal by mud were following.

There was no reason for Mel not to go himself. He would—in a moment or two; but for the second time tonight he found the airfield's loneliness, its closeness to the elemental part of aviation, a stimulus to thought.

It was here, a few hours ago, Mel remembered, that he had had an instinct, a premonition, of events moving toward some disastrous end. Well, in a way they had. The disaster had happened, though through good fortune it had been neither complete, nor had the airport's facilities—or lack of them—been directly responsible.

But the disaster *could* have involved the airport; and the airport in turn might have caused complete catastrophe—through inadequacies which Mel had foreseen and had argued, vainly, to correct.

For Lincoln International was obsolescent.

Obsolescent, Mel knew, despite its good management, and gleaming glass and chrome; despite its air traffic density, its record-breaking passenger volume, its Niagara of air freight, its expectations of even more of everything, and its boastful title, "Aviation Crossroads of the World."

The airport was obsolescent because—as had happened so often in the short six decades of modern aviation history—air progress had eclipsed prediction. Once more, expert prognosticators had been wrong, the visionary dreamers right.

And what was true here was true elsewhere.

Nationwide, worldwide, the story was the same. Much was talked about aviation's growth, its needs, coming developments in the air which would provide the lowest cost transportation of people and goods in human history, the chance these gave the nations of the world to know each other better, in peace, and to trade more freely. Yet little on the ground—in relation to the problem's size—had been done.

Well, one voice alone would not change everything, but each voice which spoke with knowledge and conviction was a help. It had come to Mel within the past few hours—he was not sure why or how—that he intended to continue speaking out the way he had tonight, the way he hadn't for so long.

Tomorrow—or rather, later today—he would begin by summoning, for Monday morning, an emergency special meeting of the Board of Airport Commissioners. When the Board met, he would urge an immediate commitment to build a new runway paralleling three zero.

The experience of tonight had strengthened, as nothing else could, the arguments for increasing runway capacity which Mel had presented long ago. But this time, he determined, he would make a fight of it—with plain, blunt words, warning of catastrophe if public safety were given lip service only, while vital operational needs were ignored or shelved. He would see to it that press and public opinion were marshaled on his side— the kind of pressure which downtown politicians understood.

After new runways, other projects, so far only talked

about or hoped for, must be pressed on; among them—
an entirely new terminal and runway complex; more
imaginative ground flow of people and freight; smaller,
satellite fields for the vertical and short takeoff aircraft
which were coming soon.

Either Lincoln International was in the jet age, or it
wasn't; if it was, it must keep pace far better than it had.

It was not, Mel thought, as if airports were an indulgence or some civic luxury. Almost all were self-sus-
taining, generating wealth and high employment.

Not all the battles for ground-air progress would be
won; they never were. But some of them could be, and
some of what was said and done here—because of Mel's
stature in airport management—could spill over into
national, even international, arenas.

If it did, so much the better! The English poet John
Donne, Mel remembered, had once written: *No man is
an island, entire of itself; every man is a piece of the
continent, a part of the main.* No airport was an island
either; those which called themselves International
should employ the kind of thinking to justify their name.
Perhaps, working with others, Mel could help to show
them how.

People who hadn't heard from Mel Bakersfeld for a
while might quickly learn that he was still around.

And intensive work, a resumption of more of his old
industry-wide interests, might help with personal problems by keeping his mind occupied. Mel hoped so,
anyway. The thought was an abrupt reminder that
sometime soon—perhaps tomorrow—he would have to
call Cindy and arrange to move out his clothes and
personal belongings. It would be an unhappy process
which he hoped the girls, Roberta and Libby, would not
be around to see. To begin with, Mel supposed, he
would move into a hotel until he had time to arrange an
apartment of his own.

But more than ever he knew that Cindy's and his own
decision for divorce had been inevitable. Both of them
had known it; tonight they merely resolved to remove a
facade behind which nothing existed any more. Neither
for themselves nor for the children could anything have
been gained by more delay.

It would still take time, though, to adjust.

And Tanya? Mel was not sure what, if anything, was ahead for them together. He thought there might be a good deal, but the time for a commitment—if there was to be one—was not yet. He only knew that tonight, before this long and complex workday ended, he craved companionship, warmth, and tenderness; and, of all the friends he possessed, Tanya had those qualities in greatest measure.

What else, between himself and Tanya, these might lead to would be known in time.

Mel put his car in gear and swung it toward the perimeter road which would take him to the terminal. Runway three zero was on his right as he drove.

Now that the runway was open, he saw, other aircraft were beginning to use it, arriving in a steady stream despite the lateness. A Convair 880 of TWA swept by and landed. Behind it, half a mile out, were the landing lights of another flight approaching. Behind the second, a third was turning in.

The fact that Mel could see the third set of lights made him aware that the cloud base had lifted. He noticed suddenly that the snowfall had stopped; in a few places to the south, patches of sky were clearing. With relief, he realized the storm was moving on.

ABOUT THE AUTHOR

ARTHUR HAILEY was born in Luton, England, in 1920. He was a flight lieutenant in World War II and served in the Royal Air Force in the Middle and Far East.

His two most recent books, *Airport* and *Hotel,* have been sensational bestsellers. His novels are published in all major languages. His plays have been performed throughout the world on television, and many of his stories have been made into successful motion pictures.

Mr. Hailey lives in California with his wife and three children.

BANTAM BESTSELLERS

OUTSTANDING BOOKS NOW AVAILABLE AT A FRACTION OF THEIR ORIGINAL COST!

If you think this book was good,
wait 'til you see what *else* we've
got in store for you!

Send for your FREE catalog of Bantam Bestsellers today!

This money-saving catalog lists hundreds of best-sellers originally priced from $3.75 to $15.00—yours now in Bantam paperback editions for just 50¢ to $1.95! Here is a great opportunity to read the good books you've missed and add to your private library at huge savings! The catalog is FREE! So don't delay—send for yours today!

Diana Wynne Jones

Castle
in the Air

A GREENWILLOW BOOK

HarperTrophy®
An Imprint of HarperCollins Publishers

Harper Trophy® is a registered trademark of
HarperCollins Publishers Inc.

Castle in the Air
Copyright © 1990 by Diana Wynne Jones
First published in Great Britain in 1990 by Methuen Children's Books.
address HarperCollins Children's Books, a division of HarperCollins Publishers,
195 Broadway, New York, NY 10007

Library of Congress Cataloging-in-Publication Data
Jones, Diana Wynne.
Castle in the air / by Diana Wynne Jones.
p.   cm.
"Greenwillow Books."
Summary: Having long indulged himself in daydreams more exciting than his mundane life
as a carpet merchant, Abdullah unexpectedly purchases a magic carpet and his life changes
dramatically as his daydreams come true and dangerous adventures become daily fare.
ISBN 0-06-029882-0 — ISBN 0-06-447345-7 (pbk.)
[1. Fantasy.] I. Title.
PZ7.J684Cau 1991   90-30266
[Fic]—dc20   CIP
                                                                                    AC

Typography by Karin Paprocki
❖
First Harper Trophy edition, 2001
Visit us on the World Wide Web!
www.harperchildrens.com

16 17 18 QGM 20 19 18 17 16

Castle
in the Air

Contents

Chapter 1

---◆---

In which Abdullah
buys a carpet

Far to the south of the land of Ingary, in the Sultanates of Rashpuht, a young carpet merchant called Abdullah lived in the city of Zanzib. As merchants go, he was not rich. His father had been disappointed in him, and when he died, he had only left Abdullah just enough money to buy and stock a modest booth in the northwest corner of the Bazaar. The rest of his father's money, and the large carpet emporium in the center of the Bazaar, had all gone to the relatives of his father's first wife.

Abdullah had never been told why his father was disappointed in him. A prophecy made at Abdullah's birth had something to do with it. But Abdullah had never bothered to find out more. Instead, from a very early age, he had simply made up daydreams about it. In his daydreams, he was really the long-lost son of a great prince, which meant, of course, that his father was not really his father. It was a complete castle in the air, and Abdullah knew it was. Everyone told him

1

he inherited his father's looks. When he looked in a mirror, he saw a decidedly handsome young man, in a thin, hawk-faced way, and knew he looked very like the portrait of his father as a young man, always allowing for the fact that his father wore a flourishing mustache, whereas Abdullah was still scraping together the six hairs on his upper lip and hoping they would multiply soon.

Unfortunately, as everyone also agreed, Abdullah had inherited his character from his mother—his father's second wife—who had been a dreamy and timorous woman and a great disappointment to everyone. This did not bother Abdullah particularly. The life of a carpet merchant holds few opportunities for bravery, and he was, on the whole, content with it. The booth he had bought, though small, turned out to be rather well placed. It was not far from the West Quarter, where the rich people lived in their big houses surrounded by beautiful gardens. Better still, it was the first part of the Bazaar the carpet makers came to when they came into Zanzib from the desert to the north. Both the rich people and the carpet makers were usually seeking the bigger shops in the center of the Bazaar, but a surprisingly large number of them were ready to pause at the booth of a young carpet merchant when that young merchant rushed out into their paths and offered them bargains and discounts with most profuse politeness.

In this way, Abdullah was quite often able to buy best-quality carpets before anyone else saw them, and sell them at a profit, too. In between buying and selling he could sit in his booth and continue with his daydream, which suited him very well. In fact, almost the only trouble in his life came from his father's first wife's relations, who would keep visiting him once a month in order to point out his failings.

"But you're not saving any of your profits!" cried Abdullah's father's first wife's brother's son, Hakim (whom Abdullah detested), one fateful day.

Abdullah explained that when he made a profit, his custom was to use that money to buy a better carpet. Thus, although all his money was bound up in his stock, it was getting to be better and better stock. He had enough to live on. And as he told his father's relatives, he had no need of more since he was not married.

"Well, you *should* be married!" cried Abdullah's father's first wife's sister, Fatima (whom Abdullah detested even more than Hakim). "I've said it once, and I'll say it again—a young man like you should have at least two wives by now!" And not content with simply saying so, Fatima declared that this time she was going to look out for some wives for him—an offer which made Abdullah shake in his shoes.

"And the more valuable your stock gets, the more likely you are to be robbed, or the more you'll lose if your booth catches fire. Have you thought of that?" nagged Abdullah's father's first wife's uncle's son, Assif (a man whom Abdullah hated more than the first two put together).

He assured Assif that he always slept in the booth and was very careful of the lamps. At that all three of his father's first wife's relatives shook their heads, tut-tutted, and went away. This usually meant they would leave him in peace for another month. Abdullah sighed with relief and plunged straight back into his daydream.

The daydream was enormously detailed by now. In it, Abdullah was the son of a mighty prince who lived so far to the east that his country was unknown in Zanzib. But Abdullah had been kidnapped at the age of two by a villainous bandit called Kabul Aqba. Kabul Aqba had a hooked nose like the beak of a vulture and wore a gold ring clipped into one of his nostrils. He carried a pistol with a silver-mounted stock with which he menaced Abdullah, and there was a bloodstone in his turban which seemed to give him more than human power. Abdullah was so frightened that he ran away into the desert, where he was found by the man he called his father now. The daydream took no account of the fact that Abdullah's father had never ventured into the desert in his life; indeed, he had often said that anyone who ventured beyond Zanzib must be mad. Nevertheless, Abdullah could picture every nightmare inch of the dry, thirsty, foot-sore journey he had made before the good carpet merchant found him. Likewise, he could picture in great detail the palace he had been kidnapped from, with its pillared throne room floored in green porphyry, its women's quarters, and its kitchens, all of the utmost richness. There were seven domes on its roof, each one covered with beaten gold.

Lately, however, the daydream had been concentrating on the princess to whom Abdullah had been betrothed at his birth. She was as highborn as Abdullah and had grown up in his absence into a great beauty with perfect features and huge misty dark eyes. She lived in a palace as rich as Abdullah's own. You approached it along an avenue lined with angelic statues and entered by way of seven marble courts, each with a fountain in the middle more precious than the last, starting with one made of chrysolite and ending with one of platinum studded with emeralds.

But that day Abdullah found he was not quite satisfied with this arrangement. It was a feeling he often had after a visit from his father's first wife's relations. It occurred to him that a good palace ought to have magnificent gardens. Abdullah loved gardens, though he knew very little about them. Most of his experience had come from the public parks of Zanzib—where the turf was somewhat trampled and the flowers few—in which he sometimes spent his lunch hour when he could afford to pay one-eyed Jamal to watch his booth. Jamal kept the fried food stall next door and would, for a coin or so, tie his dog to the front of Abdullah's booth. Abdullah was well aware that this did not really qualify him to invent a proper garden, but since anything was better than thinking of two wives chosen for him by Fatima, he lost himself in waving fronds and scented walkways in the gardens of his princess.

Or nearly. Before Abdullah was fairly started, he was interrupted by a tall, dirty man with a dingy-looking carpet in his arms.

"You buy carpets for selling, son of a great house?" this stranger asked, bowing briefly.

For someone trying to sell a carpet in Zanzib, where buyers and sellers always spoke to one another in the most formal and flowery way, this man's manner was shockingly abrupt. Abdullah was annoyed anyway because his dream garden was falling to pieces at this interruption from real life. He answered curtly. "That is so, O king of the desert. You wish to trade with this miserable merchant?"

"Not trade—sell, O master of a stack of mats," the stranger corrected him.

Mats! thought Abdullah. This was an insult. One of the carpets on display in front of Abdullah's booth was a rare floral tufted one from Ingary—or Ochinstan, as that land was called in Zanzib—and there were at least two inside, from Inhico and Farqtan, which the Sultan himself would not have disdained for one of the smaller rooms of his palace. But of course, Abdullah could not say this. The manners of Zanzib did not let you praise yourself. Instead, he bowed a coldly shallow bow. "It is possible that my low and squalid establishment might provide that which you seek, O pearl of wanderers," he said, and cast his eye critically over the stranger's dirty desert robe, the corroded stud in the side of the man's nose, and his tattered headcloth as he said it.

"It is worse than squalid, mighty seller of floor coverings," the stranger agreed. He flapped one end of his dingy carpet toward Jamal, who was frying squid just then in clouds of blue, fishy smoke. "Does not the honorable activity of your neighbor penetrate your wares," he asked, "even to a lasting aroma of octopus?"

Abdullah seethed with such rage inside that he was forced to rub his hands together slavishly to hide it. People were not supposed to mention this sort of thing. And a slight smell of squid might even improve that thing the stranger wanted to sell, he thought, eyeing the drab and threadbare rug in the man's arms. "Your humble servant takes care to fumigate the interior of his booth with lavish perfumes, O prince of wisdom," he said. "Perhaps the heroic sensitivity of the prince's nose will nevertheless allow him to show

7

this beggarly trader his merchandise?"

"Of course, it does, O lily among mackerel," the stranger retorted. "Why else should I stand here?"

Abdullah reluctantly parted the curtains and ushered the man inside his booth. There he turned up the lamp which hung from the center pole but, upon sniffing, decided that he was not going to waste incense on this person. The interior smelled quite strongly enough of yesterday's scents. "What magnificence have you to unroll before my unworthy eyes?" he asked dubiously.

"This, buyer of bargains!" the man said, and with a deft thrust of one arm, he caused the carpet to unroll across the floor.

Abdullah could do this, too. A carpet merchant learned these things. He was not impressed. He stuck his hands in his sleeves in a primly servile attitude and surveyed the merchandise. The carpet was not large. Unrolled, it was even dingier than he had thought— although the pattern was unusual, or it would have been if most of it had not been worn away. What was left was dirty, and its edges were frayed.

"Alas, this poor salesman can only stretch to three copper coins for this most ornamental of rugs," he observed. "It is the limit of my slender purse. Times are hard, O captain of many camels. Is the price acceptable in any way?"

"I'll take FIVE HUNDRED," said the stranger.

"What?" said Abdullah.

"GOLD coins," added the stranger.

"The king of all desert bandits is surely pleased to jest?" said Abdullah. "Or maybe, having found my small booth lacking in anything but the smell of frying squid, he wishes to leave and try a richer merchant?"

"Not particularly," said the stranger. "Although I will leave if you are not interested, O neighbor of kippers. It is, of course, a magic carpet."

Abdullah had heard that one before. He bowed over his tucked-up hands. "Many and various are the virtues said to reside in carpets," he agreed. "Which one does the poet of the sands claim for this? Does it welcome a man home to his tent? Does it bring peace to the hearth? Or maybe," he said, poking the frayed edge suggestively with one toe, "it is said never to wear out?"

"It flies," said the stranger. "It flies wherever the owner commands, O smallest of small minds."

Abdullah looked up into the man's somber face, where the desert had entrenched deep lines down each cheek. A sneer made those lines deeper still. Abdullah found he disliked this person almost as much as he disliked his father's first wife's uncle's son. "You must convince this unbeliever," he said. "If the carpet can be put through its paces, O monarch of mendacity, then some bargain might be struck."

"Willingly," said the tall man, and stepped upon the carpet.

9

At this moment one of the regular upsets happened at the fried food stall next door. Probably some street boys had tried to steal some squid. At any rate, Jamal's dog burst out barking; various people, Jamal included, began yelling, and both sounds were nearly drowned by the clash of saucepans and the hissing of hot fat.

Cheating was a way of life in Zanzib. Abdullah did not allow his attention to be distracted for one instant from the stranger and his carpet. It was quite possible the man had bribed Jamal to cause a distraction. He had mentioned Jamal rather often, as if Jamal were on his mind. Abdullah kept his eyes sternly on the tall figure of the man and particularly on the dirty feet planted on the carpet. But he spared a corner of one eye for the man's face, and he saw the man's lips move. His alert ears even caught the words *two feet upward* despite the din from next door. And he looked even more carefully when the carpet rose smoothly from the floor and hovered about level with Abdullah's knees, so that the stranger's tattered headgear was not quite brushing the roof of the booth. Abdullah looked for rods underneath. He searched for wires that might have been deftly hooked to the roof. He took hold of the lamp and tipped it about, so that its light played both over and under the carpet.

The stranger stood with his arms folded and the sneer entrenched on his face while Abdullah performed these tests. "See?" he said. "Is the most desperate of doubters now convinced? Am I standing in the air, or am I not?" He had to shout. The noise was still deafening from next door.

Abdullah was forced to admit that the carpet did appear to be up in the air without any means of support that he could find. "Very nearly," he shouted back. "The next part of the demonstration is for you to dismount and for me to ride that carpet."

The man frowned. "Why so? What have your other senses to add to the evidence of your eyes, O dragon of dubiety?"

"It could be a one-man carpet," Abdullah bawled, "as some dogs are." Jamal's dog was still bellowing away outside, so it was natural to think of this. Jamal's dog bit anyone who touched it except Jamal.

The stranger sighed. "Down," he said, and the carpet sank gently to the floor. The stranger stepped off and bowed Abdullah toward it. "It is yours to test, O sheikh of shrewdness."

With considerable excitement, Abdullah stepped onto the carpet. "Go up two feet," he said to it—or, rather, yelled. It sounded as if the constables of the City Watch had arrived at Jamal's stall now. They were clashing weapons and bawling to be told what had happened.

And the carpet obeyed Abdullah. It rose two feet in a smooth surge which left Abdullah's stomach behind it. He sat down rather hastily. The carpet was perfectly comfortable to sit on. It felt like a very tight hammock. "This woefully sluggish intellect is becoming convinced," he confessed to the stranger. "What was your price again, O paragon of generosity? Two hundred silver?"

"Five hundred GOLD," said the stranger. "Tell the carpet to descend, and we will discuss the matter."

Abdullah told the carpet, "Down, and land on the floor," and it did so, thus removing a slight nagging doubt in Abdullah's mind that the stranger had said something extra when Abdullah first stepped on it which had been drowned in the din from next door. He bounced to his feet, and the bargaining commenced. "The utmost of my purse is one hundred and fifty gold," he explained, "and that is when I shake it out and feel all around the seams."

"Then you must fetch out your other purse or even feel under your mattress," the stranger rejoined. "For the limit of my generosity is four hundred and ninety-five gold, and I would not sell at all but for the most pressing need."

"I might squeeze another forty-five gold from the sole of my left shoe," Abdullah replied. "That I keep for emergencies, and it is my pitiful all."

"Examine your right shoe," the stranger answered. "Four-fifty."

And so it went on. An hour later the stranger

departed from the booth with 210 gold pieces, leaving Abdullah the delighted owner of what seemed to be a genuine—if threadbare—magic carpet. He was still mistrustful. He did not believe that anyone, even a desert wanderer with few needs, would part with a real flying carpet—albeit nearly worn out—for less than 400 gold pieces. It was too useful—better than a camel, because it did not need to eat—and a good camel cost at least 450 in gold.

There had to be a catch. And there was one trick Abdullah had heard of. It was usually worked with horses or dogs. A man would come and sell a trusting farmer or hunter a truly superb animal for a surprisingly small price, saying that it was all that stood between himself and starvation. The delighted farmer (or hunter) would put the horse in a stall (or the dog in a kennel) for the night. In the morning it would be gone, being trained to slip its halter (or collar) and return to its owner in the night. It seemed to Abdullah that a suitably obedient carpet could be trained to do the same. So, before he left his booth, he very carefully wrapped the magic carpet around one of the poles that supported the roof and bound it there, around and around, with a whole reel of twine, which he then tied to one of the iron stakes at the base of the wall.

"I think you'll find it hard to escape from that," he told it, and went out to discover what had been going on at the food stall.

The stall was quiet now, and tidy. Jamal was sitting on its counter, mournfully hugging his dog.

"What happened?" asked Abdullah.

"Some thieving boys spilled all my squid," Jamal said. "My whole day's stock down in the dirt, lost, gone!"

Abdullah was so pleased with his bargain that he gave Jamal two silver pieces to buy more squid. Jamal wept with gratitude and embraced Abdullah. His dog not only failed to bite Abdullah; it licked his hand. Abdullah smiled. Life was good. He went off whistling to find a good supper while the dog guarded his booth.

When the evening was staining the sky red behind the domes and minarets of Zanzib, Abdullah came back, still whistling, full of plans to sell the carpet to the Sultan himself for a very large price indeed. He found the carpet exactly where he had left it. Or would it be better to approach the Grand Vizier, he wondered while he was washing, and suggest that the Vizier might wish to make the Sultan a present of it? That way he could ask for even more money. At the thought of how valuable that made the carpet, the story of the horse trained to slip its halter began to nag at him again. As he got into his nightshirt, Abdullah began to visualize the carpet wriggling free. It was old and pliable. It was probably very well trained. It could certainly slither out from behind the twine. Even if it did not, he knew the idea would keep him awake all night.

In the end, he carefully cut the twine away and spread the carpet on top of the pile of his most valuable rugs, which he always used as a bed. Then he put on his nightcap—which was necessary, because the cold winds blew off the desert and filled the booth with drafts—spread his blanket over him, blew out his lamp, and slept.

Chapter 2

⊷—⋈—⊶

In which Abdullah is mistaken
for a young lady

He woke to find himself lying on a bank, with the carpet still underneath him, in a garden more beautiful than any he had imagined.

Abdullah was convinced that this was a dream. Here was the garden he had been trying to imagine when the stranger so rudely interrupted him. Here the moon was nearly full and riding high above, casting light as white as paint on a hundred small fragrant flowers in the grass around him. Round yellow lamps hung in the trees, dispelling the dense black shadows from the moon. Abdullah thought this was a very pleasing idea. By the two lights, white and yellow, he could see an arcade of creepers supported on elegant pillars, beyond the lawn where he lay, and from somewhere behind that, hidden water was quietly trickling.

It was so cool and so heavenlike that Abdullah got up and went in search of the hidden water, wandering down the arcade, where starry blooms brushed his face, all white and hushed in the moonlight, and bell-like flowers breathed out the headiest and gentlest of scents. As one does in dreams, Abdullah fingered a great waxy lily here and detoured deliciously there into a dell of pale roses. He had never before had a dream that was anything like so beautiful.

The water, when he found it beyond some big fernlike bushes dripping dew, was a simple marble fountain in another lawn, lit by strings of lamps in the bushes, which made the rippling water into a marvel of gold and silver crescents. Abdullah wandered toward it raptly.

There was only one thing needed to complete his rapture, and as in all the best dreams, it was there. An extremely lovely girl came across the lawn to meet him, treading softly on the damp grass with bare feet. The gauzy garments floating around her showed her to be slender, but not thin, just like the princess from Abdullah's daydream. When she was near Abdullah, he saw that her face was not quite a perfect oval as the face of his dream princess should have been, nor were her huge dark eyes at all misty. In fact, they examined his face keenly, with evident interest. Abdullah hastily adjusted his dream, for she was certainly very beautiful. And when she spoke, her voice was all he could have desired, being light and merry as the water in the fountain and the voice of a very definite person, too.

"Are you a new kind of servant?" she said.

People always did ask strange things in dreams,

Abdullah thought. "No, masterpiece of my imagination," he said. "Know that I am really the long-lost son of a distant prince."

"Oh," she said. "Then that may make a difference. Does that mean you're a different kind of woman from me?"

Abdullah stared at the girl of his dreams in some perplexity. "*I'm* not a woman!" he said.

"Are you sure?" she asked. "You *are* wearing a dress."

Abdullah looked down and discovered that, in the way of dreams, he was wearing his nightshirt. "This is just my strange foreign garb," he said hastily. "My true country is far from here. I assure you that I am a man."

"Oh, no," she said decidedly. "You can't be a man. You're quite the wrong shape. Men are twice as thick as you all over, and their stomachs come out in a fat bit that's called a belly. And they have gray hair all over their faces and nothing but shiny skin on their heads. You've got hair on your head like me and almost none on your face." Then, as Abdullah put his hand rather indignantly to the six hairs on his upper lip, she asked, "Or have you got bare skin under your hat?"

"Certainly not," said Abdullah, who was proud of his thick, wavy hair. He put his hand to his head and removed what turned out to be his nightcap. "Look," he said.

"Ah," she said. Her lovely face was puzzled. "You have hair that's almost as nice as mine. I don't understand."

"I'm not sure I do, either," said Abdullah. "Could it be that you have not seen very many men?"

"Of course not," she said. "Don't be silly. I've only seen my father! But I've seen quite a lot of him, so I *do* know."

"But don't you ever go out at all?" Abdullah asked helplessly.

She laughed. "Yes, I'm out now. This is my night garden. My father had it made so that I wouldn't ruin my looks going out in the sun."

"I mean, out into the town, to see all the people," Abdullah explained.

"Well, no, not yet," she admitted. As if that bothered her a little, she twirled away from him and went to sit on the edge of the fountain. Turning to look up at him, she said, "My father tells me I *might* be able to go out and see the town sometimes after I'm married—if my husband allows me to—but it won't be *this* town. My father's arranging for me to marry a prince from Ochinstan. Until then I have to stay inside these walls, of course."

Abdullah had heard that some of the very rich people in Zanzib kept their daughters—and even their wives, too—almost like prisoners inside their grand houses. He had many times wished someone would keep his father's first wife's sister, Fatima, that way. But now, in this dream, it seemed to him that this custom was entirely unreasonable and not fair to this lovely girl at all. Fancy not knowing what a normal young man looked like!

"Pardon my asking, but is the Prince from Ochinstan perhaps old and a little ugly?" he said.

"Well," she said, evidently not quite sure, "my father says he's in his prime, just as my father is himself. But I believe the problem lies in the brutal nature of men. If another man saw me before the Prince did, my father says he would instantly fall in love with me and carry me off, which would ruin all my father's plans, naturally. He says most men are great beasts. Are you a beast?"

"Not in the least," said Abdullah.

"I thought not," she said, and looked up at him with great concern. "You do not seem to me to be a beast. This makes me quite sure that you can't really be a man." Evidently she was one of those people who like to cling to a theory once they have made it. After considering a moment, she asked, "Could your family, perhaps, for reasons of their own, have brought you up to believe a falsehood?"

Abdullah would have liked to say that the boot was on the other foot, but since that struck him as impolite, he simply shook his head and thought how generous of her it was to be so worried about him and how the worry on her face only made it more beautiful—not to speak of the way her eyes shone compassionately in the gold and silver light reflecting from the fountain.

"Perhaps it has something to do with the fact that you are from a distant country," she said, and patted the edge of the fountain beside her. "Sit down and tell me all about it."

"Tell me your name first," said Abdullah.

"It's rather a silly name," she said nervously. "I'm called Flower-in-the-Night."

It was the perfect name for the girl of his dreams, Abdullah thought. He gazed down at her admiringly. "My name is Abdullah," he said.

"They even gave you a man's name!" Flower-in-the-Night exclaimed indignantly. "Do sit down and tell me."

Abdullah sat on the marble curb beside her and thought that this was a very real dream. The stone was cold. Splashes from the fountain soaked into his nightshirt, while the sweet smell of rose water from Flower-in-the-Night mingled most realistically with scents from the flowers in the garden. But since it was a dream, it followed that his daydreams were true here, too. So Abdullah told her all about the palace he had lived in as a prince and how he was kidnapped by Kabul Aqba and escaped into the desert, where the carpet merchant found him.

Flower-in-the-Night listened with complete sympathy. "How terrifying! How exhausting!" she said. "Could it be that your foster father was in league with the bandits to deceive you?"

Abdullah had a growing feeling, despite the fact that he was only dreaming, that he was getting her sympathy on false pretenses. He agreed that his father could have been in the pay of Kabul Aqba and then changed the subject. "Let us get back to *your* father and his plans," he said. "It seems to me a little awkward that you should marry this Prince from Ochinstan without having seen any other men to compare him with. How are you going to know whether you love him or not?"

"You have a point," she said. "This worries me, too, sometimes."

"Then I tell you what," Abdullah said. "Suppose I come back tomorrow night and bring you pictures of as many men as I can find? That should give you some standard to compare the Prince with." Dream or not, Abdullah had absolutely no doubt that he would be back tomorrow. This would give him a proper excuse.

Flower-in-the-Night considered this offer, swaying dubiously back and forth with her hands clasped around her knees. Abdullah could almost see rows of fat, bald men with gray beards passing in front of her mind's eye.

"I assure you," he said, "that men come in every sort of size and shape."

"Then that would be very instructive," she agreed. "At least it would give me an excuse to see you again. You're one of the nicest people I've ever met."

This made Abdullah even more determined to come back tomorrow. He told himself it would be unfair to leave her in such a state of ignorance. "And I think the same about you," he said shyly.

At this, to his disappointment, Flower-in-the-Night got up to leave. "I have to go indoors now," she said. "A first visit must last no longer than half an hour, and I'm almost sure you've been here twice as long as that. But now we know each other, you can stay at least two hours next time."

"Thank you. I shall," said Abdullah.

She smiled and passed away like a dream, beyond the fountain and behind two frondy flowering shrubs.

After that the garden, the moonlight, and the scents seemed rather tame. Abdullah could think of nothing better to do than wander back the way he had come. And there, on the moonlit bank, he found the carpet. He had forgotten about it completely. But since it was there in the dream, too, he lay down on it and fell asleep.

He woke up some hours later with blinding daylight streaming in through the chinks in his booth. The smell of the day before yesterday's incense hanging about in the air struck him as cheap and suffocating. In fact, the whole booth was fusty and frowsty and cheap. And he had an earache because his nightcap seemed to have fallen off in the night. But at least, he found while he hunted for the nightcap, the carpet had not made off in the night. It was still underneath him. This was the one good thing he could see in what suddenly struck him as a thoroughly dull and depressing life.

Here Jamal, who was still grateful for the silver pieces, shouted outside that he had breakfast ready for both of them. Abdullah gladly flung back the curtains of the booth. Cocks crowed in the distance. The sky was glowing blue, and shafts of strong sunlight sliced through the blue dust and old incense inside the booth. Even in that strong light, Abdullah failed to discover his nightcap. And he was more depressed than ever.

"Tell me, do you sometimes find yourself unaccountably sad on some days?" he asked Jamal as the two of them sat cross-legged in the sun outside to eat.

Jamal tenderly fed a piece of sugar pastry to his dog. "I would have been sad today," he said, "but for you. I think someone paid those wretched boys to steal. They were so thorough. And on top of that, the Watch fined me. Did I say? I think I have enemies, my friend."

Though this confirmed Abdullah's suspicions of the stranger who had sold him the carpet, it was not much help. "Maybe," he said, "you should be more careful about whom you let your dog bite."

"Not I!" said Jamal. "I am a believer in free will. If my dog chooses to hate the whole human race except myself, it must be free to do so."

After breakfast Abdullah looked for his nightcap again. It was simply not there. He tried thinking carefully back to the last time he truly remembered wearing it. That was when he had lain down to sleep the previous night, when he was thinking of taking the carpet to the Grand Vizier. After that came the dream. He had found he was wearing the nightcap then. He remembered taking it off to show Flower-in-the-Night (what a lovely name!) that he was not bald. From then on, as far as he could recall, he had carried the nightcap in his hand until the moment when he had sat down beside her on the edge of the fountain. After that, when he recounted the history of his kidnapping by Kabul Aqba, he had a clear memory of waving both hands freely as he talked, and he knew that the nightcap had not been in either one. Things did disappear like that in dreams, he knew, but the evidence pointed, all the same, to his having dropped it as he sat down. Was it possible he had left it lying on the grass beside the fountain? In which case—

Abdullah stood stock-still in the center of the booth, staring into the rays of sunlight, which, oddly enough, no longer seemed full of squalid motes of dust and old incense. Instead, they were pure golden slices of heaven itself.

"It was *not a dream!*" said Abdullah.

Somehow his depression was clean gone. Even breathing was easier.

"It was *real!*" he said.

He went to stand thoughtfully looking down at the magic carpet. That had been in the dream, too. In which case—

"It follows that you transported me to some rich man's garden while I slept," he said to it. "Perhaps I spoke and ordered you to do so in my sleep. Very likely. I was thinking of gardens. You are even more valuable than I realized!"

26

Chapter 3

──◆──

In which Flower-in-the-Night
discovers several important facts

A bdullah carefully tied the carpet around the roof pole again and went out into the Bazaar, where he sought out the booth of the most skillful of the various artists who traded there.

After the usual opening courtesies, in which Abdullah called the artist prince of the pencil and enchanter with chalks and the artist retorted by calling Abdullah cream of customers and duke of discernment, Abdullah said, "I want drawings of every size, shape, and kind of man that you have ever seen. Draw me kings and paupers, merchants and workmen, fat and thin, young and old, handsome and ugly, and also plain average. If some of these are kinds of men that you have never seen, I require you to invent them, O paragon of the paintbrush. And if your invention fails, which I hardly think is likely, O aristocrat of artists, then all you need do is turn your eyes outward, gaze, and copy!"

Abdullah flung out one arm to point to the

teeming, rushing crowds shopping in the Bazaar. He was moved almost to tears at the thought that this everyday sight was something Flower-in-the-Night had never seen.

The artist drew his hand dubiously down his straggly beard. "For sure, noble admirer of mankind," he said, "this I can do easily. But could the jewel of judgment perhaps inform this humble draftsman what these many portraits of men are needed for?"

"Why should the crown and diadem of the drawing board wish to know this?" Abdullah asked, rather dismayed.

"Assuredly, the chieftain of customers will understand that this crooked worm needs to know what medium to use," the artist replied. In fact, he was simply curious about this most unusual order. "Whether I paint in oils on wood or canvas, in pen upon paper or vellum, or even in fresco upon a wall depends on what this pearl among patrons wishes to do with the portraits."

"Ah, paper, please," Abdullah said hastily. He had no wish to make his meeting with Flower-in-the-Night public. It was clear to him that her father must be a very rich man who would certainly object to a young carpet merchant's showing her other men besides this Prince of Ochinstan. "The portraits are for an invalid who has never been able to walk abroad as other men do."

"Then you are a champion of charity," said the artist, and he agreed to draw the pictures for a surprisingly small sum. "No, no, child of fortune, do not thank me," he said when Abdullah tried to express his gratitude. "My reasons are three. First, I have laid by me many portraits which I do for my own pleasure, and to charge you for those is not honest since I would have drawn them anyway. Second, the task you set is ten times more interesting than my usual work, which is to do portraits of young women or their bridegrooms, or of horses and camels, all of whom I have to make handsome, regardless of reality; or else to paint rows of sticky children whose parents wish them to seem like angels—again regardless of reality. And my third reason is that I think you are mad, my most noble of customers, and to exploit you would be unlucky."

It became known almost immediately, all over the Bazaar, that young Abdullah, the carpet merchant, had lost his reason and would buy any portraits that people had for sale.

This was a great nuisance to Abdullah. For the rest of that day he was constantly being interrupted by persons arriving with long and flowery speeches about this portrait of their grandmother which only poverty would induce them to part with; or this portrait of the Sultan's racing camel which happened to fall off the back of a cart; or this locket containing a picture of their sister. It took Abdullah much time to get rid of these people—and on several occasions he did actually buy a painting or drawing if the subject was a man. That, of course, kept people coming.

"Only today. My offer extends only until sunset today," he told the gathering crowd at last. "Let all with a picture of a *man* for sale come to me an hour before sunset and I will buy. But only then."

This left him a few hours of peace in which to experiment with the carpet. He was wondering by now if he was right to think that his visit to the garden had been any more than a dream. For the carpet would not move. Abdullah had naturally tested it after breakfast by asking it to rise up two feet again, just to prove that it still would. And it simply lay on the floor. He tested it again when he came back from the artist's booth, and still it just lay there.

"Perhaps I have not treated you well," he said to it. "You have remained with me faithfully, in spite of my suspicions, and I have rewarded you by tying you around a pole. Would you feel better if I let you lie free on the floor, my friend? Is that it?"

He left the carpet on the floor, but it still would not fly. It might have been any old hearthrug.

Abdullah thought again, in between the times when people were pestering him to buy portraits. He went back to his suspicions of the stranger who had sold him this carpet and to the enormous noise that just happened to break out in Jamal's stall at the precise moment when the stranger ordered the carpet to rise. He recalled that he had seen the man's lips move both times but had not heard all that was said.

"That is *it!*" he cried out, smashing his fist into his palm. "A code word needs to be spoken before it will move, which for reasons of his own—no doubt highly sinister—this man withheld from me. The villain! And this word I must have spoken in my sleep."

He rushed to the back of his booth and rummaged out the tattered dictionary he had once used at school. Then, standing on the carpet, he cried out, "Aardvark! Fly, please!"

Nothing happened, either then or for any word beginning with *A*. Doggedly Abdullah went on to *B*, and when that did no good, he went on again, through the whole dictionary. With the constant interruptions from portrait sellers, this took him some time. Nevertheless, he reached *zymurgy* in the early evening without the carpet's having so much as twitched.

"Then it has to be a made-up word or a foreign one!" he cried out feverishly. It was that or believe that Flower-in-the-Night was only a dream after all. Even if she was real, his chances of getting the carpet to take him to her seemed slimmer by the minute. He stood there uttering every strange sound and every foreign word he could think of, and still the carpet made no move of any kind.

Abdullah was interrupted again an hour before sundown by a large crowd gathering outside, carrying bundles and big flat packages. The artist had to push his way through the crowd with his portfolio of drawings. The following hour was hectic in the extreme. Abdullah inspected paintings, rejected portraits of aunts and mothers, and beat down huge prices asked for bad drawings of nephews. In the course of that hour he acquired, beside the hundred excellent drawings from the artist, eighty-nine further pictures, lockets, drawings, and even a piece of a wall with a face daubed on it. He also parted with almost all the money he had left over after buying the magic carpet—if it *was* magic. It was dark by the time he finally convinced the man who claimed that the oil painting of his fourth wife's mother was enough like a man to qualify that this was not the case and pushed him out of the booth. He was by then too tired and wrought up to eat. He would have gone straight to bed had not Jamal—who had been doing a roaring trade selling snacks to the waiting crowd—arrived with tender meat on a skewer.

"I don't know what has got into you," Jamal said. "I used to think you were normal. But mad or not, you must eat."

"There is no question of madness," Abdullah said. "I have simply decided to go into a new line of business." But he ate the meat.

At last he was able to pile his 189 pictures onto the carpet and lie down among them.

"Now listen to this," he told the carpet. "If by some lucky chance I happen to say your command word in my sleep, you must instantly fly with me to the night garden of Flower-in-the-Night." That seemed the best he could do. It took him a long time to get to sleep.

He woke to the dreamy fragrance of night flowers and a hand gently prodding him. Flower-in-the-Night was leaning over him. Abdullah saw she was far lovelier than he had been remembering her.

"You really did bring the pictures!" she said. "You are very kind."

I *did* it! Abdullah thought triumphantly. "Yes," he said. "I have one hundred and eighty-nine kinds of men here. I think this ought to give you at least a general idea."

He helped her unhook a number of the golden lamps and put them in a ring beside the bank. Then Abdullah showed her the pictures, holding them under a lamp first and then leaning them up against the bank. He began to feel like a pavement artist.

Flower-in-the-Night inspected each man as Abdullah showed him, absolutely impartially and with great concentration. Then she picked up a lamp and inspected the artist's drawings all over again. This pleased Abdullah. The artist was a true professional. He had drawn men exactly as Abdullah asked, from a heroic and kingly person evidently taken from a statue, to the hunchback who cleaned shoes in the Bazaar, and had even included a self-portrait halfway through.

"Yes, I see," Flower-in-the-Night said at last. "Men do vary a lot, just as you said. My father is not at all typical, and neither are you, of course."

"So you admit I am not a woman?" said Abdullah.

"I am forced to do so," she said. "I apologize for my error." Then she carried the lamp along the bank, inspecting certain of the pictures a third time.

Abdullah noticed, rather nervously, that the ones she had singled out were the handsomest. He watched her leaning over them with a small frown on her forehead and a curly tendril of dark hair straying over the frown, looking thoroughly intent. He began to wonder what he had started.

Flower-in-the-Night collected the pictures together and stacked them neatly in a pile beside the bank. "It is just as I thought," she said. "I prefer you to every single one of these. Some of these look far too proud of themselves, and some look selfish and cruel. You are unassuming and kind. I intend to ask my father to marry me to you, instead of to the Prince in Ochinstan. Would you mind?"

The garden seemed to swirl around Abdullah in

34

a blur of gold and silver and dusky green. "I—I think that might not work," he managed to say at last.

"Why not?" she asked. "Are you married already?"

"No, no," he said. "It is not that. The law allows a man to have as many wives as he can afford, but——"

The frown came back to Flower-in-the-Night's forehead. "How many husbands are women allowed?" she asked.

"Only one!" Abdullah said, rather shocked.

"That is extremely unfair," Flower-in-the-Night observed musingly. She sat on the bank and thought. "Would you say it is possible that the Prince in Ochinstan has some wives already?"

Abdullah watched the frown grow on her forehead and the slender fingers of her right hand tapping almost irritably on the turf. He knew he had indeed started something. Flower-in-the-Night was discovering that her father had kept her ignorant of a number of important facts. "If he is a prince," Abdullah said rather nervously, "I think it entirely possible that he has quite a number of wives. Yes."

"Then he is being greedy," Flower-in-the-Night stated. "This takes a weight off my mind. Why did you say that my marrying you might not work? You mentioned yesterday that you are a prince as well."

Abdullah felt his face heating up, and he cursed himself for babbling out his daydream to her. Though he told himself that he had had every reason to believe

35

he was dreaming when he told her, this did not make him feel any better. "True. But I also told you I was lost and far from my kingdom," he said. "As you might conjecture, I am now forced to make my living by humble means. I sell carpets in the Bazaar of Zanzib. Your father is clearly a very rich man. This will not strike him as a fitting alliance."

Flower-in-the-Night's fingers drummed quite angrily. "You speak as if it is my *father* who intends to marry you!" she said. "What is the matter? I love you. Do you not love me?"

She looked into Abdullah's face as she said this. He looked back into hers, into what seemed an eternity of big dark eyes. He found himself saying, *"Yes."* Flower-in-the-Night smiled. Abdullah smiled. Several more moonlit eternities went by.

"I shall come with you when you leave here," Flower-in-the-Night said. "Since what you say about my father's attitude to you could well be true, we must get married first and tell my father afterward. Then there is nothing he can say."

Abdullah, who had had some experience of rich men, wished he could be sure of that. "It may not be quite that simple," he said. "In fact, now I think about it, I am certain our only prudent course is to leave Zanzib. This ought to be easy, because I do happen to own a magic carpet. There it is, up on the bank. It brought me here. Unfortunately it needs to be activated by a magic word which I seem only able to say in my sleep."

Flower-in-the-Night picked up a lamp and held it high so that she could inspect the carpet. Abdullah watched, admiring the grace with which she bent toward it. "It seems very old," she said. "I have read about such carpets. The command word will probably be a fairly common word pronounced in an old way. My reading suggests these carpets were meant to be used quickly in an emergency, so the word will not be anything too out of the way. Why do you not tell me carefully everything you know about it? Between us we ought to be able to work it out."

From this Abdullah realized that Flower-in-the-Night—if you discounted the gaps in her knowledge—was both intelligent and very well educated. He admired her even more. He told her, as far as he knew them, every fact about the carpet, including the uproar at Jamal's stall which had prevented him hearing the command word.

Flower-in-the-Night listened and nodded at each new fact. "So," she said, "let us leave aside the reason why someone should sell you a proven magic carpet and yet make sure you could not use it. That is such an odd thing to do that I feel sure we should think about it later. But let us first think about what the carpet does. You say it came down when you ordered it to. Did the stranger speak then?"

She had a shrewd and logical mind. Truly he had found a pearl among women, Abdullah thought. "I am quite sure he said nothing," he said.

"Then," said Flower-in-the-Night, "the command word is only needed to start the carpet flying. After that I see two possibilities: first, that the carpet will do as you say until it touches ground anywhere or, second, that it will in fact obey your command until it is back at the place where it first started—"

"That is easily proved," Abdullah said. He was dizzy with admiration for her logic. "I think the first possibility is the correct one." He jumped on the carpet and cried experimentally, "Up, and back to my booth!"

"No, no! Don't! Wait!" Flower-in-the-Night cried out at the same instant.

But it was too late. The carpet whipped up into the air and then away sideways with such speed and suddenness that Abdullah was first thrown over on his back, with all the breath knocked out of him, and then found himself hanging half off over its frayed edge at what seemed a terrifying height in the air. The wind of its movement took his breath away as soon as he did manage to breathe. All he could do was to claw frantically for a better grip on the fringe at one end. And before he could work his way back on top of it, let alone speak, the carpet plunged downward—leaving Abdullah's newly gained breath high in the air above—barged its way through the curtains of the booth—half smothering Abdullah in the process—and landed smoothly—and very finally—on the floor inside.

Abdullah lay on his face, gasping, with dizzy memories of turrets whirling past him against a starry sky. Everything had happened so quickly that at first all he could think of was that the distance between his booth and the night garden must be quite surprisingly short. Then, as his breath did at last come back, he wanted to kick himself. What a *stupid* thing to have done! He could at least have waited until Flower-in-the-Night had had time to step on the carpet, too. Now Flower-in-the-Night's own logic told him that there was no way to get back to her but to fall asleep again and, once more, hope he chanced to say the command word in his sleep. But as he had already done it twice, he was fairly sure that he would. He was even more certain that Flower-in-the-Night would work this out for herself and wait in the garden for him. She was intelligence itself—a pearl among women. She would expect him back in an hour or so.

After an hour of alternately blaming himself and praising Flower-in-the-Night, Abdullah did manage to fall asleep. But alas, when he woke he was still facedown on the carpet in the middle of his own booth. Jamal's dog was barking outside, which

39

was what had woken him up.

"Abdullah!" shouted the voice of his father's first wife's brother's son. "Are you awake in there?"

Abdullah groaned. This was all he needed.

Chapter 4

Which concerns marriage
and prophecy

Abdullah could not think what Hakim was doing there. His father's first wife's relatives usually only came near him once a month, and they had paid that visit to him two days ago. "What do you want, Hakim?" he shouted wearily.

"To speak to you, of course!" Hakim shouted back. "Urgently!"

"Then part the curtains and come in," said Abdullah.

Hakim inserted his plump body between the hangings. "I must say, if this is your vaunted security, son of my aunt's husband," he said, "I don't think much of it. Anyone could come in here and surprise you as you slept."

"The dog outside warned me you were there," Abdullah said.

"What use is that?" asked Hakim. "What would you propose to do if I proved to be a thief? Strangle me with a carpet? No, I cannot approve the

41

safety of your arrangements."

"What do you wish to say to me?" asked Abdullah. "Or did you only come here to find fault as usual?"

Hakim seated himself portentously on a pile of carpets. "You lack your normal scrupulous politeness, cousin by marriage," he said. "If my father's uncle's son were to hear you, he would not be pleased."

"I am not answerable to Assif for my behavior or for anything else!" Abdullah snapped. He was thoroughly miserable. His soul cried out for Flower-in-the-Night, and he could not get to her. He had no patience with anything else.

"Then I shall not trouble you with my message," Hakim said, getting up haughtily.

"Good!" said Abdullah. He went to the back of his booth to wash.

But it was clear that Hakim was not going away without delivering his message. When Abdullah turned around from washing, Hakim was still standing there. "You would do well to change clothes and visit a barber, cousin by marriage," he told Abdullah. "At present you do not look a suitable person to visit our emporium."

"And why should I visit there?" Abdullah asked, somewhat surprised. "You all made it clear long ago that I am not welcome there."

"Because," said Hakim, "the prophecy made at

your birth has come to light in a box long thought to contain incense. If you care to present yourself at the emporium in proper apparel, this box will be handed over to you."

Abdullah had not the slightest interest in this prophecy. Nor did he see why he had to go himself to collect it when Hakim could just as easily have brought it with him. He was about to refuse when it occurred to him that if he succeeded in uttering the correct word in his sleep tonight (which he was confident he would, having done it twice before), then he and Flower-in-the-Night would in all probability be eloping together. A man should go to his wedding correctly clothed and washed and shaved. So since he would be going to baths and barber anyway, he might as well drop in and collect the silly prophecy on his way back.

"Very well," he said. "You may expect me two hours before sunset."

Hakim frowned. "Why so late?"

"Because I have things to do, cousin by marriage," Abdullah explained. The thought of his coming elopement so overjoyed him that he smiled at Hakim and bowed with extreme politeness. "Though I lead a busy life that has little time left in it for obeying your orders, I shall be there, never fear."

Hakim continued to frown and turned that frown on Abdullah back over his shoulder as he left.

He was obviously both displeased and suspicious. Abdullah could not have cared less. As soon as Hakim was out of sight, he joyfully gave Jamal half his remaining money to guard his booth for the day. In return, he was forced to accept from the increasingly grateful Jamal a breakfast consisting of every delicacy on Jamal's stall. Excitement had taken away Abdullah's appetite. There was so much food that in order not to hurt Jamal's feelings, Abdullah gave most of it secretly to Jamal's dog; this he did warily, because the dog was a snapper as well as a biter. The dog, however, seemed to share its master's gratitude. It thumped its tail politely, ate everything Abdullah offered, and then tried to lick Abdullah's face.

Abdullah dodged that piece of politeness. The dog's breath was laden with the scent of elderly squid. He patted it gingerly on its gnarled head, thanked Jamal, and hurried off into the Bazaar. There he invested his remaining cash in the hire of a handcart. This cart he loaded carefully with his best and most unusual carpets—his floral Ochinstan, the glowing mat from Inhico, the golden Farqtans, the glorious patterned ones from the deep desert, and the matched pair from distant Thayack—and wheeled them along to the big booths in the center of the Bazaar where the richest merchants traded. For all his excitement, Abdullah was being practical. Flower-in-the-Night's father was clearly very rich. None but the wealthiest of men could afford the dowry for marrying a prince. It was therefore clear to Abdullah that he and Flower-in-the-Night would have to go very far away, or her father could make things very unpleasant for them. But it was also clear to Abdullah that Flower-in-the-Night was used to having the best of everything. She would not be happy roughing it. So Abdullah had to have money. He bowed before the merchant in the richest of the rich booths and, having called him treasure among traders and most majestic of merchants, offered him the floral Ochinstan carpet for a truly tremendous sum.

The merchant had been a friend of Abdullah's father. "And why, son of the Bazaar's most illustrious," he asked, "should you wish to part with what is surely, by its price, the gem of your collection?"

"I am diversifying my trade," Abdullah told him. "As you may have heard, I have been buying pictures and other forms of artwork. In order to make room for these, I am forced to dispose of the least valuable of my carpets. And it occurred to me that a seller of celestial weavings like yourself might consider helping the son of his old friend by taking off my hands this miserable flowery thing, at a bargain price."

"The contents of your booth should in future be choice indeed," the merchant said. "Let me offer you half what you ask."

"Ah, shrewdest of shrewd men," Abdullah said.

"Even a bargain costs money. But for you I will reduce my price by two coppers."

It was a long, hot day. But by the early evening Abdullah had sold all his best carpets for nearly twice as much as he had paid for them. He reckoned that he now had enough ready money to keep Flower-in-the-Night in reasonable luxury for three months or so. After that he hoped that either something else would turn up or that the sweetness of her nature would reconcile her to poverty. He went to the baths. He went to the barber. He called at the scent maker and had himself perfumed with oils. Then he went back to his booth and dressed in his best clothes. These clothes, like the clothes of most merchants, had various cunning insets, pieces of embroidery and ornamental twists of braid that were not ornaments at all, but cleverly concealed purses for money. Abdullah distributed his newly earned gold among these hiding places and was ready at last. He went, not very willingly, along to his father's old emporium. He told himself that it would pass the time between now and his elopement.

It was a curious feeling to go up the shallow cedar steps and enter the place where he had spent so much of his childhood. The smell of it, the cedarwood and the spices and the hairy, oily scent of carpets, was so familiar that if he shut his eyes, he could imagine he was ten years old again, playing behind a roll of carpet while his father bargained with a customer. But with his eyes open, Abdullah had no such illusion. His father's first wife's sister had a regrettable fondness for bright purple. The walls, the trellis screens, the chairs for customers, the cashier's table, and even the cashbox had all been painted Fatima's favorite color. Fatima came to meet him in a dress of the same color.

"Why, Abdullah! How prompt you are and how smart you look!" she said, and her manner said she had expected him to arrive late and in rags.

"He looks almost as if he were dressed for his wedding!" Assif said, advancing, too, with a smile on his thin, bad-tempered face.

It was so rare to see Assif smiling that Abdullah thought for a moment that Assif had ricked his neck and was grimacing with pain. Then Hakim sniggered, which made Abdullah realize what Assif had just said. To his annoyance, he found he was blushing furiously. He was forced to bow politely in order to hide his face.

"There's no need to make the boy blush!" Fatima cried. That, of course, made Abdullah's blush worse. "Abdullah, what is this rumor we hear that you are suddenly planning to deal in pictures?"

"And selling the best of your stock to make room for the pictures," added Hakim.

Abdullah ceased to blush. He saw he had been

summoned here to be criticized. He was sure of it when Assif added reproachfully, "Our feelings are somewhat hurt, son of my father's niece's husband, that you did not seem to think *we* could oblige you by taking a few carpets off your hands."

"Dear relatives," said Abdullah. "I could not, of course, sell you my carpets. My aim was to make a profit, and I could hardly mulct you, whom my father loved." He was so annoyed that he turned around to go away again, only to find that Hakim had quietly shut and barred the doors.

"No need to stay open," Hakim said. "Let us be just family here."

"The poor boy!" said Fatima. "Never has he had more need of a family to keep his mind in order!"

"Yes, indeed," said Assif. "Abdullah, some rumors in the Bazaar state that you have gone mad. We do not like this."

"He's certainly been behaving oddly," Hakim agreed. "We don't like such talk connected to a respectable family like ours."

This was worse than usual. Abdullah said, "There is nothing *wrong* with my mind. I know just what I am doing. And my aim is to cease giving you any chance to criticize me, probably by tomorrow. Meanwhile, Hakim told me to come here because you have found the prophecy that was made at my birth. Is this correct, or was it merely an excuse?" He had never been so rude to his father's first wife's relations before, but he was angry enough to feel they deserved it.

Oddly enough, instead of being angry with Abdullah in return, all three of his father's first wife's relations began hurrying excitedly around the emporium.

"Now where *is* that box?" said Fatima.

"Find it, find it!" said Assif. "It is the very words of the fortune-teller his poor father brought to the bedside of his second wife an hour after Abdullah's birth. He must see it!"

"Written in your own father's hand," Hakim said to Abdullah. "The greatest treasure for you."

"*Here* it is!" said Fatima, triumphantly pulling a carved wooden box off a high shelf. She gave the box to Assif, who thrust it into Abdullah's hands.

"Open it, open it!" they all three cried excitedly.

Abdullah put the box down on the purple cashier's table and sprang the catch. The lid went back, bringing a musty smell from inside, which was perfectly plain and empty apart from a folded yellowish paper.

"Get it out! Read it!" said Fatima in even greater excitement.

Abdullah could not see what the fuss was about, but he unfolded the paper. It had a few lines of writing on it, brown and faded and definitely his father's. He turned toward the hanging lamp with it. Now that Hakim had shut the main doors, the general purpleness of the emporium made it hard to see in there.

"He can barely see!" said Fatima.

Assif said, "No wonder. There's no light in here. Bring him into the room at the back. The overhead shutters are open there."

He and Hakim took hold of Abdullah's shoulders and pushed and hustled him toward the back of the shop. Abdullah was so busy trying to read the pale and scribbly writing of his father that he let them push him until he was positioned under the big overhead louvers in the living room behind the emporium. That was better. Now he knew why his father had been so disappointed in him. The writing said:

> These are the words of the wise fortune-teller: "This son of yours will not follow you in your trade. Two years after your death, while he is still a very young man, he will be raised above all others in this land. As Fate decrees it, so I have spoken."
>
> My son's fortune is a great disappointment to me. Let Fate send me other sons to follow in my trade, or I have wasted forty gold pieces on this prophecy.

"As you see, a great future awaits you, dear boy," said Assif.

Somebody giggled.

Abdullah looked up from the paper, a little

bemused. There seemed to be a lot of scent in the air.

The giggle came again, two of it, from in front of him.

Abdullah's eyes snapped forward. He felt them bulge. Two extremely fat young women stood in front of him. They met his bulging eyes and giggled again, coyly. Both were dressed to kill in shiny satin and ballooning gauze—pink on the right, yellow on the left one—and hung with more necklaces and bracelets than seemed probable. In addition, the pink one, who was fattest, had a pearl dangling on her forehead, just below her carefully frizzed hair. The yellow one, who was only just not fattest, wore a sort of amber tiara and had even frizzier hair. Both wore a very large amount of makeup, which was, in both cases, a severe error.

As soon as they were sure Abdullah's attention was on them—and it was; he was riveted with horror—each girl drew a veil from behind her ample shoulders—a pink veil on the left and a yellow on the right—and draped it chastely across her head and face. "Greetings, dear husband!" they chorused from beneath the veils.

"What!" exclaimed Abdullah.

"We veil ourselves," said the pink one.

"Because you should not look at our faces," said the yellow one.

"Until we are married," finished the pink.

"There must be some mistake!" said Abdullah.

"Not in the least," said Fatima. "These are my niece's two nieces who are here to marry you. Didn't you hear me say I was going to look out for a couple of wives for you?"

The two nieces giggled again. "He's ever so handsome," said the yellow one.

After a fairly long pause, in which he swallowed hard and did his best to control his feelings, Abdullah said politely, "Tell me, O relatives of my father's first wife, have you known of the prophecy which was made at my birth for a long time?"

"Ages," said Hakim. "Do you take us for fools?"

"Your dear father showed it to us," said Fatima, "at the time he made his will."

"And naturally we are not prepared to let your great good fortune take you away from the family," Assif explained. "We waited only for the moment when you ceased to follow your good father's trade—this surely being the signal for the Sultan to make you a vizier or invite you to command his armies or maybe to elevate you in some other way. Then we took steps to ensure that we shared in your good fortune. These two brides of yours are closely related to all three of us. You will naturally not neglect us as you rise. So, dear boy, it only remains for me to introduce you to the magistrate, who, as you see, stands ready to marry you."

Abdullah had, up to now, been unable to look

away from the billowing figures of the two nieces. Now he raised his eyes and met the cynical look of the Justice of the Bazaar, who was just stepping out from behind a screen with his Register of Marriages in his hands. Abdullah wondered how much he was being paid.

Abdullah bowed politely to the Justice. "I am afraid this is not possible," he said.

"Ah, I *knew* he would be unkind and disagreeable!" said Fatima. "Abdullah, think of the disgrace and disappointment to these poor girls if you refuse them now! After they've come all this way, expecting to be married, and got all dressed up! How could you, nephew!"

"Besides, I've locked all the doors," said Hakim. "Don't think you can get away."

"I am sorry to hurt the feelings of two such spectacular young ladies . . ." Abdullah began.

The feelings of the two brides were hurt anyway. Each girl uttered a wail. Each put her veiled face in her hands and sobbed heavily.

"This is awful!" wept the pink one.

"I *knew* they should have asked him first!" cried the yellow one.

Abdullah discovered that the sight of females crying—particularly such large ones, who wobbled with it everywhere—made him feel terrible. He knew he was an oaf and a beast. He was ashamed. The situation

53

was not the girls' fault. They had been used by Assif, Fatima, and Hakim, just as Abdullah had been. But the chief reason he felt so beastly—and it made him truly ashamed—was that he just wanted them to stop, to shut up and stop wobbling. Otherwise he did not care two hoots for their feelings. If he compared them with Flower-in-the-Night, he knew they revolted him. The idea of marrying them stuck in his craw. He felt sick. But just because they were whimpering and sniffing and flubbering in front of him, he found himself considering that three wives were perhaps not so many, after all. The two of them would make companions for Flower-in-the-Night when they were all far from Zanzib and home. He would have to explain the situation to them and load them onto the magic carpet—

That brought Abdullah back to reason. With a bump. With the sort of bump a magic carpet might make if loaded with two such weighty females—always supposing it could even get off the ground with them on it in the first place. They were so very fat. As for thinking they would make companions for Flower-in-the-Night—phooey! She was intelligent, educated, and kind, as well as being beautiful (and thin). These two had yet to show him that they had a brain cell between them. They wanted to be married, and their crying was a way of bullying him into it. And they giggled. He had never heard Flower-in-the-Night giggle.

Here Abdullah was somewhat amazed to discover

that he, really and truly, did love Flower-in-the-Night just as ardently as he had been telling himself he did—or more, because he now saw he respected her. He knew he would die without her. And if he agreed to marry these two fat nieces, he *would* be without her. She would call him greedy, like the Prince in Ochinstan.

"I am very sorry," he said above the loud sob-bings. "You should really have consulted me first about this, O relatives of my father's first wife, O much honored and most honest Justice. It would have saved this misunderstanding. I cannot marry yet. I have made a vow."

"*What* vow?" demanded everyone else, the fat brides included, and the Justice added, "Have you registered this vow? To be legal, all vows must be registered with a magistrate."

This was awkward. Abdullah thought rapidly. "Indeed, it *is* registered, O veritable weighing scale of judgment," he said. "My father took me to a magistrate to register the vow when he ordered me to make it. I was but a small child at the time. Though I did not understand then, I see now it was because of the prophecy. My father, being a prudent man, did not wish to see his forty gold coins wasted. He made me vow that I would never marry until Fate had placed me above all others in this land. So you see"—Abdullah put his hands in the sleeves of his best suit and bowed regretfully to the two fat brides——"I cannot yet marry you, twin plums of candied sugar, but the time will come."

Everyone said, "Oh, in *that* case!" in various tones of discontent, and to Abdullah's profound relief, most of them turned away from him.

"I always thought your father was a rather grasping man," Fatima added.

"Even from beyond the grave," Assif agreed. "We must wait for this dear boy's elevation then."

The Justice, however, stood his ground. "And which magistrate was it, before whom you made this vow?" he asked.

"I do not know his name," Abdullah invented, speaking with intense regret. He was sweating. "I was a tiny child, and he appeared to me an old man with a long white beard." That, he thought, would serve as a description of every magistrate there ever was, including the Justice standing before him.

"I shall have to check all records," the Justice said irritably. He turned to Assif, Hakim, and Fatima and——rather coldly——made his formal good-byes.

Abdullah left with him, almost clinging to the Justice's official sash in his hurry to get away from the emporium and the two fat brides.

Chapter 5

Which tells how Flower-in-the-Night's father wished to raise Abdullah above all others in the land

"What a day!" Abdullah said to himself when he was back inside his booth at last. "If my luck goes on this way, I will not be surprised if I never get the carpet to move again!" Or, he thought as he lay down on the carpet, still dressed in his best, he might get to the night garden only to find that Flower-in-the-Night was too annoyed at his stupidity last night to love him anymore. Or she might love him still but have decided not to fly away with him. Or . . .

It took him a while to get to sleep.

But when he woke, everything was perfect. The carpet was just gliding to a gentle landing on the moonlit bank. So Abdullah knew he had said the command word after all, and it was such a short while since he had said it that he *almost* had a memory of what it was. But it went clean out of his head when Flower-in-the-Night came running eagerly toward him, among the white scented flowers and the round yellow lamps.

"You're here!" she called as she ran. "I was quite worried!"

She was not angry. Abdullah's heart sang. "Are you ready to leave?" he called back. "Jump on beside me."

Flower-in-the-Night laughed delightedly—it was definitely no giggle—and came running on across the lawn. The moon seemed just then to go behind a cloud because Abdullah saw her lit entirely by the lamps for a moment, golden and eager, as she ran. He stood up and held out his hands to her.

As he did so, the cloud came right down into the lamplight. And it was not a cloud but great black leathery wings, silently beating. A pair of equally leathery arms, with hands that had long fingernails like claws, reached from the shadow of those fanning wings and wrapped themselves around Flower-in-the-Night. Abdullah saw her jerk as those arms stopped her running. She looked around and up. Whatever she saw made her scream, one single wild, frantic scream, which was cut off when one of the leathery arms changed position to clap its huge taloned hand over her face. Flower-in-the-Night beat at the arm with her fists, and kicked and struggled, but all quite uselessly. She was lifted up, a small white figure against the huge blackness. The great wings silently beat again. A gigantic foot, with talons like the hands, pressed the turf a yard or so from the bank where Abdullah was still in the act of standing up, and a

leathery leg flexed mighty calf muscles as the thing—
whatever it was—sprang upright. For the merest
instant Abdullah found himself staring into a hideous
leathery face with a ring through its hooked nose and
long, upslanting eyes, remote and cruel. The thing
was not looking at him. It was simply concentrating
on getting itself and its captive airborne.

The next second it was aloft. Abdullah saw it
overhead for a heartbeat longer, a mighty flying djinn
dangling a tiny, pale human girl in its arms. Then the
night swallowed it up. It all had happened unbeliev-
ably quickly.

"After it! Follow that djinn!" Abdullah ordered
the carpet.

The carpet seemed to obey. It bellied up from the
bank. Then, almost as if someone had given it
another command, it sank back and lay still.

"You moth-eaten doormat!" Abdullah screamed
at it.

There was a shout from farther down the garden.
"This way, men! That scream came from up there!"

Along the arcade Abdullah glimpsed moonlight
on metal helmets and—worse still—golden lamplight on swords and crossbows. He did not wait to
explain to these people why he had screamed. He
flung himself flat on the carpet.

"Back to the booth!" he whispered to it. "Quickly!
Please!"

This time the carpet obeyed, as quickly as it had the night before. It was up off the bank in an eye blink and then hurtling sideways across a forbiddingly high wall. Abdullah had just a glimpse of a large party of northern mercenaries milling around in the lamp-lit garden before he was speeding above the sleeping roofs and moonlit towers of Zanzib. He had barely time to reflect that Flower-in-the-Night's father must be even richer than he had thought—few people could afford that many hired soldiers, and mercenaries from the north were the most expensive kind—before the carpet planed downward and brought him smoothly in through the curtains to the middle of his booth.

There he gave himself up to despair.

A djinn had stolen Flower-in-the-Night and the carpet had refused to follow. He knew that was not surprising. A djinn, as everyone in Zanzib knew, commanded enormous powers in the air and the earth. No doubt the djinn had, as a precaution, ordered everything in the garden to stay where it was while he carried Flower-in-the-Night away. It had probably not even noticed the carpet, or Abdullah on it, but the carpet's lesser magic had been forced to give way to the djinn's command. So the djinn had stolen away Flower-in-the-Night, whom Abdullah loved more than his own soul, just at the moment when she was about to run into his arms, and there seemed nothing he could do.

He wept.

After that he vowed to throw away all the money hidden in his clothes. It was useless to him now. But before he did, he gave himself over to grief again, noisy misery at first, in which he lamented out loud and beat his breast in the manner of Zanzib; then, as cocks crowed and people began moving about, he fell into silent despair. There was no point even in moving. Other people might bustle about and whistle and clank buckets, but Abdullah was no longer part of that life. He stayed crouching on the magic carpet, wishing he were dead.

So miserable was he that it never occurred to him that he might be in any danger himself. He paid no attention when all the noises in the Bazaar stopped, like birds when a hunter enters a wood. He did not really notice the heavy marching of feet or the regular clank-clank-clank of mercenary armor that went with it. When someone barked *"Halt!"* outside his booth, he did not even turn his head. But he did turn around when the curtains of the booth were torn down. He was sluggishly surprised. He blinked his swollen eyes against the powerful sunlight and wondered vaguely what a troop of northern soldiers was doing coming in here.

"That's him," said someone in civilian clothes, who might have been Hakim, and then faded prudently away before Abdullah's eyes could focus on him.

"You!" snapped the squad leader. "Out. With us."

"What?" said Abdullah.

"Fetch him," said the leader.

Abdullah was bewildered. He protested feebly when they dragged him to his feet and twisted his arms to make him walk. He went on protesting as they marched him at the double—clank-clank, clank-clank—out of the Bazaar and into the West Quarter. Before long he was protesting very strongly indeed. "What is this?" he panted. "I demand . . . as a citizen . . . where we are . . . going!"

"Shut up. You'll see," they answered. They were too fit to pant.

A short while after, they ran Abdullah in under a massive gate made of blocks of stone that glared white in the sun, into a blazing courtyard, where they spent five minutes outside an ovenlike smithy loading Abdullah with chains. He protested even more. "What is this for? Where *is* this? I demand to know!"

"Shut *up!*" said the squad leader. He remarked to his second-in-command in his barbarous northern accent, "They always *winge* so, these Zanzibbeys. Got no notion of dignity."

While the squad leader was saying this, the smith—who was from Zanzib, too—murmured to Abdullah, "The Sultan wants you. I don't think much of your chances, either. Last one I chained like this got crucified."

"*But I haven't done anyth*—" protested Abdullah.

"SHUT UP!" screamed the squad leader. "Finished, smith? Right. *On* the double!" And they ran Abdullah off again, across the glaring yard and into the large building beyond.

Abdullah would have said it was impossible even to walk in those chains. They were so heavy. But it is wonderful what you can do if a party of grim-faced soldiers is quite set on making you do it. He ran, clank-chankle, clank-chankle, clash, until at last, with an exhausted jingle, he arrived at the foot of a high raised seat made of cool blue and gold tiles and piled with cushions. There the soldiers all went down on one knee, in a distant, decorous way, as northern soldiers did to the person who was paying them.

"Present prisoner Abdullah, m'lord Sultan," the squad leader said.

Abdullah did not kneel. He followed the customs of Zanzib and fell on his face. Besides, he was exhausted and it was easier to fall down with a mighty clatter than do anything else. The tiled floor was blessedly, wonderfully cool.

"Make the son of a camel's excrement kneel," said the Sultan. "Make the creature look us in the face." His voice was low, but it trembled with anger.

A soldier hauled on the chains, and two others

pulled on Abdullah's arms until they had got him sort of bent on his knees. They held him that way, and Abdullah was glad. He would have crumpled up in horror otherwise. The man lounging on the tiled throne was fat and bald and wore a bushy gray beard. He was slapping at a cushion, in a way that looked idle but was really bitterly angry, with a white cotton thing that had a tassel on top. It was this tasseled thing that made Abdullah see what trouble he was in. The thing was his own nightcap.

"Well, dog from a muck heap," said the Sultan, "where is my daughter?"

"I have no idea," Abdullah said miserably.

"Do you deny," said the Sultan, dangling the nightcap as if it were a severed head he was holding up by its hair, "do you *deny* that this is your nightcap? Your name is inside it, you miserable salesman! It was found by me——by *us* in person!——inside my daughter's trinket box, along with eighty-two portraits of common persons, which had been hidden by my daughter in eighty-two cunning places. Do you deny that you crept into my night garden and presented my daughter with these portraits? Do you deny that you then stole my daughter away?"

"Yes, I do deny that!" said Abdullah. "I do not deny, O most exalted defender of the weak, the nightcap or the pictures——although I must point out that your daughter is cleverer in hiding than you are in finding, great wielder of wisdom, for I gave her, in fact, one hundred and seven more pictures than you have discovered—but I have most certainly not stolen Flower-in-the-Night away. She was snatched from before my very eyes by a huge and hideous djinn. I have no more idea than your most celestial self where she is now."

"A likely story!" said the Sultan. "Djinn indeed! Liar! Worm!"

"I swear that it is true!" Abdullah cried out. He was in such despair by now that he hardly cared what he said. "Get any holy object you like, and I will swear to the djinn on it. Have me enchanted to tell the truth, and I will still say the same, O mighty crusher of criminals. For it is the truth. And since I am probably far more desolated than yourself by the loss of your daughter, great Sultan, glory of our land, I implore you to kill me now and spare me a life of misery!"

"I will willingly have you executed," said the Sultan. "But first tell me where she is."

"But I have *told* you, wonder of the world!" said Abdullah. "I do not know where she is."

"Take him away," the Sultan said with great calmness to his kneeling soldiers. They sprang up readily and pulled Abdullah to his feet. "Torture the truth out of him," the Sultan added. "When we find her, you can kill him, but have him linger until then. I daresay the Prince of Ochinstan will accept her as a widow if I double the dowry."

"You mistake, sovereign of sovereigns!" Abdullah gasped as the soldiers clattered him across the tiles. "I have no idea where the djinn went, and my great sorrow is that he took her before we had any chance to get married."

"What?" shouted the Sultan. "Bring him back!" The soldiers at once trailed Abdullah and his chains back to the tiled seat, where the Sultan was now leaning forward and glaring. "Did my clean ear become soiled by hearing you say you are *not* married to my daughter, filth?" he demanded.

"That is correct, mighty monarch," said Abdullah. "The djinn came before we could elope."

The Sultan glared down at him in what seemed to be horror. "This is the truth?"

"I swear," said Abdullah, "that I have not yet so much as kissed your daughter. I had intended to seek out a magistrate as soon as we were far from Zanzib. I know what is proper. But I also felt it proper to make sure first that Flower-in-the-Night indeed wished to marry me. Her decision struck me as made in ignorance, despite the hundred and eighty-nine pictures. If you will forgive my saying so, protector of patriots, your method of bringing up your daughter is decidedly unsound. She took me for a woman when she first saw me."

"So," said the Sultan musingly, "when I set soldiers to catch and kill the intruder in the garden last night, it could have been disastrous. You fool," he said to Abdullah, "slave and mongrel who dares to criticize! Of course I had to bring my daughter up as I did. The prophecy made at her birth was that she would marry the first man, apart from me, that she saw!"

Despite the chains, Abdullah straightened up. For the first time that day he felt a twinge of hope.

The Sultan was staring down the gracefully tiled and ornamented room, thinking. "The prophecy suited me very well," he remarked. "I had long wished for an alliance with the countries of the north, for they have better weapons than we can make here, some of those weapons being truly sorcerous, I understand. But the princes of Ochinstan are very hard to pin down. So all I had to do—so I thought—was to isolate my daughter from any possibility of seeing a man—and naturally give her the best of educations otherwise, to make sure she could sing and dance and make herself pleasing to a prince. Then, when my daughter was of marriageable age, I invited the Prince here on a visit of state. He was to come here next year, when he had finished subduing a land he has just conquered with those same excellent weapons. And I knew that as soon as my daughter set eyes on him, the prophecy would make sure that I had him!" His eyes turned balefully down on Abdullah. "Then my plans are upset by an insect like you!"

"That is unfortunately true, most prudent of rulers," Abdullah admitted. "Tell me, is this Prince of Ochinstan by any chance somewhat old and ugly?"

"I believe him to be hideous in the same northern fashion as these mercenaries," the Sultan said, at which Abdullah sensed the soldiers, most of whom ran to freckles and reddish hair, stiffened. "Why do you ask, dog?"

"Because, if you will forgive further criticism of your great wisdom, O nurturer of our nation, this seems somewhat unfair to your daughter," Abdullah observed. He felt the eyes of the soldiers turn to him, wondering at his daring. Abdullah did not care. He felt he had little to lose.

"Women do not count," said the Sultan. "Therefore, it is impossible to be unfair to them."

"I disagree," said Abdullah, at which the soldiers stared even harder.

The Sultan glowered down at him. His powerful hands wrung the nightcap as if it were Abdullah's neck. "Be silent, you diseased toad!" he said. "Or you will make me forget myself and order your instant execution!"

Abdullah relaxed a little. "O absolute sword among the citizens, I implore you to kill me now," he said. "I have transgressed and I have sinned and I have trespassed in your night garden——"

"Be quiet," said the Sultan. "You know perfectly well I *can't* kill you until I have found my daughter and made sure she marries you."

Abdullah relaxed further. "Your slave does not follow your reasoning, O jewel of judgment," he protested. "I demand to die now."

The Sultan practically snarled at him. "If I have learned one thing," he said, "from this sorry business, it is that even I, Sultan of Zanzib though I am, cannot cheat Fate. That prophecy will get itself fulfilled somehow, I know that. Therefore, if I wish my daughter to marry the Prince of Ochinstan, I must first go along with the prophecy."

Abdullah relaxed almost completely. He had naturally seen this straightaway, but he had been anxious to make sure that the Sultan had worked it out, too. And he had. Clearly Flower-in-the-Night inherited her logical mind from her father.

"So where is my daughter?" asked the Sultan.

"I have told you, O sun shining upon Zanzib," said Abdullah. "The djinn—"

"I do not for a moment believe in the djinn," said the Sultan. "It is far too convenient. You must have hidden the girl somewhere. Take him away," he said to the soldiers, "and shut him in the safest dungeon we have. Leave the chains on him. He must have used some form of enchantment to get into the garden, and he can probably use it to escape unless we are careful." Abdullah was unable to avoid flinching at this. The Sultan noticed. He smiled nastily. "Then," he said, "I want a house-to-house search made for my daughter. She is to be brought to the dungeon for the wedding as soon as she is found." His eyes turned musingly back to Abdullah. "Until then," he said, "I shall entertain myself by inventing new ways to kill you. At the moment I favor impaling you upon a forty-foot stake and then loosing vultures to eat bits off you. But I could change my mind if I think of something worse."

As the soldiers dragged him away, Abdullah nearly despaired again. He thought of the prophecy made at his own birth. A forty-foot stake would raise him above all others in the land very nicely.

Chapter 6

Which shows how Abdullah went from the frying pan into the fire

They put Abdullah in a deep and smelly dungeon where the only light came through a tiny grating high up in the ceiling—and that light was not daylight. It probably came from a distant window at the end of a passage on the floor above, where the grating was part of the floor.

Knowing that this was what he had to look forward to, Abdullah tried, as the soldiers dragged him away, to fill his eyes and mind with images of light. In the pause while the soldiers were unlocking the outside door to the dungeons, he looked up and around. They were in a dark little courtyard with blank walls of stone standing like cliffs all about it. But if he tipped his head tight back, Abdullah could just see a slender spire in the mid-distance, outlined against the rising gold of morning. It amazed him to see that it was only an hour after dawn. Above the spire the sky was deep blue with just one cloud standing peacefully in it. Morning was still flushing the cloud red and gold, giving it the look of a high-piled castle with golden windows. Golden light caught the wings of a white bird circling the spire. Abdullah was sure this was the last beauty he would ever see in his life. He stared backward at it as the soldiers lugged him inside.

He tried to treasure this image when he was locked in the cold gray dungeon, but it was impossible. The dungeon was another world. For a long time he was too miserable even to notice how cramped he was in his chains. When he did notice, he shifted and clanked about on the cold floor, but it did not help very much.

"I have to look forward to a lifetime of this," he told himself. "Unless someone rescues Flower-in-the-Night, of course." That did not seem likely, since the Sultan refused to believe in the djinn.

After this he tried to stave off despair with his daydream. But somehow, thinking of himself as a prince who had been kidnapped helped not at all. He knew it was untrue, and he kept thinking guiltily that Flower-in-the-Night had believed him when he told her. She must have decided to marry him because she thought he was a prince—being a princess herself, as he now knew. He simply could not imagine himself ever daring to tell her the truth. For a while it seemed to him that he deserved the worst fate the Sultan could invent for him.

Then he began thinking of Flower-in-the-Night herself. Wherever she was, she was certainly at least as scared and miserable as he was himself. Abdullah yearned to comfort her. He wanted to rescue her so much that he spent some time wrenching uselessly at his chains.

"For certainly nobody *else* is likely to try," he muttered. "I must get *out* of here!"

Then, although he was sure it was another notion as silly as his daydream, he tried to summon the magic carpet. He visualized it lying on the floor of his booth, and he called to it, out loud, over and over again. He said all the magic-sounding words he could think of, hoping one of them would be the command word.

Nothing happened. And how silly to think that it would! Abdullah thought. Even if the carpet could hear him from the dungeon, supposing he got the command word right at last, how could even a magic carpet wriggle its way in here through that tiny grating? And suppose it *did* wriggle in, how would that help Abdullah to get out?

Abdullah gave up and leaned against the wall, half dozing, half despairing. It must now be the heat of the day, when most folk in Zanzib took at least a short rest. Abdullah himself, when he was not visiting one of the public parks, usually sat on a pile of his less good carpets in the shade in front of his stall, drinking fruit juice, or wine if he could afford it, and chatting lazily with Jamal. No longer. And this is just my first day! he thought morbidly. I'm keeping track of the hours now. How long before I lose track even of days?

He shut his eyes. One good thing. A house-to-house search for the Sultan's daughter would cause at least some annoyance to Fatima, Hakim, and Assif simply because they were known to be the only family Abdullah had. He hoped soldiers turned the purple emporium upside down. He hoped they slit the walls and unrolled all the carpets. He hoped they arrested—

Something landed on the floor beyond Abdullah's feet.

So they throw me some food, Abdullah thought, and I would rather starve. He opened his eyes lazily. They shot wide of their own accord.

There, on the dungeon floor, lay the magic carpet. Upon it, peacefully sleeping, lay Jamal's bad-tempered dog.

Abdullah stared at both of them. He could imagine how, in the heat of midday, the dog might lie down in the shade of Abdullah's booth. He could see that it would lie on the carpet because it was comfortable. But how a dog—a *dog!*—could chance to say the command word was beyond him to understand entirely. As he stared, the dog began dreaming. Its paws worked. Its snout wrinkled, and it snuffled, as if it had caught the most delicious possible scent, and it uttered a faint whimper, as if whatever it smelled in the dream were escaping from it.

"Is it possible, my friend," Abdullah said to it, "that you were dreaming of me and of the time I gave you most of my breakfast?"

The dog, in its sleep, heard him. It uttered a loud snore and woke up. Doglike, it wasted no time wondering how it came to be in this strange dungeon. It sniffed and smelled Abdullah. It sprang up with a delighted squeak, planted its paws among the chains on Abdullah's chest, and enthusiastically licked his face.

Abdullah laughed and rolled his head to keep his nose out of the dog's squiddy breath. He was quite as delighted as the dog was. "So you *were* dreaming of me!" he said. "My friend, I shall arrange for you to have a bowl of squid daily. You have saved my life and possibly Flower-in-the-Night's, too!"

As soon as the dog's rapture had abated a little, Abdullah began rolling and working himself along the floor in his chains, until he was lying, propped on one elbow, on top of the carpet. He gave a great sigh. Now he was safe. "Come along," he said to the dog. "Get on the carpet, too."

But the dog had found the scent of what was certainly a rat in the corner of the dungeon. It was pursuing the smell with excited snorts. At each snort

Abdullah felt the carpet quiver beneath him. It gave him the answer he needed.

"Come along," he said to the dog. "If I leave you here, they will find you when they come to feed me or question me, and they will assume I have turned myself into a dog. Then my fate will be yours. You have brought me the carpet and revealed me its secret, and I cannot see you stuck on a forty-foot stake."

The dog had its nose rammed into the corner. It was not attending. Abdullah heard, unmistakable even through the thick walls of the dungeon, the tramp of feet and the rattle of keys. Someone was coming. He gave up persuading the dog. He lay flat on the carpet.

"Here, boy!" he said. "Come and lick my face!"

The dog understood that. It left the corner, jumped on Abdullah's chest, and proceeded to obey him.

"Carpet," Abdullah whispered from under the busy tongue. "To the Bazaar, but do not land. Hover beside Jamal's stall."

The carpet rose and rushed sideways—which was just as well. Keys were unlocking the dungeon door. Abdullah was not any too sure how the carpet left the dungeon because the dog was still licking his face and he was forced to keep his eyes shut. He felt a dank shadow pass across him—perhaps that was when they melted through the wall—and then bright sunlight. The dog lifted its head into the sunlight, puzzled.

Abdullah squinted sideways across his chains and saw a high wall rear in front of them and then fall below as the carpet rose smoothly over it. Then came a succession of towers and roofs, quite familiar to Abdullah though he had only seen them by night before. And after that the carpet went planing down toward the outer edge of the Bazaar. For the palace of the Sultan was indeed only five minutes' walk from Abdullah's booth.

Jamal's stall came into view, and beside it, Abdullah's own wrecked booth, with carpets flung all over the walkway. Obviously soldiers had searched there for Flower-in-the-Night. Jamal was dozing, with his head on his arms, between a big simmering pot of squid and a charcoal grill with skewered meat smoking on it. He raised his head, and his one eye stared as the carpet came to hang in the air in front of him.

"Down, boy!" Abdullah said. "Jamal, call your dog."

Jamal was clearly very scared. It is no fun keeping the stall next door to anyone a sultan wishes to impale on a stake. He seemed speechless. Since the dog was taking no notice, either, Abdullah struggled into sitting position, clanking, rattling, and sweating. This tipped the dog off. It jumped nimbly to the stall counter, where Jamal absently seized it in his arms.

"What do you want me to do?" he asked, eyeing the chains. "Shall I fetch a blacksmith?"

Abdullah was touched at this proof of Jamal's friendship. But sitting up had given him a view down the walkway between the stalls. He could see the soles of running feet down there and flying garments. It seemed that one boothkeeper was on his way to fetch the Watch, though there was something about the running figure that reminded Abdullah rather strongly of Assif. "No," he said. "There's no time." Clanking, he wriggled his left leg over the edge of the carpet. "Do this for me instead. Put your hand on the embroidery above my left boot."

Jamal obediently stretched out a brawny arm and, very gingerly, touched the embroidery. "Is it a spell?" he asked nervously.

"No," said Abdullah. "It's a hidden purse. Put your hand in and take the money out of it."

Jamal was puzzled, but his fingers groped, found the way into the purse, and came out as a fistful of gold. "There's a fortune here," he said. "Will this buy your freedom?"

"No," said Abdullah. "Yours. They'll be after you and your dog for helping me. Take the gold and the dog and get out. Leave Zanzib. Go north to the barbarous places, where you can hide."

"North!" said Jamal. "But whatever can I do in the north?"

"Buy everything you need and set up a Rashpuhti restaurant," said Abdullah. "There's enough gold to do it, and you're an excellent cook. You could make your fortune there."

"Really?" said Jamal, staring from Abdullah to his handful of money. "You really think I could?"

Abdullah had been keeping a wary eye on the walkway. Now he saw the space fill, not with the Watch but with northern mercenaries, and they were running. "Only if you go now," he said.

Jamal caught the clank-clank of running soldiers. He leaned out to look and make sure. Then he whistled to his dog and was gone, so swiftly and quietly that Abdullah could only admire. Jamal had even spared time to move the meat off the grill so that it would not burn. All the soldiers were going to find here was a caldron of half-boiled squid.

Abdullah whispered to the carpet. "To the desert. Fast!"

The carpet was off at once, with its usual sideways rush. Abdullah thought he certainly would have been thrown off it but for the weight of his chains, which caused the carpet to bulge downward in the center, rather like a hammock. And speed was necessary. The soldiers shouted behind him. There were some loud bangs. For a few instants two bullets and a crossbow bolt carved the blue sky beside the carpet and then fell behind. The carpet hurtled on, across roofs, over walls, beside towers, and then skimming palm trees and market gardens. Finally it shot forth into hot gray emptiness, shimmering white and yellow under a huge bowl of sky, where Abdullah's chains began to grow uncomfortably warm.

The rushing of air stopped. Abdullah raised his head and saw Zanzib as a surprisingly small clump of towers on the horizon. The carpet sailed slowly past a person riding a camel, who turned his well-veiled face to watch. It began to sink toward the sand. At this the person on the camel turned his camel, too, and urged it into a trot after the carpet. Abdullah could almost *see* him thinking gleefully that here was his chance to get his hands on a genuine, working magic carpet, and its owner in chains and in no position to resist him.

"Up, up!" he almost shrieked at the carpet. "Fly north!"

The carpet lumbered up into the air again. Annoyance and reluctance breathed from every thread of it. It turned in a heavy half circle and sailed gently northward at walking pace. The person on the camel cut across the middle of the half circle and came on at a gallop. Since the carpet was only about nine feet in the air, it was a sitting target for someone on a galloping camel.

Abdullah saw it was time for some quick talking. "Beware!" he shouted at the camel rider. "Zanzib has cast me out in chains for fear I spread this plague I have!" The rider was not quite fooled. He reined in his camel and followed at a more cautious pace, while he wrestled a tent pole out of his baggage. Clearly he intended to tip Abdullah off the carpet with it. Abdullah turned his attention hastily to the carpet. "O most excellent of carpets," he said, "O brightest-colored and most delicately woven, whose lovely textile is so cunningly enhanced with magic, I fear I have not treated you hitherto with proper respect. I have snapped commands and even shouted at you, where I now see that your gentle nature requires only the mildest of requests. Forgive, oh, forgive!"

The carpet appreciated this. It stretched tighter in the air and put on a bit of speed.

"And dog that I am," continued Abdullah, "I have caused you to labor in the heat of the desert, weighted most dreadfully with my chains. O best and most elegant of carpets, I think now only of you and how best I might rid you of this great weight. If you were to fly at a gentle speed—say, only a little faster than a camel might gallop—to the nearest spot in the desert northward where I can find someone to remove these chains, would this be agreeable to your amiable and aristocratic nature?"

He seemed to have struck the right note. A sort of smug pridefulness exuded from the carpet now. It rose a foot or so, changed direction slightly, and moved forward at a purposeful seventy miles an hour. Abdullah clung to its edge and peered backward at the frustrated camel rider, who was soon dwindling to a dot in the desert behind.

"O most noble of artifacts, you are a sultan among carpets, and I am your miserable slave!" he said shamelessly.

The carpet liked this so much that it went even faster.

Ten minutes later it surged over a sand dune and came to an abrupt stop just below the summit on the other side. Slanting. Abdullah was rolled helplessly off in a cloud of sand. And he went on rolling, clattering, jingling, bounding, raising more sand, and then—after desperate efforts—tobogganing feetfirst in a groove of sand, down to the very edge of a small muddy pool in an oasis. A number of ragged people who were crouching over something at the edge of this pool sprang up and scattered as Abdullah plowed in among them. Abdullah's feet caught the thing they were crouching over and shot it back into the pool. One man shouted indignantly and went splashing into the water to rescue it. The rest drew sabers and knives—and in one case a long pistol—and surrounded Abdullah threateningly.

"Cut his throat," said one.

Abdullah blinked sand out of his eyes and thought he had seldom seen a more villainous crew of men. They all had scarred faces, shifty eyes, bad teeth, and unpleasant expressions. The man with the pistol was the most unpleasant of the lot. He wore a sort of earring through one side of his large hooked nose and a very bushy mustache. His headcloth was pinned up at one side with a flashy red stone in a gold brooch.

"Where have you sprung from?" this man said. He kicked Abdullah. "Explain yourself."

All of them, including the man who was wading out of the pool with some kind of bottle, looked at Abdullah with expressions that said his explanation had better be good. Or else.

Chapter 7

Which introduces the genie

Abdullah blinked more sand out of his eyes and stared earnestly at the man with the pistol. The man really was the absolute image of the villainous bandit of his daydream. It must be one of those coincidences.

"I beg your pardon a hundred times, gentlemen of the desert," he said with great politeness, "for intruding on you in this manner, but am I addressing the most noble and world-famous bandit, the matchless Kabul Aqba?"

The other villainous men around him seemed astonished. Abdullah distinctly heard one say, "How did he know that?" But the man with the pistol simply sneered. It was something his face was particularly well designed to do. "I am indeed he," he said. "Famous, am I?"

It *was* one of those coincidences, Abdullah thought. Well, at least he knew where he was now. "Alas, wanderers in the wilderness," he said, "I am, like your noble selves, one who is outcast and oppressed. I have sworn revenge on all Rashpuht. I came here expressly to join with you and add the strength of my mind and my arm to yours."

"Did you indeed?" said Kabul Aqba. "And how did you get here? By dropping from the sky, chains and all?"

"By magic," Abdullah said modestly. He thought it was the thing most likely to impress these people. "I did indeed drop from the sky, noblest of nomads."

Unfortunately they did not seem impressed. Most of them laughed. Kabul Aqba, with a nod, sent two of them up the sand dune to examine Abdullah's point of arrival. "So you can work magic?" he said. "Do these chains you wear have anything to do with that?"

"Certainly," said Abdullah. "Such a mighty magician am I that the Sultan of Zanzib himself loaded me with chains for very fear of what I could do. Only strike these chains apart and undo these handcuffs and you will see great things." Out of the corner of his eye he saw the two men returning, carrying the carpet between them. He hoped very much that this was a good thing to happen. "Iron, as you know, inhibits a magician in the use of magic," he said earnestly. "Feel free to strike it off me and see a new life open before you."

The rest of the bandits looked at him dubiously. "We haven't got a cold chisel," said one. "Or a mallet."

Kabul Aqba turned to the two men with the carpet. "There was only this," they reported. "No sign of anything to ride. No tracks."

At this the chief bandit stroked his mustache. Abdullah found himself wondering if it ever got tangled with his nose ring. "Hmm," he said. "Then I'll lay odds it's a magic carpet. I'll have it here." He turned sneeringly to Abdullah. "Sorry to disappoint you, magician," he said, "but since you delivered yourself so conveniently in chains, I'm going to leave you that way and take charge of your carpet, just to prevent accidents. If you really want to join us, you can make yourself useful first."

Somewhat to his surprise, Abdullah found he was far more angry than frightened. Perhaps it was that he had exhausted all his fear that morning in front of the Sultan. Or perhaps it was just because he ached all over. He was sore and scraped from sliding down the sand dune, and one of his ankle bands was chafing brutally. "But I have told you," he said haughtily, "that I shall be no use to you until my chains are off."

"It is not magic we want from you. It is knowledge," said Kabul Aqba. He beckoned to the man who had gone wading into the pool. "Tell us what manner of thing this is," he said, "and we may let your legs loose as a reward."

The man who had been in the pool squatted down and held out a smoky blue bottle with a rounded belly. Abdullah levered himself to his elbows and looked at it resentfully. It seemed to be new. There was a clean new cork showing through the smoky glass of the neck, which had been sealed over with a stamped lead seal, again new-looking. It looked like a bottle of perfume that had lost its label. "It's quite light," said the squatting man, shaking the bottle about, "and it neither rattles nor sloshes."

Abdullah thought of a way he could use this to get himself unchained. "It's a genie bottle," he said. "Know, denizens of the desert, that it could be very dangerous. Do but take these chains from me, and I will control the genie within and make sure he obeys your every wish. Otherwise I think no man should touch it."

The man holding the bottle dropped it nervously, but Kabul Aqba only laughed and picked it up. "It looks more like something good to drink," he said. He tossed the flask to another man. "Open it." The man laid down his saber and got out a large knife, with which he hacked at the lead seal.

Abdullah saw his chance of getting unchained going. Worse, he was about to be exposed as a fraud. "It is really extremely dangerous, O rubies among robbers," he protested. "Once you have broken the seal, do not on any account draw the cork." As he spoke, the man peeled the seal away and dropped it on the sand. He began prying the cork out, while another man held the bottle steady for him. "If you must draw the cork," Abdullah babbled, "at least tap on the bottle the correct and mystical number of times and make the genie inside swear——"

The cork came out. *Pop.* A thin mauvish vapor came smoking out of the neck of the flask. Abdullah hoped the thing was full of poison. But the vapor almost instantly thickened to a cloud that came rushing out of the bottle like a kettle boiling bluish mauve steam. This steam shaped itself into a face——large and angry and blue——and arms, and a wisp of body connected to the bottle, and went on rushing forth until it was easily ten feet tall.

"I made a vow!" the face howled, in a large, windy roar. "The one who lets me out shall suffer. *There!*" The misty arms gestured.

The two men holding the cork and the bottle seemed to wink out of existence. Cork and bottle both fell to the ground, forcing the genie to billow sideways from the neck of the bottle. From the midst of his blue vapor, two large toads came crawling and seemed to gaze around in bewilderment. The genie came slowly and vaporously upright, hovering above the bottle with his smoky arms folded and a look of utter hatred on his misty face.

By this time everyone had run away except for Abdullah and Kabul Aqba, Abdullah because he could barely move in his chains and Kabul Aqba because he was clearly unexpectedly brave. The genie glowered at the two of them.

"I am the slave of the bottle," he said. "Much as I hate and detest the whole arrangement, I have to tell you that he who owns me is allowed one wish every day and I am forced to grant it." And he added menacingly, "What is your wish?"

"I wish——" began Abdullah.

Kabul Aqba quickly rammed his hand across Abdullah's mouth. "*I* am the one wishing," he said. "Get that quite clear, genie!"

"I hear," said the genie. "What wish?"

"One moment," said Kabul Aqba. He put his face close to Abdullah's ear. His breath smelled even worse than his hand, although neither, Abdullah had to admit, was a patch on Jamal's dog. "Well, magician," the bandit whispered, "you've proved you know what you're talking about. Advise me what to wish and I'll make you a free man and an honored member of my band. But if you try to make a wish yourself, I kill you. Understand?" He put the muzzle of his pistol to Abdullah's head and let go of his mouth. "What shall I wish?"

"Well," said Abdullah, "the wisest and kindest wish would be to wish your two toads turned back into men."

Kabul Aqba spared a surprised glance for the two toads. They were crawling uncertainly along the muddy edge of the pool, obviously wondering whether they could swim or not. "A waste of a wish," he said. "Think again."

Abdullah racked his brain for what might please a bandit chief most. "You could ask for limitless wealth, of course," he said, "but you would then need to carry your money, so perhaps you should first wish for a team of sturdy camels. And you would need to defend this treasure. Perhaps your first wish should be for a supply of the famous weapons of the north, or—"

"But *which?*" demanded Kabul Aqba. "Hurry. The genie is becoming impatient."

This was true. The genie was not exactly tapping his foot, since he had no feet to tap, but there was something about his looming, lowering blue face that suggested there would be two more toads by the pool if he had to wait much longer.

A very short burst of thought was enough to convince Abdullah that his situation, despite the chains, would be very much worse if he became a toad. "Why not wish for a feast?" he said lamely.

"*That's* better!" said Kabul Aqba. He clapped Abdullah on the shoulder and sprang up jovially. "I wish for a most lavish feast," he said.

The genie bowed, rather like a candle flame bending in a draft. "Done," he said sourly. "And much good may it do you." And he poured himself carefully back into his bottle again.

It was a very lavish feast. It arrived almost at once, with a dull whooping noise, on a long table with a striped awning above it for shade, and with it arrived liveried slaves to serve it. The rest of the bandits rather quickly got over their fear and came racing back to lounge on cushions and eat delicate food from golden dishes and to shout at the slaves for more, more, more! The servants were, Abdullah found when he got a chance to talk to some of them, the slaves of the Sultan of Zanzib himself, and the feast should have been the Sultan's.

This news made Abdullah feel just a little better. He spent the feast still in chains, hitched up against a handy palm tree. Though he had not expected anything better from Kabul Aqba, it was still hard. At least Kabul Aqba remembered him from time to time and, with a lordly wave of his hand, sent a slave over with a golden dish or a jug of wine.

For there was plenty. Every so often there was another muffled whoomp and a fresh course would arrive, carried by more bewildered slaves, or there would be what looked like the pick of the Sultan's wine cellar loaded onto a jeweled trolley, or an astonished group of musicians. Whenever Kabul Aqba sent a new slave over to Abdullah, Abdullah found that slave only too ready to answer questions.

"In truth, noble captive of a desert king," one told him, "the Sultan was most enraged when the first and second courses so mysteriously disappeared. On the third course, which is this roast peacock that I carry, he placed a guard of mercenaries to escort us from the kitchen, but we were snatched from beside them, even at the very door of the banquet hall, and instantly found ourselves in this oasis instead."

The Sultan, Abdullah thought, must be getting hungrier and hungrier.

Later a troupe of dancing girls appeared, snatched in the same way. That must have enraged the Sultan even more. These dancers made Abdullah melancholy. He thought of Flower-in-the-Night, who was twice as beautiful as any of them, and tears came into his eyes. As the jollity around the table grew, the two toads sat in the shallow edge of the pond, hooting mournfully. No doubt they felt at least as bad about things as Abdullah did.

The moment night fell, the slaves, the musicians, and the dancing girls all vanished, though what was left of the food and wine stayed. The bandits by then had glutted themselves and then sated themselves again after that. Most of them fell asleep where they sat. But to Abdullah's dismay, Kabul Aqba got up—a little unsteadily—and collected the genie bottle from under the table. He made sure it was corked. Then he staggered over to the magic carpet and lay down on it with the bottle in his hand. He fell asleep almost at once.

Abdullah sat against the palm tree in increasing anxiety. If the genie had returned the stolen slaves to the palace in Zanzib—and it seemed likely that he had—then someone was going to ask them angry questions. They would all tell the same story of being forced to serve a band of robbers, while a well-dressed young man in chains sat and watched from a palm tree. The Sultan would put two and two together. He was no fool. Even now a troop of soldiers could be setting out on fast racing camels to hunt the desert for a certain small oasis.

But that was not the greatest of Abdullah's worries. He watched the sleeping Kabul Aqba in even greater anxiety. He was about to lose the magic carpet and, of course, an extremely useful genie with it.

Sure enough, after about half an hour Kabul Aqba rolled over on to his back and his mouth came open. As no doubt Jamal's dog had done, as Abdullah himself must have done—but surely not so *very* loudly?—Kabul Aqba uttered an enormous rasping snore. The carpet quivered. Abdullah saw it clearly in the light of the rising moon rise a foot or so from the ground, where it hung and waited. Abdullah conjectured that it was busy interpreting whatever dream Kabul Aqba was having just then. What a bandit chief might dream about Abdullah had no idea, but the carpet knew. It soared into the air and began to fly.

Abdullah looked up as it glided over the palm

fronds above him and had one last try at influencing it. "O most unfortunate carpet!" he called out softly. "I would have treated you so much more kindly!"

Maybe the carpet heard him. Or maybe it was an accident. But something roundish and faintly glimmering rolled off the edge of the carpet and dropped with a light thunk on the sand a few feet from Abdullah. It was the genie bottle. Abdullah reached out, as quickly as he could without too much rattling and jingling of his chains, and dragged the bottle into hiding between his back and the palm tree. Then he sat and waited for morning, feeling decidedly more hopeful.

Chapter 8

In which Abdullah's dreams continue to come true

The moment the sun flushed the sand dunes with white-rosy light, Abdullah wrenched the cork out of the genie's bottle. The vapor steamed forth, became a jet, and rushed upward into the blue-mauve shape of the genie, who looked, if possible, angrier than ever. "I said one wish a day!" the windy voice announced.

"Yes, well, this is a new day, O mauve magnificence, and I am your new owner," said Abdullah. "And this wish is simple. I wish these chains of mine gone."

"Hardly worth wasting a wish on," the genie said contemptuously, and dwindled rapidly away inside the bottle again. Abdullah was just about to protest that though this wish might seem trivial to a genie, being without chains was important to *him* when he found himself able to move freely, without rattling. He looked down and found the chains had vanished.

He put the cork carefully back in the bottle and stood up. He was horribly stiff. Before he could move at all, he had to make himself think of fleet camels with soldiers on them speeding toward this oasis and then of what would happen if the sleeping bandits woke to find him standing there without his chains. That got him moving. He hobbled like an old man toward the banquet table. There, very careful not to disturb the various bandits who were asleep with their faces on the cloth, he collected food and wrapped it in a napkin. He took a flask of wine and tied it and the genie bottle to his belt with two more napkins. He took a last napkin to cover his head in case he got sunstroke—travelers had told him this was a real danger in the desert—and then he set off, as swiftly as he could limp, out of the oasis and due north.

The stiffness wore off as he walked. Walking became almost pleasant then, and for the first half of the morning Abdullah strode out with a will, thinking of Flower-in-the-Night and eating succulent meat pies and swigging from the wine flask as he walked. The second half of the morning was not so good. The sun swung overhead. The sky became glaring white, and everything shimmered. Abdullah started to wish that he had poured the wine away and filled the flask at the muddy pond instead. Wine did nothing for thirst except make it worse. He wet the napkin with wine and laid it over the back of his neck, where it kept drying out far too quickly. By midday he thought he was dying. The desert swayed about before his eyes, and the glare hurt. He felt like a sort of human cinder.

"It seems that Fate has decreed that I live through my entire daydream in reality!" he croaked.

Up till then he had thought he had imagined his escape from the villainous Kabul Aqba in masterly detail, but now he knew he had never even conceived of how horrible it was to stagger in blaring heat, with sweat running into his eyes. He had not imagined the way the sand somehow got into everything, including his mouth. Nor had his daydream allowed for the difficulty of steering by the sun when the sun was right overhead. The tiny puddle of shadow around his feet gave him no guide to direction. He had to keep looking behind to check that his line of footprints was straight. This worried him because it wasted time.

In the end, wasted time or not, he was forced to stop and rest, squatting in a dip in the sands where there was a small piece of shade. He still felt like a piece of meat laid out on Jamal's charcoal grill. He soaked the napkin in wine and spread it over his head and then watched it drip red blobs on his best clothes. The only thing that convinced him he was not going to die was that prophecy about Flower-in-the-Night. If Fate had decreed that she was to marry him, then he *had* to survive because he had not yet married her. After that he thought of the prophecy about himself, written down by his father. It could have more than one meaning. In fact, it could already have come true, for had he not risen above everyone in the land by flying on the magic carpet? Or perhaps it did refer to a forty-foot stake.

This notion forced Abdullah to get up and walk again.

The afternoon was worse still. Abdullah was young and fit, but the life of a carpet merchant does not include long walks. He ached from his heels to the top of his head—not forgetting his toes, which seemed to have worn raw. In addition, one of his boots turned out to rub where the money pocket was. His legs were so tired he could hardly move them. But he knew he had to put the horizon between himself and the oasis before the bandits started looking for him or the line of fleet camels appeared. Since he was not sure how far it was to the horizon, he slogged on.

By evening all that kept him going was the knowledge that he would be seeing Flower-in-the-Night tomorrow. That was to be his next wish to the genie. Apart from that, he vowed to give up drinking wine and swore never to look at a grain of sand again.

When night fell, he toppled into a sandbank and slept.

At dawn his teeth were chattering and he was anxiously wondering about frostbite. The desert was as cold by night as it was hot by day. Still, Abdullah knew his troubles were almost over. He sat on the warmer side of the sandbank, looking east into the golden flush of dawn, and refreshed himself with the last of his food and a final swig of the hateful wine. His teeth stopped chattering, though his mouth tasted as if it belonged to Jamal's dog.

Now. Smiling in anticipation, Abdullah eased the cork out of the genie's bottle.

Out gushed the mauve smoke and rolled upward into the genie's unfriendly form. "What are you grinning about?" asked the windy voice.

"My wish, O amethyst among genies, of color more beautiful than pansies . . ." Abdullah replied. "May violets scent your breath. I wish you to transport me to the side of my bride-to-be, Flower-in-the-Night."

"Oh, do you?" The genie folded his smoky arms and turned himself to look in all directions. This, to Abdullah's fascination, turned the part of him that was joined to the bottle into a neat corkscrew shape. "Where *is* this young woman?" the genie said irritably when he was facing Abdullah again. "I can't seem to locate her."

"She was carried off by a djinn from her night garden in the Sultan's palace in Zanzib," Abdullah explained.

"That accounts for it," said the genie. "I can't grant your wish. She's nowhere on earth."

"Then she must be in the realm of the djinns,"

Abdullah said anxiously. "Surely you, O purple prince among genies, must know that realm like the back of your hand."

"That shows how little you know," the genie said. "A genie confined to a bottle is debarred from any of the spirit realms. If that's where your girl is, I can't take you there. I advise you to put the cork back in my bottle and be on your way. There's quite a large troop of camels coming up from the south."

Abdullah sprang to the top of the sandbank. Sure enough, there was the line of fleet camels he had been dreading, speeding toward him with smooth waltzing strides. Though distance made them visible only as indigo shadows just then, he could tell from the outlines that the riders were armed to the teeth.

"See?" said the genie, bellying upward to the same height as Abdullah. "They might miss finding you, but I doubt it." The idea clearly gave him pleasure.

"You must grant me a different wish, quickly," said Abdullah.

"*Oh*, no," said the genie. "One wish a day. You've already made one."

"Certainly I did, O splendor of lilac vapors," Abdullah agreed with the speed of desperation, "but that was a wish you were unable to grant. And the terms, as I clearly heard when you first stated them, were that you were forced to *grant* your owner one wish a day. This you have not yet done."

"Heaven preserve me!" the genie said disgustedly. "The young man is a coffee shop lawyer."

"Naturally I am!" said Abdullah with some heat. "I am a citizen of Zanzib, where every child learns to guard its rights, for it is certain that no one else will guard them. And I claim you have not yet *granted* me a wish today."

"A quibble," the genie said, swaying gracefully opposite him with folded arms. "One wish has been made."

"But not granted," said Abdullah.

"It is not my fault if you choose to ask for things which are impossible," said the genie. "There are a million beautiful girls I can take you to, instead. You can have a mermaid if you fancy green hair. Or can't you swim?"

The speeding line of camels was now a good deal nearer. Abdullah said hurriedly, "Think, O puce pearl of magic, and soften your heart. Those soldiers approaching us will certainly seize your bottle from me when they reach us. If they take you back to the Sultan, he will force you to do mighty deeds daily, bringing him armies and weapons and conquering his enemies for him, most exhaustingly. If they keep you for themselves—and they might, for not all soldiers are quite honest—you will be passed from hand to hand and be made to grant many wishes each day, one for each of the squad. In either case, you will be working far harder than you will work for me, who want only one small thing."

"What eloquence!" said the genie. "Though you have a point. But have you thought, on the other hand, what opportunities the Sultan or his soldiers will give me to work havoc?"

"Havoc?" asked Abdullah, with his eyes anxiously on the speeding camels.

"I never said my wishes were supposed to do anyone any good," said the genie. "In fact, I swore that they would always do as much harm as possible. Those bandits, for instance, are now all on their way to prison or worse, for stealing the Sultan's feast. The soldiers found them late last night."

"You are causing worse havoc with me for *not* granting me a wish!" said Abdullah. "And unlike the bandits, I do not deserve it."

"Regard yourself as unlucky," said the genie. "This will make two of us. I don't deserve to be shut in this bottle, either."

The riders were now near enough to see Abdullah. He could hear shouts in the distance and see weapons being unslung. "Give me tomorrow's wish, then," he said urgently.

"That might be the solution," the genie agreed, rather to Abdullah's surprise. "What wish then?"

"Transport me to the nearest person who can help me find Flower-in-the-Night," said Abdullah, and he bounded down the sandbank and picked the bottle up. "Quickly," he added to the genie, now billowing above him.

The genie seemed a little puzzled. "This is odd," he said. "My powers of divination are usually excellent, but I can't make head or tail of this."

A bullet plowed into the sand not too far away. Abdullah ran, carrying the genie like a vast streaming mauve candle flame. "Just take me to that person!" he screamed.

"I suppose I'd better," said the genie. "Maybe you can make some sense out of it."

The earth seemed to spin past under Abdullah's running feet. Shortly he seemed to be taking vast loping strides across lands that were whirling forward to meet him. Though the combined speed of his own feet and the turning world made everything into a blur, except for the genie streaming placidly out of the bottle in his hand, Abdullah knew that the speeding camels were left behind in instants. He smiled and loped on, almost as placid as the genie, rejoicing in the cool wind. He seemed to lope for a long time. Then it all stopped.

Abdullah stood in the middle of a country road, getting his breath. This new place took a certain amount of getting used to. It was cool, only as warm as Zanzib in springtime, and the light was different. Though the sun was shining brightly from a blue sky, it put out a light that was lower and bluer than Abdullah was used to. This may have been because there were so many very leafy trees lining the road and casting shifting green shade over everything. Or it may have been due to the green, green grass growing on the verges. Abdullah let his eyes adjust and then looked around for the person who was supposed to help him find Flower-in-the-Night.

All he could see was what seemed to be an inn on a bend in the road, set back among the trees. It struck Abdullah as a wretched place. It was made of wood and white-painted plaster, like the poorest of poor dwellings in Zanzib, and its owners only seemed able to afford a roof made of tightly packed grass. Someone had tried to beautify the place by planting red and yellow flowers by the road. The inn sign, which was swinging on a post planted among the flowers, was a bad artist's effort to paint a lion.

Abdullah looked down at the genie's bottle, intending to put the cork back into it now he had arrived. He was annoyed to find he seemed to have dropped the cork, either in the desert or on the journey. Oh, well, he thought. He held the bottle up to his face. "Where is the person who can help me find Flower-in-the-Night?" he asked.

A wisp of steam smoked from the bottle, looking much bluer in the light of this strange land. "Asleep on a bench in front of the Red Lion," the wisp said irritably, and withdrew back into the bottle. The genie's hollow voice came from inside it. "He appeals to me. He shines with dishonesty."

Chapter 9

---×—×—×---

In which Abdullah encounters
an old soldier

Abdullah walked toward the inn. When he got closer, he
saw that there was indeed a man dozing on one of the
wooden settles that had been placed outside the inn.
There were tables there, too, suggesting that the place
also served food. Abdullah slid into a settle behind
one of the tables and looked dubiously across at the
sleeping man.

He looked like an outright ruffian. Even in
Zanzib, or among the bandits, Abdullah had never
seen such dishonest lines as there were on this man's
tanned face. A big pack on the ground beside him made
Abdullah think at first that he might be a tinker—
except that he was clean-shaven. The only other
men Abdullah had seen without beards or mustaches
were the Sultan's northern mercenaries. It was possible this man was a mercenary soldier. His clothes did
look like the broken-down remains of some kind of
uniform, and he wore his hair in a single pigtail down
his back in the way the Sultan's men did. This was a

fashion the men of Zanzib found quite disgusting, for it was rumored that the pigtail was never undone or washed. Looking at this man's pigtail, draped over the back of the settle where he slept, Abdullah could believe this. Neither it nor anything else about the man was clean. All the same, he looked strong and healthy, although he was not young. His hair under its dirt seemed to be iron gray.

Abdullah hesitated to wake the fellow. He did not look trustworthy. And the genie had openly admitted that he granted wishes in a way that would cause havoc. This man may lead me to Flower-in-the-Night, Abdullah mused, but he will certainly rob me on the way.

While he hesitated, a woman in an apron came to the inn doorway, perhaps to see if there were customers outside. Her clothes made her into a plump hourglass shape which Abdullah found very foreign and displeasing. "Oh!" she said, when she saw Abdullah. "Were you waiting to be served, sir? You should have banged on the table. That's what they all do around here. What'll you have?"

She spoke in the same barbarous accent as the northern mercenaries. From it Abdullah concluded that he was now in whatever country those men came from. He smiled at her. "What are you offering, O jewel of the wayside?" he asked her.

Evidently no one had ever called the woman a

jewel before. She blushed and simpered and twisted her apron. "Well, there's bread and cheese now," she said. "But dinner's doing. If you care to wait half an hour, sir, you can have a good game pie with vegetables from our kitchen garden."

Abdullah thought this sounded perfect, far better than he would have expected from any inn with a grass roof. "Then I would most gladly wait half an hour, O flower among hostesses," he said.

She gave him another simper. "And perhaps a drink while you wait, sir?"

"Certainly," said Abdullah, who was still very thirsty from the desert. "Could I trouble you for a glass of sherbet—or, failing that, the juice of any fruit?"

She looked worried. "Oh, sir, I—we don't go in much for fruit juice, and I never heard of the other stuff. How about a nice mug of beer?"

"What is beer?" Abdullah asked cautiously.

This flummoxed the woman. "I—well, I—it's, er—"

The man on the other bench roused himself and yawned. "Beer is the only proper drink for a man," he said. "Wonderful stuff." Abdullah turned to look at him again. He found himself staring into a pair of round limpid blue eyes, as honest as the day is long. There was not a trace of dishonesty in the brown face now it was awake. "Brewed from barley and hops," added the man. "While you're here, landlady, I'll have a pint of it myself."

The landlady's expression changed completely. "I've told you already," she said, "that I want to see the color of your money before I serve you with anything."

The man was not offended. His blue eyes met Abdullah's ruefully. Then he sighed and picked up a long white clay pipe from the settle beside him, which he proceeded to fill and light.

"Shall it be beer then, sir?" the landlady said, returning to her simper for Abdullah.

"If you would, lady of lavish hospitality," he said. "Bring me some, and also bring a fitting quantity for this gentleman here."

"Very well, sir," she said, and with a strongly disapproving look at the pigtailed man, she went back indoors.

"I call that very kind of you," the man said to Abdullah. "Come far, have you?"

"A fair way from the south, worshipful wanderer," Abdullah answered cautiously. He had not forgotten how dishonest the fellow had looked in his sleep.

"From foreign parts, eh? I thought you must be, to get a sunburn like that," the man observed. Abdullah was fairly sure the fellow was fishing for information, to see if he was worth robbing. He was therefore quite surprised when the man seemed to give up asking questions. "I'm not from these parts either, you know," he said, puffing large clouds of smoke from his barbarous pipe. "I'm from Strangia myself. Old soldier. Turned loose on the world with a bounty after Ingary beat us in the war. As you saw, there's still a lot of prejudice here in Ingary about this uniform of mine."

He said this into the face of the landlady as she came back with two glasses of frothing brownish liquid. She did not speak to him. She just banged one glass down in front of him before she put the other carefully and politely in front of Abdullah. "Dinner in half an hour, sir," she said as she went away.

"Cheers," said the soldier, lifting his glass. He drank deeply.

Abdullah was grateful to this old soldier. Thanks to him, he now knew he was in a country called Ingary. So he said, "Cheers," in return as he dubiously lifted his own glass. It seemed to him likely that the stuff in it had come from the bladder of a camel. When he sniffed it, the smell did nothing to dispel that impression. Only the fact that he was still horribly thirsty led him to try it at all. He took a careful mouthful. Well, it was wet.

"Wonderful, isn't it?" said the old soldier.

"It is most interesting, O captain of warriors," Abdullah said, trying not to shudder.

"Funny you should call me captain," said the soldier. "I wasn't, of course. Never made it higher than corporal. Saw a lot of fighting, though, and I did have hopes of promotion, but the enemy were all over us before I got my chance. Terrible battle it was, you know. We were still on the march. No one expected the enemy to get there so soon. I mean, it's all over now, and there's no point in crying over spilled milk; but I'll tell you straight the Ingarians didn't fight fair. Had a couple of wizards making sure they won. I mean, what can an ordinary soldier like me do against magic? Nothing. Like me to show you a plan of how the battle went?"

Abdullah understood just where the genie's malice lay now. This man who was supposed to help him was quite obviously a thundering bore. "I know absolutely nothing of military matters, O most valiant strategist," he said firmly.

"No matter," the soldier said cheerfully. "You can take it from me we were absolutely routed. We ran. Ingary conquered us. Overran the whole country. Our royal family, bless them, had to run, too, so they put the King of Ingary's brother on the throne. There was some talk of making this prince legal by having him marry our Princess Beatrice; but she'd run with the rest of her family—long life to her!—and she couldn't be found. Mind you, the new prince wasn't all bad. Gave all the Strangian army a bounty before he turned us loose. Like to know what I'm doing with my money?"

"If you wish to tell me, bravest of veterans," Abdullah said, smothering a yawn.

"I'm seeing Ingary," said the soldier. "Thought I'd take a walk through the country that conquered us. Find out what it's like before I settle down. It's a fair sum, my bounty. I can pay my way as long as I'm careful."

"My felicitations," Abdullah said.

"They paid half of it in gold," said the soldier.

"Indeed," said Abdullah.

It was a great relief to him that a few local customers arrived just then. They were farming people mostly, wearing mucky breeches and outlandish smocks that reminded Abdullah of his own nightshirt, along with great clumping boots. Very cheerful they were, talking loudly of the hay crop—which they said was doing nicely—and bashing on the tables for beer. The landlady and a little twinkling landlord, too, were kept very busy running in and out with trays of glasses because, from then on, more and more people kept arriving. And—Abdullah did not know whether to be more relieved, or annoyed, or amused—the soldier instantly lost interest in Abdullah and began to talk earnestly to the new arrivals. They did not seem to find him boring at all. Nor did it seem to worry them that he had been an enemy soldier. One of them bought him more beer at once. As more and more people arrived, he became ever more popular. Beer glasses lined up beside him. Dinner was ordered for him before long, while out of the crowd that surrounded the soldier, Abdullah kept hearing things like "Great battle . . . Your wizards gave them the advantage, see . . . our cavalry . . . folded up our left wing . . . overran us on the hill . . . we infantry forced to run . . . went on running like rabbits . . . not a bad sort . . . rounded us up and paid us a bounty . . . "

Meanwhile, the landlady came to Abdullah with a steaming tray and more beer without being asked. He was still so thirsty he was almost glad of the beer. And the dinner struck him as quite as delicious as the Sultan's feast. For a while he was so busy attending to it that he lost track of the soldier. When he next looked, the soldier was leaning forward over his own empty plate, blue eyes shining with earnest enthusiasm, while he moved glasses and plates about on the table to show his country listeners exactly where everything was in the Battle of Strangia. After a while he ran out of glasses, forks, and plates. Since he had already used the salt and the pepper for the King of Strangia and his general, he had nothing left to use for the King of Ingary and his brother or for their wizards. But the soldier did not let this bother him. He opened a pouch at his belt and took out two gold coins and a number of silver ones, which he rang down on the table to stand for the King of Ingary, his wizards, and his generals.

Abdullah could not help thinking this was extraordinarily silly of him. The two gold pieces caused quite a bit of comment. Four loutish-looking young men at a nearby table turned around on their settles and began to be extremely interested. But the soldier was deep into explaining the battle and quite unaware of it.

Finally, most of the folk around the soldier got up to go back to their work. The soldier got up with them, slung his pack on his shoulder, put on his head the dirty soldier's hat which was tucked into the top flap of his pack, and asked the way to the nearest town. While everyone was loudly explaining the way to the soldier, Abdullah tried to catch the landlady in order to pay his own bill. She was a little slow in coming. By the time she was ready, the soldier was out of sight around the bend in the road. Abdullah was not sorry. Whatever help the genie thought this man could give, Abdullah felt he could do without it. He was glad that Fate and he seemed to see eye to eye for once.

Not being a fool like the soldier, Abdullah paid his bill with his smallest silver coin. Even that seemed to be big money in these parts. The landlady took it indoors in order to get change. While he was waiting for her to come back, Abdullah could not help over-hearing the four loutish young men. They were hold-ing a swift and significant discussion.

"If we nip up the old bridle path," one said, "we

can catch him in the wood at the top of the hill."

"Hide in the bushes," agreed the second, "on both sides of the road, so we come at him two ways."

"Split the money four ways," insisted the third. "He's got more gold than he showed, that's certain."

"We make sure he's dead first," said the fourth. "We don't want him telling tales."

And "Right!" and "Right" and "Right then," the other three said, and they got up and left as the landlady came hurrying to Abdullah with a double handful of copper coins.

"I do hope this is the right change, sir. We don't get much southern silver here, and I had to ask my husband how much it was worth. He says it's one hundred of our coppers, and you owed us five, so—"

"Bless you, O cream of caterers and brewer of celestial beer," Abdullah said hurriedly, and gave her one handful of the coins back instead of the nice long chat she was obviously meaning to have with him. Leaving her staring, he set off as swiftly as he was able after the soldier. The man might be a barefaced sponger and a thundering bore, but this did not mean he deserved to be ambushed and murdered for his gold.

Chapter 10

Which tells of violence and bloodshed

Abdullah found he could not go very fast. In the cooler climate of Ingary, he had stiffened abominably while he sat still, and his legs ached from walking all the day before. The money container in his left boot proved to have made a very severe blister on his left foot. He was limping before he had walked a hundred yards. Still, he was concerned enough about the soldier to keep up the best pace he could. He limped past a number of cottages with grass roofs and then out beyond the village, where the road was more open. There he could see the soldier in the distance ahead, sauntering along toward a point where the road climbed a hill covered with the dense leafy trees that seemed to grow in these parts. That would be where the loutish young men were setting their ambush. Abdullah tried to limp faster.

An irritable blue wisp came out of the bottle bouncing at his waist. "Must you *bump* so?" it said.

"Yes," panted Abdullah. "The man you chose to

help me needs *my* help instead."

"Huh!" said the genie. "I understand you now. Nothing will stop you taking a romantic view of life. You'll be wanting shining armor for your next wish."

The soldier was sauntering quite slowly. Abdullah closed the gap between them and entered the wood not far behind. But the road here wound back and forth among the trees to make an easier climb, so that Abdullah lost sight of the soldier from then on, until he limped around a final corner and saw him only a few yards ahead. That happened to be the very moment when the louts chose to make their attack.

Two of them sprang from one side of the road upon the soldier's back. The two who jumped from the other side rushed him from in front. There was a moment or so of horrid drubbing and struggling. Abdullah hastened to help, though he hastened somewhat hesitantly because he had never hit anyone in his life.

While he approached, a whole set of miracles seemed to happen. The two fellows on the soldier's back went sailing away in opposite directions, to either side of the road, where one of them hit his head on a tree and did not trouble anyone again, while the other collapsed in a sprawl. Of the two facing the soldier, one received almost at once an interesting injury, which he doubled up to contemplate. The other, to Abdullah's considerable astonishment, rose into the air and actually, for a brief instant, became draped over the branch of a tree. From there he fell with a crash and went to sleep in the road.

At this point, the doubled-up young man undoubled himself and went for the soldier with a long, narrow knife. The soldier seized the wrist of the hand that held the knife. There was a moment of grunting deadlock, which Abdullah found he had every faith would soon be resolved in favor of the soldier. He was just thinking that his concern about this soldier had been completely unnecessary, when the fellow sprawled in the road behind the soldier suddenly unsprawled himself and lunged at the soldier's back with another long, thin knife.

Quickly Abdullah did what was needful. He stepped up and clouted the young man over the head with the genie bottle. *"Ouch!"* cried the genie. And the fellow dropped like a fallen oak tree.

At the sound the soldier swung around from apparently tying knots in the other young man. Abdullah stepped back hurriedly. He did not like the speed with which the soldier turned or the way he held his hands, with the fingers tightly together, like two blunt but murderous weapons.

"I heard them planning to kill you, valiant veteran," he explained quickly, "and hurried to warn or help."

He found the soldier's eyes fixed on his, very blue

but no longer at all innocent. In fact, they were eyes that would have counted as shrewd even in the Bazaar at Zanzib. They seemed to sum Abdullah up in every possible way. Luckily they seemed satisfied with what they saw. The soldier said, "Thanks, then," and turned to kick the head of the young man he had been tying into knots. He stopped moving, too, making the full set.

"Perhaps," suggested Abdullah, "we should report this to a constable."

"What for?" asked the soldier. He bent down and, to Abdullah's slight surprise, made a swift and expert search of the pockets of the young man whose head he had just kicked. The result of the search was quite a large handful of coppers, which the soldier stowed in his own pouch, looking satisfied. "Rotten knife, though," he said, snapping it in two. "Since you're here, why don't you search the one you clob-bered, while I do the other two? Yours looks worth a silver or so."

"You mean," Abdullah said doubtfully, "that the custom of this country permits us to rob the robbers?"

"It's no custom I ever heard of," the soldier said calmly, "but it's what I aim to do all the same. Why do you think I was so careful to flash my gold about at the inn? There's always a bad'un or so who thinks a stupid old soldier worth mugging. Nearly all of them carry cash."

He stepped across the road and began to search the young man who had fallen out of the tree. After hesitating a moment, Abdullah bent to the unpleasing task of searching the one he had felled with the bottle. He found himself revising his opinion of this soldier. Apart from anything else, a man who could confidently take on four attackers at once was someone who was better as a friend than an enemy. And the pockets of the unconscious youth did indeed contain three pieces of silver. There was also the knife. Abdullah tried breaking it on the road as the soldier had done with the other knife.

"Ah, no," said the soldier. "That one's a good knife. You hang on to it."

"Truthfully I have had no experience," Abdullah said, holding it out to the soldier. "I am a man of peace."

"Then you won't get far in Ingary," said the soldier. "Keep it, and use it for cutting your meat if you'd rather. I've got six more knives better than that in my pack, all off different ruffians. Keep the silver, too—though from the way you didn't get interested when I talked of my gold, I guess you're quite well off, aren't you?"

Truly a shrewd and observant man, Abdullah thought, pocketing the silver. "I am not so well off that I could not do with more," he said prudently. Then, feeling that he was entering properly into the spirit of things, he removed the young man's boot-laces and used them to tie the genie bottle more securely to his belt. The young man stirred and groaned as he did so.

"Waking up. We'd best be off," said the soldier. "They'll twist it around to *we* attacked *them* when they wake up. And seeing this is their village and we're both foreigners, they're the ones who'll get believed. I'm going to cut off across the hills. If you'll take my advice, you'll do likewise."

"I would, most gentle fighting man, feel honored if I could accompany you," Abdullah said.

"I don't mind," said the soldier. "It'll make a change to have company I don't have to lie to." He picked up his pack and his hat—both of which he seemed to have had time to stow tidily behind a tree before the fighting began—and led the way into the woods.

They climbed steadily among the trees for some time. The soldier made Abdullah feel woefully unfit. He strode as lightly and easily as if the way were downhill. Abdullah limped after. His left foot felt raw.

At length the soldier stopped and waited for him in an upland dell. "That fancy boot hurting you?" he asked. "Sit on that rock and take it off." He unslung his pack as he spoke. "I've got some kind of unusual first-aid kit in here," he said. "Picked it up on the battlefield, I think. Found it somewhere in Strangia, anyway."

Abdullah sat down and wrestled off his boot. The relief it gave him to have it off was quickly canceled when he looked at his foot. It *was* raw. The soldier grunted and slapped some kind of white dressing on it, which clung without needing to be tied on. Abdullah yelped. Then blissful coolness spread from the dressing. "Is this some kind of magic?" he asked.

"Probably," the soldier said. "I think those Ingary wizards gave these packs to their whole army. Put the boot on. You'll be able to walk now. We've got to be far away before those boys' dads start looking for us on horseback."

Abdullah trod cautiously into his boot. The dressing must have been magic. His foot seemed as good as new. He was almost able to keep up with the soldier—which was just as well, for the soldier marched onward and upward until Abdullah felt they had gone as far as he had walked in the desert yesterday. From time to time Abdullah could not help glancing nervously behind in case horses were now pursuing them. He told himself it made a change from camels, although it would be nice not to have someone chasing him for once. Thinking about it, he saw that even in the Bazaar his father's first wife's relatives had been pursuing him ever since his father died. He was annoyed with himself for not having seen this before.

Meanwhile, they had climbed so high that the

wood was giving way to wiry shrubs among rocks. As evening drew on, they were walking simply among rocks, somewhere near the top of a range of mountains, where only a few small, strong-smelling bushes grew, clinging to crevices. This was another sort of desert, Abdullah thought, while the soldier led the way along a narrow sort of ravine between high rocks. It did not look like a place where there was any chance of finding supper.

Some way along the ravine the soldier stopped and took off his pack. "Take care of this for a moment," he said. "There looks to be a cave of sorts up the cliff this side. I'll pop up and see if it's a good place to spend the night."

There did seem to be a dark opening in the rocks some way above their heads when Abdullah wearily looked up. He did not fancy sleeping in it. It looked cold and hard. But it was probably better than just lying down on the rock, he thought, as he ruefully watched the soldier swing easily up the cliff and arrive at the hole.

There was a noise like a mad metal pulley wheel.

Abdullah saw the soldier reel back from the cave with one hand clapped to his face and almost fall backward down the cliff. He saved himself somehow and came sliding and cursing down the rocks in a storm of rubble.

"Wild animal in there!" he gasped. "Let's move

on." He was bleeding quite badly from eight long scratches. Four of them started on his forehead, crossed his hand, and went on down his cheek to his chin. The other four had torn his sleeve open and scored his arm from wrist to elbow. It looked as if he had got his hand to his face only just in time to avoid losing an eye. He was so shaken that Abdullah had to pick up his hat and his pack and guide him on down the ravine—which he did rather hurriedly. Any animal that could get the better of this soldier was an animal Abdullah did not want to meet.

The ravine ended after another hundred yards. And it ended in the perfect camping place. They were now on the other side of the mountains with a wide view over the lands beyond, all golden and green and hazy in the westering sun. The ravine stopped in a broad floor of rock sloping gently up to what was almost another cave, where the rocks above hung over the slanting floor. Better still, there was a small stony stream babbling down the mountain just beyond.

Perfect though this was, Abdullah had no wish to stop anywhere so near that wild animal in the cave. But the soldier insisted. The scratches were hurting him. He threw himself down on the sloping rock and fetched out some kind of salve from the wizardly first-aid kit. "Light a fire," he said as he smeared the stuff on his wounds. "Wild animals are scared of fire."

Abdullah gave in and scrambled about, tearing up strong-smelling shrubs to burn. An eagle or something had nested in the crags above long ago. The old nest gave Abdullah armloads of twigs and quite a few dry branches, so that he soon had quite a stack of firewood. When the soldier had finished smearing himself with the salve, he brought out a tinderbox and lit a small fire halfway down the sloping rock. It crackled and leaped most cheerfully. The smoke, smelling rather like the incense Abdullah used to burn in his booth, drifted out from the end of the ravine and spread against the beginnings of a glorious sunset. If this really scared the beast in the cave off, Abdullah thought, it would be almost perfect here. Only *almost* perfect, because of course, there was nothing to eat for miles. Abdullah sighed.

The soldier produced a metal can from his pack. "Like to fill that with water? Unless," he said, eyeing the genie bottle tied to Abdullah's belt, "you've got something stronger in that flask of yours."

"Alas, no," Abdullah said. "It is merely an heirloom—rare fogged glass from Singispat—which I carry for sentimental reasons." He had no intention of letting someone as dishonest as the soldier know about the genie.

"Pity," said the soldier. "Fetch us water then, and I'll get on with cooking us some supper."

This made the place almost nearly perfect.

Abdullah went leaping down to the stream with a will. When he came back, he found the soldier had brought out a saucepan and was emptying packets of dried meat and dried peas into it. He added the water and a couple of mysterious cubes and set it to boil on the fire. In a remarkably short time it had turned into a thick stew. And smelled delicious.

"More wizard's stuff?" Abdullah asked as the soldier shared half the stew onto a tin plate and passed it to him.

"I think so," said the soldier. "I picked it up off the battlefield." He took the saucepan to eat from himself and found a couple of spoons. They sat eating companionably with the fire crackling between them, while the sky turned slowly pink and crimson and gold, and the lands below became blue. "Not used to roughing it, are you?" the soldier remarked. "Good clothes, fancy boots, you have, but they've seen a bit of wear and tear lately by the looks of them. And by your talk and your sunburn, you come from quite a way south of Ingary, don't you?"

"All that is true, O most acutely observant campaigner," Abdullah said cagily. "And of you all I know is that you come from Strangia and are most oddly proceeding through this land, encouraging persons to rob you by flourishing the coins of your bounty—"

"Bounty be damned!" the soldier interrupted angrily. "Not one penny did I get from either Strangia or Ingary! I sweated my guts out in those wars—we all did—and at the end of it they say, 'Right, lads, that's it, it's peacetime now!' and turn us all out to starve. So I say to myself, 'Right indeed! *Someone* owes me for all the work I've done, and I reckon it's the folk of Ingary! *They* were the ones who brought wizards in and cheated their way to victory!' So I set off to *earn* my bounty off them, the way you saw me doing it today. You may call it a scam if you like, but you saw me; you judge me. I only take money off those who up and try to rob *me!*"

"Indeed, the word *scam* never crossed my lips, virtuous veteran," Abdullah said sincerely. "I call it most ingenious, and a plan that few but you could succeed in."

The soldier seemed soothed by this. He stared ruminatively out at the blue distance below. "All that down there," he said, "that's Kingsbury Plain. That should yield me a mort of gold. Do you know, when I started out from Strangia, all I had was a silver three-penny bit and a brass button I used to pretend was a sovereign?"

"Then your profit has been great," said Abdullah.

"And it'll be greater yet," the soldier promised. He set the saucepan neatly aside and fished two apples out of his pack. He gave one to Abdullah and ate the other himself, lying stretched on his back, staring out at the slowly darkening land. Abdullah assumed he was calculating the gold he would earn from it. He was surprised when the soldier said, "I always did love the evening camp. Take a look at that sunset now. Glorious!"

It was indeed glorious. Clouds had come up from the south and had spread like a ruby landscape across the sky. Abdullah saw ranges of purple mountains flushed wine red in one part; a smoking orange rift like the heart of a volcano; a calm rosy lake. Out beyond, laid against an infinity of gold-blue sky-sea, were islands, reefs, bays, and promontories. It was as if they were looking at the seacoast of heaven or the land that looks westward to Paradise.

"And that cloud there," the soldier said, pointing. "Doesn't that one look just like a castle?"

It did. It stood on a high headland above a sky-lagoon, a marvel of slender gold, ruby, and indigo turrets. A glimpse of golden sky through the tallest tower was like a window. It reminded Abdullah poignantly of the cloud he had seen above the Sultan's palace while he was being dragged off to the dungeon. Though it was not in the least the same shape, it brought back his sorrows to him so forcefully that he cried out.

"O Flower-in-the-Night, where *are* you?"

Chapter 11

———— ✦ ————

In which a wild animal causes
Abdullah to waste a wish

The soldier turned on his elbow and stared at Abdullah.

"What's that supposed to mean?"

"Nothing," said Abdullah, "except that my life has been full of disappointments."

"Tell," said the soldier. "Unburden. I told you about me, after all."

"You would never believe me," said Abdullah. "My sorrows surpass even yours, most murderous musketeer."

"Try me," said the soldier.

Somehow it was not hard to tell, what with the sunset and the misery that sunset brought surging up in Abdullah. So, as the castle slowly spread and dissolved into sandbars in the sky-lagoon and the whole sunset faded gently to purple, to brown, and finally to three dark red streaks like the healing claw marks on the soldier's face, Abdullah told the soldier his story. Or at any rate, he told the gist of it. He did not, of course, tell anything so personal as his own daydreams or the uncomfortable way they had of coming true lately, and he was very careful to say nothing at all about the genie. He did not trust the soldier not to take the bottle and vanish with it during the night, and he was helped in this editing of the facts by a strong suspicion that the soldier had not told his whole story, either. The end of the story was quite difficult to tell with the genie left out, but Abdullah thought he managed rather well. He gave the impression he had escaped from his chains and from the bandits more or less by willpower alone, and then that he had walked all the way north to Ingary.

"Hmm," said the soldier when Abdullah had done. Musingly he put more spicy bushes on the fire, which was now the only light left. "Quite a life. But I must say it makes up for a good deal, being fated to marry a princess. It's something I always had a fancy to do myself—marry a nice quiet princess with a bit of a kingdom and a kindly nature. Bit of a daydream of mine, really."

Abdullah found he had a splendid idea. "It is quite possible you can," he said quietly. "The day I met you I was granted a dream—a vision—in which a smoky angel the color of lavender came to me and pointed you out to me, O cleverest of crusaders, as you slept on a bench outside an inn. He said that you could aid me powerfully in finding Flower-in-the-Night. And if you did, said the angel, your reward would be that you would marry another princess yourself." This was—or would be—almost perfectly true, Abdullah told himself. He had only to make the correct wish to the genie tomorrow. Or rather, the day *after* tomorrow, he reminded himself, since the genie had forced him to use tomorrow's wish today. "Will you help me?" he asked, watching the soldier's firelit face rather anxiously. "For this great reward."

The soldier seemed neither eager nor dismayed. He considered. "Not sure quite what I could do to help," he said at last. "I'm not an expert on djinns, for a start. We don't seem to get them this far north. You'd need to ask some of these damn Ingary wizards what djinns do with princesses when they steal them. The wizards would know. I could help you squeeze the facts out of one, if you like. It would be a pleasure. But as for a princess, they don't grow on trees, you know. The nearest one must be the King of Ingary's daughter, way off in Kingsbury. If she's what your smoky angel friend had in mind, then I guess you and me'd better walk down that way and see. The king's tame wizards mostly live down that way, too, so they tell me, so it seems to fit in. That idea suit you?"

"Excellently well, military friend of my bosom!" said Abdullah.

"Then that's settled, but I don't promise anything, mind," said the soldier. He fetched two blankets out of his pack and suggested that they build up the fire and settle down to sleep.

Abdullah unhitched the genie bottle from his belt and put it carefully on the smooth rock beside him on the other side from the soldier. Then he wrapped himself in the blanket and settled down for what proved to be rather a disturbed night. The rock was hard. And though he was nothing like as cold as he had been yesterday night in the desert, the damper air of Ingary made him shiver just as much. In addition, the moment he closed his eyes he found he became obsessed with the wild beast in the cave up the ravine. He kept imagining he could hear it prowling around the camp. Once or twice he opened his eyes and even thought he saw something moving just beyond the light from the fire. He sat up each time and threw more wood on the fire, whereupon the flames flared up and showed him that nothing was there. It was a long time before he fell properly asleep. When he did, he had a hellish dream.

He dreamed that around dawn a djinn came and sat on his chest. He opened his eyes to tell it to go away and found it was not a djinn at all, but the beast from the cave. It stood with its two vast front paws planted on his chest, glaring down at him with eyes that were like bluish lamps in the velvety blackness of its coat. As far as Abdullah could tell, it was a demon in the form of a huge black panther.

He sat up with a yell.

Naturally nothing was there. Dawn was just breaking. The fire was a cherry smudge in the grayness of everything, and the soldier was a darker gray hump, snoring gently on the other side of the fire. Behind him the lower lands were white with mist. Wearily Abdullah put another bush on the fire and fell asleep again.

He was woken by the windy roaring of the genie. "Stop this thing! *Get it OFF me!*"

Abdullah leaped up. The soldier leaped up. It was broad daylight. There was no mistaking what they both saw. A small black cat was crouching by the genie bottle, just beside the place where Abdullah's head had been. The cat was either very curious or convinced there was food in the bottle, for it had its nose delicately but firmly in the neck of the flask. Around its neat black head the genie was gushing out in ten or twelve distorted blue wisps, and the wisps kept turning into hands or faces and then turning back to smoke again.

"Help me!" he yelled in chorus. "It's trying to *eat* me or something!"

The cat ignored the genie entirely. It just went on behaving as if there were a most enticing smell in the bottle.

In Zanzib everyone hated cats. People thought of them as very little better than the rats and mice they ate. If a cat came near you, you kicked it, and you drowned any kittens you could lay hands on. Accordingly Abdullah ran at the cat, aiming a flying kick at it as he ran. *"Shoo!"* he yelled. *"Scat!"*

The cat jumped. Somehow it avoided Abdullah's lashing foot and fled to the top of the overhanging rock, where it spat at him and glared. It was not deaf then, Abdullah thought, staring up into its eyes. They were bluish. So *that* was what had sat on him in the night! He picked up a stone and drew back his arm to throw it.

"Don't do that!" said the soldier. "Poor little animal!"

The cat did not wait for Abdullah to throw the stone. It shot out of sight. "There is nothing poor about that beast," he said. "You must realize, gentle gunman, that the creature nearly took your eye out last night."

"I know," the soldier said mildly. "It was only defending itself, poor thing. Is that a genie in that flask of yours? Your smoky blue friend?"

A traveler with a carpet for sale had once told Abdullah that most people in the north were unaccountably sentimental about animals. Abdullah shrugged and turned sourly to the genie bottle, where the genie had vanished without a word of thanks. This would have to happen! Now he would have to watch the bottle like a hawk. "Yes," he said.

"I thought it might be," said the soldier. "I've

heard tell of genies. Come and look at this, will you?"
He stooped and picked up his hat, very carefully,
smiling in a strange, tender way.

There seemed definitely to be something wrong
with the soldier this morning, as if his brains had
softened in the night. Abdullah wondered if it was
those scratches, although they had almost vanished by
now. Abdullah went over to him anxiously.

Instantly the cat was standing on the overhanging
rock again, making that iron pulley noise, anger and
worry in every line of its small black body. Abdullah
ignored it and looked into the soldier's hat. Round blue
eyes stared at him out of its greasy interior. A little
pink mouth hissed defiance as the tiny black kitten
inside scrambled to the back of the hat, whipping its
minute bottle brush of a tail for balance.

"Isn't it *sweet?*" the soldier said besottedly.

Abdullah glanced at the wauling cat on top of the
rock. He froze, and looked again carefully. The thing
was huge. A mighty black panther stood there, baring
its big white fangs at him.

"These animals must belong to a witch, courageous companion," he said shakily.

"If they did, then the witch must be dead or
something," the soldier said. "You saw them. They
were living wild in that cave. That mother cat must
have carried her kitten all the way here in the night.
Marvelous, isn't it? She must have *known* we'd help

her!" He looked up at the huge beast snarling on the rock and did not seem to notice the size of it. "Come on down, sweet thing!" he said wheedlingly. "You know we won't hurt you or your kitten."

The mother beast launched herself from the rock. Abdullah gave a strangled scream, dodged, and sat down heavily. The great black body hurtled past above him——and to his surprise, the soldier started to laugh. Abdullah looked up indignantly to find that the beast had become a small black cat again, and was most affectionately walking about on the soldier's broad shoulder and rubbing herself on his face.

"Oh, you're a wonder, little Midnight!" The soldier chuckled. "You know I'll take care of your Whippersnapper for you, don't you? That's right. You purr!"

Abdullah got up disgustedly and turned his back on this love feast. The saucepan had been cleaned out very thoroughly in the night. The tin plate was burnished. He went and washed both, meaningly, in the stream, hoping the soldier would soon forget these dangerous magical beasts and begin thinking about breakfast.

But when the soldier finally put the hat down and tenderly plucked the mother cat off his shoulder, it was breakfast for cats that he thought about. "They'll need milk," he said, "and a nice plate of fresh fish. Get that genie of yours to fetch them some."

A jet of blue-mauve spurted from the neck of the bottle and spread into a sketch of the genie's irritated face. "Oh, no," said the genie. "One wish a day is all I give, and he had today's wish yesterday. Go and fish in the stream."

The soldier advanced on the genie angrily. "There won't be any fish this high in the mountain," he said. "And that little Midnight is starving, and she's got her kitten to feed."

"Too bad!" said the genie. "And don't you try to threaten me, soldier. Men have become toads for less."

The soldier was certainly a brave man—or a very foolish one, Abdullah thought. "You do that to me, and I'll break your bottle, whatever shape I'm in!" he shouted. "I'm not wanting a wish for *myself!*"

"I prefer people to be selfish," the genie retorted. "So you *want* to be a toad?"

Further blue smoke gushed out of the bottle and formed into arms making gestures that Abdullah was afraid he recognized. "No, no, stop, I implore you, O sapphire among spirits!" he said hastily. "Let the soldier alone, and consent, as a great favor, to grant me another wish a day in advance, that the animals might be fed."

"Do *you* want to be a toad, too?" the genie inquired.

"If it is written in the prophecy that Flower-in-the-Night shall marry a toad, then make me a toad,"

Abdullah said piously. "But first fetch milk and fish, great genie."

The genie swirled moodily. "Bother the prophecy! I can't go against that. All right. You can have your wish, provided you leave me in peace for the next two days."

Abdullah sighed. It was a dreadful waste of a wish. "Very well."

A crock of milk and an oval plate with a salmon on it plunked down on the rock by his feet. The genie gave Abdullah a look of huge dislike and sucked himself back inside the bottle.

"Great work!" said the soldier, and proceeded to make a large pother over poaching salmon in milk and making sure there were no bones the cat might choke on.

The cat, Abdullah noticed, had all this while been peacefully licking at her kitten in the hat. She did not seem to know the genie was there. But she knew about the salmon all right. As soon as it started cooking, she left her kitten and wound herself around the soldier, thin and urgent and mewing. "Soon, soon, my black darling!" the soldier said.

Abdullah could only suppose that the cat's magic and the genie's were so different that they were unable to perceive each other. The one good thing he could see about the situation was that there was plenty of salmon and milk for the two humans as well. While the cat daintily guzzled, and her kitten lapped, and sneezed, and did his amateur best to drink salmon-flavored milk, the soldier and Abdullah feasted on porridge made with milk and roast salmon steak.

After such a breakfast Abdullah felt kinder toward the whole world. He told himself that the genie could not have made a better choice of companion for him than this soldier. The genie was not so bad. And he would surely be seeing Flower-in-the-Night soon now. He was thinking that the Sultan and Kabul Aqba were not such bad fellows either when he discovered, to his outrage, that the soldier intended to take the cat and her kitten along with them to Kingsbury.

"But, most benevolent bombardier and considerate cuirassier," he protested, "what will become of your scheme to earn your bounty? You cannot rob robbers with a kitten in your hat!"

"I reckon I won't need to do any of that now you've promised me a princess," the soldier answered calmly. "And no one could leave Midnight and Whippersnapper to starve on this mountain. That's cruel!"

Abdullah knew he had lost this argument. He sourly tied the genie bottle to his belt and vowed never to promise the soldier anything else. The soldier repacked his pack, scattered the fire, and gently picked up his hat with the kitten in it. He set off downhill beside the stream, whistling to Midnight as if she were a dog.

Midnight, however, had other ideas. As Abdullah set off after the soldier, she stood in his way, staring meaningly up at him. Abdullah took no notice and tried to edge past her. And she was promptly huge again. A black panther, if possible even larger than before, was barring his way and snarling. He stopped, frankly terrified. And the beast leaped at him. He was too frightened even to scream. He shut his eyes and waited to have his throat torn out. So much for Fate and prophecies!

A softness touched his throat instead. Small, firm feet hit his shoulder, and another set of such feet pricked his chest. Abdullah opened his eyes to find that Midnight was back to cat size and clinging to the front of his jacket. The green-blue eyes looking up into his said, "Carry me. Or else."

"Very well, formidable feline," Abdullah said. "But take care not to snag any more of the embroidery on this jacket. This was once my best suit. And please remember that I carry you under strong protest. I do not love cats."

Midnight calmly scrambled her way to Abdullah's shoulder, where she sat smugly balancing while Abdullah plodded and slithered his way down the mountain for the rest of that day.

Chapter 12

In which the law catches up with Abdullah and the soldier

By evening Abdullah was almost used to Midnight. Unlike Jamal's dog, she smelled extremely clean, and she was clearly an excellent mother. The only times she dismounted from Abdullah were to feed her kitten. If it had not been for her alarming habit of turning huge at him when he annoyed her, Abdullah felt he could come to tolerate her in time. The kitten, he conceded, was charming. It played with the end of the soldier's pigtail and tried to chase butterflies—in a wobbly way—when they stopped for lunch. The rest of the day it spent in the front of the soldier's jacket, peeping eagerly forth at the grass and the trees and at the fern-lined waterfalls they passed on their way to the plains.

But Abdullah was entirely disgusted at the fuss the soldier made about his new pets when they stopped for the night. They decided to stay in the inn they came to in the first valley, and here the soldier decreed that his cats were to have the best of everything.

141

The innkeeper and his wife shared Abdullah's opinion. They were lumpish folk who had, it seemed, been put in a bad mood anyway by the mysterious theft of a crock of milk and a whole salmon that morning. They ran about with dour disapproval, fetching just the right shape of basket and a soft pillow to put in it. They hurried grimly with cream and chicken liver and fish. They grudgingly produced certain herbs which, the soldier declared, prevented canker in the ears. They stormily sent out for other herbs which were supposed to cure a cat of worms. But they were downright incredulous when they were asked to heat water for a bath because the soldier suspected that Whippersnapper had picked up a flea.

Abdullah found himself forced to negotiate. "O prince and princess of publicans," he said, "bear with the eccentricity of my excellent friend. When he says a bath, he means, of course, a bath for himself and for me. We are both somewhat travel-stained and would welcome clean hot water—for which we will, of course, pay whatever extra is necessary."

"What? Me? Bath?" the soldier said when the innkeeper and his wife had stumped off to put big kettles to boil.

"Yes. You," said Abdullah. "Or you and your cats and I part company this very evening. The dog of my friend Jamal in Zanzib was scarcely less ripe to the nose than you, O unwashed warrior, and

Whippersnapper, fleas or not, is a good deal cleaner."

"But what about my princess and your sultan's daughter if you leave?" asked the soldier.

"I shall think of something," said Abdullah. "But I should prefer it if you got into a bath and, if you wish, took Whippersnapper into it with you. That was my aim in asking for it."

"It weakens you—having baths," the soldier said dubiously. "But I suppose I could wash Midnight as well while I'm at it."

"Pray use both cats as sponges if it pleases you, infatuated infantryman," Abdullah said, and went off to revel in his own bath. In Zanzib people bathed a lot because the climate was so hot. Abdullah was used to visiting the public baths at least every other day, and he was missing that. Even Jamal went to the baths once a week, and it was rumored that he took his dog into the water with him. The soldier, Abdullah thought, becoming soothed by the hot water, was really no more besotted with his cats than Jamal was with his dog. He hoped that Jamal and his dog had managed to escape and, if they had, that they were not at this moment suffering hardships in the desert.

The soldier did not appear any weaker for his bath, although his skin had turned a much paler brown. Midnight, it seemed, had fled at the mere sight of water, but Whippersnapper, so the soldier claimed, had loved every moment. "He played with the soap bubbles!" he said dotingly.

"I hope you think you're worth all this trouble," Abdullah said to Midnight as she sat on his bed delicately cleaning herself after her cream and chicken. Midnight turned and gave him a round-eyed scornful look—of *course* she was worth it!—before she went back to the serious business of washing her ears.

The bill, next morning, was enormous. Most of the extra charge was for hot water, but cushions, baskets, and herbs figured quite largely on the list, too. Abdullah paid, shuddering, and anxiously inquired how far it was to Kingsbury.

Six days, he was told, if a person went on foot.

Six days! Abdullah nearly groaned aloud. Six days at this rate of expense, and he would barely be able to afford to keep Flower-in-the-Night in the state of direst poverty when he found her. And he had to look forward to six days of the soldier's making this sort of fuss about the cats, before they could collar a wizard and even *start* trying to find her. No, Abdullah thought. His next wish to the genie would be to have them all transported to Kingsbury. That meant he would only have to endure two more days.

Comforted by this thought, Abdullah strode off down the road with Midnight serenely riding his shoulders and the genie bottle bobbing at his side. The sun shone. The greenness of the countryside was a pleasure to him after the desert. Abdullah even began to appreciate the houses with their grass roofs. They had delightful rambling gardens and many of them had roses or other flowers trained around their doors. The soldier told him that grass roofs were the custom here. It was called thatch, and it did, the soldier assured him, keep out the rain, though Abdullah found this very hard to believe.

Before long Abdullah was deep in another daydream, of himself and Flower-in-the-Night living in a cottage with a grass roof and roses around the door. He would make her such a garden that it would be the envy of all for miles around. He began to plan the garden.

Unfortunately, toward the end of the morning, his daydream was interrupted by increasing spots of rain. Midnight hated it. She complained loudly in Abdullah's ear.

"Button her in your jacket," said the soldier.

"Not I, adorer of animals," Abdullah said. "She loves me no more than I love her. She would doubtless seize the chance to make grooves in my chest."

The soldier handed his hat to Abdullah with Whippersnapper in it, carefully covered with an unclean handkerchief, and buttoned Midnight into his own jacket. They went on for half a mile. By then the rain was pouring down.

The genie draped a ragged blue wisp over the side of his bottle. "Can't you *do* something about all this water that's getting in on me?"

Whippersnapper was saying much the same at the top of his small, squeaky voice. Abdullah pushed wet hair out of his eyes and felt harassed.

"We'll have to find somewhere to shelter," said the soldier.

Luckily there was an inn around the next corner but one. They squelched thankfully into its taproom, where Abdullah was pleased to discover that its grass roof was keeping the rain out very well.

Here the soldier, in the way Abdullah was getting used to, demanded a private parlor with a fire, so that the cats could be comfortable, and lunch for all four of the party. Abdullah, in the way that he was also getting used to, wondered how much the bill would be this time, although he had to admit the fire was very welcome. He stood in front of it and dripped, with a glass of beer—in this particular inn the beer tasted as if it had come from a camel that was rather unwell—while they waited for lunch. Midnight washed the kitten dry, then herself. The soldier stretched his boots to the fire and let them steam, while the genie bottle stood in the hearth and also steamed faintly. Even the genie did not complain.

They heard horses outside. This was not unusual. Most people in Ingary traveled on horseback if they could. Nor was it surprising that the riders seemed to be stopping at the inn. They must be wet, too.

Abdullah was just thinking that he should firmly have asked the genie to provide horses instead of milk and salmon yesterday when he heard the horsemen shouting at the innkeeper outside the parlor window.

"Two men—a Strangian soldier and a dark chap in a fancy suit—wanted for assault and robbery—have you seen them?"

Before the riders had finished shouting, the soldier was over by the parlor window, with his back to the wall so that he could look sideways through the window without being seen, and somehow he had his pack in one hand and his hat in the other.

"Four of them," he said. "They're constables, by the uniform."

All Abdullah could think to do was stand gaping in dismay, thinking that this was what came of fussing for cat baskets and bath-water and giving innkeepers reason to remember you. *And* demanding private parlors, he thought, as he heard the voice of this innkeeper in the distance saying smarmily that yes, indeed, both fellows were here, in the small parlor.

The soldier held out his hat to Abdullah. "Put Whippersnapper in here. Then pick up Midnight and be ready to get out of the window as soon as they come into the inn."

Whippersnapper had chosen that moment to go exploring under an oak settle. Abdullah dived after

147

him. As he backed out on his knees with the kitten squirming in his hand, he could hear distant boots clumping into the taproom. The soldier was undoing the latch on the window. Abdullah dropped Whippersnapper into his outstretched hat and turned around for Midnight. And saw the genie bottle warming on the hearth. Midnight was up on a high shelf across the room. This was hopeless. The boots were now much nearer, tramping toward the parlor door. The soldier was banging at the window, which seemed to be stuck.

Abdullah snatched up the genie bottle. "Come *here*, Midnight!" he said, and ran toward the window, where he collided with the soldier backing away.

"Stand clear," said the soldier. "Thing's stuck. Have to kick it."

As Abdullah staggered aside, the parlor door was flung open and three large men in uniform plunged into the room. At the same instant the soldier's boot met the window frame with a bang. The casement burst open, and the soldier went scrambling out over the sill. The three men shouted. Two made for the window, and one dived for Abdullah. Abdullah overturned the oak settle in front of all of them and then sprinted for the window, where he hurdled the sill out into the drenching rain without pausing to think.

Then he remembered Midnight. He turned back. She was huge again, larger than he had ever seen her, looming like a great black shadow in the space below the window, with her immense white fangs bared at the three men. They were falling over one another to get away backward through the door. Abdullah turned and ran after the soldier, gratefully. He was pelting toward the far corner of the inn. The fourth constable, who was outside holding the horses, started to run after them, then realized that this was stupid and ran back to the horses, which scattered away from him as he ran at them. As Abdullah bounded after the soldier through a sopping kitchen garden, he could hear the shouting of all four constables as they tried to catch their horses.

The soldier was an expert at escapes. He found a way from the vegetable garden into an orchard and from there a gate into a wide field, all without wasting an instant. A wood stood across the field in the distance like a promise of safety, veiled in rain.

"Did you get Midnight?" gasped the soldier as they trotted through the soaking grass of the field.

"No," said Abdullah. He had no breath to explain.

"*What?*" exclaimed the soldier. He stopped and swung around.

At that moment the four horses, each with a constable in the saddle, came jumping over the orchard hedge into the field. The soldier swore violently. He and Abdullah both sprinted for the wood. By the time they reached its bushy outskirts, the horsemen were well over halfway across the field. Abdullah and the soldier crashed through the bushes and leaped onward into open woodland, where, to Abdullah's amazement, the ground was thick with thousands upon thousands of bright blue flowers, growing like a carpet into far blue distance.

"What . . . these flowers?" he panted.

"Bluebells," said the soldier. "If you've lost Midnight, I'll kill you."

"I haven't. She'll find us. She grew. Told you. Magic," Abdullah gasped.

The soldier had never seen this trick of Midnight's. He did not believe Abdullah. "Run faster," he said. "We'll have to circle back and collect her."

They rushed forward, crunching bluebells, suffused with the strange wild scent of them. Abdullah could have believed, but for the gray, pouring rain and the shouts of the constables, that he was running over the floor of heaven. He was rapidly back in his daydream. When he made his garden for the cottage he would share with Flower-in-the-Night, he would have bluebells in it by the thousand, like these. But this did not blind him to the fact that they were leaving a trampled trail of broken white stems and snapped-off flowers as they ran. Nor did it deafen him to the cracking of twigs as the constables shoved their horses into the wood behind them.

"This is hopeless!" said the soldier. "Get that genie

of yours to make the constables lose us."

"Point out . . . sapphire of soldiers . . . no wish . . . day after tomorrow," Abdullah panted.

"He can give you one in advance again," said the soldier.

Blue steam fluttered angrily from the bottle in Abdullah's hand. "I gave you your last wish only on condition you left me alone," said the genie. "All I ask is to be left to sorrow alone in my bottle. And do you let me? No. At the first sign of trouble, you start wailing for extra wishes. Doesn't anyone consider *me* around here?"

"Emergency . . . O hyacinth . . . *bluebell* among bottled spirits," Abdullah puffed. "Transport us . . . far off—"

"Oh, no, you don't!" said the soldier. "You don't wish us far off without Midnight. Have him make us invisible until we find her."

"Blue jade of genies—" gasped Abdullah.

"If there's one thing I hate," interrupted the genie, bellying forth in a lavender cloud, "more than this rain and being pestered for wishes in advance all the time, it's being *coaxed* for wishes in flowery language. If you want a wish, talk straight."

"Take us to Kingsbury," puffed Abdullah.

"Make those fellows lose us," the soldier said at the same moment.

They glared at each other as they ran.

"Make up your minds," said the genie. He folded his arms and streamed contemptuously out behind them. "It's all one to me what you choose to waste another wish on. Just let me remind you that it will be your last one for two days."

"I'm not leaving Midnight," said the soldier.

"If we are . . . waste a wish," panted Abdullah, "then should . . . usefully . . . foolish fortune hunter . . . forward our . . . quest . . . Kingsbury."

"Then you can go without me," said the soldier.

"The horsemen are only fifty feet away," remarked the genie.

They looked over their shoulders and discovered this was quite true. Abdullah hurriedly gave in. "Then make them unable to see us," he panted.

"Have us unseen until Midnight finds us," added the soldier. "I know she will. She's that clever."

Abdullah had a glimpse of an evil grin spreading on the genie's smoky face and of smoky arms making certain gestures.

There followed a wet and gluey strangeness. The world suddenly distorted around Abdullah and grew vast and blue and green and out of focus. He crawled, in a slow and toilsome crouch, among what seemed to be giant bluebells, placing each huge and warty hand with extreme care because, for some reason, he could not look downward—only up and across. It was such hard work that he wanted to stop and crouch where he was, but the ground was shaking most terribly. He could feel some gigantic creatures galloping toward him, so he crawled on frantically. Even so, he barely got out of their way in time. A huge hoof, as big as a round tower, with metal underneath it, came smashing down just beside him as he crawled. Abdullah was so frightened by it that he froze and could not move. He could tell that the enormous creatures had stopped, too, quite close. There were loud, annoyed sounds that he could not hear properly. These went on for some time. Then the smashing of hooves began again, and went on for some time, too, trampling this way and that, always rather near, until, after what seemed most of the day, the creatures seemed to give up looking for him and went crashing and squelching away.

Chapter 13

⊰—◆—⊱

In which Abdullah challenges Fate

Abdullah crouched for a while longer, but when the creatures did not come back, he began crawling again, in a vague, vain way, hoping to discover what had happened to him. He knew *something* had happened, but he did not seem to have much of a brain to think with.

While he crawled, the rain stopped. He was rather sad about that, since it was wonderfully refreshing to the skin. On the other hand— A fly circled in a shaft of sunlight and came to sit on a bluebell leaf nearby. Abdullah promptly shot out a long tongue, whipped up that fly, and swallowed it. *Very* nice! he thought. Then he thought: But flies are unclean! More troubled than ever, he crawled around another bluebell clump.

And there was another one just like himself.

It was brown and squat and warty, and its yellow eyes were at the top of its head. As soon as it saw him, it opened its wide, lipless mouth in a bray of horror and began to swell up. Abdullah did not wait to see more. He turned and crawled off as fast as his distorted legs could take him. He knew what he was now. He was a toad. The malicious genie had fixed things so that he would be a toad until Midnight found him. When she did, he was fairly sure she would eat him.

He crawled under the nearest overarching bluebell leaves and hid. . . .

About an hour later the bluebell leaves parted to let through a monster black paw. It seemed interested in Abdullah. It kept its claws sheathed and patted at him. Abdullah was so horrified that he tried to hop away backward.

Whereupon he found himself lying on his back among the bluebells.

He blinked up at the trees first, trying to adjust to the way he suddenly had thoughts in his head again. Some of those thoughts were unpleasant ones, about two bandits crawling beside an oasis pool in the shape of toads and about eating a fly and being nearly trodden on by a horse. Then he looked around and found the soldier crouching nearby, looking as bewildered as Abdullah felt. His pack was beside him, and beyond that, Whippersnapper was making determined efforts to climb out of the soldier's hat. The genie bottle stood smugly beside the hat.

The genie was outside the bottle in a small wisp like the flame of a spirit lamp, with his smoky arms propped on the neck of the bottle. "Enjoy yourselves?" he asked jeeringly. "I got you there, didn't I? That'll teach you to pester me for extra wishes!"

Midnight had been extremely alarmed by their sudden transformation. She was in a small angry arch, spitting at both of them.

The soldier stretched out his hand to her and made soothing noises. "You frighten Midnight again like that," he told the genie, "and I'll break your bottle!"

"You said that before," retorted the genie, "and you couldn't, worse luck. The bottle's enchanted."

"Then I'll make sure his next wish is that *you* turn into a toad," the soldier said, jerking his thumb at Abdullah.

The genie shot Abdullah a wary look at this. Abdullah said nothing, but he saw it was a good idea and might keep the genie in order. He sighed. One way and another, he just could not seem to stop wasting wishes.

They picked themselves and their belongings up and resumed their journey. But they went much more cautiously. They kept to the smallest lanes and footpaths they could find, and that night, instead of going to an inn, they camped in an old empty barn. Here Midnight suddenly looked alert and interested and shortly slipped away into the shadowy corners. After a while she came trotting back with a dead mouse, which she laid carefully in the soldier's hat for Whippersnapper. Whippersnapper was not very sure what to do with it. In the end he decided it was the kind of toy you leaped on fiercely and killed. Midnight prowled off again. Abdullah heard the small sounds of her hunting most of the night.

In spite of this, the soldier worried about feeding the cats. Next morning he wanted Abdullah to go to the nearest farm and buy milk.

"You do it if you want it," Abdullah said curtly.

And somehow he found himself on the way to the farm with a can from the soldier's pack on one side of his belt and the genie bottle bumping at the other.

Exactly the same thing happened the next two mornings, too, with the small difference that they slept under haystacks both those nights and Abdullah bought a beautiful fresh loaf one morning and some eggs on the next. On the way back to the haystack that third morning he tried to work out just why he was feeling increasingly bad-tempered and put-upon.

It was not just that he was stiff and tired and damp all the time. It was not just that he seemed to spend such a lot of time running errands for the soldier's cats, though that had something to do with it. Some of it was Midnight's fault. Abdullah knew he ought to be grateful to her for defending them from the constables. He *was* grateful, but he still did not get on with Midnight. She rode his shoulder disdainfully every day and contrived to make it quite clear that as far as she was concerned, Abdullah was only a sort of horse. It was a bit hard to take from a mere animal.

Abdullah brooded on this and other matters all that day, while he tramped country lanes with Midnight draped elegantly around his neck and the soldier trudging cheerfully ahead. It was not that he did not like cats. He was used to them now. Sometimes he found Whippersnapper almost as sweet as the soldier did. No, his bad humor had much more to do with the way the soldier and the genie between them kept contriving to postpone his search for Flower-in-the-Night. If he was not careful, Abdullah could see himself tramping country lanes for the rest of his life, without ever getting to Kingsbury at all. And when he did get there, he still had to locate a wizard. No, it would not do.

That night they found the remains of a stone tower to camp in. This was much better than a haystack. They could light a fire and eat hot food from the soldier's packets and Abdullah could get warm and dry at last. His spirits rose.

The soldier was cheerful, too. He sat leaning against the stone wall with Whippersnapper asleep in his hat beside him and gazed out at the sunset. "I've been thinking," he said. "You get a wish from your misty blue friend tomorrow, don't you? You know the most practical wish you could make? You should wish for that magic carpet back. Then we could really get on."

"It would be just as easy to wish ourselves straight to Kingsbury, intelligent infantryman," Abdullah pointed out—a little sullenly, if the truth be told.

"Ah, yes, but I've got that genie's measure now, and I know he'd mess that wish up if he possibly could," the soldier said. "My point is, you know how to work that carpet, and you could get us there with much less trouble *and* a wish in hand for emergencies."

This was sound sense. Nevertheless, Abdullah only grunted. This was because the way the soldier put his advice had made Abdullah suddenly see things a whole new way. Of course, the soldier had got the genie's measure. The soldier was like that. He was an expert in getting other people to do what he wanted. The only creature that could make the soldier do something he did not want was Midnight, and Midnight did things *she* did not want only when Whippersnapper wanted something. That put the kitten right at the top of the pecking order. A kitten! thought Abdullah. And since the soldier had the genie's measure, and the genie was very definitely on top of Abdullah, that put Abdullah right down at the bottom. No wonder he had been feeling so put-upon! It did not make him feel any better to realize that things had been exactly the same way with his father's first wife's relations.

So Abdullah only grunted, which in Zanzib would have counted as shocking rudeness, but the soldier was quite unaware of it. He pointed cheerfully at the sky. "Lovely sunset again. Look, there's another castle."

The soldier was right. There was a glory of yellow lakes in the sky, and islands and promontories, and one long indigo headland of cloud with a frowning square cloud like a fortress on it. "It is not the same as the other castle," Abdullah said. He felt it was time he asserted himself.

"Of course not. You never get the same cloud twice," said the soldier.

Abdullah contrived to be the first one awake the next morning. Dawn was still flaring across the sky when he sprang up, seized the genie bottle, and took it some distance away from the ruins where their camp was. "Genie," he said. "Appear."

A flutter of steam appeared at the mouth of the bottle, grudging and ghostly. "What's this?" it said. "Where's all the talk about jewels and flowers and so forth?"

"You told me you did not like it. I have discontinued it," said Abdullah. "I have now become a realist.

The wish I want to make is in accordance with my new outlook."

"Ah," said the wisp of genie. "You're going to ask for the magic carpet back."

"Not at all," said Abdullah. This so surprised the genie that he rose right out of the bottle and regarded Abdullah with wide eyes, which in the dawnlight looked solid and shiny and almost like human eyes. "I shall explain," said Abdullah. "Thus. Fate is clearly determined to delay my search for Flower-in-the-Night. This is in spite of the fact that Fate has also decreed that I shall marry her. Any attempt I make to go against Fate causes you to make sure that my wish does no good to anyone and usually also ensures that I get pursued by persons on camels or horses. Or else the soldier causes me to waste a wish. Since I am tired both of your malice and of the soldier's so continually getting his own way, I have decided to challenge Fate instead. I intend to waste every wish deliberately from now on. Fate will then be forced to take a hand, or else the prophecy concerning Flower-in-the-Night will never be fulfilled."

"You're being childish," said the genie. "Or heroic. Or possibly mad."

"No—realistic," said Abdullah. "Furthermore, I shall challenge *you* by wasting the wishes in a way that might do good somewhere to someone."

The genie looked decidedly sarcastic at this.

"And what is your wish today? Homes for orphans? Sight for the blind? Or do you simply want all the money in the world taken away from the rich and given to the poor?"

"I was thinking," said Abdullah, "that I *might* wish that those two bandits whom you transformed into toads should be restored to their own shape."

A look of malicious glee spread over the genie's face. "You might do worse. I could grant you that one with pleasure."

"What is the drawback to that wish?" asked Abdullah.

"Oh, not much," said the genie. "Simply that the Sultan's soldiers are camped in that oasis at the moment. The Sultan is convinced that you are still somewhere in the desert. His men are quartering the entire region for you, but I'm sure they will spare a moment for two bandits, if only to show the Sultan how zealous they are."

Abdullah considered this. "And who else is in the desert who might be in danger from the Sultan's search?"

The genie looked sideways at him. "You *are* anxious to waste a wish, aren't you? Nobody much there except a few carpet weavers and a prophet or so—and Jamal and his dog, of course."

"Ah," said Abdullah. "Then I waste this wish on Jamal and his dog. I wish that Jamal and his dog both be instantly transported to a life of ease and prosperity as—let me see—yes, as palace cook and guard dog in the nearest royal palace apart from Zanzib."

"You make it very difficult," the genie said pathetically, "for that wish to go wrong."

"Such was my aim," said Abdullah. "If I could discover how to make *none* of your wishes go wrong, it would be a great relief."

"There is one wish you could make to do that," said the genie.

He sounded rather wistful, from which Abdullah realized what he meant. The genie wanted to be free of the enchantment that bound him to the bottle. It would be easy enough to waste a wish that way, Abdullah reflected, but only if he could count on the genie's being grateful enough to help him find Flower-in-the-Night afterward. With *this* genie, that was most unlikely. And if he freed the genie, then he would have to give up challenging Fate. "I shall think about that wish for later," he said. "My wish today is for Jamal and his dog. Are they now safe?"

"Yes," the genie said sulkily. From the look on his smoky face as it vanished inside the bottle, Abdullah had an uneasy feeling that he had somehow contrived to make this wish go wrong, too, but of course, there was no way to tell.

Abdullah turned around to find the soldier watching him. He had no idea how much the soldier had overheard, but he got ready for an argument.

But all the soldier said was "Don't quite follow your logic in all that," before suggesting that they walk on until they found a farm where they could buy breakfast.

Abdullah shouldered Midnight again, and they trudged off. All that day they wandered deep lanes again. Though there was no sign of any constables, they did not seem to be getting any nearer to Kingsbury. In fact, when the soldier inquired from a man digging a ditch how far it was to Kingsbury, he was told it was four days' walk.

Fate! thought Abdullah.

The next morning he went around to the other side of the haystack where they had slept and wished that the two toads in the oasis should now become men.

The genie was very annoyed. "You heard me say that the first person who opened my bottle would become a toad! Do you want me to undo my good work?"

"Yes," said Abdullah.

"Regardless of the fact that the Sultan's men are still there and will certainly hang them?" asked the genie.

"I think," said Abdullah, remembering his experiences as a toad, "that they would rather be men even so."

"Oh, very well then!" the genie said angrily. "You realize my revenge is in ruins, don't you? But what do *you* care? I'm just a daily wish in a bottle to you!"

Chapter 14

Which tells how the magic carpet reappeared

Once again Abdullah turned around to find the soldier watching him, but this time the soldier said nothing at all. Abdullah was fairly sure he was simply biding his time. That day, as they trudged onward, the ground climbed. The lush green lanes gave way to sandy tracks bordered with bushes that were dry and spiny. The soldier remarked cheerfully that they seemed to be getting somewhere different at last. Abdullah only grunted. He was determined not to give the soldier an opening.

By nightfall they were high on an open heath, looking over a new stretch of the plain. A faint pimple on the horizon was, the soldier said, still very cheerful, certainly Kingsbury. As they settled down to camp, he invited Abdullah, even more cheerfully, to see how charmingly Whippersnapper was playing with the buckles on his pack.

"Doubtless," said Abdullah. "It charms me even less than a lump on the skyline that may be Kingsbury."

There was another huge red sunset. While they ate supper, the soldier pointed it out to Abdullah and drew his attention to a large red castle-shaped cloud. "Isn't that beautiful?" he said.

"It is only a cloud," said Abdullah. "It has no artistic merit."

"Friend," said the soldier, "I think you are letting that genie get to you."

"How so?" said Abdullah.

The soldier pointed with his spoon to the distant dark hummock against the sunset. "See there?" he said. "Kingsbury. Now, I have a hunch, and I think you do, too, that things are going to start moving when we get there. But we don't seem to get there. Don't think I can't see your point of view: You're a young fellow, disappointed in love, impatient; naturally you think Fate's against you. Take it from me, Fate doesn't care either way most of the time. The genie's not on anyone's side any more than Fate is."

"How do you make that out?" asked Abdullah.

"Because he hates everyone," said the soldier. "Maybe it's his nature—though I daresay being shut in a bottle doesn't help any. But don't forget that whatever his feelings, he's always got to grant you a wish. Why make it hard for yourself just to spite the genie? Why not make the most useful wish you can, get what *you* want out of it, and put up with whatever he does to send it wrong? I've been thinking this through, and it seems to me that *whatever* that genie does to send it wrong, your best wish is still to ask for that magic carpet back."

While the soldier was speaking, Midnight—to Abdullah's great surprise—climbed to Abdullah's knees and rubbed herself against his face, purring. Abdullah had to admit he was flattered. He had been letting Midnight get to him as well as the genie and the soldier—not to speak of Fate. "If I wish for the carpet," he said, "I am prepared to bet that the misfortunes the genie sends with it will far outweigh its usefulness."

"You bet, do you?" said the soldier. "I never resist a bet. Bet you a gold piece the carpet will be more use than trouble."

"Done," said Abdullah. "And now you have your own way again. It perplexes me, my friend, that you never rose to command that army of yours."

"Me, too," said the soldier. "I'd have made a good general."

Next morning they woke into a thick mist. Everywhere was white and wet, and it was impossible to see beyond the nearest bushes. Midnight coiled against Abdullah, shivering. The genie's bottle, when Abdullah put it down in front of them, had a distinctly sulky look.

"Come out," said Abdullah. "I need to make a wish."

"I can grant it quite as well from in here," the genie retorted hollowly. "I don't like this damp."

"Very well," said Abdullah. "I wish for my magic carpet back again."

"Done," said the genie. "And let that teach you to make silly bets!"

For a while Abdullah looked up and around expectantly, but nothing seemed to happen. Then Midnight sprang to her feet. Whippersnapper's face came out of the soldier's pack, ears cocked sideways to the south. When Abdullah gazed that way, he thought he could just hear a slight whispering, which could have been the wind or something moving through the mist. Shortly the mist swirled—and swirled harder. The gray oblong of the carpet slid into sight overhead and glided to the ground beside Abdullah.

It had a passenger. Curled up on the carpet, peacefully asleep, was a villainous man with a large mustache. His beak of a nose was pressed into the carpet, but Abdullah could just see the gold ring in it, half hidden by the mustache and a dirty drape of headcloth. One of the man's hands clutched a silver-mounted pistol. There was no question that this was Kabul Aqba again.

"I think I win the bet," Abdullah murmured.

Even that murmur—or maybe the chilliness of the mist—set the bandit stirring and muttering fretfully.

The soldier put his finger to his lips and shook his head. Abdullah nodded. If he had been on his own, he would have been wondering what on earth to do now, but with the soldier there he felt almost equal to Kabul Aqba. As quietly as he could, he made a gentle snoring noise and whispered to the carpet, "Come out from underneath that man and hover in front of me."

Ripples ran down the edge of the carpet. Abdullah could see it was trying to obey. It gave a strong wriggle, but Kabul Aqba's weight was evidently just too much to allow it to slide out from under him. So it tried another way. It rose an inch into the air, and before Abdullah realized what it intended to do, it had darted out from under the sleeping bandit.

"No!" said Abdullah, but he said it too late. Kabul Aqba thumped down on to the ground and woke. He sat up, waving his pistol and howling in a strange language.

In an alert, leisurely sort of way, the soldier picked up the hovering carpet and wrapped it around Kabul Aqba's head. "Get his pistol," he said, holding the struggling bandit in both brawny arms.

Abdullah plunged to one knee and grasped the strong hand waving the pistol. It was a *very* strong hand. Abdullah could do nothing about taking the pistol away. He could only hang on and go crashing to and fro as the hand tried to shake him off. Beside him the soldier was also crashing to and fro. Kabul

Aqba seemed quite amazingly strong. Abdullah, as he was battered about, tried to take hold of one of the bandit's fingers and uncurl it from around the pistol. But at this Kabul Aqba roared and rose upward, and Abdullah was flung off backward with the carpet somehow wrapped around *him* instead of around Kabul Aqba. The soldier hung on. He hung on even though Kabul Aqba went on rising upward, roaring now like the sky falling, and the soldier from gripping him around the arms went to gripping him around the waist and then around the top of the legs. Kabul Aqba shouted as if his voice were the thunder itself and rose up bigger yet, until both his legs were too big to hold at once, and the soldier slid down until he was grimly clutching one of them, just below its vast knee. That leg tried to kick the soldier loose and failed. Whereupon Kabul Aqba spread enormous leathery wings and tried to fly away. But the soldier, though he slid downward again, hung on still.

Abdullah saw all this while he was struggling out from under the carpet. He also caught a glimpse of Midnight standing protectively over Whippersnapper, larger even than she had been when she faced the constables. But not large enough. What stood there now was one of the mightiest of mighty djinns. Half of him was lost upward in the mist, which he was beating into swirling smoke with his wings, unable to fly because the soldier was anchoring one of his enormous taloned feet to the ground.

"Explain yourself, mightiest of mighty ones!" Abdullah shouted up into the mist. "By the Seven Great Seals, I conjure you to cease your struggling and explain!"

The djinn stopped roaring and halted the violent fanning of his wings. "You conjure me, do you, mortal?" the great sullen voice came down.

"I do indeed," said Abdullah. "Say what you were doing with my carpet and in the form of that most ignoble of nomads. You have wronged me at least twice!"

"Very well," said the djinn. He began ponderously to kneel down.

"You can let go now," Abdullah said to the soldier, who, not knowing the laws that governed djinns, was still hanging on to the vast foot. "He has to stay and answer me now."

Warily the soldier let go and mopped sweat from his face. He did not seem reassured when the djinn simply folded his wings and knelt. This was not surprising, because the djinn was high as a house even kneeling, and the face coming into view through the mist was hideous. Abdullah had another glimpse of Midnight, now normal size again, scurrying for the bushes with Whippersnapper dangling from her mouth. But the face of the djinn took up most of his attention. He had seen that blank brown glare and the gold ring through that hooked nose—albeit briefly—before, when Flower-in-the-Night was carried off from the garden.

"Correction," Abdullah said. "You have wronged me *three* times."

"Oh, more than that," the djinn rumbled blandly. "So many times that I have lost count."

At this Abdullah found himself angrily folding his arms. "Explain."

"Willingly," said the djinn. "I was indeed hoping to be asked by someone, although I had supposed the questions most likely to come from the Duke of Farqtan or the three rival princes of Thayack, rather than from you. But none of the rest has proved determined enough—which surprises me somewhat, because you were certainly never my main irons in the fire, either of you. Know then that I am one of the greatest of the host of Good Djinns, and my name is Hasruel."

"I didn't know there *were* any good djinns," said the soldier.

"Oh, there are, innocent northerner," Abdullah told him. "I have heard this one's name spoken in terms that place him nearly as high as the angels."

The djinn frowned—an unpleasant sight. "Misinformed merchant," he rumbled. "I am *higher* than some angels. Know that some two hundred angels of the lesser air are mine to command. They serve as guards to the entrance of my castle."

Abdullah kept his arms folded and tapped with his foot. "This being the case," he said, "explain why you have seen fit to behave toward me in a manner so far from angelic."

"The blame is not mine, mortal," said the djinn. "Need spurred me on. Understand all, and forgive. Know that my mother, the Great Spirit Dazrah, in a moment of oversight allowed herself to be ravished by a djinn of the Host of Evil some twenty years ago. She then gave birth to my brother Dalzel, who—since Good and Evil do not breed well together—proved weak and white and undersized. My mother could not tolerate Dalzel and gave him to me to bring up. I lavished every care upon him as he grew. So you can imagine my horror and sorrow when he proved to inherit the nature of his Evil sire. His first act, when he came of age, was to steal my life and hide it, thereby making me his slave."

"Come again?" said the soldier. "You mean you're *dead?*"

"Not at all," said Hasruel. "We djinns are not as you mortals, ignorant man. We can die only if one small portion of us is destroyed. For this reason all djinns prudently remove that small part from our persons and hide it. As I did. But when I instructed Dalzel how to hide his own life, I lovingly and rashly told him where my life was hidden. And he instantly took my life into his power, forcing me to do his bidding or die."

"Now we come to it," said Abdullah. "His bidding was to steal Flower-in-the-Night."

"Correction," said Hasruel. "My brother inherits a grandeur of mind from his mother, Great Dazrah. He ordered me to steal every princess in the world. A moment's thought will show you the sense in this. My brother is of an age to marry, but he is of a birth so mixed that no female among djinns will countenance him. He is forced to resort to mortal women. But since he is a djinn, naturally only those females of the highest blood will serve."

"My heart bleeds for your brother," remarked Abdullah. "Could he not be satisfied with less than all?"

"Why should he be?" asked Hasruel. "He commands my power now. He gave the matter careful thought. And seeing clearly that his princesses would not be able to walk on air as we djinns do, he first ordered me to steal a certain moving castle belonging to a wizard in this land of Ingary in which to house his brides, and then he ordered me to commence stealing princesses. This I am now engaged in doing. But naturally at the same time I am laying plans of my own. For each princess that I take, I arrange to leave behind at least one injured lover or disappointed prince, who might be persuaded to attempt to rescue her. In order to do this, the lover will have to challenge my brother and wrest from him the secret hiding place of my life."

"And is this where I come in, mighty machinator?" Abdullah asked coldly. "I am part of your plans to regain your life, am I?"

"Just barely," answered the djinn. "My hopes were more upon the heirs of Alberia or the Prince of Peichstan, but both these young men have thrown themselves into hunting instead. Indeed, all of them have shown remarkable lack of spirit, including the King of High Norland, who is merely attempting to catalog his books on his own, without his daughter's help, and even he was a likelier chance than you. You were, you might say, an outside bet of mine. The prophecy at your birth *was* highly ambiguous, after all. I confess to selling you that magic carpet almost purely out of amusement—"

"*You* did!" Abdullah exclaimed.

"Yes—amusement at the number and nature of the daydreams proceeding from your booth," said Hasruel. Abdullah, despite the cold of the mist, found his face was heating up. "Then," continued Hasruel, "when you surprised me by escaping from the Sultan of Zanzib, it amused me to take on your character of Kabul Aqba and to force you to live out some of your daydreams. I usually try to make appropriate adventures befall each suitor."

Despite his embarrassment, Abdullah could have sworn that the djinn's great gold-brown eyes slanted toward the soldier here. "And how many disappointed princes have you so far put in motion, O subtle and jesting djinn?" he asked.

"Very nearly thirty," Hasruel said, "but as I said, most of them are not in motion at all. This strikes me as strange, for their birth and qualifications are all far better than yours. However, I console myself with the thought that there are still one hundred and thirty-two princesses left to steal."

"I think you might have to be satisfied with me," Abdullah said. "Low as my birth is, Fate seems to want it so. I am in a position to assure you of this, since I have recently challenged Fate on this very point."

The djinn smiled—a sight as unpleasant as his frown—and nodded. "This I know," he said. "This is the reason I have stooped to appear before you. Two of my servant angels returned to me yesterday, having just been hanged in the shape of men. Neither was wholly pleased by this, and both claimed it was your doing."

Abdullah bowed. "Doubtless when they consider, they will find it preferable to being immortal toads," he said. "Now tell me one last thing, O thoughtful thief of princesses. Say where Flower-in-the-Night, not to speak of your brother Dalzel, may be found."

177

The djinn's smile broadened, making it even more unpleasant, for this revealed a number of extremely long fangs. He pointed upward with a vast spiked thumb. "Why, earthbound adventurer, they are, naturally, in the castle you have been seeing in the sunset these last few days," he said. "It used, as I said, to belong to a wizard of this land. You will not find it easy to get there, and if you do, you will do well to remember that I am my brother's slave and forced to act against you."

"Understood," said Abdullah.

The djinn planted his enormous taloned hands on the ground and began to lever himself up. "I must also observe," he said, "that the carpet is under orders not to follow me. May I depart now?"

"No, wait!" cried the soldier. Abdullah, at the same moment, remembered one thing he had forgotten and asked, "And what of the genie?" but the soldier's voice was louder and drowned Abdullah's. "WAIT, *you monster!* Is that castle hanging around in the sky here for any particular reason, monster?"

Hasruel smiled again and paused, balanced on one huge knee. "How perceptive of you, soldier. Indeed, yes. The castle is here because I am preparing to steal the daughter of the King of Ingary, Princess Valeria."

"My princess!" said the soldier.

Hasruel's smile became a laugh. He threw back

his head and bellowed into the mist. "I doubt it, soldier! Oh, I doubt it! This princess is only four years old. But though she is of little use to you, I trust that you are going to be of great use to me. I regard both you and your friend from Zanzib as well-placed pawns on my chessboard."

"How do you mean?" the soldier asked indignantly.

"Because the two of you are going to help me steal her!" said the djinn, and sprang away upward into the mist in a whirl of wings, laughing hugely.

Chapter 15

In which the travelers arrive at Kingsbury

"If you ask me," said the soldier, moodily dumping his pack on the magic carpet, *"that creature is as bad as his brother—if he *has* a brother, that is."*

"Oh, he has a brother. Djinns do not lie," said Abdullah. "But they are always prone to see themselves as superior to mortals, even the good djinns. And Hasruel's name *is* on the Lists of the Good."

"You could have fooled me!" said the soldier. "Where's Midnight got to? She must have been frightened to death." He made such a pother over hunting for Midnight in the bushes that Abdullah did not try to explain any more of the lore concerning djinns, which every child in Zanzib learned at school. Besides, he feared the soldier was right. Hasruel might have taken the Seven Vows that made him one of the Host of the Good, but his brother had given him the perfect excuse to break all seven of them. Good or not, Hasruel was clearly enjoying himself hugely.

Abdullah picked up the genie bottle and put it on the carpet. It promptly fell on its side and rolled off. "No, no!" the genie cried out from inside. "I'm not going on *that!* Why do you think I fell off it before? I hate heights!"

"Oh, don't *you* start!" said the soldier. He had Midnight wrapped around one arm, kicking and scratching and biting, and demonstrating in every way she could that cats and flying carpets do not mix. This in itself was enough to make anyone irritable, but Abdullah suspected that most of the soldier's ill humor had to do with the fact that Princess Valeria was only four years old. The soldier had been thinking of himself as engaged to Princess Valeria. Now, not unnaturally, he was feeling a fool.

Abdullah seized the genie bottle, very firmly, and settled himself on the carpet. Tactfully he said nothing about their bet although it was fairly clear to him that he had won it hands down. True, they had the carpet back, but since it was forbidden to follow the djinn, it was no use at all for rescuing Flower-in-the-Night.

After a prolonged struggle the soldier got himself and his hat and Midnight and Whippersnapper more or less securely on the carpet, too. "Give your orders," he said. His brown face was flushed.

Abdullah snored. The carpet rose a gentle foot in the air, whereupon Midnight howled and struggled and the genie bottle shook in his hands. "O elegant tapestry of enchantment," Abdullah said, "O carpet compiled of most complex cantrips, I pray you to move at a sedate speed toward Kingsbury, but to exercise the great wisdom woven into your fabric to make sure that we are not seen by anyone on the way."

Obediently the carpet climbed through the mist, upward and south. The soldier clamped Midnight in his arms. A hoarse and trembling voice said from the bottle, "Do you *have* to flatter it so disgustingly?"

"This carpet," said Abdullah, "unlike you, is of an ensorcellment so pure and excellent that it will listen only to the finest of language. It is at heart a poet among carpets."

A certain smugness spread through the pile of the carpet. It held its tattered edges proudly straight and sailed sweetly forward into the golden sunlight above the mist. A small blue jet came out of the bottle and disappeared again with a yip of panic. "Well, *I* wouldn't do it!" said the genie.

At first it was easy for the carpet not to be seen. It simply flew above the mist, which lay below them white and solid as milk. But as the sun climbed, golden-green fields began to appear shimmeringly through it, then white roads and occasional houses. Whippersnapper was frankly fascinated. He stood at the edge staring downward and looked so likely to tip off headfirst that the soldier kept one hand strongly around his small, bushy tail.

This was just as well. The carpet banked away toward a line of trees that followed a river. Midnight dug all her claws in, and Abdullah only just saved the soldier's pack.

The soldier looked a little seasick. "Do we have to be this careful not to be seen?" he asked as they went gliding beside the trees like a tramp lurking in a hedge.

"I think so," said Abdullah. "In my experience, to see this eagle among carpets is to wish to steal it." And he told the soldier about the person on the camel.

The soldier agreed that Abdullah had a point. "It's just that it's going to slow us down," he said. "My feeling is that we ought to get to Kingsbury and warn the King that there's a djinn after his daughter. Kings give big rewards for that kind of information." Clearly, now he had been forced to give up the idea of marrying Princess Valeria, the soldier was thinking of other ways of making his fortune.

"We shall do that, never fear," said Abdullah, and once again did not mention their bet.

It took most of that day to reach Kingsbury. The carpet followed rivers, slid from wood to forest, and only put on speed where the land below was empty. When, in the late afternoon, they reached the city, a wide cluster of towers inside high walls that was easily three times the size of Zanzib, if not larger, Abdullah directed the carpet to find a good inn near the King's palace and to set them down somewhere where no one would suspect how they had traveled.

The carpet obeyed by sliding over the great walls like a snake. After that it kept to the roofs, following the shape of each roof the way a flounder follows the sea bottom. Abdullah and the soldier and the cats, too, stared down and around in wonder. The streets, wide or narrow, were choked with richly dressed people and expensive carriages. Every house seemed to Abdullah like a palace. He saw towers, domes, rich carvings, golden cupolas, and marble courts the Sultan of Zanzib would have been glad to call his own. The poorer houses—if you could call such richness poor—were decorated with painted patterns quite exquisitely. As for the shops, the wealth and quantity of the wares they had for sale made Abdullah realize that the Bazaar at Zanzib was really shabby and second-rate. No wonder the Sultan had been so anxious for an alliance with the Prince of Ingary!

The inn the carpet found for them, near the great marble buildings at the center of Kingsbury, had been plastered by a master in raised designs of fruit, which had then been painted in the most glowing colors with much gold leaf. The carpet landed gently on the sloping roof of the inn stables, hiding them cunningly beside a gold spire with a gilded weathercock on the top. They sat and looked around at all this magnificence while they waited for the yard below to be empty. There were two servants down there, cleaning a gilded carriage, gossiping as they worked.

Most of what they said was about the landlord of this inn, who was clearly a man who loved money. But when they had finished complaining how little they were paid, one man said, "Any news of that Strangian soldier who robbed all those people up north? Someone told me he was heading this way."

To this the other replied, "He's sure to make for Kingsbury. They all do. But they're watching for him at the city gates. He won't get far."

The soldier's eyes met Abdullah's.

Abdullah murmured, "Do you have a change of clothes?"

The soldier nodded and dug furiously in his pack. Shortly he produced two peasant-style shirts with smocked embroidery on the chests and backs. Abdullah wondered how he had come by those.

"Clothesline," murmured the soldier, bringing out a clothes brush and his razor. There, on the roof, he changed into one of the shirts and did his best to brush his trousers without making a noise. The noisiest part was when he was trying to shave without anything but the razor. The two servants kept glancing toward the dry scratching from the roof.

"Must be a bird," said one.

Abdullah put the second shirt on over his jacket, which was by now looking like anything but his best one. He was rather hot like that, but there was no way he could remove the money hidden in his jacket without letting the soldier see how much he had. He brushed his hair with the clothes brush, smoothed his mustache—it now felt as if there were at least twelve hairs there—and then brushed his trousers with the clothes brush, too. When he was done, the soldier passed Abdullah the razor and silently stretched out his pigtail.

"A great sacrifice, but a wise one, I think, my friend," Abdullah murmured. He sawed the pigtail off and hid it in the golden weathercock. This made quite a transformation. The soldier now looked like a bushy-headed prosperous farmer. Abdullah hoped he would pass for the farmer's young brother himself.

While they were doing this, the two servants finished cleaning the carriage and began pushing it into the coach house. As they passed under the roof where the carpet was, one of them asked, "And what do you think of this story that someone's trying to steal the Princess?"

"Well, I think it's true," the other one said, "if that's what you're asking. They say the Royal Wizard risked a lot to send a warning, poor fellow, and he's not the kind to take a risk for nothing."

The soldier's eyes met Abdullah's again. His mouth formed a hearty curse.

"Never mind," Abdullah murmured. "There are other ways to earn a reward."

They waited until the servants had gone back across the yard and into the inn. Then Abdullah requested the carpet to land in the yard. It glided obediently down. Abdullah picked the carpet up and wrapped the genie bottle inside it, while the soldier carried his pack and both cats. They went into the inn trying hard to look dull and respectable.

The landlord met them there. Warned by what the servants had said, Abdullah met the landlord with a gold piece casually between his finger and thumb. The landlord looked at that. His flinty eyes stared at the gold piece so fixedly that Abdullah doubted if he even saw their faces. Abdullah was extremely polite. So was the landlord. He showed them to a nice spacious room on the second floor. He agreed to send up supper and provide baths.

"And the cats will need—" the soldier began.

Abdullah kicked the soldier's ankle, hard. "And that will be all, O lion among landlords," he said. "Although, most helpful of hosts, if your active and vigilant staff could provide a basket, a cushion, and a dish of salmon, the powerful witch to whom we are to deliver tomorrow this pair of exceptionally gifted cats will undoubtedly reward whoever brings these things most bountifully."

"I'll see what I can do, sir," the landlord said. Abdullah carelessly tossed him the gold piece. The man bowed deeply and backed out of the room, leaving Abdullah feeling decidedly pleased with himself.

"There's no need to look so smug!" the soldier said angrily. "What are we supposed to do now? I'm a wanted man here, and the King seems to know all about the djinn."

It was a pleasant feeling to Abdullah to find that he was in command of events instead of the soldier. "Ah, but does the King know that there is a castle full of stolen princesses hovering overhead to receive his daughter?" he said. "You are forgetting, my friend, that the King cannot have had the advantage of speaking personally to the djinn. We might make use of this fact."

"How?" demanded the soldier. "Can you think of a way to stop that djinn stealing the child? Or a way to get to the castle, for that matter!"

"No, but it seems to me that a wizard might know these things," said Abdullah. "I think we should modify the idea you had earlier. Instead of finding one of this King's wizards and strangling him, we might inquire which wizard is the best and pay him a fee for his help."

"All right, but you'll have to do that," said the

soldier. "Any wizard worth his salt would spot me for a Strangian at once and call the constables before I could move."

The landlord brought the food for the cats himself. He hurried in with a bowl of cream, a carefully boned salmon, and a dish of whitebait. He was followed by his wife, a woman as flinty-eyed as himself, carrying a soft rush basket and an embroidered cushion. Abdullah tried not to look smug again. "Generous thanks, most illustrious of innkeepers," he said. "I will tell the witch of your great care."

"That's all right, sir," the landlady said. "We know how to respect those that use magic, here in Kingsbury."

Abdullah went from smug to mortified. He saw he should have pretended to be a wizard himself. He relieved his feelings by saying, "That cushion *is* stuffed only with peacock feathers, I hope? The witch is most particular."

"Yes, sir," said the landlady. "I know all about that."

The soldier coughed. Abdullah gave up. He said grandly, "As well as the cats, my friend and I have been entrusted with a message for a wizard. We would prefer to deliver it to the Royal Wizard, but we heard rumors on the way that he has met with some sort of misfortune."

"That's right," said the landlord, pushing his wife

aside. "One of the Royal Wizards *has* disappeared, sir, but fortunately there are two. I can direct you to the other one—Royal Wizard Suliman—if you want, sir." He looked meaningly at Abdullah's hands.

Abdullah sighed and fetched out his largest silver piece. That seemed to be the right amount. The landlord gave him very careful directions and took the silver piece, promising baths and supper shortly. The baths, when they came, were hot, and the supper was good. Abdullah was glad. While the soldier was bathing himself and Whippersnapper, Abdullah transferred his wealth from his jacket to his money belt, which made him feel much better. The soldier must have felt better, too. He sat after supper with his feet up on a table, smoking that long clay pipe of his. Cheerfully he untied the bootlace from the neck of the genie bottle and dangled it for Whippersnapper to play with.

"There's no doubt about it," he said. "Money talks in this town. Are you going to talk to the Royal Wizard this evening? The sooner, the better, to my mind."

Abdullah agreed. "I wonder what his fee will be," he said.

"Big," said the soldier. "Unless you can work it that you're doing *him* a favor by telling him what the djinn said. All the same," he went on thoughtfully, whisking the bootlace out of Whippersnapper's pouncing paws, "I reckon you shouldn't tell him about the genie or the carpet if you can help it. These magical gentlemen love magical items the way this innkeeper loves gold. You don't want him asking for those for his fee. Why don't you leave them here when you go? I'll look after them for you."

Abdullah hesitated. It seemed sound sense. Yet he did not trust the soldier.

"By the way," said the soldier, "I owe you a gold piece."

"You do?" said Abdullah. "Then this is the most surprising news I have had since Flower-in-the-Night told me I was a woman!"

"That bet of ours," said the soldier. "The carpet brought the djinn, and he's even bigger trouble than the genie usually manages. You win. Here." He tossed a gold piece across the room at Abdullah.

Abdullah caught it, pocketed it, and laughed. The soldier *was* honest, after his own fashion. Full of thoughts of being soon on the trail of Flower-in-the-Night, Abdullah went cheerfully downstairs, where the landlady caught him and told him all over again how to get to Wizard Suliman's house. Abdullah was so cheerful that he parted with another silver piece almost without a pang.

The house was not far from the inn, but it was in the Old Quarter, which meant that the way was mostly through confusing small alleys and hidden courts. It was twilight now, with one or two large liquid stars already in the dark blue sky above the domes and towers, but Kingsbury was well lit by big silver globes of light, floating overhead like moons.

Abdullah was looking up at them, wondering if they were magical devices, when he happened to notice a black four-legged shadow stealing along the roofs beside him. It could have been any black cat out for a hunt on the tiles, but Abdullah knew it was Midnight. There was no mistaking the way she moved. At first, when she vanished into the deep black shadow of a gable, he supposed she was after a roosting pigeon to make another unsuitable meal for Whippersnapper. But she reappeared again when he was halfway down the next alley, creeping along a parapet above him, and he began to think she was following him. When he went through a narrow court with trees in tubs down the center and he saw her jump across the sky, from one gutter to another, in order to get into that court, too, he knew she was certainly following him. He had no idea why. He kept an eye out for her as he went down the next two alleys, but he saw her only once, on an arch over a doorway. When he turned into the cobbled court where the Royal Wizard's house was, there was no sign of her. Abdullah shrugged and went to the door of the house.

It was a handsome narrow house with diamond-paned windows and interwoven magic signs painted on its old irregular walls. There were tall spires of yellow flame burning in brass stands on either side of the front door. Abdullah seized the knocker, which was a leering face with a ring in its mouth, and boldly knocked.

The door was opened by a manservant with a long, dour face. "I'm afraid the wizard is extremely busy, sir," he said. "He is receiving no clients until further notice." And he started to shut the door.

"No wait, faithful footman and loveliest of lackeys!" Abdullah protested. "What I have to say concerns no less than a threat to the King's daughter!"

"The wizard knows all about that, sir," said the man, and went on shutting the door.

Abdullah deftly put his foot in the space. "You must hear me, most sapient servant," he began. "I come——"

Behind the manservant a young woman's voice said, "Just a moment, Manfred. I know this is important." The door swung open again.

Abdullah gaped as the servant vanished from the doorway and reappeared some way back in the hall inside. His place at the door was taken by an extremely lovely young woman with dark curls and a vivid face. Abdullah saw enough of her in one glance to realize that in her foreign northern way, she was as beautiful as Flower-in-the-Night, but after that he felt bound to look modestly away from her. She was very obviously going to have a baby. Ladies in Zanzib did not show themselves in this interesting condition. Abdullah scarcely knew where to look.

"I'm the wizard's wife, Lettie Suliman," this young woman said. "What did you come about?"

Abdullah bowed. It helped to keep his eyes on the doorstep. "O fruitful moon of lovely Kingsbury," he said, "know that I am Abdullah, son of Abdullah, carpet merchant from distant Zanzib, with news that your husband will wish to hear. Tell him, O splendor of a sorcerous house, that this morning I spoke with the mighty djinn Hasruel concerning the King's most precious daughter."

Lettie Suliman was clearly not at all used to the manners of Zanzib. "Good heavens!" she said. "I mean, how *polite!* And you're speaking the exact truth, aren't you? I think you ought to talk to Ben at once. Please come in."

She backed away from the doorway to give Abdullah room to enter. Abdullah, still with his eyes modestly lowered, stepped forward into the house. As soon as he did, something landed on his back. Then it took off again with a heavy rip of claws and went sailing over his head to land with a thump on Lettie's prominent front. A noise like a metal pulley filled the air.

"Midnight!" Abdullah said crossly, staggering forward.

"*Sophie!*" screamed Lettie, staggering backward with the cat in her arms. "Oh, Sophie, I've been worried *sick!* Manfred, get Ben at once. I don't care what he's doing. This is *urgent!*"

Chapter 16

---※---

In which strange things befall Midnight and Whippersnapper

There was a great deal of confusion and rushing about. Two other servants appeared, followed by first one and then a second young man in long blue gowns, who seemed to be the wizard's apprentices. All these people ran about, while Lettie ran back and forth in the hall with Midnight in her arms, screaming orders. In the midst of it all, Abdullah found Manfred showing him to a seat and solemnly giving him a glass of wine. Since this seemed what he was expected to do, Abdullah sat down and sipped the wine, rather bemused by the confusion.

Just as he was thinking it was going to go on forever, it all stopped. A tall, commanding man in a black robe had appeared from somewhere. "What on *earth* is going on?" said this man.

Since this summed up Abdullah's feelings entirely, he found himself rather taking to this man. He had faded red hair and a tired, craggy face. The black robe made Abdullah certain that this must be

Wizard Suliman; he would have looked like a wizard whatever he was wearing. Abdullah rose from his chair and bowed. The wizard shot him a look of craggy mystification and turned to Lettie.

"He's from Zanzib, Ben," said Lettie, "and he knows something about the threat to the Princess. And he brought Sophie with him. She's a *cat*! Look! Ben, you've got to change her back at *once*!"

Lettie was one of those ladies who look lovelier the more distraught they get. Abdullah was not surprised when Wizard Suliman took her gently by the elbows and said, "Yes, of course, my love," and followed that by kissing her forehead. It made Abdullah wonder miserably whether he would ever have a chance to kiss Flower-in-the-Night like that, or to add, as the wizard added, "Calm down——remember the baby." After this the wizard said over his shoulder, "And can't someone shut the front door? Half Kingsbury must know what's happened by now."

This endeared the wizard to Abdullah more than ever. The one thing that had prevented him getting up and shutting the door was a fear that it might be the custom here to leave your front door open in a crisis. He bowed again and found the wizard swinging around to face him.

"And what *has* happened, young man?" asked the wizard. "How did you know this cat was my wife's sister?"

Abdullah was somewhat taken aback by this question. He explained—several times—that he had had no idea Midnight was human, let alone that she was the Royal Wizard's sister-in-law, but he was not at all sure that anyone listened. They all seemed so glad to see Midnight that they simply assumed that Abdullah had brought her to the house out of pure friendship. Far from demanding a large fee, Wizard Suliman seemed to think that *he* owed Abdullah something, and when Abdullah protested that this was not so, he said, "Well, come along and see her changed back, anyway."

He said this in such a friendly and trusting way that Abdullah warmed to him even more and let himself be swept along with everyone else to a large room that *seemed* to be at the back of the house—except that Abdullah had a feeling that it was somehow somewhere else entirely. The floor and the walls sloped in a way that was not usual.

Abdullah had never seen any working wizardry before. He gazed around with interest, for the room was crowded with intricate magical devices. Nearest to him were filigree shapes with delicate smokes wreathing about them. Beside that, large and peculiar candles stood inside complicated signs, and beyond those were strange images made of wet clay. Farther off he saw a fountain of five jets that fell in odd geometric patterns and that half hid many much odder things, crowded into the distance beyond.

"No room to work in here," Wizard Suliman said, sweeping through. "These should hold by themselves while we set up in the next room. Hurry, all of you."

Everyone whirled on into a smaller room beyond, which was empty apart from some round mirrors hanging on the walls. Here Lettie set Midnight carefully down on a blue-green stone in the middle, where she sat seriously washing the inside of her front legs and looking totally unconcerned, while everyone else, including Lettie and the servants, worked away feverishly at building a sort of tent around her out of long silver rods.

Abdullah stood prudently against the wall, watching. By now he was rather regretting assuring the wizard that he owed him nothing. He should have taken the opportunity to ask how to reach the castle in the sky. But he reckoned that since nobody seemed to have listened to him then, it was better to wait until things calmed down. Meanwhile, the silver rods grew into a pattern of skeletal silver stars, and Abdullah watched the bustle, somewhat confused at the way the scene was reflected in all the mirrors, small and busy and bulging. The mirrors bent as oddly as the walls and floors did.

At length Wizard Suliman clapped his large, bony hands. "Right," he said. "Lettie can help me here. The rest of you get to the other room and make sure the wards for the Princess stay in place."

The apprentices and the servants hurried away. Wizard Suliman spread his arms. Abdullah intended to watch closely and remember clearly what happened. But somehow, as soon as the magic working started, he was not at all sure what was going on. He knew things were happening, but they did not *seem* to happen. It was like listening to music when you were tone-deaf. Every so often Wizard Suliman uttered a deep, strange word that blurred the room and the inside of Abdullah's head with it, which made it even harder to see what was happening. But most of Abdullah's difficulty came from the mirrors on the walls. They kept showing small, round pictures that looked like reflections but were not—or not quite. Every time one of the mirrors caught Abdullah's eye, it showed the framework of rods glowing with silvery light in a new pattern—a star, a triangle, a hexagon, or some other symbol angular and secret—while the real rods in front of him did not glow at all. Once or twice a mirror showed Wizard Suliman with his arms spread when, in the room, his arms were by his sides. Several times a mirror showed Lettie standing still with her hands clasped, looking vividly nervous. But each time Abdullah looked at the real Lettie, she was moving about, making strange gestures and perfectly calm. Midnight never appeared in the mirrors at all. Her small black shape in the middle of the rods was oddly hard to see in reality, too.

Then all the rods suddenly glowed misty silver and the space inside filled with a haze. The wizard spoke a final deep word and stepped back.

"Confound it!" said someone inside the rods. "I can't smell you at all now!"

This made the wizard grin and Lettie laugh outright. Abdullah looked for the person who was amusing them so and was forced to look away almost at once. The young woman crouching inside the framework, understandably enough, had no clothes on at all. The glimpse he caught, told him that the young woman was as fair as Lettie was dark but otherwise quite like her. Lettie ran to the side of the room and came back with a wizardly green gown. When Abdullah dared to look, the young woman was wearing the gown like a dressing gown, and Lettie was trying to hug her and help her out of the framework at the same time.

"Oh, *Sophie!* What *happened?*" she kept saying.

"One moment," gasped Sophie. She seemed to have difficulty balancing on two feet at first, but she hugged Lettie and then staggered to the wizard and hugged him, too. "It feels so odd without a tail!" she said. "But thanks awfully, Ben." Then she advanced on Abdullah, walking rather more easily now. Abdullah backed against the wall, afraid she was going to hug him, too, but all Sophie said was "You must have wondered why I was following you. The truth is, I *always* get lost in Kingsbury."

"I am happy to have been of service, most charming of changelings," Abdullah said rather stiffly. He was not sure he was going to get on with Sophie any more than he had got on with Midnight. She struck him as uncomfortably strong-minded for a young woman—almost as bad as his father's first wife's sister, Fatima.

Lettie was still demanding to know what had turned Sophie into a cat, and Wizard Suliman was saying anxiously, "Sophie, does this mean that Howl's wandering about as an animal, too?"

"No, no," Sophie said, and suddenly looked desperately anxious. "I've no idea where Howl is. He was the one who turned me into a cat, you see."

"*What?* Your own husband turned you into a cat!" Lettie exclaimed. "Is this another of your quarrels, then?"

"Yes, but it was all perfectly reasonable," said Sophie. "It was when someone stole the moving castle, you see. We only had about half a day's notice, and that was only because Howl happened to be working on a divining spell for the King. It showed something very powerful stealing the castle and then stealing Princess Valeria. Howl said he'd warn the King at once. Did he?"

"He certainly did," said Wizard Suliman. "The

Princess is guarded every second. I invoked demons and set up wards in the next room. Whatever being is threatening her has no chance of getting through."

"Thank goodness!" said Sophie. "That's a weight off my mind. It's a djinn, did you know?"

"Even a djinn couldn't get through," said Wizard Suliman. "But what did Howl do?"

"He swore," said Sophie. "In Welsh. Then he sent Michael and the new apprentice away. He wanted to send me away, too. But I said if he and Calcifer were staying, then so was I, and couldn't he put a spell on me that would simply make the djinn not notice I was there? And we argued about that—"

Lettie chuckled. "Now, why doesn't that surprise me?" she said.

Sophie's face became somewhat pink, and she put her head up defiantly. "Well, Howl would keep saying I'd be safest right out of the way in Wales with his sister, and he *knows* I don't get on with her, and I kept saying I'd be more use if I could be in the castle without the thief noticing. Anyway"—she put her face in her hands—"I'm afraid we were still arguing when the djinn came. There was an enormous noise, and everything went dark and confused. I remember Howl shouting the words of the cat spell—he had to gabble them in a hurry—and then yelling to Calcifer—"

"Calcifer's their fire demon," Lettie explained politely to Abdullah.

"—yelling to Calcifer to get out and save himself because the djinn was too strong for either of them," Sophie went on. "Then the castle came off from on top of me like the lid off a cheese dish. Next thing I knew, I was a cat in the mountains north of Kingsbury."

Lettie and the Royal Wizard exchanged puzzled looks over Sophie's bent head. "Why those mountains?" Wizard Suliman wondered. "The castle wasn't anywhere near there."

"No, it was in four places at once," Sophie said. "I think I was thrown somewhere midway between. It could have been worse. There were plenty of mice and birds to eat."

Lettie's lovely face twisted in disgust. *"Sophie!"* she exclaimed. "Mice!"

"Why not? That's what cats eat," Sophie said, lifting her head defiantly again. "Mice are delicious. But I'm not so fond of birds. The feathers choke you. But"—she gulped and put her head in her hands again—"but it happened at a rather bad time for me. Morgan was born about a week after that, and of course, he was a kitten—"

This caused Lettie, if possible, even more consternation than the thought of her sister eating mice. She burst into tears and flung her arms around Sophie. "Oh, Sophie! What did you *do?*"

"What cats always do, of course," Sophie said.

"Fed him and washed him a lot. Don't worry, Lettie. I left him with Abdullah's friend the soldier. That man would kill anyone who harmed his kitten. But," she said to Wizard Suliman, "I think I ought to fetch Morgan now so that you can turn him back, too."

Wizard Suliman was looking almost as distraught as Lettie. "I wish I'd known!" he said. "If he was born a cat as part of the same spell, he may be changed back already. We'd better find out." He strode to one of the round mirrors and made circular gestures with both hands.

The mirror—all the mirrors—at once seemed to be reflecting the room at the inn, each from a different viewpoint, as if they were hanging on the wall there. Abdullah stared from one to the other and was as alarmed at what he saw as the other three were. The magic carpet had, for some reason, been unrolled upon the floor. On it lay a plump, naked pink baby. Young as this baby was, Abdullah could see he had a personality as strong as Sophie's. And he was asserting that personality. His legs and arms were punching the air, his face was contorted with fury, and his mouth was a square, angry hole. Though the pictures in the mirrors were silent, it was clear that Morgan was being very noisy indeed.

"Who is that man?" said Wizard Suliman. "I've seen him before."

"A Strangian soldier, worker of wonders," Abdullah said helplessly.

"Then he must remind me of someone I know," said the wizard.

The soldier was standing beside the screaming baby, looking horrified and useless. Perhaps he was hoping the genie would do something. At any rate, he had the genie bottle in one hand. But the genie was hanging out of the bottle in several spouts of distracted blue smoke, each spout a face with its hand over its ears, as helpless as the soldier.

"Oh, the poor darling child!" said Lettie.

"The poor blessed soldier, you mean," said Sophie. "Morgan's furious. He's never *been* anything but a kitten, and kittens can do so much more than babies can. He's angry because he can't walk. Ben, do you think you can—"

The rest of Sophie's question was drowned in a noise like a giant piece of silk tearing. The room shook. Wizard Suliman exclaimed something and made for the door—and then had to dodge hastily. A whole crowd of screaming, wailing *somethings* swept through the wall beside the door, swooped across the room, and vanished through the opposite wall. They were going too fast to be seen clearly, but none of them seemed to be human. Abdullah had a blurred glimpse of multiple clawed legs, of something streaming along on no legs at all, of beings with one wild eye and of others with many eyes in clusters. He saw fanged heads, flowing tongues, flaming tails. One, moving swiftest of all, was a rolling ball of mud.

Then they were gone. The door was thrown open by an agitated apprentice. "Sir, sir! The wards are down! We couldn't hold—"

Wizard Suliman seized the young man's arm and hurried him back into the next room, calling over his shoulder, "I'll be back when I can! The Princess is in danger!"

Abdullah looked to see what was happening to the soldier and the baby, but the round mirrors now showed nothing but his own anxious face, and Sophie's and Lettie's, all staring upward into them.

"Drat!" said Sophie. "Lettie, can you work them?"

"No. They're Ben's special thing," said Lettie.

Abdullah thought of the carpet unrolled and the genie bottle in the soldier's hand. "Then in that case, O pair of twinned pearls," he said, "most lovely ladies, I will, with your permission, hasten back to the inn before too many complaints are made about the noise."

Sophie and Lettie replied in chorus that they were coming, too. Abdullah could scarcely blame them, but he came precious near it in the next few minutes. Lettie, it seemed, was not up to hurrying through the streets in her interesting condition. As the three of them rushed through the jumble and chaos of broken spells in the next room, Wizard Suliman spared a second from frantically setting up new things in the ruins to order Manfred to get the carriage out. While Manfred raced off to do that, Lettie took Sophie upstairs to get her some proper clothes.

Abdullah was left pacing the hall. To everyone's credit, he only waited there less than five minutes, but during that time he tried the front door at least ten times, only to find there was a spell holding it shut. He thought he would go mad. It seemed like a century before Sophie and Lettie came downstairs, both in elegant going-out clothes, and Manfred opened the front door to show a small open carriage drawn by a nice bay gelding, waiting outside on the cobbles. Abdullah wanted to take a flying leap into that carriage and whip up that gelding. But of course, that was not polite. He had to wait while Manfred helped the ladies up into it and then climbed to the driver's seat. The carriage set off smartly clattering across the cobbles while Abdullah was still squeezing himself into the seat beside Sophie, but even that was not quick enough for him. He could hardly bear to think of what the soldier might be doing.

"I hope Ben can get some wards back on the Princess soon," Lettie said anxiously as they rolled spankingly across an open square.

The words were scarcely out of her mouth when

there came a hurried volley of explosions, like very mismanaged fireworks. A bell began to ring somewhere, dismal and hasty—gong-gong-gong.

"What's all that?" asked Sophie, and then answered her own question by pointing and crying out, "Oh, confound it! Look, look, look!"

Abdullah craned around to where she pointed. He was in time to see a black spread of wings blotting out the stars above the nearest domes and towers. Below, from the tops of several towers, came little flashes and a number of bangs as the soldiers there fired at those wings. Abdullah could have told them that that kind of thing was no use at all against a djinn. The wings wheeled imperturbably and circled upward and then vanished into the dark blue of the night sky.

"Your friend the djinn," Sophie said. "I think we distracted Ben at a crucial moment."

"The djinn intended that you should, O former feline," Abdullah said. "If you recollect, he remarked as he was leaving that he expected one of us to help him steal the Princess."

Other bells around the city had joined in ringing the alarm now. People ran into the streets and stared upward. The carriage jingled on through an increasing clamor and was forced to go more and more slowly as more people gathered in the streets. Everyone seemed to know exactly what had happened. "The Princess is gone!" Abdullah heard. "A devil has stolen Princess Valeria!" Most people seemed awed and frightened, but one or two were saying, "That Royal Wizard ought to be hanged! What's he *paid* for?"

"Oh, dear!" said Lettie. "The King won't believe for a moment how hard Ben's been working to stop this from happening!"

"Don't worry," said Sophie. "As soon as we've fetched Morgan, I'll go and tell the King. I'm good at telling the King things."

Abdullah believed her. He sat and jittered with impatience.

After what seemed another century but was probably only five minutes, the carriage pushed its way into the crowded innyard. It was full of people all staring upward. "Saw its wings," he heard a man saying. "It was a monstrous bird with the Princess clutched in its talons."

The carriage stopped. Abdullah could give way to his impatience at last. He sprang down, shouting, "Clear the way, clear the way, O people! Here are two witches on important business!" By repeated shouting and pushing, he managed to get Sophie and Lettie to the inn door and shove them inside. Lettie was very embarrassed.

"I wish you wouldn't *say* that!" she said. "Ben doesn't like people to know I'm a witch."

"He will have no time to think of it just now,"

Abdullah said. He pushed the two of them past the staring landlord and to the stairs. "Here are the witches I spoke to you about, most heavenly host," he told the man. "They are anxious about their cats." He leaped up the stairs. He overtook Lettie, then Sophie, and raced on up the next flight. He flung open the door of the room. "Do nothing rash—" he began, and then stopped as he realized there was complete silence inside.

The room was empty.

Chapter 17

In which Abdullah at last reaches the castle in the air

There was a cushion in a basket among the remains of supper on the table. There was a rumpled dent in one of the beds and a cloud of tobacco smoke above it, as if the soldier had been lying there smoking until very recently. The window was closed. Abdullah rushed toward it, intending to fling it open and look out—for no real reason except that it was all he could think of—and found himself tripping over a saucer full of cream. The saucer overturned, slewing thick yellow-white cream in a long streak across the magic carpet.

Abdullah stood staring down at it. At least the carpet was still there. What did that mean? There was no sign of the soldier and certainly no sign of a noisy baby anywhere in the room. Nor, he realized, turning his eyes rapidly toward every place he could think of, was there any sign of the genie bottle.

"Oh, *no!*" Sophie said, arriving at the door. "Where *is* he? He can't have gone far if the carpet's still here."

Abdullah wished he could be so certain of that. "Without desiring to alarm you, mother of a most mobile baby," he said, "I have to observe that the genie appears to be missing also."

A small vague frown creased the skin of Sophie's forehead. "What genie?"

While Abdullah was remembering that as Midnight, Sophie had always seemed quite unaware that the genie existed, Lettie arrived in the room, too, panting, with one hand pressed to her side. "What's the matter?" she gasped.

"They're not here," said Sophie. "I suppose the soldier must have taken Morgan to the landlady. She must know about babies."

With a feeling of grasping at straws, Abdullah said, "I will go and see." It was always just possible that Sophie was right, he thought as he sped down the first flight of stairs. It was what most men would do faced with a screaming baby suddenly—always supposing that man did not have a genie bottle in his hand.

The lower flight of stairs was full of people coming up, men wearing tramping boots and some kind of uniform. The landlord was leading them upward, saying, "On the second floor, gentlemen. Your description fits the Strangian if he had cut off his pigtail, and the younger fellow is obviously the accomplice you speak of."

Abdullah turned and ran back upstairs on tiptoe, two stairs at a time.

"There is general disaster, most bewitching pair of women!" he gasped to Sophie and Lettie. "The landlord—a perfidious publican—is bringing constables to arrest myself and the soldier. Now what can we do?"

It was time for a strong-minded woman to take charge. Abdullah was quite glad that Sophie was one. She acted at once. She shut the door and shot its bolt. "Lend me your handkerchief," she said to Lettie, and when Lettie passed it over, Sophie knelt and mopped the cream off the magic carpet with it. "You come over here," she told Abdullah. "Get on this carpet with me, and tell it to take us to wherever Morgan is. You stay here, Lettie, and hold the constables up. I don't think the carpet would carry you."

"Fine," said Lettie. "I want to get back to Ben before the King starts blaming him, anyway. But I'll give that landlord a piece of my mind first. It'll be good practice for the King." As strong-minded as her sister, she squared her shoulders and stuck out her elbows in a way that promised a bad time for the landlord and the constables as well.

Abdullah was glad about Lettie, too. He crouched on the carpet and snored gently. The carpet quivered. It was a reluctant quiver. "O fabulous fabric, carbuncle and chrysolite among carpets," Abdullah said, "this miserable clumsy churl apologizes profoundly for spilling cream upon your priceless surface—"

Heavy knocking came at the door. "Open, in the King's name!" bellowed someone outside.

There was no time to flatter the carpet any further. "Carpet, I implore you," Abdullah whispered, "transport myself and this lady to the place where the soldier has taken the baby."

The carpet shook itself irritably, but it obeyed. It shot forward in its usual way, straight through the closed window. Abdullah was alert enough this time actually to see the glass and the dark frame of the window for an instant, like the surface of water, as they passed through it and then soared above the silver globes that lit the street. But he doubted if Sophie was. She clutched Abdullah's arm with both hands, and he rather thought her eyes were shut.

"I hate heights!" she said. "It had better not be far."

"This excellent carpet will carry us with all possible speed, worshipful witch," Abdullah said, trying to reassure her and the carpet together. He was not sure it worked with either of them. Sophie continued to cling painfully to his arm, uttering little, short gasps of panic, while the carpet, having made one brisk, giddy sweep just above the towers and lights of Kingsbury, swung dizzily around what seemed to be the domes of the palace and began on another circuit of the city.

"What is it *doing?*" gasped Sophie. Evidently her eyes were not quite shut.

"Peace, most serene sorceress," Abdullah reassured her. "It does but circle to gain height as birds do." Privately he was sure the carpet had lost the trail. But as the lights and domes of Kingsbury went by underneath for the third time, he saw he had accidentally guessed right. They were now several hundred feet higher. On the fourth circuit, which was wider than the third—though quite as giddy—Kingsbury was a little jeweled cluster of lights far, far below.

Sophie's head bobbed as she took a downward peep. Her grip on Abdullah became even tighter, if that was possible. "Oh, goodness and awfulness!" she said. "We're still going *up!* I do believe that wretched soldier has taken Morgan after the djinn!"

They were now so high that Abdullah feared she was right. "He no doubt wished to rescue the Princess," he said, "in hope of a large reward."

"He had no business to take my baby along, too!" Sophie declared. "Just wait till I see him! But how did he *do* it without the carpet?"

"He must have ordered the genie to follow the djinn, O moon of motherhood," Abdullah explained.

To that Sophie said again, "What genie?"

"I assure you, sharpest of sorcerous minds, that I

owned a genie as well as this carpet, though you never appeared to see it," Abdullah said.

"Then I take your word for it," said Sophie. "Keep talking. Talk—or I shall look down, and if I look down, I *know* I'll fall off!"

Since she was still clinging mightily to Abdullah's arm, he knew that if she fell, then so would he. Kingsbury was now a bright, hazy dot, appearing on this side and then on that, as the carpet continued to spiral upward. The rest of Ingary was laid out around it like a huge dark blue dish. The thought of plunging all that way down made Abdullah almost as frightened as Sophie. He began hastily to tell her all his adventures, how he had met Flower-in-the-Night, how the Sultan had put him in prison, how the genie had been fished out of the oasis pool by Kabul Aqba's men—who were really angels—and how hard it was to make a wish that the genie's malice did not spoil.

By this time he could see the desert as a pale sea south of Ingary, though they were so high that it was quite hard to make out anything below. "I see now that the soldier agreed I had won that bet in order to convince me of his honesty," Abdullah said ruefully. "I think he always meant to steal the genie and prob-ably the carpet, too."

Sophie was interested. Her grip on his arm relaxed slightly, to Abdullah's great relief. "You can't blame that genie for hating everyone," she said. "Think how you felt shut in that dungeon."

"But the soldier—" said Abdullah.

"Is another matter!" Sophie declared. "Just *wait* till I get my hands on him! I can't *abide* people who go soft over animals and then cheat every human they come across! But to get back to this genie you say you had, it looks as if the djinn meant you to have it. Do you think it was part of his scheme to have disappointed lovers help him get the better of his brother?"

"I believe so," said Abdullah.

"Then, when we get to the cloud castle, *if* that's where we're going," Sophie said, "we might be able to count on other disappointed lovers arriving to help."

"Maybe," Abdullah said cautiously. "But I recollect, most curious of cats, that you were fleeing to the bushes while the djinn spoke, and the djinn expected only myself."

Nevertheless, he looked upward. It was growing chilly now, and the stars seemed uncomfortably close. There was a sort of silveriness to the dark blue of the sky which suggested moonlight trying to break through from somewhere. It was very beautiful. Abdullah's heart swelled with the thought that he might be, at last, on the way to rescue Flower-in-the-Night.

Unfortunately Sophie looked up, too. Her grip on his arm tightened. "Talk," she said. "I'm terrified."

"Then you must talk, too, courageous caster of spells," said Abdullah. "Close your eyes and tell me of the Prince of Ochinstan, to whom Flower-in-the-Night was betrothed."

"I don't think she could have been," Sophie said, almost babbling. She was truly terrified. "The King's son is only a baby. Of course, there's the King's *brother*, Prince Justin, but *he* was supposed to be marrying Princess Beatrice of Strangia—except that she refused to hear of it and ran away. Do you think the djinn's got her? I think your Sultan was just after some of the weapons our wizards have been making here—and he wouldn't have got them. They don't let the mercenaries take them south when they go. In fact, Howl says they shouldn't even send mercenaries. Howl . . ." Her voice faded. Her hands on Abdullah's arm shook. "Talk!" she croaked.

It was getting hard to breathe. "I barely can, strong-handed Sultana," Abdullah gasped. "I think the air is thin here. Can you not make some witchly weaving that might help us to breathe?"

"Probably not. You keep calling me a witch, but I'm really quite new to it," Sophie protested. "You saw. When I was a cat, all I could do was get larger." But she let go of Abdullah for a moment in order to make short, jerky gestures overhead. "Really, air!" she said. "This is disgraceful! You are going to have to let us breathe a bit better than this or we won't last out.

Gather around and let us breathe you!" She clutched Abdullah again. "Is that any better?"

There really did seem to be more air now, though it was colder than ever. Abdullah was surprised, because Sophie's method of casting a spell struck him as most unwitchlike—in fact, it was not much different from his own way of persuading the carpet to move—but he had to admit that it worked. "Yes. Many thanks, speaker of spells."

"Talk!" said Sophie.

They were so high that the world below was out of sight. Abdullah had no trouble understanding Sophie's terror. The carpet was sailing through dark emptiness, up and up, and Abdullah knew that if he had been alone, he might have been screaming. "You talk, mighty mistress of magics," he quavered. "Tell me of this Wizard Howl of yours."

Sophie's teeth chattered, but she said proudly, "He's the best wizard in Ingary or anywhere else. If he'd only had time, he would have defeated that djinn. And he's sly and selfish and vain as a peacock and cowardly, and you can't pin him down to anything."

"Indeed?" asked Abdullah. "Strange that you should speak so proudly such a list of vices, most loving of ladies."

"What do you mean, vices?" Sophie asked angrily. "I was just *describing* Howl. He comes from another world entirely, you know, called Wales, and I refuse to believe he's dead——ooh!"

She ended in a moan as the carpet plunged upward into what had seemed to be a gauzy veil of cloud. Inside the cloud the gauziness proved to be flakes of ice, which peppered them in slivers and chunks and rounds like a hailstorm. They were both gasping as the carpet burst upward out of it. Then they both gasped again, in wonder.

They were in a new country, which was bathed in moonlight——moonlight that had the golden tinge of a harvest moon to it. But when Abdullah spared an instant to look for the moon, he could not see it anywhere. The light seemed to come from the silver-blue sky itself, studded with great limpid golden stars. But he could only spare that one glance. The carpet had come out beside a hazy, transparent sea and was laboring alongside soft rollers breaking on cloudy rocks. Regardless of the fact that they could see through each wave as if it were gold-green silk, its water was wet and threatened to overwhelm the carpet. The air was warm. And the carpet, not to speak of their own clothes and hair, was loaded with piles of melting ice. Sophie and Abdullah, for the first few minutes, were entirely occupied in sweeping ice over the edges of the carpet into the translucent ocean, where it sank through into the sky beneath and vanished.

When the carpet bobbed up lighter and they had a chance to look around, they gasped again. For here were the islands and promontories and bays of dim gold that Abdullah had seen in the sunset, spreading out from beside them into the far silver distance, where they lay hushed and still and enchanted like a vista of Paradise itself. The pellucid waves broke on the cloud shore with only the faintest of whispers, which seemed to add to the silence.

It seemed wrong to speak in such a place. Sophie nudged Abdullah and pointed. There, on the nearest cloudy headland, stood a castle, a mass of proud, soaring towers with dim silvery windows showing in them. It was made of cloud. As they looked, several of the taller towers streamed sideways and shredded out of existence, while others shrank and broadened. Under their eyes, it grew like a blot into a massive frowning fortress and then began to change again. But it was still there and still a castle, and it seemed to be the place where the carpet was taking them.

The carpet was going at a swift walking pace, but gently, keeping to the shoreline as if it were not at all anxious to be seen. There were cloudy bushes beyond the waves, tinged red and silver like the aftermath of sunset. The carpet lurked in the cover of these, just as it had lurked behind trees in Kingsbury Plain, while it circled the bay to come to the promontory.

As it went, there were new vistas of golden seas, where far-off smoky shapes moved that could have been ships or may have been cloudy creatures on business of their own. Still in utter, whispering silence, the carpet crept out onto the headland, where there were no more bushes. Here it slunk close to the cloudy ground, much as it had followed the shapes of the roofs in Kingsbury. Abdullah did not blame it. Ahead of them, the castle was changing again, stretching out until it had become a mighty pavilion. As the carpet entered the long avenue leading to its gates, domes were rising and bulging, and it had protruded a dim gold minaret as if it were watching them coming.

The avenue was lined with cloudy shapes, which also seemed to watch them coming. The shapes grew out of the cloud-ground in the way that one often sees a tuft of cloud curl upward out of the main mass. But unlike the castle, they did not change shape. Each one ramped proudly upward, somewhat in the shape of a sea horse or the knights in a game of chess, except that their faces were blanker and flatter than the faces of horses and surrounded by curling tendrils that were neither cloud nor hair.

Sophie looked at each one as they passed it with increasing disfavor. "I don't think much of his taste in statues," she said.

"Oh, hush, most outspoken lady!" Abdullah whispered. "These are no statues, but the two hundred attendant angels spoken of by the djinn!"

The sound of their voices attracted the attention of the nearest cloudy shape. It stirred mistily, opened a pair of immense moonstone eyes, and bent to survey the carpet as it slunk past it.

"Don't you dare try to stop us!" Sophie said to it. "We're only coming to get my baby."

The huge eyes blinked. Evidently the angel was not used to being spoken to so sharply. Cloudy white wings began to spread from its sides.

Hastily Abdullah stood up on the carpet and bowed. "Greetings, most noble messenger of the heavens," he said. "What the lady says so bluntly is the truth. Pray forgive her. She is from the north. But she, like me, comes in peace. The djinns are minding her child, and we do but come to collect him and render them our most humble and devout thanks."

This seemed to placate the angel. Its wings melted back into its cloudy sides, and though its strange head turned to watch them as the carpet slunk on, it did not try to stop them. But by now the angel across the way had its eyes open, too, and the two next were turned to stare as well. Abdullah did not dare sit down again. He braced his feet for balance and bowed to each pair of angels as they came to it. This was not easy to do. The carpet knew how dangerous the angels could be as well as Abdullah did, and it was moving faster and faster.

Even Sophie realized that a little politeness would help. She nodded to each angel as they whipped past. "Evening," she said. "Lovely sunset today. Evening." She had not time for more because the carpet was fairly scuttling up the last stretch of avenue. When it reached the castle gates, which were shut, it dived through like a rat up a drainpipe. Abdullah and Sophie were suffused with foggy damp and then out into calm goldish light. They found they were in a garden. Here the carpet fell to the floor, limp as a dishrag, where it stayed. It had little shivers running through the length of it, as a carpet might that was shaking with fear, or panting with effort, or both.

Since the ground in the garden was solid and did not seem to be made of cloud, Sophie and Abdullah cautiously stepped onto it. It was firm turf, growing silver-green grass. In the distance, among formal hedges, a marble fountain played. Sophie looked at this, and looked around, and began to frown.

Abdullah stooped and considerately rolled the carpet up, patting it and speaking soothingly. "Bravely done, most daring of damasks," he told it. "There, there. Never fear. I will not allow any djinn, however mighty, to harm so much as a thread of your treasured fabric or a fringe from your border."

"You sound like that soldier making a fuss of Morgan when he was Whippersnapper," Sophie said. "The castle's over there."

They set off toward it, Sophie staring alertly around and uttering one or two snorts, Abdullah with the carpet tenderly over his shoulder. He patted it from time to time and felt the quivers die out of it as they went. They walked for some time, for the garden, although it was not made of cloud, changed and enlarged around them. The hedges became artistic banks of pale pink flowers, and the fountain, which they could see clearly in the distance all the time, now appeared to be crystal or possibly chrysolite. A few steps more, and everything was in jeweled pots, and frondy, with creepers trained up lacquered pillars. Sophie's snorts became louder. The fountain, as far as they could tell, was of silver inset with sapphires.

"That djinn has taken liberties with a person's castle," Sophie said. "Unless I'm entirely turned around, this used to be our bathroom."

Abdullah felt his face heat up. Sophie's bathroom or not, these were the gardens out of his daydreams. Hasruel was mocking him, as he had mocked Abdullah all along. When the fountain ahead turned to gold, glinting wine dark with rubies, Abdullah became as annoyed as Sophie was.

"This is not the way a garden should be, even if we disregard the confusing changes," he said angrily. "A garden should be natural-seeming, with wild sections, including a large area of bluebells."

"Quite right," said Sophie. "Look at that fountain now! *What* a way to treat a bathroom!"

The fountain was platinum, with emeralds.

"Ridiculously flashy!" said Abdullah. "When I design *my* garden—"

He was interrupted by a child's screaming. Both of them began to run.

Chapter 18

◆──❦──◆

Which is rather full of princesses

The child's screams rose. There was no doubt about the direction. As Sophie and Abdullah ran that way, along a pillared cloister, Sophie panted, "It's not Morgan; it's an older child!"

Abdullah thought she was right. He could hear words in the screams, although he could not pick out what they were. And surely Morgan, even howling his loudest, did not possess big enough lungs to make this kind of noise. After getting almost too loud to bear, the screams became grating sobs. Those sank to a steady, nagging "Wah-wah-wah!" and just as that sound became truly intolerable, the child raised his or her voice into hysterical screams again.

Sophie and Abdullah followed the noise to the end of the cloister and out into a huge cloudy hall. There they stopped prudently behind a pillar, and Sophie said, "Our main room. They must have blown it up like a balloon!"

It was a very big hall. The screaming child was in

the middle of it. She was about four years old, with fair curls and wearing a white nightdress. Her face was red, her mouth was a black square, and she was alternately throwing herself down on the green porphyry floor and standing up in order to throw herself down again. If ever there was a child in a temper, it was this one. The echoes in the huge hall yelled with it.

"It's Princess Valeria," Sophie murmured to Abdullah. "I thought it might be."

Hovering over the howling princess was the huge dark shape of Hasruel. Another djinn, much smaller and paler, was dodging about behind him. "*Do* something!" this small djinn shouted. Only the fact that he had a voice like silver trumpets made him audible. "She's driving me insane!"

Hasruel bent his great visage down to Valeria's screaming face. "Little princess," he boomingly cooed, "stop crying. You will not be hurt."

Princess Valeria's answer was first to stand up and scream in Hasruel's face, then to throw herself flat on the floor and roll and kick there. "Wah-wah-*wah!*" she vociferated. "I want *home!* I want my *dad!* I want my *nurse!* I want my *Uncle Ju-ustin!* WaaaAH!"

"Little princess!" Hasruel cooed desperately.

"Don't just *coo* at her!" trumpeted the other djinn, who was clearly Dalzel. "Work some magic! Sweet dreams, a spell of silence, a thousand teddies, a ton of toffee! *Anything!*"

Hasruel turned around on his brother. His spread wings fanned agitated gales, which flapped Valeria's hair and fluttered her nightdress. Sophie and Abdullah had to cling to the pillar, or the force of the wind would have blown them backward. But it made no difference to Princess Valeria's tantrum. If anything, she screamed harder.

"I have *tried* all that, brother of mine!" Hasruel boomed.

Princess Valeria was now producing steady yells of "MOTHER! MOTHER! THEY'RE BEING *HORRID* TO ME!"

Hasruel had to raise his voice to a perfect thunder. "Don't you know," he thundered, "that there is almost no magic that will stop a child in this kind of temper?"

Dalzel clapped his pale hands across his ears—pointed ears, with a look of fungus to them. "Well, I can't stand it!" he shrilled. "Put her to sleep for a hundred years!"

Hasruel nodded. He turned back to Princess Valeria as she screamed and thrashed upon the floor and spread his huge hand above her.

"Oh, dear!" said Sophie to Abdullah. "*Do* something!"

Since Abdullah had no idea what to do, and since he privately felt that *anything* that stopped this horrible noise was a good idea, he did nothing but edge uncertainly away from the pillar. And fortunately, before Hasruel's magic had any noticeable effect on Princess Valeria, a crowd of other people arrived. A loud, rather rasping voice cut through the din.

"What is all this noise about?"

Both djinns started backward. The new arrivals were all female, and they all looked extremely displeased; but when you had said that, you seemed to have said the only two things they had in common. They stood in a row, thirty or so of them, glaring accusingly at the two djinns, and they were tall, short, stout, skinny, young and old, and of every color the human race produces. Abdullah's eyes scudded along the row in amazement. These must be the kidnapped princesses. That was the third thing they had in common. They ranged from a tiny, frail, yellow princess nearest to him, to an elderly, bent princess in the mid-distance. And they were wearing every possible kind of clothing, from a ball dress to tweeds.

The one who had called out was a solidly built middle-sized princess standing slightly in front of the rest. She was wearing riding clothes. Her face, besides being tanned and a little lined from outdoor activity, was downright and sensible. She looked at the two djinns with utter contempt. "Of all the ridiculous things!" she said. "Two great powerful creatures like you, and you can't even stop a child crying!" And she stepped up to Valeria and gave her a sharp slap on her

231

thrashing behind. "Shut up!"

It worked. Valeria had never been slapped in her life before. She rolled over and sat up as if she had been shot. She stared at the downright princess out of astonished, swollen eyes. "You *hit* me!"

"And I shall hit you again if you ask for it," said the downright princess.

"I shall scream," said Valeria. Her mouth went square again. She drew a deep breath.

"No, you won't," said the downright princess. She picked Valeria up and bundled her briskly into the arms of the two princesses behind her. They, and several more, closed around Valeria in a huddle, making soothing noises. From the midst of the huddle Valeria began screaming again, but in a way that was not quite convinced. The downright princess put her hands on her hips and turned contemptuously to the djinns.

"See?" she said. "All you need is a bit of firmness and some kindness, but neither of you can be expected to understand *that!*"

Dalzel stepped toward her. Now that he was not so anguished, Abdullah saw with surprise that Dalzel was beautiful. Apart from his fungoid ears and taloned feet, he could have been a tall, angelic man. Golden curls grew on his head, and his wings, though small and stunted-looking, were golden, too. His very red mouth spread into a sweet smile. Altogether he had an unearthly beauty that matched the strange cloud kingdom where he lived. "Pray take the child away," he said, "and comfort her, O Princess Beatrice, most excellent of my wives."

Downright Princess Beatrice was gesturing to the other princesses to take Valeria away anyway, but she turned back sharply at this. "I've told you, my lad," she said, "that *none* of us is any wife of yours. You can call us that until you're blue in the face, but it won't make the slightest difference. We are *not* your wives, and we never will be!"

"Exactly!" said most of the other princesses, in a firm but ragged chorus. All of them, except for one, turned and swept away, taking the sobbing Princess Valeria with them.

Sophie's face was lit with a delighted smile. She whispered, "It looks as if the princesses are holding their own!"

Abdullah could not attend to her. The remaining princess was Flower-in-the-Night. She was, as always, twice as beautiful as he remembered her, looking very sweet and grave, with her great dark eyes fixed seriously on Dalzel. She bowed politely. Abdullah's senses sang at the sight of her. The cloudy pillars around him seemed to sway in and out of existence. His heart pounded for joy. She was safe! She was here! She was speaking to Dalzel.

"Forgive me, great djinn, if I remain to ask you a

question," she said, and her voice, even more than Abdullah remembered it, was melodious and merry as a cool fountain.

To Abdullah's outrage, Dalzel reacted with what seemed to be horror. "Oh, not *you* again!" he trumpeted, at which Hasruel, standing like a dark column in the background, folded his arms and grinned maliciously.

"Yes, it is I, stern stealer of the daughters of sultans," Flower-in-the-Night said with her head bowed politely. "I am here merely to ask what thing it was which started the child crying."

"How should *I* know?" Dalzel demanded. "You're always asking me questions I can't answer! Why are you asking this one?"

"Because," Flower-in-the-Night answered, "O robber of the offspring of rulers, the easiest way to calm the child is to deal with the cause of her temper. This I know from my own childhood, for I was much given to tantrums myself."

Surely not! Abdullah thought. She is lying for a purpose. No nature as sweet as hers could ever have screamed for anything! Yet, as he was outraged to see, Dalzel had no difficulty believing this.

"I'll *bet* you were!" Dalzel said.

"So what was the cause, bereaver of the brave?" Flower-in-the-Night persisted. "Was it that she wishes to be back in her own palace or to have her own particular doll, or was she simply frightened by your face or—"

"I'm not sending her back if that's what you're aiming for," Dalzel interrupted. "She's one of my wives now."

"Then I adjure you to find out what set her off screaming, raptor of the righteous," Flower-in-the-Night said politely, "for without that knowledge, even thirty princesses may not silence her." Indeed, Princess Valeria's voice was rising again in the distance—"wah-wah-WAH!"—as she spoke. "I speak from experience," Flower-in-the-Night observed. "I once screamed night and day, for a whole week, until my voice was gone, because I had grown out of my favorite shoes."

Abdullah could see Flower-in-the-Night was telling the exact truth. He tried to believe it, but try as he might, he just could not imagine his lovely Flower-in-the-Night lying on the floor, kicking and screaming.

Dalzel again had no difficulty at all. He shuddered and turned angrily to Hasruel. "Think, can't you? You brought her in. You must have noticed what set her off."

Hasruel's great brown visage crumpled helplessly. "Brother mine, I brought her in through the kitchen, for she was silent and white with fear, and I thought maybe a sweetmeat would make her happy. But she threw the sweetmeats at the cook's dog and remained silent. Her cries only began, as you know, after I placed her among the other princesses, and her screams only when you had her brought—"

Flower-in-the-Night raised a finger. "Ah!" she said.

Both djinns turned to her.

"I have it," she said. "It must be the cook's dog. It is often an animal with children. She is used to being given all she wants, and she wants the dog. Instruct your cook, king of kidnappers, to bring his animal to our quarters, and the noise will cease, this I promise you."

"Very well," said Dalzel. "*Do* it!" he trumpeted at Hasruel.

Flower-in-the-Night bowed. "I thank you," she said, and turned and walked gracefully away.

Sophie shook Abdullah's arm. "Let's follow her."

Abdullah did not move or reply. He stared after Flower-in-the-Night, hardly able to believe he was really seeing her and equally unable to believe that Dalzel did not fall at her feet and adore her. He had to admit that this was a relief, but all the same—

"She's yours, is she?" Sophie said after one look at his face. Abdullah nodded raptly. "Then you've got good taste," said Sophie. "Now come *on* before they notice us!"

They edged behind the pillars in the direction

Flower-in-the-Night had gone, keeping a wary eye on the huge hall as they went. In the far distance Dalzel was moodily settling into an enormous throne at the top of a flight of steps. When Hasruel returned from wherever the kitchens were, Dalzel motioned him to kneel by the throne. Neither looked their way. Sophie and Abdullah tiptoed to an archway where a curtain was still swaying after Flower-in-the-Night had lifted it to go through. They pushed the curtain aside and followed.

There was a large, well-lit room beyond, confusingly full of princesses. From somewhere in the midst of them Princess Valeria sobbed, "I want to go home now!"

"Hush, dear. You shall soon," someone answered.

Princess Beatrice's voice said, "You cried beautifully, Valeria. We're all proud of you. But do stop crying now, there's a good girl."

"Can't!" sobbed Valeria. "I'm in the *habit!*"

Sophie was staring around the room in growing outrage. "This is our *broom* cupboard!" she said. "Really!"

Abdullah could not attend to her because Flower-in-the-Night was quite near, softly calling, "Beatrice!"

Princess Beatrice heard and plunged out of the crowd. "Don't tell me," she said. "You did it. Good. Those djinns don't know what hits them when you get after them, Flower. Then things are coming along beautifully if that man agrees——" At this point she noticed Sophie and Abdullah. "Where did you two spring from?" she said.

Flower-in-the-Night whirled around. For a moment, when she saw Abdullah, there was everything in her face he could have wished for: recognition, delight, love, and pride. "I knew you'd come to rescue me!" said her big dark eyes. Then, to his hurt and perplexity, it all went. Her face became smooth and polite. She bowed courteously. "This is Prince Abdullah from Zanzib," she said, "but I am not acquainted with the lady."

Flower-in-the-Night's behavior shook Abdullah from his daze. It must be jealousy of Sophie, he thought. He, too, bowed and made haste to explain. "This lady, O pearls in many a king's diadems, is wife to the Royal Wizard Howl and comes here in search of her child."

Princess Beatrice turned her keen, weathered face to Sophie. "Oh, it's *your* baby!" she said. "Howl with you, by any chance?"

"No," Sophie said miserably. "I hoped he'd be here."

"Not a trace of him, I'm afraid," said Princess Beatrice. "Pity. He'd be useful even if he did help conquer my country. But we've got your baby. Come this way."

Princess Beatrice led the way to the back of the

room, past the group of princesses trying to comfort Valeria. Since Flower-in-the-Night went with her, Abdullah followed. To his increasing distress, Flower-in-the-Night was now barely looking at him, only inclining her head politely at each princess they passed. "The Princess of Alberia," she said formally. "The Princess of Farqtan. The Lady Heiress of Thayack. This is the Princess of Peichstan, and beside her the Paragon of Inhico. Beyond her, you see the Damoiselle of Dorimynde."

So if it was not jealousy, what *was* it? Abdullah wondered unhappily.

There was a wide bench at the back of the room with cushions on it. "My oddments shelf!" Sophie growled. There were three princesses sitting on the bench: the elderly princess Abdullah had noticed before, a lumpish princess swaddled in a coat, and the tiny yellow princess perched in the middle between them. The tiny princess's twiglike arms were wrapped around the chubby pink body of Morgan.

"She is, as far as we can pronounce it, High Princess of Tsapfan," Flower-in-the-Night said formally. "On her right is the Princess of High Norland. On her left the Jharine of Jham."

The tiny High Princess of Tsapfan looked like a child with a doll too big for her, but in the most expert and experienced way, she was giving Morgan a feed from a large baby bottle.

"He's fine with her," said Princess Beatrice. "Good thing for her. Stopped her moping. She says she's had fourteen babies of her own."

The tiny princess glanced up with a shy smile. "Boyth, all," she said, in a small, lisping voice.

Morgan's toes and hands were curling and uncurling. He looked the picture of a satisfied baby. Sophie gazed for a moment. "Where did she get that bottle?" she asked, as if she were afraid it might be poisoned.

The tiny princess looked up again. She smiled and spared a minute finger to point.

"Doesn't speak our language very well," Princess Beatrice explained. "But that genie seemed to understand her."

The princess's twiglike finger was pointing to the floor by the bench, where, below her small, dangling feet, stood a familiar blue-mauve bottle. Abdullah dived for it. The lumpish Jharine of Jham dived for it at the same moment, with an unexpectedly big, strong hand.

"Stop it!" the genie howled from inside as they tussled for it. "I'm *not* coming out! Those djinns will kill me this time for sure!"

Abdullah took hold of the bottle in both hands and jerked. The jerk caused the swaddling coat to fall away from the Jharine. Abdullah found himself looking into wide blue eyes in a lined face inside a bush of grizzled hair. The face wrinkled innocently as the old soldier gave him a sheepish smile and let go of the genie bottle.

"You!" Abdullah said disgustedly.

"Loyal subject of mine," Princess Beatrice explained. "Turned up to rescue me. Rather awkward, actually. We had to disguise him."

Sophie swept Abdullah and Princess Beatrice aside. "Let me get at him!" she said.

Chapter 19

In which a soldier, a cook, and a carpet seller all state their price

There was a brief time of noise so loud that it drowned Princess Valeria completely. Most of it came from Sophie, who started with mild words like *thief* and *liar* and worked up to screaming accusations at the soldier of crimes Abdullah had never heard of and perhaps even the soldier had never thought to commit. Listening, Abdullah thought the metal pulley noise Sophie used to make as Midnight was actually nicer than the noise she was making now. But some of the noise came from the soldier, who had one knee up and both hands in front of his face and was bellowing, louder and louder, "Midnight—I mean, madam! Let me *explain*, Midnight—er—madam!"

To this Princess Beatrice kept adding raspingly, "No, let *me* explain!"

And various princesses added to the clamor by crying out, "Oh, *please* be quiet or the djinns will hear!"

Abdullah tried to stop Sophie by shaking imploringly at her arm. But probably nothing would have stopped her had not Morgan taken his mouth from the bottle, gazed around in distress, and started to cry, too. Sophie shut her mouth with a snap then and then opened it to say, "All right, then. Explain."

In the comparative quiet the tiny princess hushed Morgan, and he went back to feeding again.

"I didn't mean to bring the baby," said the soldier.

"*What?*" said Sophie. "You were going to desert my—"

"No, no," said the soldier. "I told the genie to put him where someone would look after him and take me after the Princess of Ingary. I won't deny I was after a reward." He appealed to Abdullah. "But you know what that genie's like, don't you? Next thing I knew, we were both here."

Abdullah held the genie bottle up and looked at it. "He got his wish," the genie said sulkily from inside.

"And the infant was yelling blue murder," said Princess Beatrice. "Dalzel sent Hasruel to find out what the noise was, and all I could think of to say was that Princess Valeria was having a tantrum. Then, of course, we had to get Valeria to scream. That was when Flower here started to make plans."

She turned to Flower-in-the-Night, who was obviously thinking of something else—and that something else had nothing to do with Abdullah, Abdullah noted dismally. She was staring across the room. "Beatrice, I think the cook is here with the dog," she said.

"Oh, good!" said Beatrice. "Come along, all of you." She strode toward the middle of the room.

A man in a tall chef's hat was standing there. He was a seamed and hoary fellow with only one eye. His dog was pressed close to his legs, growling at any princess who came near. This probably expressed the way the cook was feeling, too. He looked thoroughly suspicious of everything.

"Jamal!" shouted Abdullah. Then he held the genie bottle up and looked at it again.

"Well, it *was* the nearest palace that wasn't Zanzib," the genie protested.

Abdullah was so delighted to see his old friend safe that he did not argue with the genie. He barged past ten princesses, entirely forgetting his manners, and seized Jamal by the hand. "My friend!"

Jamal's one eye stared. A tear came out of it as he wrung Abdullah's hand hard in return. "You are safe!" he said. Jamal's dog bounced to its hind legs and planted its front paws on Abdullah's stomach, panting lovingly. A familiar squiddy breath filled the air.

And Valeria promptly began screaming again. "I don't want that doggy! He SMELLS!"

"Oh, hush!" said at least six princesses. "Pretend, dear. We need the man's help."

"I . . . DON'T . . . WANT . . ." yelled Princess Valeria.

Sophie tore herself away from where she was leaning critically over the tiny princess and marched down upon Valeria. "Stop it, Valeria," she said. "You remember me, don't you?"

It was clear Valeria did. She rushed at Sophie and wrapped her arms around her legs, where she burst into much more genuine tears. "Sophie, Sophie, Sophie! Take me *home!*"

Sophie sat down on the floor and hugged her. "There, there. Of course, we'll take you home. We've just got to arrange it first. It's very odd," she remarked to the surrounding princesses. "I feel quite expert with Valeria, but I'm scared stiff of dropping Morgan."

"You'll learn," said the elderly Princess of High Norland, sitting stiffly down beside her. "I'm told they all do."

Flower-in-the-Night stepped to the center of the room. "My friends," she said, "and all three kind gentlemen, we must now put our heads together to discuss the plight in which we find ourselves and make plans for our early release. First, however, it would be prudent to put a spell of silence upon the doorway. It would not do for our kidnappers to overhear." Her eyes, in the most thoughtful and neutral way, went to the genie bottle in Abdullah's hand.

"No!" said the genie. "Try to make me do anything and you're all toads!"

"I'll do it," said Sophie. She scrambled up with Valeria still clinging to her skirts and went over to the doorway, where she took hold of a handful of the curtain there. "Now, you're not the kind of cloth to let any sound through, are you?" she remarked to the curtain. "I suggest you have a word with the walls and make that quite clear. Tell them no one's going to be able to hear a word we say inside this room."

A murmur of relief and approval came from most of the princesses at this. But Flower-in-the-Night said, "My pardon for being critical, skillful sorceress, but I think the djinns should be able to hear *something* or else they will become suspicious."

The tiny princess from Tsapfan wandered up with Morgan looking huge in her arms. Carefully she passed the baby to Sophie. Sophie looked terrified and held Morgan as if he were a bomb about to blow up. This seemed to displease Morgan. He waved his arms. While the tiny princess was laying both small hands on the curtain, several looks of utter distaste chased themselves across his face. *"Burp!"* he remarked.

Sophie jumped and all but dropped Morgan. "Heavens!" she said. "I'd no idea they did that!"

Valeria laughed heartily. "My brother does—all the time."

The tiny princess made gestures to show that she

had now dealt with Flower-in-the-Night's objection. Everyone listened closely. In the distance somewhere they could now hear the pleasant ringing hum of princesses chatting together. There was even an occasional yell that sounded like Valeria.

"Most perfect," said Flower-in-the-Night. She smiled warmly at the tiny princess, and Abdullah wished she would only smile like that at him. "Now if every person could sit down, we can lay some plans to escape."

Everyone obeyed in his or her own way. Jamal squatted with his dog in his arms, looking suspicious. Sophie sat on the floor with Morgan clumsily in her arms and Valeria leaning against her. Valeria was quite happy now. Abdullah sat cross-legged beside Jamal. The soldier came and sat about two places away, whereupon Abdullah took tight hold of the genie bottle and gripped the carpet over his shoulder with the other hand.

"That girl Flower-in-the-Night is a real marvel," Princess Beatrice remarked as she sat herself between Abdullah and the soldier. "She came here knowing nothing unless she'd read it out of a book. And she learns all the time. Took her two days to get the measure of Dalzel; wretched djinn's scared stiff of her now. Before she arrived, all I'd managed was to make it clear to the creature that we weren't going to be his wives. But she thinks big. Had her mind on escaping right from the start. She's been plotting all along to get that cook in to help. Now she's done it. Look at her! Looks fit to rule an empire, doesn't she?"

Abdullah nodded sadly and watched Flower-in-the-Night as she stood waiting for everyone to get settled. She was still wearing the gauzy clothes she had been wearing when Hasruel snatched her from the night garden. She was still as slim, as graceful, and as beautiful. Her clothes were now crushed and a little tattered. Abdullah had no doubt that every crease, every three-cornered tear, and every hanging thread meant some new thing that Flower-in-the-Night had learned. Fit to rule an empire indeed! he thought. If he compared Flower-in-the-Night with Sophie, who had displeased him for being so strong-minded, he knew Flower-in-the-Night had twice Sophie's strength of mind. And as far as Abdullah was concerned, this only made Flower-in-the-Night more excellent. What made him wretched was the way she carefully and politely avoided singling him out in any way. And he wished he knew *why*.

"The problem we face," Flower-in-the-Night was saying when Abdullah started to attend, "is that we are in a place where it does no good simply to get *out*. If we could sneak out of the castle without the djinns' becoming aware of it or the angels of Hasruel's preventing us, we should only sink through the clouds and fall heavily to earth, which is a very

248

long way below. Even if we can overcome those difficulties in some way"——here her eyes turned to the
bottle in Abdullah's hand and, thoughtfully, to the
carpet over his shoulder, but not, alas, to Abdullah
himself——"there seems nothing to stop Dalzel from
sending his brother to bring us all back. Therefore,
the essence of any plan we make has to be the defeat
of Dalzel. We know that his chief power derives from
the fact that he has stolen the life of his brother
Hasruel, so that Hasruel must obey him or die. So it
follows that in order to escape, we must find
Hasruel's life and restore it to him. Noble ladies,
excellent gentlemen, and esteemed dog, I invite your
ideas on this matter."

Excellently put, O flower of my desire! Abdullah
thought sadly as Flower-in-the-Night gracefully sat
down.

"But we still don't know where Hasruel's life can
be!" bleated the fat Princess of Farqtan.

"Exactly," said Princess Beatrice. "Only Dalzel
knows that."

"But the beastly creature's always dropping hints,"
complained the blond princess from Thayack.

"To let us know how clever he is!" the dark-
skinned Princess of Alberia said bitterly.

Sophie looked up. "What hints?" she said.

There was a confused clamor as at least twenty
princesses all tried to tell Sophie at once. Abdullah

was straining his ears to catch at least one of the hints and Flower-in-the-Night was getting up to restore order when the soldier said loudly, "Oh, shut up, the lot of you!"

This caused complete silence. The eyes of every single princess turned to him in freezing royal outrage.

The soldier found this very amusing. "Hoity-toity!" he said. "Look at me how you please, ladies. But while you do, think whether I ever agreed to help you escape. I did not. Why should I? Dalzel never did me any harm."

"That," said the elderly Princess of High Norland, "is because he's not found you yet, my good man. Do you wish to wait and see what happens when he does?"

"I'll risk it," said the soldier. "On the other hand, I *might* help—and I reckon you won't get too far if I don't—provided one of you can make it worth my while."

Flower-in-the-Night, poised on her knees ready to stand, said with beautiful haughtiness, "Worth your while in what way, menial mercenary? All of us have fathers who are very rich. Rewards will shower on you once they have us back. Do you wish to be assured of a certain sum from each? That can be arranged."

"And I wouldn't say no," said the soldier. "But that's not what I meant, my pretty. When I started on this caper, I was promised I'd get a princess of my own out of it. That's what I want—a princess to marry. One of you ought to be able to accommodate me. And if you can't or won't, then you can count me out and I'll be off to make my peace with Dalzel. He can hire me to guard you."

This caused a silence, if possible more frozen, outraged, and royal than before, until Flower-in-the-Night pulled herself together and rose to her feet again. "My friends," she said, "we all need the help of this man—if only for his ruthless, low cunning. What we do not want is to have a beast like him set over us to guard us. Therefore, I vote that he be allowed to choose a wife from among us. Who disagrees?"

It was clear that every other princess disagreed mightily. Further freezing looks were turned on the soldier, who grinned and said, "If I go to Dalzel and offer myself to guard you, rest assured you'll *never* get away. I'm up to every trick. Isn't that true?" he asked Abdullah.

"It is true, most cunning corporal," Abdullah said.

There was a small murmuring from the tiny princess. "She says she's married already—those four-teen children, you know," said the elderly princess, who seemed to understand the murmur.

"Then let all who are as yet unmarried please raise their hands," said Flower-in-the-Night, and most determinedly, raised her own.

Waveringly, reluctantly, two-thirds of the other princesses put their hands up, also. The soldier's head turned slowly as he looked around them, and the look on his face reminded Abdullah of Sophie when, as Midnight, she was about to feast on salmon and cream. Abdullah's heart stood still as the man's blue eyes traveled from princess to princess. It was obvious he would choose Flower-in-the-Night. Her beauty stood out like a lily in the moonlight.

"You," said the soldier at last, and pointed. To Abdullah's astonished relief, he was pointing at Princess Beatrice.

Princess Beatrice was equally astonished. "*Me?*" she said.

"Yes, you," said the soldier. "I've always fancied a nice bossy, downright princess like you. Fact that you're a Strangian, too, makes it ideal."

Princess Beatrice's face had become a bright beety red. It did not improve her looks. "But—but—" she said, and then pulled herself together. "My good soldier, I'll have you know I'm supposed to be marrying Prince Justin of Ingary."

"Then you'll just have to tell him you're spoken for," said the soldier. "Politics, wasn't it? It seems to me you'll be glad to get out of it."

"Well, I—" began Princess Beatrice. To Abdullah's surprise, there were tears in her eyes, and she had to start again. "You don't *mean* it!" she said. "I'm not good-looking or any of those things."

"That suits me," said the soldier, "down to the ground. What would I do with a flimsy, pretty little princess? I can see you'd back me up whatever scam I got up to—and I bet you can darn socks, too."

"Believe it or not, I can darn," said Princess Beatrice. "*And* mend boots. You *really* mean it?"

"Yes," said the soldier.

The two of them had swung around to face each other, and it was clear that both were entirely in earnest. And the rest of the princesses had somehow forgotten to be frozen and royal. Every one of them was leaning forward to watch with a tender, approving smile. There was the same smile on Flower-in-the-Night's face as she said, "Now may we continue our discussion, if no one else objects?"

"Me. I do," said Jamal. "I object."

All the princesses groaned. Jamal's face was almost as red as Princess Beatrice's, and his one eye was screwed up; but the soldier's example had made him bold.

"Lovely ladies," he said, "we are frightened, me and my dog. Until we got snatched away up here to do your cooking for you, we were on the run in the desert with the Sultan's camels at our heels. We don't want to be sent back to that. But if all you perfect princesses get away from here, what *do* we do? Djinns don't eat the kind of food I can cook. Meaning no disrespect to anyone, if I help you to get away, my dog and I are out of a job. It's as simple as that."

"Oh, dear," said Flower-in-the-Night, and seemed not to know what else to say.

"Such a shame. He's a very good cook," remarked a plump princess in a loose red gown, who was probably the Paragon of Inhico.

"He certainly is!" said the elderly Princess of High Norland. "I shudder to remember the food those djinns kept stealing for us until he came." She turned to Jamal. "My grandfather once had a cook from Rashpuht," she said, "and until you got here, I'd never tasted anything like that man's fried squid! And yours is even better. You help us to escape, my man, and I'll employ you like a shot, dog and all. But," she added as a grin brightened on Jamal's leathery face, "please remember that my old father only rules a very small principality. You'll get board and lodging, but I can't afford a big wage."

The grin remained broadly fixed on Jamal's features. "My great, great lady," he said, "it is not wages I want, only safety. For this I will cook you food fit for angels."

"Hmm," said the elderly princess. "I'm not at all sure what those angels eat, but that's settled then. Does either of you other two want anything before you'll help?"

Everyone looked at Sophie.

"Not really," Sophie said rather sadly. "I've got Morgan, and since Howl doesn't seem to be here, there's nothing else I need. I'll help you, anyway."

Everyone looked at Abdullah then.

He rose to his feet and bowed. "O moons of many monarchs' eyes," he said, "far be it from one as unworthy as me to impose any kind of condition for my help on such as you. Help freely given is best, as the books tell us." He had got this far in his magnificent and generous speech when he realized it was all nonsense. There *was* something he did want—very much indeed. He hastily changed his tack. "And freely given my help will be," he said, "as free as air blows or rain bedews the flowers. I will work myself to extinction for your noble sakes and crave only in return one small boon, most simply granted——"

"Get *on* with it, young man!" said the Princess of High Norland. "What *do* you want?"

"Five minutes' talk in private with Flower-in-the-Night," Abdullah admitted.

Everyone looked at Flower-in-the-Night. Her head went up, rather dangerously.

"Come off it, Flower!" said Princess Beatrice. "Five minutes won't kill you!"

Flower-in-the-Night seemed fairly clear that it *might* kill her. She said, like a princess going to her execution, "Very well," and, with a more than usually freezing look in the direction of Abdullah, she asked, "Now?"

"Or sooner, dove of my desire," he said, bowing firmly.

Flower-in-the-Night nodded frigidly and stalked away to the side of the room, looking positively martyred. "Here," she said as Abdullah followed her.

He bowed again, even more firmly. "I said, in private, O starry subject of my sighs," he pointed out.

Flower-in-the-Night irritably twitched aside one of the curtains hanging beside her. "They can probably still hear," she said coldly, beckoning him after her.

"But not see, princess of my passion," Abdullah said, edging behind the curtain.

He found himself in a tiny alcove. Sophie's voice came to him clearly. "That's the loose brick where I used to hide money. I hope they have *room*." Whatever the place once had been, it now seemed to be the princesses' wardrobe. There was a riding jacket hanging behind Flower-in-the-Night as she folded her arms and faced Abdullah. Cloaks, coats, and a hooped petticoat that evidently went under the loose red garment worn by the Paragon of Inhico dangled around Abdullah as he faced Flower-in-the-Night. Still, Abdullah reflected, it was not much smaller or more crowded than his own booth in Zanzib, and that was usually private enough.

"What did you want to say?" Flower-in-the-Night asked freezingly.

"To ask the reason for this very coldness!" Abdullah answered heatedly. "What have I done that you will barely look at me and barely speak? Have I not come here, expressly to rescue you? Have I not, alone of all the disappointed lovers, braved every peril in order to reach this castle? Have I not gone through the most strenuous adventures, allowing your father to threaten me, the soldier to cheat me, and the genie to mock me, solely in order to bring you my aid? What more do I have to do? Or should I conclude that you have fallen in love with Dalzel?"

"*Dalzel!*" exclaimed Flower-in-the-Night. "Now you insult me! Now you add insult to injury! Now I see Beatrice was right and you do indeed not love me!"

"*Beatrice!*" thundered Abdullah. "What has *she* to say how I feel?"

Flower-in-the-Night hung her head a little, although she looked more sulky than ashamed. There was a dead silence. In fact, the silence was so *very* dead that Abdullah realized that the sixty ears of all the other thirty princesses—no, sixty-*eight* ears, if you counted Sophie, the soldier, Jamal, and his dog and assumed Morgan was asleep—anyway, that all these ears were at that moment focused entirely upon what he and Flower-in-the-Night were saying.

"Talk among yourselves!" he shouted.

The silence became uneasy. It was broken by the elderly princess saying, "The most distressing thing about being up here above the clouds is that there is no *weather* to make conversation out of."

Abdullah waited until this statement was followed by a reluctant hum of other voices and then turned back to Flower-in-the-Night. "Well? What *did* Princess Beatrice say?"

Flower-in-the-Night raised her head haughtily. "She said that portraits of other men and pretty speeches were all very well, but she couldn't help noticing you'd never made the slightest attempt to kiss me."

"Impertinent woman!" said Abdullah. "When I first saw you, I assumed you were a dream. I assumed you would only melt."

"But," said Flower-in-the-Night, "the second time you saw me, you seemed quite sure I was real."

"Certainly," said Abdullah, "but then it would have been unfair because, if you recall, you had then seen no other living men but your father and myself."

"Beatrice," said Flower-in-the-Night, "says that men who do nothing but make fine speeches make very poor husbands."

"*Bother* Princess Beatrice!" said Abdullah. "What do *you* think?"

"I think," said Flower-in-the-Night, "I think I

want to know why you found me too unattractive to be worth kissing."

"*I DIDN'T find you unattractive!*" bawled Abdullah. Then he remembered the sixty-eight ears beyond the curtain and added in a fierce whisper, "If you must know, I——I had never in my life kissed a young lady, and you are far too beautiful for me to want to get it wrong!"

A small smile, heralded by a deep dimple, stole across Flower-in-the-Night's mouth. "And how many young ladies have you kissed by now?"

"None!" groaned Abdullah. "I am still a total amateur!"

"So am I," admitted Flower-in-the-Night. "Though at least I know enough not to mistake you for a woman now. That was very stupid!"

She gave a gurgle of laughter. Abdullah gave another gurgle. In no time at all, both of them were laughing heartily, until Abdullah gasped, "I think we should practice!"

After that there was silence from behind the curtain. This silence went on so long that all the princesses ran out of small talk, except Princess Beatrice, who seemed to have a lot to say to the soldier. At length Sophie called out, "Are you two finished?"

"Certainly," Flower-in-the-Night and Abdullah called out. "Absolutely!"

"Then let's make some plans," said Sophie.

Plans were no problem at all to Abdullah in the state of mind he was in just then. He came out from behind the curtain holding Flower-in-the-Night's hand, and if the castle had chanced to vanish at that moment, he knew he could have walked on the clouds beneath or, failing that, on air. As it was, he walked across what seemed a very unworthy marble floor and simply took charge.

Chapter 20

——※※——

In which a djinn's life is found and then hidden

Ten minutes later Abdullah said, "There, most eminent and intelligent persons, are our plans laid. It only remains for the genie—"

Purple smoke poured from the bottle and trailed in agitated waves along the marble floor. "You do *not* use me!" cried the genie. "I said toads, and I *mean* toads! Hasruel put me in this bottle, don't you understand? If I do anything against him, he'll put me somewhere even worse!"

Sophie looked up and frowned at the smoke. "There really is a genie!"

"But I merely require your powers of divination to tell me where Hasruel's life is hidden," Abdullah explained. "I am not asking for a wish."

"*No!*" howled the mauve smoke.

Flower-in-the-Night picked the bottle up and balanced it on her knee. Smoke flowed downward in puffs and seemed to try to seep into the cracks in the marble floor. "It stands to reason," Flower-in-the-Night said, "that since every man we asked to help has had his price, then the genie has his price, also. It must be a male characteristic. Genie, if you agree to help Abdullah in this, I will promise you what logic assures me is the correct reward."

Grudgingly the mauve smoke began to seep backward toward the bottle again. "Oh, very well," said the genie.

Two minutes after this the charmed curtain in the doorway to the princesses' room was swept aside, and everyone streamed out into the great hall, clamoring for Dalzel's attention and dragging Abdullah in their midst, a helpless prisoner.

"Dalzel! Dalzel!" clamored the thirty princesses. "Is *this* the way you guard us? You ought to be ashamed of yourself!"

Dalzel looked up. He was leaning over the side of his great throne to play chess with Hasruel. He blanched a bit at what he saw and signed to his brother to remove the chess set. Fortunately the crowd of princesses was too thick for him to notice Sophie and the Jharine of Jham huddled in the midst of it, though his lovely eyes did fall on Jamal and narrow with astonishment. "What is it *now?*" he said.

"A *man* in our room!" screamed the princesses. "A terrible, awful *man!*"

"What man?" trumpeted Dalzel. "What man would dare?"

"This one!" shrieked the princesses. Abdullah was dragged forward between Princess Beatrice and the Princess of Alberia, most shamefully clothed in almost nothing but the hooped petticoat that had hung behind the curtain. This petticoat was an essential part of the plan. Two of the things underneath it were the genie's bottle and the magic carpet. Abdullah was glad he had taken these precautions when Dalzel glared at him. He had not known before that a djinn's eyes could actually flame. Dalzel's eyes were like two bluish furnaces.

Hasruel's behavior made Abdullah even more uncomfortable. A mean grin spread over Hasruel's huge features, and he said, "Ah! You again!" Then he folded his great arms and looked very sarcastic indeed.

"How did this fellow get in here?" Dalzel demanded in his trumpet voice.

Before anyone could answer, Flower-in-the-Night performed her part in the plan by bursting out from among the other princesses and throwing herself gracefully down on the steps of the throne. "Have mercy, great djinn!" she cried out. "He only came to rescue me!"

Dalzel laughed contemptuously. "Then the fellow's a fool. I shall throw him straight back to earth."

"Do that, great djinn, and I shall never leave you in peace!" Flower-in-the-Night declared.

She was not acting. She really meant it. Dalzel knew she did. A shiver ran through his narrow, pale body, and his gold-taloned fingers gripped the arms of the throne. But his eyes still flamed with rage. "I shall do what I want!" he trumpeted.

"Then desire to be merciful!" cried Flower-in-the-Night. "Give him at least a chance!"

"Be quiet, woman!" trumpeted Dalzel. "I haven't decided yet. I want to know how he managed to get in here first."

"Disguised as the cook's dog, of course," said Princess Beatrice.

"And quite naked when he turned into a man!" said the Princess of Alberia.

"Shocking business," said Princess Beatrice. "We had to put him in the Paragon's petticoat."

"Bring him closer," commanded Dalzel.

Princess Beatrice and her assistant lugged Abdullah toward the steps of the throne, Abdullah walking with little mincing steps that he hoped the djinns would put down to the petticoat. The reason, in fact, was that the third thing under the petticoat was Jamal's dog. It was gripped rather firmly between Abdullah's knees in case it escaped. This part of the plan made it necessary to be minus one dog, and none of the princesses had trusted Dalzel not to send Hasruel looking for it and prove that everyone was lying.

Dalzel glared down at Abdullah, and Abdullah hoped very much that Dalzel truly had almost no powers of his own. Hasruel had called his brother weak. But it occurred to Abdullah that even a weak djinn was several times stronger than a man. "You came here as a dog?" Dalzel trumpeted. "How?"

"By magic, great djinn," Abdullah said. He had intended to make a detailed explanation at this point, but under the Paragon's petticoat, a hidden struggle was developing. Jamal's dog turned out to hate djinns even more than it hated most of the human race. It wanted to go for Dalzel. "I disguised myself as the dog of your cook," Abdullah began to explain. At this point Jamal's dog became so eager to go for Dalzel that Abdullah was afraid it would get loose. He was forced to grip his knees together tighter yet. The dog's response was a huge, snarling growl. "Your pardon!" panted Abdullah. Sweat was standing on his brow. "I am still so much of a dog that I cannot refrain from growling from time to time."

Flower-in-the-Night recognized that Abdullah was having problems and burst into lamentations. "O most noble prince! To suffer the shape of a dog for my sake! Spare him, noble djinn! Spare him!"

"Be quiet, woman," said Dalzel. "Where is that cook? Bring him forward."

Jamal was dragged forward by the Princess of Farqtan and the Heiress of Thayack, wringing his hands and cringing. "Honored djinn, it was nothing to do with me, I swear!" Jamal wailed. "Do not hurt me! I never knew he was not a real dog!" Abdullah could have sworn that Jamal was in a state of true terror. Maybe he was, but he had the presence of mind, all the same, to pat Abdullah on the head. "Nice dog," he said. "Good fellow." After that he fell down and groveled on the steps of the throne in the manner of Zanzib. "I am innocent, great one!" he blubbered. "Innocent! Harm me not!"

The dog was soothed by its master's voice. Its growls stopped. Abdullah was able to relax his knees a little. "I am innocent, too, O collector of royal maidens," he said. "I came only to rescue the one I love. You must surely feel kindly toward my devotion, since you love so many princesses yourself!"

Dalzel rubbed his chin in a perplexed way. "Love?" he said. "No, I can't say I understand love. I can't understand how *anything* could make someone put himself in your position, mortal."

Hasruel, squatting vast and dark beside the throne, grinned more meanly than ever. "What do you want me to do with the creature, brother?" he rumbled. "Roast him? Extract his soul and make it part of the floor? Take him apart?"

"No, no! Be merciful, great Dalzel!" Flower-in-the-Night promptly cried out. "Give him at least a chance! If you do, I will never ask you questions, or complain, or lecture you again. I will be meek and polite!"

Dalzel grasped his chin again and looked uncertain. Abdullah felt much relieved. Dalzel was indeed a weak djinn—weak in character, anyway. "If I were to give him a chance——" he began.

"If you'll take my advice, brother," Hasruel cut in, "you won't. He's tricky, this one."

At this Flower-in-the-Night raised another great wail and beat her breast. Abdullah cried out through the noise, "Let me try to guess where you hid your brother's life, great Dalzel. If I fail to guess, kill me. If I guess right, let me depart in peace."

This amused Dalzel highly. His mouth opened, showing pointed silvery teeth, and his laughter rang around the cloudy hall like a fanfare of trumpets. "But you'll never guess, little mortal!" he said as he laughed. Then, as the princesses had repeatedly assured Abdullah, Dalzel was unable to resist giving hints. "I've hidden that life so cleverly," he said gleefully, "that you can look at it and not see it. Hasruel can't see it, and he is a djinn. So what hope have you? But I think for the fun of it I will give you three guesses before I kill you. Guess away. Where *have* I hidden my brother's life?"

Abdullah shot a swift look at Hasruel in case Hasruel decided to interfere. But Hasruel was simply squatting there, looking inscrutable. So far the plan was succeeding. It was in Hasruel's interest not to interfere. Abdullah had been counting on that. He took a firmer grip on the dog with his knees and hitched at the Paragon's petticoat, while he pretended to think. What he was really doing was jogging the genie bottle. "For my first guess, great djinn . . ." he said, and stared at the floor as if the green porphyry might inspire him. Would the genie go back on his word? For one scared and miserable moment Abdullah thought that the genie had let him down as usual and that he was going to have to risk guessing on his own. Then, to his great relief, he saw a tiny tendril of purple smoke creep out from under the Paragon's petticoat, where it lay, still and watchful, beside Abdullah's bare foot. "My first guess is that you hid Hasruel's life on the moon," Abdullah said.

Dalzel laughed delightedly. "Wrong! He would have found it there! No, it's much more obvious than that, and much *less* obvious. Consider the game of hunt the slipper, mortal!"

This told Abdullah that Hasruel's life was here in the castle, as most of the princesses had thought it was. He made a great show of thinking hard. "My second guess is that you gave it to one of the guardian angels to keep," he said.

"Wrong again!" said Dalzel, more delighted than ever. "The angels would have given it back straightaway. It's *much* cleverer than that, little mortal. You'll never guess. It's amazing how no one can see what's under his own nose!"

At this, in a burst of inspiration, Abdullah was sure he knew where Hasruel's life really was. Flower-in-the-Night loved him. He was still walking on air. His mind was inspired, and he *knew*. But he was mortally afraid of making a mistake. When the time shortly came when he had to take hold of Hasruel's life himself, he knew he would have to go straight to it because Dalzel would give him no second chance. That was why he needed the genie to confirm his guess. The tendril of smoke was still lying there, near invisible, and if Abdullah had guessed, surely the genie knew, too?

"Er . . ." Abdullah said. "Um . . ."

The tendril of smoke crept noiselessly back inside the Paragon's petticoat and bellied up inside, where it must have tickled the nose of Jamal's dog. The dog sneezed.

"Atishoo!" cried Abdullah, and almost drowned the thread of the genie's voice whispering, *"It's the ring in Hasruel's nose!"*

"Atishoo!" said Abdullah, and pretended to guess wrong. This was where his plan was distinctly risky. "Your brother's life is one of your teeth, great Dalzel."

"Wrong!" trumpeted Dalzel. "Hasruel, roast him!"

"Spare him!" wailed Flower-in-the-Night as

Hasruel, with disgust and disappointment written all over him, began to get up.

The princesses were ready for this moment. Ten royal hands instantly pushed Princess Valeria out of the crowd to the steps of the throne.

"*I want my doggy!*" Valeria announced. This was her big moment. As Sophie had pointed out to her, she had found thirty new aunties and three new uncles and all of them had begged her to scream as hard as she could. No one had ever *wanted* her to scream before. In addition, all the new aunties had promised her a box of sweets if she made this a really good tantrum. Thirty boxes. It was worth the best she could do. She made her mouth square. She expanded her chest. She gave it everything she had. "I WANT MY DOGGY! I DON'T WANT ABDULLAH! I WANT MY DOGGY BACK!" She hurled herself at the throne steps, fell over Jamal, threw herself to her feet again, and flung herself at the throne. Dalzel hastily jumped onto the throne seat to get out of her way. "GIVE ME MY DOGGY!" Valeria bellowed.

At the same moment the tiny yellow Princess of Tsapfan gave Morgan a shrewd nip, just in the right place. Morgan had been asleep in her tiny arms, dreaming he was a kitten again. He woke with a jump and found he was still a helpless baby. His fury knew no bounds. He opened his mouth, and he roared. His feet pedaled with anger. His hands pumped. And his roars were so lusty that had it been a competition between himself and Valeria, Morgan might have won. As it was, the noise was unspeakable. The echoes in the hall picked it up, doubled the screams, and rolled it all back at the throne.

"Echo at those djinns," Sophie was saying in her conversational magical way. "Don't just double it. *Treble* it."

The hall was a madhouse. Both djinns clapped their hands over their pointed ears. Dalzel hooted, "Stop it! Stop them! Where did that baby come from?"

To which Hasruel howled, "Women have babies, fool of a djinn! What did you expect?"

"I WANT MY DOGGY BACK!" stated Valeria, beating the seat of the throne with her fists.

Dalzel's trumpet voice fought to be heard. "*Give* her a doggy, Hasruel, or I'll kill you!"

At this stage in Abdullah's plans he had confidently expected—if he had not been killed by then—to be turned into a dog. It was what he had been leading up to. This, he had calculated, would also have released Jamal's dog. He had counted on the sight of not one dog but two, dashing from beneath the Paragon's petticoat, to add to the confusion. But Hasruel was as distracted by the screams, and the triple echoes of screams, as his brother was. He turned this way and that, clutching his ears and yelling with pain, the picture of a djinn at his wits' end. Finally he folded his great wings and became a dog himself.

He was a very huge dog, something between a donkey and a bulldog, brown and gray in patches, with a golden ring in his snub nose. This huge dog put its gigantic forepaws on the arm of the throne and stretched an enormous slavering tongue out toward Valeria's face. Hasruel was trying to seem friendly. But at the sight of something so big and so ugly, Valeria, not unnaturally, screamed harder than ever. The noise frightened Morgan. He screamed harder, too.

Abdullah had a moment when he was quite at a loss what to do, and then another moment when he was sure no one would hear him shout. *"Soldier!"* he roared. "Hold Hasruel! Someone hold Dalzel!"

Luckily the soldier was alert. He was good at that. The Jharine of Jham vanished in a flurry of old clothes, and the soldier leaped up the steps of the throne. Sophie rushed after him, beckoning to the princesses. She threw her arms around Dalzel's slender white knees, while the soldier wrapped his brawny arms around the neck of the dog. The princesses stampeded up the steps behind them, and most of them threw themselves on Dalzel, too, with the air of princesses badly in need of revenge—all except Princess Beatrice, who dragged Valeria out of the brawl and began the difficult task of shutting her up.

The tiny Princess of Tsapfan meanwhile sat calmly on the porphyry floor, rocking Morgan back to sleep.

Abdullah tried to run toward Hasruel. But no sooner did he move than Jamal's dog seized its chance and got away. It burst out from under the Paragon's petticoat to see a fight in progress. It loved fights. It also saw another dog. If anything, it hated dogs even more than djinns or the human race. No matter what size the dog was. It sped, snarling, to the attack. While Abdullah was still trying to kick his way out of the Paragon's petticoat, Jamal's dog sprang for Hasruel's throat.

This was too much for Hasruel, already beset by the soldier. He became a djinn again. He made an angry gesture. And the dog went sailing away, end over end, to land with a yelp on the other side of the hall. After that Hasruel tried to stand up, but the soldier was on his back by then, preventing him spreading his leathery wings. Hasruel heaved and surged.

"Hold your head down, Hasruel, I conjure you!" Abdullah shouted, kicking free of the Paragon's petticoat at last. He leaped up the steps, wearing nothing but his loincloth, and seized hold of Hasruel's great left ear. At this Flower-in-the-Night understood where Hasruel's life was, and to Abdullah's great joy, she jumped up and hung on to Hasruel's right ear. And there they hung, raised in the air from time to time when Hasruel got the better of the soldier, and slammed to the floor when the soldier got the better of Hasruel, with the soldier's straining arms wrapped around the djinn's neck just beside them and Hasruel's great snarling face between them. From time to time Abdullah caught glimpses of Dalzel standing on the seat of his throne under a pile of princesses. He had spread his weak golden wings. They did not seem much use for flying with, but he was battering at the princesses with them and shouting to Hasruel for help.

Dalzel's trumpet shouts seemed to inspire Hasruel. He began to get the better of the soldier. Abdullah tried to get a hand loose so that he could reach out to the golden ring, dangling just by his shoulder, under Hasruel's hooked nose. Abdullah freed his left hand. But his right hand was sweating and slipping off Hasruel's ear. He grabbed—desperately—before he slipped off.

He had reckoned without Jamal's dog. After lying dazed for most of a minute, it stood up, angrier than ever and full of hatred for djinns. It saw Hasruel and knew its enemy. Back across the hall it raced, hackles up and snarling, past the tiny princess and Morgan, past Princess Beatrice and Valeria, through the princesses eddying around the throne, past the crouching figure of its master, and sprang at the easiest piece of djinn to reach. Abdullah snatched his hand away just in time.

Snap! went the dog's teeth. *Gulp* went the dog's throat. After that, a puzzled look crossed the dog's face, and it dropped to the floor, hiccuping uneasily. Hasruel howled with pain and sprang upright with both hands clapped to his nose. The soldier was hurled to the floor. Abdullah and Flower-in-the-Night were flung off to either side. Abdullah dived for the hiccuping dog, but Jamal got there first and picked it up tenderly.

"Poor dog, my poor dog! Better soon!" he crooned to it, and carried it carefully away down the steps.

Abdullah dragged the dazed soldier with him and put them both in front of Jamal. "Stop, everyone!" he shouted. "Dalzel, I conjure you to stop! We have your brother's life!"

The struggle on the throne stilled. Dalzel stood with spread wings and his eyes like furnaces again. "I don't believe you," he said. "Where?"

"Inside the dog," said Abdullah.

"But only until tomorrow," Jamal said soothingly, thinking only of his hiccuping dog. "It has an irritable gut from eating too much squid. Be thankful——"

Abdullah kicked him to shut him up. "The dog has eaten the ring in Hasruel's nose," he said.

The dismay on Dalzel's face told him that the genie had been right. He had guessed correctly. "Oh!" said the princesses. All eyes turned to Hasruel, huge and bowed over, with tears in his fiery eyes and both hands clasped to his nose. Djinn blood, which was clear and greenish, dripped between his great horned fingers.

"I should hab dode," Hasruel said dismally. "It wad right udder by dose."

The elderly Princess of High Norland detached herself from the crowd around the throne, felt in her sleeve, and reached up to Hasruel with a small lacy handkerchief. "Here you are," she said. "No hard feelings."

Hasruel took the handkerchief with a grateful "Thang you" and pressed it to the torn end of his nose. The dog had not really eaten much except the ring. Having mopped the place carefully, Hasruel knelt ponderously down and beckoned to Abdullah up the steps of the throne. "What would you have me do now I am good again?" he asked mournfully.

Chapter 21

---❦---

In which the castle comes down to earth

Abdullah did not need to give Hasruel's question much thought. "You must exile your brother, mighty djinn, to a place from which he will not return," he said.

Dalzel at once burst into melting blue tears. "It's not *fair!*" He wept and stamped his foot on the throne. "Everyone's always against me! You don't love me, Hasruel! You cheated me! You didn't even try to get rid of those three people hanging on to you!"

Abdullah was sure Dalzel was right about that. Knowing the power a djinn had, Abdullah was sure Hasruel could have flung the soldier, not to speak of himself and Flower-in-the-Night, to the ends of the earth if he had wanted to.

"It wasn't as if I was doing any harm!" Dalzel shouted. "I have a right to get married, don't I?"

While he shouted and stamped, Hasruel murmured to Abdullah, "There is a wandering island in the ocean to the south, which is only to be found once in a hundred years. It has a palace and many fruit trees. May I send my brother there?"

"And now you're going to send me away!" Dalzel screamed. "None of you care how lonely I shall be!"

"By the way," Hasruel murmured to Abdullah, "your father's first wife's relatives made a pact with the mercenaries, which allowed them to flee from Zanzib to escape the Sultan's wrath, but they left the two nieces behind. The Sultan has locked the unfortunate girls up, they being the nearest of your family he could find."

"Most shocking," Abdullah said. He saw what Hasruel was driving at. "Perhaps, mighty djinn, you might celebrate your return to goodness by fetching the two damsels here?"

Hasruel's hideous face brightened. He raised his great clawed hand. There was a clap of thunder, followed by some girlish squealing, and the two fat nieces stood before the throne. It was as simple as that. Abdullah saw that Hasruel had indeed been holding back his strength before. Looking into the djinn's great slanting eyes—which still had tears in the corners from the dog's attack—he saw that Hasruel knew he knew.

"Not *more* princesses!" Princess Beatrice said. She was kneeling by Valeria, looking rather harassed.

"Nothing of the sort, I assure you," said Abdullah.

The two nieces could hardly have looked less like

princesses. They were in their oldest clothes, practical pink and workaday yellow, torn and stained from their experiences, and the hair of both had come unfrizzed. They took one look at Dalzel stamping and weeping above them on the throne, another look at the huge shape of Hasruel, and then a third look at Abdullah wearing nothing but a loincloth, and they screamed. Then each tried to hide her face in the other's plump shoulder.

"Poor girls," stated the Princess of High Norland. "Hardly royal behavior."

"Dalzel!" Abdullah shouted up at the sobbing djinn. "Beauteous Dalzel, poacher of princesses, be peaceful a moment and look upon the gift I have given you to take with you into exile."

Dalzel stopped in mid-sob. "Gift?"

Abdullah pointed. "Behold two brides, young and succulent and sorely in need of a bridegroom."

Dalzel wiped luminous tears from his cheeks and surveyed the nieces in much the same way that Abdullah's cannier customers used to inspect his carpets. "A matching pair!" he said. "And wonderfully fat! Where's the catch? Are they perhaps not yours to give away?"

"No catch, shining djinn," said Abdullah. It seemed to him that, now the girls' other relatives had deserted them, they were surely his to dispose of. But to be on the safe side, he added, "They are yours for the stealing, mighty Dalzel." He went up to the nieces and patted each on her plump arm. "Ladies," he said. "Fullest moons of Zanzib, pray forgive me that unfortunate vow which prevents me forever from enjoying your largeness. Look up instead and behold the husband I have found you in my place."

The heads of both nieces came up as soon as they heard the word *husband*. They gazed at Dalzel. "He's ever so handsome," said the pink one.

"I like them with wings," said the yellow one. "It's different."

"Fangs are rather sexy," mused the pink one. "So are claws, provided he's careful with them on the carpets."

Dalzel beamed wider with each remark. "I shall steal these at once," he said. "I like them better than princesses. Why didn't I collect fat ladies instead, Hasruel?"

A fond smile bared Hasruel's fangs. "It was your decision, brother." His smile faded. "If you are quite ready, it is my duty to send you into exile now."

"I don't mind so much now," Dalzel said, with his eyes still on the two nieces.

Hasruel stretched out his hand again, slowly, regretfully, and slowly, in three long rolls of thunder, Dalzel and the two nieces faded out of sight. There was a slight smell of the sea and a faint noise of sea gulls. Both Morgan and Valeria started crying again.

Everyone else sighed, Hasruel deepest of all. Abdullah realized with some surprise that Hasruel truly loved his brother. Although it was hard to understand how anyone could love Dalzel, Abdullah could hardly blame him. Who am I to criticize? he thought, as Flower-in-the-Night came up and put her arm through his.

Hasruel heaved up an even heavier sigh and sat down on the throne, which fitted his size far better than Dalzel's, with his great wings drooping sadly to either side. "There is other business," he said, touching his nose gingerly. It seemed to be healing already.

"Yes, there certainly *is!*" said Sophie. She had been waiting on the throne steps for her chance to speak. "When you stole our moving castle, you disappeared my husband, Howl. Where is he? I want him back."

Hasruel raised his head sadly, but before he could reply, there were alarmed noises from the princesses. Everyone at the bottom of the steps retreated from the Paragon's petticoat. It was bulging and bellying up and down on its hoops like a concertina. "Help!" cried the genie inside. "Let me out! You promised!"

Flower-in-the-Night's hand leaped to her mouth. "Oh! I clean forgot!" she said, and darted away from Abdullah, down the steps. She threw aside the petticoat in a roll of purple smoke. "I wish," she cried out, "that you be released from your bottle, genie, and be free forevermore!"

As usual the genie did not waste time in thanks. The bottle burst with a resounding smack. Inside the rolls of smoke a decidedly more solid figure climbed to its feet. Sophie gave a scream at the sight. "Oh, bless the girl! Thank you, *thank you!*" She arrived in the vanishing smoke so fast that she nearly knocked the solid man there over. He did not seem to mind. He picked Sophie up and swung her around and around. "Oh, why didn't I *know?* Why didn't I *realize?*" Sophie panted, staggering about on broken glass.

"Because that was the enchantment," Hasruel said gloomily. "If he was known to be Wizard Howl, someone would have released him. You could not know who he was, nor could he tell anyone."

The Royal Wizard Howl was a younger man than Wizard Suliman, and a good deal more elegant. He was richly dressed in a suit of mauve satin, against which his hair showed a rather improbable shade of yellow. Abdullah stared at the wizard's light eyes in the wizard's bony face. He had seen those eyes clearly, one early morning. He felt he should have guessed. He felt himself altogether in an awkward position. He had used the genie. He felt he knew the genie very well. Did that mean he also knew the wizard? Or not?

For this reason, Abdullah did not join in when everyone, including the soldier, gathered around Wizard Howl, exclaiming and congratulating him. He watched the tiny Princess of Tsapfan walk quietly among the exclaiming crowd and gravely put Morgan into Howl's arms.

"Thanks," said Howl. "I thought I'd better bring him along where I could keep an eye on him," he explained to Sophie. "Sorry if I gave you a fright." Howl seemed more used to holding babies than Sophie was. He rocked Morgan soothingly and stared at him. Morgan stared, rather balefully, back. "My word, he's ugly!" Howl said. "Chip off the old block."

"*Howl!*" said Sophie. But she did not sound angry.

"One moment," said Howl. He advanced to the steps of the throne and looked up at Hasruel. "Look here, djinn," he said, "I've a bone to pick with you. What do you mean by pinching my castle and shutting me up in a bottle?"

Hasruel's eyes lit to an angry orange. "Wizard, do you imagine your power is equal to mine?"

"No," said Howl. "I just want an explanation." Abdullah found himself admiring the man. Knowing what a coward the genie had been, he had no doubt that Howl was a jelly of terror inside. But he showed no sign of it. He hoisted Morgan over his mauve silk shoulder and glared back at Hasruel.

"Very well," said Hasruel. "My brother ordered me to steal the castle. In this I had no choice. But Dalzel gave no orders concerning you, except that I ensure you could not steal the castle back again. Had you been a blameless man, I would simply have transported you to the island where my brother is now. But I knew you had been using your wizardry to conquer a neighboring country—"

"That's not fair!" said Howl. "The King *ordered* me!" He sounded for a moment just like Dalzel, and he must have realized that he did. He stopped. He thought. Then he said ruefully, "I daresay I could have redirected His Majesty's mind if it had occurred to me. You're right. But don't ever let me catch you where I can put *you* in a bottle, that's all."

"That I might deserve," Hasruel agreed. "And I deserve it the more as I took pains to let everyone involved meet with the most fitting fate I could devise." His eyes slanted toward Abdullah. "Did I not?"

"Most painfully, great djinn," Abdullah agreed. "*All* my dreams came true, not only the pleasant ones."

Hasruel nodded. "And now," he said, "I must leave you when I have performed one more small, needful act." His wings rose, and his hands gestured. Instantly he was in the midst of a swarm of strange winged shapes. They hovered over his head and around the throne like transparent sea horses, completely silent except for the faint whisper of their whirling wings.

"His angels," Princess Beatrice explained to Princess Valeria.

Hasruel whispered to the winged shapes, and

they departed from him as suddenly as they had appeared, to reappear in the same swarm, whispering around Jamal's head. Jamal backed away from them, horrified, but it did no good. The swarm followed him. One after another, the winged shapes went to perch on different parts of Jamal's dog. As each landed, it shrank and disappeared among the hairs of the dog's coat, until only two were left.

Abdullah suddenly found these two shapes hovering level with his eyes. He ducked, but the shapes followed. Two small, cold voices spoke, in a way that seemed for his ears alone. "After long thought," they said, "we find we prefer this shape to that of toads. We think in the light of eternity, and we therefore thank you." So saying, the two shapes darted away to perch on Jamal's dog, where they, too, shrank and disappeared into the gnarled skin of its ears.

Jamal stared at the dog in his arms. "Why am I holding a dog full of angels?" he asked Hasruel.

"They will not harm you or your beast," said Hasruel. "They will simply wait for the gold ring to reappear. Tomorrow, I believe you said? You must see that I am naturally anxious to keep track of my life. When my angels find it, they will bring it to me wherever I am." He sighed, heavily enough to stir everyone's hair. "And I do not know where I shall be," he said. "I shall have to find some place of exile in the far deeps. I have been wicked. I cannot again join the

285

ranks of the Good Djinns."

"Oh, come now, great djinn!" said Flower-in-the-Night. "It was taught to me that goodness is forgiveness. Surely the Good Djinns will welcome you back?"

Hasruel shook his great head. "Intelligent Princess, you do not understand."

Abdullah found that he understood Hasruel very well. Perhaps his understanding had something to do with the way he had been less than polite to his father's first wife's relatives. "Hush, love," he said. "Hasruel means that he enjoyed his wickedness and does not regret it."

"It is true," said Hasruel. "I had more fun these last months than I had in many hundreds of years before that. Dalzel taught me this. Now I must go away for fear I start having the same fun among the Good Djinns. If I only knew where to go."

A thought seemed to strike Howl. He coughed. "Why not go to another world?" he suggested. "There are many hundreds of other worlds, you know."

Hasruel's wings rose and beat with excitement, whirling the hair and dresses of every princess in the hall. "There are? Where? Show me how I may get to another world."

Howl put Morgan into Sophie's awkward arms and bounded up the steps of the throne. What he showed Hasruel was a matter of a few strange gestures and a nod or so. Hasruel seemed to understand perfectly. He nodded in return. Then he rose from the throne and simply walked away, without another word, across the hall and through the wall as if it were so much mist. The huge hall suddenly felt empty.

"Good riddance!" said Howl.

"Did you send him to *your* world?" Sophie asked.

"No way!" said Howl. "They've got enough to worry about there. I sent him in the opposite direction. I took a risk that the castle wouldn't just disappear." He turned around slowly, staring out at the cloudy reaches of the hall. "It's all still here," he said. "That means Calcifer must be here somewhere. He's the one who keeps it going." He gave out a ringing shout. *Calcifer! Where are you?*

The Paragon's petticoat once more seemed to take on a life of its own. This time it bowled away sideways on its hoops to let the magic carpet float free of it. The carpet shook itself, in rather the same way as Jamal's dog was now doing. Then, to everyone's surprise, it flopped to the floor and began to unravel. Abdullah nearly cried out at the waste. The long thread whirling free was blue and curiously bright, as if the carpet were not made of the usual wool at all. The free thread, darting back and forth across the carpet, rose higher and higher as it grew longer, until it was stretched between the high cloudy ceiling and the almost bare canvas it had been woven into. At last, with an impatient flip, the other end tore free from the canvas and shrank upward into the rest, where it spread in a flickering sort of way, and shrank again, and finally spread into a new shape like an upside-down teardrop or maybe a flame. This shape came drifting downward, steadily and purposefully. When it was near, Abdullah could see a face on the front of it composed of little purple or green or orange flames. Abdullah shrugged fatalistically. It seemed that he had parted with all those gold pieces to buy a fire demon and not a magic carpet at all.

The fire demon spoke, with a purple, flickering mouth. "Thank goodness!" it said. "Why didn't someone call my name before? I *hurt*."

"Oh, poor Calcifer!" said Sophie. "I didn't *know!*"

"I'm not speaking to you," retorted the strange flame-shaped being. "You stuck your claws into me. Nor," it said as it floated past Howl, "to you, either. You let me in for this. It wasn't me that wanted to help the King's army. I'm only speaking to *him*," it said, bobbing up beside Abdullah's shoulder. He heard his hair frizzle gently. The flame was hot. "He's the only person who ever tried to flatter me."

"Since when," Howl asked acidly, "have you needed flattery?"

"Since I discovered how nice it is to be told I'm nice," said Calcifer.

"But I don't think you are nice," said Howl. "*Be* like that, then!*" He turned his back on Calcifer with a fling of mauve satin sleeves.

"Do you want to be a toad?" Calcifer asked. "You're not the *only* one who can do toads, you know!"

Howl tapped angrily with one mauve-booted foot. "Perhaps," he said, "your new friend might ask you to get this castle down where it belongs then."

Abdullah felt a little sad. Howl seemed to be making it plain that he and Abdullah did *not* know each other. But he took the hint. He bowed. "O sapphire among sorcerous beings," he said, "flame of festivity and candle among carpets, magnificent more by a hundred times in your true form than ever you were as treasured tapestry—"

"Get *on* with it!" muttered Howl.

"—would you graciously consent to re-place this castle on earth?" Abdullah finished.

"With pleasure," said Calcifer.

They all felt the castle going down. It went so fast at first that Sophie clutched Howl's arm and a number of princesses cried out. For as Valeria loudly said, a person's stomach got left behind in the sky. It was possible that Calcifer was out of practice after being in the wrong shape for so long. Whatever the reason was, the descent slowed after a minute and became so gentle that everyone hardly noticed it. This was just as well, because as it descended, the castle became notice-ably smaller. Everyone was jostled toward everyone else and had to fight for room in which to balance. The walls moved inward, turning from cloudy porphyry to plain plaster as they came. The ceiling moved down, and its vaulting turned to large black beams, and a window appeared behind the place where the throne had been. It was shadowy at first. Abdullah turned toward it eagerly, hoping for one more glimpse of the transparent sea with its sunset islands, but by the time the window was a real solid window, there was only sky outside, flooding the cottage-sized room with clear yellow dawn. By this time princess was crowded against princess, Sophie was squashed in a corner, grasping Howl in one arm and Morgan with the other, and Abdullah found himself squeezed between Flower-in-the-Night and the soldier.

The soldier, Abdullah realized, had not said a word in a very long time. In fact, he was behaving decidedly oddly. He had pulled his borrowed veils back over his head and was sitting bowed over on a small stool which had appeared beside the hearth as the castle shrank.

"Are you quite well?" Abdullah asked him.

"Perfectly," said the soldier. Even his voice sounded odd.

Princess Beatrice pushed her way through to him. "Oh, *there* you are!" she said. "Whatever is the matter with you? Afraid I'm going to go back on my promise now we're getting back to normal? Is that it?"

"No," said the soldier. "Or rather, yes. It'll bother you."

"It will bother me not at all!" snapped Princess Beatrice. "When I make a promise, I keep it. Prince Justin can just go to . . . whistle."

"But I *am* Prince Justin," said the soldier.

"What?" said Princess Beatrice.

Very slowly and sheepishly the soldier put away his veils and looked up. It was still the same face, with the same blue eyes that were either utterly innocent or deeply dishonest, or both, but it was a smoother and more educated face. A different sort of soldierliness looked out of it. "That damned djinn enchanted me, too," he said. "I remember it now. I was waiting in a wood for the search parties to report back." He looked rather apologetic. "We were hunting for Princess Beatrice—er, you, you know—without much luck, and suddenly my tent blew away and there was the djinn, squeezing himself in among the trees. 'I'm taking the Princess,' he said. 'And since you defeated her country by unfair use of magic, you can be one of the defeated soldiers and see how *you* like it.' And next thing I knew, I was wandering about on the battlefield, thinking I was a Strangian soldier."

"And did you hate it?" asked Princess Beatrice.

"Well," said the Prince, "it was hard. But I sort of

got on with it and picked up everything useful I could and made a few plans. I see I shall have to do something for all those defeated soldiers. But"——a grin that was purely that of the old soldier spread across his face—"to tell the truth, I enjoyed myself rather a lot, wandering through Ingary. I had fun being wicked. I'm like that djinn, really. It's getting back to ruling again that's depressing me."

"Well, I can help you there," said Princess Beatrice. "I know the ropes, after all."

"Really?" said the Prince, and he looked up at her in the same way that as the soldier he had looked at the kitten in his hat.

Flower-in-the-Night nudged Abdullah, softly and delightedly. "The Prince of Ochinstan!" she whispered. "No need to fear him!"

Shortly after that the castle came to earth as lightly as a feather. Calcifer, floating against the low beams of the ceiling, announced that he had set it down in the fields outside Kingsbury. "And I sent a message to one of Suliman's mirrors," he said smugly.

This seemed to exasperate Howl. "So did I," he said angrily. "Take a lot on yourself, don't you?"

"Then he got two messages," said Sophie. "What of it?"

"How stupid!" said Howl, and began to laugh. At that Calcifer sizzled with laughter, too, and they seemed to be friends again. Thinking about it,

Abdullah could see how Howl felt. He had been bursting with anger all the time he was a genie, and he was still bursting with anger now, with no one except Calcifer to take it out on. Probably Calcifer felt the same. Both of them had magic that was too powerful to risk being angry with ordinary people.

Clearly both messages had arrived. Someone beside the window shouted, "Look!" and everyone crowded to it to watch the gates of Kingsbury opening to let the King's coach hasten out behind a squad of soldiers. In fact, it was a procession. The coaches of numerous ambassadors followed the King's, emblazoned with the arms of most of the countries where Hasruel had collected princesses.

Howl turned toward Abdullah. "I feel I got to know you rather well," he said. They looked at each other awkwardly. "Do you know me?" Howl asked.

Abdullah bowed. "At least as well as you know me."

"That's what I was afraid of," Howl said ruefully. "Well, then, I know I can rely on you to do some good fast talking when it's needed. When all those coaches get here, it may be necessary."

It was. It was a most confusing time, during the course of which Abdullah grew rather hoarse. But the most confusing part, as far as Abdullah was concerned, was that every single princess, not to speak of Sophie, Howl, and Prince Justin, insisted on telling the King how brave and intelligent Abdullah had been. Abdullah kept wanting to put them right. He had not been brave—just walking on air because Flower-in-the-Night loved him.

Prince Justin took Abdullah aside, into one of the many antechambers of the palace. "Accept it," he said. "Nobody ever gets praised for the right reasons. Look at me. The Strangians here are all over me because I'm giving money to their old soldiers, and my royal brother is delighted because I've stopped making difficulties about marrying Princess Beatrice. Everyone thinks I'm a model prince."

"*Did* you object to marrying her?" asked Abdullah.

"Oh, yes," said the Prince. "I hadn't met her then, of course. The King and I had one of our quarrels about it, and I threatened to throw him over the palace roof. When I disappeared, he thought I'd just gone off in a huff for a while. He hadn't even started to worry."

The King was so pleased with his brother, and with Abdullah for bringing Valeria and his other Royal Wizard back, that he ordered a magnificent double wedding for the next day. This added a great deal of urgency to the confusion. Howl hurriedly made a strange simulacrum—constructed mostly of parchment—of a King's Messenger, which was sent by magic to the Sultan of Zanzib, to offer him transport to his daughter's wedding. This simulacrum came back half an hour later, looking decidedly tattered, with the news that the Sultan had a fifty-foot stake ready for Abdullah if he ever showed his face in Zanzib again. This being so, Sophie and Howl went and talked to the King. The King created two new posts called Ambassadors Extraordinary for the Realm of Ingary and gave those posts to Abdullah and Flower-in-the-Night that same evening.

The wedding of the Prince and the Ambassador made history, for Princess Beatrice and Flower-in-the-Night had fourteen princesses each as bridesmaids and the King himself gave the brides away. Jamal was Abdullah's best man. As he passed Abdullah the wedding ring, he reported in a whisper that the angels had departed earlier that morning, taking Hasruel's life with them.

"And a good thing, too!" Jamal said. "Now my poor dog will stop scratching."

Almost the only persons of note who did *not* attend the wedding were Wizard Suliman and his wife. This had only indirectly to do with the King's anger. It seemed that Lettie had spoken so strong-mindedly to the King, when the King wished to arrest Wizard Suliman, that she had gone into labor rather earlier than her time. Wizard Suliman was afraid to leave her side. But on the very day of the wedding Lettie gave birth to a daughter with no ill effects at all.

"Oh, good!" said Sophie. "I knew I was cut out to be an aunt."

The first task of the two new ambassadors was to conduct numbers of the kidnapped princesses to their homes. Some of them, like the tiny Princess of Tsapfan, lived so far away that their countries had barely been heard of. The ambassadors had instructions to make trading alliances and also to note all other strange places on the way, with a view to later exploration. Howl had talked to the King. Now, for some reason, all Ingary was talking about mapping the globe. Exploring parties were being chosen and trained.

What with journeying, and pampering princesses, and arguing with foreign kings, Abdullah was somehow always too busy to make his confession to Flower-in-the-Night. It always seemed that there would be a more promising moment the next day. But at last, when they were about to arrive in far-distant Tsapfan, he realized that he could delay no longer.

He took a deep breath. He felt the color leave his face. "I am not really a prince," he blurted out. There. It was said.

Flower-in-the-Night looked up from the map she was drawing. The shaded lamp in the tent made her face almost more beautiful than usual. "Oh, I know *that*," she said.

"What?" whispered Abdullah.

"Well, naturally, while I was in the castle in the air, I had plenty of time to think about you," she said. "And I soon realized you were romancing, because it was so like *my* daydream, only the other way around. I used to dream that I was just an ordinary girl, you see, and that my father was a carpet merchant in the Bazaar. I used to imagine that I managed the business for him."

"You are a marvel!" said Abdullah.

"Then so are you," she said, and went back to her map.

They returned to Ingary in due time with an extra packhorse loaded with the boxes of sweets the princesses had promised Valeria. There were chocolates and candied oranges and coconut ices and honeyed nuts, but the most wonderful of all were the sweets from the tiny princess—layer upon layer of paper-thin candy that the tiny princess called Summer Leaves. These came in a box so beautiful that Valeria used it for jewelry when she grew older. Strangely enough, she had almost given up screaming. The King could not understand it, but as Valeria explained to Sophie, when thirty people all tell you you've *got* to scream, it rather puts you off the whole idea.

Sophie and Howl were living—somewhat quarrelsomely, it must be confessed, although they were said to be happiest that way—in the moving castle again. One of its aspects was a fine mansion in the

Chipping Valley. When Abdullah and Flower-in-the-Night returned, the King gave them land in the Chipping Valley, too, and permission to build a palace there. The house they had built was quite modest—it even had a thatched roof—but their gardens soon became one of the wonders of the land. It was said that Abdullah had help in their design from at least one of the Royal Wizards, for how else could even an Ambassador have a bluebell wood that grew bluebells all the year around?